SISTERS OF BATTLE
THE OMNIBUS

Others stories featuring the Sisters of Battle

SHROUD OF NIGHT
A novel by Andy Clark

CULT OF THE WARMASON
A novel by CL Werner

IMPERIAL CREED
A novel by David Annandale

REBIRTH
A novel by Nick Kyme

THE DEATH OF ANTAGONIS
A novel by David Annandale

BLOOD OF ASAHEIM
A novel by Chris Wraight

REDEMPTION CORPS
A novel by Rob Sanders

DAEMONIFUGE
A graphic novel by Jim Campbell and Kev Walker

SISTERS OF BATTLE

THE OMNIBUS

JAMES SWALLOW

BLACK LIBRARY

*For Mandy; my Faith and my Fire and
for Sarah; a Sister among the Brothers.*

A BLACK LIBRARY PUBLICATION

Red & Black first published as an audio drama in 2011.
Faith & Fire first published in 2006.
Hammer & Anvil first published in 2011.
Heart & Soul first published in 2017.
This edition published in Great Britain in 2018 by
Black Library,
Games Workshop Ltd.,
Willow Road,
Nottingham, NG7 2WS, UK.

10 9 8 7 6 5 4

Produced by Games Workshop in Nottingham.
Cover illustration by Slawomir Maniak.

Sisters of Battle: The Omnibus © Copyright Games Workshop Limited 2018. Sisters of Battle: The Omnibus, GW, Games Workshop, Black Library, The Horus Heresy, The Horus Heresy Eye logo, Space Marine, 40K, Warhammer, Warhammer 40,000, the 'Aquila' Double-headed Eagle logo, and all associated logos, illustrations, images, names, creatures, races, vehicles, locations, weapons, characters, and the distinctive likenesses thereof, are either ® or TM, and/or © Games Workshop Limited, variably registered around the world.
All Rights Reserved.

A CIP record for this book is available from the British Library.

ISBN 13: 978 1 78496 572 3

No part of this publication may be reproduced, stored in a retrieval system, or transmitted in any form or by any means, electronic, mechanical, photocopying, recording or otherwise, without the prior permission of the publishers.

This is a work of fiction. All the characters and events portrayed in this book are fictional, and any resemblance to real people or incidents is purely coincidental.

See Black Library on the internet at

blacklibrary.com

Find out more about Games Workshop
and the world of Warhammer 40,000 at

games-workshop.com

Printed and bound by CPI Group (UK) Ltd, Croydon, CR0 4YY

It is the 41st millennium. For more than a hundred centuries the Emperor has sat immobile on the Golden Throne of Earth. He is the Master of Mankind by the will of the gods, and master of a million worlds by the might of his inexhaustible armies. He is a rotting carcass writhing invisibly with power from the Dark Age of Technology. He is the Carrion Lord of the Imperium for whom a thousand souls are sacrificed every day, so that he may never truly die.

Yet even in his deathless state, the Emperor continues his eternal vigilance. Mighty battlefleets cross the daemon-infested miasma of the warp, the only route between distant stars, their way lit by the Astronomican, the psychic manifestation of the Emperor's will. Vast armies give battle in His name on uncounted worlds. Greatest amongst his soldiers are the Adeptus Astartes, the Space Marines, bioengineered super-warriors. Their comrades in arms are legion: the Astra Militarum and countless planetary defence forces, the ever-vigilant Inquisition and the tech-priests of the Adeptus Mechanicus to name only a few. But for all their multitudes, they are barely enough to hold off the ever-present threat from aliens, heretics, mutants – and worse.

To be a man in such times is to be one amongst untold billions. It is to live in the cruellest and most bloody regime imaginable. These are the tales of those times. Forget the power of technology and science, for so much has been forgotten, never to be re-learned. Forget the promise of progress and understanding, for in the grim dark future there is only war. There is no peace amongst the stars, only an eternity of carnage and slaughter, and the laughter of thirsting gods.

CONTENTS

Introduction	9
Red & Black	13
Faith & Fire	57
Hammer & Anvil	367
Heart & Soul	709

INTRODUCTION

In a universe where the darkness is eternal and ever-encroaching, someone has to bring the fire to beat back the night – and in the distant gothic future of Warhammer 40,000, there are none who embody that ideal more than the Sisters of Battle.

Their look is immediately arresting: warrior-women archetypes in robes and armour, reminiscent of ancient war-queens or swift and deadly Valkyries, marching to victory with burning zeal in their eyes and hymnals in their hearts. They are a force of nature, undaunted and unstoppable. So it's little wonder that their stories have struck a chord with so many readers over the years.

But bringing the Adepta Sororitas to prose didn't happen swiftly. Perhaps fittingly, they had to fight for it. Back in 2004, after the success of my first Blood Angels duology, the editorial team at Black Library asked me what I'd like to write next, and the Sisters of Battle were at the top of my list. The brilliant *Daemonifuge* comic serialised in *Warhammer Monthly* had been their first outing in fiction, and I wanted to give the Sisters their own novel, but there was some reticence at first. At the time, Warhammer 40,000's fan-base was predominantly male and there was some concern that a full-length novel featuring a nearly all female cast of characters might not find its readership – but I was convinced it was a strong concept. Not just because of the surface appeal of "nuns with guns", but because writing about the Sororitas could allow us to tell a story of the 41st millennium through a new lens. In the past, we'd seen stories told through the eyes of Space Marines, Imperial Guardsmen and Inquisitors, but the Sisters of Battle had something different to offer. Over the last decade, as Black Library's output has grown, we've continued to work to narrow that gender imbalance as much as possible, and as such it seems right that the Imperium's most fearsome and faithful women have carried the torches to light the way.

For me, what makes the Adepta Sororitas such incredible protagonists for a Warhammer 40,000 tale is the central pillar of what makes them who they are: their *belief*. Like the Space Marines of the Adeptus Astartes, the Sisters of Battle regularly go to war against all the horrific foes that the grim dark future can throw at them, be they aliens, mutants or witches. The Sororitas may carry powerful flamers and deadly boltguns, wear powered armour and utilise heavy combat vehicles, but unlike their gene-engineered counterparts, if you strip that away, beneath it all they are still just ordinary human beings. The one thing that sets them apart is their spirit – the singular unswerving power of their faith in the Emperor of Mankind, and that immediately makes them interesting to write about. Because, as the real world shows us, while faith and belief in a higher ideal can create amazing things and be a true force for good, the dark side of that kind of zealotry can lead even the most principled of souls down a road to damnation.

Conflict, nobility, sacrifice, humanity – all these grand themes are marbled through the Sisters of Battle from the very start, and in the arena of the 41st millennium they can be opened out into epic, mythic tales.

The omnibus collection you hold in your hands includes two novels, *Faith & Fire* and *Hammer & Anvil*. My original concept for the first Sisters novel would actually end up becoming the plot for the second book in the series. My inspiration for that storyline came from a small piece of colour text in the 3rd edition version of *Codex: Necrons*, a diary entry by one Canoness Sepherina detailing a Sororitas mission to the convent on Sanctuary 101, sent there to re-consecrate it after it had been destroyed by the deadly xenos species. As so often happens writing in this universe, it's the dangling threads of tales left unfinished that entice us writers into wanting to follow up on them, and this time was no exception. But after some consideration, Black Library decided that they wanted the first ever Sisters of Battle novel to show the Sororitas fighting not aliens, but their more "traditional" foes – rogue psykers and heretics. And so the Sanctuary 101 story became the second adventure, while *Faith & Fire*'s narrative shifted to one pitting the battle-hardened Sister Miriya and her reluctant companion, the Sister-Hospitaller Verity, against a band of murderous pyrokinetics and a conspiracy among one world's ruling ecclesiarchy. *Faith & Fire* debuted in 2006 and became a hit with readers, allowing me in 2011 to tell the Sanctuary story in *Hammer & Anvil*, and create a prequel to *Faith & Fire* as part of Black Library's audio range in the tale *Red & Black*.

What I found was that my Sisters of Battle stories brought me a whole new readership. Miriya and Verity became fan favourites, and at events and book signings, I got – and still get – two distinct types of readers for the Sororitas novels; some are men who bought the books for their significant other, often to prove to them that the worlds of Warhammer could also feature dynamic female characters as well as male ones; and some are women who were delighted to see the Sisters getting their own novels. One of the coolest things about writing for this universe is hearing a reader say they were so inspired by your work that it made them want to build those characters into an army with which to play the game, or produce fan-art based on the stories. For a writer, there's little that is more rewarding than knowing your story has encouraged others to go out and create something of their own.

And then there's the question I am often asked, whenever the subject of these novels comes up. *Is this the last we will see of Sister Miriya and Sister Verity? Are their stories over, or are there more to come?*

To that I simply say this: *Have faith.*

James Swallow
London, November 2016

RED & BLACK

And so it was decreed, in the wake of the Age of Apostasy. So it was said by the High Lords of Terra, that the Ecclesiarchy, the great church of the Imperium, founded on the worship of the God-Emperor of Mankind, would never be granted the use of "men under arms", lest the temptation be too great for cardinals of weak character and high ambition.

The Ecclesiarchy; the guardians of the Imperial Creed and the celestial truth of the Emperor's divinity, whose sole purpose was to regulate the veneration of millions across the galaxy. And in a universe so harsh, where heathen alien life, heretic witch-psychics and the forces of Chaos laid their threat, the church could not go undefended.

No "men under arms"; so the very letter of the edict was adhered to, and thus rose the Orders Militant of the Adepta Sororitas – the Sisters of Battle. Some called them fanatics. Warrior-women spiritually betrothed to their religion, clothed in powered armour, cleansing the unbelievers with flamer and boltgun. The Celestians; the Seraphim; the Repentia, Dominions and Retributors, called to castigate those who defied the Emperor's divine will. The great work of the Battle Sisters never ended, for there were always Wars of Faith to be won, always more heretics for the pyre. They were the line of fire between the anarchy of the infidel and the bulwark of pure devotion. The red against the black. For millennia they had been the burning sword and holy shield for humankind.

Few exemplified such devotion more than Sister Miriya, a ranked Celestian Eloheim of the Order of our Martyred Lady, although she would never have been so arrogant as to say such a thing herself. Under the flickering light of electro-candles, she walked the length of the penitent corridor on Zhodon Orbital, voicing the words of holy catechism amid the echoes of her footfalls.

'*A spiritu dominatus. Domine, libra nos. A morte perpetua. Domine, libra nos. Ave, Imperator. Domine, libra nos.*' The phrases in High Gothic fell from her lips easily, with rote precision, whispering off the stone walls.

Like many of the citadel stations across human space, Zhodon resembled an ancient cathedral ripped free of the land and cast into the darkness. Spires and naves spread like the points of a morningstar, plasma lanterns burning behind mile-high stained-glass windows. Located on the pilgrim route to the Segmentum Solar, the platform was a way-point for travellers and a barracks for the Witch Hunters of the Ecclesiarchy.

Miriya approached the iron gate that closed off the sanctum of the prioress, the mistress of this place. She slowed and dwelt a little, taking a moment to study the complex devotional sculptures in the walls. Above was a rendering of Saint Katherine, first mistress of her order, whose brutal death gave them their title. Miriya bowed in respect, crossing her hands across her chest, forming the holy shape of the Imperial Aquila. 'In your name,' she said aloud. 'Grant me your wisdom and clarity.'

After a moment, she rose to look upon the statue. Like the saint, Miriya's face bore the ancient mark of the *fleur de lys*, tattooed in blood-red on her cheek. Her hair was a cascade of black, falling to the neck of her battle gear.

Saint Katherine was shown as she had been in battle, her mail and plate little different from Miriya's, even though centuries separated them. Sigils of the aquila, purity seals and rosaries decorated the armour, and a chaplet hung from her neck. Miriya's hand rose to her own, resting on a string of adamantine beads. Each one of the beads represented an act of devotion to the Imperial church.

She wondered if her next duty would warrant a new link in the chain. Prioress Lydia had been unusually circumspect on the details, a fact that concerned Miriya greatly. Secrets were not the currency of the Sisterhood, and she disliked anything that smacked of the clandestine. The Imperial Creed was the God-Emperor's Light, and so all deeds done in His name were never to be committed in shadow.

Miriya knocked twice on the heavy iron door and from beyond it, a voice bid her to enter. She strode in, her eyes downcast as protocol demanded, and bowed. 'Your Grace. As you order, so shall I be ready.'

'Look at me. Let me see your face.' Miriya did as she was ordered and raised her head. The prioress was two hundred solar years old, but kept to the appearance of a woman a quarter of that age by juvenat treatments. Lydia had been a prioress before Miriya had been inducted as a novice, and she would likely remain one for decades more. She was arrow-sharp and uncompromising, a masterful tactician and commander of the Orders Militant in the local sector of space. Miriya heard it said that the prioress had burned a thousand witches, and fought alongside saints. The steel in Lydia's eyes gave truth to it. 'You believe you are prepared for the task I will set you, Sister Celestian?' She smiled slightly. 'We shall see.'

The faint edge of mockery in the prioress' tone made Miriya's lips thin. 'My squad stand willing to meet the enemy,' she replied, with stiff formality. 'If you doubt their skills, mistress, I would ask why you summoned me and not another of our Sisterhood.'

Lydia studied the other woman intently. 'We are the weapons of the God-Emperor's church, Miriya. But we are more than that. We are His banner-bearers, the spear-tip that brings the rod of truth behind it. We must never lose sight of this. For each heretic we put to the sword, we must welcome another soul into the glory of Imperial Truth.'

Miriya frowned. 'Is that not the work of preachers and iterators?'

'Yes.' She inclined her head. 'But in some instances, it is ours as well. The Adepta Sororitas must inspire, Sister, and not just fear, but *love*. Not every test the church faces can be dealt with by bullet or blade's edge.'

The conversation was not progressing as Miriya had expected. Instead of a *mission*, the prioress seemed intent on giving her a *lesson*. She chafed under the thought. Miriya was a battle-tested veteran, not some callow noviciate. Lydia seemed to sense her thoughts, and went on.

'I summoned you specifically, Sister Miriya, because the duty I am about to set will require a mind clear and uncluttered by doubt. But also one that is willing to question.'

Lydia's words carried the slightest hint of challenge. Miriya's reputation preceded her; in an army where obedience was the watchword, the Celestian had often earned censure from her commanders because she frequently dared to exhibit an independent streak.

Her tolerance for the prioress' obfuscation was quickly thinning. 'I would ask you illuminate me, mistress. I do not follow your meaning.'

'You will, Sister,' offered Lydia, rising stiffly from her chair. She beckoned with one augmetic hand, the entire forearm replaced by a machine-proxy in the wake of an old battle wound. 'Come with me. And know that what I am about to show you must be veiled by the utmost secrecy.'

She followed. They travelled into the lower levels of Zhodon Orbital, to sections of the station that Miriya had never entered, past reliquaries and sacred compartments open only to nobles and cardinals. The prioress used blood-locks to bypass thick steel doors etched with hexagrammic wards, until at last they emerged in a chamber that was part prison, part hospice. The metallic space had a cold and clinical ambience. A cluster of watchful arco-flagellants stood sentinel before a wall of opaque armoured glass. They had once been men, each a heretic damned for their defiance of the church, now repurposed in its service. Their bodies were augmented with weapons, brains controlled by lobotomaic taps and hymnal implants. For now, they were docile, but if activated they would become vicious berserkers.

Miriya ignored them and peered at the dark barrier. She could not help but wonder what manner of prisoner required such guardians. A psyker mind-witch? A xenos beast? Perhaps even... a *daemon*? Her hand fell to the holster at her hip, where her plasma pistol lay ready.

Prioress Lydia halted before the panel and glanced at the Battle Sister. 'A question for you. The Hollos star system. Do you know the name?'

Miriya paused for a moment, drawing on mnemonic memory programmes from the hypnogogic training regimens of her time as a novice. Hollos; the name rose up from depths of her thoughts, dragging recollection with it. 'Aye. It is a vanished domain, cut off from the rest of the sector by violent warp-storms in the 38th millennium. Vessels avoid the quadrant around it like the plague.'

Lydia nodded. 'Correct. An Imperial colony world in unremembered space, unreachable for more than two thousand years. The storms killed any ships that attempted passage. The Imperial Navy and the Adeptus Terra declared Hollos to be lost...'

'But now something has changed?'

'You are perceptive, Sister,' noted the other woman. 'It is indeed so. Over the past year, the storms about Hollos have finally abated and the space beyond them has once again become navigable. Contact with this errant daughter-world has at long last been re-established.'

'Praise the Throne,' Miriya began.

'Not just yet,' warned the prioress. 'The nature of that contact has given the Ecclesiarchy great cause for concern.'

Two millennia was a long time to be alone in the darkness.

Miriya wondered what kind of changes could be wrought to a world, a society, a people, over so many years. The return of a lost colony to the Emperor's Light should have been a joyous occasion, but all too often such things only ended in bloodshed and pain.

'A warship intercepted a small vessel a few light years from the Hollos system,' Lydia went on. 'There was a lone crew member on board. A messenger, of sorts.'

Something in the prioress' tone gave Miriya pause. 'Human?'

Lydia raised an eyebrow. 'See for yourself, Sister.' The prioress gave a command and the misted glass became clear. Beyond it, Miriya saw a sparse dormitory chamber, furnished with a simple pallet, a fresher unit and a small, makeshift shrine venerating the God-Emperor.

But it was the cell's lone occupant that made every muscle in her body tense. It was humanoid in form and female, after a fashion. The being's skin was milk-pale and dressed with peculiar striations that at first seemed like tattoos. Tall and athletic in build, but not willowy like the alien eldar, it was clearly human, and yet it was *not*. Miriya's combat training immediately took hold, and she found herself evaluating the way it moved about the cell, looking at it for points of weakness and wondering how it might be killed.

Her eye was drawn by its innate grace and poise. The Battle Sister studied it and a strange thought occurred to her. The creature seemed almost *engineered* in its perfect symmetry. Beneath a cowl of close-cut white hair, eyes of stark violet glanced up to peer at her, then looked away.

Miriya shot the prioress a wary look. 'What in Terra's name is it?'

'She is not aware of us,' said Lydia, without answering immediately. 'The glass does not allow her to see through it.'

'If this thing were xenos or a mutant, you would have executed it,' noted the Battle Sister. 'So, then... I would hazard a guess that it is a breed of abhuman.'

'In a way,' allowed the prioress. 'What you see before you is not a subspecies like the ogryn or a gene-altered human like the Adeptus Astartes. No, she is a synthetic creation, grown of cultured stock from blood and flesh. Tests conducted by adepts of the magos biologis confirm it. She is an artificially manufactured organic being.'

'A... replicae?' The old word felt strange to say aloud. 'A cloned life grown from human cells?' Miriya shook her head. 'Such technology does not exist!'

'Not so,' Lydia corrected. 'Such technology does not exist *anymore*. But the God-Emperor, His light find us, created many miracles such as this. It is the tragedy of our age that they have been lost to the Imperium of Man.' The prioress moved closer to the glass, watching the prisoner carefully. 'Our guest speaks a common dialect of Imperial Gothic. Her ship and its systems are comparable to those of ours. She calls herself "Rho", and all gene-scans indicate that she is as much of human stock as you or I.' She gave that slight smile again. 'Outward appearances notwithstanding, of course.'

Miriya found it difficult to accept Lydia's words. Gene-forged beings and modified humans were a common thing in the Imperium, from the warriors of the Space Marines, to helots and cherubim, and even the arco-flagellants... But what the prioress described was an order of magnitude more complex. And certainly, if this "Rho" was indeed a replicae, it deserved to be no more than a menial, a servitor at best.

Then the being did something that made Miriya's breath catch in her throat. Rho bent down before the brass shrine in the cell wall and made the exact, correct stations of obeisance before an icon of the God-Emperor, crossing her long-fingered hands over her chest, just as the Battle Sister had done in the corridor before Saint Katherine's icon.

'It... It is praying!' It shocked Miriya to see the being doing something so sacred to her, an act that only a human was permitted to perform.

'Yes, she is,' said Lydia. 'And to *our* deity.'

They returned to the sanctum in silence, and along the way Miriya struggled to interpret what she had seen.

The prioress saw the conflict in her expression. 'It is quite shocking, is it not? A being born from an artificial womb, something that cannot possess an immortal soul, and yet she kneels before the Emperor's grace like one of us.'

'It is mimicry of some sort,' Miriya began. 'I've seen aliens that imitate human behaviours.'

Lydia shook her head. 'You are mistaken, Sister. The clone, Rho... She is not some mindless, drooling servitor commanded by punch-cards and neuro-stimms. She is a thinking, reasoning being. What she does is a learned behaviour, not one copied from observing one of us. I am certain of this.'

'You have spoken to it?' Miriya could not overlook how the prioress continued to refer to the replicae using the female pronoun.

'I have spoken to *her*, yes,' she insisted. 'When Rho saw the sign of the holy aquila upon my robes, she was elated. The replicae worships the God-Emperor of Mankind as her creator and master. She claims her mission from Hollos was begun in His name, to serve His will.'

It was difficult for Miriya to accept what she was hearing. It was enough that her view of the universe had been challenged by the mere existence of such a being, and now she was to believe that it could know the magnificence of the Imperial Creed? It went against the order of things, and she almost said as much aloud.

She held her tongue, and at length the prioress came to the full explanation of why Miriya had been summoned to Zhodon Orbital. 'Your mission, Sister, will be to seek the truth of this,' began Lydia. 'You will travel across the unmapped zone to the Hollos colony. There, you and your squad of Sister Celestians will ascertain what has transpired during the time of isolation. It will fall to you to determine if the populace has retained its true faith in the God-Emperor.'

She nodded, accepting the command. 'But, mistress... The replicae. If it exists, then–'

The prioress cut her off. 'Rho will go with you. Take your Sisters and do as I order.'

'And what shall I do if we find more of them?' Miriya's eyes narrowed. 'What if they are all that is left on Hollos?'

The prioress did not answer her question. Instead, she pushed a pict-slate across her desk towards the Battle Sister. Miriya gathered it up and saw dense text outlining her new orders. It bore the seal of the High Lords of Terra.

'You will not be alone,' said the other woman. 'Due to the unusual nature of the emissary from Hollos, the Adeptus Mechanicus have taken a direct interest in the situation. An agent of their magos biologis will also be accompanying you.'

Miriya paged through the contents of the slate. The Adeptus Mechanicus, the guardians of all technology within the Imperium of Man, were well known to her, and Lydia's statement came as no surprise. Every scrap of science and learning was jealously hoarded by them, from their master forges on Mars to the countless manufactoria worlds across a thousand star systems. A discovery like Rho – a living, functioning clone – would be like nectar to the adepts of the biologis. She came across a data panel showing a name and visual profile of the agent who would be joining the mission; Genus Nohlan, a questor, one of countless adepts who scoured the galaxy for lost scraps of technology, missing since the Age of Old Night.

She glanced up at the prioress. 'Command of this mission is mine, yes? I will not brook interference from the hand of the Mechanicum. If certain choices need to be made about the fate of Hollos and its people...' She trailed off, unwilling to finish the sentence.

The prioress did not seem to notice. 'Nohlan has been instructed to obey your orders. You may do whatever is required to retain the sanctity of church and Imperium.'

'Even if that requires the death of a world?'

Lydia turned away, dismissing her with the motion. 'It would not be the first time, Sister Miriya.'

The warship *Coronus* knifed through the void of deep space, a sword-blade prow leading towers of iron and steel, the wicked maws of lance cannons and massed laser batteries decorating the flanks. The ship was by no means the largest of the God-Emperor's fleet, but it was still powerful. The weapons it carried could rain death from high orbit and crack continents.

The ultimate sanction lay nestled within the warheads of a dozen cyclonic torpedoes. The command need only be given – *Exterminatus* – and the planet Hollos would die.

Sister Miriya had prayed each day of the journey that she would not be called upon to speak that word, but she had beseeched her saint and her God-Emperor to give her the strength to do so, if the moment came.

For despite the size of the Imperial church, despite the millions of loyal, devout souls in its service, its faith was a delicate and fragile thing, in constant need of protection. One single thread of poison could be enough to let rot set in. The Sisters of Battle were ever vigilant, always watching for heathens, witches and betrayers cloaked in the mantle of friendship. Put in such terms, the mission seemed clear, but Miriya knew that was a falsehood. There were no simple choices in the eternal service to the God-Emperor. Only in death did duty end, and until that time, Miriya would do as her oath demanded.

The voyage would be over soon, and she welcomed it. Her Celestians – Sisters Lethe, Cassandra, Isabel, Portia and Iona – were troubled by their orders. The presence of the replicae Rho had divided them. Some considered the clone to be an aberration, something that should be destroyed out of hand for daring to ape humanity, but they had not seen the curious, affecting sight of Rho at prayer. Try as she might, Miriya could not shake that image from her thoughts.

In the end, it was inevitable that she would seek to better understand the messenger from the lost colony.

She found Questor Nohlan where he had been for the duration of the voyage, prowling the observation chamber before Rho's cell, his mechanical limbs clicking and whirring.

Through means Sister Miriya was not privy to, the entire

compartment had been shifted from Zhodon Orbital to a bay aboard the *Coronus*, so strict was the security around the clone envoy. Nohlan had not moved from there, conducting scans and taking reams of notes on the humanoid, as if he were a collector with a newly discovered species of animal.

Rho's odd, bird-like movements were visible through the armoured glass, and as Miriya approached, she saw Nohlan copy them, as if attempting to understand the replicae.

'Honoured questor.' She gave him a shallow bow of greeting. 'You should prepare. We have emerged from the warp and the ship is making its approach to Hollos.'

'Oh. Sister Celestian!' Nohlan flinched, surprised by her arrival. 'Forgive me. I am deep in my analysis. Processing. Processing.' His vox-processed voice had an officious quality to it, but that couldn't hide his captivation with the subject of his study.

The adept was a typical example of his kind. Beneath voluminous crimson robes, the remnants of a human being lay among numerous bio-mechanical enhancements, implants and cybernetics. Serpentine mechadendrites wandered across the deck near his clawed feet, or wavered in the air like fronds in a breeze. A whiff of ozone and scented machine oil was always present around him. What she could see of his face beneath his hood had too many eyes, all of them red-lit and set in brass.

Miriya looked away towards the glassy wall. 'You have been here for days. Tell me, adept, do you ever sleep?'

'Praise the Omnissiah, but that need was edited from my body many years ago, four-point-two recurring,' he explained. 'It is quite liberating.'

'What have you learned about...' Miriya paused, mentally correcting. 'About *her*?'

'Much indeed, forty giga-quads of data, still rising.' Nohlan became enthused. 'I admit to being both fascinated and unnerved by the very presence of such a being as designate: Rho. She stimulates emotional responses in me that are rare occurrences. I am quite inspired!'

'The clone is what it seems, then?'

Nohlan's hooded head bobbed. 'Affirmative. The ideal of a genetically-engineered, vat-grown "perfect human" has hitherto been a myth. Now it is fact. She is fact. Ninety-seven point six per cent.' He paused. 'However... I admit to some concern over her unusual neurological development.'

Miriya watched Rho pick carefully at a data-slate she had been given, a simple child's primer on the glory of the Golden Throne. 'She seems as intelligent as you or I.'

Nohlan nodded again. 'My point *exactly*. The records of the magos biologis note that replicae were designed to be a replacement for machine-life, automata and the like. Great creations indeed, but made to be the servants of mankind. Loyal slave-warriors for our wars. Not our equals.' He shook his head. 'Error condition noted.'

On the other side of the glass, Rho put down the slate and closed her eyes. The clone's head was cocked and her lips were moving. 'What is she doing?'

'Singing,' said the adept. 'I have observed her doing so on several occasions. Parsing the audial portion, it appears to be a variant of the Oleon Anthem, probability factor plus or minus two per cent.'

'I know it well.' Miriya recalled the hymnal from her orphan youth in the Schola Progenium, and in that moment she made a decision. 'Open the chamber, adept. I want to look her in the eye.'

Nohlan hesitated, uncertain if she was serious, before finally obeying her order. 'As you wish...' A mechadendrite snaked out across the floor before rising up to tap out a code on a panel in the wall.

The glass wall shifted and retracted into the deck, and Miriya caught a brief snatch of Rho's faint and eerie singing before she fell silent. With pause, the Battle Sister strode into the compartment and stood before the clone, daring it to speak. Those odd violet eyes measured her, sweeping across to Nohlan and then back.

'I do not blame you,' said Rho. Her words were gentle and

breathy. 'I understand why you have kept me confined here. But I forgive it. You fear me.'

'I am Sister Miriya of the Order of Our Martyred Lady,' she replied, 'and you are nothing to be afraid of.'

Rho blinked slowly. 'The actions of your prioress would seem to suggest otherwise.' She went on before Miriya could respond. 'But it is of no consequence. I sense we grow nearer to my home world with each passing second. You have brought me back. Thank you, Miriya.' Rho bowed to her. 'Truly, the God-Emperor has smiled upon us.'

'You believe so?' Now she heard the clone-being say the words, Miriya wanted to challenge her. 'How can you know His will?'

'I do not presume to,' she replied. 'I am only His servant. But there can be no other explanation. You and I are here by His design. All that has happened is the wish of the Great Progenitor.'

At closer quarters, Miriya could better see the replicae's shape and form. While slight, Rho's body was all engineered muscle, without a single iota of useless flesh. Her looks belied a hidden strength, and the Battle Sister imagined that in combat Rho would be formidable indeed. Yet she radiated an air of calm stillness.

She tried a different tack. 'Your world has been isolated from the Imperium for two millennia. You are a living example of that fact.'

'Yes,' Rho said sadly. 'Can you imagine such pain, Sister? To be surrounded by a veil of madness for century upon century? Some began to fear that the universe had been destroyed in a great cataclysm, and only cruel fate had left our worlds untouched. Others believed we were the playthings of the Ruinous Powers. But not I. I have always known the truth. It is why I was chosen to be the messenger.'

Miriya took a step closer. 'What is the truth you speak of?'

When Rho replied, her eyes were shining and her words were those of a true zealot. She reached up and clasped Miriya's hand. 'It was His doing. The God-Emperor isolated

Hollos in order to *test* us. To keep us *pure*. And our faith in Him has finally been rewarded. The veil has fallen.'

'The veil... You mean the warp storms?'

Rho nodded. 'Aye. Now, after so long, we are free and ready to return. Our world has endured... It has prospered! I cannot wait for you to see it!'

'Nor I,' said Miriya, unable to keep the wariness from her tone.

The engines of the Arvus-class shuttle hummed as it dropped towards the capital of Hollos, and the sound kindled old battle-memory in Sister Miriya. Many times she had deployed into combat from a craft such as this, and it took a near-physical effort to remind herself of an important truth.

'This is a mission of words,' she muttered to herself. 'Not warfare.'

'Not yet.' The warrior seated in the crash-couch at her side gave the reply with a grim nod, and Miriya glanced at her

'Did I voice my thoughts aloud, Sister Lethe?'

The other woman gave a nod. 'You did, Eloheim. But trust we are all ready with hymnal and bolter, sword and scripture alike, should either be needed.'

Miriya gave a thin smile. Lethe was her strong right arm, second-in-command of her unit and a trusted comrade. They had fought many Wars of Faith side by side, and this day they shared the same silent concerns. 'Ready the Celestians, Sister. We will make planetfall soon, and I wish to be prepared.' She got out of her couch and made her way to the back of the shuttle; she didn't need to make sure Lethe was following her orders. The gruff, dour Battle Sister was already immediately snapping out commands to Sister Iona and Sister Portia to secure their weapons, and calling upon Sister Cassandra and Sister Isabel to prepare for a security sweep across the landing site on touchdown.

Miriya left her second to her work and moved forward to find Adept Nohlan and the replicae near the bow of the vessel, peering out through a wide viewport.

'Look there,' Rho was saying, picking out points of interest with her long, delicate fingers. 'Can you see? That is the hive-tower of Solasian. To the west, beneath the photon sails, our farmlands. And the White Plains. A world living under the Great Progenitor's munificence.'

'Ah, "The Great Progenitor",' Nohlan echoed her words. 'This is your local designation for the God-Emperor?'

Rho gave a nod. 'It reflects His position as the forge-master of all that we have and all that we are.'

'Indeed,' he mused. 'Processing...'

Miriya watched the interaction between the clone and the adept with a cold eye. Nohlan seemed to have no trouble adjusting to the abhuman's appearance, but then she imagined his interest in the replicae and the technology that had made it overrode any other intentions.

'Initial scans indicate that this region of the planet appears to be stable,' he went on. 'Data collation in progress.'

Rho seemed uncertain what to make of that reply. 'Hollos has its problems, like any world. But they have not dimmed our faith. We strive to improve our lot with each new day.' She glanced up as Miriya approached.

'Tell us about the council we are to meet on our arrival,' said Miriya. 'They have the authority to speak for all citizens of Hollos?'

Rho nodded again. 'I am one of their number. We are the legal government of our planet. Some of us have held high office for more than seven hundred Terran years! It is through the council's guidance that we have developed a benign, enduring society.'

Nohlan caught the inference and immediately seized upon it. 'Interrogative: beings like you, the replicae. In this culture you are the serviles, the soldiers, the protectors, yes?'

'The protectors... Yes,' Rho replied, but cautiously.

The shuttle's winglets bit into the air as it turned on a final approach and Miriya felt a vibration shiver up through the deck. Behind her, she heard Lethe calling the other Sisters to readiness and unbidden, her hand once more slipped towards the holster of her plasma pistol.

'This is a historic day!' Rho's violet eyes grew wide with something like joy. 'There will be celebrations!'

We shall see, Miriya told herself. Hard-earned experience had shown here that even the most benign of missions could twist into something dangerous if one were not ever-watchful.

Like a spire of sculpted ice, the white stone citadel of Hollos rose up above the planetary capital, catching the dazzling light of the day. It towered over a broad marble plaza dotted with ornamental fountains and gardens, filled with ornate statuary that rose at all points of the compass, the sculpted figures standing proudly and gazing up into the sky. Tallest among them was a rendering of the God-Emperor in the garb of an ancient knight, the stone inlaid with jewels and platinum.

The Arvus landed atop a granite rose tiled into the stonework, and past the distant lines of crowd barriers, a throng of Hollosi citizens raised their voices in cheers of happiness and a rolling fanfare blared from golden trumpets. Floating drone-birds wheeled overhead, camera-eyes feeding images to the crowds and the world beyond.

But as the shuttle's hatch hissed open, the music and the voices ebbed and the first silent note of dread lingered in the air. The Battle Sisters were the first to disembark, moving in cautious lock-step. Lethe led them forward, and each cradled her Godwyn-De'az pattern boltgun in a low, unthreatening carry, but each woman was primed to bring them to combat ready if the slightest threat presented itself.

Miriya exited last with Rho and the questor, taking in the scope of the place. Hollos' air smelled of blossoms and morning rain, clean and welcoming.

Eight figures stood waiting at the foot of the Emperor's statue, and Miriya threw Lethe a nod. As one, the Sisters paused to bow in the direction of the great effigy before proceeding.

Nohlan leaned in to speak to the Celestian as the group approached them. 'Analysing. The council... It would appear that only two of them are–'

She cut him off. 'Humans. Yes.' Miriya could not conceal a

frown of dismay at the presence of six other replicae among the planet's ruling body.

Rho stepped forward, beaming and excited, and addressed her people. 'I have returned, my fellow arbiters, and with great tidings! The Imperium endures, just as we have! I bring these emissaries from the God-Emperor's church to reunite with us! We are delivered!' Her words brought a new wave of applause and cheering from the crowd, but the goodwill did not spread to shift the mood of the Battle Sisters.

'Look sharp,' grated Lethe, glancing to her commander. 'Do you see them, Eloheim? The clones are *everywhere*.'

Miriya nodded. The replicae were not just part of the Hollosi Council, but also visible in the crowds, standing on the battlements and out amid the gardens. She estimated there was at least one of them for every two humans in sight. 'Stay your hand, Sister,' she warned Lethe. 'The ways of this world are unknown to us. Caution is our watchword.'

'They are garbed in such finery,' remarked Nohlan. 'Hypothesis – the clone-beings appear to be the ruling class in this culture. Further study is warranted.'

The adept's theory gave Miriya pause, but before she could consider it further, Rho was turning towards her and gesturing to the air. 'Allow me to present Sister Miriya, Celestian Eloheim of the Adepta Sororitas, and Questor Nohlan of the magos biologis!' Her smile took them both in as she and the council members bowed. 'Welcome our first visitors in thousands of years! This is truly a glorious day. Let us give praise to the Great Progenitor for His munificence. We welcome our kindred to our home!'

'Kindred?' Lethe muttered, as if she were insulted to be considered the same manner of being as the replicae.

Miriya silenced her with a look, and instead she returned the bow, looking up to find the faces of the humans who stood alongside the line of clones, both of them dressed in the same robes of office. One was an older male who seemed fatigued and distracted, but the other was a woman of Miriya's age and returned her gaze intently.

The Sister took a breath. 'Well met, arbiters. I bring greetings from the Ecclesiarchy of Holy Terra. Know that we are heartened to see that your...' She searched for the right word. 'Your disconnection from the Imperium did not break your faith.'

'Of course,' said Rho. 'We are an elected leadership, selected by our people to embody their faith and service to the greater community. The council has managed the affairs of Hollos for centuries, Sister Miriya. Through it, our world has become the ideal you see around you.'

The human arbiter suddenly broke her silence. 'Our replicae partners have held their roles for many, many years. In that time they have guided us... to a kind of prosperity.' Her words were neutral, but Miriya sensed something unsaid lurking just beneath their surface.

'Indeed so, dear Ahven,' continued Rho. 'Together, we are all children of the God-Emperor of Mankind.' She beckoned the group to follow her. 'Come, kindred. We will receive your mission in the great hall.'

Miriya gave a nod, but paused to give new orders to her second. 'Lethe. You and Isabel remain in the plaza until I summon you. Keep the shuttle secure.'

Lethe accepted the command with a nod, but not with silence. 'Eloheim. I don't like what I see here. Synthetics lording it over humans? It's not right. It goes against the natural order.'

Part of Miriya agreed with her, but she pushed that thought away. 'Perhaps so... But we cannot rush to judge these people by our lights.'

Lethe's eyes narrowed. 'Forgive my presumption, Sister, but I assumed that the very reason we are here is to pass judgement.'

Miriya found she had no reply and set off towards the white tower, the other woman's words dogging her all the way.

In the citadel's great hall, an arc of dark wood rose from a massive stone dais, and behind it each of the council members took up a station as another formal fanfare piped them to their places. Looking around, Miriya saw paintings worked into the walls, the floor and the ceiling. All of them were detailed landscapes of Holy Terra, Ophelia, Evangelion and other planets with great religious significance. Her eye was drawn to a set of tall panels that showed an unfolding narrative, apparently the history of Hollos itself.

Rho nodded sagely as she saw Miriya studying them. 'The chronicle, yes. I imagine you have many questions about what became of our world after the monstrous veil fell between us.'

The first illustration showed a recognisable depiction of an Adeptus Mechanicus explorator base, and Miriya said as much.

Nohlan confirmed her thoughts. 'Affirmative. That appears to be a Type-Zed embedded test and research colony. I have recovered what data remains of that endeavour from the Mechanicum's knowledge pool.'

'Hollos was originally an outpost dedicated to studying the science that birthed me,' explained Rho. 'You call it "replicae". But after the warp storms came and we were alone in the void, the surface of the planet was ravaged by lashes of dark energy.' She indicated the next few panels. Miriya saw paintings of terrible tempests sweeping across the landscape, and of desperate battles against the elements and other, more unnatural forces.

'Those creatures depicted there,' said the Battle Sister. 'The monsters...'

'*Daemons.*' Rho's bright and open face was momentarily darkened by the shadow of an old, deep fear as she uttered the word. Some of the Hollosi within earshot reflexively spat at the mention of it and made the sign of the aquila. 'The storms spilled out foul warp spawn upon the land,' continued Rho. 'The colonists fought, but they were pushed to the verge of extinction. Isolated and alone, with no hope of rescue, they reached out to the only ones who could save them.'

'The replicae.' Nohlan studied the images on the next panel

of the chronicle, parsing the images. 'Processing. The survivors decanted the prototype soldier clones to help them fight off the archenemy, and keep their world alive.'

Miriya walked along the line of the panels, watching the images shift from those of warfare and desolation, first to hardship and adversity, and finally to a bold new rebirth. It was a pretty tale, she had to admit.

'We drew Hollos back from the brink of destruction,' said Rho. 'We turned away the tide of the warp and held it at bay. And over the centuries, we – the replicae – evolved beyond our simplistic warrior natures into something superior.'

That last word caused Miriya to give the clone a sharp look. 'Superior to what?'

Rho returned her gaze. 'To what we once were. Little more than organic machines, tools and cannon fodder. We unlocked our potential.' She indicated the last few panels of the chronicle. 'Eventually, the colonists decided to cede governance of Hollos to us. We are tireless, virtually immortal. And under our stewardship, this world has thrived.'

'You must be very proud of your accomplishments.' Miriya kept her tone level.

Rho didn't respond to the implicit judgement in the Battle Sister's words. 'It is only by the will of the God-Emperor that we have endured. Without Him, we would be ashes. But instead, we are a peaceful world ready and willing to return to the Imperial fold...' Suddenly she faltered, as if a terrible possibility had occurred to her. 'That is... if you will have us? If you still want us?'

The ready desperation in Rho's strange eyes gave Miriya a moment of pause. 'I... *We* will need to be certain,' she said.

'Of what? Do you fear we are tainted by the warp?' Rho came closer and placed a hand on the vambrace of Miriya's power armour. 'I swear on my honour it is not so! We have purged our planet of such things!'

Beneath his hooded head, Nohlan's artificial eyes clicked as they focused on her. 'The way of Chaos is insidious,' he intoned. 'Are you sure? Probability factors unclear.'

'In the God-Emperor's name, yes!' Rho drew herself up. 'Hollos is at peace! A replicae has no need to raise arms! We have embraced pacifism and transcended our violent roots. There is no warfare here!'

'You truly have been isolated.' Miriya felt a moment of genuine pity for the clone. 'The rest of the galaxy has not been so lucky.'

Rho looked stricken, and turned to her fellow replicae as if she were seeking support, and then without warning, a distant explosion sounded out beyond the windows of the citadel, swiftly followed by the rattle of bolter-fire.

'Analysing,' said Nohlan, instantly parsing the noise of the discharge. 'Chemical explosive detonation, high yield, close proximity.'

In the same moment, Sister Lethe's voice issued out from the vox-bead in Miriya's ear. *'Eloheim! We have multiple attackers pushing through the crowd, armed with ballistic weapons and grenades! They're killing anything that moves!'*

'Move to cover and stand by,' Miriya ordered, then turned on the arbiters, her eyes flashing. 'What is the meaning of this?'

That same flash of cold fear she had seen on Rho's face moments before now rushed back as the replicae female shrank back. 'Oh, Imperator, no... It must be the *Red*... But they have been silent for so long...'

'Explain!' barked Miriya, reaching for her pistol. *'Now!'*

'Please, you must believe me, this is not our doing!' Rho grabbed at her in sudden panic, but the Battle Sister shrugged her hand from her arm and turned to her squad, an old and familiar sensation filling the Celestian's thoughts.

'Sister Iona will remain here with the questor.' The pale, morose Sororitas accepted Miriya's command with a nod. 'Cassandra, Portia, remove the peace-bonds from your weapons and come with me.' The women did as they were ordered, ripping off the ceremonial ribbons and racking the slides of their bolters.

Nohlan held up a metal-fingered hand. 'What are you doing?'

She ignored him, tapping the vox-bead to re-open the channel to the rest of her squad. 'Lethe! Assume defensive formation! We're on our way to you.'

'*Aye, Sister,*' came the reply, followed by the crackle of gunfire. A split-second later, the same sound reached the windows of the citadel.

'Stay here,' Miriya told the adept, meeting his gaze. 'And trust nothing.'

By the time the Battle Sisters reached the plaza, the crowd was a seething mass of terror as the Hollosi citizens crushed each other in their heedless attempts to flee. Miriya sprinted out from an ornate arcade and across the glittering marble, her steel boots clattering across the stone. Smoke and blood wafted on the breeze.

She heard Lethe calling out orders to Isabel. '*Target to your right, moving behind the pergola!*' The other Battle Sister shifted up ahead and let off a burst of bolter fire; Miriya could not see the target from where she was, but she heard it die with a feral screech.

Lethe was in cover behind the shuttle, furiously reloading her weapon. 'In Katherine's name, what are these things?'

'Report!' snapped Miriya, as she slid in next to her.

'They came out of nowhere,' said Lethe. 'One moment, all was serene. The next, the citizens were like panicked cattle!'

'What are we dealing with?'

Lethe eyed her. 'Combat replicae. Or something very similar.'

'More clone-forms?' Miriya peered out from behind the cover of the shuttle and got her first clear look at the attackers.

There were a dozen of them, moving with incredible speed across the plaza, dodging from side to side to avoid the shots from the Battle Sisters. They resembled Rho and the other clones, but these new beings were wild and savage. An aura of feral brutality and vicious, animal anger spread before them. Their flesh was a livid crimson the colour of blood.

'Rho... She called them the *Red*...'

'They're like beasts!' spat Lethe, firing towards the advancing creatures. 'They fight with fury and no heed to danger!'

With each passing second, the attackers were closing in, and the turmoil of screaming and gunfire grew louder and louder. 'So much for promises of a world at peace,' Miriya said bitterly. Her next act was now cast in stone, and she called out over the vox-net. '*Sororitas*! In the Emperor's name, destroy them!'

The Celestians were no strangers to conflict, and as one they laid a wall of shots upon the enemy. Miriya aimed her plasma pistol and sent sun-bright streaks of burning death into the advancing ranks.

Crimson-skinned replicae became shrieking torches, burning to ruin on the marble square. But their comrades did not falter and did not slow, still coming onwards, hurling grenades and firing blindly with heavy stub-guns. Luckless civilians caught in their path went down, lives brutally snuffed out in moments.

'We can't break the line!' Lethe spat out a gutter curse. 'They keep coming!'

Miriya saw movement behind her and realised that Rho had followed them out to the plaza. The pale female cowered behind a planter, her face a picture of raw fear. Miriya dashed across the space between them and grabbed her by the shoulder. 'Where are your soldiers?' she demanded. 'These creatures will overwhelm us if your kind do not fight!'

'No.' Rho shook her head. 'No. We cannot. We reject warfare!'

The idea that a sentient being would rather embrace inaction and certain death than fight to survive was anathema to Miriya's character. 'You were born a clone-warrior!' She shook Rho hard. 'That is your template, your birth right! You have the skills! Pick up a weapon and defend yourself!'

'*No!*' For a brief instant, Miriya saw anger in Rho's eyes, but then it was gone again, and she cowered as shots whined off the stonework around them.

'More of them coming in!' called Lethe. 'We can't take them all!'

'Damn this...' Miriya released her grip on Rho and turned her back on the clone. Lethe was right. As formidable as the Sisters of Battle were, the numbers of the attackers were swelling as more of them poured into the plaza from the surrounding gardens. The Celestians were just one squad, and if the tide of this fight did not turn now, they would be overrun.

A change in tactics was required.

'Lethe!' Miriya marshalled her strength. 'Cover me!' The Celestian broke into a sprint and raced across the plaza to the rear of the shuttle, stubber shells cracking at her heels every step of the way, bolter rounds flashing back the other way as her Sisters met the enemy approach.

She threw herself up the ramp of the shuttle and vanished inside, and when Miriya emerged from the Arvus once more, her plasma pistol was holstered. In her hands, she cradled the hissing bulk of an Inferus Infinitas-pattern heavy flamer drawn from the vessel's weapons locker.

Filling her lungs with air, she let out a furious battle cry that carried across the plaza and echoed off the walls of the citadel. *'With Faith and Fire!'*

Her finger tightened on the igniter, and jets of burning liquid promethium lashed out like flaming whips, snaking across the enemy advance and stopping it dead. Miriya's squad-mates formed up behind her and followed their commander's lead.

'It's working!' shouted Lethe. 'They're falling back!'

The searing heat washed over Miriya's face as she advanced. 'Drive them into the ground, Sisters! Show them the folly of their heresy!'

Before the cleansing flame, the enemy line fell in disarray. Leaving the corpses of their dead behind, the red-skinned attackers broke apart and scattered, some fleeing down hatches into the sewers, others disappearing across the ruined gardens and into smoky side streets.

* * *

'You... You killed so many of them...' Rho staggered through the coils of haze wreathing the bodies of the dead, aghast at the carnage. In the aftermath of the brutal, bloody fight, the opulent plaza resembled a war grave, littered with the dead and the dying.

'We *stopped* them,' Miriya corrected. 'Now you will tell me what they were! You lied to me. You said Hollos was at peace.'

'It is! We are!' Rho tried to recover her composure, but failed. 'The Red... They're not like the rest of us.'

'You will explain it to me,' Miriya's voice was iron hard.

Rho seemed to wilt before her eyes and she looked at the ground, nodding once.

'Sister Miriya.' She turned as Lethe approached, reloading her bolter. 'It's over. The enemy have fled.'

'Status of the squad?' asked Miriya.

Lethe jerked a thumb over her shoulder. 'Cassandra was injured, but her armour took the brunt of the damage. She remains combat-ready. Other wounds were minor and of no concern. The total of civilian dead is still incomplete, but it is estimated to be in the hundreds. We tally nineteen replicae corpses. Questor Nohlan came down from the citadel... He insisted on examining them.'

'Very well.' Miriya sensed there was more Lethe wanted to say, and inclined her head, giving her permission to continue.

'I have contacted the *Coronus*,' added the other woman. 'They stand ready to deploy additional squads to the surface at your command.'

At first glance, it seemed like the right thing to do. Representatives of the Imperium of Man had been threatened, and the standard response would be to answer that attack with the maximum available force. But there were still too many variables at play here, still too many questions unanswered. 'Not yet,' she told her. 'We did not come here to invade this world, Lethe.'

Lethe scowled. 'They attacked us. We are the scions of the Imperial church on this world. That makes it an act of Holy War.'

'Perhaps,' she admitted. 'But I will not respond in kind without an understanding of the situation. Too many conflicts have begun that way.'

Lethe shot a look at the replicae, who stood by silent and unmoving. 'The truth is being kept from us. That's reason enough. There is more than meets the eye at work here.'

'All the more reason for the full truth to be uncovered.' Before her second-in-command could speak further to the matter, Miriya gave out her orders. 'Carry on here. I will return to the citadel and determine our next course of action.'

'As you command,' snapped Lethe, giving Rho one last lingering glare before stalking away.

'She looks at me as if she wishes to kill me,' the clone said softly.

Miriya rounded on her. 'Give me a reason she should not, Rho. Those beings who attacked us, they were replicae. Like you.'

'I told you, they are not like me! The Red are... *throwbacks*. They are an aberration among our kind, violent and consumed by destructive emotions. We have tried to re-educate them, rehabilitate them... But we cannot. Nothing works. They are... irredeemable.' Slowly, reluctantly, Rho explained that in every generation of clones, some would exhibit the reddening of their flesh and a marked predilection for aggression and violence. The council, reluctant to cull what they considered to be innocent beings with no control over their baser natures, exiled the Red to an outlying island continent. But somehow, they returned to plague the peaceful cities of Hollos.

'You kept this from us,' said Miriya. 'How can we trust anything you say now?'

'You must understand,' insisted Rho, 'the Red are an isolated problem. They are not responsible for what they do.'

Miriya considered that. 'Like a rabid animal?'

'Yes.'

She tapped the butt of her plasma pistol. 'Where I come from, violent beasts are put down, not given free reign to go where they wish! How often do these attacks occur?'

'Rarely.' Rho's answer was too quick, too practised. After a moment, she went on. 'Not as rarely as they used to be, I must admit. But they are like tempests, Sister Miriya. They come and we weather them, and they pass. We endure. We rebuild–'

Miriya nodded towards the shrouded corpses being gathered up from the bloodied grassland of the ornamental gardens. 'Tell that to your people who died today.' A weary sigh escaped her. 'I will speak with your arbiters. And then I must confer with my ship.'

'What are you going to do?' Rho could not keep the fear from her words.

'That remains to be seen,' she replied. But in truth, the Celestian knew that her options were already beginning to narrow.

She strode back into the council chamber, her temper only held in check by the oath to this duty she had sworn to Prioress Lydia, but the corridors of the citadel were in disarray, the servants and the counsellors scattered and missing, frightened by the massed assault on their most sacred building. It seemed that they had retreated to safe havens and left the Sororitas to oppose the Red alone. Only Rho had shown any courage to join them and look the assault in the eye.

Miriya cast around, frowning. Were these people so weak that they fled at the first sign of battle? How had they managed to survive in a universe as hostile as this one? There was no place for the pacifist way in Miriya's world. There was only war, and the need to fight to live.

'Arbiters!' she called out across the empty chamber. 'Where are you? I would speak with–'

The words died in her throat. The Battle Sister heard the clumsy, inexpert approach, a sudden and furtive movement nearby, boots scraping on flagstones. Someone was attempting to flank her, figures moving unseen in the shadows beyond the light thrown from the tall stained-glassaic windows that dominated the chamber. She relied on instinct, turning as the inevitable attack came.

Darts arrowed from the depths of the shadows, whistling through the air like lazy hornets. The first flew wide as she dodged away, but the second came at her from another direction and she was distracted for long enough, for one tiny moment. Enough for the dart to bury itself in the bare flesh of her neck. Gasping as the chilling flood of a neurotoxin flashed through her veins, Miriya seized the dart and yanked it out, tossing it away.

'Who... dares...?' she snarled, but her throat was closing up and it was a monumental effort just to speak. The rush of blood in her ears rose to a thunder. Even as she pulled her plasma pistol, the Celestian felt the tranquilising agent passing into every part of her body. Her hands felt heavy and numb.

The Battle Sister resisted, fighting against the void coiling at the edges of her vision, cursing her assailant through gritted teeth. 'Damn... you...'

'Shoot her again, you fools!' The voice was distant and distorted, but she knew it. She had heard it before, in this very room...

More buzzing shots lanced into her and she gave a strangled cry, stumbling to the ground. Miriya fell, cursing herself as her body refused to answer her commands. The pistol was dead weight in her hands, her legs turning to water. The glittering tiles of the council chamber floor rose up to meet her, turning black and dark, opening up to swallow her whole.

She rose back to wakefulness with a choking gasp.

Miriya could not reckon the passing of time. It seemed like an instant, but it could have been days. The Battle Sister awoke, resting in a heavy wooden chair, and found her armour untouched but her pistol absent from its holster. She had expected restraints, but there were none.

Her eyes adjusted to the dimness. Her new surroundings were a cellar of some sort, lit by dull bio-lumes, damp and chilly. And there, standing before her in a loose group, were five hooded figures in heavy cloaks.

One of them detached from the group and came forward, rolling back the hood to reveal the face beneath. 'Sister Miriya,' began Arbiter Ahven, 'I must apologise for–'

The Celestian did not let her finish. The grave mistake these fools had made was now fully revealed to them as Miriya became a blur of black and crimson armour, crossing the chamber in the blinking of an eye. Her gauntlet clamped about the throat of the other woman and she lifted her off her feet, scattering the rest of the group.

Miriya slammed her captor into the stone wall and hissed in fury. 'You have attacked the God-Emperor's Sororitas! You will answer for that!'

The other hooded figures drew weapons – common blades and stubber guns – but Ahven desperately waved them away, gasping for air. 'No! No! Stop! Miriya, *please*! Let me explain!'

It was a long moment before the Battle Sister released her grip and the arbiter dropped to the floor. 'Speak,' she said coldly.

'I... I am sorry,' Ahven managed, recovering as her cohorts helped her to her feet. 'I deserved that. But you must understand, I had no choice...'

'I have had my fill of this world's lies and half-truths.' Miriya's reply was icy. 'You will explain yourself to me *now*, or I swear by dawn Hollos will be *ashes*.'

The threat hung in the dank air between them, and no one doubted that it was genuine. 'I could not take the chance you would refuse me. This was the only way to be sure we could speak alone.' She massaged her bruised throat and coughed. 'We are in the sewers beneath the citadel. This is the only place where we can meet without fear of being overheard by the replicae.' At a nod from Ahven, the rest of the group revealed their faces. They were all normal humans. 'You have seen a glimpse of our society,' she went on. 'You see how the replicae have made themselves the supreme power on our planet. They allow two of us to sit on their precious council, but they ignore everything we say! They know better than we natural-borns! They are superior!' She turned her head and spat in disgust. 'But there are many who reject their rule.'

Miriya scanned the faces of the others in her group as they nodded and mutter their agreement with Ahven's words. 'And you speak for them?'

The arbiter nodded. 'In secret, I lead a sect who oppose Rho and her vat-bred freaks. We have been working against them for years, waiting for the opportunity... And now you are here!' She exchanged a look with her co-conspirators. 'It is time. The stars are right.'

'What are you saying, Ahven?' Miriya found her plasma pistol sitting undamaged atop a low wall and returned it to her holster. 'That you wish the support of the Imperium in your plans for a coup?'

'Will you stand with us?' Ahven took a step towards her, her tone shifting towards entreaty. 'Human and human against synthetic? You have seen them! Weak-willed and pathetic, working against the order of things. They have no right to rule us! The replicae are supposed to be our servants, not our masters!'

'On that point, I may agree,' allowed the Battle Sister. 'And what of these... Red? Did you summon them to attack the plaza today?'

Ahven stiffened, becoming defensive. 'In every revolution blood must be spilled. The Red are what the replicae should be, slave-warriors. But today's attack was not directed against you!'

Miriya eyed her. 'You bring me here by force. You attack civilians and cause bloodshed. And now you dare to petition my church for help?'

When Ahven spoke again, her eyes were alight with a passion. 'I remember the words of the Codex Imperialis! The words of the Ecclesiarchy, left behind two millennia ago! *No heretic, no mutant, no xenos can be suffered to live!* What are these replicae if not inhuman?'

The ferocity of the arbiter's words gave Miriya pause. 'I will consider your request,' she said after a long moment.

* * *

Night had fallen across the capital as Miriya returned to the plaza before the citadel, and she sought out Questor Nohlan, picking her way through the rubble and the churned earth of destroyed flowerbeds.

Beneath a floating lumoglobe, the adept was bent over the burned remains of one of the Red, his machine-enhanced hands and a trio of mechanical limbs prodding and poking at the innards of the attacker. He seemed quite enthused by his grisly work, oblivious of the stark horror before him. With the bright, buzzing edge of a laser scalpel, Nohlan painstakingly flensed strips of skin from the dead replicae, all the while talking to himself in quiet, sing-song tones. 'Processing. Oh, how interesting... Processing.' He froze mid-action as Miriya came into the glow from the lume and offered her something approximating a smile. 'Sister Miriya! You've been off the vox for hours, where were you? Sister Lethe was quite perturbed.'

'It is of no consequence,' she told him, deflecting the question. 'Have these corpses provided you with any new information?'

'Oh, indeed...' His head bobbed. 'The locals were reluctant to let me examine them, but Sister Iona can be quite persuasive. Processing.'

'What have you learned?' She came closer, eyeing the corpse with mild disgust.

'Cross-referencing. Original files from Mechanicum colony Hollos Seven-Nine-Seven. I have formed a hypothesis about the variant strains of replicae we have seen here. The Red and the, uh, others.' He cocked his head. 'You see, the brain tissue of the violent clones shows evidence of a distinct neuro-chemical signature not present in the tissue of Rho and her kind.

'You performed an autopsy on one of the... normal replicae as well?'

He nodded. 'I did it without informing the locals. I thought it best not to ask permission. I imagine they would have been opposed to the idea,' Nohlan added airily.

'Quite.' Miriya put aside the adept's cavalier attitude to the sanctity of the dead for a moment and went on. 'So, this chemical... Is it artificial? A virus?'

'Negative. Sister Miriya, it is the *absence* of the chemical that is artificial.'

She glanced around, to be certain that none of the replicae were within earshot of their conversation. 'What are you saying? That Rho and her kind have been biologically altered in some fashion?'

'Remnants of the original gene-template for the replicae from the Hollos Seven-Nine-Seven remain in my databanks,' explained the adept. 'They show the missing neuro-chemical as a 'bio-trigger'. A genetic control mechanism implanted by their creators, if you will.'

'Implanted by the Imperium,' Miriya corrected.

'Affirmative. But clones like Rho and the others we have met in the city, those without the bio-trigger, have free will. I believe they have *deliberately* re-engineered themselves to switch off the production of the neuro-chemical. They... evolved.'

Nohlan's theory, if it were true, suggested a heretical act that would incur grave consequences. 'How could that happen, unless they defied the orders of the gene-smiths who made them? Unless the slaves defied their rightful masters?'

'There is another possibility,' offered the adept. 'It may have occurred naturally, without external interference.' He spread his machine-hands. 'Perhaps it is the will of the God-Emperor? Remember, not all of the replicae have been granted this... *gift*.'

'A gift, or a curse?' She wondered aloud. 'No. I do not see His hand in this, questor. I see division and violence on the horizon. This planet is on the verge of a revolution. And I must decide if I am to stop it, or allow Hollos to be engulfed by war.'

It was Nohlan's turn to be a step behind. 'What are you saying, Sister Miriya?'

'Prepare for greater violence,' she told him. 'No matter what happens, I fear it is inevitable.'

A new dawn rose, and it was as if the attack had never occurred. Overnight, human workers had washed away all traces of spilled blood and mended every last broken stone, until the plaza was spotless.

Miriya led her Battle Sisters to the council chamber, where Rho and the others were waiting. For a moment, Miriya's gaze dwelled on Arbiter Ahven, but the other woman showed no reaction to her scrutiny. The Celestian moved to stand in the centre of the room, the squad in guardian stances and Nohlan at her side. After the events of the previous day, the peace-bonds on their weapons had not been restored.

Rho stood up and bowed to the room. 'Honoured representatives of the Imperial church. You have our deepest regrets. We hoped that you would not be touched by our internal social problems. That you were dragged into such a lamentable incident shames all of Hollos. We beseech you and ask that you understand we meant no artifice in this matter. The... embarrassment of the Red is a problem we are working to bring to an end. We hope it will not sour your feelings towards our world.'

Miriya gave a nod, her expression cold and steady. 'I understand. Know this, people of Hollos. The Imperial church will welcome you back to the rule of Holy Terra.' There was a murmur of approval from the council, but they fell silent once more as the Celestian continued to speak. 'I have communicated via astropathic signal to my superiors regarding the situation on this world. The ships of the Ministorum are already on their way. But be clear, there will be changes ahead. For many of you, the... re-integration with the Imperium will be difficult.' The mood of the room changed, as her words made the council become wary.

'What changes do you refer to, Sister Miriya?' said Rho.

Miriya met the gaze of the arbiter, knowing that her next words would change the fate of a world forever. 'It is with regret I must inform you that all replicae on Hollos will fall under the jurisdiction of the magos biologis, the gene-smiths of the Adeptus Mechanicus.'

The clone-beings on the council reacted with open shock and dismay. Rho raised a hand to quiet them. 'If you please, what does that mean, exactly?'

'Confirming,' noted Nohlan. 'As artificially created life forms, clones have no rights to citizenship in the Imperium of Mankind.'

A bleak silence fell in the wake of the adept's words, and when Rho finally broke it, it was with anger. 'You cannot expect us to accept that! We, who have protected this planet for twenty of your lifetimes? We, who made Hollos a near-utopia?' Her pale face darkened to a rosy shade. 'How dare you make such demands?'

'It is as the Imperial church has decreed,' she said sadly.

Miriya saw a smile bloom on Ahven's face, and the human arbiter suddenly rushed to her feet, waving Rho aside. 'Be silent, vat-born,' she snapped. 'Your weakling reign is at an end, as it should be!'

All too soon, Miriya realised that she had handed the woman exactly what she wanted. 'Ahven, no! You will not be allowed to–'

But the arbiter ignored her, instead snarling into a vox-bead hidden in her collar. 'Now! The time is *now*! Begin the revolt! The Red Sect rises this day!'

'What are you doing?' Rho reached out a hand to the other arbiter. 'Ahven, please...'

'I told you to be silent!' Ahven spat the words at the replicae and then struck her across the face with a vicious backhand blow. Beyond the smack of flesh on flesh, there came another sound, the same that had rocked the citadel only hours ago. The distant rumble of explosions and the chatter of gunfire. Ahven tore a weapon from the folds of her robes, and from the corridors leading into the chamber came dozens of humans wearing clothes streaked with blood-red dye.

The Battle Sisters instinctively raised their weapons, drawing into a combat wheel formation, but Miriya stepped away, approaching the council. 'Stay your hands,' she demanded. 'I did not do this for you, Ahven! I gave this decree to stop any further bloodshed!'

'It's too late for that!' Ahven shook her head, aiming her gun in Rho's direction. 'Today, we show our true colours. We show our secret sign, hidden for so long...' The arbiter tore open her tunic, bearing her breast, and her action was mirrored by her followers. 'We show our unity!'

What the Celestian saw branded into their flesh made her blood chill. Each of the Red Sect bore a mark – a disc and a line bisecting two arcs. It was a symbol of the Ruinous Powers, of Chaos itself.

Nohlan recoiled from the sight as if he had been physically struck. 'The mark of the daemon Tzeench!' It cost him just to say the name of the horror. 'Terra protect us, they are a Cult of Change!'

The Sororitas raised brought their weapons to bear, but Ahven seemed shocked that fellow humans would threaten her. 'What are you doing? We are the same! We have followed the words of the old books since before the fall of the veil! We have been loyal! Why do you turn against us?'

'Because you are tainted.' The words were ashes in Miriya's mouth. Her thoughts raced as she took aim with her plasma pistol. What she had feared all along was so. During its great isolation, Hollos had been tainted by the touch of the Dark Gods lurking in the warp, so deeply and so insidiously that those perverted by it were not even aware that they had been kneeling before a corrupting power.

'Why do you take *their* side, Miriya?' Ahven slammed her fist against her chest. 'We are both human! The clones are the enemy, they are the ones who are unclean and tainted! The Red are the way of new change! We are the secret truth!'

'No.' Miriya shook her head gravely. 'You have been deceived. You are pawns of Chaos and as the God-Emperor wills, we cannot suffer you to live.'

As the last words left her lips, Lethe and the other Battle Sisters cut down the Red Sect members in a brutal hail of bolter rounds. Ahven and her cohorts died screaming, their blood spattering across the chamber floor.

'The bodies will need to be burned,' said Lethe.

Miriya nodded. 'And more besides.'

'They... They're all dead...' Rho's delicate hands flew to cover her mouth.

'Not yet,' said Nohlan. 'Look, out in the streets.' He pointed towards the glassaic windows, where flashes of yellow light marked the flares of gun muzzles. The anarchy of the battle in the courtyard was dwarfed by the conflict now erupting in the city. Staring down, Miriya glimpsed dozens of the feral replicae the Battle Sisters had faced before, laying waste beyond the plaza, and killing without pause.

Down in the vast courtyard, the carnage was horrific to behold. The numbers of the Red dwarfed those that had attacked the previous day, with legions of them running riot through the streets, an army of cloned berserkers emerging from the underground sewer system where Ahven's cult had been containing them in preparation for this day.

Miriya watched them killing their way through the civilian populace, human and replicae alike. It was less a battle, more a cull, and the grim mathematics of war were abundantly clear to her. 'We cannot fight such numbers.'

At her side, Lethe gave a nod of agreement. 'Aye, Eloheim. Five squads more, even ten would be hard-pressed to match them.' She looked up into the sky. 'So, then. The ship. If we have the *Coronus* deploy their lance cannons from orbit, the gunners could wipe out the insurgents within moments. Contain this before it spreads beyond the city limits.'

'The collateral damage would be immense. Hundreds of thousands of civilians dead. And the capital would be nothing but a smoking crater.' She shook her head. 'No, Sister. There's another way.' Miriya turned to Rho. Along with the other council members, she had followed them down into the plaza to witness the bloody destruction of their metropolis. 'I will ask once again, replicae,' she began. 'Help us to fight these creatures. You are gene-engineered with superior strength, superior speed! If you fight back, you can defeat your savage equivalents... If you will not take up arms and defend your world, I will be forced to destroy it!'

Once more, Rho shook her head. '*No*! We have foresworn conflict. We excised the ability to kill from ourselves, forever. We are passive... Even if we wished to do so, the ability to take life is no longer a part of us!'

Nohlan gave the clone a measured look. 'Error,' he said. 'That statement is incorrect.' The adept gestured with a cyber-limb. 'I have computed the nature of the... mutation that separates the Red strain of the replicae from Rho and her kind... Those who consider themselves pacifists. In the past, they changed themselves to expunge their warrior natures. Error. They have only *deactivated* that part of themselves. It still remains.'

Rho blinked, not comprehending his meaning. 'That was all so long ago, before I was decanted...'

'I can undo the alteration,' Nohlan explained. 'It is, in fact, a very simple task to accomplish. An aerosolised viral form of the correct neuro-chemical, synthesised by my internal bio-fac module.' He presented a nozzle at the tip of his cyber-limb, one of a dozen micro-tools built into his augmetic form. His clicking lens-eyes studied Rho sadly. 'It will regress all of them to their default warrior-helot nature.'

The naked shock on Rho's face was an awful sight on so gentle an aspect. 'God-Emperor, no! You would rob us of our reason, our very freedom?'

'You don't have any freedom,' Lethe said grimly. 'You are slaves. That's how you were made.'

With an expression of pure, undiluted horror, Rho turned to Miriya, pleading with her. 'Sister, please! Tell me you will not do this!'

It took an effort of will to look away from her. 'How would it work, questor?'

'Once released, it will reproduce very rapidly, moving from clone to clone.' Nohlan's limbs whirred as he drew them back. 'Infecting them. Reactivating the dormant neural links. Effect would be near-instantaneous. All replicae would revert to type. All humans would be unaffected.' He paused. 'But you must understand, Sister Celestian, this is a grave act. It is irreversible. Once implemented, all that the altered replicae are would be lost to them. Memories, personality, self... *Erased.*'

'In the name of Holy Terra,' Rho cried, her panic rising. 'I beg of you! Do not consider this!' She tried to reach out for Miriya, but Isabel and Cassandra moved to block her way.

'I will not let a world fall to the taint of Chaos.' Miriya turned back to look Rho in the eye. 'Not one single world. Never, as long as I draw breath. If I must sacrifice some to save others... I will do whatever is required to retain the sanctity of church and Imperium.' She shut away the sorrow that threatened to rise in her chest before it could fully form.

'You... have destroyed us,' wept Rho.

'Do it,' Miriya told the adept.

Nohlan gave a curt, solemn nod. 'As you command, Sister Celestian.'

The scream that tore from Rho's lips was the agony of a soul thrown into the darkest reaches of torment, drowned out for a moment by the shrieking hiss of the neuro-chemical dispersing from the adept's bio-fabricator. Rho and the other replicae around them moaned and wept, collapsing to the ground. It was a sickening sight. But then an eerie silence descended on them as their cries died off to nothing.

The change flooded over the replicae like a storm cloud blotting out the sun. Miriya watched Rho's pale flesh grow darker, becoming a deep, sullen crimson.

'Throne and Blood,' whispered Lethe. 'It's working. All of them, they're becoming like the others...'

Miriya approached Rho as she rose shakily to her feet once more. Her eyes were dull and lifeless now, the spark of intelligence that had animated them before sniffed out. 'Rho. Do you hear me?'

'I hear you.' The reply was hollow and distant, like the rote speech of a machine-vox.

Nohlan studied Rho carefully, then nodded once. 'Confirmed. Balance is restored. The pacifist replicae are as they once were. Ready for your battle orders.'

'Rho. Heed me.' Miriya pointed down towards the lower city, where the turmoil was in full force. 'Gather your kindred and take weapons. Destroy the Red Sect and the clones they control.'

'As you command.' They were the last words she would ever say to Miriya. Without pause or hesitation, Rho and the other replicae stormed across the plaza in the direction of the conflict. They moved as automatons, fast and lethal, striding into battle in silent formation.

'Now we have a chance to save this planet,' said Lethe. 'In an hour, we'll have an army of them.'

'And what has it cost?' Miriya severed the treacherous train of thought that would lead her toward doubt and sadness with a near-physical effort. She drew her plasma pistol and pointed after the replicae. 'Sisters! Follow them in!' Miriya broke into a run, blotting out all other concerns for the glory and the fire of battle. It was all that mattered; it was all she was.

She let out a shout that rang across the conflict unfolding before her. 'Ave Imperator!'

In the aftermath, there finally came a moment for her to reflect.

From the observation gallery of the *Coronus*, Sister Miriya watched the planet turn beneath her feet. Lines of black strayed across the surface of Hollos, the wind carrying plumes of smoke from the burning capital and out across the plains.

The Celestian saw shuttles passing back and forth through the atmosphere, and sharing the warship's high orbit, the massive slab-sided forms of other Imperial vessels drifted like great iron monoliths. Summoned by Questor Nohlan, the Adeptus Mechanicus had arrived in force. Even now they were down there, gathering up every last clone that had survived the uprising, plundering all remnants of the lost technology that had created them.

And with every cargo that left the planet, Ministorum preachers and iterators were being deposited in their place. The confessors and the firebrand priests of the Imperial church would take the reins of Hollos and fill the gap left by the planet's ruling council. With their words and deeds, in a few years the locals would forget their former leaders and embrace the same monumental, unbending worship that lived in the chapels of thousands of worlds.

Sister Miriya's mission was complete. The lost had been returned to the fold. The price of it no longer mattered. 'It is done,' she said to herself, recalling an ancient catechism in High Gothic. '*Omnis Vestri Substructio. Es Servus, Ad Nobis.*'

She did not turn as mechanical footsteps approached from behind her. At length, Questor Nohlan spoke. 'I believe we destroyed something unique on this world, Sister Celestian. It troubles me.'

'We did it to save them,' she replied. 'For church and Imperium.'

'Fortunate for us, that we have such ironclad justification to absolve all doubts,' he noted. 'If we did not... One might go quite mad.'

She turned to the adept, her eyes dark and weary with the weight of what she had done. 'They were not human, and only the God-Emperor has the divine right to create new life. They allowed Chaos to take root among them during their stewardship. These are all reasons enough.'

'Are you certain?' Nohlan asked gently. 'We have taken vital, intelligent beings, and reduced them to little more than walking weapons. Is that right?'

'Rho said they wanted to act in the Emperor's name. To serve His will.' She turned her back on the adept and once again allowed her gaze to be drawn down to the newly scarred planet below. 'And now they shall, in the manner they were created for.' She found a transport ship leaving the atmosphere, a cargo carrier taking whatever was left of Rho's kind so they might be studied, understood, dissected and replicated, all in the name of the God-Emperor's eternal wars.

'In battle,' said the Sororitas. '*Unto death.*'

FAITH & FIRE

CHAPTER ONE

From his high vantage point, the Emperor of Mankind looked down upon Miriya where she knelt. His unchanging gaze took in all of her, the woman's bowed form shrouded in blood-coloured robes. In places, armour dark as obsidian emerged from the folds of the crimson cloth. It framed her against the tan stonework of the chapel floor. She was defined by the light that reflected upon her from the Emperor's eternal visage; all that she was, she was only by His decree.

Miriya's lips moved in whispers. The Litany of Divine Guidance spilled from her in a cascading hush. The words were such a part of her that they came as quickly and effortlessly as breathing. As the climax of the declaration came, she felt a warm core of righteousness establish itself in her heart, as it always did, as it always had since the day she had discarded her noviciate cloak and taken the oath.

She allowed herself to look up at Him. Miriya granted herself this small gesture as a reward. Her gaze travelled up the altar, drinking in the majesty of the towering golden idol. The Emperor watched her over folded arms, across the inverted hilt of a great burning sword. At His left shoulder stood Saint Celestine, her hands cupped to hold two stone doves as if she were offering them up. At His right was Saint

Katherine, the Daughter of the Emperor who had founded the order that Miriya now served.

She lingered on Katherine's face for a moment: the statue's hair fell down over her temple and across the fleur-de-lys carved beneath her left eye. Miriya unconsciously brushed her black tresses back over her ear, revealing her own fleur tattoo in dark red ink.

The armour the stone saint wore differed from Miriya's in form but not function. Katherine was clad in an ancient type of wargear, and she bore the symbol of a burning heart where Miriya wore a holy cross crested with a skull. When the saint had been mistress of her sect, they had been known as the Order of the Fiery Heart – but that had been decades before Katherine's brutal ending on Mnestteus. Since that date, for over two millennia they had called themselves the Order of Our Martyred Lady. It was part of a legacy of duty to the Emperor that Sister Miriya of the Adepta Sororitas had been fortunate to continue.

With that thought, she looked upon the effigy of Him. She met the stone eyes and imagined that on far distant Terra, the Lord of Humanity was granting her some infinitely small fraction of His divine attention, willing her to carry out her latest mission with His blessing. Miriya's hands came to her chest and crossed one another, making the sign of the Imperial aquila.

'In Your name,' she said aloud. 'In service to Your Light, grant me guidance and strength. Let me know the witch and the heretic, show them to me.' She bowed once again. 'Let me do Your bidding and rid the galaxy of man's foe.'

Miriya drew herself up from where she knelt and moved to the font servitor, presenting the slave-thing with her ornate plasma pistol. The hybrid produced a brass cup apparatus in place of a hand and let a brief mist of holy water sprinkle over the weapon. Tapes of sanctified parchment stuttered from its lipless mouth with metallic ticks of sound.

She turned away, and there in the shadows was Sister Iona. Silent, morose Iona, the patterned hood of her red robe forever deepening the hollows of her eyes. Some of the Battle Sisters disliked the woman. Iona rarely showed emotion, never allowed herself to cry out in pain when combat brought her wounds, never raised her voice in joyous elation during the daily hymnals. Many considered her flawed, her mind so cold that it was little more than the demi-machine inside the skull of the servitor at the font. Miriya had once sent two novice girls to chastisement for daring to voice such thoughts aloud. But those who said these things did not know Iona's true worth. She was as devout a Sororitas as any other, and if her manner made some Sister Superiors reluctant to have her in their units, then so be it. Their loss was Miriya's gain.

'Iona,' she said, approaching. 'Speak to me.'

'It is time, Sister,' said the other woman, her milk-pale face set in a frown. 'The witch ship comes.'

In spite of herself, Miriya's hand tensed around the grip of her plasma pistol. She nodded. 'I am prepared.'

Iona returned the gesture. 'As are we all.' The Sister clasped a small fetish in her gloved grip, a silver icon of the Convent Sanctorum's Hallowed Spire on Ophelia VII. The small tell was enough to let Miriya know the woman was concerned.

'I am as troubled as you,' she admitted as they crossed the chancel back towards the steel hatch in the chapel wall.

Iona opened it and they stepped through, emerging into the echoing corridor beyond. Where the stone of the church ended, the iron bones of the starship around it began. Once, the chapel had been earthbound, built into a hill on a world in the Vitus system, now it existed as a strange transplanted organ inside the metal body of the Imperial Naval frigate *Mercutio*.

'This vexes me, Sister Superior,' said Iona, her frown deepening beneath her hood. 'What is our cause if not to take the psyker to task for his witchery, to show the Emperor's displeasure?' She looked as if she wanted to spit. 'That we are called upon to... to *associate* with this mutant is enough to make my stomach turn. There is a part of me that wants to contact the captain and order him to take that abomination from the Emperor's sky.'

Miriya gave her a sharp look. 'Have a care, Sister. You and I may detest these creatures, but in their wisdom, the servants of the Throne see fit to use these pitiful wretches in His name. As much as that may sicken us, we cannot refuse a command that comes from the highest levels of the Ecclesiarchy.'

The answer was not nearly enough to satisfy Iona's disquiet. 'How can such things go on, I ask you? The psyker is our mortal enemy–'

Iona's commander silenced her with a raised hand. 'The *witch* is our enemy, Sister. The psyker is a *tool*. Only the untrained and the wild are a threat to the Imperium.' Miriya's eyes narrowed. 'You have never served as I have, Iona. For two full years I was a warden aboard one of those blighted vessels. On the darkest nights, the things I saw there still haunt me so…' She forced the memories away. 'This is how the God-Emperor tests the faithful, Sister. He shows us our greatest fears and has us overcome them.'

They walked in silence for a few moments before Iona spoke again. 'We are taught in the earliest days of our indoctrination that those cursed with the psychic mark in their blood are living gateways to Chaos. All of them, Sister Superior, not just the ones who eschew the worship of the Golden Throne. One single slip and even the most devout will fall, and open the way to the warp!'

Miriya raised an eyebrow. It was perhaps the most passion she had ever seen the dour woman display. 'That is why we are here. Since the Age of Apostasy, we and all our Sister Sororitas have stood at the gates to hell and barred the witchkin. As the mutant falls, so does the traitor, so does the witch.' She placed a hand on Iona's shoulder. 'Ask yourself this, Sister. Who else could be called forth to accomplish what we shall do today?' Miriya's face split in a wry smile. 'The men of the Imperial Navy or the Guard? They would be dead in moments from the shock. The Adeptus Astartes? Those inhuman brutes willingly welcome psykers into their own ranks.' She shook her head ruefully. 'No, Iona, only we, the Sisters of Battle, can stand sentinel here.' The woman patted her pistol holster. 'And mark me well, if but one of those misbegotten wretches steps out of line, then we will show them the burning purity of our censure.'

The sound of her voice drew the attention of Miriya's squad as she approached. They did not exchange the curt bows or salutes that were mandatory in other Sororitas units. Sister Miriya kept a relaxed hand on her warriors, preferring to keep them sharp in matters of battle prowess rather than parade ground niceties.

'Report,' she demanded.

Her second-in-command Sister Lethe cleared her throat. 'We are ready, Sister Superior, as per your command.'

'Good,' Miriya snapped, forestalling any questions about their orders before they could be uttered. 'This will be a simple matter of boarding the ship and securing the prisoner.'

Lethe threw a look at the other members of the Celestian squad. Usually deployed for front line combat operations, the Celestians were known as the elite troops of the Adepta Sororitas and such a simple duty as a prisoner escort could easily be considered beneath them. Celestians were used to fighting at the heart of heretic confrontations and mutant uprisings, not acting like mere line officer enforcers.

Miriya saw these thoughts in the eyes of Lethe and the other Sisters. She knew the misgivings well, as they had been her own after the orders had first been delivered by astropathic transfer from Canoness Galatea's adjutant. 'Any duty in the Emperor's name is glorious,' she told them, a stern edge to her words, 'and we would do well to remember that.'

'Of course,' said Lethe, her expression contrite. 'We obey.'

'I share your concern.' Miriya admitted, her voice lowered. 'Our squad has never been the most favoured of units–' and with that the other women shared a moment of grim amusement, '–but we will do as we must.'

'There,' Sister Cassandra called, observing through one of the crystalline portholes in the corridor wall. 'I see it!'

Miriya drew closer and peered through the thick lens. For a moment, she thought her Battle Sister had been mistaken, but then she realised that the darkness she saw beyond the hull of the *Mercutio* was not the void of interstellar space at all, but the flank of another craft. It gave off no light, showed no signals or pennants. Only the faint glow of the frigate's own portholes and beacons illuminated it – and then, not the whole vessel but only thin slivers of it caught in the radiance.

'A Black Ship,' breathed Iona. 'Emperor protect us.'

In two by two overwatch formation, their bolters at the ready, Miriya's squad made their way up the corded flex-tube that had extended itself from one of the *Mercutio*'s outer airlocks. At their head, the Sister Superior walked with her own weapon holstered, but her open hand lay flat atop the knurled wood grip. The memories spiked her thoughts again, taking her back to the first time she had stepped into the dark iron heart of an Adeptus Astra Telepathica vessel.

No one knew how many craft there were in the fleets of the Black Ships. Some spoke of a secret base on Terra, sending out droves of ebon vessels to scour the galaxy for psykers. Others said that the ships worked in isolation from one another, venturing back and forth under psychic directives sent by the Emperor himself. Miriya did not know the truth, and she did not want to.

Whenever a potent psyker was discovered, the Black Ships would come for them. Some, those with pure hearts and wills strong enough to survive the tests the adepts forced upon them, might live to become servants to the Inquisition or the astropathic colleges. Most would be put to death in one manner or another, or granted in sacrifice to the Emperor so that he might keep alight the great psychic beacon of the Astronomicon.

The Battle Sisters entered an elliptical reception chamber carved from iron and whorled with hexagrammic wards. Strips of biolume cast weak yellow light into the centre of the space and hooded figures lingered at the edges, orbiting the room with silent footsteps. Lethe and the others automatically fell into a combat wheel formation, guns covering every possible angle of attack. Miriya watched the shrouded shapes moving around them. The Adeptus Astra Telepathica had their own operatives but by Imperial edict they were not allowed to serve as warders upon their own vessels; it was too easy for a malignant psyker to coerce another telepath. Instead, Sisters of Battle or Inquisitorial Storm Troopers served in the role of custodian aboard the Black Ships, their adamantine faith protecting them from the predations of the mind-witches they guarded.

Footsteps approached from the gloomy perimeter of the chamber. Her eyes had grown accustomed to the dimness now, and she quickly picked out the figures filing from an iris hatch on the far wall. Two of them were Sister Retributors, armed with heavy multi-meltas, and another a Celestian like herself. The other Battle Sisters wore gunmetal silver armour and white robes, with the sigil of a haloed black skull on their shoulder pauldrons. There were more behind them, but they remained in the shadows for now.

The Celestian saluted Miriya and she returned the gesture. 'Miriya of the Order of Our Martyred Lady. Well met, Sister.'

'Dione of the Order of the Argent Shroud,' said the other woman. 'Well met, Sister.' Miriya was instantly struck by the look of fatigue on Dione's face, the tension etched into the lines about her eyes. Her fellow Sororitas met her gaze and a moment of silent communication passed between them. 'The prisoner is ready. It is my pleasure to have rid of him.' She beckoned forward hooded men and the two Retributors turned their guns to draw a bead on them.

The adepts brought a rack in the shape of a skeletal cube, within which sat a large drum made of green glass. There was a man inside it, naked and pale in the yellow illumination. His head was concealed beneath a metal mask festooned with spikes and probes. 'Torris Vaun,' Miriya said his name, and the masked man twitched a little as if he had heard her. 'A fine catch, Sister Dione.'

'He did not go easily, of that you can be sure. He killed six of my kith before we were able to subdue him.'

'And yet he still draws breath.' Miriya studied the huge jar, aware that the man inside was scrutinising her just as intently with other, preternatural senses. 'Had the choice been mine, this witch would have been shot into the heart of a star.'

Dione managed a stiff nod. 'We are in agreement, Sister. Alas, we must obey the Ministorum's orders. You are to deliver this criminal to Lord Viktor LaHayn at the Noroc Lunar Cathedral on the planet Neva.' A hobbling servitor approached clutching a roll of parchment and a waxy stick of data-sealant. Dione took the paper and made her mark upon it. 'So ordered this day, by the authority of the Ecclesiarchy.'

Miriya followed suit, using the sealant to press her squad commander signet into the document. From behind her, she heard Lethe think aloud.

'He seems such a frail thing. What crime could a man like this commit that would warrant our stewardship?'

Dione took a sharp breath. Clearly she did not allow her troops to speak without permission as Miriya did. 'The six he murdered were only the latest victims of his violence. This man has sown terror and mayhem on a dozen worlds across this sector, all in the name of sating his base appetites. Vaun is an animal, Sister, a ruthless opportunist and a pirate. To him, cruelty is its own reward.' Her face soured. 'It disgusts me to share a room with such an aberrance.'

Miriya shot Lethe a look. 'Your candour is appreciated, Sister Dione. We will ensure the criminal reaches Neva without delay.'

More servitors took up the confinement capsule and marched into the tunnel back to the *Mercutio*. As Vaun was taken away, Dione relaxed a little. 'Lord LaHayn was most insistent that this witch be brought to his court for execution. It is my understanding the honoured deacon called in several favours with the Adeptus Terra to ensure it was so.'

Miriya nodded, recalling the message from Galatea. The Canoness would be waiting in Noroc City for their arrival with the criminal. 'Vaun is a Nevan himself, correct? One might consider it just that he be put to the sword on the soil of his birthworld, given that he created so much anarchy there.' She threw a glance at Lethe, and her second marshalled the rest of the Celestians to flank the prisoner as he vanished into the docking tube. Miriya turned to follow. 'Ave Imperator, Sister.'

Dione's armoured gauntlet clasped Miriya's wrist and held her for a moment. 'Don't underestimate him,' she hissed, her eyes glittering in the murkiness. 'I did, and six good women paid the price.'

'Of course.'

Dione released her grip and faded back into the blackness.

From the rendezvous point, the *Mercutio* came about and made space for the Neva system. The Black Ship vanished from her sensorium screen like a lost dream, so quickly and so completely that it seemed as if the dark vessel had never been there.

The frigate's entry to the empyrean went poorly, and a momentary spasm in the warship's Geller Field killed a handful of deckhands on the gunnery platforms. The crew spoke in hushed tones behind guarded expressions, never within earshot of the Battle Sisters. None of them knew what it was that Miriya's squad had brought back from the Black Ship, but all of them were afraid of it.

Over the days that followed, prayer meetings in the frigate's sparse chapel had a sudden increase in attendance and there were more hymns being played over the vox-nets on the lower decks. Most of the crew had never seen Battle Sisters in the flesh before. In dozens of ports across the sector they had heard the stories about them, just like every other Navy swab. There were things that men of low character would think of women such as these, thoughts that ran the spectrum from lustful fantasy to violent distrust. Some said they lived off the flesh of the males they killed, like a jungle mantis. Others swore they were as much concubines as they were soldiers, able to bring pleasure and damnation to the unwary in equal measure. The crewmen were as scared by the Sororitas as they were fascinated by them, but there were some who watched the women wherever they went, compelled by something deeper and darker.

Lethe glanced up as Miriya entered the cargo bay, stepping past the two gun servitors at the hatch to where she and Cassandra stood on guard by the glass capsule.

'Sister Superior,' she nodded. 'What word from the captain?'

Miriya's frown was answer enough. 'He tells me the Navigator is troubled. The way through the warp is turbulent, but he hopes we will arrive at Neva in a day or so.'

Lethe glanced at the capsule and saw that Cassandra was doing the same.

'The prisoner cannot be the cause,' Miriya answered the unspoken question. 'I was assured the nullifying mask prevents any exercise of witchery.' She tapped her finger on the thick glass wall.

Sister Lethe fingered the silver rosary chain she habitually wore around her neck. She was not convinced. 'All the same, the sooner this voyage concludes, the better. This inaction chafes at my spirit.'

Miriya found her head bobbing in agreement. She and Lethe had served together for the longest span among this squad and often the younger woman was of one mind with her unit's commander. 'We have endured worse, have we not? The ork raids on Jacob's Tower? The Starleaf purge?'

'Aye, but all the same, the waiting gnaws at me.' Lethe looked away. 'Sister Dione was correct. Being in the presence of this criminal makes my very soul feel soiled. I shall need to bathe in sanctified waters after this mission is at an end.'

Cassandra tensed suddenly, and the reaction brought the other women to attention. 'What is it?' Miriya demanded.

The Battle Sister stalked towards a mess of metal girders heaped in one corner of the cargo bay. 'Something...'

Cassandra's hand shot out and she dragged a wriggling shape out of the darkness. 'Intruder!'

The gun servitors reacted, weapons humming up to firing position. Miriya sneered as Cassandra hauled the protesting form of a deckhand into the centre of the bay. 'What in the Emperor's name are you?' she demanded.

'M-Midshipman. Uh. Vorgo. Ma'am.' The man blinked wet, beady eyes. 'Please don't devour me.'

Lethe and Cassandra exchanged glances. 'Devour you?'

Miriya waved them into silence. 'What are you doing here, Midshipman Vorgo? Who sent you?'

'No one!' He became frantic. 'Myself! I just... just wanted to see...' Vorgo extended a finger towards the glass capsule and just barely touched its surface.

The Sister Superior slapped his hand away and he hissed in pain. 'Idiot. I am within my rights to have you thrown into the void for this trespass.'

'I'm sorry. I'm sorry!' Vorgo fell to his knees and made the sign of the aquila. 'Came in through the vent... By the Throne, I was only curious–'

'That will get you killed,' said Lethe, her bolter hovering close to his head.

Miriya stepped away and made a terse wave of her hand. 'Get this fool out of here, then have the engineseers send a helot to seal any vents in this chamber.'

Cassandra hauled the man to his feet and propelled him out of the cargo bay, his protests bubbling up as he went. Lethe followed, hesitating on the cusp of the hatch. 'Sister Superior, shall I remain?'

'No. Have Isabel join me here forthwith.' Vorgo's protesting form between them, the Battle Sisters closed the hatch behind them.

The cargo bay fell quiet. Miriya listened to the faint, irregular tick of metal flexing under the power of the frigate's drives, the humming motors of the servitors, the murmur of bubbles in the tank. A nerve in her jaw twitched. She smelled a thick, greasy tang in the air.

'Alone at last.'

For a moment, she thought she had imagined it. Miriya turned in place, eyeing the two gun slaves. Had one of them spoken? Both of them peered back at her with blank stares and dull, doll-like sensor apertures, lines of drool emerging from their sewn lips. Impossible: whatever intelligence they might have once possessed, the machine-slaves were nothing but automatons now, incapable of such discourse.

'Who addresses me?'

'Here.' The voice was heavy with effort. 'Come here.'

She spun in place. There before her was the capsule, the ebony metal frame about it and the spidery, hooded man-shape adrift within. The Battle Sister drew her pistol and thumbed the activation rune, taking aim at the glass tank. 'Vaun. How dare you touch me with your witchery!'

'Have a care, Sister. It would go badly for you to injure me.' The words came from the air itself, as if the psyker was forcing the atmosphere in the chamber to vibrate like a vox diaphragm.

Miriya's face twisted in revulsion. 'You have made a foolish mistake, criminal. You have tipped your hand.' She crossed to a pod of arcane dials and switches connected to the flank of the glass container. Rods and levers were set at indents indicating the amounts of sense-deadening liquids and contrapsychic drugs filling Vaun's cell. The Battle Sister was no tech-priest, but she had seen confinement frames of this design before. She knew how they worked, pumping neuropathic philtres into the lungs and pores of particularly virulent psykers to stifle their mutant powers. She adjusted the rods and fresh splashes of murky fluid entered the tank. 'This will quiet you.'

'Wait. Stop.' Vaun's body jerked inside the capsule, a pallid hand pressing on the inside of the thick glass. 'You do not understand. I only wanted… to talk.'

Another dial turned and darts of electricity swam into the liquid. 'No one here wants to listen, deviant.'

The words became vague, laboured, fading. 'You… mistaken… will regret…'

Miriya rested the barrel of her plasma weapon on the glass. 'Heed me. If one breath more of speech comes from that cesspool you call a mind before I deliver you to Neva, I will boil you in there like a piece of rotten meat.'

There was no reply. Torris Vaun hung suspended in the foggy solution, slack and waxy.

With a shudder, Sister Miriya muttered the Prayer of Virtue and fingered the purity seals on her armour.

Mercutio fell from the grip of the warp and pushed into the Neva system at full burn, as if the ship itself were desperate to deposit the cargo it carried. As the capital planet orbiting fourth from its yellow-white star swelled in the frigate's hololiths, a small and quiet insurrection began on *Mercutio*'s lower decks.

Men from the labourer gang on the torpedo racks came to the brig where Midshipman Vorgo was confined, and in near silence they murdered the armsmen guarding him. When they freed Vorgo, he didn't thank them. In fact, he said hardly anything but a few clipped sentences, mostly to explain where the gun servitors were placed in the cargo bay, and how the Battle Sisters had behaved towards him.

Vorgo's liberators were not his friends. Some of them were men who had actively disliked him in the past, picking on him in dark corridors and shaking him down for scrip. There was a common denominator between them all, but not one of the men could have spoken of it. Instead, they went their separate ways, each moving with the same hushed purpose and blank expression.

In the generarium where the *Mercutio*'s reactor-spirits coiled inside their cores and bled out their power to the vessel's systems, some of the quiet men walked up to the service gantries over the vast cogwheels of the coolant arrays. They waited for a count of ten decimals from the turning discs and then leapt in groups of three, directly into the teeth of the mechanism. Of course, they were crushed between the cogs, but the pulpy mess of their corpses made the workings slip and seize. In moments, vital flows of chilling fluid were denied to the reactors and alarms began to wail.

Vorgo and the rest of the men went to the cargo decks, meeting more of their number along the way. The new arrivals had cans of chemical unguent taken from the stores of the tech-priests who ministered to the lascannons. Applied in a vacuum, the sluggish fluid could be used to keep the wide glassy lenses of the guns free from micro-meteor scarring and other damage, but on contact with air, the unguent had a far more violent reaction.

After the incident with the midshipman, Sister Miriya had demanded and been given a third gun servitor from the ship's complement to guard the prisoner. Miriya made sure that no member of her squad was ever alone again with Vaun, pairs of the Celestians watching him around the clock in shifts.

Lethe and Iona were holding that duty when the hatch exploded inward. The machine-slaves stumbled about, their autosenses confused by the deafening report of the blast. The muzzles of weapons dallied, unable to find substantial targets to lock on to.

The Battle Sisters had no such limitations. The men that pushed their way in through the ragged hole in the wall, heedless of the burns the hot metal gave them, were met with bolter fire. Lethe's Godwyn-De'az pattern weapon chattered in her gloved grip. The gun's fine tooling of filigree and etching caught the light, catechisms of castigation aglow upon its barrel and breech. Iona's hand flamer growled as puffs of orange fire jetted across the bay, licking at the invaders and immolating them, but there were many, clasping crude clubs and metal cans. She spied Vorgo among them, throwing a jar of thick fluid at a servitor. The glass shattered on the helot's chest and the contents flashed magnesium-white. Plumes of acrid grey smoke spat forth as acids chewed up flesh and implanted machinery alike.

'Sisters, to arms!' Lethe shouted into the vox pickup on

her armour's neck ring, but her voice was drowned out by the keening wail of the *Mercutio*'s general quarters klaxon. She couldn't know it from here, deep inside the hull, but the frigate was starting to list as the heat build-up in the drives baffled the ship's cogitator systems.

A scrum of deckhands piled atop another gun servitor, forcing it down, choking the muzzles of its guns with their chests and hands, muffling shotgun discharges with the meat of their bodies. Lethe's face wrinkled in grim disgust and it was then she noticed that the men did not speak, did not cry out, did not howl in frenzy. Doe-eyed and noiseless, they let themselves die in order to suffocate the prisoner's guardians.

Another chemical detonation signalled the destruction of the last servitor and then the attackers surged forward over the bodies of their crewmates, ten or twenty men moving in one great mass. Sister Lethe saw Iona reel backwards, choking and strangling on clouds of foul air from the makeshift acid bombs. The bleak woman's face sported chemical burns and her eyes were swollen. Unlike the superhuman warriors of the Adeptus Astartes, the Sororitas did not possess the altered physiognomies that could shrug off such assaults.

Lethe's lungs gave up metallic, coppery breaths as the bitter smoke scarred her inside. The silent mob moved to her, letting the Battle Sister waste her ammunition on them. When the magazine in her bolter clicked empty, they pounced and beat her to the ground, the sheer weight of them forcing her to her knees.

Time blurred in stinking lurches of pungent fumes, fogging her brain. The toxic smoke made thinking difficult. Through cracked and seared lips, Lethe mouthed the Litany of Divine Guidance, calling to the Emperor to kindle the faith in her heart.

She forced herself up from the decking. Her gun was missing from her grip and she tried to push the recollection of where it had gone to the front of her mind but the smoke made everything harsh and rough, each breath like razorwool in her throat, each thought as heavy and slow as a glacier.

She focused. Vorgo had loops of cable and odd metal implements in his hands, all of them still wet with greenish liquid where they had been immersed in the tank. He was struggling to breathe, but the midshipman's eyes were distant and watery. Behind the portly deckhand, a naked man was clothing himself in a dirty coverall, running a scarred hand through a fuzz of greying hair. He seemed to sense Lethe's scrutiny and turned about to face her.

'Vaun,' she choked. His reply was a cold smile and a nod at the broken capsule, thick neurochemical soup lapping out of the crack in its flank. Lethe's eyes were gritty and inflamed, making it hard to blink. 'Free...'

'Yes,' His voice was cool and metered. Under the right circumstances, it would have been playful, even seductive. He patted Vorgo on the shoulder and gestured towards the torn doorway. 'Well done.'

'Traitor,' Lethe managed.

Vaun gave a slow shake of the head. 'Be kind, Sister. He doesn't know what he's doing.' A brief smile danced on his lips. 'None of them do.'

'The others will be here soon. You will die.'

'I'll be long gone. These matters were prepared for, Sister.' The psyker crossed to Iona, where the injured woman lay gasping in shallow breaths. Lethe tried to get to her feet and stop him from whatever it was he was doing, but the deckhands punched and kicked her back to the floor, boots ringing off her armour.

Vaun whispered things in Iona's ear, brushing his hands over her blonde hair, and the Battle Sister began to weep brokenly. Vaun stood up and rubbed his hands together, amused with himself.

'You can't escape,' Lethe said thickly. 'It will take more than this to stop us. My Sisters are loyal. They will never let you get away from this vessel!'

He nodded. 'Yes, they are loyal. I saw that.' The criminal took a barbed knife from one of his erstwhile rescuers and came closer. Vorgo and the others held Lethe down in anticipation. 'That kind of loyalty breeds passion. It makes one emotional, prone to recklessness.' He turned the blade in his hand, letting light glint off it. 'Something that I intend to use to my advantage.'

Lethe tried to say something else, but Vaun tipped back her head with one hand, and used the other to bury the knife in her throat.

CHAPTER TWO

The Corolus was a starship in only the very loosest sense of the word. It didn't possess warp drives, it was incapable of navigating across the vast interstellar distances as its larger brethren could. And where the majority of vessels in service to humankind had some degree of artistry, however brutal, to their design, *Corolus* was little more than an agglomeration of spent fuel tanks from sub-orbital landers, lashed together with pipework and luck. Fitted with a simple reaction drive and a bitter old enginarium from a larger vessel now centuries dead, the cargo scow plied the sub-light routes across the Neva system from the core worlds to the outer manufactory satellites with loads of chemicals and vital breathing gases. The ship was slow and fragile and utterly unprepared for the fury that had suddenly been turned upon it.

There was a matter of communication that had not been acted on quickly enough, then thunderous flares of laser fire from an Imperial frigate had set *Corolus* dead in space while razor-edged boarding pods slashed into her hull spaces.

If the ship had a captain, it was Finton. He owned *Corolus*, after a fashion, along with most of the crew thanks to a network of honour-debts and punitive indenture contracts. He floundered around the cramped, musty bridge space, his hand constantly straying to and from the ballistic pistol on his hip. Over the intercom he kept hearing little snatches of activity – panic, mostly, along with bursts of screaming and the heavy rattle of bolt-fire. Piece by piece, his ship was slipping out of his grasp and into the hands of the Navy.

He'd dealt with Naval types a hundred times before. They were never this fast, never this good. Finton was entertaining a new emotion inside his oily, calculating mind. He was *afraid*, and when the bridge door went orange and melted off its hinges, he very nearly lost control of his bodily functions.

Figures in black armour came into the chamber, iron boots clanging off the patched and rusty deck plates. They wore dark helmets bannered with white faceplates, eyes of deep night-blue crystal that searched every shadowed corner of the bridge. Movement for them was graceful and deadly, not a single gesture or motion wasted. One of them noticed him for the first time and Finton saw a difference: this one had a brass shape on the front of its helmet, a dagger-shaped leaf.

'Oh, Blood's sake,' whispered the captain, and he fumbled at his belt. The next sound on the bridge was the thud of Finton's holster and weapon hitting the deck. He bent his knees, hesitated, and then raised his hands, unsure if he should kneel or not.

As one, the invaders threw back their heads and the helmets snapped open. Their short, bobbed hair, framed eyes that were hard and flinty. The leader came forward to Finton in two quick steps and gripped him by a fistful of his jacket.

'Where is he?' growled Miriya, lifting the man off the deck.

Finton licked his lips. 'Sister, please! What have I done to displease the Sororitas?'

'Search this tier,' she shouted over her shoulder. 'Leave no compartment unchecked. Vent the atmosphere if you have to!'

'No, please–' said the captain. 'Sister, what–'

Miriya let him drop to the deck and kicked him hard in the gut. 'Don't play games with me, worm. You measure your life in ticks of the clock.' The Sister Superior carefully placed her armoured boot on Finton's right leg and broke it.

Behind her, Sister Isabel directed the other women to their tasks, then began a search of the bridge's control pits, pushing her way past doddering servitors and aged cogitator panels. 'As before, there is nothing here.'

'Keep searching.' Miriya presented her plasma pistol to Finton's face, the neon glow of the energy coils atop it washing him with pale illumination. 'Where is Vaun, little man?' she spat. *'Answer me!'*

'Who?' The word was drawn out like a moan.

'You are testing my patience,' snapped the Sister Superior. 'Half your crew is dead already from resisting us. Unless you wish to join them, tell me where the heretic hides!'

In spite of his pain, Finton shook his head in confusion. 'But... but, no. We left the commerce station... You came after us, fired on us. Our communications were faulty.' He waved feebly at a jury-rigged console across the chamber. 'We couldn't reply...'

'Liar!' Miriya's face twisted in anger and she released a shot from the plasma weapon into a support stanchion near Finton's head. The captain screamed and shoved himself away from the corona of white-hot vapour, dragging his twisted leg behind him. Miriya tracked him across the floor with the gun muzzle.

Finton tried to make the sign of the aquila. 'Please don't kill me. It was just some smuggling, nothing more, a few tau artefacts. But that was months ago, and they were all fake anyway.'

'I don't care about your petty crimes, maggot.' Miriya advanced on him. 'I want Torris Vaun. The *Corolus* was the only interplanetary ship to leave Neva's orbital commerce platform.' She bit out each word, as if she were explaining something to a particularly backward child. 'If Vaun was not on the station, then here is the only place he could be.'

'I don't know any Vaun,' screamed Finton.

'Lies!' The Battle Sister fired again, striking a dormant servitor and killing it instantly.

Finton coiled into a ball, sobbing. 'No, no, no...'

'Sister Superior,' began Isabel, a warning tone in her voice.

Miriya did not choose to hear it. Instead, she knelt next to the freighter captain and let the hot metal of the plasma pistol hover near his face. The heat radiating from the muzzle was enough to sear his skin.

'For the last time,' said the woman, 'where have you hidden Torris Vaun?'

'He's not here.'

Miriya blinked and looked up. It was Isabel who had spoken.

'Vaun was never aboard this vessel, Sister Miriya. These cogitator records show the manifest.' She held a spool of parchment in her grip. 'They match the dockmaster's datum for the *Corolus*.'

'The datum is wrong,' Miriya retorted. 'Would you have me believe that Vaun used his witchery to simply teleport himself to safety, Sister? Did he beg the gods of the warp to give him safe passage somewhere else?'

Isabel coloured, afraid to challenge her squad commander when her ire was so high. 'I have no answer to give you, Sister Superior, save that this wretch does not lie. Torris Vaun never set foot on this trampship.'

'No,' Miriya growled, 'that will not stand. He must not escape us–'

A hollow chime sounded from the vox bead in the Battle Sister's armour. 'Message relay from *Mercutio*,' began the flat, monotone voice. 'By direct order of Her Eminence Canoness Galatea, you are ordered to cease all operations and make planetfall at Noroc City immediately. Ave Imperator.'

'Ave Imperator,' repeated the women.

With effort, Miriya holstered her pistol and turned away, her head bowed and eyes distant. The rage she displayed moments earlier had drained away.

'Sister,' said Isabel. 'What shall we do? With him, with this ship?'

Miriya threw a cold glance at Finton and then looked away.

'Turn this wreck over to the planetary defence force. This crew are criminals, even if they are not the ones we seek.'

At the hatch stood Sister Portia and Sister Cassandra. Their expressions confirmed that they too had found nothing of the escaped psyker in their search.

Portia spoke. 'We heard the recall from Neva. What does it mean? Have they found him?'

Miriya shook her head. 'I think not. Our failure is now compounded, my Sisters. Blame... must be apportioned.'

There had been Adepta Sororitas on Neva for almost as long as there had been Adepta Sororitas. A world of stunning natural beauty, the planet's history vanished into the forgotten past of the Age of Strife, into the dark times when the turbulent warp had isolated worlds across the galactic plane, but unlike those colonies of man that had embraced the alien or fallen into barbarism, Neva had never given up its civilisation. Throughout the millennia, it had been a place where art and culture, theology and learning had been ingrained in the very bones of the planet. From a military or economic standpoint, Neva had little to offer – all her industry existed on the outer worlds of the system, on dusty, dead moons laced with ores and mineral deposits – but she remained rich in the currency of thought and ideas. Grand museum-cities that were said to rival the temples of Terra reached towards the clouds, and in the streets of Noroc, Neva's coastal capital, every street was blessed with its own murals drawn from the annals of Imperial Earth and Nevan chronicles spanning ten thousand years of history.

There had been a time, after the confusion wrought by the Horus Heresy, when Neva had become lost once again to the Imperium at large. Warp storms the like of which had not been seen for generations cut the system off from human contact and the Nevans feared a second Age of Strife would follow, but this was not to be their fate. When the day came that the storms lifted, as silently as they had first arrived, Neva's sky held a new star – a mighty vessel that had lost its way crossing the void.

Aboard that ship were the Sisters of Battle, and with them came the Living Saint Celestine. Golden and magnificent in her heraldry, Celestine and her cohorts had embarked on a War of Faith to chastise the heretical Felis Salutas sect, but fate had brought them here by the whim of the empyrean. It was said by some that Celestine remained only long enough to allow her Navigators to establish a fresh course before leaving Neva behind, but for the planet it was deliverance from a servant of the Emperor Himself.

Internecine conflicts and the wars of assassination that had riven Neva's theocratic barony during the isolation years were instantly nulled. Chapels and courts and universities dedicated to the Imperial Cult flourished as never before. New purpose came to the planet, and that purpose was pilgrimage.

The Order of Our Martyred Lady was not the only order of the Adepta Sororitas to have a convent on Neva, but theirs was the largest and by far the most elaborate. The tower was cut from stone of a hue found only in Neva's equatorial desert, a honeyed yellow that made the building glow when the rays of the sunset crossed it. From the highest levels of the convent, an observer could look down along the graceful curve of Noroc City's bay, following the lines of the snow-white sand that mirrored the bowed streets and boulevards.

On any other day, the beauty of it might have struck a chord in Sister Miriya, but at this moment her heart was immune to the sight. From the battlements, she stared out over Noroc's cathedrals and habitat clutches without really seeing them, watching the day dissipate, observing nothing but the moments fading away from her in the march of shadows over the city's giant sundial.

A grim smile rose and fell on her lips as she recalled her words to the trampship's captain. *You measure your life in ticks of the clock.* Perhaps she had meant that as much to herself as to him. The time fast approached when she would be called to the Canoness and made to answer for her errors.

Miriya's gaze dropped to the plaza beyond the convent's gates. There were penitents there, robed in hair shirts and cloaks of fishhook barbs. Some of them moaned and growled their way through verses of Imperial dogma, while others took to picking out hapless members of the public who tarried too long, for shouted condemnation and censure. There were flagellators who whipped at children wearing the wrong kinds of hood, and men bearing spears that ended in festoons of candles.

She frowned. Parts of the rites at play down there were known to her. The Battle Sister recognised the Commemoration of the Second Sacrifice of the Colchans, the Litany Against Fear and one of the Lesser Prayers to Saint Sabbat – but there were other cantos that seemed strange and hard against her ears. The iconography the penitents bore brimmed with images of wine-dark blood, and unbidden the stark, lifeless face of Lethe rose to the surface of her thoughts, the dead woman's throat open like a second raw mouth.

'They do things differently here,' Cassandra's voice drifted to her on the evening breeze as she approached. The woman threw a nod at the people in the plaza. 'I've not seen the like on other worlds.'

Miriya made an effort to shake off her black mood. 'Nor I. Like you, this is my first venture to Neva. But each planet beneath the Emperor's light embraces Him in its own way.'

'Indeed.' Cassandra joined her at the balcony's edge. 'But some embrace with more fervour than others.'

The Sister Superior eyed her. 'Do I detect a note of disquiet in your tone?'

From a different squad leader, such a comment might have been a caution but from Miriya it was an invitation. Cassandra's commander demanded and respected honesty in the women who served the church with her. 'It troubles me to hear, but I have been told that in some of Noroc's less... civilised districts, there are women who will mutilate and murder their third child if it is revealed to be a female whilst still unborn. This is done in the name of some aged, arcane idolatry.'

'It is not our place to question their ways,' said Miriya. 'The Ecclesiarchy works to ensure that the veneration of the God-Emperor meshes with the doctrine of each and every planet. Some distasteful anomalies of belief are inevitable.'

'Fortunate then that our order is here to show the Nevans the way.'

'I have never believed in fortune,' Miriya said distantly. 'Faith is enough.'

'Not enough to find Vaun,' replied Cassandra in a morose voice. 'He tricked us, played us for fools.'

Miriya looked at her squadmate. 'Aye. But do not punish yourself, Sister. Canoness Galatea will wish to reserve that pleasure.'

'You know her of old, yes?'

A nod. 'She was once my Sister Superior as I am yours. An unparalleled warrior and a true credit to the legacy of Saint Katherine, but perhaps a touch too inflexible for my liking. We would often disagree on matters of our credo.'

Cassandra could not keep the fear from her voice. 'What do you think will become of us?'

'There will be a cost for our lapse, of that you may have no doubt.' Inwardly, Miriya was already rehearsing the plea she would enter, offering to fall on her sword and take all the blame for Vaun's escape rather than drag Cassandra, Portia, Isabel and poor Iona down with her.

Her Sister gripped the edge of the stone battlements tightly, as if she could squeeze an answer from them. 'This apostate torments me, Sister Superior. By the Throne, how could he have simply vanished into thin air? The escape pod Vaun stole from the *Mercutio* was found on the commerce station, witnesses saw him there. But the only ship he could have been on was that rattletrap scow we boarded.' She shook her head. 'Perhaps... perhaps he hides still on the orbital platform? Waiting for a warp-capable craft to leave?'

'No.' Miriya pointed at the ground. 'Sub-orbital craft are plentiful on the station. Vaun took one and made planetfall. He came *here*. It is the only explanation.'

'To Neva? But that makes no sense. The man is a fugitive, his face is infamous on every world in this system. Any rational person would find the first route out of this sub-sector as fast as possible.'

'It makes sense to Vaun, Sister. The witch's arrogance is so towering that he believes he can hide in plain sight. Mark me well, I tell you that Torris Vaun never had any intention of escaping from Neva. He wanted to come here.'

Cassandra shook her head. 'Why? Why take such a risk of discovery?'

The sun dropped away behind the Shield Mountains and Miriya turned from the balcony. 'When we learn the answer to that, we will find him.' She beckoned her Battle Sister. 'Come. The Canoness will be waiting.'

The boat rode in the swell, making good speed across the narrows, the lights of Noroc long since vanished over the stern. The first mate rose into the untidy flying bridge and gave the sailor on watch a jut of the chin, like a nod.

'Asleep,' he whispered, and the sailor knew who he meant. 'Fast asleep but still I'm adrift around him.'

The sailor licked his dry lips, chancing a look back through the open hatch at the shape beyond, hidden under the rough-hewn blankets. The atmosphere on the little fishing cutter had turned stale and leaden the moment they'd taken the passenger aboard. 'Wish I could sleep,' he muttered. 'Men been getting bad dreams since we left port, is what they say. Seeing things. Reckon he's a witchkin, I do.'

The first mate blinked owlishly. He was tired too. 'Don't you be saying what you're thinking. Keep a course and stay silent, lad. Better that way. Get us there quick-like, all be gone and over.'

'Oh aye–' The words died in the sailor's parched throat. Out of the windscreen, across the bow of the cutter, there was a dark shape rising from the ocean. A razormaw, ugly as Chaos and twice as hungry. He'd never seen a fish so large, not even a deader like in the docker pubs where big stuffed heads and jawbones decorated the walls.

The sailor threw the wheel about in a panic, turning the boat on a hard arc away from the razormaw's grinning mouth. Ice water pooled in his gut. The thing was going to swallow them whole.

'You wastrel throwback, what are ye doing?' The first mate smacked him hard about the temple and shoved him away from the helm. 'Trying to capsize us?'

'But the razor–' he began, stabbing his finger at the sea. 'Do you not see it?'

'See what? There's nothing out there but ocean, boy.'

The sailor pressed his face to the window. No razormaw floated, arch-backed and ready to chew the boat apart. There were only the waves, rising and falling. He spun about, glaring at the sleeping man alone on the cot. For a moment, he thought he heard soft, mocking laughter.

'Witchkin,' repeated the sailor.

As the rituals demanded, each of them surrendered their weapons to a grey-robed novice before they entered the chapel. The noviciates were just girls, barely out of the schola progenium on Ophelia VII, and they sagged beneath the weight of the heavy firearms. As Celestians, and with that rank, privileged, Sister Miriya and her unit were gifted with superior, master-crafted guns that resembled a votive icon more than a battlefield weapon, but as with all elements of the Adepta Sororitas's equipment, from the power armour that protected them to their chainswords and Exorcist tanks, every piece of the order's machinery was as much a holy shrine as the place in which they now stood.

The convent's chapel was high and wide, encompassing several floors of the building's shell keep design. Up above, where the pipes of the organ ended and biolume pods hovered on suspensors, cherubim moved in lazy circuits, handing notes to one another as they passed, the sapphire of their optic implants glittering in the lamplight.

The four women advanced across the chancel to where their seniors awaited them, falling as one into a kneeling position before the vast stone cross-and-skull that dominated the chapel altar.

'In the name of Katherine and the Golden Throne,' they intoned, 'we are the willing daughters of the God-Emperor. Command us to do His bidding.'

It was customary for the senior Battle Sister present to let the new arrivals stand after the ritual invocation, but Galatea did not. Instead, she stepped forward from the pulpit and took up a place before the altar. Her dark eyes flashed amid the frame of her auburn hair. 'Sister Superior Miriya. When Prioress Lydia informed me that it would be your Celestians bringing the witch to us, I confess I was surprised. Surprised that so sensitive a prisoner be given to a woman of your reputation.'

Miriya spoke without looking up. 'Sister Lydia showed great faith in me.'

'She did,' Galatea let the breach of protocol go unmentioned. 'How shameful for her now, given your unforgivable lapse of judgement aboard the *Mercutio*.'

'I...' Miriya took a shuddering breath. 'There is no excuse. The culpability is mine alone to shoulder, Canoness. I had the opportunity to terminate the psyker Vaun and I chose not to. His escape falls to me.'

'It does.' Galatea's cold, strong voice echoed in the chapel's heavy air. 'You have lived a charmed life, Sister Miriya. Circumstances have always conspired to save you from the small transgressions you have made in the past, minor as they were. But this... I ask you, Sister. What would you do, if you were me?'

After a moment she replied. 'I would not presume to have the wisdom for such a thing, Canoness.'

Galatea showed her teeth in an icy smile. 'How very well said, Miriya. And now I find myself on the horns of a dilemma. A dangerous warlock is loose on this world and I need every able-bodied Battle Sister I can field to corral him yet the more severe interpretations of our doctrines would seem to insist that you be made to atone. Perhaps in the most *final* of ways.'

Miriya looked up, defiant. 'If the Emperor wills.'

The Canoness leaned forward and her voice dropped to a whisper. 'You do presume, Miriya. You always have.'

'Then kill me for it, but spare my Sisters.'

Galatea gave a grim smile. 'I'm not going to make you a martyr. That would excuse you, and I am not in a forgiving mood–'

The rest of the Canoness's words were lost in a sudden crash of sound as the chapel doors slammed open. A commotion spilled into the room as a troop of armsmen and clerics marched through. At their head was a tall rail of a man, draped in fine silks and priestly regalia. Red and white purity seals hung off him like the medals of a soldier, and the rage on his face matched the crimson of his robes. In one fist he clasped a heavy tome bound in rosaries, in the other there was the clattering blade of a gunmetal chainsword, the adamantine teeth spinning and ready.

'Which of them is the one?' he bellowed, pointing across the book at Miriya's squad. 'Which of these wenches is the fool who lost me my prize?'

Galatea held out a hand to stop him, her face tight with annoyance. 'Lord LaHayn, you forget yourself. This is a place of worship. Shoulder your weapon!'

'You dare defy me?' The high priest's colour darkened, the mitre on his head bobbing.

'Aye,' Galatea shot back. 'This place is the sacred house of Saint Katherine and the God-Emperor. I should not need to remind you of that!'

There was a moment when LaHayn's wiry muscles bunched around the sword, as if he were preparing to strike but in the next the anger dropped from him and he stiffly forced the blade into the hands of a subordinate dean at his side. 'Yes, yes,' he said, after a long silence. 'Forgive me, Canoness. I allowed my baser instincts to overrule the better angels of my nature.' He gave a low bow that was echoed by all of his retinue. When he came up, he was looking into Galatea's eyes with a piercing, steely gaze. 'My question, however, still stands. You will answer it.'

'Vaun's escape is not so simple a matter that it can be laid at the feet of these women,' said the Canoness, each word carefully balanced and without weight. 'An investigation must take place.'

'The enforcers have begun an analysis,' noted the dean.

Galatea ignored him, concentrating on LaHayn. 'This cannot be left to the enforcers or the Imperial Navy. Torris Vaun was the responsibility of the Adepta Sororitas, and we will find him.'

The priest-lord's gaze drifted to Miriya and her troops. 'Unsatisfactory. While I applaud your determination to amend the oversights of your Battle Sisters, necessity demands consequences.' He took a step forward. 'In all things. Did not Celestine's arrival teach us that?' LaHayn smoothly shifted into a mode of speech better suited to a church mass with the common folk. 'This is a universe of laws. Actions beget reactions. For all things, there are costs and penalties.' His lined, hard face loomed over Galatea. 'There must be reciprocity.'

'Lord deacon, I would ask that you speak plainly.' The Canoness did not flinch from his gaze.

LaHayn showed a thin smile. 'The few survivors of the witch's escape, the man Vorgo and the others, they are to be taken to the excruciators to become object lessons. It occurs to me that perhaps a contrite Battle Sister should join them, as an example of your order's devotion.'

'One of my kinswomen has already perished in the unfolding of this sorry matter,' snapped Galatea. 'You would ask me to give you another?'

'The dead one... Sister Lethe, yes? She is the most blameless of all, falling in honourable conflict to the heretic. Her sacrifice is not enough.'

Miriya began to rise to her feet. 'I shall–'

'*You will kneel, Sister!*' The voice of the Canoness hammered about the chamber like a cannon shot, and by sheer force it pushed Miriya to her knees once more. Galatea's expression hardened. 'My Sisters are the most precious resource of my order, and I will not squander them to appease your displeasure, my lord priest.'

'Then what will you do, Sister Galatea?' He demanded.

Finally, the Canoness looked away. 'I will give you your sacrifice.' She gestured to her aide, a veteran Sororitas. 'Sister Reiko. Summon Sister Iona.'

A gasp of surprise slipped from Portia's lips and Miriya shot her a look to silence her, but in truth, the Sister Superior was just as shocked to hear their errant squadmate's name spoken. From the dim shade of a sub-chancel, the woman called Reiko returned with Iona following behind. Her pale face looked down at the floor, her hair lank and unkempt. She seemed like a faint ghost of her former self, a faded copy worn thin through age and neglect.

In the aftermath of Vaun's escape, it was Isabel who had found Iona alone in the cargo decks of the *Mercutio*. Her eyes were faraway and vacant, and the cool, intense will she had always shown in the Emperor's service was gone. Iona's physical injuries were slight, but her mental state... That was a raw, gaping wound, ragged and bleeding where the psyker had pillaged her mind to exercise his powers. It was not until much later that Miriya had understood what the witch had been doing when he casually despoiled Iona's psyche. Vaun had used her to test the gallows, and left her alive as a warning.

None of them had expected to see Iona again. Her bouts of uncontrolled weeping and self-mutilation marked her as irreparably broken. Yet here she stood, still clad in her wargear.

'What is this?' LaHayn asked.

'Tell him,' said Galatea.

Iona looked up and blinked. 'I... I am far from absolution. Lost to any exculpation. I offer myself to repentance.'

'*No...*' Miriya was surprised by the denial that fell from her mouth. At her side, Portia's hand flew to her lips. Only

Cassandra dared to whisper the terrible truth that all of them suddenly realised.

'She is invoking the Oath of the Penitent...'

Iona shrugged off her red robe and let it drop to the stone floor in a heap. Behind her, Sister Reiko silently gathered it up, never once looking upon the other woman as she trembled.

'Before the Emperor I have sinned.' Iona's voice found a brittle strength and swelled to fill the chapel. 'Beyond forgiveness. Beyond forbearance.' She blinked back tears. 'Beyond mercy.'

Miriya looked to the Canoness, a pleading expression on her face. Galatea gave her a tiny nod and the Celestians came to their feet, moving to surround Iona. All of them knew the pattern of the ritual by heart.

Miriya, Portia, Cassandra and Isabel each took an item of Iona's wargear and armour, detaching it and casting it aside. As one they spoke the next verse of the catechism. 'We turn our backs upon you. We cast off your armour and your arms.'

'I leave this company of my own free will,' Iona continued, 'and by my will shall I return.' Behind her, Reiko used a rough-hewn blade to rip the Sister's discarded robe into strips that Portia and Isabel tied over Iona's bare arms and legs. Cassandra strung barbed expiation chains across her torso and pressed seals bearing the words of the oath into her stripped tunic. 'I shall seek the Emperor's forgiveness in the darkest places of the night,' intoned the woman.

Sister Reiko bent forward with the knife and reached for a hank of Iona's hair, but Miriya took the blade from her with a stony countenance. The Sister Superior leaned close and whispered in her friend's ear.

'You do not have to do this.'

Iona looked back at her. 'I must. With just one touch he hollowed me out, did such horrific things... I cannot rest until I cleanse myself.'

Miriya nodded once and said the next stanza aloud. 'When forgiveness is yours, we shall welcome you back.'

With sharp, hard motions, she cut off Iona's straw-coloured tresses until her scalp was bare and dashed with shallow scratches. 'Until such time you are nameless to us.'

With that, the oath was sealed, and the Battle Sisters took two steps back before turning away from her. Miriya was the last to do so, gripping the paring knife in her hand.

'See me and do not see,' Iona sighed, speaking the final verse. 'Know me and know fear, for I have no face today but this one. I stand before you a Sister Repentia, until absolution finds me once more.'

'So shall it be.' Galatea bowed her head, and all others in the chapel did the same. Iona walked past them all, into the stewardship of a lone Battle Mistress at the chapel doors. The Mistress carried a pair of matched neural whips that crackled and hummed with deadly power. In her hand she held a ragged red hood. Iona donned it, and then they were gone.

LaHayn broke the silence with a grunt of contentment. 'Not quite the price I would have demanded, but it will do.' He gave a shallow bow and snapped his fingers to summon the dean. 'Until the Blessing, then, Canoness?'

Galatea returned his bow. 'Until then, lord deacon. His light be with you.'

'And you.' The priest's delegation filed out, leaving the Battle Sisters alone again.

The Canoness made a dismissive gesture. 'Leave me now. I will deal with your dispensation later.'

The rest of the Celestians did as they were commanded, but Miriya remained, still kneading the grip of the knife. 'Iona was unfit to take the oath,' she said without preamble. 'It is a death sentence for her.'

Galatea snatched the blade from her grip. 'Fool! She saved your life with her sacrifice, woman. You and all your unit.'

'It is not right.'

'It was her choice. Willingly taking up the mantle of the Repentia is a rarity, you know that. Even Lord LaHayn could not deny the piety and strength of zeal Iona showed today.

Her gesture casts away any doubt on the devoutness of your squad and our order...' Galatea looked away. 'And what other path was open to her? After suffering so terribly at the hands of that monster... Honourable death was her only option.'

'What did Vaun do to her?' Miriya swallowed hard. Even thinking about such a thing made her feel ill. 'What horrors must he have conjured to breach her shield of faith?'

'The witch's way sees into the very core of a human soul. It finds the flaws that all of us hide and cracks them wide open. Pity your Sister, Miriya, and pray to Katherine that you never have to face what she did.'

When she was alone, Miriya knelt before the altar and offered up an entreaty to the Saints and the God-Emperor to keep Iona safe. To become a Sister Repentia was to throw away all thought of survival and fight possessed by a righteous passion. Ushered into battle by the whips of the harsh Mistress, the Repentia were the fiercest and most brutal of the Battle Sisters. Enemies lived in dread of their fearless assaults as their mighty eviscerator chainblades blazed through heretic lines, and only in death or forgiveness would their duty to the Emperor end. Some said that they lived in a state of grace that all aspired to reach, yet few had the purity of heart to attain. Each day, each breath for these women was an act of self-punishment and penance in honour of the Golden Throne – and they turned their righteousness into a weapon as keen as their killing swords.

Miriya had seen the Repentia on the field of battle in the past, but she had never expected to count one of her own among them. The purity of Iona's sacrifice stabbed at her heart; it would take much to prove herself worthy of it. The Sister Superior resolved then and there that Torris Vaun would be brought to justice, or she would forfeit her life in the attempt.

CHAPTER THREE

The hatch fell open like a drawbridge, allowing a perfumed gust of Neva's pre-dawn air to sweep in and scour the transport's cargo bay. The shuttle pilot eyed the three women standing on the lip of the hatch and rubbed at his face. He was wondering if there was some sort of special dispensation he could get from the Blessing for carrying Adepta Sororitas down from orbit. There had to be a little value to it, he reasoned. They were holy women, after all. That had to count for something towards his yearly tithes.

The tallest of the three, the ebony-skinned one with the curly hair, gave him a warning glance with her dark eyes. The pilot was smart enough to read it and pretended to make himself busy with a cargo web that was hanging loose. Better to let them complete their business without interfering. When she turned away again, the pilot stole another look at the trio. They had kept to themselves all the way down, talking in hushed voices at the back of the compartment while he had navigated the flight corridors to Noroc's port complex. Now and then, the winsome-looking one with the brown hair would sob a little, and the other one, tawny of face and elegant – by his lights, the prettiest of the three – would comfort her with whispers.

He would never have even dared to stay in the same room with them had they been Battle Sisters, but the Adepta Sororitas had many faces to it, and these three were just nurses. Sisters Hospitaller, they called themselves. The pilot amused himself thinking of how he might like them to comfort him in bed one night.

As if she smelled the notion in his brain, the tall woman broke away and came over to him. 'Could you give us a few moments, please? In private.'

'Uh, well.' He stalled. 'The thing is, you said this would be quick. I've got a perishable load waiting on the dock up at the commerce station, bound for the epicurias in Metis City.' The pilot gave a vague wave in the direction of the ocean. 'I can't spare the time.'

'No,' said the woman firmly, 'you can. And you will. I am a servant of the Divine Imperial Church. Do you know what that means?'

'That... I have to... do what you say?'

'I'm glad we understand each other.' She turned her back on him and returned to her Sisters, who were walking out on to the starport apron.

'Are you sure you don't want Sister Zoë or me to go with you? You do not have to bear this sorrow alone, Verity.'

The girl swallowed hard, watching the first rays of sunlight cresting the mountains in the distance. She could smell the salt of the sea in the cool air. 'Inara, no. You have already done enough.' Verity forced a weak smile. 'This is something that I must attend to myself. It is a matter of family.'

'We are all family,' Zoë said gently. 'All Sisters by duty if not by blood.'

Verity shook her head. 'I thank you both for accompanying me, but our order's work on the outer moons is more important. The Palatine might bear to lose me for a time, but not you two as well.' She took up her bag from Zoë and gave them both a curt bow. 'Ave Imperator, Sisters.' With finality, the Hospitaller withdrew a black mourning shawl from her pocket and tied it about her neck.

Inara said her farewell with a light touch on her arm. 'We will pray for her,' she promised, 'and for you.'

'Ave Imperator,' said Zoë, as the hatch began to rise up again.

Verity made her way down from the landing pad, turning back just once to see the cargo shuttle throw itself up into the lightening sky on plumes of dirty smoke. She brushed dirt from the ruby hem of her robes and set off across the port, a fistful of papers and consent seals in her hand.

She found a stand of cable-carriages outside the port proper, where the hooded drivers congregated in clusters under clouds of tabac smoke. Verity had Imperial scrip with which to pay, but none of them would even meet her gaze. Instead, the driver at the head of the group pulled a mesh veil down over his eyes and beckoned her towards his vehicle. With a rattle of gears, he worked the lever on the carriage's open cockpit and the boxy vehicle moved off along the wide, curved boulevard.

Trenches set into the surface of the roadway crisscrossed every major artery in the city, through which lines of cable rolled on endless loops. The carriages had spiked cogs in their wheel wells that bit into the cables and locked, allowing the vehicles to move about with no power source of their own. It kept the city's air clean of combustion fumes and engine noise, replacing it with the constant hiss and clatter of cabs jumping slots and passing over points. The metal landaus that travelled Noroc's streets varied in size from small taxis to large flatbed haulers and triple-decker omnibuses. Only the wealthy and the church had their own.

Verity understood from her indoctrination assemblies that Neva's laws forbade everyone but the agents of the Emperor himself – and by that they meant the Arbites, Imperial Guard and Ecclesiarchy – the use of a vehicle with any true freedom of movement.

She had never been on Neva Prime before. In all the months that the Order of Serenity had been in service to the poor and wretched of the outer moons, Verity had never once come to the world those innocents served. The moons were desolate places, each and every one of them. Whole planetoids given over to open cast mines or deep-bore geothermal power taps, riven with sickness from the polluting industry that controlled them. It was no wonder that Neva itself was such a jewel of a world, she reflected, when every iota of its effluent and engineering had been transplanted to the satellite globes about it.

She caught reflections of her face in the windows of shops as they trundled through the vendor district. Her flawless skin and amber hair did nothing to hide the distance in her eyes; what beauty she had was ruined by the sadness lurking there. Stallholders were already erecting their pitches, piling high stacks of fat votive candles, cloth penitent hoods, paper offerings and icons cast out of resin. Once or twice there was the crack of a whip on the wind, but that might have just been the cables. The cable-carriage clanked past a flatbed piled high with what seemed to be hessian corpse sacks, there and then gone. At an interchange, a train of teenagers, ashen, shaven-headed and sexless, were led across the avenue by priests in bright regalia. Then the cab was moving again, the driver plucking at the wires in the road to steer it.

Verity sighed, and it felt like knives in her chest. Gloom crowded her. She was hollow and echoing within, as if everything that had made her who she was had been scooped out and destroyed. Once again, tears prickled at her eyes and she gasped, trying to hold them back and failing.

Through the gauzy muslin curtains across the carriage she saw the Convent of Saint Katherine emerging in the distance, and presently the woman surrendered herself to the grief that churned within her, muffling her sobs in the folds of her black shawl.

* * *

They buried Sister Lethe in the memorial garden, a space of light and greenery on the southern face of the convent. It grew out of the side of the building in a flat disc-shaped terrace, emerging from the wide portal doors of the chapel. The garden was dominated by a statue of Saint Katherine, dressed in the armour of a Sister Seraphim. She stood as if ready to leap off her plinth and take to the air, carved coils of flame and smoke licking from the jump pack on her back.

In keeping with her new status and penances, Iona was not permitted to attend the funeral. Instead, Cassandra walked ahead of the pallbearer helots in their white robes, a censer of votive oils burning as she swung it back and forth like a pendulum. Miriya, Isabel and Portia followed the cloaked body, their black Celestian armour polished to a mirror-bright sheen. In accordance with the rites of the order, cloths of red silk were tied across the barrels of their guns to signify the silence of the weapons in this moment of reflection.

Reiko, the veteran Sister Superior who served Canoness Galatea as her aide, conducted the ceremony in a correct but not heartfelt manner. A scattering of other Battle Sisters, women that Miriya did not know by sight – most likely members of the Convent's garrison – paid their respects as they were wont to do. Yet, not one of them had known Lethe, none of them had fought alongside her against traitors and xenos, none of them had bled red for the same patches of accursed ground.

Miriya grimaced. She had lost women under her command before, in circumstances much worse than this one, and yet the simple and utterly brutal manner of Lethe's murder weighed her down with guilt. It was all the Sister Superior could do to hold back the tirade of inner voices that would willingly blame her for her error aboard the *Mercutio*.

In her mind's eye she saw herself again, in that moment when she placed the plasma pistol against Vaun's capsule and threatened to kill him. *Why didn't I do it? Then Lethe would still be alive, Iona would still be one of us...* But to do so would have been to disobey a direct command from her church. Miriya had often been called to account for her frequently 'creative' interpretations of instructions from her seniors, but she had never defied a superior; such an idea was anathema to a Sororitas. Her gaze dropped to the stone path beneath her feet. Sister Dione had warned her not be complacent, and she had not fully heeded that warning until it was too late. *I will make those responsible pay*, she vowed.

An oval slot in the stony path of the garden was open to the air, revealing a vertical silo a few metres deep. Reiko brought the Litany of Remembrance to a close, and the white-clad servitors tipped Lethe's body into the space and filled it with earth. As the Nevans did with all their dead, they buried her standing up with her face tilted back towards the sky. It was for the deceased to see the way back to Terra, and to the path that led them to the right hand of the Emperor, so their clerics said.

'In His name, and by the sanction of Our Martyred Lady, we commit our Sister Lethe Catena to the earth. There to rest until the Divine One calls upon His fallen to rise once more.' Reiko bowed her head, and the others did the same. Miriya hesitated for a second, catching the eye of a young Sister wearing the robes of a different order. She gave the Celestian a look loaded with pain and anger.

'Praise the Emperor, for in our resolve we only reflect His purpose of will,' intoned Reiko. 'So shall it be.'

'So shall it be,' they chorused.

Drawn inexorably to the place where Lethe lay, Miriya approached the woman kneeling there even though part of her knew only ill could come of it. Closer, and she recognised the unbroken circle symbol on the girl's robes, the mark of the Order of Serenity. Like the Order of Our Martyred Lady, the Sisters Hospitaller who served in the name of Serenity came from the Convent Sanctorum on Ophelia VII. Hospitaller orders were, by Imperial law, non-militant, but that by no means meant their ranks were filled with weaklings.

These women were chirurgeons and nurses of expert skill and great compassion, serving the warriors of the Imperial military machine on countless thousands of worlds. They were also full trained in the arts martial, and were fully able to take action if circumstances demanded it. No planet that dared to consider itself civilised was without a hospice or valetudinarium staffed by such Sisters.

The woman stood and met Miriya's gaze. She seemed on the verge of tears, but her hands were balled into fists. 'You... You are Lethe's commander. Sister Miriya.'

'I had that honour,' Miriya replied carefully.

The words seemed to pain the girl. 'You. Let her die.'

'Lethe ended her life as she lived it, in battle against the heretic and the witchkin.' Miriya replied, taken aback by the young woman's grief.

'I want to know how it happened,' snapped the Hospitaller. 'You must tell me.'

Miriya gave a slow shake of the head. 'That is a matter for the Orders Militant, not for you.'

'You have no right to keep it from me.' Tears streaked the woman's face. 'I am her sister!'

Miriya's gesture took in the whole of the convent. 'We are all her Sisters.'

The Hospitaller pulled at her collar and tugged out a length of intricate silver chain: a rosary, the like of which Miriya had only ever seen worn by one other person. 'Where did you get that?'

'I am Sister Verity Catena of the Order of Serenity,' said the girl. 'Sibling to Sister Lethe of the Order of Our Martyred Lady, orphan of the same mother.' She grabbed Miriya's wrist. 'Now you will tell me how my only blood kin was killed, or by the Golden Throne I'll claw it from you!'

She saw it instantly: the same curve of the nose, the eyes and the determination burning behind them. The moment stretched taut in the silence, Verity's anger breaking against the cold dejection that cloaked Miriya.

'Very well,' said the Celestian, after a long silence. 'Sit with me, Sister Verity, and I will tell you the hard and unforgiving truth.'

The skinny youth rolled the lit candle between his fingers, playing with the soft tallow, tipping it so the rivulets of molten wax made coiled tracks around its length.

'Nervous?' asked Rink, balancing on the edge of the table.

Ignis glanced up at the other man. 'Are you asking me or telling me?' Rink hadn't been able to sit still for five minutes since they arrived in the saloon, and even now in this secluded back room, he was constantly in motion. As if to illustrate the point, Rink fingered the tin cup of recaf on the table and licked his lips.

'I'm not nervous.' The large guy said it with such bland innocence that it made Ignis smirk. 'I just... don't like this place.'

'You'll get no argument from me,' said the youth, teasing the flame along the candle's wick. He shook his head. 'Ach. I can't believe we're even here.'

'My point,' retorted Rink, putting the cup down again. 'Maybe we should just give this up as a bad job and–'

'And what?' A hooded figure pushed open the bead curtain cordoning off the room from the rest of the saloon. 'Whistle down a starship to come get you?'

Rink gaped like a fish and Ignis got to his feet, a grin springing to life on his lips. 'By all that's holy, is it you?'

Torris Vaun returned the smile. 'Oh yes, it's me. In the flesh.' He patted both of the men on their shoulders. 'Bet you never thought you'd see this face again, eh?'

'Well, uh, no, to be honest,' admitted Rink. 'After them nuns took you in the nets on Groombridge, we reckoned that was it. All over.'

'*Some* of us did,' Ignis added, with a pointed look.

'They were a bit rough with me, but nothing I wasn't ready for.' Vaun helped himself to a cup of recaf and sweetened it generously with the brandy bottle on the table. 'Got a smoke?' he asked, off-handedly. 'I'm gasping.'

Rink nodded and fished out a packet of tabac sticks. Vaun made a face at the label – it was a cheap local brand that smelled like burning sewage – but he took one just the same. 'Your hand is shaking, Rink,' noted the criminal. 'You're not happy to see me?'

'I'm... uh...'

'He's nervous,' explained Ignis. 'Honestly, Vaun, I'm in there with him on that. Coming here... Well, there's been talk it was a mistake.'

'Mistake?' Vaun repeated. He tapped the end of the cigarillo with the flat of his finger and it puffed alight. 'Who has been saying that?'

The two other men exchanged glances. 'Some people. They didn't come.'

'Like?'

'Gibbin and Rox. Jefter, too.' Rink sniffed.

Vaun made a dismissive gesture. 'Ah, the warp take them. Those bottom-feeders never had the eye for a big score, anyway.' He smiled. 'But you boys came, didn't you? That warms my heart.' The tip of the tabac stick glowed orange.

'The others are scattered about. Lying low,' noted Ignis. 'But we all came.'

'Even though you didn't want to,' Vaun voiced the unspoken part of the sentence. 'Because you're asking yourself, what in Hades made Torris Vaun think he could get free from the Adepta Sororitas?'

'Yeah,' said Rink, 'and the message. Didn't even know the twerp who brought it, some moneyed little fig with his hands all high.'

'You still came, though. That's good. Even though LaHayn's dogs and every city watch on Neva will be sniffing for us, you still came.' He exhaled sweet smoke. 'You won't regret it.'

Ignis blinked. 'We're not staying here... Vaun, tell me we're not gonna stay on this churchy prayer-pit one second longer.' His voice went up at the end of the sentence.

'Watch it,' said Vaun, amused. 'This is my homeworld you're disparaging. But yes, we're staying. There's a big prize here,

Ig. Bigger than you can imagine. With the help of my, ah, moneyed friends, we're going to have it, and more besides.'

'More?' asked Rink. 'What like?'

'Like revenge, Rink. Bloody revenge.' Vaun's eyes glittered with violence.

Ignis looked away. He toyed with the candle some more, making the flame change shape. 'Who are these friends of yours, then? Highborns and top caste lackwits? Why do we need them?'

'For what they can give us, boy. You know the way it is, rich folk only want to be richer. They don't know what it's like to be poor and powerless, and they're terrified of falling to it. Makes them predictable, and fat for the gutting.'

The youth frowned. 'I don't like the way the people around about look at me. Like they see the mark on me. Every time I'm walking down the street, I think I see folks on the vox to the ordos, calling out... "Come and get him. Witchboy!" I don't want to stay here.' The candle burned brightly, licking his fingers. Ignis seemed not to notice.

Vaun took a long draw on the tabac. 'How about you, Rink? You have a complaint, too?'

'Don't like the priests,' said the big man at length. 'They beat me when I was a nipper.'

A slow smile crossed Vaun's face. 'Aren't we all the wounded little birds? Listen to me, lads, when I tell you there's no man alive who hates Neva more than I do. But I have unfinished business here, and with the good grace of the Sisters of Our Martyred Lady, I am now delivered back to my place of birth to conclude it.' He waved the cigarillo in a circle. 'For starters, we're going to light some fires back in Noroc and give the goodly lord deacon the hiding he so richly deserves. Then we'll move on to the main event.' A smile crossed his lips. 'When we're done, this entire damned planet will be burning.'

Ignis perked up at those words. 'I'd like that.'

'Wait and see,' promised Vaun. 'Just you wait and see.'

* * *

The prison was a monument to deterrence. There were no windows of any kind along its outer facia, nothing but the thin slits where cogitator-controlled autoguns peeked out at the open plaza around it. The brassy weapons hummed and clicked as people passed beneath their sights, ever prepared to unleash hails of bullets into escapees or troublemakers.

There was never any of either, of course. Noroc's central district was a model of pious and lawful behaviour, and had it not been for the less salubrious activities of the commoners in the outer zones of the city, the local enforcers precinct would have had little to do but polish their power mauls and take part in parades. Part of the strength that kept the citizenry quiet came from buildings like the prison. One only had to raise one's head and look to see the cone-shaped construction, with the relief of brutal carvings that covered its every surface.

The reformatory, as it was known, was a propagandist artwork on a massive scale. Each level showed sculptures of the Emperor's agents – Adeptus Arbites, Space Marines, inquisitors, Battle Sisters and more – killing and purging those who broke Imperial law and doctrine. Crimes as base as rape and child-murder were there, along with petty theft, lying and tardiness. Each and every perpetrator was shown in the moment of their guilt, suffering the full weight of retribution upon them. At the very top of the conical construct, loud hailers broadcast stern hymns and blunt sermons on the nature of crime. Everything about the building was a threat to those who would entertain thoughts of malfeasance.

Sister Miriya approached the prison across the plaza, with Cassandra at her side and the Hospitaller Verity a step or two behind.

'Is her presence really necessary, Sister Superior?' Cassandra asked from the side of her mouth.

'Another pair of eyes is always useful,' replied Miriya, but in truth that was a poor justification. Had she wanted another observer, it would have been a simple matter for her to summon Isabel or Portia to accompany them. She was conflicted by Verity, pressured by a sense of obligation to her comrade Lethe. In some way Miriya felt as if she owed the Hospitaller a debt of closure. *Or is it my own guilt she reflects back upon me?* The Sister Superior shook the thought away. Verity wanted to see the men who had aided Vaun in murdering her sibling, and Miriya could think of no good reason to refuse her.

An enforcer with veteran sergeant chevrons on his duty armour was waiting for them at the gate, and with grim purpose the enforcer ushered the three of them in through the prison's layers of security. Other enforcers stopped what they were doing to watch the Sisters passing by. They did not look at them with reverence or respect; the lawmen half-hid smirks or sneers and muttered among themselves, quietly mocking the women who had so publicly lost the notorious psyker.

Cassandra's lip curled and Miriya knew she was on the verge of snapping out an angry retort, but the Sister Superior silenced such thoughts in her with a brief shake of the head. They had more serious concerns than the opinions of a few common police troopers.

'We've got them segregated,' said the enforcer sergeant. 'A couple have died since we got them here.'

'How?' piped Verity.

He gave her an arch look. 'Wounds, I imagine. Fell down the stairs.'

'Have you interrogated them?' Miriya studied the line of cell doors as they passed into the holding quadrant.

'Couldn't get much sense out of them,' admitted the enforcer. 'Crying for their wives and kids, mostly.' He grimaced. 'Big men, some wetting their britches and wailing like newborns. Pathetic.'

'They know the price they will pay for turning on the Emperor's benificence,' said Cassandra. 'They have nothing to look forward to but death.'

The sergeant nodded. 'You want to see them all, or what? You won't learn anything of use, I'll warrant.' He handed a fan of punch cards to Miriya and signalled another enforcer trooper to open the heavy steel door to an interrogation chamber.

She scanned the names. 'This one,' said Miriya after a moment, tapping her finger on a worn card. 'Bring him to us.'

The sergeant and the trooper returned with Midshipman Vorgo strung between them like a side of meat. The sailor's face was all pallid skin and fresh bruising, but even a swollen-shut eye was not enough to hide the look of abject terror that appeared when he saw the Battle Sisters. Vorgo made weak mewling noises as the enforcer shackled him into the stained bronze restraint harness, above the drainage grate in the centre of the room.

Miriya gave Verity a sideways look. The Sister Hospitaller's expression was conflicted, compassion at the wretched man's mien warring with anger at his misdeeds. The Sister Superior stepped closer, into the circle of light cast by the biolumes overhead. 'You remember my face, don't you?'

Vorgo gave a jerky nod.

'Let me explain what is going to happen to you. There will be no court of law, no appeals, no due process.' She took in the lawmen and the prison with a wave of her hand. 'You will not be heard by the enforcers judges, you will not submit to a captain's mast aboard the *Mercutio*.' Miriya studied him gravely. 'You have aided and abetted in the murder of a Sororitas, colluded in the escape of a terrorist witch. You belong to the Sisters of Battle for us to persecute as we see fit. You have no rights, no voice, and no recourse. All that remains to be decided is how you will perish.'

Vorgo emitted a whimper and said something unintelligible.

'Have you ever seen an arco-flagellant, Vorgo?' Miriya signalled to Cassandra and the other Battle Sister dropped her bolter into a ready stance. 'Let me tell you about them.' Her voice took on a cold, steely quality. 'As the Emperor wills, those who are found guilty of heresy and crimes of similar gravity are taken into the service of we who hunt the witch-kin. Chirurgeons and Hospitallers adapt them to this new life with surgery and conditioning, implanting pacifier helms and lobotomaic taps in their brains.'

For emphasis, she tapped Vorgo's forehead with a finger. 'Imagine that. Your limbs removed, replaced with spark-whips and nests of claws. Eyes bored from your skull and stained glass in their places. Your heart and organs fixed with stimm injectors and neuropathic glands. And then, proud in your new body, what remains of your drooling waste of a mind will be turned to the good of the Imperium. With a word of my command, you'll willingly fling yourself into the jaws of hell, a berserk flesh-machine bound for a long, long death.' When she threw Cassandra a nod, the Battle Sister took aim at Vorgo's head. 'There is a cleaner, quicker way... but only for the repentant.' Miriya paused in front of the restraint rig. 'I will give you that gift if you tell me who you were working for. What compelled you to free Torris Vaun?'

'Who?' said Vorgo, pushing the word out of his mouth. 'I don't know any Vaun.'

'Are you playing games with me?' Miriya growled. 'There are others I can offer my mercy to. Now answer me, why did you free Vaun?'

'Don't know Vaun.' The sailor shouted suddenly. 'My daughter. What have you done to my daughter, you bitch?'

'What is he talking about?' asked Verity.

The enforcer sergeant shifted and frowned. 'This again. Like I said, crying for his family, like all of them. Can't get a proper answer from any of these wastrels.'

Verity took the punch card that showed Vorgo's record and held it up to the light. 'The Imperial census notation here shows this man has no family. No daughter.'

'You can read the machine dialect?' asked Cassandra.

The Hospitaller nodded. 'A little. I have worked closely with Sisters of the Orders Dialogous in the past. Some of their skills are known to me.'

'I love my daughter.' spat the sailor, desperation making him lunge at the manacles. 'And you took her and put her in that glass jar. You black-hearted whores–'

Miriya slapped him with the flat of her ceramite gauntlet, knocking out a couple of teeth and silencing him for the moment. 'He thinks our prisoner was his daughter? What idiocy is this?'

'Why in Terra's name would he think we had his non-existent child as our prisoner?' Cassandra shook her head. 'This man was *there*. He saw the capsule's occupant first hand. He freed Vaun from the pskyer hood himself.'

Miriya cupped the prisoner's chin in her hand. 'Who was in the capsule, Vorgo?'

'My daughter...' He sobbed. 'My beautiful daughter.'

'What is her name?' asked Verity, the question cutting through the air. 'What does she look like?'

Something went dark behind the sailor's eyes. 'Wh-what?' His face became slack and pasty.

'Her name, Vorgo,' repeated the Hospitaller. 'Tell us your daughter's name, and we'll bring her back to you.'

'I... I don't... remember...'

'Just tell us, and we'll let you go free.' Verity took a step closer. 'You *do* know the name of your own daughter, don't you?'

'I... I...' From nowhere, the midshipman let out a piercing scream of agony, throwing his head from side to side. Vorgo wailed and his eyes rolled back in their sockets, blood streaming from his nose and ears. Verity ran to him as the man went limp against the rack.

After a moment she shook her head. 'Dead. A rupture within his brain, I believe.'

'The psyker did that to him?' asked the enforcer with disgust.

'Impossible,' Miriya shook her head. 'Vaun's witchery is all brute strength and violence. He lacks the subtlety for something like this.'

'He would not have been able to control this man's mind from inside the capsule,' added Cassandra, 'and certainly not the minds of a dozen men.'

Verity looked at the sergeant. 'The others from the *Mercutio* who helped Vaun escape, you say they are all calling for their loved ones?'

A nod. 'Like lost children.'

The Hospitaller turned to face Miriya. 'Sister Superior, your prisoner did not escape of his own accord. Someone freed him, someone who used these weak men like regicide pawns. They were compelled to believe that a person they cared for deeply was in your custody.'

The sergeant snorted. 'You're an inquisitor now as well as a nurse, then, Sister?' He snapped his fingers at the dead man and the trooper at his side took the corpse away. 'Please excuse me if I don't take the word of a dozen lying traitors as to why they took it into their heads to free a mass-murderer. These men are bilge-scum, plain as nightfall. They reckoned they might earn some gratitude from Vaun, so they busted him out. There's no witch-play or magic about it, pardon me for my impertinence!' He said the last words in a way that clearly showed he didn't mean them.

'The simplest explanation is usually the right one,' admitted Cassandra, and Verity looked at the floor, crestfallen.

'When one deals with witches, nothing is simple,' commented the Sister Superior.

CHAPTER FOUR

The Canoness did a poor job of hiding her dismay as Miriya entered her chambers, frowning deeply over the pict-slate in her hand. The Sister Superior gave a contrite bow.

'Your eminence. I would speak with you.'

Galatea did not offer her the room's only vacant chair. Instead, she placed the slate on her wide wooden desk and rolled back the sleeves of her day robe. 'I knew, Miriya. I knew it, somewhere deep in my marrow, from the moment the astropaths brought me the message from Prioress Lydia. When I saw your name on the document, I knew this day would not run smoothly.' She gave a bitter laugh. 'I was in error, it seems. I underestimated considerably.'

Miriya scowled. 'You and I have always read from different pages of the Emperor's book, but you understand me, Sister. We have fought the foe and prayed together afterwards a hundred times. You know I am not so lax that I would have let this happen–'

'But you did,' Galatea insisted, 'through your fault or not, Vaun's escape was on your watch and so you bear responsibility. And as our order's prime representative on this planet, by extension so do I. You have brought disgrace to Saint Katherine's name.'

'Don't you think I am aware of that?' Miriya snapped angrily. 'Don't you think I would take my own life here and now if that could undo what happened? I lost two comrades to that monster, one buried, one broken.'

The Canoness nodded. 'And more will die before Vaun is made to answer for his crimes, that much is certain.' She turned to study the view through the room's stained glass window. 'You have given me a bloody mess to clean up, Miriya.'

'Let me do something about it.' The Celestian took a step forward. 'No one on this world wants Vaun to pay more than I do. I want your permission to pursue my investigation of the fugitive.'

'He will be found. Neva is sealed tight. Vaun will never make it offworld alive.' Galatea shook her head. 'His arrogance in coming home will be his undoing.'

'Vaun's not going to leave,' insisted Miriya. 'Not until he gets what he wants.'

'Oh?' The Canoness threw an arch look at her. 'Suddenly you are an expert on this man? You have some inner knowledge of his thoughts and desires? Pray tell, Sister, of your belated insight.'

She ignored the thinly veiled sarcasm. 'He's a brute, a thief and a corsair drawn only to what makes him richer or more powerful. He came to Neva because he wants something that is here.'

'Vaun came to Neva because he was captured, not of his own will.'

'Did he?' It was Miriya's turn to sneer. 'Or perhaps he allowed himself to be caught, knowing full well he would be freed.'

Galatea returned to her pict-slate, her attention fading with every moment. 'Oh, this is the theory advanced by the Hospitaller, yes? What is her name? Verana?'

'Sister Verity,' corrected Miriya, 'of the Order of Serenity.'

'An order not known for its expertise in martial matters,' commented Galatea, dryly.

Miriya suppressed a snarl. 'She may not be a Battle Sister, but she has a keen mind and a strong heart. Her skills could prove useful to us.'

'Indeed? Or is it merely that you feel an obligation for letting her sibling perish?'

She looked away. 'There is some truth in that, I will not deny it. But still I stand by what I have said. I... I trust her.' The admission surprised her as much as it did the Canoness.

Galatea shook her head again. 'Be that as it may, Sister Verity has no place here. Her dispensation to visit Neva extended only to the duration of Lethe's funerary service. The Order of Serenity has its works to perform on the outer moons with the sick and the diseased. It is my understanding that the workers there suffer in their service to the Imperium...'

'You outrank the Palatine leading the mission on the moons,' noted Miriya. 'You would be within your remit to order Verity to linger here, if you wished it.'

'*If* I wished it,' repeated Galatea. 'I'm not convinced there is any value to having her remain. It's enough that you, a senior Battle Sister, have allowed your emotions to cloud your judgement on this matter. What can I expect of a mere medicae like Verity, a woman unused to the violence and trials that we will be facing?'

'The same as any one of us,' Miriya said grimly, 'that we embrace the passion and do the Emperor's will.' She advanced as close as she could and laid her hands flat upon the Canoness' desk. 'Give me this, Galatea. I will ask you for nothing else, but give me this chance to make amends.'

The weight and intensity behind the Sister Superior's words gave her pause, and the two women studied each other for a long moment, measuring each other's resolve. Finally, Galatea broke the stalemate and gathered up a fresh data-slate and an electro-quill. 'Despite what you may think of me, Miriya, I have always considered you to be an exemplary warrior. Because of that, and that alone, I'll grant you the freedom to pursue this.' She scratched out a line of words, the glassy plate turning her flowing script into precise letters as she wrote. 'But understand, you have no margin for error. If you do not bring Vaun to book, it will be the end for you – and you will drag the Hospitaller down as well.' The slate gave a soft, melodic chime as the messenger program within came to an end.

Miriya gave a low bow. 'Thank you, Sister Canoness. I promise you, we will see the witch burn for his transgressions.'

Galatea smiled a crooked smile. 'It is not me that you need to convince, Sister Superior. The esteemed Deacon Lord LaHayn is watching our convent like a hawk. I'm certain he will want to know every detail of how you plan to locate the psyker.'

'I do not understand.'

'You shall. The Blessing of the Wound begins at eight-bell today, and tradition requires that our order be in attendance at the fête of observance in the Lunar Cathedral.' She made a dismissive gesture with her hand. 'You will accompany my party. Dress robes and full honours, Sister. Inform your squad.'

In the streets, children who were too young to understand the true nature of an adult's penance ran alongside the flagellatory wagons and threw loose cobbles at the moaning, soiled people inside. Drawn down in cattle-shuttles from the penitentiary mines and work camps on the moons, the remorseful were brought to Neva by the promise of time deducted from their indentures or sentences, should they survive the great games of the festival. The ones who were already broken in will were of no use; those were kept on the moons to work until they died. Only the men and women who still held a living spark of inner strength were allowed to sacrifice themselves to the machine of the church in this great annual celebration.

So the priests and clerics in the chapels told it, everyone was remorseful. To be human was to be born that way, already alive only at the sufferance of the Emperor, but hard graft and piety were a good salve, and only the truly low were irredeemable. Criminals and heretics, dissidents and slaves, only they had no voice in the church – and as such, they were the best sacrifices for the Blessing of the Wound. Persistent rumours said that they would be joined by innocents who spoke too loudly about the church's severe rule or the flaccid, ineffectual regime of the planetary governor; the festival was always a good time to rid the city of unmutual thinkers.

On other Imperial worlds, there would be harvest celebrations and burnt offerings, great hymnal concerts, sometimes fasting or dancing. A million planets and billions of people celebrated the greatness of the Master of Mankind in their own sanctioned ways, and here, on this world of theologians and rigid dogma, there was no dividing line between zealous penance and devout worship.

This year Noroc was alive with chatter on the streets and in the pulpits, even among the youths spilling out of the seminaries and schola. The lord deacon had promised the death of a witch to cap the festival's commencement this year, not a make-believe one using fireworks and lightning guns like they'd seen before, but a real live psyker. Now that was not going to come to pass, and rumours ran about the city like mice in the walls.

The barony and the moneyed castes looked on at the commoners and pretended they knew what was to be done instead, but they were just as ignorant – save for the knowledge that Lord LaHayn and Governor Emmel would have to collude to create something of equal spectacle to placate the people. All across the metropolis, individuals donned their ritual wear or chose their costumes if they were lucky enough to have received a blood red summons paper. The icon sellers filled their stalls and emptied them, filled and emptied them again, taking in fists of Imperial scrip and church-certified tithe beads.

This year, it was the new cotton shirts adorned with a gold-thread aquila that were the must-have item, and the enforcers had already broken up a minor fracas in the linen quarter after stock had sold out. Elsewhere, devotional parades where local girls painted themselves sun-yellow and wore wings, celebrated the passing of Celestine. In other districts there were gleeful, impromptu stonings for those whose petty crimes had gone unpunished by the judges. The mood was a strange, potent mix of the buoyant and the fierce, with the lust for hard violence hovering just beneath the surface. You could see it in the eyes of the running children, on the faces of their parents, reflected in the fervour of the city's thousands of clerics.

The carriages jumped cables and fell down the gentle incline towards the grandest of Noroc's basilicas, the lofty pinnacle of the Lunar Cathedral. From a distance, the cathedral resembled a tall cone with geometric scoops cut from its flanks. In fact, these carefully assembled voids were aligned with the complex orbital paths of Neva's many moons, and during midnight mass it was often possible for parishioners inside to see the pinprick lights of fusion furnaces on the surfaces of the distant, blackened spheres.

Below the church was the oval ring of the amphitheatre from which LaHayn himself sometimes held sermons. The ancient power of the great hololithic projectors ringing the edges turned him into a glowing ghost ten storeys tall, the ornate brass horns of a thousand vox-casters throwing his voice across the city. For now, the arena was quiet, but that would soon change. Already, the shapes of elaborate scenery flats and large sections of stage set were coming together, casting alien shadows beneath the crackling yellow floodlights that hung from gas balloons. Once the carriages disgorged their cargoes of conscript actors, once the guns were charged and the mesh-weave costumes donned, the great performances of the day would begin in earnest.

Verity's first glimpse of the Lunar Cathedral's great chamber came over the shoulder of Sister Miriya's power armour, the high vault of the white stone ceiling rising away from her.

The rock had a peculiar glitter about it where flecks of bright mica were caught in its matrix. Lights seemed to dance and play in the heights, and it was a far cry from the close, introspective feel of the convent. The Hospitaller had never seen so much gold in one place. It was on every surface, worked in lines across the mosaics on the floor, climbing up the columns in coils of High Gothic script, fanning in thick cables like a vast, honeyed web.

The people here were just as gilded as the cathedral interior. She passed by women with arch expressions and a sense of disdain that seemed so deeply ingrained that it must have been bred into them. Their clothes mimicked the cut of Inquisitorial robes or, among the more daring, the garb of living saints. They fanned themselves with tessen, semicircles of thin jade that could double as an edged weapon in a fight.

Verity doubted that any of these perfumed noble ladies would ever do anything so base, though. There were troupes of elaborate servitors hovering about each of them, some peeling grapes, some tasting wines for their mistresses. Each of the helots was probably armed with all manner of discreet – but lethal – firepower. She watched the machine-slaves drift to and fro, and observed the way the women edited their servants from their world: they never looked directly at them, never spoke to them. They ignored their very existence, and yet depended entirely upon it.

One of the more audacious of the ladies said something whispered behind her fan and set a clutch of her friends giggling. Verity, the smallest and plainest thing for what must have been kilometres around, instantly knew the insult was directed at her.

At her side, the Battle Sister called Cassandra caught the ripple of spiteful amusement and made a show of sniffing, before turning a soldier's eye on the servitors. 'A passable combat construct,' she noted to no one in particular, 'but I imagine any attacker would be turned back before these slaves could be called to arms.'

'How so?' asked Sister Portia.

'Even a Space Marine would find those fragrances an irritant,' she replied, her voice low – but not *that* low. 'I suspect a crop-duster was used to apply them.'

Verity couldn't help but snatch a look back at the noblewomen, and the pink blushes colouring their faces.

They walked on, the rolling murmur of the fête rising and falling as merchants and theologians made their small talk in drifting shoals of conversation. The Hospitaller kept in line with Miriya and her unit, as Miriya in turn followed the Canoness Galatea and her adjutant Sister Reiko. Verity saw dozens of priests of ranks too numerous to tally, all in various cuts of crimson and white. A very few wore gold and black, and the men in red congregated around them, pups before pack leaders. Verity bowed whenever one of them crossed the orbit of the Adepta Sororitas contingent, but she suspected that her presence was not even noticed. She allowed herself to survey the edges of the gathering as they crossed beneath a great silver glow-globe hanging on suspensors in the chancel. There were a few Sisters from other orders here, representatives of the Orders Famulous and Dialogous. She shared looks with those women, curt nods that carried a dozen subtle signals.

The mix of the pious and the laity was about even. The cream of Neva's magnate class preened in their copious robes, and something of the arrogance of it made Verity uncomfortable. This was, after all, a place of the Emperor's worship, not a ballroom for foppish merchants. The men – they were almost all male – proudly displayed the sigils of their noble houses on medallions, tabards and tunics. The Hospitaller reflected: the last time she had seen many of those symbols, they had been rendered as livid brands burnt into the flesh of indentured workers, or carved across the smoke-belching stacks of manufactories, as an undisciplined child might daub their name on a wall.

Their procession stopped with such abruptness that Verity was jolted from her thoughts and almost walked into the back of Sister Isabel. She recovered quickly, frowning at her lack of focus.

It took a moment for Verity to recognise the man that Galatea stood before, a stiff salute in her pose. She had seen his placid, patrician face on billboards out at the port, and on some of the moons, on posters drawn over with rude graffiti.

'Governor Emmel, are you well?' asked the Canoness.

He presented an expression of theatrical sadness. 'As well as can be expected, my dear lady. It has been explained to me that my festival's star attraction will not be appearing.' Verity could tell from his tone of voice that Emmel was more distressed about the prospect of throwing a poor festival than he was that Torris Vaun was at large among his people.

'The Adepta Sororitas will ensure that your distress will be short-lived,' Galatea replied smoothly. 'The matter is in hand.'

That seemed to be enough to satisfy the planetary ruler, his gaze already wandering to the perfumed women congregating at the wine fountain. 'Ah, good. I know I can place my trust in the Daughters of the Emperor...'

From the edge of her vision came a cluster of other aristocrats, buoyed up on drink and sweet tabac smoke. 'With all due respect, that may not be an entirely good idea.' This new arrival was of the same stock as Emmel, but he had the look about him of a hunting dog. He was lean and spare, and hungry with it. The analytical part of Verity's mind automatically noticed the telltale yellowing around the edges of his eyelids common to those who smoked kyxa. The plant extract from worlds in the Ultima Segmentum was a mild narcotic and aphrodisiac, far too costly for the common folk.

Governor Emmel gave a shallow bow. 'My honoured Baron Sherring, your counsel is welcome at all times. There is an issue you wish to bring to my attention?'

Sherring glanced at Galatea and the assembled Sisters, then away again. 'I would not be so bold as to cast doubt on the dedication of these fine women, but voices are raised in chambers, governor. My fellow barons wonder if our personal guards might not take up the hunt for this Vaun fellow.'

Miriya spoke for the first time since they had entered the

room. At first she seemed apologetic. 'Begging the baron's pardon, but you overlook a matter of some importance.'

'Does he?' piped Emmel, drawing a goblet from a passing cherubim. 'Do tell.'

'Torris Vaun was loose on this planet for a full two solar years before he ventured offworld to further his criminal career. In that time, the soldiers of your noble houses utterly failed to effect the witch's capture.' She laid a cool eye on Sherring. 'But forgive me. I am not party to the radical, sweeping changes in combat doctrine that you must have instilled in your guards since then.'

Sherring covered his annoyance with a puff from a tabac stick, and Emmel tapped his lips thoughtfully. 'I don't recall any changes,' he said aloud. 'Perhaps there were and I was not informed?'

The baron bowed and made to leave. 'As I said, it was a suggestion, nothing more. Clearly the Battle Sisters have everything in hand.' Sherring retreated back into the gathering, bidding farewell with a plastic smile.

Emmel found Verity watching him and he threw her a slightly boozy wink. 'Good old Holt. Stout fellow, if a bit ambitious.' He glanced at Miriya. 'Sister, your forthrightness is refreshing. A good trait for a warrior.' The governor leaned closer to her, and in that moment his mask of affable geniality slipped. 'But I will be disappointed if that is the only arrow in your quiver.' Then the smirk was back and he was drifting away, draining the goblet to the dregs.

In his place appeared an officer of the planetary guard garrison, bearded and furrow-browed. The man wore the local uniform of grass green and black, dotted with highly polished decorations of many kinds. At his waist was a ceremonial lasgun made of glass and a scimitar. 'The lord deacon asks that you attend him on the tier.' His voice was flat.

'I would be glad to do so, Colonel Braun,' began Galatea, but the officer gave a slow shake of the head.

'Lord LaHayn wishes to address Sister Miriya.' Braun looked at Verity. 'And the Hospitaller as well.'

The Canoness covered a twitch of annoyance. 'Of course.' She nodded, but the colonel was already walking.

Verity felt her throat go dry as she fell into step with Miriya. It took her a moment to find her voice. 'What do I tell him?'

Miriya's expression remained rigid. Her distaste for these people was more potent than the perfumes. 'Whatever he wants to hear.'

The Tier of Greatest Piety extended out like a jutted lip from the cathedral tower at its thickest point, high up over the teeming masses below. While white noise generators kept the genteel music inside the chapel, out here on the crescent-shaped terrace the night seemed to float on waves of cheering and hymnals. There were ranks of illuminators everywhere, but none of them were operating at the moment. The only light came from below, from the floodlamps and the uncountable numbers of electro-candles in the hands of the amphitheatre audience. Braun guided them between busy lines of servitors preparing hololith lenses and nets of vox cabling. At the raised edge of the terrace, the great Lord Deacon of Neva, Viktor LaHayn, sat atop a stone battlement watching the crowd, apparently unaffected by the dizzying view.

He had to raise his voice a little to be heard. 'They can't see us up here yet,' began the priest-lord. 'We are dark. Anyone who looks up will miss the words and that would be unforgivable.'

Miriya saw down below where vast turning boards made of small painted shutters flapped and clacked into words in High Gothic. The lyrics to the hymns rolled over them for the massive crowd to see. 'Surely, lord, they should know the words by heart?'

LaHayn threw an amused look to the dean at his side. 'Spoken like a true Sororitas, eh Venik?'

The other man just nodded, and then gestured to Braun. Without words, the colonel gave a shallow bow and retreated into the company of a dozen armsmen near the chapel door.

It became clear to Miriya that the deacon was waiting for the soldiers to be out of earshot.

'Those who cannot read, learn by rote,' said LaHayn. 'In this way, the word of the God-Emperor is never lost to us. It remains unalterable, inviolate, eternal.'

'Ave Imperator.' The ritual coda slipped from her mouth without conscious thought.

'Indeed,' said the priest-lord, and he smiled again. 'Sisters Miriya and Verity, I hope you will not think ill of me for my display in the convent. Understand that the zeal the Emperor imbues me with is sometimes more than an old man may conduct. In the matter of the criminal Vaun, I am most ardent.'

'His light touches all of us in its own way,' piped Verity, keeping her eyes lowered.

'And you share my passion for this mission, yes?' LaHayn's voice was casual, level, but aimed like a laser at the Sister Superior.

'How could I not?' she replied. 'The man took the life of one of my most trusted comrades, a decorated Sister who devoted her entire existence to our church, and for that alone he should die a hundred deaths.' She kept her voice steady with effort. 'His violation of Sister Iona's mind blackens him further still. If it is in my power, I should like to present the wastrel to her so that she might be the one to strike his head from his neck.'

Dean Venik raised an eyebrow, but LaHayn's expression did not alter. 'It pleases me to hear you say those words. I prayed for Sister Iona's soul today at my private mass. I hope that in the grace of the Condicio Repentia she might find the solace she seeks.'

A nerve jumped in Miriya's jaw. Iona might never have taken the terrible exile of the repentant had it not been for LaHayn's demands for contrition. That simple fact seemed to escape the priest-lord.

'Honoured Sisters, I require you to keep the dean appraised of your investigations at all times. I'm sure you understand that Governor Emmel and the planetary congress have their issues with your continued involvement, but I have ensured that you may progress without undue censure.'

'His lordship has instructed me to open my office to you during your hunt for the criminal,' added Venik. 'You may petition me directly on any matters that fall outside your purview.'

'You are most generous,' added Verity.

'Tell me,' the priest-lord said in a confidential tone. 'I understand you conducted an interro-gation at the reformatory. What did you discover?'

'I have no conclusions to offer at this stage, lord,' Miriya spoke quickly, pre-empting anything that Verity might say. 'But I fear that the orchestration of Vaun's escape was not mere opportunism. There is a plan at work here.'

'Indeed? We must consider that carefully.' Something below in the arena made the crowd cry out in awe and it caught LaHayn's attention for a moment. He studied Miriya. 'Vaun is no easy prey, Sister. He is elusive and deadly, but brilliant with it.'

'He's a thug,' she grated, a growing sense of irritation building in her.

The priest seemed not to notice. 'Only on the outside. I've met him face to face, my dear, and he can be charming when he wants to be.'

'If you were close enough to look him in the eye, why is he not dead?' Venik inhaled sharply and shot her a warning glare, but Miriya ignored it. 'I find myself wondering why a creature such as he was not gathered up as a youth for the harvest of the Black Ships.'

'Torris Vaun is wily,' noted LaHayn. 'Compassion and love are absent from his heart. He burns cold, Sister.'

Verity studied his face as he spoke. 'You sound as if you admire him, lord.'

The priest snorted lightly. 'Only as one might admire the function of a boltgun or the virulence of a disease. Believe me, there is no one on Neva who will be more content than I when Vaun meets the end I have planned for him.'

The dean made to dismiss them, but Miriya stood her ground. 'If it pleases the deacon, you have not answered my questions.'

LaHayn stood, brushing a speck of dust from the rich crimson and gold fabric of his robes. 'Sometimes, death alone is not enough to satisfy the Emperor's decree.' He was terse now, each word sharp and hard. 'As to the inner workings of the Adeptus Astra Telepathica, that is something that I am pleased to be untouched by.' The priest-lord gave the two women a long, calculating look. 'Let me ask you something. Do you fear the witch?'

'The psyker is the gate through which Chaos enters. Only by sacrament and denial can those cursed with the witch-sight hope to live and serve Terra.' Verity repeated the words from the Liturgy of Retribution.

'Well said, but now it is *you* who does not answer *my* question.' He stared at Miriya. 'Answer me, Sister. Do you fear the witch?'

She didn't hesitate to respond. 'Of course I do. Verity is right in what she says, the witchkin would destroy mankind if left unchecked. They are as great a foe as the mutant and the heretic, the alien and daemon. Our fear makes us strong. It is the spur that takes us to destroy these monsters. If I had no fear of these things, I would have nothing to fight for.'

'Just so,' LaHayn nodded. 'If there were any doubts in my mind that you are the one to catch this pestilent, they have fled.' He bowed to them. 'Now, forgive me, but the bell comes close to ringing and I have a sermon to deliver.' The priest-lord took in the crowds below with a sweep of his arms.

As Venik ushered them away, Miriya halted and turned back to face LaHayn. 'Begging your pardon, deacon. There is one other question I wish to pose to you.'

'If you are quick about it.'

She bowed again. 'While we have focused on the incidence of Vaun's escape, a single factor eludes me. The criminal had the chance to go where he wanted, to strike out for a hundred worlds other than this one. Why, in the Emperor's name, did he elect to return to a planet where his face and his villainy are so well known? What possible bounty could exist on Neva that he would risk all for it?' Miriya became aware that Verity was watching both of them very closely.

LaHayn's face became very still. 'Who can fathom the mind of a madman, Sister? I confess I have no answer for you.'

Miriya bowed once more and let Venik hand them off to Colonel Braun, who in turn led them down a few levels to the viewing galleries. Verity was quiet, her face pale and her gaze turned inward.

'What say you?' she asked.

Verity took her time answering. 'I... am mistaken,' said the Hospitaller, the words difficult for her to give voice to. 'For a moment, I thought... the dilation of his eyes, the blush response...'

Miriya leaned in close, so that only the two of them could hear one another. 'Say it.'

'No.' Verity shook her head. 'I am in error.'

'*Say it*,' repeated the Battle Sister. 'Tell me so I know I am not alone in my thoughts.'

Verity met her gaze. 'When you asked him about Vaun's reasons... he lied to us.'

'Just so,' said Miriya. 'But to what end?'

When the lamps illuminated him, LaHayn felt as if he were being projected upward into the stars, cutting free of the confines of his human meat and becoming something greater and more ephemeral – something linked directly to the bright supernova that was the Light of the God-Emperor. It never failed to elate him.

There was an old saying on Neva, that all men born there had the calling. Indeed, every male child was required to take a term in the seminary to see if they were suitable for the planet's massive caste of clerics. It had been under such simple circumstances that Viktor LaHayn had come into the orbit of the Church of Terra, and in those gloomy cloisters, among the grim-faced adepts and the priests alight with brimstone oratory, he had truly found his first vocation. The mere thought of those days brought a smile to his face. Those were less complicated times, when the word and deed of persecution were all that occupied his mind, when all he needed was the chainsword in his strong right hand and the Book of the Fated in his left.

The roaring crowd filled his senses and he welcomed them in, raising his hands in the age-old sign of the aquila, the divine two-headed eagle. Blind and yet not blind, forward looking yet knowing the past, wings unfurled to shield humanity.

In moments of introspection like this one, LaHayn wondered what he would say if he were able to step back into the past and meet his younger self in those lost days. What would he have told him? Could he have stood to whisper the secrets that would later be revealed to him? How could he, when to do so would deny that callow youth the shattering, soul-blazing revelation that his later years brought?

LaHayn watched his hololithic image grow to giant proportions and drank in the awe of his congregation. If his first calling had taken him to a vast, new world in the Emperor's service, then his second had pressed him to the very foot of the Golden Throne. None of them down there in the amphi-theatre could see it, but they sensed it in the words he spoke, in the touch he laid on them. They knew, in their hearts, just as he did, never doubting, unflinching in his righteousness.

The final pieces were coming together. Lord Viktor LaHayn was the hand of the God-Emperor, and His will would be done. Nothing would be allowed to prevent it.

CHAPTER FIVE

The Imperial Church was an engine fuelled by devotion, a machine lubricated by the blood of its faithful, and across a hundred thousand stars, the temples and spires of the God-Emperor's spirit cast long shadows. As each planet and populace was distinctive, so each society took the worship of the Lord of Mankind and made it their own. On feral planets like Miral, the primitive natives saw Him as a great animal stalking the stygian depths of their forests. The forge world Telemachus revered Him as the Great Blacksmith, the Moulder of All Things, and the people of Limnus Epsilon believed He lived in their sun, breathing radiance down upon them.

The church had learned in the days of the Great Crusade that enforcing its will on worlds by eradicating their belief systems and starting from scratch was a lengthy and troublesome process. Instead, the Ecclesiarchy worked by coercion and change, turning native religions to face Holy Terra and showing them the great truth of the universe – that all gods were the God-Emperor of Man in one guise or another.

On a world such as Neva, where dogma and creed were irreversibly threaded through every single aspect of its civilisation, wars had been fought over single verses in holy tracts, over the smallest points in the reading of prayers. Barons and city-lords had put each other to the sword when interpretations of credo boiled into violent discord. On such a planet, where every man, woman and child prayed to Terra in fear of their immortal souls, there was friction and dangerous strife over the meaning and the matter of the church's word.

To end such disharmony, Neva required a miracle, and by the grace of the God-Emperor, it received one. The people called it the Blessing of the Wound.

Lord LaHayn did not speak or gesture for the crowds to become silent. He merely watched and waited, his aspect neutral and his hands clasped behind his back. The tall hololithic ghost projection glittered beneath him, hovering over the stage sets mounted in the amphitheatre's dirt arena. He allowed his visage to turn gently this way and that, the image's eyes scanning the people with a cool, unwavering stare. LaHayn had long ago mastered the ability to address a crowd and have each person in it think that it was only they to whom he was speaking.

When they were quiet, he gave them a shallow bow. 'Sons and daughters of Neva. We are blessed.' The priest-lord felt the gaze of thousands upon him, thousands of breaths held in tight throats. 'The path towards a better tomorrow stretches out before us, towards a future that is golden and eternal, but our journey together must cross a wilderness of hardship and struggle.'

He bowed his head. 'Each year we gather here and ask for the Blessing, and we are granted it. Why? Because we are humanity. Because we are the children of the God-Emperor, the most supreme man that ever drew breath. Through His servants, we know Him and we know His words. We understand what is expected of us. Our duties, to be strong, to never weaken, to purge the xenos, the mutant, the heretic from our ranks.' The priest looked up again. 'We know that the price of all things is not gold, not uranium, not diamonds. It is *faith unfailing*. And that price is paid with blood.'

* * *

When Saint Celestine's warfleet had appeared in Neva's orbit to herald the passing of the warp storm that had isolated the system, the churches across the planet were filled to bursting. Lives were lost in some places when chapels, overflowing with worshippers, collapsed under their own weight. According to some records from that time, the living saint herself made planetfall at the Discus Rock some kilometres from Noroc – although log-tapes from the warrior's flagship never fully corroborated this incident, leading some historians on other worlds to doubt the words of the Nevan priests. But true or not, the saint's passage under Neva's sun changed the planet forever. The monks living in the monastery that stood at Discus now guarded the spot. Ringed with brass electro-fences there was a shallow imprint in the flat stone, allegedly marking the place where Celestine's golden boot first touched the surface of Neva. The very richest and most favoured of the planet's noble castes were allowed to kneel there and kiss the mark. Some would ritually cut themselves and offer a few drops of blood to the footprint, if they were highborn enough.

Saint Celestine, the Hieromartyr of the Palatine Crusade, was second only to the Emperor in the number of Nevan chapels dedicated to her name. Her face adorned coins, icons and devotional artworks, and in every one, the man who had come to be known as Ivar of the Wound attended at her feet.

The priest gathered the people in with his open arms. 'I am humbled by the magnificent example that you, my congregation, have set. The workers and artisans among you who toil and ask not for acclaim, but accept the honour of our noble Governor Emmel. The soldiers and warriors who burn with cold fire and unyielding resolve, never flinching before the threat of the heretical and unmutual. The pastors and clerics who hold the very soul of our people in their hands, shielding it from the lies of the treacherous and disloyal. You seek reward in service alone.' He made the sign of the aquila once more. 'I am forever in awe of you.' After a long moment, he spoke again, but now the warmth in his voice was bleeding out, changing to something cold and hard. 'The greatest pride of the Nevan people is order and yet there are those among us who seek only chaos and destruction. As a chirurgeon might sever a limb to excise a lethal cancer, we must do the same. Our society offers so much to those who follow the rule of law, and yet these criminals want only discord and anarchy. To be pious is to be strong and never yield to such offenders. Remember! The stalwart will inherit tomorrow; the weak will be buried today. We must protect our children and our nation from the malignancy of rebellion. In Ivar's name, they must know the cost. They must know it!'

Ivar's story was famous to every Nevan, taught in crèches and re-told to them again and again throughout their lives. There were books of his life, heavy with garish illustrations and few words for the simple-minded and the young, or dense with layers of interpretation for the thinker. Each year the church had the public vox networks produce a lavish viddy-drama biography. He was celebrated in song and his patrician profile adorned murals across the planet.

An ordinary soldier in Noroc's city guard, Ivar had witnessed first-hand the arrival of Celestine in those turbulent days, and when the shadow of her starship quieted the assassin-wars and dismissed the warp storm, he was so moved by the event that he gathered a legion of warriors and followed the saint on her War of Faith. He called it a payment in return for Celestine's rescue of his homeworld, and so in the months that ensued Ivar and his men pledged themselves as militia in the service of the Adepta Sororitas. Ivar's soldiers fought with the passion of true zealots, their numbers thinning through attrition until at last only Ivar himself was still alive.

Finally, on the battlefields of the Kodiak Cluster where Celestine's force had engaged an eldar conclave, the living saint was drawn into close combat with an alien warlord. Ivar, attempting to prove his devotion, tried and failed to strangle the warlord with his bare hands, and instead found himself taken as a human shield by the xenos creature. Confronting Celestine, the alien believed that she would never willingly kill a member of her own species in cold blood but Ivar called out for the saint to sacrifice him in order to destroy the eldar commander. Celestine plunged the burning tip of her Ardent Blade through Ivar's chest, running him through and cleaving the heart of the alien behind him, but when the sword was withdrawn, by some miracle Ivar still lived.

'Zeal. Purity. Duty. The pillars of the church are the platform on which we stand, unbreakable and unending. We look to the future that only we can achieve. As Ivar showed us, history does not long entrust the care of freedom to the weak or the timid.' LaHayn gently returned to the smooth, careful cadence of his earlier words. 'Each of you shares in the greatest glory of them all – you are the truly virtuous. We, who are ruthless to those who oppose our vision, masters of those we defeat, unflinching in the face of adversity. I pity all those who are not born beneath our skies, for they will never know the touch of righteousness as we do.'

The crowd roared its approval, and LaHayn gave it a fatherly smile. 'The path we have chosen is not an easy one. Struggle is the parent of all things and true virtue lies in bloodshed. But we will not tire, we will not falter, we will not fail. In the blood of our children comes the price we must pay. Blood alone moves the wheels of history, and we will be resolute, we will fear no sacrifice, and surmount every difficulty to win our just destiny. Redemption is within your grasp. The Emperor rewards His children who show courage and fidelity, just as He rejects those without it!' The amphitheatre exploded with sound, cheers pealing off the walls and booming across the city in waves of sound. Across Noroc and across the planet, the priest-lord's sermon reached the ears of Neva's faithful and they loved him for it.

* * *

The sword cut in Ivar's chest never healed. In honour of his great courage, Saint Celestine released him from his obligation to her and bid him return to Neva, there to serve the will of the God-Emperor among his people. From that day until the end of his life, Ivar's holy wound never closed, and despite the constant agony it brought him, he wore it as a badge of honour. It was said that those anointed with a drop of blood from Ivar's cut were blessed, and the bandages with which he wrapped it were held to this day as sacred relics. Ivar rose to the rank of lord deacon and founded the construction of the great Lunar Cathedral. His legacy of willing sacrifice, penitence, bloodshed and pain became the foundations on which the Nevan sect of the Imperial Church stood – and with his guidance, the Blessing of the Wound took its place as the most important religious ceremony in the planet's calendar.

Miriya and Verity stood at the lip of the gallery's fluted balcony, watching the riot of activity at the edges of the arena. LaHayn's hololithic image bowed and faded into the evening, a great cry rising from the audience as it went. Below, figures in all kinds of gaudy costumes were streaming out of hidden gates, forming up into ragged skirmish lines or gadding about in peculiar, directionless dances. Just beneath the level of the observation galleries, there were catwalks and gantries made of thin steel, painted in neutral shades so as not to stand out beneath the floodlamps. The Celestian and the Hospitaller could see people in grey coveralls working feverishly at cables and pulleys, making parts of the wooden sets below shift and move in time to the building hum of choral chants.

Verity blinked at the figures in the amphitheatre. 'Those are... They are just children.'

Miriya followed her gaze towards a group of youngsters and her brow furrowed. They were clad in crude approximations of Adepta Sororitas wargear, but made from simple cloth and cardboard instead of ceramite and flexsteel. One of the teenagers stumbled, clutching at her head to hold a wig of straw-like white hair that mimicked the traditional cut of the Battle Sisters.

'I... I saw those youths in the street, when I was travelling to the convent. Is this some sort of game?'

Miriya gave a nod. 'The Games of Penance, as they are known. A reconstruction of great events from Saint Celestine's Wars of Faith. I have never seen them myself...'

'Look, there,' Verity pointed. 'Do you see those players on the stage? What are they supposed to be?'

'Eldar,' Miriya observed, recognising the rudimentary capes and plumes adorning the fake armour of the actors. 'They are playing at the battle for Kodiak Prime, or something like it.' She failed to keep a grimace from her face. The whole performance was a caricature, a ridiculous spectacle that might have been comic if she had not found it so offensive. Miriya had faced the xenos in battle, and the eldar she had fought were terrifying, deadly killers full of powerful grace and unstoppable speed – these moronic mimics in the amphitheatre were blundering jesters in comparison, exaggerated and simplistic parodies of the real thing.

The crowd did not share her low opinion, however. The locals were chanting and whooping, spinning celebratory banners over their heads or letting off small screamer fireworks. Over the loud hailers in the stadium the opening bars of the Palatine March issued forth, and the two sides in the imitation battle rushed at one another, screaming incoherent war cries.

'This is a mockery,' growled Miriya.

'It is... disturbing,' admitted Verity, 'but not to the Nevans. This is their way of honouring the living saint.'

The Battle Sister's rejoinder was silenced as a clatter of gunfire rose up from the amphitheatre. Miriya's gauntleted hands tensed automatically at the sound of a hundred ballistic stubbers going off in ragged succession. All of the participants in the ersatz skirmish were firing on one another, but where she had expected them to knock each other down with paint shells and powder rounds, there was the flat crackle of bullets.

'They are using live weapons...' As the Sister Superior watched, one of the youths dressed as a Sororitas inexpertly discharged a salvo of shots into a boy on stubby stilts, the heavy rounds ripping through the wood and cloth imitations of eldar armour. Blood was already pooling on the arena's sands where figures from both sides had been cut down.

'Holy Terra!' gasped Verity, her hand flying to her mouth in shock.

Close by, one of the merchantmen from the cathedral clapped and let out a guffaw. 'What a magnificent effort this year. This Blessing will be one for the ages.'

Miriya rounded on him. 'They're killing each other.'

The portly man's expression shattered under the Battle Sister's leaden stare. 'But... But of course they are. That's how it is done...' He forced a smile. 'Ah, of course. Forgive me. You must both be off-worlders, yes? You are both new to Neva and the festival?'

'What kind of blessing demands you force your people to kill one another?' challenged Miriya.

'F-force?' said the merchant. 'No one is forced, honoured Sister.' He fumbled in the folds of his robes and recovered a fold of long papers from a hidden pocket. 'The participants in the reconstruction are all willing... Well, except for a few irredeemables from the reformatory and some asylum inmates.' One of the papers was a dark crimson, and he peeled it from the pack to wave it at her. 'Every citizen who received one of these dockets in the clerical lottery knows they are obligated to take part in the great re-enactment. We are all more than ready to do our part in penance!'

Miriya snatched the red paper from him. 'Then tell me, sir, why are you here and not down there?' She jerked a thumb at the melee below them.

The merchant's face coloured. 'I... I was happy to present the church with a substantial forfeit donation in my stead!'

'You bought your way out with coin? How lucky for you

that your coffers are deep enough,' she sneered. 'If only others were so fortunate!'

'Now see here,' the noble retorted, attempting to maintain a level of superiority. 'Those who endure the Blessing are praised and rewarded. Our finest chirurgeons attend them in the aftermath, and those whose fortitude is lesser are buried with honours!'

Barely able to contain her anger, Miriya turned away, her hand dropping unconsciously to the grip of her holstered plasma pistol. The sound and fury of the confrontation set her teeth on edge, triggering old, ingrained battle instincts.

'Celestine. *Celestine*!' The cry came from one of the merchant's retinue, and the name was picked up and repeated by the crowd.

From a hidden hatch in the walls of the cathedral, a winged figure in gold emerged to fly over the amphitheatre, swooping like a bird of prey.

Verity watched the girl garbed as the living saint race over the blood-stained sands, a fat set of pulley-wheels in the small of her back connected by glassy cables to a rig on the suspended catwalks. The grey-suited workers pulled at levers and tugged spindles to work her like a puppet, and in turn her wings of paper feathers fluttered and snapped through the air. A heavy brass halo hung about her head, decorated with yellowish biolumes, and she had an oversized replica of the Celestine's blessed weapon, the Ardent Blade, secured to one hand by tethers.

A dispenser tucked under her waist spat out a stream of paper slips, each one printed with a devotional message and a tithe voucher. People in the crowds tussled and snatched at the air trying to pull them from the night winds.

The psuedo-saint fell low and her sword clipped the heads and torsos of a dozen men in eldar costume. The blade was just for show and too blunt to sever a limb; those it struck were concussed or reeled away with broken bones.

Verity watched, and she felt queasy. It was not that she was frail or unused to the sight of spilt blood, but the malicious theatre with which this spectacle was unfolding made her uncomfortable. On the moons where she served in the wards of the hospices, there had been stories of the things done in the Emperor's name on Neva – but there were always such stories on the outer worlds, and Sister Verity was never one to place too much credence in rumour and insinuation. She wished now that she had paid greater mind. The wanton disregard for human life at play here jarred with the very core of Verity's vow to the Order of Serenity and her life's work as a Sister Hospitaller. The oath she had sworn the day she entered the Sisterhood returned to her: *First, do no harm to the Emperor's subjects. Take pain from those who revere Him, inflict it only on those who stand against His Light.*

'This is a harsh universe,' she heard the merchant remark to one of his cronies. 'It is not by chance that our church and our festival reflect the truth of that. After all, if no blood were shed this day, in what possible way could we hope to show the Emperor our devotion?'

A flurry of motion drew her eye. On the gantry a few metres below, the men in grey were panicking. Aged, overworked metal snapped with a percussive crash and cables whipped free, slashing one man across the chest and throwing another over the catwalk's rail and down to his death. The girl playing Celestine was suddenly jerked out of her pattern of flight and reeled upward like a hooked fish. The sword dangled from her fingers, and in horror, Verity saw where the glass cables looped about her head and neck. If the crowds in the stands understood or even cared what had happened, the Hospitaller had no idea but she saw clear as day the face of the costumed girl in abject terror as she started to choke.

Sister Verity reacted without conscious thought, and vaulted over the edge of the balcony. Boots scraping on stone, she slipped down the sheer face of the cathedral and landed on the catwalk. She was running to the trapped girl before she was even aware of Miriya calling after her.

* * *

The merchant and his troupe of perfumed dandies actually broke out in laughter when the Hospitaller jumped, and it took much of Miriya's self-control not to toss one of them after her. Shooting them an iron-hard glare, she followed the woman down to the gantry, shouting her name, but Verity did not seem to hear her, intent instead on the luckless girl caught up in the wires beneath the catwalk.

The workers who had not been struck insensate or dead by the broken cables were of little use, and she forced them aside. The catwalk squealed and complained beneath her every footfall, flecks of dust trickling off ancient joints. The shattered pulley mechanism lowed like a dying animal, and Miriya's hand shot out to grab a support as the decking began to tilt. The framework was rife with rust and decay.

'Verity! We are not safe here.'

The Hospitaller was already pulling the girl up. She was ashen-faced as she worked to unwind the cabling from the youth's pale, bruised neck. 'I think she may still live...'

In reply, the catwalk let out a shriek of buckling steel and listed sharply. All at once, the costumed girl fell away from Verity's grip and Miriya bounded forward to snag the Sister Hospitaller before she went along with her. Their hands met, the Battle Sister clutching a handful of Verity's robes and then the gantry broke apart.

It was centuries old, and maintained as well as it could have been, but artisans and technicians were not the most favoured of castes on Neva and even in the amphitheatre of the Lunar Cathedral, there were never enough skilled hands to service all of the church's machinery. Steel and bodies fell through the air and crashed into the wood and fibre of the false eldar domes, straight into the middle of the arena.

Galatea's knuckles turned white where she gripped the stone balustrade. 'In Katherine's name, what is she doing?'

At her side, Sister Reiko peered through a small monocular. 'An accident, Canoness? I do not think this was intentional–'

'Now, this is an interesting development.' Governor Emmel's

words cut off Reiko's speech as he approached, his retinue trailing behind him and the lord deacon at his side. 'My dear Canoness, if your Battle Sister wished to take part in the games, she had only to ask.'

'Governor, I fear that a mistake has been made,' Galatea spoke quickly. 'Perhaps if you would consider a pause in the proceedings?'

Emmel made a face. 'Ah, that would not be prudent. The rules of the fête are quite clear on these matters. The re-enactment must be played out to its conclusion without interruption. There would be much discord if I tried to halt it.'

'Perhaps even a riot,' ventured Dean Venik.

The governor cupped his ear. 'Listen, Canoness. Do you hear? The people are enraptured. They must think this is some surprise performance in lieu of the witch they were promised.'

'Perhaps not a mistake after all,' added LaHayn. 'The God-Emperor moves in mysterious ways.'

Emmel nodded and clapped his hands. 'Oh, yes, yes. You may be right!' His eyes sparkled with the idea of it. 'I wonder, an actual Sister of Battle on the field? What a game that will be!'

'With respect, governor, Sister Miriya may be injured, and she was not alone. Sister Verity is a Hospitaller, not used to combat.' Galatea's words were intense.

LaHayn accepted this with a dismissive nod. 'I am sure the Emperor will extend to her the protection her vocation merits.'

Miriya hauled herself out of the ruins of the wooden set and winced in pain: her right arm was dislocated. Gritting her teeth, she gripped her right wrist with her left hand and yanked. A sickening snap and a moment of sharp agony resonated through the Battle Sister's frame. She shook off the pain and coughed out metallic spittle.

A groan drew her to where Verity lay. The Hospitaller was

uninjured but dazed, and Miriya pulled her unsteadily to her feet.

'The... the girl...' began Verity, but she fell silent when the other woman pointed a gloved finger at the wreckage. The teenager dressed as Celestine had broken the Hospitaller's fall and rested there in an untidy heap. Sightless, dull eyes looked up into the night sky. Verity knelt and closed the dead girl's eyelids, whispering a verse of funerary rites over her body.

The roaring of the audience crashed around them, loud as ocean breakers on a storm-tossed shore. In among the players fighting the mock battle, several of the imitation eldar had been startled by the sudden cacophony of metal that had dropped from the air, and they milled about, unsure of themselves. This close to them, Miriya could see that the weapons they bore were actually common projectile rifles and shotguns disguised to resemble the alien shuriken projectors. The Battle Sister knew the look in their eyes all too well. She had seen it before on the faces of heretic vassals and slave-troopers, on cultists whipped into frenzy by their demagogues.

'Stay close to me,' she hissed to Verity. 'They're going to fire on us.'

The Hospitaller shook her head. 'But why?'

Miriya ignored her and advanced, stepping off the pile of wreckage and holding up one hand, palm flat in a warding gesture. 'We have no part in your games,' she said aloud, in a clear, level voice. 'Stand aside.'

The costumed men were all dressed in the same warped outfits, so it was unclear if there were any ranks or hierarchy among them. They shot nervous glances at the women and at each other. Miriya saw a path she could take, up and behind the wreckage of the stage to where the gates in the arena walls would lead to safety.

'Don't run,' she whispered. 'If we run, they'll attack.'

'They're just ordinary people,' insisted Verity.

Miriya made eye contact with one of the alien-attired men,

catching sight of his gaze through the triangular slits in his plumed helmet. 'That doesn't matter.'

She saw the thought forming in his mind before the man was even aware of it, her hand tearing away the peace-bond ribbon wrapped around her pistol holster. A dozen camouflaged weapons came about to bear on them and Miriya shoved Verity out of the firing line, her gun clearing its leather as shot and shell spat into the air.

'Death to the humans!' The call exploded from the lips of the false eldar, and the crowd watching them roared once again.

Automatic training born from decades of hard, unswerving service in the name of the Emperor took over. Miriya's gun barked, the ear-splitting shriek of supeheated plasma bolts drowning out the dull rattle of lead shot. It became a rout, every trigger-pull marking a critical hit, no single charge from the energy pistol wasted as the costumed men screamed and died. Paper and cloth in garish oranges and greens were stained with dark arterial crimson. Helmets made out of softwood splintered and broke.

The Battle Sister heard the pellets clattering off her power armour, as ineffectual as hailstones against the black ceramite sheath. A chance ricochet nicked a line of stinging pain across her cheek and she ignored it, turning and firing again in a single fluid motion.

When all the assailants lay dead or bleeding their last into the dust, Miriya closed her eyes and prayed for silence but she was denied it, the air about her filled to overflowing with the deafening adulation of the congregation.

Verity grabbed at her arm and turned her about. The Hospitaller was furious. 'You didn't need to kill them!' she shouted, her voice barely audible above the crowd. 'Why did you do that?'

The other players in the reconstruction were gathering to them, pathetic remnants in their tattered and bloody costumes. Some dragged injured comrades with them, others limped and showed wounds that were wet and ragged. Miriya shook off Verity's grip with an angry snarl and jerked her chin at the penitents. 'Help them.'

The Hospitaller left her there and took to ripping bandages from torn robes. Miriya surveyed the dead arranged around her, Verity's question ringing in her mind. What madness was this, that these people would force her to end their lives, all in the name of a brutal game? There were other ways to show devotion to the Golden Throne that did not require such a wasteful sacrifice. Was life valued so little on Neva?

The vox speakers struck up again with a fresh barrage of song, beginning with a stern rendition of the grand hymnal from Enoch's Castigations. Miriya cast her gaze upward, searching the dark sky for some sign, some explanation. Her thoughts were a churn of confusion, a state that was unacceptable for a Sister of Battle. Her skin crawled, and she found that all she wanted at this moment was to purify herself with a purgatory oil and take prayer in the convent's chapel. *What cursed luck has brought me to this madhouse,* she asked herself?

A handful of bright dots crossed the night above the amphitheatre, moving with purpose and great speed towards the towering Lunar Cathedral. Just as it had moments before when she locked gazes with the gunmen, Miriya's honed combat sense rang a warning in her mind. 'Aircraft,' she said aloud, 'in attack formation.'

As if they had been waiting for her to voice her thoughts, the flyers suddenly split apart and swept away in pairs towards different points of the compass. The closest duo dipped low and came into the nimbus of the floating lamp-blimps. They were coleopters, vessels with a ring-shaped fuselage enclosing a large spinning fan that kept them airborne. The unmistakable shapes of boxy weapons pods hung on stubby winglets.

No alarm cry would have warned the people in the crowds, and they watched the flyers with disbelief, perhaps believing them to be yet another surprise addition to the Games of Penance. In the next second panic and terror rose up in a wave as fountains of firebombs spat from the coleopters and fell in orange trails towards the stadium. Everywhere they landed, great balls of black smoke and yellow flame bloomed, immolating hundreds. The aircraft wove through the mayhem they seeded, strafing the panicked people, while above them another lone ship dropped out of sight on the Tier of Greatest Piety. Whoever these killers were, they were landing men on the upper levels of the church tower.

Lasers lanced out of the observation galleries, questing after the darting ships and missing. Miriya assumed the shots were being fired by the gun servitors she had seen serving the nobles earlier. She swore a gutter oath recalled from her childhood. How in Terra's name had such a thing been allowed to happen? Were the planetary defence forces stationed in Noroc so lax that any terrorist could idle into the city's airspace unchallenged?

Unbidden, another, darker thought rose to the surface of her mind. Was this some other part of Neva's dogma of atonement and suffering, a random attack thrown at the innocent as some kind of penance? She shook the idea away and sprinted towards the arena's edge, where elevator cages would carry her back up to the galleries of the cathedral.

Verity came after her. 'Where are you going?'

'To fight a real enemy,' she retorted. 'You may join me, if you can stomach it!'

CHAPTER SIX

The men of the Noroc city watch would later report that the terrorist coleopters had come from the south and the west, flying in the nap of the earth along valleys or over the scudding white tops of shallow waves. Too low to the ground for detection by conventional sensors, hulls daubed with black paint and running lights blinded, the aircraft threaded into the air over Noroc and went about their business. In the throes of the festival, where sacramental wines were flowing freely and hymns were blotting out the sound of everything else, not many eyes turned from their devotions to maintain watchfulness. In the days that followed, the enforcers would have their hands full, in both matters of arrest and punishment as well as purging its own officers guilty of inattention.

A good percentage of the men in the flyers had previously visited Noroc, some had even been born there. All of them were chosen because they knew the city well enough to wound it. Torris Vaun had gathered them all in the hold of a chilly, echoing transport barge as they crossed the coastal waters, goading them into readiness. Some of these men brought their own codes and morals to the fight, with big talk of striking against the moneyed theocrats in the name of the people, but most of them, like Vaun himself, were in the game for the fire and the havoc. They wanted anarchy for the sport of it, because they thrived on it.

The rockets dropped from the coleopters were stolen from Imperial Guard regiments, elderly area denial munitions pilfered from bunkers where they waited for rebellions and uprisings that never came... until now. The warheads broke open in bright plumes that made miniature daybreaks wherever they struck, and where people did not die from smoke and flame, they smothered each other in panic.

The air inside the Lunar Cathedral was hot with terror. Many of the nobles had fled to the lower levels to find their carriages and draymen destroyed by explosion and firestorm, and they milled about and became frantic, some of them starting small scuffles as their frustrations boiled over. On the higher levels, in the vaulted space of the chapel proper and the galleries that ranged above it, barons and upper echelon priests took to gathering in small, terrified packs with their gun servitors surrounding them, bleakly waiting for invasion, destruction or salvation.

The flyer that approached the Tier of the Greatest Piety executed a running touch-and-go, its wheels barely kissing the careworn granite for ten seconds before it took off again, thrusting away to enter a wide, lazy orbit of the conical tower. It left behind a squad of rag-tag men with no single uniform or look to them. All that united these killers was a callous, predatory anticipation, that and the absolute loyalty they showed to their leader.

Vaun dropped a pair of battered night vision goggles from his eyes and pointed with both hands. 'Get in there, and make some trouble.'

The men obeyed with harsh laughter and ready violence.

Rink jogged to keep up with him. 'We gonna kill them here, then?'

'Patience,' replied the other man. 'It's a nice evening. We'll see how things play out.'

The big thug's eyes glittered. 'I wanna do the priest.'

Vaun shot him a hard look. 'Oh no. That one's for me. I *owe* him.' The criminal's hand strayed to an old, hateful scar beneath his right ear. 'But don't worry, I've got something in mind for you.'

The rattling cage was little more than a basket of steel mesh, but it clambered doggedly up the stone wall of the cathedral, cogged teeth picking their way past oval service hatches cast from fans of brassy leaves. Oil and sparks spat at them as the elevator slowed and halted, presenting them to the observation level. Miriya came through the hatch leading with her pistol, and Verity was close behind, virtually throwing herself out of the lift. The clattering machine seemed to have unnerved the Hostpitaller – and after the accident with the falling catwalk, it was perhaps no surprise that she was newly afraid of Neva's ill-maintained mechanisms.

There were bodies. Mostly they were servitors, and by the pattern of the kill shots they had been targeted by weapons aimed from a moving platform beyond the balconies. Miriya recognised the distinctive wound patterns of shells from Navy-issue heavy bolters. The bodyguards had died under the guns of the coleopter as it strafed the tower with random cascades of fire. With a degree of delicacy that seemed out of place among the carnage, Verity stepped lightly over the bodies of a few aristocrats, giving each a murmured prayer verse.

The Celestian saw one of the perfumed women they had crossed earlier in the evening, her only bouquet now the copper of spilt blood.

'Sister, how many times have you given last rites?' The question came from nowhere.

Verity gave her an odd look. 'There was once a time when I kept a count. I decided to stop when the number brought me to tears.'

'Take comfort then that those you attended are at the Emperor's side now.'

The Hospitaller gestured to the dead servitors. 'But not all.'

'No,' agreed Miriya. 'Not all.'

From the inner halls of the gallery at the back of the platform a figure approached, a sharp-edged shadow where the dying glow of broken biolumes struck it. 'Stand and be recognised!' called a voice.

Miriya returned a nod. 'Sister Isabel, is that you?'

Isabel emerged into the flickering light cast from the fires down in the amphitheatre, throwing the screaming crowds a cursory look. 'Sister Superior, it's good to see you're still with us. The Canoness bid me to scout this tier for any fresh threats, but these cloisters are like a maze...'

'Where are the other Battle Sisters?'

'Below in the chapel. It is pandemonium in there. The cathedral has been compromised. Invaders are abroad.'

'I saw their aircraft land,' said Miriya. 'Not a large ship. Less than ten men, I'd warrant.'

'Very likely, but we have barely that number of able fighters here–' A crashing salvo of bolt fire from the floors below them cut into Isabel's words and her eyes went wide.

The Sister Superior spoke into the vox pickup on her armour's neck ring. 'This is Sister Miriya, report. Who is firing?'

'He's here,' Galatea snarled in her ear bead speaker. 'Vaun. Warp curse him, the witch is here!'

Across the mosaic floor of the chapel the fleeing, shrieking nobles fled back and forth, clouding Galatea's line of sight and that of every other Battle Sister in the chamber. Fallen braziers knocked askew in the panic had set light to tapestries as old as the city itself, filling the vaulted chamber with thick, choking smoke. The Canoness wished that she had ordered her women to bring their helmets: the optical matrix of Sabbat-pattern Sororitas headgear had a full-spectrum capacity that would render the darkest clouds transparent. But then, they had not expected to face a terrorist attack on this, the most sacred of Neva's holidays, and by the order of the High Ecclesiarch they had only been allowed to carry token weapons into the house of the God-Emperor.

She glimpsed Vaun and his killers as they moved and fired. They had no need to pick their targets, discharging streams of stubber rounds into silk-clad torsos, firing without aiming. Behind her, the floating illuminator that dominated the centre of the chapel took a shot in the heart and exploded, showering her with glass fragments and curls of hot brass.

'The governor,' she snapped. 'Where is he?' It did not occur to her to ask after the ecclesiarch. Lord LaHayn was more able to defend himself than the fragile politician ever could be. Years in service to the church had taught LaHayn how to fight against the enemies of order. But Emmel… He was another case entirely. Born of Neva's best noble stock, he fancied himself a man of action, but the reality was far less flattering. He was a peacock among peacocks, as much as he played at being a hawk, and was certainly no match for a killer of Torris Vaun's calibre.

Sister Portia was close by, clearing a fouled cartridge from her bolter. The ritual cloth of ceremony that chapel law required she wrap about her gun had tangled in the mechanism, stopping her from shooting back at the attackers. 'I last saw the governor in the company of Baron Sherring, a moment before the firing started.'

Galatea's adjutant, Sister Reiko, nodded. 'Aye. The baron and his retinue were making for the east terrace.' She was armed only with an ornate dress sword, and chafed at being pinned down by the terrorist weapons, unable to return fire.

The Canoness saw motion as some of Vaun's men dug themselves in behind the ranks of heavy oak pews. The psyker himself was disappearing into a side corridor.

'He must be stopped. Miriya, do you hear me? Vaun is on the loose inside the tower. He may be moving towards the upper tiers!'

As if it were drawn by the sound of her voice, gunfire came her way, clipping at the ancient mosaics in the floor near Galatea's feet.

'Quickly, quickly!' snapped Emmel, his hands darting around the folds of his brocade coat. His spindly fingers clutched at a small, fat orb of gold inlaid with ruby studs – a needler pistol from the defunct workshops of the Isher Studio, an antique that dated back to the thirty-ninth millennium. Passed down through the generations, the governor had only killed with it once in his life, when he had accidentally shot a playmate at the age of eleven. The sense of the object in his hand made clear the understanding of how dangerous his situation was. He barked out more commands to a pair of his elite guardsmen and they in turn shoved forwards past Baron Sherring's gaggle of lackeys, pushing through the people blocking the corridor.

'Please, governor,' said Sherring, an arch lilt to his voice. 'My flyer is just a little further. It will be my honour to convey you away from this fracas.'

'Yes, yes, hurry up.' Privately, Emmel was already entertaining the idea of leaving the ambitious baron on the landing terrace and taking his aircraft to flee to the safety of the impregnable Governmental Citadel. Unless the men sowing chaos throughout Noroc had stoneburners, he would be totally protected there.

'Such luck,' piped one of Sherring's friends, 'such good grace that you thought to bring an aeronef with you, my dear Holt.'

'Indeed,' said the baron. 'Lucky.'

The clanking servitor leading them through the warren of passageways turned a corner and scraped to a juddering halt that sent everyone behind it scattering. There was scarce illumination in these narrow cloisters, but the governor's eyesight was keen enough to see the liquid arc of something thick and oily spurt from the machine-slave's neck. A sound like a sack of wet meal being torn open accompanied it. The servitor gave a peculiar ululating wail and sank to its knees.

'Back!' called Emmel's guardsman. 'Get back, sir.'

New shapes emerged around the corner, jamming the corridor with blades and guns. At their head was the witch.

'Good evening, gentlefolk,' he grinned. 'Ivar's blessing be on you all. I am afraid your flight has been cancelled. An accident with fire has occurred.'

'Kill him!' Emmel shouted, somewhat redundantly as his men were already firing.

There was a horrible moment when the air about Torris Vaun's body bowed and lensed like a heat haze, and fizzing spurts of molten lead spat away from him. Vaun raised a hand in a blasé wave and the two guardsmen began to twitch and scream. Emmel had personally chosen these two from the ranks of his private sentry force for their devotion and fortitude, but that counted for nothing as he watched them die on their feet. Heat radiated from them, along with the burnt-skin smell of overcooked meat. Thin plumes of fatty smoke streamed from their nostrils and mouths, while the decorative festival ribbons in their hair and beards caught fire in puffs of ignition. Swelling with internal combustion, the guards dropped to the stone floor, burning from the inside out.

Some of Sherring's retinue fled, and they were burned down by the men who followed Vaun. The baron and his closest companion stumbled backwards, bumping into the horror-stricken governor. Emmel was jerked from his shock and fumbled with the orb-gun. It had been so long, he couldn't remember how to use it.

Vaun came closer. 'You don't dare harm me,' Emmel bleated. 'I am a supreme agent of the Emperor's–'

The psyker killed Sherring's pale-faced friend with a needle of yellow flame, the psi-discharge punching the body away down the corridor. He seemed to relish it.

There was a big man at Vaun's back and he nodded at the baron with a strange grin on his face. 'What about this one?'

Sherring blinked and his mouth worked in silence. Vaun leaned in close to the baron and looked him over, as if the noble was a helot on the auction block for purchase. He brought up the still-flaming tips of his fingers and touched them to Sherring's sweaty cheek. The wet skin sizzled and the baron bit back a cry of anger and pain.

'Just a small fish,' Vaun smirked, then with a sudden savage rush, he clubbed Sherring about the head and left him sprawled on the floor.

The big man took the inert gun from Emmel's fingers and tossed it away. 'I am very rich,' pleaded the governor. 'I can pay you a lot of money.'

Vaun nodded. 'I don't doubt it.' He nodded to the other man. 'Rink, take his lordship up to the tier and wait. Raise Ignis on the vox and tell him we're going to pull out. I want the other ships departing in the next ten minutes.'

'And you?'

Vaun glanced back over his shoulder. 'I've come all this way. I can't leave without paying my respects to the lord deacon.'

Emmel tried to resist the big man's iron grip. 'I will not go with you.'

In reply, Rink gave him a careless shove and the governor slammed into the stone wall. He stumbled, dazed and bleeding.

LaHayn propelled himself up to the chapel's pulpit. Smoke hung in thick drifts at head height, masking the disorder spreading around the chamber. The priest-lord drew in a deep breath of tainted air and roared into the vox set into the golden angel on the podium's crest.

'Do not have fear. Heed me, my friends. Discord is what these brutes want from us, do not give them their desire!' Some of the speakers secreted in gargoyles on the walls were still functioning, and they carried his words about the chapel like low thunder. 'Rally to the altar here, let the noble guardsmen and the steadfast Sisters of Battle be our shield and sword!'

The aristocrats were a fickle lot, but every one of them had been attending LaHayn's weekly sermons for years, and his words of command were enough to break through their terror and be acted upon. He ignored the grimace that Canoness Galatea shot at him, and from the corner of his eye he saw the Battle Sister snap out orders to the handful of surviving bodyguards, gun servitors and her own Sororitas warriors. A desultory rattle of bolt fire echoed through the chapel from the far nave, lost behind the grey fumes. The attackers had broken off for the moment, probably regrouping.

'All we need do is keep faith and hold, my friends,' he told the congregation. 'Even as I speak, detachments of enforcers and Imperial Guard are on their way here to rescue you.' In fact, Lord LaHayn had no way of knowing if that were true or not – but the Lunar Cathedral represented the greatest concentration of Nevan nobility on the planet, and he expected – he *demanded* – nothing less than the full might of the military to be turned to the matter of their protection.

Beneath his pulpit, the nervous barons and titled aristocrats clustered in his shadow, around the wrecked tables where earlier there had been piles of the finest foods and rarest liquors. Some of the fountains still frothed and bubbled with heady, pungent wines.

'They're coming,' LaHayn caught Galatea's words at the edge of his hearing. 'Stay alert.'

'Have faith in the Golden Throne,' shouted LaHayn. 'The Emperor protects!' From the depths of the smoke, the priest saw shapes moving, and a voice he had hoped never to hear again came with them, mocking and insolent.

'The Emperor protects?' said Vaun. 'Not here, He doesn't. Not *tonight*.'

Rink threw Emmel to the floor and placed a large booted foot upon his neck. 'You try to run, and I'm gonna break you.' The governor whimpered something, but Rink didn't care to listen. He raised a small vox transmitter to his lips. 'Ig? Ig, you little firebug, can you hear me?' He glanced around the Tier of the Greatest Piety, at the dead servitors and smashed machinery. All about the bowl-shaped terrace were glowing threads of smoke from the cathedral below.

After a couple of seconds there came a reply, laden with the crackle of interference. 'Bit busy at the moment. Wait. Wait.' On the night air Rink's ears caught the distant concussion of something very large and very flammable combusting, somewhere in the heart of the city. Over the static-choked channel Ignis gave a wordless sigh of rapture. 'Better. What is it?'

'Playtime is over. Vaun wants us to start heading home.'

'Aw. So soon? I was just warming up.'

Rink sniffed. 'You know what he said. Main event's still to come.'

'Yeah,' Ignis didn't sound happy. 'I'm doing it. We lost one 'copter over the jackyards but that's all. I'll pass word. Hold tight, Rink. I'm coming to you.'

'Don't make me wait.' He flicked off the device and dropped it in a pocket.

Emmel sniffed and tried to move. 'Please, listen to me. Let me speak a language you will understand. Money.'

Rink showed crooked teeth. 'Go on then.'

'I can pay you...'

'How much? A thousand in gold? Ten thousand? A million?'

'Yes.' The governor squirmed.

'Got it on you?' Rink bent low and spoke to Emmel's face. 'Right now?'

'Uh. Well, no, but...'

'Outta luck, then.'

'I don't want to die!' wailed the nobleman.

'And I don't want to be poor,' smirked Rink. 'You can see the nuisance of it.'

'Even gold will turn black in hands as corrupted as yours.'

Rink spun at the shouted words, grasping for his gun. 'Aw, warpshit.'

Miriya stepped slowly across the terrace, her plasma pistol aimed at the big man. From the corner of her eye she saw Isabel doing the same. Verity hung back in the archway, trying to keep out of sight. 'Listen to me,' said the Celestian. 'You are bound by law to stand down and surrender Governor Emmel. Release him or die.'

'And then what? You'll let me go on my way, like, with a kiss on the cheek?' He dragged Emmel to his feet, using the man like a human shield. 'No, you get lost, doxy, else I ventilate this runt!'

'This is your last chance,' said Isabel. 'Your one opportunity to accept the Emperor's light or die in its shadow.'

Rink's face creased with anger. 'What? What does that mean, eh? I hate you church bitches. But you can't beat Rink now, can ya? Can ya?' With a roar, he threw Emmel at the edge of the tier and fired at Isabel with his laser. Miriya vaulted into a dive, rolling hard on one shoulder. She was dimly aware of her Battle Sister trading fire with the thug, but her attention was on Emmel, sliding across blood-slick stone towards a drop that would smash him against the amphitheatre floor far below. Her gun discarded in her headlong flight, she fell upon the governor as he slipped over the edge and caught a handful of his heavy coat in her hands.

Emmel's jacket ripped but it held enough to keep him hanging there, suspended hundreds of metres above the burning stadium. The muscles in her arms bunching, Miriya dragged him back up. The effort of it dazed her, and she cast around.

Isabel had fallen against a dead servitor. She seemed injured. Miriya could not see Verity anywhere... and the big man...

She rolled on to her back as fresh wreaths of smoke coiled over the terrace, and the criminal was there, leering over her.

He fell on her with a bone-crushing impact, slamming her against the inside of her ceramite armour. Miriya's teeth rattled in her head and she tasted copper in her mouth.

A grinning face, breath stinking of tabac, pressed into hers. She struggled against him. He was twice her size and all of it was hard, packed muscle. The sheer weight of the man was enough to force the breath from her lungs.

'Give Rink a kiss, little Sister,' he hissed, licking her cheek. 'Come on. Don't be shy.'

Her punches to his ribs and groin brought grunts of pain but nothing more. Rink's eyes narrowed and he surrounded her throat with thick hands big enough to crush her skull.

She could not pant or gasp. He was going to kill her with her own silence. Miriya tried to dislodge his hands without success.

'Heh,' he smirked. 'No sermons for me now, eh?'

Rink bent forward to lick her again, and with one last effort, the Celestian butted him in the nose. She felt the big man's bone crack and blood spurt, but it seemed to do little more than annoy him. Rink's grip tightened still further and the colour drained from Miriya's vision. Everything changed to a gauzy, charcoal sketch, becoming grey and distorted.

A woolly, indistinct noise like the bark of a dog reached her ears, and then Rink rolled off her. It took a long moment for Miriya to realise that there was sticky, wet matter coating her face and torso. She sat up and unceremoniously used her robes to mop the thick offal away. The Battle Sister shook off her daze and realised that Rink, lying there on the tier next to her, was without his head.

Verity emerged from the haze with Isabel's bolter in her hands, vapour coiling from the barrel. The gun looked wrong in her grip, the shape of it there almost obscene against the virginal white of the Hospitaller's garb.

'Is he...?'

'Dead?' Miriya got to her feet with a wince. 'I should think so.' She staggered a little and Verity put the gun aside to steady her. 'Where is Sister Isabel?'

'Wounded.' Verity did not look away from the headless man.

'Is this the first time you have taken a life, Sister?'

'I...' Her eyes were glassy and hollow, her gaze locked on the corpse. 'I have given the Emperor's Peace to those who need it many times... But never... I have never...'

'Never killed with a weapon in your hand, in the heat of battle?' Miriya coughed and spat. 'Fortunate for me then that you still remember your training. A little to the left and that shot would have found me, not him.' With gentle force, the Celestian guided her away to where Governor Emmel lay on the stonework.

On more familiar ground, Verity became efficient and quick of hand, using an auspex-like device to divine the man's well-being, touching him to feel a pulse. She frowned. 'We cannot take him from this place, Sister. He has internal injuries that will worsen if we move him.'

'We can't leave him here, it's not safe.'

'You should summon a rescue flyer to recover him and take him to a hospice. Unless a chirurgeon sees to him, he could perish.' The Hospitaller nodded in the direction of the cathedral. 'Go for help. I will remain here. I can keep him stable.'

Dragging her injured leg as she walked, a pale-faced Isabel approached them. 'She is right, Sister Superior. The psyker witch is still loose in the tower. While we tarry here, his every breath is an affront to the God-Emperor.'

'Can you fight?' asked Miriya, eyeing her.

'Need you ask?' Isabel glanced at the bloody laser wound on her thigh. 'A mere flea bite. It appears worse than it is.'

'Then what of you?' Sister Miriya turned back to Verity. 'You won't catch Vaun unawares like his thug here. You can't engage him.'

The Hospitaller gave her a defiant look. 'Then be quick, and I will have no need to.'

Miriya accepted that with a nod, and then recovered the dead thug's lasgun. 'Take this until we can find you a better weapon,' she said, handing it to Verity. 'Use it if you must.'

'But you said I would not be able to fight Vaun.'

The Celestian shook her head. 'There are only two charges left in the weapon. If Vaun comes, I would suggest you use them to grant the Emperor's Peace to the good governor here and yourself.' She gathered up her fallen plasma pistol and walked away. 'It is a better fate than letting that beast lay open your mind.'

The witch melted out of the mist choking the chapel with bubbles of burning air dancing about his fingers. He tossed streamers of fire at the aristocrats and swept them around, using them as a Repentia Mistress would a neural whip.

Wherever the flames touched skin or cloth, people were instantly flashed into screeching torches. Behind Vaun came his men, spreading further the touch of witchfire.

'Here they come,' Galatea snapped. 'All guns to bear.' She led the Sisters in a quick subvocalised litany, each of them murmuring prayers of blessing to their firearms.

Portia brought up her bolter and Reiko – who had liberated a clumsy ornamental rifle from a dead honour guard – did as she ordered, but the gun servitors and the other men at arms fell apart in a rout. The servitors, too slow of brain to react with anything other than brute reflex, marched into Vaun's firecasts and burnt to death standing up. Internal ammunition magazines cooked off in wailing cracks as limbs and torsos were shattered. The bodyguards and sentries lost their nerve when they were confronted by a psyker of Vaun's deadly prowess, breaking ranks and making themselves perfect targets for his men.

Fire-streaks buzzed past Galatea's head like hoverflies, humming and slow in the melee. The Battle Sisters had come with little to replenish their weapons, and where Vaun's killers fired for effect, the Canoness and her fighters paced their shots. Each had to be certain death for the target. They could not afford to spend more than one precious bolt shell on each attacker.

Vaun's flame-whips guttered out and the psyker dropped low, masking himself and minimising his target silhouette. An eerie glow cast about from the witchkin's eyes. Galatea had seen the like before on those kissed by Chaos or touched by the sign of the mutant.

'By Katherine's heart, what is he doing?' Portia hesitated, trying and failing to get a good firing angle on the crouching man.

From behind her where the liquor fountains gurgled and frothed, Galatea heard the squeal of building pressure and a rush of hot bubbles. Suddenly she understood. 'Get down. Get down!' she shouted, throwing herself into Portia and Reiko.

Vaun released a 'Ha!' of effort and threw a spear of psionic force into the wine drums. Superheated by his mindfire, the volatile alcohols combusted and shattered their wood and iron kegs. With a whoop of air, the atomised liquids turned a pocket of atmosphere into an inferno. A miniature tidal wave of burning Nevan whisky and foaming spice wine threw itself across the cowering nobles. The searing flood boiled them red and screaming, the agony of it so fierce that some of the merchants died instantly.

LaHayn clung to the pulpit as it rocked and sank into the burning tide around it. Before him, striding across the flaming pool without a hint of discomfort, Vaun met his eyes and gave the priest a theatrically contrite bow of the head.

'Forgive me, father, for I have sinned.' The last word was drawn out and sibilant, turning into a harsh smile. 'Hello, Viktor. I'm willing to bet that this isn't how you had imagined things would go when we met again.' With a callous kick, he shoved a wailing noblewoman out of his path. 'It's time for you to reap the whirlwind, old man.'

'You will regret your arrogance, creature,' spat the priest. 'I will see to it!'

Vaun snorted. 'You?' He opened his arms. 'Look around, Viktor. The wastrels you surrounded yourself with are dead or dying. Even your precious Sororitas lie defeated by me.' He pointed at the spot where Galatea and the other women lay wounded and unmoving. 'Meet your end with some decorum, dear teacher. If you ask me nicely, I may even let you spout off some prayers first to your precious god.'

'You dare not speak the name of the Lord of Mankind!' LaHayn's rage rolled across his aspect in a dark thunderhead. 'Pirate. Petty thief and brigand. Your tiny mind lacks even the smallest inkling of my unity with Him!' The ecclesiarch stabbed an accusing finger at the psyker. 'You could have been great, Torris. You could have known glory the likes of which have not been seen in ten thousand years. But now you are fit only to die, remembered only as an anarchist and a criminal!'

Vaun let out a laugh. 'And who will kill me, you decrepit fool?' He drew back his hands and cupped the air between them. The molecules of smoke and haze he held there flickered and condensed, catching fire. 'This ridiculous monument of yours will be your funeral pyre – and once you are ashes I'll plunder your dirty little secrets for myself.'

He was close enough now, reasoned the priest. Close enough to be certain. 'I think not, child,' said LaHayn, and from his voluminous sleeves he produced an ornamental box that ended in a finely tooled argentium muzzle. He squeezed the device and it shrieked, projecting a mid-calibre bolt shell at the witch's chest.

The recoil from the weapon was so strong it almost broke the priest's wrist, but the gun was just the means to deliver the shell to the target. The bolt itself was not the typical carbide-fusion matrix bullet that issued forth from countless Astartes and Sororitas weapons – the very matter of the round was impregnated with psionic energy, culled from the minds of dying heretics. Each molecule of it reeked with mental anguish, pain and psychic terror imprinted on the shell down to the atomic level. These munitions were very rare, but Lord Viktor LaHayn had taken a long time to build up the position he now held, and along the way many such items had come into his possession.

The psycannon bolt struck Torris Vaun in the chest, tearing through the heat-wards that had turned the lesser shots of other men, and spent its massive kinetic energy punching through the flexsteel armour of his battle vest. The impact threw him back into the puddles of burning liquor, ripples of contained psy-force licking around him, fading. He coughed hard and brought up a mist of blood.

'Fool,' growled the priest. 'Did you think I would go about unprepared when I knew that you were on the loose?' He holstered the spent weapon, massaging his throbbing wrist. 'Now I will have the prisoner I promised for this day.' LaHayn glanced down as Miriya and Isabel entered the chamber, guns questing for a target. 'What perfect timing,' he remarked. 'Here, sisters. Here is your witch, ready for the cages–'

A whooshing jet of fire erupted from where Vaun had fallen, pushing the criminal back to his feet. Curls of heat enveloped him and he bared his teeth, chewing on new pain. 'Well played, Viktor,' spat the psyker. 'But I'm not beaten just yet.'

LaHayn's world turned red as the pulpit burst into flames about him.

'Take him!' screamed Miriya, her voice streaming into the concussive blast of noise from her plasma pistol. Isabel fired with her, both of the Battle Sisters throwing their shots at Torris Vaun, knocking him back off his stance.

The psyker stumbled and snarled at them, blood from broken capillaries in his eyes trickling down his face in red tracks. The glowing brand where the psycannon shot had struck him still flickered with desultory glimmers of blue-white energy, and Vaun picked at it with sweat-slick fingers, using his other hand in a warding gesture to banish the incoming bolts. The rounds struck the heat-wall conjured by his mind and deflected, some breaking and melting, others skipping away, but Miriya could see the agony caused by the injury LaHayn had inflicted was taking its toll. Vaun met her gaze for a split second and she knew he realised it too.

'I won't let you run again,' she spat. 'Take the witch!'

Groggy and wounded, Portia dragged herself into the fight alongside her squadmates. Near the wrecked pews, Galatea, a shock of her perfect auburn hair crisped into white ash from the fires, stumbled up from where she lay bearing Reiko on one shoulder.

'You should not have come back,' shouted LaHayn. 'Now you will pay for daring to defy the church.' The priest pointed at the corpses of the raiders where Galatea and the other Battle Sisters had terminated them along the way. 'All your reavers and cutthroats have fled or died, fiend. You are alone and naked before the God-Emperor's righteous vengeance!'

'Always the lectures with you, eh?' Vaun barked out a harsh laugh and shook the sleeve of his coat, revealing a bulbous, ornate device of jewels and metals wrapped about his wrist. 'You make the same mistakes over and over again, Viktor. You never fail to underestimate me.' The psyker squeezed a triangular emerald switch and delicate, century-old microcircuits sent an activation signal.

The Battle Sisters heard a chug of static across their vox channels. Instants later, the shaped charges of detonite that Vaun's men had secreted all about the cathedral exploded. Under cover of the fires and the panic they had gone unnoticed. Still, there were enough in place to do what Vaun wished of them.

The coughing crashes of noise blew out stained glass windows and threw doors off their hinges. They cut through support pillars as saws might fell trees, or dashed ancient pews and unlucky people about the place in clouds of vapour.

Stonework from the upper tiers dropped to punch ragged holes through the mosaic floors, and Lord LaHayn threw himself off the pulpit just as a granite angel smashed the thing to matchwood. Blinking through brick dust and pain, the priest cursed the psyker's name as Vaun's mocking laughter echoed back at him.

CHAPTER SEVEN

The Tier of Greatest Piety shuddered beneath Verity's feet and she sprawled, falling away from where Governor Emmel lay. His skin was waxy and sallow, and death was close to him. The Hospitaller heard the sounds of rock grinding on rock, and in horror she saw the high spire of the Lunar Cathedral above her twitch and break off, cascading down past the terrace. Growing up on the sturdiness of Ophelia VII, Verity had never experienced earthquakes, and the occurrence of a solid, rooted building shifting around her was new and terrifying. The thunder of explosions from the lower level set the whole church humming, and the woman threw a fearful look to the smoke-choked sky. Where was the rescue ship? If she were here much longer, Emmel would be dead from his injuries or she would perish with him when the great terrace crumbled.

From above, a narrow-beamed spotlight suddenly stabbed down at the tier, probing at the cluttered space. Verity leapt to her feet, the weapon in her hand forgotten, and waved. 'Here. Here!' The sound of ducted rotors reached her ears and in the thick of the haze she saw the dark shape of a coleopter moving against the night sky.

The spotlight passed over her, lingered for a moment and

then moved on, tracing towards the entrance arch that led down into the chapel. A figure emerged into the sodium glare, dark coat and tunic spattered with fresh blood, shielding his eyes from the light. The beam faded away and the 'copter swept about for another pass. With a great chill the woman realised that the flyer was one of the ships she had seen strike at the cathedral.

Torris Vaun walked painfully towards the middle of the terrace and halted there, panting hard. For a moment, Verity was struck dumb by the sight of him. The psyker examined the red on his hands and returned to cupping the wound on his chest, sparing her gun a quick look. 'Are you going to use that, nursemaid?'

Verity tried to speak, but no words came. Vaun stepped closer.

'How is the esteemed governor?' He peered at the injured man lying in the shadows. 'Dead, or near enough? Pity. I wanted to use him a little before he died. Oh well.' A rueful smile crossed his lips. 'Plans change.'

The Hospitaller gulped air. Where were Miriya and the others?

'I know what you are thinking–' he began.

'Stay out of my mind,' shouted the woman. More used to handling a boltpistol, she brought up the lasgun in a clumsy stance.

Vaun gave a hollow chuckle and winced in slight pain. 'There's no need for me to exercise my attributes to know your thoughts, Sister. You know what fate befell poor Sister Iona on the *Mercutio*, yes? You are wondering, if he could do that so easily to a hardened warrior like her, what chance does my fragile little mind have?'

'I will kill you.'

He raised an eyebrow, amused. 'You don't have that in you. I think perhaps you wish that you did, but you don't.'

'I killed your man,' she retorted, jerking her head at Rink's remains. 'I can end you too.'

'Oh.' Vaun eyed the dead body. 'Impressive. Perhaps I was

wrong about you.' He coughed a little. 'Go on then, shoot me if you dare, little nursemaid.'

Verity took careful aim at the psyker, and she was rewarded by the very slightest twitch of dismay on Vaun's smug face. 'Do not profess to know me when you do not. Your arrogance is sickening. How *dare* you dismiss me, you heartless fiend!' The safety catch flicked off beneath her thumb. 'Any other soul, and perhaps I might have felt distress at taking their life, but you? One look at your face and I am willing to throw away every oath to ethics I have ever sworn!'

The criminal was very still now, watching her carefully. 'Then before you do, I would ask you grant me one thing. Tell me what I have done that has earned such enmity.'

She gasped. 'You... You don't even know? Does killing mean so little to you that you dismiss it from your mind with every murder?'

'For the most part, yes,' Vaun noted. 'Let me see if I can guess. A father? Or a brother, perhaps?'

'My sister,' she snarled. 'Lethe Catena, of the Order of Our Martyred Lady, dead by your blade.' A sob caught in her chest. 'You ended her like some common animal!'

'Ah.' He nodded. 'Of course. There's a bit of a family resemblance between you, isn't there?'

His words were enough. '*Die*! In Terra's name, die,' she bellowed, and jerked the trigger of the gun.

'No,' said Vaun, and snapped his fingers at her. Before the lasing crystal in the slender pistol could even energise, the psyker caused the molecules of the emitter matrix to superheat and fracture. Verity knew nothing of this until the gun became red-hot and sizzled against the flesh of her hand. By reflex, the Hospitaller threw the weapon away and cried out. Her shriek was drowned by the thrum of coleopter blades as the flyer banked around and dropped towards the terrace. The Hospitaller fell to her knees, clutching her scarred hand to her chest.

'Keep that as a reminder not to test your betters.' Vaun's voice was an icy whisper in her ears, pushing into her thoughts. 'You are a foolish, maudlin child. I killed your sister because I had to, not because I took pleasure in it. She was an obstacle to me, nothing more than that. Don't complicate matters by making it personal.'

'Emperor curse you...' sobbed the woman.

The psyker reached up to grab a dangling tether as the coleopter dipped low. The noise of it was deafening, but still she heard his words as clear as day. 'This is not about you, Verity. You have no comprehension of what is hidden on this planet, you or that other wench. Your simple minds, stifled by dogma, cannot grasp the notion of anything beyond your experience.'

Verity screamed. *'Get out of my head!'*

'Let me leave you with this. My crimes are legion, of that you may have no doubt, but even in my worst excesses, nothing I have ever done can hold a candle to the sins of Viktor LaHayn.' Hate oozed from the mindspeech. 'You have impeded me tonight, but in the end nothing will stop me from paying back tenfold what that whoreson owes me. *I swear it.'*

Vaun's last words struck her like a physical blow, and she doubled over and vomited.

The coleopter fled into the night, leaving the Sister Hospitaller and the comatose governor for the medicae to find when the aeronefs finally arrived.

Dawn brought rain with it from the sea, a cold and lonely downpour that was grey with spent smoke and powdered stone. The smell of blackened wood was dense in the air.

The eventual arrival of units of Guard and enforcers came too late to save the lives of many a noble, although by the grace of the Golden Throne there were barely a quarter of the city's highly ranked pastors lying dead as the sun rose. Those who had passed away were laid out in the viewing galleries of the central hospice, where their parishioners could file in and out and pay respects to the men and women who had led them to the light of the Emperor.

Miriya found visitors clogging entranceways to the upper floors of the building. She was given to understand that many of the sobbing mourners had also lost family members, but in accordance with Nevan church mandates the funeral rites of priests took precedence over those of all other citizens.

Noroc was as wounded as her people. The stark light of day showed the places where rockets from the air attack had burnt out apartment warrens and gutted hundreds of chapels. In some places, where broken street cables meant the fire engines could not reach, pits of ruined ferrocrete still smouldered. Miriya had seen the same scene repeated on every street corner as she rode to the hospice. Anguish, blank fear, terror on every face.

The Battle Sister's countenance was set in a frown. Twice now, she had laid Torris Vaun beneath her gunsight and twice he had escaped her. The thought of it made her stomach churn, and in darker moments she caught herself feeling the weight of all the turmoil around her. Had she stopped him back there on the *Mercutio*, none of this horror would have come to pass. Her mood dark as the stormy sky, Miriya pressed on to find her way to the cubicle where Sister Verity was being attended.

'Of course you understand the deacon's concerns,' said Dean Venik, looming over the serf boy ministering to the bandage on Verity's forearm. 'I do not mean to imply that is not so, Sister Hospitaller, but nevertheless it is important to ensure a full and correct picture of the witch's intentions.'

'How can I know that?' Verity replied. She found the man to be intimidating, in his arch, unctuous way.

'What did the criminal say to you?' Venik looked her in the eye. 'Did he speak of anything... untoward? Did he take the names of Lord LaHayn or the God-Emperor in vain?'

'It happened very quickly. He... He used his power...' She held up the livid, inflamed hand, flesh scabbed with new scarring peeking through the white gauze. 'I was unable to prevent his escape.'

'A pity.' Venik nodded to himself. 'I imagine you would have liked to take a part in Vaun's downfall, after what transpired with your sibling.'

Sister Miriya entered behind the cleric, startling the man. 'There's still time.' She made the sign of the aquila. 'Lord dean. If it pleases you, I would speak to my fellow Sororitas.'

'Sister Superior,' Venik returned the gesture. 'Of course. I have completed my interview and there are others with whom I must speak, to gather information for the lord deacon.'

'Sir, a moment,' said Verity. 'What of Governor Emmel? Does he still live?'

The dean flashed a brief, shallow smile. 'By the God-Emperor's grace, he does. It is my understanding that the governor is being attended by ten of the finest medicae in Noroc.'

'Ten?' Miriya eyed him. 'Does one man need so many healers, especially on a day such as this?'

'I am not an apothecary, Sister, I cannot answer to that. I know only that he may never fully regain his faculties after such a brutalisation,' sniffed Venik.

'Who governs Neva now, then?' asked the Hospitaller.

Venik arched an eyebrow. 'His lordship the ecclesiarch, of course. It is only right that in this time of moral outrage the church take the whip hand.' He turned to leave. 'Lord LaHayn's first edict in his new capacity was to reinforce the order for Vaun's capture. The witch is to be taken alive.'

'Dean, perhaps you might furnish us with solutions to another matter.' Verity's nervous voice wavered. 'There are records within the halls of Noroc's Administratum librarium that might assist in tracking the fugitive Vaun. With your permission, I should like to examine them...'

Venik gave a cold smile. 'The enforcers have already performed a thorough check of those documents. All information gleaned will be acted upon.'

'Nevertheless...'

'Attend to your recovery, Sister Verity,' snapped the dean. 'Don't expend energy on pointless endeavours.' He glanced at Miriya. 'I'm sure there are many avenues of investigation to follow in this affair.' With a sniff of finality, he manoeuvred past the other woman and out into the corridor.

The Hospitaller waved away the boy and patted the bandage on her forearm. The youth bowed as low as he could without touching his forehead to the floor and averted his eyes. The Battle Sister in turn dismissed him with a curt gesture and the two women were alone.

'You are unhurt,' said Verity. 'And the other Celestians?'

'As well as can be expected,' Miriya frowned. 'Canoness Galatea was burned, but she bears the pain with a fortitude typical of her.' She paused. 'I come to you to apologise for an error, Sister Verity. I pressed the Canoness to have you remain here on Neva and in doing so exposed you to a threat you should never have faced.'

'No,' Verity shook her head. 'You hold no blame. In some strange way I am pleased that I could look Vaun in the eye. At least now I can give a form to the pain in my heart.'

'You should return to the mission of the Order of Serenity. Last night's attack will change things here, and I foresee that the bloodshed and turmoil will only increase.'

'Thank you for your concern, Sister Miriya, but I refuse. Don't think me a delicate flower just because I bear no sword or bolter in my duties. My Order has served on hundreds of hell-worlds and battlefields. I know the face of horror well enough.'

The other woman's head bobbed. 'As you wish.' For a moment she was silent, studying the Hospitaller. 'But Vaun... He *did* speak to you, didn't he? Your answer to Venik's question–'

'I was not entirely forthcoming.' Verity looked away. 'Yes. He... He told me Lethe's death was just a matter of course. Nothing personal.'

'A convenient excuse for his kind. How else could he commit such acts of barbarity and continue unfettered by guilt?'

Verity looked up at her, at eyes that were surprisingly gentle in such a hard face. 'But you have killed... And now so have I.'

'And look how keenly we feel it, Sister. This is what separates us from the heretic, the alien. We fight and kill because we must, not for glory or the sport of it. Each death we inflict serves a greater cause.'

The Hospitaller nodded. 'Of course, you are right. Forgive me if I seem irresolute, it is just that… these days have been most testing for me.'

Miriya extended a hand to the younger woman. 'Look to the Emperor, Sister. Whatever clouds your vision, He will be there.'

Verity's gaze turned inward. 'If there was ever a day I needed His guidance, this would be it. There is more that I did not reveal to Dean Venik. Vaun gave me a warning before he fled.'

The Battle Sister sneered. 'His threats hold little sway over me.'

'No, you misunderstand. He spoke of the lord deacon. Vaun said that Lord LaHayn was guilty of crimes far worse than any he had committed.'

'Sedition and lies,' Miriya spat out the denial instantly, although with less conviction than she should have. 'The witch was trying to sow dissent in your thoughts.'

Verity met her gaze. 'I have attended many interrogations in my service and seen many confessions and denials. I know lies when I hear them. What I saw from Torris Vaun was the truth, at least from his point of view. He *believed* it.'

'What a heretic believes counts for nothing,' said the Battle Sister, 'and were you to speak of this to the dean or anyone else, you might find an interrogator turning his skills to you.'

'I have considered that, even entertained the idea that Vaun might have forced some seed of doubt into my mind with his freakish abilities. But all I can think of is that this witch spoke the truth to me while Lord LaHayn did the opposite at the cathedral.'

Her words brought Miriya up short and her eyes narrowed. 'He is a high priest of the Imperial Church, the voice of the Holy Synod. It is within Lord LaHayn's remit to deny us whatever facts or truths he feels are in our best interests.'

Despite her reply, Verity could tell that the other woman was not convinced by her own argument.

'Why do that when by his own command he charged us to pursue this man? You heard the dean a moment ago. We are promised help in one breath and denied it in the next. Make no mistake, I want Vaun to pay for his misdeeds – but I cannot escape the fear that there is much more at play in this matter than we know of. There are falsehoods and secrets shrouding us, Miriya. I know you think the same.'

For a long moment, Verity was afraid the Battle Sister would give a sharp denial or censure her for such doubts, but instead the Celestian's head bobbed in regretful agreement. 'Aye. Curse me, but aye, I feel it as well. There are too many questions unanswered here, too many things averted from close scrutiny.'

Verity sighed. 'I am conflicted, Sister. Where does our duty lie?'

'To the church and the God-Emperor, as it always was. But I see the real question you are asking – does Neva's deacon serve Him as well, or is there another agenda at hand?'

She shuddered. 'I dare not even voice such a thing.'

'Then prepare yourself,' Miriya said darkly, 'for a time may come when you must do more than that. Never forget that the price of vigilance requires we watch those who march under our banner as well as those who stand against it.'

'I pray it will not be so.' Verity got to her feet, testing her injured arm. 'What are we to do now?'

'I believe you said something about the Administratum?' The Battle Sister raised an eyebrow.

'But the dean said the enforcers–'

'The enforcers are nothing more than armour-clad night watchmen. The day I accept the second-hand words of their investigators is the day that Sol burns cold in the sky.' She walked away. 'I must attend to the welfare of my squad. In the meantime, I suggest you might use the confusion of the day to visit the halls of records and look for these facts that may help us find our quarry.' Miriya paused on the threshold. 'That is, if you truly do wish to remain here?'

'You ask me to defy the dean.'

Miriya gave her a quizzical look. 'I have done no such thing. The dean merely said that the enforcers have already checked the records. What harm can come from a second examination? Just to be sure?'

Verity threw her a wooden nod. For better or worse, she suddenly understood that a choice had been made in this small room that could damn them both.

With a sharp backhand slap, Vaun sent the medicae scuttling away from him. 'Go on with yourself, now. I've had enough of your fussing.' He tested the places on his face where small cuts were daubed with blobs of healing gel. 'Like a thousand paper cuts,' he grimaced, glancing up as Ignis approached him from the creaking gloom of the barge's hold. 'What now?'

The younger man saw the thought forming in his mind and handed him a lit tabac stick. Ignis had been muted since they returned to the boat, ill at ease over Rink's sudden absence. The two of them had been friends, or close enough. 'He's here,' said the youth, without preamble. 'Brought his aeronef right down on the deck.' He pointed at the steel roof above.

Vaun took a long, hissing drag on the tabac and stood up. 'That was what all the commotion was about, was it?' Here in the barge's makeshift sickbay, Vaun had heard the clatters and shouts of the crewmen. They were all afraid to be carrying the witch and his cohorts but they had been paid very well. He spat, hard. 'Idiot. Why can't he just be a good little snob and play his role?'

Heavy footsteps were descending from the upper deck and Vaun sneered, taking another puff. 'Watch me now,' he told Ignis. 'This is how to handle this kind of man.'

The sickbay hatch came open with difficulty, creaking and moaning. The new arrival was in disarray, his fine robes smeared with soot and a little blood. He found Vaun and shook a fist at him. 'What... What was all that?'

The psyker put on a neutral face. 'All what, milord?'

The other man stamped forward. 'Don't you *milord* me, Torris. You talked to me about speed, about clean kills and surgical attacks. That...' He pointed in the vague direction of Noroc. 'That was nothing short of a military strike!'

Vaun threw Ignis an amused, comradely look. 'What did you expect? A few discreet murders and some swinging from chandeliers in the chapel, perhaps some disquieting deaths for the servants but nothing more?' In a rush, his face darkened and he swept towards the noble, bunching the cigarillo in his fist. 'You wanted power? Power has to be taken. Perhaps if your ridiculous legions of spies and soldiers had an ounce of sense, last night might have gone all the way. The church's stranglehold on Neva broken, LaHayn dead along with Emmel–'

'Emmel lives,' spat the man. 'You couldn't even give me that!'

'Huh.' Vaun paused, considering. 'But he'll be in no state to govern. I don't doubt LaHayn will finish the job for me.' He sighed. 'How amusing.'

'*Amusing*?' The dam holding back the nobleman's rage broke. 'You wreak havoc and leave me exposed, and call it *amusing*? You crooked witch-freak, you have jeopardised everything–'

Vaun crossed the distance between them in a flash, swatting the man to the floor. The noble squealed and clutched at his cheek, where a fresh burn wound lay. 'The only thing in jeopardy is your complacency, baron. For too long you've played your stupid little rivalry with LaHayn like some regicide game, all polite rules and how-do-you-dos.' He stamped out the tabac stick. 'It's not a silly diversion any more, Holt. I've taken it up a notch. Now it's a fistfight, a stabbing. A real feud.'

'I'm not ready,' whimpered the noble. 'There will be killing. War.'

'Yes,' agreed Vaun, 'and when it's done, when Viktor LaHayn is crucified in Judgement Square and you are in the governor's palace signing my pardon for all the good I've done for Neva, on that day you will be thanking me for making it happen.' He leaned closer to Baron Sherring's face. 'For freeing you.' After a moment he stepped back. 'Get to your 'nef and start making plans. It's time to tell the world what a bad man the dear old deacon is.'

The baron got to his feet and shuffled away. 'I... I'll see you in Metis?'

Vaun bowed. 'You can count on it.'

Sherring left them, a shadow of the man who had blasted into the room moments earlier. Ignis tapped his lips with a finger. 'Did you push him there to make him fold? In the brain, like?'

'Not a bit of it. There are easier ways to coerce men than to use a mind-touch on them. I just gave him what he wanted.'

From above, the whir of airship rotors started up. 'And what was that, then?'

'Freedom from blame. Sherring has always dreamed of setting fire to that pious old braggart and his holy churches. I did it for him, and now he's free to step up to the fight without the guilt of being the one who started it.'

Ignis let out a laugh. 'He... He thinks you're doing this all for him? Ha!'

Vaun nodded. 'He'll find out that's not the way of it. Probably just before he dies.'

Verity could see little but the long river of illumination that pooled either side of the walkway bisecting the librarium. The edges of shelves vanished into the darkness towards the unseen walls of the long bunker. The morose logistoras who had accompanied her down to this level rattled off a few cursory facts about the place, like a tourist's data-plate. He spoke of how many hundreds of metres they were below the streets of Noroc, of how many more levels were below this one. In the middle distance, the Hospitaller could hear the oiled clanking of huge brass cogs as one of the room's mobile decks dropped away into the storage tiers. She stopped to watch the empty space, as big as a scrumball pitch. After a moment, another deck clattered up to replace it, a piece of a huge library rolling into position complete with endless racks of papers and bookish little men working the aisles. Automatically, a flight of tarnished silver servo-skulls dipped out from the eaves over her head and began patrolling the canyons of books. Whole floors of the librarium were moving with ponderous speed, tiles in a puzzle slate for giant hands.

The logistoras, his ink-stained robe large on his wiry frame, peered at her through augmented eyes. 'You understand, we don't often see representatives of your orders in these halls.' He attempted something like a smile. 'The Sisters Dialogous of the Quill and the Sacred Oath do visit us at times. I cannot recall a Sister Hospitaller in my tenure.' His gaze turned inward. 'Perhaps I should begin a statistical check into that datum–'

'Perhaps you should,' Verity broke in, 'but in the interim, there are the matters of which I spoke to you?'

'Yes. Crew records for the warship *Mercutio*. I have not forgotten.' He beckoned. 'Follow.' The clerk-priest ambled on along the walkway. 'I'm curious as to why the Order of Serenity would require such information.'

In the dimness, Verity felt her cheeks go hot. That she had come this far without undue challenge was luck, and with each further step the Sororitas feared her presence here would be found out and declared fraudulent. She floundered for an instant, unsure of how to reply. How would Sister Miriya answer him, she wondered? She'd probably threaten to injure him. I can do better than that.

Verity sucked in a breath of parchment-dry air. 'Is it necessary that you know why I require this datum in order to find it for me?' She pitched her voice in the same lecturing tone she'd heard her Palatine use on wayward novices.

'Well, uh, no.' The logistoras blinked brass lashes. 'I was merely–'

'Curious, yes. But forgive me, I was given to understand that curiosity is not a trait that the Adeptus Ministorum wishes to cultivate in its librarians. Is it not an article of faith that you may never read from the books you collate, lest you come into contact with material of an unmutual nature?'

That weak smile again. 'I have never been tempted, Sister.' He threw a nervous look up at the servo-skulls buzzing above them, the thin tubes of lasers hanging from their lipless mouths. 'To do so would incur the ultimate penalty.' He halted at a side gantry and removed a chain-link closing off the section. 'Here we are. The cogitator will provide you with the datum.' He bowed and backed away. 'I hope you will forgive my injudicious use of words earlier. It is just, that with the incident on the night of the Blessing...'

Verity smiled back. 'We are all shaken, priest. Fortunately, the Emperor gives His light to guide us.'

The logistoras bowed again and left her there with the ancient thinking machine, the brassy coils and silver-rope filigree inside it ticking and tocking as it churned out the lives of Midshipman Vorgo and the men who had freed Torris Vaun.

There were wide webs of girders, loops of greasy cable and cogworks everywhere inside the librarium, almost all of them perpetually in the darkness. The meagre glow of the photon candles about the underground hall never reached into the thick ebon shadows that collected at the edges of the corridors. Many of the papers held here were so old that they would wilt beneath hard light, and in some sectors the servitors that ministered to the books operated totally on infrared wavelengths. In such a place, the act of concealment was almost welcoming.

Verity's shadow watched her from the hex-frame supporting part of the ferrocrete roof above the Hospitaller's head. The shadow was molten darkness, merged there into the black with such skill that even the vigilant skulls with their tiny red eyes looked straight at it and passed on, unaware. Verity's shadow watched and listened to her, measuring and considering where the day would take the pretty Sororitas. The certainty began to build in the shadow's thoughts that the woman would not see daylight again and in the interests of preparation, the shadow readied its ghost pistol to kill her.

CHAPTER EIGHT

Verity pressed her fingers to the place where her brow met her nose and pinched the skin there, trying to massage some sort of life back into her face. She stifled a yawn and blinked eyes that were tired and gritty. On an oaken desk and in neat piles around the cogitator's marble plinth, fan-folds of yellow-brown parchment displayed acres of text in High Gothic, machine dialect and the local Nevaspreche tongue. Many of them sported red tags bearing a tiny rendition of the enforcer shield, along with a text string showing a precinct house number. They represented the places where the investigators had pored over the papers, the point at which they had completed their searches. Verity had read all the same files, up to the red markers and then further back, probing for some connection, some small suspicion of a link between the men who had freed Miriya's prisoner.

She sighed, a heavy dejection threatening to overcome her. There were no timepieces anywhere in sight here inside the librarium, and so she had no idea how long she had been confined in this dark chamber, fingers tracing over page after page beneath the flicker of photon candles. Her lips were dry and she felt a little sick. The libations the medicae had given her after the incident in the cathedral were fading away, and

Verity's body was sending her mixed messages for sleep and for sustenance. Her chest felt tight with the dust of old books.

'This is a waste of time...' she murmured, 'all for nothing...'

At the sound of her voice, the cogitator's pewter mask-speaker turned on oiled spindles to face the woman. It was a morose thing, worked out of metal to resemble the aspect of an exalted tech-priest some centuries dead. Bellows and tiny chimes in the throat of the device huffed and rattled, creating a sound that resembled human speech. 'To find clarity, it will be necessary to repeat your request.'

'I wasn't talking to you,' Verity retorted, her frustration and weariness snapping in her voice. 'Be quiet.' For the first few hours, the cogitator had taken to breaking the silence at regular intervals by intoning random church-approved axioms designed to reinforce piety and clarity of thought. The Hospitaller had swiftly tired of repeated assertions that 'A closed mind is never open to heresy' and that 'Death is the currency of traitors'.

'By your command.' The machine clicked and whirred, turning away again. Through the blank gaps of the mask's mouth and eyes, the Sororitas could make out the dim shape of a mottled glass orb and the form of turning grey spools within, pierced by thousands of gold filaments. She understood little of how the cogitators worked, but found her mind wandering to thoughts of the components that formed it. Had they originated inside some ancient scholar-machine on Terra, one so old and learned that it could not be allowed to cease its service?

She shook the thought away and frowned at the ancient apparatus, as if it were to blame for her lack of success. The fatigue she felt was making it difficult for her to concentrate, and she fingered the silver rosary at her neck to focus. The lives of Midshipman Vorgo and a dozen other deckhands from the warship *Mercutio* lay strewn about her on paper and punch card, everything from birth certifications to notices of indenture, stipend accounts and disciplinary warrants.

Verity ran her finger over the raised studs on the index of a man named Priser. It was remarkable how such a small piece of cardboard could so encapsulate the life of a person. She lingered over a blank spot on the index. Just one accidental nick of her fingernail, a dot of spilled ink on the wrong page, and Priser could find himself penniless or declared dead. Such was the monumental inertia of the Imperium's monolithic bureaucracy that the word of these documents was law, and these flawed, impossibly old machines were the custodians of it all. It was a sobering thought to imagine all the things – people, ships, perhaps even entire worlds – that could go missing just for the sake of a wrongly placed decimal point.

Verity realised that she had been staring at the same document for several minutes, reading and re-reading the same line of text in Priser's file without actually taking it in. She sighed, and read it again.

It was a reference code to an incident in the man's service record, some weeks before the *Mercutio* had departed Neva to pick up Miriya's Celestians prior to their rendezvous with the Black Ship. Verity blinked. She had seen this number before.

The woman took up another file and found the same index point. The code was there as well. It was the same in a third, in a fourth. All of them, including Vorgo, sported the same numerical reference, and it lay in place below the red tags placed by the enforcers. A rush of sudden excitement flooded Verity, making her giddy. She tapped the front of the cogitator to attract its attention.

'This code,' she said, showing the eyeless mask the paperwork. 'What does it refer to?'

Clockwork twittered and clicked. 'Your forbearance. Your answer will attend forthwith.' After a few moments, the device made a sucking noise and a vacuum tube in its chest opened, revealing a coiled parchment. 'Sacrifice is the most noble worship.'

She read quickly. The papers were a mimeographed copy of a report from the Naval attaché's office, explaining how a transport tender taking some of the *Mercutio*'s crew on liberty to Noroc had been diverted by a malfunction. The shuttle had been forced to put down in the city-state of Metis and eventually returned to orbit with its passengers intact a day later. There were one or two additional names, but without exception, every man who had a hand in Vaun's escape had been on that transport. Verity looked for the crewmen who had been aboard but hadn't joined Vorgo and the others. None of them were still alive. On a ship as large as the *Mercutio*, deaths by misadventure and accident were a daily occurrence, but the pattern made the Sister's skin crawl. The others had died before the rendezvous.

Gathering up her data-slate, Verity made swift notes with an electroquill. She thought about Vorgo, there in the confinement cell, screaming for a daughter that he never had, and reached for his papers.

Her eyes narrowed. According to the Naval renumary, Vorgo and his shipmates had been given their usual stipend of Imperial scrip to spend during their leave in Noroc – but not a single note of it had been exchanged. That seemed impossible. Metis was notorious for taverns and salacious diversions. Any visiting swabbie with a pocket full of unspent pay would return to ship with nothing to show for it but a hangover and some interesting social diseases.

'What happened in Metis?' Verity asked the question to the air, and suddenly she was very, very awake.

Her shadow cocked its head and wondered at the words the young woman spoke. It had already noted and logged the paperwork she had been interested in for later evaluation by its master. Verity's body language had changed radically in the last few moments. Before, she seemed to be on the verge of physical exhaustion, but now the shadow could see the spark of adrenaline in her eyes, could almost smell it in the oily air.

The killer weighed this new information carefully, briefly entertaining the idea of terminating the girl now, but years of servitude in Neva's assassin wars had left an indelible mark on the shadow. Haste was the enemy of the invisible murder. It was only certainty that made the single shot, the killing blow perfect. The shadow elected to wait a little longer. Another figure was within the target envelope, and it might become necessary to end more than just the girl's life.

The ghost pistol moved a few degrees. The age and origin of the killer's weapon was unknown. Some had said it was of xenos manufacture, others that it dated back to the black period known as the Dark Age of Technology. The shadow liked it for its silence. Inside the non-reflective matter of the breech, single dart-shaped projectiles nestled and waited. These were made by hand, crafted by sightless tech-priests specially blinded for just that purpose. When fired, they left the ghost pistol with no ejecta, no sound or report of fire. Not even the whispering air about the flying darts could give away their passage, and the material they and the gun were made from was utterly energy-inert. Any senses, from an auspex to a psyker's witchsight, could not see it.

There were many darts in the gun, but one would be enough.

With a heavy clank, the gantry leading to the main walkway locked into place and the library platform shuddered slightly. Verity looked up to see another logistoras picking his way down towards her. This one was of a lower rank than the adept who had escorted her into the hall, a mere quillan with less than a dozen service buttons. The clerk-priest bowed and pointed a finger at the scattered papers. He seemed rather distressed that the files were displayed in so imprecise a manner.

'I need to revise,' he hissed. 'You have to let me proceed.'

'Revise what?'

The logistoras ambled forward on roller-ball feet and took up the first file that came to hand. Paper looped from a dispenser reel at his hip, a device fashioned to look like a closed book. He shot Verity a glance. 'Certification. After the attack, there's been a lot to do.' A grey tongue drooped from his lips and he licked the paper with it. With a swift motion, the quillan pasted the label to the file and folded it away. He began to repeat the procedure.

Verity took the altered file and studied it. The new addition was a finger's length of black-bordered ticket bearing a date, time and identifier code. In red letters, one word stood out like a livid brand. *Deceased*.

'What is going on?' Verity demanded, turning on the logistoras.

He blinked and recoiled a little. The quillan seemed nervous of her. 'Last night? The attack?' He licked another label and stuck it on Priser's file card. 'Some of the rockets fired struck the reformatory. Many prisoners were killed in the conflagration that ensued.' The clerk paused and gestured around at the files with a metal hand, steel pen nibs for fingers. 'All these men are dead. The files must be revised to reflect the new truth.'

Verity let the logistoras complete his work without interruption. The adept kept stealing sidelong glances at her when he thought she wasn't looking at him, and finally she blew out a breath. 'Do you have something to say to me?'

Another owlish blink. 'I... I know you. Your ident crossed my work queue recently, Sister Verity. I know of your involvement in the Vaun investigation.'

Something in the logistoras's tone gave her pause. 'Yes,' she said carefully. 'I am gathering information on the witch to aide in his capture.'

The clerk-priest paused, his task at an end. 'I have never been commissioned to engage in a criminal investigation.' There was an air of wistful hope in his voice. 'My works are purely administrational. I often wonder what it would be like to–'

Verity took a chance. 'Perhaps you might assist me now?'

The quillan froze. 'It would be my honour. How might I be of help, Sister?'

The Hospitaller's mind whirled. The question danced on her lips. 'I... I want to see the files you have on Torris Vaun.'

'That datum is restricted.' The logistoras eyed her. 'But

should I assume you have the requisite sanction from the office of the lord deacon?'

Sister Verity kept all emotion from her face, afraid of giving it away with a simple tell but then the clerk-priests were a sheltered lot not often given to contact with other humans, and she doubted he would be able to spot a lie on her lips. 'You may assume that,' she told him.

The quillan bowed and led her deeper into the librarium.

They descended through a series of hatches into an iron cupola, which in turn crossed between the slow-turning cogs to another platform, filled with books that were chained to their racks. The logistoras extruded a key mechanism from his palm and granted them entrance. He glanced over his hunched shoulder at Verity.

'It occurs to me, I have not given you my identity. I am Quillan Class Four Unshir, cutter of paper and copy maker.' He bowed a little. 'Pardon me if I seem forward, but if you could see your way to highlight my co-operation in this matter to my savant senioris–'

She threw him a quick, fake smile. 'Of course. Your assistance will be rewarded.' Verity disliked lying, even to a demi-human such as Unshir, but she had committed herself now. 'Emperor forgive me,' she whispered. 'This I do in Your name.'

The quillan glanced at her. 'Did you address me, Sister?'

'No,' she snapped, a little too quickly. 'Vaun's records. Show them to me.'

He bowed. 'Of course.'

Unshir used the keys to unlock a tome sheathed in light-absorbing obsidian, touching a ring of code-spots on the cover to open it. He whispered something that sounded like birdsong into a grille on the book's spine and it obediently opened by itself, pages moving on armatures in a blur. With a snap, the book laid itself flat in Unshir's hands and he turned, presenting it to her. 'The pages are made of a psycho-active papyrus,' he said reverently. 'Don't touch them with naked skin.'

Verity nodded and began to read. These were the books of the tithe kept to record the comings and goings of the Adeptus Astra Telepathica in the Neva system. Whenever a person was found bearing the stigma of a psyker, their name was entered here along with a preliminary record of the abilities they exhibited. In time, when the Black Ships came to claim them, the witchkin would be transferred from the deep cells in Neva's Inquisitorial dungeons to the mysterious vessels, never to be seen again.

And there was Torris Vaun's name. The records were sketchy: apparently sold into slavery as a child, the youth's psychic talents had come to the attention of the Ecclesiarchy's agents – and tellingly, Viktor LaHayn himself, at the time a senior confessor. There were several notes in florid prose on the matter of Vaun's unholy capabilities. He was seen to have committed acts of wilful telepathy, shriving and extreme feats of pyrokene mastery. Verity thought of the fire that burnt in the witch's eyes and gave an involuntary shudder.

'As you can see, the files remain intact.' Unshir nodded to himself. 'Are you satisfied?'

The Hospitaller ignored him. She knew what to look for now, and kept searching the tight scrawl of luminous text for discrepancies. 'The dates...' Verity said at length, marshalling her thoughts aloud. 'The sequence is incorrect.'

The logistoras flinched as if she had struck him. 'You are mistaken. We care for these documents as if they were the words of the God-Emperor Himself. Nothing is wrong.'

'Vaun's detection and capture. There is a gap here, a missing datum.'

'Impossible.' Unshir's pale face flushed red.

'The file jumps from the date he was captured to the notation of his escape from Neva. Where was he during the intervening time? Where was he held? The page says nothing.'

'You are misreading it,' the clerk-priest exclaimed, suddenly irritated.

'See for yourself.'

'No,' Unshir shivered. 'It is forbidden for us to look upon

the pages that we write and protect. Our cognitive functions are compartmentalised so that we cannot understand the words which we transcribe.'

'There must be other records of Vaun,' she demanded. 'Where are they?'

'There are no others,' he spluttered, as if the very idea of information residing anywhere but within these walls was a joke. But in the next instant, the logistoras's face clouded. 'Wait. If the lord deacon sent you on an errand, why would you say such a thing? Is this some sort of test? Or perhaps not?'

'I...' Caught unawares, Verity's fragile cloak of deception disintegrated with a single look. 'No, I was sent–'

At last he saw the lie on her face. 'Charlatan. You have *misinformed* me!' Unshir spat the words like a curse. 'You have no right to be here.' Anger and then terror crossed the priest's face as he realised that it was his inattention that had allowed Verity to gain access where she was not meant to. 'Alarm. Alarm!' he called, lurching away towards a control grille on one of the support girders.

From above, the Sororitas heard the keening hum of servo-skulls swooping down from the heights. The quillan's pen-nib fingertips scratched at the security buzzer panel, but then his head ripped open with a noise like tearing cloth and the clattering clerk fell dead to the deck.

Verity thought she saw the shape of something dark moving in among the gantries overhead. Somewhere up there, fizzing sparks of colour cast brief flashes as a trio of servo-skulls were pierced with razored metal darts. The Hospitaller ran, her heart hammering against her chest.

The shadow was not in the business of hunting, the assassin did not enjoy the thrill of the chase, the hot rush of pursuit as a target fled in fear of its life. Rather, the shadow's way was one of stealth. The killer strove never to race after a mark, but instead be there when the target was least suspecting, to plant a silent dart in their soft flesh and have them perish never knowing where death had come from. But the Sister Hospitaller had disrupted that plan by deviating from ascribed behaviour patterns. It was unexpected that the woman took the bold step of lying to the hapless quillan, and even more so that she would dare to delve into sealed church records. If there had been an iota of uncertainty that Verity's death was required, it was with that action that she removed any doubt in the assassin's mind.

But then the logistoras buffoon had over-reacted and his murder became necessary, then too the elimination of the servo-skull scouts before they could relay any alarm to the tech-guards on the upper tiers.

The gloom of the librarium was rendered bright by the preysight mechanism within the sealed helm the shadow wore. Ahead, the assassin saw the heat blob that was Sister Verity lurching from one canyon of books to another, directionless and terrified. A frown formed behind the faceplate. In her panic, it was making it impossible to draw a bead on the woman, so that a fatal shot might be taken. This was not acceptable.

The killer surveyed the library platform and found a hod of heavy books suspended over one of the wide metal shelves. There were volumes covering matters of decrepit old history, awaiting return to their rightful place by some minor functionary like the late Unshir. With care, the shadow aimed at the cable holding the book carriage up and shot it away.

Huge black slabs of the gloom above her detached from the darkness and crashed down around Verity, the heavy books striking the mesh decking about her with ringing impacts. One of the tomes slammed into her and sent the woman sprawling. Verity screamed, colliding with the bookshelves and spinning about. The blow knocked the wind from her lungs and she felt her precious data-slate fall from her fingers. She heard a smash of broken plastics as another weighty volume landed squarely on the little device and crushed it into fragments.

The carriage's load gone, the frame itself dropped from the cable overhead and fell, tumbling end over end. Verity tried to get away, but the hems of her robe snarled about her feet and she came to her knees. The carriage came down on her, trapping her legs beneath it.

Through the veil of preysight, Sister Verity's cry of pain was a bloom of hot orange air in the cool, dry voids of the librarium. The assassin was aware of confusion and noise from the other gantries in the hall. The clerk-priests were becoming aware that something was amiss, the colours of their bodies moving and swarming closer. There was little time. The killing of the Hospitaller had to be now.

Careful, deft fingers dialled the barrel of the ghost pistol to maximum dilation and the shadow racked a dart into the breech. A sensor pit on the tip of the gun relayed information to the preysight, highlighting the shape of organs inside Verity's shuddering frame. There was the throbbing orb of her heart, nestled beneath the crosshairs. The assassin's finger tightened on the trigger.

She fired blindly.

From the connecting gantry, Miriya had seen the book hod fall. She had heard the death scream of Unshir and the pops of detonation as the servo-skulls were obliterated. Her plasma pistol was singing in her hand and she broke into a run, disciplined muscle-memory taking over. In the shade of the towering bookcases she caught a glimpse of flapping robes as Verity fell. The Sister's cry was full of fear.

Miriya fired, releasing a salvo of quick energy bolts up into the steel rafters. She could not see the attacker, but the Celestian's mind operated on an instinctual, instantaneous level. There was some part of her consciousness calculating angles and likely points of attack, aiming at the places where she herself might have hidden in order to kill the girl.

And *there*! For a fraction of a second, backlit by a streak of sun-bright gaseous plasma, a man-shape recoiling in the girders.

The black-suited figure switched targets and shot back at the Battle Sister. Miriya threw herself across the deck in a tuck-and-roll as darts, invisible in the gloom, smashed into supports or punched holes in the covers of rare manuscripts.

Her opponent moved and fired again. The accuracy of the near-hits was punishing, forcing her on the defensive, and it was instantly clear to Miriya that the assassin possessed some form of enhanced senses.

'Preysight,' she reasoned, shaking off her cloak to gain greater freedom of movement. The woman knew of the arcane technology that rendered night into day – the Sabbat helmets of the Adepta Sororitas had similar capacity – but she also understood its limitations. Miriya aimed low, not at the place where the shadowy killer was lurking, but at the racks of ancient papers beneath. The plasma pistol shrieked and cast flares of brilliant white light into the aged, dry tomes. The conflagration was instant, sending a sheet of fire up towards the rafters.

A scream pealed through the air, and there atop the racks was the assassin, framed by orange flames, clutching at its face. Miriya had only a moment. The machine-spirits of the librarium would not stand to let a fire rage for more than a second or two, lest it spread across the entire complex. There were networks of pipes that delivered inert, suffocating gases to such outbreaks – if the flames died, then so would she and Verity.

The Battle Sister's weapon howled.

A fist of gaseous matter as hot as the core of a star ripped into the shadow's left arm, just above the elbow. Everything below the joint exploded from the touch of the incredible heat, and the hydrostatic shock of boiling blood sent a hammer blow racing through the killer's body. The assassin tumbled from the bookcases, falling to the decks through wreaths of fire-retardant mist.

Plasma weapons were designed not to target un-armoured forms like the shadow, but to melt their way through ceramite or hull metal. Used on flesh, they were a blowtorch turned upon wax. The pain of the hit was of such intensity that the killer's heart was stopped by it, and in turn, this factor triggered the compact denial charge of hexogen that was implanted beneath the shadow's ribcage. The assassin's patron was not in the business of letting discarded tools fall into the wrong hands.

With a wet crack, the shadow blew apart in mid-air.

Flecks of burnt matter, some of it flesh, some unidentifiable, scattered down around them in a macabre rain. Disgust churned in Miriya's gullet as she batted the burning remains from her cloak. Nearby, Verity extracted herself from beneath the fallen book carriage, favouring her leg. She eyed the black scorch mark, waving away the acrid puffs of extinguisher gas. Nothing recognisable as human remained of the assassin.

Miriya saw the glitter of glass and holstered her gun. There, lost to the shadow when she had taken her kill, was the murderer's arcane weapon. The Battle Sister picked it up and turned it over in her gauntleted hands, running a practiced eye over the deadly lines of the pistol. 'Mark me, what is this?' Her hand found the knurled porcelain butt and the gun fell into her grip by reflex. Through the clear ammunition store drum she could see the wicked barbs of the dart loads.

'You saved my life,' managed Verity.

'Thank the Emperor for placing me here where I was needed most,' said Miriya. 'You have been in here for the better part of a day. I was concerned and so I came to find you. Had I not...'

'Vaun. He must have known,' husked Verity, her throat raw from the vapours of the dead fire. 'Wanted to keep me from finding out...'

Miriya's eyes never left the gun. 'He had ample chance to murder you in the Lunar Cathedral.'

'What are you saying?' The Hospitaller's voice was high with emotion.

'I've never seen the like of this before. I do not think that a corsair like Vaun would be able to field a weapon and an agent such as this.' She weighed the weapon in her hand, gingerly running her thumb over the setting studs. 'The value of this pistol alone could probably buy him the loyalty of a dozen men...'

'Then who–' Verity's words were cut off by a fizzing spit of noise from the ghost pistol's breech. Suddenly the gun went red hot, the structure of it warping and distending.

'Get down!' Miriya drew back her arm and threw the pistol away into the dark with all her might. She heard it clatter against metal walls then in the next moment there was a crash of detonation. The Battle Sister felt, rather than heard, one of the freed darts streak past her face to embed itself in a rack of books. Suspicion sent a cold sensation crawling over her skin. Such an assassin, such weaponry was far beyond the capabilities of a renegade like Vaun. Only someone with influence, with connections that stretched all over Neva and beyond, could have sent the shadow to silence the Hospitaller.

Miriya glanced up and unconsciously traced the silver fleur-de-lys between her armoured breasts.

'This is outrageous!' Venik's voice was almost a scream, his tirade roaring about the Canoness's chambers. 'I do not know where to begin with this litany of misdeeds and insubordination!' He whirled about, his red cloak flaring, to stab a finger at Miriya and Verity. The Hospitaller's head was bowed, but the Battle Sister did little to show any contrition before the furious dean. 'This presumptuous wench dares to go against my explicit orders, against the word of the lord deacon and lie her way into the librarium – and then your Celestian commits an act of horrific vandalism. Hundreds of Neva's most precious manuscripts, the works of a thousand dedicated lexmechanics turned to ashes!'

Standing at the side of Galatea's wide desk, Sister Reiko cleared her throat. 'The term "precious" is an interesting choice of words, Dean Venik. I understand that the papers destroyed were those relating to crop rotations on the Pirin island chain. Considering that archipelago sank into the ocean during the thirty-fourth millennium, one might ask why they might be considered of more value than the life of Sister Verity.'

'The Sister Superior discharged a weapon inside a holy shrine of the Adeptus Ministorum.'

Miriya fixed him with a hard stare. 'Indeed I did, in the defence of a fellow Sororitas, against an intruder who had already murdered an innocent savant. An intruder whom the librarium's guardians failed to detect or apprehend.'

Canoness Galatea steepled her fingers and said nothing, content to watch the interplay with a neutral, measuring expression.

Venik paused, gathering himself. 'Very well. Then, for the sake of argument, let us dismiss the matter of the books and your wanton gunplay, and consider this errant Hospitaller.' He took a step closer to Verity. 'Did I not say to you in no uncertain terms that the enforcers investigation precluded the need for further enquiry? Were my words unclear? Or are the Sisters of the Order of Serenity given to ignoring the commands of their superiors?' The dean was almost shouting again.

Galatea caught Miriya's eye, and the Battle Sister felt the Canoness searching her soul with that level, unflinching stare. At length, she spoke. 'Verity was acting under my command.'

Venik spun to face the older woman, his face tight with anger. 'What did you say?'

'I ordered Verity to proceed to the librarium, despite your words to her. She was there on my authority.'

Unseen by the dean, Verity and Miriya exchanged glances. Galatea had known nothing of the Hospitaller's venture into the hall of records until after the commotion there. *She is vouching for us...*

'Did you?' Venik seemed unconvinced. 'Yet you did not consider informing my office of that fact?'

Galatea gave an off-hand wave. 'I have many duties to

attend to in the convent, my honoured dean. I apologise for giving the matter a lower priority.'

Venik glared at Miriya. If he knew the Canoness was providing a way out for the Sisters, there was no way he could challenge her on it. The ranks they held in the church hierarchy were roughly analogous, with neither holding seniority over the other. 'So be it. I hope then, after all that has transpired, that Sister Verity's impromptu venture yielded something of value. Speak, girl,' he snapped. 'Tell us what great revelation you found among the burning books and corpses.'

With a tremor in her voice, Verity explained the datum she had uncovered in the remunery files and the correlation between the mutineers on the *Mercutio*. Venik listened with a sneer on his lips, but Galatea was evaluating every word, and Reiko followed with swift entries on her data-slate.

'This is all you have? Malfunctioning shuttles and unspent money?' snapped Venik. 'Circumstantial hearsay, nothing more.'

'Men have been put to the sword for less,' Miriya said darkly.

'The city-state of Metis is under the governance of Baron Holt Sherring,' noted Sister Reiko. 'The baron's considerable fortune comes from his family's holdings in Neva's transport and shipping guilds. It was a vessel under Sherring's livery that was diverted on that day.'

Galatea nodded. 'And let us not forget, the good baron is a major shareholder in the consortium that controls the orbital commerce station where the witch made his escape.'

Venik's mood changed abruptly. 'You... You are suggesting that a member of Neva's aristocrat caste aided and abetted a known criminal? That he somehow engineered the escape of Torris Vaun?' He snorted. 'These are serious charges.'

'How hard would it be to coerce members of a transport crew or commerce station staff, especially if the pressure came from a noble?' Galatea replied. 'It is well known that Baron Sherring is a ruthless and ambitious man. His numerous contentions with the planetary governor are a matter of record.'

'It is my belief that the mutineers were somehow... *conditioned* by an unknown agency while in Metis,' said Verity. 'I would suggest some form of post-hypnotic suggestion, perhaps keyed to a certain event or stimulus that would trigger a programmed set of behaviour. Such things are medically possible with the correct devices.'

Galatea came to her feet. 'Reiko, prepare my personal Immolator. Dean Venik, you will accompany me to a meeting with the lord deacon. I will demand a warrant to prepare a pogrom against Sherring. If the criminal Vaun has gone to ground in Metis–'

The heavy door to the chambers burst open to admit Sister Cassandra. The woman was flushed with effort. 'Canoness. Forgive my intrusion.'

'I left orders not to be disturbed.'

Cassandra nodded. 'Indeed, but matters require your immediate attention. A communiqué from Lord LaHayn has arrived... There is an incident in Metis...'

'Metis?' Venik repeated, shooting a look at Verity. 'Explain!'

'At five-bell today, the public vox network broadcast a signal from the baron's mansion. Sherring himself has declared secession from Governor Emmel's rule and the law of the Ecclesiarchy. He claims that the lord deacon is guilty of crimes against the Imperium.'

'Impossible,' breathed Venik. 'He has signed his city's death warrant!'

Cassandra continued. 'Lord LaHayn ordered the mobilisation of a reprisal force immediately. We are tasked to march on Metis and censure the baron for his heresy.'

Reiko frowned. 'If Verity is correct and Vaun is hiding out under Sherring's protection, the baron may have more than just some misguided guardsmen at his side.'

'It appears that events have overtaken us,' said the Canoness grimly. 'My orders are revised. Mobilise the Sisterhood. Metis will surrender to us, or we will raze it to ashes.'

CHAPTER NINE

The assault force left the highway as the gates of the Staberinde Pass loomed large through the forest. Forward scouts reported that Sherring's Household Cavalry had placed explosive charges on the sheer walls of the cutting, and Canoness Galatea was in no mood to give them cause to use such a crude tactic. With clipped orders, she sent her commands down the line to the Rhinos, Repressors, Exorcists and Immolators. In slow precision, the armoured vehicles proceeded to force their way through the trees. From the brass grilles of a dozen winged speaker horns came the opening cantos of the Fede Imperialis, the battle hymn of the Adepta Sororitas.

Miriya crouched on the roof of the Canoness's transport, the view through her magnoculars bobbing as the tracked tank rode over the dark earth. They were advancing up a gentle incline, passing through the collar of trees that surrounded Metis City in a thick ring. At first glance, the settlement appeared to be a formidable target: Metis was built into the basalt bowl of a dead volcano, a caldera-city encircled by a natural shield wall. There were few points of entry, and huge gates guarded each one, but on closer inspection, there were myriad weaknesses. In places the stone walls were thinner, thin enough that a sustained missile barrage would be able to crack them.

The Metiser soldiery, although noted for their fine uniforms and skills with ornamental cutlasses, were ill-trained to face armoured assaults and zealous attackers. Baron Sherring's troops were largely local fops with just a handful of Imperial Guardsmen grown fat in a comfortable posting. The Sisters of Battle did not expect to be challenged here.

The Celestian's viewpoint drifted down to the upper edge of the timberline, to where the drum-shaped defence bunkers studded the lower slopes of the city wall. Dean Venik had provided intelligence records showing that the baron's pillboxes were only manned by automated gun servitors. Miriya wondered idly why the church felt the need to keep detailed tactical data on Metis. Clearly Lord LaHayn had long suspected that Sherring might one day secede.

The glass dome of the gunnery hatch levered upward to allow an armoured figure to present itself. Canoness Galatea turned in place, sharing watchful, comradely nods to the Sisters marching beside her Immolator. Pooled about her shoulders and cascading down her back was a lustrous cape made from night-black velvet and stark white fur. The Cloak of Saint Aspira was one of the Neva convent's most sacred artefacts, blessed in the great Eccleisarchal Palace on Terra itself. The mantle was fabricated with a strange mesh-like metal beneath the finery, a form of near-weightless armour the creation of which was lost to the ages. It was said that the sanctified cape could turn away a killing shot by the Emperor's will.

The Canoness caught her awed gaze. 'I dislike the pageantry of this,' she said in a low voice, fingering the cloak. 'Such a relic is too holy to be dragged into battle with so unworthy a foe.'

Miriya holstered her magnoculars. 'The power of an artefact is not only in its physical strength, honoured Sister. To see the cloak upon you gives courage to our kinswomen and sows doubt in the mind of our opposition.'

Galatea sniffed. 'It is beneath us. The honour of this mantle is cheapened.'

'Only if we are not victorious.'

The Canoness laid a hand on the twin mutli-melta cannons at the hatch. 'Interesting days, Miriya. You have brought me interesting days, yet again.'

'I could not foresee–'

'That Vaun's escape would spark a revolt?' snapped Galatea. 'Of course not. To you, the mission was simply to take a criminal into your custody. How were you to understand the web of politics and subterfuge that thunders unseen over everything on Neva?' She shook her head. 'I have served the order here for years and still the secret contests of kingdom and society on this world are clouded to me. Sherring, LaHayn, Vaun… All of them are cards in some peculiar tarot.'

Despite herself, Miriya bristled. 'We are Daughters of the Emperor, not tokens on some game board.'

Galatea smiled. 'Exactly, Sister Superior. And that is why this will be an interesting day.'

The column mounted a shallow rise and they were quiet for a moment, the Fede Imperialis sounding about them. At last, Miriya leaned closer to the Canoness and spoke in low, serious tones. 'The issue of Sister Verity. You vouched for her before Dean Venik even though you knew nothing of her venture into the librarium.'

'If you have to ask me why I protected her, then perhaps your understanding of our sisterhood is unclear, Miriya.' She surveyed the horizon. 'Venik has never been a friend to the Adepta Sororitas. He would prefer that men of the Nevan PDF or his frateris militia defend his chapels, soldiers more directly influenced by his will than the word of the God-Emperor. He is like every cleric born under Neva's sky, ambitious and narrow in view. I would not give him opportunity to oppose us.'

Miriya blew out a breath. 'I will speak plainly, Canoness. This artifice, the doubletalk and power play surrounding every word and deed, it chafes at me. I have but one mission and that is to bring Torris Vaun to justice – I have no wish to be come ensnared in politics.' The Celestian's face wrinkled in disgust at the very thought of it.

Galatea gave a rueful smile. 'Then I would advise you, Sister, never to allow yourself to advance beyond your current rank. I have learned to my cost that of all the challenges to the power of His Word, it is the obfuscation of those who claim to serve Him that vexes me the most.' She looked away. 'The rigour of honest battle is a welcome respite.'

'This Sherring... If his sway over Metis is so strong, how was he ever allowed to gain such a position of authority? Surely his tendency to sedition should have been noted?' asked Miriya.

'Neva's nobility have always engaged in skirmishes and duels. Baron Sherring's avarice is no different from others of his kind.'

'Except he has made a pact with a witch.'

'If Sister Verity is correct, so it would seem.'

From below, Miriya caught the crackling hum of an open vox channel then Sister Reiko's voice hissed in her ear bead. 'Canoness, your pardon, but I think you ought to hear this.'

'What concerns you, Reiko?' Galatea looked towards the head of the formation, to where her adjutant rode in a Rhino with the banner bearers.

'A blasphemous broadcast is being sent on the general frequency. I believe it is directed at the defenders of Metis.'

The Canoness gave Miriya a look. 'Let me listen.'

There was a bark of static that shifted into the sound of a man's voice, strong with emotion. '...love for my citizens. And with that ideal, I cannot in good conscience continue to pledge the loyalty of my house and citizenry to a man whose abuse of the Imperial Church knows no bounds. It has been made clear to me that the self-declared Lord Viktor LaHayn is abusing his posting as lord deacon of Neva's diocese. My sources have brought me evidence that he and his corrupt lackeys pay fealty not to Holy Terra, but to a plan of such staggering disloyalty that I dare not utter it aloud. Even now, our sanctuary of Metis is threatened by LaHayn's misguided servants, blinded by their own shortsightedness. We do not wish open war, but that is what has been forced upon us. For our future, for our Emperor, we must reject the twisted rule of the traitor priest. Our city must be a torch of light in this darkness. We must fight and expunge this contagion. *We must fight!*'

Miriya recognised Baron Sherring's voice at once but the arch confidence he had exuded in the Lunar Cathedral was gone now, replaced with a kind of manic intensity. 'He's afraid,' she thought aloud.

'Yes,' agreed Galatea, 'and so he should be.' She tapped the vox tab on her armour's neck ring and silenced the babbling feed from the city. 'Reiko, sound the alert. He's whipping those poor fools into battle frenzy. The battle will not be long in coming.' The Canoness beckoned Miriya. 'Come below, Sister. We should take a moment to bless our ammunition before we engage them.'

Verity looked up with a start as the Rhino lurched to a halt, reflexively clutching at the medicus ministorum case on her lap. As the order had begun its gathering for the advance on Metis, Reiko had come to Verity and offered her the sanctuary of the convent until the matter of Sherring's insurrection had been dealt with.

Her answer had come swiftly, without conscious thought. She believed that the baron was conspiring with Torris Vaun, even more so now that the city-lord had openly defied the church. In her heart she knew that if Vaun were anywhere, he would be behind the black stone walls of the caldera. It seemed impossible for her to be elsewhere. Verity had no choice but to see this chain of events through to its conclusion. Sister Reiko did not challenge her on her choice – instead, she entered the Hospitaller's name on the roll of battle and found her a post. One more medicae in the assault force would be welcome.

Securing her gear, she pushed past the Battle Sisters crowded into the transport with her and pressed her face to a firing slot in the thick armoured hull. Her eyes were drawn instantly to a troop of women who moved in a tight flock, their heads bowed and hidden beneath makeshift hoods cut from rags of old battle cloak material, tatters of broken armour barely covering the pale nakedness of their bodies.

The Hospitaller's heart leapt into her throat; she had never seen the Sisters Repentia at such close hand before. They walked like women condemned, arms folded at their chests to hold their lethal-looking chainswords as a priest might carry a cross or totem. She saw the blink of black iron chains around their limbs and torsos, some with fan-folds of sanctified parchment drooping from their backs like diseased wings. Each of the faceless Repentia bore the marbling of countless scars across her bare flesh, some self-inflicted and others given in ritual before battle. Verity could not help but shudder as her mind connected this sight with the horrors she had witnessed during the Games of Penance.

The vicious, snake-hiss crack of neural whips gave her a start. The Repentia Mistress advanced through the midst of her charges, calling out a litany. 'If I must die,' she snarled. 'I shall welcome death.'

'I shall welcome death as an old friend,' chorused the Repentia, 'and wrap mine arms about it.'

'Only in death does duty end.' The Mistress crossed her hands and let the neural whips in her hands flick over the exposed skin of her Sisters, kindling the holy hate and righteous zeal within them.

The devotion of the Repentia was at once awe-inspiring and terrible. The Hospitaller could sense the burning need in them for the virtuous glory of unfettered combat. Other Sisters of Battle parted without words and without looking upon them, allowing the Mistress to guide her cadre forward. Even among the Sororitas, the respect the Repentia were shown was rooted as much in fear as it was in esteem. All Sisters in service to the Emperor aspired to the same purity of fervour, but only a few could truly surrender themselves to the terrible power of it as these women had.

One of the Repentia turned her head and from rips in her crimson hood, ice blue eyes in a pale face looked out at

Verity. The Hospitaller gasped then the woman turned away again and went on with the rest of the squad.

With a rumble, the Rhino began to move again, following the Repentia towards the battle lines. On the wind, Verity heard war cries and the report of gunfire.

The Metis Household Cavalry had laid an ambush for the Order of Our Martyred Lady. Just beyond the places where chokepoints had been planted with stands of tough trees to slow any armoured advance, a squad of Salamander scout mobiles was concealed beneath camouflage netting, ranged optics peeking out of the fake leaf-pattern material to spy on the Battle Sisters.

A few officers in Sherring's soldiery had raised questions when told their guns were to turn on the Adepta Sororitas. Those men had been the first casualties of the conflict, quietly killed and replaced with captains who better understood the nature of loyalty to the barony.

As one, the Salamanders discharged their primary armaments, a spread of punishing autocannon fire ripping through their temporary cover to strike at the Battle Sisters' forward line. Women died in streaks of orange fire, and back behind the copse, the scout commander ordered his units to fire up their engines and start the retreat. The cavalry tanks fired again as they moved, lining the perimeter with falling steel.

'Incoming fire!' Reiko's voice called from the vox. Aboard Galatea's Immolator, Miriya shook as the driver crashed the gears, splitting from the skirmish line to minimise any splash damage. The Canoness was pressed to a complex device that mingled a periscope scanner with an auspex and targeting cogitator. 'Beyond that thicket,' she grated, 'scouts on the move.' She glanced back over her shoulder at Miriya. 'Exorcists. I want that tree line burnt off. All units, pitch to attack posture and advance!'

The Battle Sister heard the prayers of acknowledgement from the missile-carrying units ranged behind them and she hauled herself up the short ladder and into the vehicle's empty cupola. Miriya was in time to hear the hoots and clarion chimes from the launch tubes of the Exorcist tanks behind them.

Built, like so many of the Imperium's armoured vehicles, upon the standard template construct that formed the basis of the Rhino, Exorcists were among the longest serving tactical units in existence. Almost all of them dated back to the turbulent years of the Age of Apostasy, when they travelled the battle zones of the Wars of Faith as mobile shrines-cum-attack units. Where most of the order's war vehicles were liveried in reds, blacks and whites, many Exorcist units had gold and silver about them in infinite detail. Their planes of ablative armour were worked with inlaid castings, and sprouting from the rear of some were towering organ pipes stained copper in the light of the Nevan sun. From these instruments came not music, but judgement and destruction. With shrieks of fire at their tails, fountains of missiles emerged from the launch tubes, describing an arc up from the launchers, then down upon the Salamanders and the intractable trees. The hardy trees were split apart or felled, clearing the way for Sisters and Retributors to advance. With them came the spike-mawed prows of a dozen Repressors and Immolators.

A second barrage was unnecessary. The surviving Salamanders fled in full retreat, random snaps of laser fire lancing back from men in the cockpits who dared to test the patience of the Sisterhood. Galatea's tank circled about one of the enemy units. The scout car had been flipped on to its side by a near miss, and Miriya caught the vague noise of movement inside as they passed. She paid little mind to it. Her Sisters on foot would deal with any survivors. The Immolator's gun turret turned easily, letting her track the fat-barrelled meltaguns back and forth across the horizon. The Salamanders were quick off the mark, and there was a chance they would get out of range before the Sororitas could find a clear shot.

'They're trying to draw us into the teeth of those emplaced

weapons,' Miriya noted. 'Perhaps we might seek a place to breach the shield wall elsewhere?'

'I do not concur,' replied Galatea. 'The West Gate is on this axis. We will collapse it and progress into the city.'

A lasgun beam flew wide of the tank, striking a tree and making it a torch. Miriya cranked the meltas to track the culprit, dialling in the focal length and waiting for the right moment. 'With respect, a breach would be the swifter option. The Exorcists could–'

'My orders are cast, Sister Superior.' The Canoness's tone brooked no argument. 'You are correct, but this is a matter of show as much as it is of tactics. If Baron Sherring's hold over this city is to be broken, we must be seen to penetrate his strongest bulwark, not to enter by guile. The gate will fall, and for that the guns will need to be silenced. Press on.'

'Ave Imperator,' said the Celestian, and squeezed the twin firing bars on the turret. Four lines of shimmering energy burst from the melta cannons and came together, falling like arrows of pure heat. The microwave blasts struck the rear of the trailing Salamander and excited the molecular structure of the scout in nanoseconds. Metal warped and outgassed, while inside men screamed as searing fumes tore their lungs. The Salamander veered sharply off course and collided with a grove of trees.

Miriya threw a look over her shoulder at the force riding up behind them. At their backs there were dirty clouds of grey smoke coiling into the air. Small blazes started in the woodlands by indirect fire were taking hold.

The hatch was twisted on its mounts, so it took the driver four attempts to kick the thing open. His limbs were trembling and he couldn't see very well, so touch and a little sight were all he really had to go on. The missile salvos had rocked the Salamander like a dinghy in a storm, and along the way he had planted his head on the metal walls a half-dozen times. He was deaf now. There was nothing but a curious squealing going on inside his skull. Just to make sure he could still speak, the driver let out a couple of curses worthy of a day in the stockade, and picked his way out past the wet paste of remains that was all that was left of his crewmates.

The broken hatch let him out close to the churned dark mud and he scrambled wildly, adding more streaks of soil to the rust-brown, red and oil-black coating the busy heraldry of his cavalryman's uniform. He had lost his stubber pistol somewhere inside the upturned tank, and after finally rolling down a little incline, he came to rest face up.

When the man wiped the blood from his eyes, he saw the circle of women about him, and cried out. They all wore death's head hoods the colour of new blood and were dressed in rags. One of them leaned down to examine him, as a child might consider an insect beneath a magnifying glass.

'Puh-please,' the driver managed to spit out. 'Emperor, please. I am no heretic!'

The woman's lips moved and he struggled to understand what she was saying to him. Finally, the hooded female snatched his hand and pressed it flat to her bare chest so he could feel the vibration as she spoke. He struggled in her grip as he realised she was not speaking, but singing.

'A morte perpetua, domine, libra nos,' intoned Sister Iona. 'That thou wouldst bring them only death, that thou shouldst spare none, that thou shouldst pardon none.'

He saw the glitter of the eviscerator chainsword as she raised it, and then his body lit with pain as she used it to sever the hand pressed to her torso. The driver reeled away and screamed as the rest of the Repentia brought down their blades and cut him apart.

The turret emplacements were hungry for them, and across the open killing zone before the western gate autocannon tracer left purple dashes in the air, chopping at the boots of the Battle Sisters as they used a grounded Salamander for cover. Spent rounds rattled off the armoured scout, clattering like stones in a tin cup.

Glassy cogitator eye-lenses on iron stalks extended from the tops of the flat turrets and there were wires connecting some of them together so that the servitor-minds inside each could share target data. The guns were elderly and ponderous, but still their accuracy was enough to rip apart Sisters who dared to press too far forward, too quickly. The surviving Salamanders retreated behind the lines of the guns, past trenches where heavy stubber cannon were being belt-fed by more of Sherring's overdressed soldiers. The occasional laser bolt showed where Imperial Guard troopers had joined the cavalry in the ill-informed defence of Metis.

Sister Reiko directed the women under her direct command to zero in on the las-fire and kill the guardsmen first. Their training was better than the second-rate locals, whose martial skills turned mostly to parade ground drills and regimented displays. Precise shots on the turncoat guards also had a demoralising effect on the cavalrymen, letting them watch the abrupt and brutal death that they themselves faced if they continued to fight.

Canoness Galatea did not halt the advance. The momentum behind the Sisters of Battle was high, and foolishly Sherring's commanders had staked their tactics on using that against the women, but these were not the common soldiers from other city-states that the Household Cavalry had faced in years past. The Order of Our Martyred Lady moved with the speed of passion, divine zeal welling up in all their hearts.

'Light of the Emperor upon us,' cried Reiko. 'Censure the fallen and chastise!' Her flamer shrieked as she leapt from the hatch of her Rhino, and at her side came a banner bearer showing the hallowed standard of Saint Katherine. Rolling through the broken landscape surrounding the gate, a phalanx of Immolators swept in behind Reiko's unit and a squad of Sister Retributors.

The Retributors were faceless valkyries, their helmets sealed against the smoke and fury of the battle. Many of them carried the bulky slabs of heavy bolters and multi-meltas. Reiko urged them on with a sharp gesture from her flamer, writing a sweep of orange fire across the enemy lines. As one, they unleashed the force of their guns, fording the spines of steel tank traps and pouring death into the outer trench lines. Blunt-nosed bullets from the ballistic stubber rifles came off the armour of the Battle Sisters in clatters, falling away like hail. Reiko gave flame in return, torching men too slow to run. Some dropped to their knees and begged. Those she killed as well, her face turned away in disgust as she granted them absolution.

Repressors in the front rank nosed into the tank traps and shoved them aside with steady progress. The rusted metal caltrops left gouges in the roadway as they tumbled, rolling into muddy gullies like jacks discarded by a giant child. The Exorcists continued a steady fusillade at the gates, setting the broad metal doors ringing with every solid impact. The Immolators were the edge of the spearhead, fire bolts and microwave energy lances blanketing the ferrocrete until it began to warp and boil.

Miriya heard the clanking of her tank's rear hatch and felt the vehicle rock as the Canoness leapt up on to the dorsal surface. Galatea held in her hand a war-worn volume of *The Rebuke*, one of the many books of sanctified combat doctrine adhered to by the Sisters of Battle. The woman held it high, so that every Sororitas on the field would be able to look up and catch sight of the shimmer-ink illuminations on the open pages. 'We are the reproach of Holy Terra, cut from burning steel,' she roared. 'Show these wastrels the edge that never dulls. The flame's eternal kiss!'

The war cry was old, but it still touched the Celestian as if it were new to her ears, sparking a vicious elation inside her. Her blood singing in her veins, Miriya placed the tank guns on deserving foes and disintegrated them.

The autocannon fire from the turrets hummed through the air as the tanks came into their range, shells punching fists of black earth into slurry.

* * *

The city-lord's residence was based on an ancient royal house from the distant past of Terra. Wide and low, the front of Baron Sherring's home presented a dozen tall windows of armoured glass to the ornamental grounds beyond and the shadow of the caldera wall. The baron himself continued as he had for the last few hours, orbiting between the windows and the collection of monitor tubes inset by the bookshelves of his chambers. The door banged open to admit Vaun, who had ignored Sherring's insistence that he don a cavalry uniform and instead remained cloaked in a tunic and trousers of deep midnight blue.

'My lord baron, still pacing? You will wear a trench in that expensive carpet.'

Sherring flushed red with anger and almost threw the monocular in his hand at the psyker. The baron's bodyguards tensed, unwilling to draw weapons against Vaun without a direct command from their employer.

Vaun gave a rude wink to the three figures that followed him into the chambers. Sherring knew the young lad with the unruly ginger hair – Ignis, he was called – but the rat-like woman and the hooded man, these other two were just more nameless hooligans from the corsair's gang of thugs.

'The engagement is not progressing well,' snapped the baron. 'Your estimates of the Sororitas numbers in Noroc was low. You told me they would not commit so much of their order's forces!'

Vaun gave an off-hand nod. 'Yes. The Order of Our Martyred Lady has been most devout in its deployment. I understand they sent almost everything they have in this region. The women of the Ermina Mantle have remained to defend Noroc in their stead, so Canoness Galatea might come here and *chastise* you.' A smirk threatened to rise on his face.

'Do you find this amusing?' spat Sherring. 'We are embarking on a battle for the very soul of this planet, against an enemy that you and your cadre are all victims of.' He swept his hand over Ignis and the other two. 'Emperor's blood, there is no more serious a matter!'

Vaun gave a contrite bow. 'Forgive me, baron. I meant no disrespect. It pleases me that I have been able to light the path to bring you to this most important decision.'

Sherring's train of thought faltered for a moment. 'The Sisterhood is more dangerous than I expected. They advance without fear...'

'Yes,' agreed Vaun. 'Zeal is a powerful weapon, isn't it?'

'If only I could show them what lies LaHayn makes them fight for–'

'That would be a mistake,' snapped the psyker. 'As much as it pains us to take the lives of these dedicated servants of the God-Emperor, their misguided faith has blinded them to the truths that we have uncovered. They would never accept your word on the lord deacon's perfidy.' He nodded to himself. 'Take heart in the fact that they will go to the Golden Throne with honour, for their only error is to believe too blindly in the church.'

'This course I have taken...' Sherring's words were leaden with effort. 'I pray that the Ecclesiarchy will see the merit of it, or else we will all be damned as traitors.'

'I am convinced of it, baron. The Ordo Hereticus will call you a hero for the stand you dare to take today.'

Sherring eyed him. 'And you? What of the help that you promised me? Where are the weapons of LaHayn's own creation you said we would turn on him?'

'Here,' smiled Vaun, gesturing at the woman and the man. 'Presenting my comrades Abb the Blinded and the girl Suki.'

It was the baron's turn to be amused. 'Surely you jest? A skinny female and a sightless man? What use are they?'

Vaun inclined his head. 'Show our friend Holt, will you?'

Suki shrank in on herself, and for a moment Sherring thought she might vomit on his rich carpets but then she let out a deep-throated yowl from her mouth and brought a gout of stinking fire along with it. The nearest of his bodyguards was caught in the nimbus of her dragon breath and he died on his feet.

The second guardian had his gun in his hand as the blind

man pointed a crooked finger at him. Milky eyes surveyed the room as if they could still see, centring on Sherring's man. Veins on Abb's brow throbbed and the soldier screamed. Smoke plumed from his nostrils and mouth, and he fell to the floor, roasting from within.

'Terra protect me,' whispered the baron. 'Pyrokenes!'

Vaun's smile grew. 'Impressive, yes? I'm granting you the service of these two as a gesture of solidarity.'

'Of... of course...' Sherring recoiled, the smell of burnt human meat sickening in his nostrils.

They sent in the flyers to strafe the Sisterhood's war machines, the same flight of oval coleopters that Vaun had used to sweep into Noroc during the Blessing of the Wound. That night, the capital's city guard had been slack and paid for its inattention with death, but Galatea's troops were more than ready for an aerial bombardment. Baron Sherring's affection for flyers and aeronefs was well documented, and the Sisters of Battle had come prepared.

The coleopters thrummed through the cowl of smoke growing up about Metis's tall West Gate, lighting up the slow-moving lines of tanks with bolter shells and laser fire. They came in low, counting on surprise, but that tactic had already been exhausted of its value.

Units of Sister Dominions, the special weapons caste of the Sororitas, switched targets from the turret emplacements and gun servitors of the cavalry. Storm bolters and meltaguns converged and brought the first of the disc-shaped aircraft out of the sky, shedding turbine blades and hull metal as it tumbled end over end into the smouldering tree line. The flames outside Metis were spreading now, coiled around the southern and western slopes in a flickering orange torc about the neck of the city.

Two more of the ships collided in panic as their pilots realised too late that the Sisters were not the easy targets they had bombed in Noroc. A third, burning fuel trailing out behind it in a blazing comet tail, turned into the line of armoured Rhinos, and metal met ceramite plate as the two vehicles collided.

The blast made the ground ripple and twitch. The shockwave of the explosion fanned up the hillside and tucked under the rear quarter of the Rhino where Sister Verity rode. Her world turned about as the steel box suddenly rotated around her, throwing the women and hardware inside into disarray. Blood streaked her vision as Verity's head rang off the decking and she was whipped about. The clinical, detached part of her mind caught the sound of somebody's neck snapping as one of the Battle Sisters with her was struck by a loose ammunition crate. A warm darkness stole the rest of the dizzying impacts from her and then abruptly, with no apparent dislocation between moments, the young woman found herself lying in the ankle-length grass, her body tight with dozens of new bruises.

Verity moved and took a wave of agony from her joints. A strong set of hands cupped under her armpits and helped her to her feet. She blinked, blurred vision clearing gradually to reveal a flock of red-pink shapes. There was a peculiar noise hereabouts, a tinny insect buzzing.

'Hospitaller, heal thyself,' she mumbled thickly, the words bubbling up with an edge of hysteria. She struggled to make her eyes see properly and when they snapped back into focus, she regretted it. There before her was the wreckage of the Rhino, volatile promethium fuel pooling beneath it amid a paste of Sororitas corpses. Her gut turned over and she gasped.

'The Emperor watches over you,' said a voice close to her ear. 'He has a plan for you, Sister. No other survived from that transport.'

Verity focused on the speaker, the grogginess in her mind fading with every passing second. She looked down to see a pale, scarred hand holding her up. She followed it to a face beneath a torn red hood and choked out a breath. 'Repentia...'

'By the Emperor's grace,' replied Iona, hefting her idling eviscerator chainblade. 'Your life will be forfeit if you remain here. He did not spare you so that could happen.'

The Mistress, a dark armoured figure with neural whips heavy in her hands, rose into sight and pointed towards the melee. 'The medicae is in our care. Take heed as we press forward. Her life is to be protected!'

Then they were advancing forwards, women in red rags and high rage all about her as the battle swung closer.

CHAPTER TEN

A backwash of raw heat seared Sister Miriya's cheek and she leaned into the firing controls, bringing the turret ring of the Immolator about in a hard arc. In the lee of the closest autocannon emplacement, a cavalryman with more bravery than intellect worked at a portable mortar, jamming a fresh shell into the breech. The Battle Sister lit up the meltas and drew a line of wavering heat across the ferrocrete and mud to where he stood, burning him down in a flashing scar of detonation.

Attracted by the activity, the cogitator brain in the turret began a ponderous turn to bear on the tank. Miriya kicked at a control switch by her feet and spoke a quick prayer to the God-Emperor and His tech-priests. The switch brought the blessing of power to a single-shot tube launcher that clung to the flank of the Immolator. Words of consecration wrapped about it on streams of parchment and the shapes of holy seals in red and white wax sheathed its exhaust vents.

Miriya pointed at the gun emplacement and glanced at the Canoness. 'With your permission, honoured Sister?'

'You may remove the obstacle,' nodded Galatea. 'The hunter is yours to command.'

'Aye.' Miriya needed no more encouragement, turning an ornate brass key inset on the turret's dashboard.

The tube chugged out a fat flower of white smoke, and from the middle of that bloom came a wicked projectile, the tip saw-toothed and barbed. Through a means that was beyond Sister Miriya's understanding, the hunter-killer missile spoke directly to the machine spirit of the Immolator and its auspex, there in the few seconds between leaving its birth chamber and turning to its target. The rocket went up into the grey air as a salmon leaps from a river, then turned about its own axis and penetrated the top of the autocannon turret.

The gun emplacement burst open in a black and red flash, unspent shells ripping the air as they ignited in the inferno. Along the line of enemy turrets, a ripple of electric shock streaked through the cables connecting the servitor-brains inside each, and the maws of guns twitched in confusion.

'Press the attack,' screamed Galatea, vox microphones in her armour taking her words and amplifying them through the loud hailers of her tank.

'Faith unfailing.' Every sister on the field replied in kind, backing up their war cry with bolt shell, fire and fury. The Exorcists and Immolators angled and fired upon the mechanical gun bunkers one by one, opening them so that the butchered masses of once-human brains within were boiled into the air.

The echo of multiple detonations sank into the smoke, falling at the feet of the charging Adepta Sororitas. In their trenches and boltholes beyond the towers of the West Gate, soldiers broke and ran at the sight of the women. Red cloaks snapped at the backs of the Battle Sisters and what faint sunlight made it through the war mist flashed off their black power armour. Those who were unhooded showed faces of wrath framed by tresses in ashen or jet. The passion of the God-Emperor was among them, the spirit of Katherine the Martyr their shield and their sword.

The defenders of Metis gave return fire but on came the women, a force of nature made manifest.

* * *

The Repentia carried Verity with them as a wave might have carried a piece of driftwood out to sea. She was beyond her own control, guided and pushed by the hands of the red hoods and their Mistress, inside but isolated from their small band. The Hospitaller pulled her own robes around her, better to cover her face from the roaring madness of the battle. There was nowhere she could look that the bloody ruin of war was not laid out for her to see. Here, the illustration from a medicae script made real, where the shattered glass egg of a servitor was spread about the ferrocrete; there, a man cored like an apple, bones white in a red mass of singed meats. Verity had come across wounds as savage as these and more so, but those had always been at a distance. She had seen the dead and the dying once removed from the field of conflict, the thought of where those wounds had originated some abstract, dislocated concept. Now, she watched the inflicting of those damages, she smelled the familiar burnt-copper aroma made new and horrible by those sights.

Verity staggered and the Mistress caught her arm and stopped her from falling. The Sisters Repentia stormed on before them, throwing themselves heedlessly over barbed wire bales and into the depths of trenches behind. Lesions covering them across every centimetre of skin, the Repentia called down death in banshee wails. Their heavy eviscerator chainswords made short work of the men, spinning razors of teeth shredding flesh, bone and cloth on the down stroke, the blunt iron edge on the weapon's other face caving in skulls and ribcages on the upswing.

The one called Iona, the woman that had invoked the Catechism of the Penitent after failing to save Lethe from death, worked at the craft of killing with blank frenzy. Verity watched her drive her sword through the sternum of a screaming cavalry officer, and found the most terrible thing to behold was the empty, doll-like glaze in Iona's eyes. The Hospitaller felt the conflict of emotions returning, the same hurricane of anger, sorrow and regret that had taken her the day she arrived on Neva. Had Iona felt the same? Had she been so scarred by Lethe's brutal killing, that all she could do was throw herself to the mercy of a blood-spattered redemption? Verity was troubled to realise that on some level, she could empathise with the pale woman.

'Advance!' screamed the Mistress. 'Take only sins, not prisoners. Leave only flesh, not corruption. Onward. *Onward!*'

Verity was taken with them, into the trenches and tunnels that led to the city.

Local legends said that the West Gate of Metis had been forged from the hull metal of the first human colony ship to arrive on Neva, back in the time of expansion when the stars were new to mankind's touch. They were, in their own way, relics of great import to the people of this planet, but the gate dared to bar the way of the God-Emperor's chosen agents. The steel which had travelled a million light years from the place of its forging was shattered by a hundred Sororitas guns, and with a sound like the collapse of heaven, the four-storey gate was felled.

The razor-prowed Repressors bit into the debris scattered across the highway, tracks spinning as they fought to gain purchase on the ferrocrete. Dead men and killed machines were forced into gutters as the Daughters of the Emperor marched in skirmish lines behind an armoured fist of tanks. Their blood was up, and down the streets before them the wind carried their hymnals.

The last line of defence left by panicked officers, laser-armed snipers in the outer buildings stitched crimson threads into the Sisters. Miriya and the other women in the tank turrets paid them back tenfold with plasma and rockets, tearing the upper floors from stone tenements and razing the wood and tile of others. At their backs, the fires from the forest advanced in with them, the curling smoke and flames hissing over the bloody trenches.

Metis was a city of riches. Like so many conurbations on Neva, the scars of poverty and lawlessness that touched the faces of many hive worlds and colonies were absent, or, at least they were *elsewhere*, shifted to the factory moons where the poor and the desperate could be corralled. The most down-market districts were veritable palaces compared to the rat-warren hovels that Sister Miriya had seen on some rim worlds. Still, they burned just as well. A bow wave of civilians, new refugees made this day by the arrival of the Sororitas, raced from their homes as the Immolators tore past them. Those that dared to stand in defiance to the Sisters of Battle were given the ritual censure of holy shot. Those that made proper obeisance were left by the roadside.

The Canoness rode tall atop her tank at the head of the castigation legion, the cloak of Saint Aspira billowing out behind her and snapping in the breeze. She coiled her book in one hand, directing the Dominions in the forward lines to places where errant cavalrymen challenged their procession. Some of the baron's soldiers threw down their arms and prayed for mercy when they saw the Sororitas coming. Men twice Miriya's age mewled like children as they met her gaze, finally understanding what crime they had committed. Some of them laid eyes on Galatea's cloak and knew it for what it was, a holy relic touched by the aura of their Eternal Lord. The Canoness was the Emperor's avatar, swift and terrible with her justice.

Miriya could read the questions they asked of themselves in their faces – How could we ever have thought to defy the church? What will become of us? Will we be forgiven? The staccato cracks of bolt pistols answered for her. Those in Sherring's brocade and brass-button finery were being culled for their disloyalty.

'From the lightning and the tempest, our Emperor, deliver us.' Galatea quoted the verse from the battle prayer by rote. 'From plague, deceit, temptation and war, our Emperor, deliver us.'

Sister Miriya tasted cordite and burnt wood in the air and turned away to run her gaze over the Sororitas lines surrounding the slow-moving tank. On foot, Reiko caught her eye and gave her a grave nod. The veteran Superior walked with Isabel and Portia at her side and a wounded banner bearer behind. Among the red robes, Miriya realised that she saw no sign of the Hospitaller Verity, and on reflex she made the sign of the aquila. 'Terra protects the faithful,' she whispered, watching the newly dead roll by beneath the Immolator's treads.

'Torris!' Ignis's strident voice carried along the marble corridors and stopped the psyker dead in his tracks. Vaun turned on his heel, clasping a pict-slate in his hand.

'Calm down, boy, you'll catch something alight. What's the panic?'

The ginger-haired youth gulped air. 'The baron is coming apart at the seams in there.' He jerked a thumb at the door to the chambers. 'He sent me to find you.'

Vaun tapped his lips with a forefinger. 'It's my estimation that our welcome is about to be worn out for good. It's time to take steps.' He glanced around. There were no guards in earshot, as one of Sherring's first frantic orders had been to send all available men to fortify the mansion house gates. 'Where are those bloody nuns?'

'West Gate's been breached, all vox traffic from that quarter is nothing but dead air or weeping. Fires are spreading, too.'

'This isn't a raid of punishment, then,' the criminal replied. 'The Sisterhood won't leave a stick unburnt here. Our dear pal Holt is going to be made an example of.'

Ignis's fingers crawled over his shirt and plucked nervously at his collar. 'I don't want to be here when they arrive.'

Vaun shrugged. 'Who does? Don't worry, we'll be long gone by then. In my capacity as the baron's "special consultant" I'm going to have his racing 'nef fuelled and put on the roof pad. Once we see the tanks rolling up the mall we'll kite out of here and go for the keep.'

The youth's eyes went wide with surprise. 'The keep? You found it?'

The psyker waved the pict-slate at him. 'Not me, boy. Sherring did. All part of the agreement I made with him. This is his price for my good company.'

'But how? That old bastard LaHayn kept it hid–'

'Doesn't matter how, Ig, just matters that we know where it is. The honourable lord deacon's dirty little secret is ours now, and it's ripe to be plundered. Sherring was busy while we were off planet – sure, he's an oily little tick, but he's connected on Neva. Must have cost him big to get this.' He weighed the slate in his hand. It seemed such a small thing to be so important, and yet inside the primitive bio-cell memory of the device were strings of numbers that meant more to Torris Vaun than any other prize he had taken.

'Sherring won't just let us go.' Ignis frowned. 'We're supposed to help him win this battle.'

'Yes. How sad.' Vaun pocketed the slate. 'That just shows how big a fool he really is. Beneath all the braggadocio, the airs and graces, Sherring doesn't see past the end of his own nose. So while his back is turned, while he's making enough noise to wake the dead, we take what we want from him and slip away real quiet, like.'

A smirk flickered on Ignis's face. 'You set him and LaHayn at each other like dogs. All this kicking and screaming, Metis seceding and all, this is just your smokescreen!'

'You're learning, that's good. Best way to get men to work for you is to have them think the job is their idea.' Vaun patted him on the shoulder. 'It's all about weakness. You find it in your mark, then you break them with it.' The sound of distant shellfire reached them, rumbling through the walls and setting the molycrystal chandeliers above their heads twittering with vibration. 'This little bloodbath is going to cover our tracks nicely. By the time the confessors and the cardinals are through sifting the ashes of Metis, we'll be kings of the Null Keep and everything in it. And then... then, Ig, we'll cut our names into the galaxy.'

'Do you think... Could we destroy a planet, maybe?'

The psyker smiled. 'You know, I've always wondered how that would feel. It's going to be interesting to find out.' Vaun gestured down the corridor. 'Go keep the baron busy. You'll know when it's time to go.' He was two steps away when the younger man's question came after him.

'What about the others? They're still out there in the thick of it. Abb and Suki, I mean.'

'I know who you mean.' Vaun said, without turning around. 'There are always sacrifices to be made, Ignis. You know that.'

'But we lost Rink already. If there's just us two–'

'There'll be plenty of new recruits in the keep,' he snapped, 'more than enough.' He threw a hard look over his shoulder. 'Do as I said. I can't afford to play favourites, not this late in the game.'

Vaun stalked away, leaving Ignis rubbing gingerly at the scarring behind his ear, and remembering.

The central avenue from the breached gate guided the Sisterhood to Metis's grand plaza, within the confines of which stood the fenced grounds of the baron's stately mansion. The circular city was arranged like a wheel, with spokes radiating out from the centre and concentric rings of boulevards growing ever smaller as they contracted inwards. At some of the crossroads along the line of the advance, the armoured vehicles and the Battle Sisters met makeshift barricades that were stormed by concentrated attacks, or hastily emplaced Leman Russ tanks drawn from the token Imperial Guard garrison. The line soldiers who had agreed to stand against the Sisterhood were ritually burnt alive, denied even the mercy of a bolter shell. They moved on, ever on, leaving the tanks afire or in fragments.

From giant speaker horns hung from the city's boxy buildings, Baron Sherring's hysterical speeches played in loops, his words nearly shrieks. Galatea ordered each one of them destroyed with rocket or laser, and in turn made the loud hailers on the Sororitas vehicles broadcast songs of penitence and admonishment. Panic warred with the Battle Sisters for mastery of the streets as they moved ever closer to the core of Metis, like a slow arrow towards its heart. The edges of the caldera were enveloped in fire now, and to observers on ships in orbit the plume of smoke appeared as if the dead volcano had returned to life.

* * *

Crossing into the outer gardens of the plaza, Miriya saw flashes of red in the near distance and caught the whirring of eviscerators. The Repentia had pressed on and taken the first kills of Sherring's personal guard, the golden sashes and ribbons the men wore soaking up their blood as the tireless blades took them. Galatea leapt down from the back of the Immolator, and Miriya dropped back through the turret hatch to follow her out into the battle. *I've ridden long enough*, she told herself, *it is time to face the traitors close at hand.*

Desultory laser fire and bolt shots hissed through the air around them, missing cleanly as the baron's men tried to beat the women back. Galatea was snapping out orders. 'Sister Reiko, take the Retributors and assault the southern flank. Sister Miriya, have your Celestians come together and follow in the path cut by our Repentia.'

'Aye,' chorused Reiko and Miriya, saluting with a balled fist to the fleur-de-lys on their chest armour.

A jerk of motion from Portia caught Miriya's eye. The Battle Sister was looking skyward, and she pointed with her gun, her tawny face split in a grimace. 'Dominica's Eyes. What is *that*?'

There was a shape coming towards them, swooping low through the drifts of haze. It was a woman, arms open to them, buoyed up on thin sheets of orange fire. Portia did not wait for an answer to her question and fired at the apparition. The flying woman brought her hands close to her chest and forced a gaseous breath from her lungs. She spat choking flames down at the Sisters with a rattling crackle of noise.

Miriya reeled away, the stench of burning bile washing over her. She felt acid mist prickle her eyes and ground the heels of her hands into them, throwing herself as far as she could from the blast.

Portia and Reiko fired, lancing shots after the woman. 'Witchkin,' spat the veteran Battle Sister. 'A psyker freak!'

Blinking the stinging miasma away, Miriya drew her plasma pistol and threaded hot flares of white light at the dragon-breath woman. The psy-witch described a lazy loop in the misty air and dropped to the ground in a crouch, rolling to avoid bolt fire. Miriya saw a second figure now, a portly little man, advancing with purposeful steps from the smoke. He raised stubby fingers in a claw-like gesture, humming to himself. 'Careful, Reiko!'

Her warning had scarcely left her lips when the veteran superior turned her bolter on the fat man. The air about him wavered and the shots deflected away. It was the same trick that Vaun had used to protect himself during the attack on the Lunar Cathedral.

Around the man's feet, circles of coloured ornamental grass and flowerbeds crisped and wilted. His face turned florid with hard effort and sweat beaded on his broad brow. All in the space of moments, the psyker who called himself Abb used his preternatural talent to excite the molecules inside the sickle magazine of Sister Reiko's boltgun. In a throaty roar of detonation, every shell in Reiko's weapon exploded at once. The crash of flame took off her gun arm and ripped away most of her breastplate and the flesh beneath. The woman was punched back into Miriya and the Celestian was thrown against a stone plinth.

The aromas of ash and cooked flesh filled Miriya's senses. She pushed Reiko off her and the woman's head lolled to one side, a ruined face in mute shock. In that moment, as she clutched at her Sister, the light faded from Reiko's eyes and she went slack. Cursing, Miriya let the body slip away and stepped forward, leading with her plasma pistol.

Abb saw her coming and marshalled his power again, drawing from the pool of inhuman energies at the heart of his psyche. For Miriya, it was as if she had suddenly stepped into an oven, the dreary, moist warmth of the day crushed under a punishing heat. The Celestian had a moment of old sense-memory from a battle in the deserts of Ariyo, as if a pitiless sun had turned its full might upon her in that single instant.

The plasma pistol sang in her mailed grip, the bright blue-white emitter coils along the breech sparking wildly with eager power. Plasmatic energy weapons were infamous for inopportune failures and catastrophic overheats, but in all the years that Miriya had used this handgun, she had never once had cause to regret it. It was a daily ritual of hers to pray over the firearm and ask the Emperor's forbearance in its use, so that she might employ it to exercise His displeasure.

'With this flame, I purify,' she murmured through dry lips.

Abb screamed as he forced the charge of burning energy from his mind, turning the power on the Battle Sister. Miriya's finger twitched on the trigger plate and the plasma pistol obeyed her. Psy-force and superheated, sun-hot plasma crossed in the air and split the day with thunder. The Sororitas reeled back, burnt and snarling. Abb became a thing of smouldering black meat, dying as the energy shot enveloped him.

The stench of the psyker-woman's coarse exhalations turned on the wind and Miriya followed her Sisters as they engaged Vaun's pyrokene killer in combat. Portia, Isabel and a dozen other line Sororitas stitched bolt shells in the air as the witch threw herself here and there, bobbing and weaving on pinions of fire. A fresh gushing spew of loathsome, steaming bile splattered among them. Miriya marvelled that so dainty a frame could continue to emit tides of flaming vomit. The foetid dragon-breath claimed the life of another Sister as she watched, cutting off her screams as it melted away the meat of her throat.

'Converge,' cried Portia. 'All guns to bear on the psy-whore!'

It was difficult to predict where the sylph-like girl was going to go next, the glowing flex of her fire wings confusing the eye of the shooters. For a moment, Miriya wondered if the venerable Sister Seraphim would be needed to down her, but the order's swift attack cadre was elsewhere in the battle, engaging the few remaining flyers still circling high above. Taking heed of Portia's cry, the Battle Sisters turned on the psyker, and in seconds she ran out of places to fly. Shots from Isabel's gun, Galatea's inferno pistol and the bolters of a dozen keen women crossed at a point where the witch's flight took her, and ripped her open in mid-air. The fiery toxins in her chest ignited and she blew apart, raining down gobbets of torn flesh.

Miriya averted her eyes and shielded her face. She had no desire to become dirtied by the fallout from the death of such a creature.

'Suffer not the witch to live,' Isabel spoke the words with grim finality.

'Aye,' said the Canoness, 'but there are more than these two to bring to their end. My orders have been given. Advance and take the mansion.'

'Are we free to kill Vaun?' Miriya asked, a little too eagerly.

'The lord deacon's commands were clear. Torris Vaun is to be taken alive.' She turned away. 'Baron Sherring and any other conspirators are to share the fate of these mutant freaks.'

All the watchtowers of Metis had been cut down or torched, and the overcomplicated pipeworks that controlled the city's rainbirds – the water nozzles for damping down the dry season – were severed. There remained nothing but wells and water buckets left to quench the encroaching fires, and those too were soon abandoned when the people understood that the conflagration would not be beaten. Sherring's subjects fled, choking the main avenues to the gates, but they streamed out into the woodlands only to find the trees ablaze there as well, the crackling necklace of heat beating at them with heavy hands. The Sisters of Our Martyred Lady had come to bring fire to the faithless, and they would only quit this blighted place when every building in Metis was ash. The flames reached high into the darkening sky, fingers of orange and black rising like hands in supplication and prayer. The city cried out for forgiveness, begging the Throne on distant Terra for respite that would never come.

Deep in the centre of the caldera, the Sisterhood heard the calls and closed their ears to them. Baron Holt Sherring had disobeyed the Nevan diocese, and so by order of Lord

LaHayn, he was declared excommunicatus. The Ecclesiarchy had signed the warrant at dawn, charging that Sherring had turned his face from the Imperial Church and made a myriad of false accusations. No matter how strong his belief might be, no matter how misguided, Sherring was a traitor and a heretic in the eyes of the Sisterhood – and in the object lesson that would be his death, LaHayn had ordered that the baron's citizens share in his punishment.

Metis burned, the city slowly surrendering to the unstoppable flames as street after street turned to hell.

Sister Miriya led with Cassandra, Portia and Isabel at her side, moving low and swift across the gentle rise of the ornamental lawns. The rattle of shots came from somewhere ahead of them, and the Celestian saw puffs of exhaust gas lick out from arrow slots in the walls of the mansion house. She surveyed the structure, looking for a means of approach, for a place where a breach might be made.

Cassandra was turning over the same thought, her eyes pressed to her magnoculars. 'There, the two ornate doors. Do you see them?'

Miriya nodded. 'Heavily guarded, though. I see stubbers. We'll need to take those down before we can enter the building.'

Further up the rise shapes in red and black emerged from the smoke and charged at the cavalrymen's barricade. 'What in the name of Celestine is that?' Isabel pointed a finger. 'Look there, do you see them?'

Cassandra gasped. 'The Repentia. By my blood, they're attacking them with just their blades!'

Miriya sprang to her feet. 'We'll not let them throw their lives away. To arms. Follow them!'

The Battle Sisters scrambled to take up the slack behind the red-hooded fighters, adding bolt and plasma to the chorus of strident death that came from the chainswords. Ahead of them, Miriya saw streaks of firepower from the stubbers hammer into the Repentia women. Some of them were killed instantly, others wounded mortally, but only those who died faltered. Their Mistress cracked her whips at their backs or turned the punishing neural lash on the enemy.

Isabel and Portia took up a flanking position while Miriya and Cassandra fell in behind the Mistress. The Sister Superior marvelled once more at the righteous fury the Repentia exhibited, the masked women beheading and gutting any one of Sherring's soldiers too slow to avoid their ceremonial eviscerators. Backing them with gunfire, the two units quickly made short work of the barricade's defenders. The cavalrymen were wheat before the scythe of their holy vengeance.

Stepping over the broken barrier, Miriya saw a Repentia drenched in blood as she struggled to get to her feet, the stuttering blade of her chainsword still buried in the skull of a turncoat officer. By reflex she extended a hand and helped the woman stand. The face shadowed by the red hood turned to hers and she saw pale skin dotted with scarlet, shaved straw-blonde hair fine against a scarred scalp. 'Iona?'

'Sister Miriya...'

The harsh sting of a neural whip darted at Iona's back and she stiffened, but did not cry out. 'You will not speak,' shouted the Repentia Mistress. 'The edicts forbid communion with those of your life before the oath!'

Miriya's hand shot out and caught the end of the whip, the barbed tip spitting out pain through her armoured glove. She jerked it, hard. 'What say you?'

The Mistress tore her lash from the Sister Superior's grip. 'You know the lore as well as any of us, Miriya. She may not speak to you!'

The Celestian opened her mouth to spit out some rebuke, but one look from Iona's hollow gaze silenced it. 'Yes. Of course.' She turned away and let the Mistress reassemble her women.

Cassandra was speaking into the vox pickup on her armour. 'Canoness. The way into the mansion lies open at the doors beside the gardens.' She flinched; there was a livid laser wound along her forearm.

'Sweep and clear,' Galatea's voice crackled through a dozen ear beads. 'Find Vaun. No survivors.'

Miriya acknowledged the command with a nod and glanced at her second's injury. 'Can you fight with that?'

'I will compensate–' began Cassandra.

'Let me help,' the new voice brought the Celestians to a halt, and Sister Verity emerged from her concealment in the lee of an overturned half-track. Miriya was without words for a moment. Verity's eyes were haunted, and there was blood of many hues across her robes even though she appeared to be unhurt.

'You should not be here,' snapped Portia.

'They brought me,' said the Hospitaller, indicating the Repentia.

'A miracle she lives still,' said Isabel in a low voice.

'Yes,' agreed Miriya, 'a miracle.' She stooped and found a boltgun close to the slashed corpse of a Sister who had once owned it. She offered it to Verity. 'We shall not test the whims of the fates further. Defend yourself.'

The Hospitaller shook her head. 'I'm not a combatant.' She clasped the scentwood case of her medicus ministorum to her chest to make more of the point.

'It was not a request,' said Miriya, an edge in her tone. 'Take the gun. I cannot have a Sister at my side who will not fight.'

'In the God-Emperor's name, my remit is to save life, not destroy it.' Verity's voice was quiet but it was as steady as a rock.

'Even traitors such as these?' The Sister Superior swept her hands about at the dead men. 'Their lives are forfeit. The Emperor's church has declared it so.'

The other woman nodded. 'That is true. But still, I am not an instrument to bring death.' She met Miriya's gaze. 'That is your job.'

Miriya's eyes narrowed. 'It is. But perhaps you have been spending too much time carrying out more secular duties. You forget yourself. Vaun and his traitors will not make so keen a definition between a Sister Hospitaller and a Sister Militant.'

'That is why the Emperor has you walk with me,' replied the nurse.

'Take the gun,' repeated the other woman.

For a moment, it seemed as if Verity would deny her again, but instead, she took the boltgun and tucked it into her habit.

The Repentia Mistress's call to arms stopped the Celestian from answering. 'A spiritu dominatus. Domine, libra nos. Death to the heretic and witchkin!'

Miriya held her plasma pistol high and pointed after the raging Repentia. She could think of no battle cry, no stirring quote at that moment. In silence, the Battle Sisters followed their hooded kin into the echoing halls.

CHAPTER ELEVEN

The words pressed into Ignis's brain like burning darts. *Now's the time, lad. We're casting off. Get to the roof pad, fast.*

The youth clutched at his head and staggered, a thin trickle of blood leaking out of his nose. He bumped into the chart table that dominated the centre of the baron's chambers, setting the confusion of markers and tiny flags upon it tumbling.

'What are you doing?' snapped Sherring, pushing past one of his soldiers. 'Answer me. What is going on?' His expression was taut with anxiety.

Ignis waved a vague hand at the nobleman. 'I... I have to go...' He shook his head to rid it of the after-effect of Vaun's telepathic touch. Bile rose in his throat and he coughed.

Sherring grabbed his arm as the youth tried to make for the door. 'Stop where you are!' He pulled Ignis around to face him, pinched and furious. 'Where is Vaun? He's abandoned me. Tell me where he is!'

'I'll go look for him–'

Quick! came the mind-speech, and a fresh wash of nausea washed over Ignis. *The Sororitas are here! We can't tarry!*

'Can't tarry...' Ignis echoed the words under his breath.

The baron saw the moment of glazing in the young man's eyes and understood what was unfolding. 'You hear him, don't you? Damned witchkin can know each other's thoughts, eh? Where is he? What is he doing?' He shook Ignis violently. 'Tell me now, you worthless gutter rat.'

'Get off me,' Ignis retorted, fighting to free himself from Sherring's frantic grip. 'I'll bring him to you–'

'Liar,' roared the baron. 'He used me. You did this to me, made me ruin my beautiful city!' Sherring's free hand came up with an ornamental dagger in it. 'I'll kill you!'

'No!' Ignis shouted, and the word hammered at the air in the room. In the echo of his cry, every photon candle and view-tube spat sparks and burst into flames.

Sherring shrank backwards in shock, still brandishing the gold blade. 'You... You can't defy me. I am your better!'

'Shut up, you pathetic lackwit,' Ignis spat back at him. 'All the money in the galaxy isn't going to save you now. You were played. You're just a mark!' With each word, the sputtering electrical fires pulsed with flashes of heat.

The baron shot imploring looks at his men. 'Slay the witch. Destroy him. I order you.'

The cavalrymen had their guns in their hands, but they were pointed at the floor. The officers exchanged glances: all of them had seen Sherring's rapid deterioration over the past hours, and none had the desire to cross the psyker on the baron's word. Outside, beyond the tall glass windows, Metis was hidden beneath a curtain of smoke, and through the walls came the sounds of gunfire and men dying. The soldiers watched in silence, waiting for the battle to end. In their eyes was the mute knowledge that they had already lost.

'We are leaving, baron,' sneered Ignis, 'and there's nothing you can do to stop us.' The youth turned and strode towards the doors.

'You will not.' Sherring threw himself at the boy and buried the knife in his back. Ignis was caught unawares and collapsed to the floor. He tried to drag himself away, the little fires around the room throbbing with his heartbeat. 'You will not,' shrieked the baron again, his lips trembling with agitation.

Something hissed and spat outside the sealed security doors to the chamber, then in the next second a flat report of sound tore through the air and the heavy wooden portal crashed open.

Wreathed in smoke, Sister Miriya and her cohorts strode into the room. Sherring baulked as he caught sight of the remaining Repentia, scarred and soaked in the blood of his men.

'Too late...' whispered Ignis, reaching with trembling fingers towards the knife in his back.

'Baron Holt Sherring, city-lord of Metis and its territories, you are bound by Imperial law.' The Battle Sister advanced, her plasma pistol aimed at his chest. 'Your crime is heresy, declared and made known by the Lord Deacon Viktor LaHayn.'

Sherring raised his hands in a halting motion. They were wet with the youth's blood. 'Wait. Please. You don't understand, it's LaHayn who is the heretic. You don't know what he has been doing. He wants to usurp the Golden–'

'The sentence is death, to be carried out with all due alacrity.' Miriya raised the pistol to come level with his face.

The baron threw Ignis a pleading look. 'Please!'

Verity caught the gesture and her heart went cold. 'Miriya, the boy–'

Ignis was as quick as lightning. His eyes flashed and the guttering fires about the room erupted like blowtorches. In a split-second the chamber's walls were yellow with streaks of conjured flame, licking up at the opulent tiles and scrollwork of the mansion's ceiling.

Bedlam broke out among the cavalrymen, some of them diving for cover beneath the chart table, others turning their guns on the Battle Sisters. Isabel and Portia shot back, but the blaze funnelled out under the psyker youth's control, ripping into a burning tornado. Verity was shouldered to the floor by Iona as the flames spiralled past her. Ignis sent the column of fire into the Repentia Mistress and the other hooded woman, setting them alight. Their death screams were piercing, the flames carrying them out into the open as the back draft shattered the chamber's armoured windows.

A tail of trailing heat slammed into Miriya and sent her flying across the room, smashing her into a cogitator bank and spinning her about like a top. A streak of energy from her pistol went wide, knocking down one of the cavalry officers with the force of its plasma nimbus.

Iona pushed away and threw herself at Ignis, brandishing her eviscerator, the ragged red hood flying from her shoulders. The psyker was on his feet, marshalling the fire into a spinning shield of flames, burning the chart table and the heavy brocade curtains. A wordless cry of vengeance on her lips, Iona charged him and thrust herself through the heart of the firewall. Her clothing and armour combusted about her, the incredible heat controlled by the boy burning off layers of her skin as she cut through it. Streamers of blackened flesh curled off her as she fell on him.

Ignis raised his arms to ward her off, but the chainsword came down upon him with an executioner's hand upon the hilt. The spinning tungsten-carbide teeth ripped into the bone and matter of his shoulder and cut into the youth's chest. Rendered nerves firing for the last time, the boy grabbed at the Repentia as she buried her blade in him, and took her in a burning embrace. Ignis perished drawing his witch-fire into himself, and his blackened corpse crashed through the chart table with Iona in a fatal grip. The Repentia wailed as she followed the psyker into death. They were a monstrous parody of two lovers, melded as one in a halo of orange flames.

Without the psyker to keep the inferno alive with his unholy power, the guttering fires shrank and spat, crawling like fat insects over the walls. It took a monumental effort for Verity to turn her face from the carnage. She attended to Miriya, pulling barbed injectors from the depths of her medicus ministorum.

Nearby, Cassandra spoke a few words of the Oath of Katherine over the dead Repentia. 'You are redeemed,' she told the corpses. 'Go to the next life free of your burden.' With a flick of her wrist, the Battle Sister salted the body of the psyker with drops from a vial of holy water. The liquid hissed into steam where it met the heated bones.

The Hospitaller frowned and applied a brass syrette to Miriya's jugular vein, forcing the injector rod into her skin. The Celestian twitched with shock as the chemical philtre charged her bloodstream, fighting off the hydrostatic shock from Ignis's psy-strike. After a long moment, Miriya blinked and opened her eyes.

'What... did you give to me?' she demanded.

'A restorative,' said Verity. 'A blend of witch-bane and tetraporfaline, blessed by the apothecarium. You should rest a moment, you are bleeding.'

Miriya pushed her aside and dragged herself to her feet. 'I have no time to shed blood for traitors.' The Celestian found Sherring on his knees, cowering by his desk. 'Where were we?' she asked him. The drug in her system made the pain of her wounds seem distant and unimportant.

'I am not the enemy,' whispered the baron. 'The deacon is the devil.'

'If that is true,' she told him in a low voice, 'then when the time comes I will judge him as harshly as I have judged you.' Miriya pulled the trigger and vaporised the upper torso of the kneeling man with a single shot. Bolter fire joined her from the guns of the other Battle Sisters as they executed the remaining men in Sherring's chambers.

Vaun felt Ignis die like a light going out in his mind, and he swore violently. In the control cupola of the aeronef, the baron's tech-priest gave him a worried look. The psyker had already killed the two comrades of the adept as a show of force and the priest was fearful he would be next if he displeased the criminal in the slightest.

'Don't stare at me,' growled Vaun. 'You have a job to do. Get this thing airborne.'

The tech-priest blinked tin eyelids with a clicking noise. 'But, there was another to come? You said we should wait.'

Vaun tugged the escape ladder and the metal frame folded up into the belly of the sleek airship racer. 'I changed my mind. We're going now.' He strode over to the cowering adept and thrust a data-slate under his nose. 'You know where these co-ordinates are?'

Cogs inside the tech-priest's elongated skull case clicked and whirred as he stored the numbers on the slate in a datum buffer. 'Yes, but that zone is restricted. It is a geologically unstable region, dangerous volcanic flows and sulphur swamps–'

'Take me to it,' Vaun stabbed a finger at the smoke-filled sky. 'Now.'

'It's a toxic wasteland,' the adept twittered. 'We will die there!'

Vaun gripped the tech-priest's robes and squeezed. 'You'll die here unless you get this 'nef moving, understand?'

The adept nodded and began to work the controls. With clanks of oiled steel, Baron Sherring's personal flyer detached from the tethers holding it to the roof and unfurled its sails. The powerful thermals blooming up from the burning city took hold of the craft and guided it skyward.

'Honoured Canoness, this is Sister Miriya.' The Celestian spoke into her vox. 'I have bestowed the Emperor's justice upon Baron Sherring.'

'I understand,' Galatea's voice crackled through her ear bead. 'We are delayed. A pocket of the turncoat Guard has decided to make a stand in the glasshouses. Secure the mansion and find Vaun.'

'Your will.' Miriya cut the communication and glanced at Verity. The Hospitaller was bent over the burnt remains of the psyker and poor Iona. 'Stand away,' the Celestian snapped, suddenly angered by the woman's lack of respect for the dead.

Verity did not obey, and instead crouched close to the blackened skull of Ignis. 'There is something here.'

'It is not your place to interfere with the departed–' began

Cassandra, but Miriya waved her to silence and crossed the chamber, laying a heavy hand on Verity's shoulder.

'Desist.'

'I do no dishonour to Iona,' retorted the Hospitaller. 'I imagine each of you owes her a debt from her time in your squad. Know then that she saved my life today as well. It is the witch that interests me.' She used a stylus to point at something in among the bones and charred meat of the dead man. 'Look here. Do you see?'

Miriya studied the object. It was a pewter half-orb, as small as a tikkerbird egg, fused to the curve of Ignis's skull. Wires as thin as human hairs spooled out from it along the inside of the bone. 'A bionic implant? I've never seen the like.' She ran a finger behind her right ear, touching the place where the device had been rooted in the psyker's body.

'Curious,' said Verity. 'The bone has partly covered the metal. This was grafted to him several years ago. It appears to be Imperial technology, not xenos or traitor-made. As to the purpose, I cannot fathom it.'

'Perhaps some device to conjure his witch-fire?' Portia made a disgusted face.

'Very advanced,' added the Hospitaller, and she looked up at Miriya. 'Far beyond the acumen of a thug like Vaun.'

A silent communication went between them, the recollection of the shadowy assassin in the Noroc librarium.

At the broken windows, Isabel reacted with a start. 'Listen. Do you hear that?'

'Just shelling–' began Cassandra.

'No. Rotors!' Isabel pointed as a silhouette moved over the glass. 'There!'

The wind changed then all the women heard it, the thrumming chop of propeller blades slicing through the thick air. Miriya sprinted to the windows in time to see the sleek bullet-shape of Sherring's gaudy aeronef passing over the mansion. The prow of the airship dipped and then rose, angling away from them.

'It's *him*,' spat the Celestian, and she threw herself out of the oval of shattered glass, landing heavily in the torn gardens below. The flyer cast a dark pool of shadow beneath it, and Miriya ran to keep below it. Her training took over from her conscious mind, compartmentalising the pain from her injuries and the adrenaline rush in her bloodstream. Her vision caught on a trailing tether dragging down the ornamental steps where it hung from the aeronef's underside. With every passing second the cable was drawing shorter as the craft gained height.

Ignoring the gunfire that lanced past her, Miriya leapt at the tether and caught it in the grip of her armoured gauntlets. No sooner had she done so than the aeronef's props pitched up in tone and the airship pushed away at great speed. Suddenly, the Battle Sister was hanging suspended beneath the vessel as the mansion grounds flashed by beneath her feet. With dogged and relentless determination, Miriya pulled herself up, hand over hand, towards the passenger cupola beneath the gas envelope.

'Is this the best speed you can muster from this craft?' demanded Vaun, menacing the adept. 'It's supposed to be a racer.'

With visible effort, the tech-priest found his voice. 'The weight distribution is in error.'

Vaun prodded him with a finger. 'Perhaps I should lighten the load, then? I'll start with your corpse.'

'No,' screeched the adept. 'The correct prayers must be offered to the machine-soul. I will compensate.'

'Bah!' The psyker shoved him back at the console and turned away, steadying himself on the listing deck as the priest mumbled and made symbols in the air over the navigational console. 'Get us some more altitude, at least. I don't want to be in range of those Exorcist tanks.'

The front quarter of the aeronef's cupola was made from a skeleton of girders and a cowl of armourglass, so that the late baron and his cronies could view the landscape below the aerial yacht. Now all that lay beneath the flyer was streets choked with dead or dying, burning buildings and the debris of a murdered city.

A fitting epitaph for a braggart and a fool like Sherring, considered the psyker. He was sure that the baron, with his overblown sense of grandeur, would have enjoyed the idea that his precious Metis would not endure without him. Playing Sherring had been easy. Like every one of these idiot nobles, he had thought that his little world, his tiny games of empire, were the only things that were of any import. It mattered nothing to the rich men of Neva that on other planets there were creatures of such alien nature that they would devour whole worlds, or that there were places where the raw stuff of Chaos itself came to life. The universe began and ended at the edge of the Nevan solar system, and they cared nothing for the greater galaxy beyond, as long as it didn't interfere with them and their asinine festivals.

Vaun thought differently. It was ironic, really. There was only one other man he knew who was native-born to this pretentious and grandiose planet, but who saw the wider view as he did, and Torris Vaun hated Viktor LaHayn with every fibre of his being.

It was that hate that had first brought Sherring into the psyker's orbit. Vaun had seen the avaricious desire in the baron's eyes, the need for power in the man that overwhelmed everything else. Vaun had aided the baron in strengthening his position and in turn Sherring had helped Vaun break the chains that bound him to the deacon. But while the nobleman had craved position and title, Vaun played – and was *still* playing – a far longer game. And now, at last, after Vaun had been forced to spend years on the run here and in deep space, the loathsome prig had finally made good on his promises.

'And for that, I pay you in immortality,' whispered the psyker, catching sight of a hobbled statue of the baron as the aeronef passed over the city. 'No one on Neva will ever forget the name of Holt Sherring,' he told the effigy. 'You'll go down in history as a traitor and a fool.' Vaun spat at the statue and turned away, his resentment kindling.

The data-slate was there in his pocket, heavy with the price he had paid to get it. Oh, of course he had never intended to keep those wastrels Abb and Suki around. Had they survived, he would have just found another way for them to serve as fodder for the cannon. After all, their talents were hard to control and unpredictable. Vaun had only recruited them because they were all he could find.

But the boy... That made him angry. Ignis was a sharp lad, and he had real potential. Vaun had seen in him someone worthy to be his protégé, a psyker with ability, but nicely untroubled by such clutter as ethics or morality. It annoyed him to have to lose so promising a tool before he could bring its potential to bear.

With a snort, he dismissed the thought. At the keep he'd find all the raw material he needed to start afresh, and then maybe he would blow Neva apart, just like the lad had wanted.

A creaking noise in the deck plates drew his eyes from the window and set the killer's nerves on edge. They were not alone. Vaun spun, calling fire to him.

A shape in black armour and red robes threw itself into the cupola from the rearward compartment, crashing through the hatchway. The psyker's face twisted in a grimace as he recognised the woman.

'You again,' he said, with loathing. 'This is becoming tiresome.'

'How did she get aboard?' asked the tech-adept, cowering at the helm.

'Be silent,' Miriya broke in. 'You'll have time to speak for your crimes soon enough.'

'Crimes?' bleated the priest. 'He forced me. He killed my brethren.'

'You should have died with them. That would have shown dedication. Now you are guilty of collusion with a criminal.'

Vaun smiled, amused by her. 'Don't be so hard on the poor wretch, Sister. I can be very persuasive, if I've a mind to be.'

'Your co-conspirator Baron Sherring is dead,' Miriya told him. 'This vessel is being tracked by units of the Order of Our Martyred Lady. You have no way to escape the church's reprisal.'

'Oh,' sniffed the psyker, his voice taking on an arch tone. 'Perhaps I should bow down and surrender? Yes, should I do that and beg for a swift and merciful death?' He gave a derisive snort. 'You dare not fire that weapon inside this vessel. One misplaced shot could sever a fuel line or puncture the gasbag. You'd kill us all.'

'You do not understand my devotion to the God-Emperor, witch. My life counts for naught if you still draw breath. If the price I must pay to have you dead is my own blood, then I do so willingly.' She fired, the plasma pistol cutting hot light across the cabin.

Vaun threw himself away from the stanchion where he had been standing, the haze of rippling heat from the discharge searing his face. He cried out in pain and threw back a trio of flaming darts. The bolts missed the Sororitas and blew out an ornate windowpane. 'You mad, blinkered bitch,' he swore. 'Stupid little wind-up toy. You have no idea what is really going on here, do you? LaHayn is the worst traitor of them all.'

'When I read your crimes to the quill servitors, I will be sure to add defamation to the list.' Miriya stroked an indent on the plasma pistol's breech and dialled the weapon's emitter nozzle to a narrow beam setting. Ducking from behind a support pillar, she fired again, slashing through a tertiary cogitator console.

A sudden thermal made the aeronef lurch to starboard and both the combatants were knocked off balance. The tech-priest wailed, his voice like a warning siren.

Vaun's next flurry of psi-fire hit home close to the woman, one glancing dart of burning air searing her shoulder plate and carving a scar across the wood panelling behind her.

Miriya snarled and fired again. The plasma weapon turned a steel stanchion to hot slag and sent flame licking up to the ceiling of the compartment.

'I should have known better than to expect intelligence from a servant of your corrupt religion!' Vaun called out to her from behind cover. 'I may be a thief and a killer, but at least I am true to myself. I don't do the bidding of ancient, crooked clerics!' He gave a harsh, mocking laugh. 'Tell me, Sister, have you never questioned? Have you always been the same trained mongrel, just a dog on some priest's leash?'

Miriya said nothing, moving carefully towards the sound of his voice. She placed each footfall with absolute care, keeping herself steady as the airship listed. The walls of the caldera drifted by below them, hazed by the smoke from the burning forest.

'If only you knew what I know,' continued Vaun. 'If only you could see the horrors that Viktor LaHayn has perpetrated over the years. You think I am a threat to your precious law and order? *Ha*. My plans are just for money and mayhem. The deacon intends nothing less than the unseating of your god!' His voice was thick with hate. 'My crimes are a child's compared to his madness.'

The Celestian hardened her heart against the psyker's words, forcing herself to put aside her doubts. He was very close now, a few hand spans away, crouched behind a recliner couch in rich groxblood leather. Miriya took careful aim.

'I know you don't trust him. You and the nursemaid both, there's something that gnaws at your thoughts. If you kill me, by the time you understand it will be too late. LaHayn will take the Imperium for himself. I'm the only one who can stop him. That's why he's so desperate to capture me.' The psyker seemed to be struggling with the effort of speaking. 'He needs me to complete his plan.'

The woman cared nothing for that order now, she would finish this wastrel and weather the ire of the deacon later. 'In the God-Emperor's name–' Miriya threw herself around the couch and levelled the gun – at *nothing*. 'Vaun? Where?'

'Here.' From behind her, the hot claws of his burning hand pressed into the flesh of the Battle Sister's neck.

'How...?'

Vaun chuckled. 'It's not just a matter of throwing balls of fire and the like, Sororitas. Being a witch brings certain other talents to the table. Misdirection, among others.' He blinked sweat from his eyes. 'Quite tasking, though.'

'Kill me then, if you dare,' she growled. 'For my death there will be ten Sisters to take my place.'

Contempt dripped from Vaun's words. 'You foolish women are so predictable. So desperate to throw your life away in service to the church, you practically beg to be killed. It's what you want, isn't it? To become a tragic martyr like your beloved Saint Katherine, to perish on a heretic's blade and earn your place in the pathetic annals of some forgotten convent?'

Miriya's gaze remained locked forwards. Ahead of her she could see the adept cowering at the helm, his spidery brass limbs working the tiller.

The criminal pressed harder. 'Would you like to die now, Sister? Would it assuage the guilt you carry like a millstone about your neck? Far easier to end your life in a futile gesture than to live on in pain, isn't it?'

'Vaun,' said the woman, gently turning her hand to aim her pistol, 'you talk too much.' Miriya pulled the trigger and the plasma pistol spat flame across the cabin. The gaseous plume melted the helm into runnels of liquid metal and sent the tech-priest screaming away, his robes on fire and his augmetics twisted by the heat surge.

The aeronef's deck pitched hard, throwing the two combatants apart and slamming them into the wall. The Battle Sister tasted blood as her head rebounded off a support girder. She heard Vaun shouting a string of inventive curses and her vision blurred for a second.

When she blinked it clear, Miriya saw the blackened forest rising up to fill the airship's windscreen, fire-stripped trees reaching up to snatch at the flyer.

* * *

Night had fallen by the time they located the crash site in the woodlands south of Metis. Sister Verity had expected to find a field of wreckage, but Baron Sherring's aeronef was intact for the most part. The elegant bullet shape of the airship's gas envelope was dirty and discoloured, some of the cells torn open and flaccid. The craft had cut through a burnt copse and landed at a tilt towards its starboard side, exposing the passenger cupola to the air. The front of the compartment was a mess of broken glassteel and twisted girders.

At her side, Sister Portia consulted an auspex and frowned. 'The device's machine-ghost speaks of lives still inside, but the glyphs are contradictory.'

'Heat from the fires,' said Cassandra, approaching the downed ship with her bolter held ready. 'The warmth radiates up from the ground. It confuses the sense-taker.'

Verity picked her way through a trail of shredded hull plates and bits of ornate furniture that had been ejected during the landing. Her boots crunched crystal droplets from a chandelier into the ashen earth, and she stepped around a stool detailed in red leather, that had landed intact and incongruous in this black setting.

From the corner of her vision she saw Isabel stoop and recover something from the dirt. 'The Sister Superior's weapon.' She held up the plasma pistol by its barrel. 'If it fell from her grasp...' The unspoken words curdled in her throat.

Cassandra shot her a look. 'Keep searching.'

Verity saw a flicker of motion among the disorder of wreckage and called out. 'Here. Someone alive!' The other women were at her side in an instant, working together to lift away a metal panel the size of a dining table. It was still warm to the touch, and had they not been wearing gauntlets, their hands would have been scorched raw.

From under the panel emerged a crooked man, almost strangling under the weight of his own robes. Brassy claw-hands, hooked and spindly where they were half-melted, snapped and clicked. 'Hello?' His voice was laden with static, like a poorly tuned vox.

'Tech-priest,' said Isabel with more than a little disappointment. 'Where are Vaun and Sister Miriya?'

'Thank you.' The adept pointed back at the grounded airship. 'Inside, I believe. Thank you.' He gave a metallic cough and tapped the vocoder implant in his throat. Verity remained a moment to examine him as Cassandra led the other women on in a steady, weapons-high approach.

She glanced around, taking in the desert of burnt land and skeletal trees, the towering plume of smoke issuing from the caldera-city dark against the night sky. Verity felt leaden and heavy with disgust at the sight. How many thousands had died today in order to punish Baron Sherring's stupidity? The unfettered carnage sickened her, and the Hospitaller found herself entertaining an almost treasonable anger towards the lord deacon. LaHayn had shown callous disregard for the people of Metis, not all of whom were to blame for their city-lord's foolish choices. With effort, she forced the thoughts away.

A sudden commotion near the wreck snapped her back from her reverie. Cassandra had a man by the scruff of the neck, dragging him out of the cupola. *Vaun*.

The Sister of Battle applied a vicious kick to the back of the psyker's legs and sent him sprawling to the ground. As Verity gingerly approached, she could see he was badly wounded, his face crosshatched with new scars caused by flying fragments of glass. He managed a bloody smile.

'Ah. Nursemaid. Kind of you to come and minister to me.'

Without a word of command between them, Cassandra, Isabel and Portia all pointed their guns at his head.

Vaun blinked. 'Oh. Viktor has changed his mind, then? I'm to die now?'

Verity strained to master her loathing of the man. 'Your execution will be at the lord deacon's pleasure.'

His smile widened. 'Lucky me. How frustrated you must all be, little sisters, to find me alive and your harlot Miriya not. Worse still, that you must keep me so.'

Verity looked at Cassandra. 'Miriya is dead?'

'There was no sign of her body in the aeronef.'

Vaun's head bobbed. 'Dead. She fell. So sad.'

Skin met skin with a loud smack and before she even realised it, Verity was looking at her hand, at the red mark where she had slapped him.

Real anger flashed in Vaun's eyes.

'Careful,' he said, in a voice low and rich with menace. 'You mustn't damage me further.'

'To hell…' The words were a ragged gasp. 'To hell with that.' Verity turned with a start as Miriya approached from the tree line, carrying herself awkwardly. The Hospitaller instantly recognised the signs of broken ribs, contusions and minor wounds. The Sister Superior marched as best she could into the circle of women, taking her pistol from the hand of a stunned Isabel.

'In Terra's name, how did you survive?' whispered the Battle Sister.

'As the witch said,' Miriya nodded at the psyker, making signs over her gun, 'I fell. By the grace of the Golden Throne, I did not die.'

Even Vaun was lost for words in that moment, but then Miriya thumbed the activation stud on her plasma weapon and he knew what she was going to do next. 'No, no,' he blurted. 'You can't kill me here. On the 'nef, no one would know, but here, these ones will see you. You can't disobey the deacon in front of them.'

'The deacon be damned.' Those words alone were enough to earn Miriya a thousand lashes. 'Die, witch.'

'Miriya…' There was a warning in Verity's tone. 'Our orders…'

The Sister Superior didn't seem to hear her. Miriya's entire world had collapsed to the space between the muzzle of her gun and Vaun's head. 'You are trying to marshal your witchfire, but the pain hobbles you. You know that I hold your life in my grip, Vaun. How does it feel to be the victim? Can you taste it?'

Then, slowly and inexorably, the psyker's eyes went cold. 'The deacon be damned,' he repeated. 'My own thoughts,

Sister. Shall I tell you why? If my death is but a heartbeat away, then let me give you a gift before I go. Let me tell you why Viktor LaHayn deserves damnation, more than I, more than any sinner you have ever sent to his grave. Let me do this small thing.'

Verity saw Miriya's finger tighten on the trigger – but not enough. As she watched, the Hospitaller heard her own voice rise in the silence.

'Let him speak.'

CHAPTER TWELVE

Vaun was not smiling now. 'Your curiosity is all that keeps me breathing, isn't it?' He moved his head slightly to look at Sister Verity. 'I thank you for these additional moments of life.'

'He has nothing to give us,' Cassandra murmured irritably. 'Sister Superior, if you will break the lord deacon's edict to keep this witch alive, then do it now, before he tries to talk us to death.'

Vaun blinked at Miriya, and she searched his face for truth and lies. The psyker's aspect was one she had never seen on him before, without masks or artifice. In his way, he was naked to her. 'Is it absolution you want?' she asked him. 'Will you confess your sins to me?'

'Oh, there shall be a confession,' he nodded, 'but not mine. I'll give you LaHayn's in proxy. Tell you the secrets.' Vaun raised a bloodied hand and tapped a spot at the base of his skull. 'Show you things.'

Miriya's eyes narrowed as she remembered the strange device Verity had found implanted in the head of Vaun's cohort Ignis. With a quick motion, she holstered her plasma pistol.

A moment of relief crossed Vaun's face. 'You've seen the value in my words.'

The Sororitas shook her head. 'I have learnt that every sentence you utter is just one more gambit in the strategies you spin.' She looked at the other women. 'Hold him down.'

Before Vaun could struggle, Cassandra and Isabel took Vaun's wrists and pressed him against a slab of hull metal. Portia kept her gun on him. The psyker blinked, trying to muster his powers, but his injuries had made him weak and tired.

Salvaging a turn of ragged, sharp-edged wire from the wreck, Miriya fashioned a makeshift binding to hold the criminal's wrists together. She glanced at Verity. 'You have a sanguinator in your medicus kit, and neuropathic drugs. Show them to me.'

The Hospitaller did as she was asked. 'What do you want me to do?'

'Sedate him.' There was a long moment before Verity understood that Miriya was not telling her but ordering her to do it.

Vaun struggled. 'I told you, I will freely explain everything!'

The Sister Superior gave him a measuring stare. 'I must be convinced.' She pointed at his arm, and Verity reluctantly discharged the glass injector into the psyker's clammy skin.

The rush of chemicals struck his bloodstream. He let out moans and the occasional coughing yelp, the sounds rolling about the burnt landscape. Now and then, small fires puffed into life around the clearing as Vaun's pain exhibited itself through his witchery. The whites of his eyes showed. Like the fluids that had contained him in the glass prison capsule on the Black Ship, the potent philtre robbed him of the will to create his mindfire. He became groggy and pallid.

Finally, when she was sure he was quietened and unable to attack them, Miriya allowed him to answer questions. 'You have your audience,' she told him, 'now enlighten us.'

Verity gently cleaned the dirtied sanguinator. 'How did you escape custody?'

Vaun sniffed wetly. 'Unimportant. You know the answer to that already.'

'You were in league with Sherring. He brought the men of the *Mercutio* to Metis and coerced them.'

'Clever, clever Holt. Too clever for his own good. Yes, a simple task, really. With the reach his clan gave him, to the shipping guilds and the commerce station, he found it easy. A man's mind can be moulded quite quickly, if one has the right tools and is untroubled by morals. Those that did not take to the imprinting... They were allowed to die. The others he made my erstwhile saviours, although they would never know it, seeds of my control sleeping in their heads.' The psyker coughed and spat. 'The one who came to the cargo bay...? He carried the order in his unconscious, then spoke it to all the others.'

Cassandra's lip curled. 'You expect us to believe that you allowed yourself to be captured on Groombridge? Just so you could be brought to Neva?' She snorted. 'There must be simpler ways to come home.'

The ghost of a smile emerged. 'Indeed. But I am such a slave to my sense of drama.' His self-amusement faded. 'I wanted to make sure Viktor would let his guard down. I knew his arrogance would make him complacent and careless, but for that to happen, he had to believe he had beaten me.' Vaun's teeth flashed. 'All to give him a greater height to fall from!'

'Your hate for him must consume you,' said Verity, pity in her words.

He glared at her. '*Hate*? There's not a word strong enough to describe my loathing for your precious deacon. A million deaths won't pay back the years he took from me, the life he stole.'

'Explain, witch,' demanded Miriya. 'I grow weary of your obtuseness.'

'Ask yourself this, Sister. If my talents were so deadly, then why was I not surrendered to Black Ships whilst I was still a mere child? Why was I not put down? What happened to me between then and now?'

'The datum,' said Verity quietly. 'The records of the librarium. There were missing pieces...'

'Years!' spat Vaun. 'Made into an experiment for him, a tool, a *plaything*! He took only those he could conceal, only those with the strongest potential. Broke us like animals, used us!' With a savage yank, Vaun tore a clutch of hair from the back of his head to reveal the distortion where a metal implant lay under his skin. 'This was just one of his gifts!'

'Like the pyrokene in Sherring's mansion,' said Isabel.

'Yes. We were all his playthings, doctored and neutered by LaHayn's secret scheming.' His eyes were wide and manic. 'Do you see now, Sister? Can you begin to understand? His agenda is not that of your church – it is not even that of your god. With his puppet governor and willing slaves in one hand, and those blind and hidebound to your dogma in the other, LaHayn does as he wishes. He plays his long game–'

'Must we listen to any more of this?' Portia growled. 'We have dallied long enough with this wastrel. Canoness Galatea must be informed of his capture, and the witch must be processed.'

'Aye,' added Cassandra. 'Can any of these creature's ramblings be corroborated? Is there more evidence than his treasonable spewing?'

'There is,' said Verity, after a long moment. 'In the deeps of Noroc's librarium, I found facts that back up what he has told us. I am certain there would be more to find, if only we could search deeper.'

'Facts? Enough to take the word of a witch over that of a High Ecclesiarch?' demanded Portia. 'I imagine not.'

'But there is doubt, yes?' Vaun broke in. 'You must have seen the edges of LaHayn's grand falsehood, you felt it out there. I know you have, else your Sister Superior would have executed me the moment I was pulled from the airship. You want to know, don't you? You have to be sure!'

'Doubt is the cancer in the minds of the unrighteous,' said Portia, quoting a dictum from the *Cardinae Noctum*.

'Only the certain can know faith. Only they are fit to judge,' countered Miriya.

'Whose words are those?' asked Verity.

'The great Sebastian Thor's, from his speech at New Hera during the Age of Apostasy.' She turned a penetrating stare on Portia. 'Are *you* sure, Sister? Beyond all shadow of uncertainty?' Portia's silence was answer enough.

'Heh,' managed the psyker. 'As entertaining as it is to listen to you cite your turgid scripture at one another, may I continue?' Vaun blinked. 'By your own admission, the Canoness knows nothing of my survival as yet. Keep that silence for me and in return I will open the doors of the deacon's duplicity to you. Better than that, I will take you to the site of his blackest and most mendacious secret.' He took a breath, his eyes glittering. 'I will take you to the Null Keep, and you will see for yourself.'

'A covenant with a witch?' Miriya made a disgusted face. 'You would dare to utter such a suggestion to a Sister of Battle?'

The man gave a sigh of false contrition. 'It is your choice, Sister Superior. But you know as well as I do that the moment I leave your sight, it will be my death and you shall never have the answers you want. You will never know why I came here, or what it was that the Hospitaller's sibling perished for.' He ignored Verity's sharp intake of breath and focused all his attention on Miriya. 'By the time you realise that I speak the truth, all the scripture in the galaxy won't be able to stop Viktor LaHayn from ripping your precious Imperium apart.'

'And what would you gain from this selfless act?' demanded the Battle Sister.

'The satisfaction of watching you realise that I do not lie. It will be sweet to see you recognise the betrayal of your own priest-lord.'

None of the women spoke, and the moment seemed to stretch out into hours. Only the crackle of distant fires on the wind crossed between them. Then at last, Sister Miriya cast a glance at the tech-priest, where the adept stumbled around the damaged aeronef.

She called out to him. 'You, cleric. Will the flyer be able to make sky again?'

The priest gave a jerky nod. 'Many systems were damaged, but the machine-spirit is well. It will fly once more, although without such grace as before.'

'Make it ready to lift.' She turned on Vaun. 'This Null Keep of which you speak, this place of secrets. Where does it lie?'

'A few hours by 'nef. I was on my way there myself when you, uh, joined me.'

'You will take us to it.'

A chorus of disbelief erupted from the other Battle Sisters, but Miriya silenced them with a stern gesture.

'Galatea will not allow this,' said Cassandra. 'Her orders were most emphatic.'

'I know what her orders were,' Miriya replied, 'but I also know that since we arrived on Neva, at all turns we have been confounded by a bodyguard of lies. I want the truth, and if it takes this blasphemy to lead us to it, so he will.' She beckoned the psyker up from where he lay. 'No word of Vaun's capture will go beyond the five of us. We shall not return to Noroc, nor surrender our prisoner to the church. These are my orders, and you will obey them, if not for me then to honour the sacrifices of Lethe and Iona.' She cast her gaze upon them all, and one by one the women returned nods of agreement. Portia was the last, but finally she bowed her head.

'You shall not regret this,' said Vaun, a razor behind his smile.

'You know nothing of regret,' she told him, and shoved the witch towards the damaged aeronef.

Galatea stepped over the debris of a broken window and surveyed Sherring's chambers with a cold eye. The baron's centre of operations was a poor attempt at a war room, something that an armchair warrior might create in order to play the role of general. A group of Battle Sisters had already been detailed to isolate and attend to the corpses, placing strips of sanctified parchment over the dead men that bore warnings not to approach the bodies of the traitors.

The heavy stink of cooked meat still hung about them, mingled with the omnipresent musk of burnt wood from the city. It occurred to the Canoness that she had not taken a single breath of clear air for hours, since the advance into Metis had begun. With sadness, she watched two women carefully wrap a dead Repentia in a funerary cloth.

'My lady.' A veteran of the Seraphim corps entered the room and gave a short bow.

'Sister Chloe? What is it?'

'We have completed our sweep of the mansion house grounds and put the disloyal to the sword.' The powerful Seraph-pattern jump pack on Chloe's back made her seem taller and broader across the shoulders than the rest of the women in the room. Galatea knew her from campaigns of old, where the arrow-faced warrior had led her unit on pillars of orange jet flame through throngs of heretics. 'Evidence of the baron's treachery is being gathered as we speak.'

The Canoness nudged Sherring's corpse with her boot. The fact that Chloe had not told her the news she wanted to hear was confirmation enough, but she asked the next question anyway. 'And the witch Torris Vaun?'

'No trace. The baron's personal aircraft was seen departing the mansion's grounds. It is likely the witchkin fled, my lady. A unit of Sisters went in pursuit.'

'Whose?' she demanded.

'Unverified at present. Several units have yet to respond to status queries.'

'Miriya...' said the Canoness, under her breath. She waved Chloe away. 'Keep me apprised. You are dismissed.'

The Sister Seraphim rocked on her heels, self-consciously. 'With respect, Canoness, there is another matter. I also bear a message from one of the adepts in the command vehicles. The lord deacon's office has been attempting to contact you for the last hour. They seem most vexed.'

Galatea concealed a wan smirk. 'Of course. I would imagine so.' The Battle Sister had purposely tuned her vox frequencies to take in only local signals immediate to the engagement at hand, not the high channel communiqué links that would connect Lord LaHayn to her ear. She wanted little distraction, reasoning that anything of great import would be relayed to her eventually. Galatea hooked her fingers over indents in the neck ring of her Sororitas power armour and was rewarded by an answering chime in her ear bead relay. 'Canoness Galatea, returning to network,' she announced.

Within seconds, the even voice of the PDF officer Colonel Braun came to her. 'Honoured Sororitas,' he began, an edge of irritation creeping into his words, 'at last. Stand ready. I have the Governmental Palace for you.' No doubt the soldier chafed at being ordered to sit by a vox and wait for Galatea to come back on stream.

A message from the Governmental Palace? The Canoness pursed her lips in thought. Had Emmel recovered enough to resume his duties already?

The next voice she heard answered that question immediately. 'Canoness, this is Dean Venik. Thank you for your attention. We have been observing the confrontation via scrye-scans from the *Mercutio* in orbit. Lord LaHayn demands a report on the situation there.'

'Put him on,' she replied, walking out into the halls and atria of the mansion. 'I'll brief him myself.'

There was a miniscule pause. 'The lord deacon is... indisposed. You may brief me in his stead.'

'Indisposed? I had thought he would wish to hear of the witch's fate first-hand.' She frowned. 'No matter. My honoured dean, please let the deacon know that by his decree, Metis is burning and all who stood against the rule of the Emperor have been made to show due contrition... or they have died. Baron Holt Sherring and his city cabinet have been terminated, as have a number of pyrokenes that we encountered acting in his employ.'

'Vaun?' demanded Venik impatiently.

Galatea thought it curious that Venik showed no concern over her mention of the other fire-witches they had dispatched. 'Status unknown, presumed at large. The Sisterhood is engaged in a search for him.'

Fury erupted from the dean. 'You burn a city and still you cannot cage this creature? Lord LaHayn's disappointment will be great.'

'I will explain it to him—'

'I told you, Sororitas, he is unavailable.'

'And why might that be?' snapped Galatea, the tension from the day's fight and her dislike of the dean breaking the veneer of her civility. 'What is of such import that he cannot speak to me himself? Is he even there in the palace with you?'

She could almost hear Venik's look of shock at her retort. 'The... The deacon does not have to justify his movements to you, Sister Galatea.'

The woman waved her hand, as if she were dismissing a nagging insect. 'Yes, of course. Permit me then to inquire after the health of the noble Governor Emmel. Is he recovering?'

Venik's voice changed in a moment, from irksome to disingenuous. 'Ah, yes, but of course. You would not have heard. It saddens me to report that the governor passed away a few hours ago. The deacon was there at the time to administer last rites and the Emperor's blessing.'

'Dead?' Galatea weighed this in her mind. 'Then who presides over the government now?' She racked her brain for the name of Neva's sub-viceroy and Emmel's second, a large fellow and the scion of a family of Imperial Guardsmen. 'Baron Preed, is it not?'

'It is not,' replied Venik with more than a little swagger. 'The lord deacon determined that for the best of the Nevan people in this time of great moral and spiritual crisis, the Imperial Church should take a more direct role in the management of the planet. Until further notice, I have taken on the honour of assuming the governorship.'

The Canoness fell silent. Such a decision was unprecedented in the modern Imperium. Since the Age of Apostasy, when the High Ecclesiarch Goge Vandire had tried to turn the galaxy to his rule, the separation of church and state in the ruling of human worlds had become an unbreakable dictum; a dictum that LaHayn had swept away while the Sisters of Battle were deep in the thick of the fighting. Galatea frowned. While she believed utterly in the church's rightness in all things, this was a development that did not sit well with her, but it would do her no good to let Venik know her mind. Finally she spoke. 'My congratulations to you on your new duties, honoured dean. May they bring you what you deserve.' She turned back to the burnt-out chambers. 'I will contact you again once Vaun is ours.' Before Venik could speak further, she deactivated the link studs on her vox control and walked away, brooding.

Once the aeronef had reached its optimal altitude, the ship's nature as a racing yacht came to bear. Even with the damage it had suffered, even with only the lone, twitchy tech-priest at its controls, Sherring's airship cut through the clouds of Neva's skies with the swiftness of a raptor, at times riding on the rapid jet streams of the planet's upper atmosphere as fast as a cruising Thunderhawk.

Verity watched the landscape below alter as they travelled further north. The habitable zones of countryside gave way to valleys choked with dense grey snows and these to chains of black, basalt hills. In among them, stubby volcanic peaks spat desultory chugs of ash, and in many places there were thin streams of lava. Neva was at its most geologically active in this region, riven with small earthquakes and outgassings of fumes. Nothing lived here beyond the hardiest plant life and a few dogged invertebrate life forms. So the mythology of the planet said, the toxic lands would have one day expanded to engulf the entire world if not for the arrival of the Emperor of Mankind, who, with a gesture to His magnificent technologies, halted the march of the volcanoes and reined them in. The blighted landscape remained now as a reminder of the planet's turbulent core and one more example of Neva's unanswerable debt to the God-Emperor.

Behind her, Cassandra was in hushed discussion with

Miriya. 'This is a pointless voyage,' she growled. 'We've been travelling all night and for nothing. Vaun is lying to us.'

'That much is certain,' replied Miriya, 'but we must know for sure. We shall give him enough rope to hang himself.'

'I can hear every word you are saying,' said the psyker from across the cupola. 'And it makes me sad. Is there not even the smallest iota of trust in you? In anyone?' He looked directly at Verity. 'Even the nursemaid?'

'It would be easier to give you some credence if you could reveal this mystery destination of yours,' said the Hospitaller. 'Come now, Vaun. How much further do you expect us to go?'

The man threw her a weak smile and glanced at a chronograph on the 'nef's bulkhead. 'No further,' said Vaun. 'We're here.' He nodded to the tech-priest. 'Take us down, cogboy, nice and easy. And douse the lumes. They'll be watching.'

'Who will be watching?' asked Miriya, striding forwards to where the naked sky peeked into the wrecked cabin.

'LaHayn's dogs.' He pointed into the darkness. 'What do you see?'

Verity squinted. 'Only the volcanoes.'

Vaun nodded. 'As you are meant to. That is the outermost lie.' The aeronef dropped quickly, just a few metres from the ground now. With his bound hands, the psyker took the adept's claw and turned it so the flyer's tiller moved. In return, the ship wavered sideways. 'The battlements are cloaked with clever designs, the points of entry disguised. Look now. Do you see?'

The Sister Hospitaller did and she gasped as a string of casements seemed to appear from nowhere along the surface of the tallest ashen crag.

'The Null Keep,' smiled Vaun. 'I've been away too long.'

From afar, no human eye or auspex scan would ever have considered the towering structure to be anything other than what it first appeared to be: one more huge volcanic tor, seething with roils of dirty steam and clogged rivulets of sluggish lava. Yet the closer one came to the mount, the more it changed to resemble a citadel rather than a natural form. At one time, centuries, perhaps millennia ago, the craggy basalt peak had been untouched by the devices of human technology, but now it was a masterpiece of clandestine engineering, a castle made by stealth that stood undetected in this barren arroyo. Shafts had been bored into the thick walls of the rock face, connecting the magma voids in the same manner as ants and termites lived within their earthen colonies. These open chambers had been emptied of molten stone, sealed seamlessly with a science that was lost to humans in this age, and made habitable. Some of the voids were small things, perhaps the size of a few rooms. Others were large enough to accommodate an Imperial Navy corvette, layered with decking, corridors and internal crawlways.

The slumbering volcanic shaft at the axis of the citadel provided tireless reserves of geothermal energy from mechanisms sunk into the liquid mantle of Neva, venting excess gouts of superheated steam from conduits about the surface of the tower.

Battlements and window slits looked out on the approaches. Cunningly fashioned from the cut of the rock itself, these openings appeared to be natural formations. Only on closer examination could the dim glow of biolumes be seen behind them. Spines of obsidian glass and petrified trees masked clusters of armoured sensor vanes and vox antennae. There were even dock platforms, planes of flat stone that extended out far enough to accommodate something the size of a coleopter or a land speeder.

Every shadowed hollow in the sheer face of the mountainside could be home to a watching sense-engine or a concealed weapon emplacement. It was an oppressive edifice, black and leaking menace into the hot, sulphurous air. The endeavour to create such a structure, the will to hide a secret tower in this barren landscape, dwarfed the palaces and temples of Noroc. The construction's original purpose was lost to antiquity, but whatever it had been made for, it had been born in secrecy. The walls of the inner chambers masked everything that took place within, patterned with exotic ores that defied the study of the few tech-adepts allowed to survey them. Nothing, no wavelength of radiation, not even the warped energy of the human psyche, could escape the walls of the tower. The silence of the Null Keep was deeper than the vacuum of space.

They left the aeronef in a steep-walled chasm, the nervous and shifty Mechanicus priest chained to the landing skid in case his curiosity got the better of him. When the Battle Sisters had secured the adept, Miriya's intent look at Verity sparked a pre-emptive denial from the Hospitaller.

'Do not ask me to remain here, Sister Superior. I have no intention of staying in this lightless cabin while you venture out.'

'I have only your safety in mind,' began Miriya, but Verity shook her head.

'I have come this far. I will see this road to its end.'

Vaun snorted. 'Ah, bravo, nursemaid. You have such tenacity.'

Miriya turned her ire on the psyker, barely moderating the tremor in her gun hand. 'We are here, witch. Now tell us, what is this place?'

'You cannot simply be told what the Null Keep is,' Vaun said darkly. 'You must see it for yourself.'

Portia snorted. 'For Katherine's sake. For all we know, this could be some elaborate trap. We'll venture inside and find a horde of mutant psykers baying for our blood!'

'If I wanted to kill you, Sister, it would have been simple to reduce this aircraft to ashes.' Sweat beaded his brow and with an effort Vaun managed to make a puff of flame snap from his fingertip. 'No, I *want* you to see this. It will please me no end to watch the truth barge its way into your shuttered minds. Even if you gun me down then and there, you'll never escape the fact that I was right... and your precious church is wrong!'

The woman pulled her bolter, but Miriya held up a warning

hand. 'You know better than to let a witch goad you, Portia. Recite the Saint's Lament and reflect upon it.'

Her face soured, but the dark-skinned Battle Sister did as she was asked, turning away to mumble the prayer under her breath. Miriya looked to Vaun once more. She could see the neuropathic drugs were beginning to wear off, and she knew that Verity had no more.

'She has a valid point. Why should I trust you, witch?'

'Nothing I have ever said to you has been a lie, Sister Miriya,' he replied. 'I see no need to change that now.' He paused. 'The keep is the covert domain of Lord LaHayn. It is here that I spent those lost years of my life—' Vaun threw a look at Verity, '—here that your precious deacon's schemes are incubating. As the nursemaid said, this place is the end of the road. For all of us.'

Miriya accepted this with a nod, then with her hands she made a couple of sharp sign-gestures, battle language directives that the other Sisters instantly reacted to. The woman took her plasma pistol from its holster and spoke the Litany of Activation to it. She approached Vaun and gave him a level stare. 'You will have heard this from me before, but it bears repeating before we go forward. If you betray us, your life will be forfeit. All that keeps air in your lungs is my desire for the truth. Give me cause to doubt you, and I will give you the screaming, bloody end that you so richly deserve.'

'Such a compelling argument,' he teased, 'and pray tell, if I do indeed give you the truths you seek, what then? What gift do I get?'

'A chance to repent and a quick end.'

'Well,' Vaun smirked mockingly. 'I'm convinced. Shall we go?'

There were entrances to the Null Keep, but none of them were less than four hundred metres above the level of the valley floor. Instead, Vaun led them to a place where the oval mouths of steam tunnels opened to the cloudy sky. 'This is the manner in which I exited the citadel on the day I escaped.

Many had attempted it before me and all had been brought back for us to see, their bodies bloated by scalding and their skin falling off in sheets.'

'You speak of this place as if it were a prison,' said Cassandra.

'It is that, and it is other things as well. A honeycomb of cells exists within these walls, dungeons cut in the solidified magma bubbles, rooms impossible to gain purchase upon…' He shuddered at the memory.

Isabel gingerly peered over the lip of the tunnel and ducked back with a start, blinking furiously. 'Ach. The heat. It will roast any exposed flesh!'

Miriya traced the fleur-de-lys on her chest plate. 'Don your helmets. Our power armour will protect us.'

Isabel pointed at Vaun. 'What about him? What about the Hospitaller?'

The psyker shook his head. 'There is a routine to the outgassing from the core. The temperature falls and rises in a precise rhythm, which I can predict. Keep close to me and I will guide you through, but do not dally. Hesitate in the wrong place and you'll be cooked.' Like a suitor asking for a courtly dance, Vaun offered his hand to Verity. 'Stay by my side, dear nursemaid.' He ended the sentence with a leer.

'Verity,' Miriya nodded. It was as much an order as she was going to give.

Loathing rose on the Hospitaller's face as she gingerly approached him. 'Have no fear, Sister,' said Vaun in a silky voice. 'I promise I will be the consummate gentleman.'

The girl closed her eyes, fighting down the disgust that she felt, and Miriya gave Vaun one final look of warning. 'Portia, with me. Cassandra, the rear. Isabel, you will keep our erstwhile guide honest. If you so much as suspect he is leading us astray or performing a foul act upon Sister Verity's mind, you have my consent to kill him where he stands.'

In a ragged line, they entered the tunnel and ventured inside. Boiling hot streams of scorching air rumbled past them, fogging the visors of their Sabbat-pattern helms with condensation. Miriya toyed with the preysight setting, but the colours were a riot of tumbling reds, whites and oranges, and she quickly became disoriented.

Blinking sweat from her lashes, she pushed on, conscious of the suit's internal mechanisms labouring to keep her body cool. The tiny fusion core apparatus in her power armour's backpack showed warning glyphs at the corner of her vision, the temperature gauge rising quickly towards the red line.

The Battle Sister kneaded the grip of her gun and pondered Portia's words again. For all she knew, Vaun was leading them into a pit of boiling lava – but to have brought them this far only to take them to certain death? It was not his way. In the days since his escape aboard the *Mercutio*, Sister Miriya found she was coming ever closer to understanding the mind of the aberrant. Vaun's ego was his driving force, and to merely end her life and that of her squad would not be satisfactory for him. He wanted them to admit *he* was in the right before they died.

In the back of her mind, a small voice asked the question: *and what if he is?* Miriya shook the thought away and kept moving.

After what seemed like hours of walking in a doubled-over crouch, they reached an intersection festooned with service walkways. Vaun sagged a little, but directed them on to a service hatch. Portia ventured through and beckoned them into a maintenance room. Relief welled up in each of them as the Battle Sisters took a moment to remove their helmets. Verity was pale and her habit was drenched with sweat. She drained most of her water bottle before she administered a potion to each of them that would restore the balance of their bodies.

There was another door in the room and Vaun walked across to it, peering through a barred slit. The strength that had been missing from his gait was starting to return. 'Here we are,' he said, a curious sadness in his tone that Miriya had not heard before.

The Sister Superior took a look herself, and gasped.

CHAPTER THIRTEEN

It was a gallery of obscenities.

The window slit looked out across the inside of a wide-open chamber, criss-crossed with the webwork of a hundred catwalks and pipeways. Complex loops of cabling went this way and that, similar to those in the streets of Noroc but far more sophisticated. Dangling from them were hooked arms, some empty, some bearing the weight of platforms or aged metal cubes as big as a tank. Many hung suspended, while others moved in trains towards unknown destinations. Among the constant rumble of activity there were odd sounds that might have been screams or electric discharges – it was hard to be sure. As far as Sister Miriya could see, the outer walls of the decks that dropped away into the depths were ringed with cell after cell of greenish, murky glass, the same sort of capsule that Vaun had been sealed in when he was brought to the *Mercutio*. An irritable sensation crawled over her skin and she tasted an indefinable tang on the air, a thick, greasy aroma. She wrinkled her face in a grimace.

'You can sense it, can't you?' Vaun asked in a low voice. 'The despair and pain of a thousand psychics, living and dead. The walls of the citadel are imprinted with it, stained by their anguish.' He shook his head. 'Imagine how it feels to me.'

'My heart bleeds for your suffering, witchkin,' she said with disdain.

Human shapes moved on some of the levels. Sister Miriya craned her neck to get a better look, but she was too high up for proper scrutiny. She could make out the doddering metal-meat amalgams of servitor drones, blinded men in what might have been Mechanicus robes, but most of the figures wore habits of drab grey, loose garb that swaddled them and became a blank moon-faced mask over their heads.

Vaun saw where her attention was directed. 'The tenders. Such a horrible joke, a soft and compassionate appellation perverted by these heartless cretins.'

The Sororitas considered the witch at her side. Now was the time to be the most watchful of him. By his own admission he had wanted to gain entry to this place, and she had facilitated that for him. Vaun's need to remain in her company was likely waning by the moment, and when the opportunity presented itself, she had no doubt that he would attempt to flee.

The other women had taken water and a brief moment for prayer. Cassandra approached, her face conflicted. 'Sister Superior, is there any sign of alarm? I am concerned, even though Portia found nothing to indicate any sense-engines that might alert the... the inhabitants.'

'Delicate machines do not last long in the humidity of the tunnels,' answered the psyker, 'and besides, the Null Keep's lines of defence are designed to keep people from leaving, not entering. Unless you decide to clatter about on the lower levels or deliver a sermon, we should remain undetected.'

Miriya gestured to her Sisters to ready themselves. 'We are intruders in this place, so be wary. Until we are sure of what practices are at hand within these walls, we must conceal ourselves.' She holstered her pistol. 'If the need comes, silent weapons only, clear?'

'Ave Imperator,' chorussed the women.

The Sister Superior shoved Vaun in the back, towards the

door. 'Come, then, heretic. Let us see what spectacle you were so eager to lay your eyes upon.'

The psyker gave her a venomous snarl in return. 'My pleasure. I'm sure you'll find it most educational.'

Verity let herself be shepherded between Isabel and Cassandra, moving with all the care she could muster through the myriad pools of shadow on the upper tiers of the chamber. Her mind flashed back to Iona and the Sisters Repentia at Metis: they had done the same, protecting her with calm and flawless skill. But Iona was dead, a torched skeleton, and the rest of the Repentia had fallen alongside her. The Hospitaller felt a hard stab of guilt in her chest. She did not want the same fate to befall these women.

Part of her railed at herself from within. Why could she not have simply remained behind on the aeronef? Or back in Noroc? Better still, why had she not paid her respects to Lethe and then returned to her order's works on the outer moons? Verity felt empty and incomplete, grasping for some intangible form of closure that would heal the wound left by her sibling's death, but as events continued to unfold around her, more and more she was beginning to realise that nothing, not even the contrition and execution of Torris Vaun, would close that void. *Emperor, grant me guidance*, she prayed silently, *I beg of you, deliver me from this*.

'Observe,' Isabel said, pointing. 'The open area below. It appears to be an exercise yard…'

An actinic green flash blinked down in the enclosure and Verity shuddered as a thin screech filtered up a moment later. 'They killed someone.'

Miriya brought them to a halt and observed the area through her magnoculars. She was silent for a while, as if she were trying to make sense of what she was seeing. Verity strained to look with the naked eye, but all she could determine were ant-sized dots moving and swarming – and once in a while the blink of a lasgun discharge.

'A training squad,' said Miriya at length. 'There are…

helots, perhaps? They are being used as targets for the ones in chains. Those robed in grey are directing the proceedings.'

'The chains are made of phase-iron,' said Vaun, his hand straying to his opposite wrist, rubbing at the site of an old injury in recollection. 'It sears the skin when psychic energies are used.'

Verity nodded. 'I have heard of this material. It is a rarity, a relic from the Dark Age of Technology.'

Vaun sniffed. 'It is not a rarity here, nursemaid. LaHayn has it in abundance.' He gestured around at the walls. 'Imagine acid boring into you every time you tried to speak, or breathe, or eat. That's what that damned metal feels like.'

The Sister Superior put away her scope and drew back from the edge of the deck. 'We move on.'

'What is going on down there?'

'A live fire exercise. The captive witches are being taught to kill with their minds.' The thought of such a thing clearly disgusted her.

Deeper in the shadows, Vaun pointed towards a section of the chamber walled off into compartments. 'This way. There used to be laboratories and chirurgeries on this level, before the fire.'

'Fire?' echoed Cassandra.

Vaun just smiled and kept walking.

On they went, trailing behind the amoral corsair in a wary line. Verity fingered her silver rosary chain, tracing the careworn letters etched into the surface of the bright metal. She ducked to step through a distorted hatch that had been warped by a massive discharge of heat. The carved black stone and steel plate of the outer chamber gave way to the same kind of design the Hospitaller had seen in dozens of space vessels and Imperial buildings. The crenellated columns and arched, rivet-dotted beams would have been just as familiar on a Navy starship as they were here.

She caught glimpses of disused laboratories, some with patches of dark colour spattered about the walls and the moribund air of decay within. Weaves of gauzy spider webs coated many of the objects inside, sealing them in the past. Other doors were of heavier gauge metal than the hatchways and set with oculus slits and heavy, ponderous gates: confinement cells. The woman found herself unwilling to peer inside, for fear of what she might see.

Ahead of her, Isabel's body language altered slightly. The Battle Sister was on more familiar ground, the shape of the corridors known to her. Verity had no doubt that Isabel, Portia and the others had been trained to fight inside such confines. Parts of the floor were uneven, deformed by the same heat-blast as the hatch, and her arm shot out to grab a stanchion to stop her from tripping over. The Hospitaller's hand came back to her coated with a thick layer of slimy ash. She knew at once that it was organic residue from an immolated body. With exaggerated care, she wiped the matter away and shot Vaun a disgusted glare. If he sensed it, he gave no indication.

Portia held a small beam lantern in her fist like a club, using the stark yellow ray it cast to probe into places where the overhead biolumes could not reach. Some of the side compartments of the corridor were pitch dark. The light glittered off things made of glass, sometimes across sluggish pools of stagnant liquid. Verity's impression was one of neglect, of abandonment.

'The witch spoke truthfully,' said Portia. 'I see operating tables and medicae devices. Perhaps the Hospitaller could tell us more?'

Verity bobbed her head in acknowledgment and stepped forward. 'If you could bring your lamp–' A scrape of metal on metal silenced her with a start, and the Battle Sisters froze.

'Someone there,' murmured Vaun in faint anticipation.

Portia pressed the lantern into Verity's trembling fingers and gave Miriya a questioning look. The Sister Superior returned a nod and the other woman slid out of the corona of light and into the darkness. There was another noise, and this time it was unmistakable: the sound of human footsteps, a dithering, unsure movement.

An indistinct outline, no more than the Hospitaller's height, wavered at the corner of Verity's eye, there in the gloom of the chirurgery chamber. Her automatic reaction was to turn the torch beam upon it. A blank, doll-like face blinked into solidity before her, with black circles for eyes and a slot for a mouth. The white mask merged into the figure's shabby grey over-robes. Caught in the light, the tender threw itself across the room at a panel on the far side of the chamber.

Startled by the apparition, Verity could do little but track the robed shape. One hand was within a finger's length of touching the console when Portia faded out of the dark and caught the tender. It happened so quickly the Hospitaller had only flashes: the wet snap of bone as the tender's arm was ruined; a rustle of clothing and the glint of a weapon; glossy black Sororitas armour glittering like an insect's carapace; the ripping crack of a neck breaking, a coughing gasp and a falling body.

'Forgive me,' said Portia to the Sister Superior. 'He was attempting to reach this vox lectern. I reacted to stop him raising an alert.'

'You acted properly,' noted Miriya.

Verity swallowed hard. The moment of death had taken hardly a blink.

Portia took the beam lantern back from her rigid grip and turned it on the dead man, using her free hand to peel back the blank mask. A rather ordinary face looked back up at them, the expression of faint surprise still there.

'Hmph. Nobody I know,' Vaun interjected. 'Good kill, though. Very nice technique.'

Portia did not look up from her examination of her victim. 'It would be my pleasure to demonstrate it to you at close quarters, maleficent.' She pulled at a line of buttons and the over-robes fell open. 'This mantle is lined with a ceramite weave.'

'Body armour,' offered Cassandra, 'in case their charges get too boisterous.'

'The clothing beneath...' Portia fingered a garment in rich red material. 'This is the attire of a cleric.' She found the dead man's necklace: it was a string of onyx beads ending in a golden aquila, an affectation of the Nevan branch of the Imperial Cult.

Vaun laughed softly. 'How troubling. Now, what would a pious servant of the God-Emperor be doing here, I wonder?'

Miriya rounded on the criminal. 'You knew. You knew and yet you let her end the life of a priest and said nothing,' she spat. 'His blood is on your hands!'

'Along with hundreds of others,' retorted Vaun, his amusement gone in an instant, 'not that I care.'

'You'll be made to,' vowed the Celestian. 'You have my word on it.'

The man made an annoyed snarl. 'Ach, look beyond that, woman,' he snapped, pointing at the corpse. 'Don't you understand what it means?'

Isabel was examining the consoles in the chamber. 'I am no tech-adept, but I believe he appeared to be attempting to perform a prayer-diagnostic on these devices.' She ran her hands over a set of tarnished brass dials and a wavering hololithic screen hummed to life. The image was leached of colour, but it clearly showed the activities of a group of similarly dressed figures working at a body on an operating dais. Verity watched for a moment before realising two things: the body was a person still alive, conscious and unanaesthetised, and the display was a visual record of something that had taken place in this very room. The screen threw more light about the chamber, illuminating the white porcelain dais and the dark stains of dried vitae about the blood gutters.

Vaun craned his neck to get a better look at the activity on the hololith. 'Now, her I *do* know,' he noted, 'or rather, I did. Kipsel, her name was.' He looked away. 'She died of that.'

'Of what?' Verity asked, in a dull voice.

Vaun tapped the lump behind his ear. 'Of this.'

Isabel scrutinised a ticking display rotor in High Gothic. 'Kipsel. That name is here in the recording. Dates, as well.'

The Hospitaller looked over her shoulder. The dates fell squarely in the time period where Vaun's librarium files were empty. She looked up at the screen and her eyes widened. 'Can you halt the progress of the image?'

The Battle Sister turned a control and the recording slowed down to a stop. 'What is it, girl?'

Verity pointed at the corner of the hololith, her finger breaking the surface of the ghost image. 'It's him. It's both of them.'

'Holy Terra... Yes, I see it.' Isabel worked the controls again, making the image shift to bring that section of the picture forward.

Verity and the other women saw several men, garbed in the same robes as the dead priest, but with their hoods down. Two men in particular were at the core of the group, the others around them showing obvious deference. Their profiles were unmistakable, even though time and the poor recording marred the likenesses.

Vaun indicated the men with a theatrical sweep of his hand. 'Honoured Sisters, may I present his most loathsome self, the Lord Viktor LaHayn and his lickspittle Venik.'

Miriya ordered her Celestians to sweep the operating theatre and the anterooms that spread off from it. It appeared that the dead priest had been in the process of surveying the contents – perhaps in preparation to return them to use, she wondered – and one of the rooms contained a wheeled cargo lighter, stacked with spools of glittering wire. Verity identified it as a variety of datum storage media, the same as the hololithic screen used to replay the images of LaHayn and the ill-fated Kipsel. There were uncountable hours of footage here, and Emperor-knew how many recordings of witches undergoing the same brutal violations.

The Sister Superior considered the spools with dispassion. She had no sympathy for the psykers, but the eager, almost wanton manner in which the woman Kipsel had been desecrated struck a chord in her mind. The church did not torture and maim without good cause, and it gnawed at her that she did not know what Lord LaHayn's motives were.

'This must have been going on for decades,' murmured Cassandra, 'and yet I have never heard of the like.'

Miriya wondered if the Imperial Inquisition might have had a hand here, but there was nothing to indicate the presence of the Ordo Malleus or any other branch of the God-Emperor's inquest. In her experience, inquisitors were only too pleased to trumpet their deeds to the church. No, the studied and careful concealment of what was taking place in the Null Keep made her seasoned warrior's mind taut with suspicion.

Verity examined the operating dais. There were tools, now rusted and dull, still stored in drawers set into the cracked porcelain frame. From a tray connected by a corroded servitor-arm, she plucked out a silvery orb and held it up to the torchlight. Miriya exchanged a look with the Hospitaller as they both recognised the same design of implant device from the inside of Ignis's skull.

In another anteroom there were objects that were undeniably of inhuman origin. Suspended in tanks of thin oil, Portia turned her torch to illuminate steely constructs mated with rods of green-hued glass, all long lines and right angles. Next to this, a curved hollow of yellowed bone marked with purple eldar runes, its purpose unguessable, and finally a grotesque hydrocelaphic ork skull, bloated beyond normal size by the touch of mutation.

'Viktor always had eclectic tastes,' noted Vaun archly. 'There's no avenue of investigation he won't venture down.'

Something inside Miriya's iron-hard resolve snapped and she backhanded the psyker with a savage, lightning-fast blow. Vaun stumbled away, clutching at a bleeding cut on his cheek as she drew her plasma pistol. 'I have reached my limit with your games, creature. I want no more of your half-truths and obfuscations!'

Vaun spat blood on the tiled floor. 'You pull that trigger, wench, and the whole keep will know it. You'll never get out of here alive!'

'I'll take that chance.' The collimator coils atop the gun hummed and glowed. 'No more games, no more wordplay, no more circumlocution. You'll tell me the truth now, or else I will gun you down and tear it from these black walls myself!'

The psyker dabbed at the wound on his face, measuring the moment. 'Very well. It seems I have no choice.' He sighed. 'It's an interesting story.'

Torris Vaun had been no more than a youth when he discovered that the cleric in his settlement had contacted the capital and told them of his 'talents'. In a fit of directionless anger, the boy had burned the church to the ground with the humming, electric potency that lurked behind his eyes. The cleric, his dirty habit smouldering, had made it into the graveyard before he set him alight too, and Vaun had stood and listened to the crisping crackle of flaming human meat.

Not a single soul in the town would come near him as he waited by the chapel arch, watching his handiwork. They were too scared to approach for fear he would do the same to them. As he listened to the townspeople point and whisper, Vaun decided that he would have to leave this place and strike for bigger, greater things. Of late, the settlement had grown stifling, the challenge of terrorising the little township ever less interesting.

Presently a man arrived, a swift coleopter depositing him on the hill. Another priest, Vaun noted. He began to muster his powers in preparation to kill again. But when the newcomer came close enough, Torris could see he was laughing. The black humour was infectious, soon the youth was laughing too. And there, in the glow of the burning church, the new arrival offered him his hand and a chance for fortune and glory the likes of which Vaun had only dreamed.

'You know the story of the Wound, of Saint Celestine and the Passing of her Glory?' Vaun waved his hand. 'Of course you do. But Neva's past holds more to it than that, or the ridiculous games fought by the nobles with assassins and cat's-paws. You just have to look deeper. Much deeper.' The psyker righted a fallen chair and sat upon it, warming to his subject. 'Celestine's coming cleared the warpstorm that had shrouded this planet and for that she was duly enshrined in its miserable annals. But that occurrence was not the first time the clouds of the empyrean had converged on Neva. You see, such a thing has happened here dozens of times, as far back as the Age of Strife.' He paused, fishing a battered tin box from his pocket. 'May I take a cigarillo?' Vaun asked Miriya. 'It's been a while–'

Cassandra reached down and slapped the box from his hand, sending it skittering away into the shadows.

'Ah. That would be a no, then?'

'Keep talking,' growled Miriya.

'Very well. The storms. While some worlds that felt the touch of the warp were destroyed or worse, fell bodily into the realm of Chaos, Neva was not one of them. No, instead the caress of the immaterium was subtler, more insidious. Like a taint upstream flowing down a river, the warp left a mark on this world. It turned the bloodlines of every living soul upon it, just a little.' The man held up his thumb and forefinger a few centimetres apart. 'But just enough. Tell me, Sister Superior, how many psykers are there for every normal human in the Imperium?'

'One or two in every hundred thousand births, perhaps less.'

Vaun nodded. 'On Neva the number would probably be closer to five times that.' He ignored the looks of incredulity on the women's faces. 'Neva's brush with warp space means that its people are more attuned to the psychic realm. Most of them never know it, they just get "feelings" or have strange dreams. But many of us exhibit the more, shall I say, *unique* properties.'

'Impossible,' snapped Portia.

'Short-sighted as ever,' retorted Vaun. 'Think, dullard. Neva is not the only world to have such a blessing. What of Magog, or Prospero, the holdfast of the Thousand Sons? Those planets were rich in preternatural power.'

'Magog obliterated itself,' said Verity, 'and the Space Marines of the Thousand Sons turned to Chaos. Prospero vanished into the Eye of Terror.'

Vaun dismissed her words with a wave of the hand. 'Details, mere details. The fact remains. The bloodlines of Neva are laced with metapsychic potential. I am living proof.'

'What does this mad theory have to do with LaHayn and this place?' demanded Miriya.

'Everything.'

The cleric – he was an arch-confessor then, of high rank among the diocese and not yet the *Lord* Viktor LaHayn – took him to a dark castle and made him play with his ability. Vaun excelled, untroubled by moral concerns and other petty things, and LaHayn saw potential in him for greatness. He hadn't known it at the time, but now Vaun understood: LaHayn, a normal, pathetic dead-mind like all the others, was jealous of him. He craved the power that came so easily to Torris, and when he couldn't engender it in himself, he worked to make himself master of those who had it.

LaHayn had had his pet adepts place things inside Vaun, opening up his brain and doctoring it. The agonies were fierce, worse than any thing a non-psyker could ever have imagined, but they also opened the floodgates to stronger wells of burning power within him. Vaun's mindfire blossomed, and in the service of his new master, he was compelled to fight in the secret wars that raged beneath the placid surface of Neva's society. But as Vaun's ability and prowess grew, so did his resentment.

The day came when Vaun crossed paths with an avaricious baron named Holt Sherring. The baron had only fragments of the story of the Null Keep and Neva's dark secret, but it was enough to make him a player in LaHayn's game. When Vaun was sent to kill him, Sherring offered the psyker a way to smash his enforced habituation and set himself free. There was no hesitation in Vaun's agreement – but he no more wanted to be a pawn of the baron than the deacon, and as soon as he was able to break free, Vaun fled to the stars to carve a reputation for himself, and brood on a reprisal.

'The Null Keep was created in the deep past as a bulwark against the daemons of the warp, and LaHayn took it for himself. It was an ideal location for his works, isolated, invisible. He kept his dark machinations concealed so they could not taint his public image, just as Neva's people moved their polluting industry to the outer moons.' Vaun tapped his knuckles on the wall, remembering. 'This was my home, my prison, my torture-house. All of us, the pieces in the lord deacon's games. After I broke free, I swore I would come back to obliterate this place. And bless poor, stupid Holt, but he found it for me.'

'I do not understand,' said Isabel. 'If you were held here for so long, why did you need Baron Sherring to find the location for you?'

He pointed at the implant. 'Viktor's adepts are very talented. The implants they created place blocks on the mind. I can no more hold the location of this place in my head than I can count the number of stars in the galaxy.' He snorted. 'It's all blurs. A clever way to stop any escapees from returning to plague him. Or so he thought.'

'You learned to break your conditioning?'

A nod. 'You see, LaHayn learned the secret of Neva as an initiate, from a secret sect of Gethsemenite monks. He told me that it was a revelation for him.' Vaun smiled coldly. 'Years later, he had me hunt down and kill every one of them, burn their monastery, destroy their manuscripts.'

'You were his weapon...' said Miriya.

'I was his slave.' The brittle ice of his smile shattered. 'He compelled me, made me kill for him, all so that he could cement his position in the hierarchy. I helped keep this secret, you see. If an inquisitor got too close, or some cleric who knew too much grew a conscience, it was I that barred the way. The burned dead in the name of LaHayn's grand scheme grew large in number.' He looked at the floor. 'For a time I liked it. I was his red right hand, his sly agent of menace. But I knew that one day I would outlive my usefulness to him.'

Vaun took a long breath. 'While I guarded his secrets, LaHayn worked diligently at his endeavours. He gathered those with the psychic gift and made sure that the tithes to the Black Ships were just as they should be. He threw them the weak ones, the lesser and broken minds, all the while skimming off the cream for his own private cadre here at the keep. Slowly and surely, he has been experimenting on my kind, peeling back the secrets of the mind with ancient technology and callous resolve. All the while, building an army, keeping them asleep until he needs them. For when his invasion begins.'

'Invasion?' echoed Cassandra. 'What do you speak of, criminal?'

'The invasion of Terra, of course. The lord deacon intends nothing less than to destroy the Golden Throne of Earth.'

The Aquila-class shuttle carved a supersonic path through the roiling black clouds of the wastelands, tipping up on the edge of a wing to skirt about the plumes of toxic gas issuing from the muttering chains of volcanoes. Designed to resemble the Imperial eagle with its wings outstretched, the craft was swift and capable: an icon of the Emperor's will made manifest in steel and ceramite. There were only a few of the ships in service on Neva, and only one dedicated exclusively to the use of a single man. In the passenger compartment, Lord LaHayn ignored the buffeting of the flight and replaced his empty amasec glass in a receptacle before him. An enunciator on the bulkhead shaped like a choral mask gave a peep of sound. 'Great Ecclesiarch,' came the voice of the pilot servitor. 'We are approaching the keep. Please prepare yourself for landing.'

'Good,' replied the deacon with a nod, and he pressed

himself back into his sumptuous acceleration chair. His outwardly calm demeanour masked the churn of his inner thoughts. The course of events was in serious danger of spiralling out of control, and LaHayn feared that the tighter he made his grip, the more threads would slip through his fingers. It was imperative for the Great Work that he personally took command of things – and there was no place better suited than his sanctum sanctorum, his perfect retreat and workshop here in the Null Keep. The lord deacon had left Venik behind, preening at his new role as Neva's interim governor. The haughty dean would give the nobles and the people something to focus on while LaHayn worked behind the scenes. With luck, he would have everything on an even keel in time for the state funeral of poor, stupid Emmel.

At the edges of his thoughts, a doubt unfurled. Who was to blame for this turn of events? In the cold light of truth, the blame could easily lie at his feet. Had he not been so rigid in his orders, had he been willing to let the Battle Sisters terminate Vaun on sight, then none of his carefully wrought schemes would be so close to discovery. He dismissed the thought with a grimace. This was not the place for uncertainty. No, the woman Miriya, it was with her that the blame rested. Her stupidity in letting the witch escape to wreak havoc... The priest glanced out of the viewport as the keep hove into view and smiled thinly. Still, some good had come of this comedy of errors. Vaun's covert contact with Sherring had become obvious and that had allowed him to eradicate a rival. Now all that remained was to complete the circle with Vaun himself.

The shuttle dipped towards the peak of the towering volcanic cone, passing through dark, ashen smoke, and LaHayn pondered on the matter of his former protégé. Vaun would come to the keep, of that he had no doubt. From the moment he had heard of the escape and flight to Neva, he had known what destination Torris sought. It was only a matter of time until teacher and student faced each other again.

'And this time, there will be an end to it,' he said aloud.

* * *

A cloister bell tolled through the decks of the Null Keep and reached to the upper tiers where the Sisters concealed themselves.

'Perfect timing,' grinned Vaun. 'Viktor does have an excellent sense of theatre. I've always admired that about him.'

At the hololithic lectern, Isabel manipulated the controls to gain some sense of what was transpiring. 'A general alert, Sister Miriya,' she said reading the glyphs. 'A ship is landing at one of the docking platforms.'

'I could show you,' offered Vaun. 'The screens link into a central nexus web. The tenders used them to broadcast those dreary hymns. With your permission, of course.'

'Do it,' ordered Miriya.

'Excuse me...' The psyker moved around Isabel and altered the setting of the device. The image changed to become an exterior view of a flat, glassy landing pad. After a moment, an honour guard of robed tenders marched up in a line as a shuttle dropped into view. There was no sound. The aircraft's wings folded upwards and claw-like landing skids deployed before it settled to the ground. Miriya looked closer. The man descending the ramp from the shuttle was unmistakably Viktor LaHayn.

'Now do you accept the veracity of what I told you?' demanded Vaun. He drifted away from the console, moving slowly out of the nimbus of light.

'There may be some truth in it.' Cassandra's admission was grudging.

Miriya glanced at the witch, then back at the hololith. It was the moment that the man had been watching for, the single instant when all the Sisters had turned their attention from him. Finding such a point in time was the mark of a true genius, Viktor had always told him. 'The key to greatness,' he had pontificated, 'is to know patience, to know when the tipping point is before you. Strike then, and you will leave your adversary in disarray.'

Just so. Vaun had let them push him about, abuse him and deride him since the moment they had found him in the wreckage, and all of it had been a play leading to this instant. Even the watchful, shrewd Sisters of Our Martyred Lady were not infallible, and it would be his pleasure to show them that fact.

Two things happened at once. The mindfire that Vaun had been carefully marshalling for the last few hours erupted into the room, the air igniting. The women were punched down by the back draft. At the same time, he was at the vox lectern, slamming home the punch-switch that sounded the alert klaxon.

Shot and shell came snapping at his heels as he threw himself out of the derelict operating theatre and into the ruined corridors. Vaun ran and found his old hiding places, laughing silently as the tenders came swarming upward.

CHAPTER FOURTEEN

Miriya's rage knew no limit. Howling like a wildcat, she stood in the throat of the oncoming firestorm and sent streaks of killing fire back towards the aggressors. Her fury was a terrible thing to see unleashed, and her anger – directed at herself as much as at the enemy – lit the corridor around her with plasma flames.

The Battle Sisters left the decrepit medicae lab behind as the tenders came to suppress them. The initial group deposited by the cable-lifts fired first, unwilling to do anything but attack the group of intruders. They were easily dispatched, no match for the Sisters of Katherine when their blood was up. But these were only the first. More men in grey robes came, and this time they brought bloodhounds. The brains of the bound psy-slaves had been reduced to animalistic levels, and they scuttled on all fours, howling as they threw wild darts of psychokinetic force about them.

The tenders were well armed for priests. What they lacked in the cold application of soldiery exhibited by the Sisters, they made up for with their rare bolter-crossbow weapons, glittering with artificer filigree. Humming electro-stakes as long as Miriya's arm rained down the open hallway, rebounding off the steel walls in sparks of searing blue light. The

Celestian heard an irate curse behind her as Isabel took a stake in the shoulder, spinning her around like a top. The priest-troopers and their cohorts came on, pressing the attack, pushing the women deeper into the iron compartments.

Portia was at her side, snarling over the noise of her bolter. 'What now, Sister Superior?' she demanded, placing a scathing emphasis on Miriya's rank. 'Our means of entry is cut off, and these clerics outnumber us more and more with each passing moment!'

Miriya ducked behind a burning console to collect her thoughts. The plasma weapon in her hand was glowing cherry red with discharge, and she could feel the heat of it through her gloves. Damn Vaun, she railed at herself. Damn the witch and his lies. My foolish curiosity has led my cohort to ruin!

'Sister,' snapped Portia. 'What are your orders?' The smell of hot metal issued from the breech of her gun as she retreated into the lee of a stanchion to reload a spent sickle magazine.

Miriya glared at her. 'We quit this place. A higher authority must intervene here. I will contact the Canoness!'

Another electro-stake whistled through the air above them. 'Vox signals. Blocked,' came Isabel's voice, each word tight with pain. 'I can't get a message out.'

'Even if we could get a communication through the walls of this blighted tower, Galatea will execute us for disobeying her orders,' retorted Portia.

'There will be a transceiver array in this place. We will find it and sound a clarion.' Miriya stared at her gun, metering her rage. 'I will take whatever punishment the Canoness decrees – but she will see my transgressions as miniscule when she understands what we have discovered here!'

'Aye, providing she's willing to take the testimony of a corsair over the lord deacon. We have only Vaun's word–'

'You saw the same as I,' snapped Miriya. 'LaHayn has a secret agenda in this place, and that cannot be denied.'

'*Mercutio* should blast this crag from orbit,' spat Isabel, returning fire with her uninjured arm. 'Accursed pastors. You dare attack the Daughters of the Emperor?'

Shot and stake crossed each other in the enclosed space. The stink of spent cordite and scorched steel cut the women's throats with every breath. Miriya glanced back at Isabel, and saw Verity tending to her injury even as the Battle Sister worked at her bolter, reloading the weapon one-handed. Behind them, Cassandra stabbed a finger into the melee.

'Something's coming…'

The words had barely left her mouth before the deck plates beneath their feet began to shudder with dozens of heavy footfalls. Miriya turned back to see the tenders and their hound-psykers parting to allow a trio of heavy gun servitors to approach the firing line. Almost the size of dreadnoughts, the flesh-metal amalgams stomped dead clerics into slime beneath their clawed feet as they shouldered forward. Meltaguns whined up to full capacity and oily snaps of sound announced the unlocking of multi-barrelled stubber cannon.

'Fall back,' she shouted, hurling herself from her cover just as the machine slaves filled the passageway with a screaming riot of gunfire.

She saw Cassandra grab a handful of Verity's cloak and bodily throw the slighter-framed girl back down the corridor. Portia tossed a krak grenade at the servitors and then joined Isabel in shooting. Miriya paced shots into the stumbling, inexorable man-shapes, her plasma pistol cooking off a drum of battery acids in an acrid slam of concussion that doubled with the blast of the grenade. One of the servitors tripped and fell, making the deck plates twitch again with the force of its collapse, but there were more than just these three. The Celestian saw four more piston-legged monstrosities lurching out of the gun smoke.

'Back. Back. Find a branch corridor, a vent grille, anything!'

'Nothing!' came Verity's panicked voice. 'This is a dead end. We are boxed in.'

Isabel growled with every step she took, the stake still embedded in her arm clearly grinding against the bone as she moved. Miriya felt a sting of pride as her Sister did not let it slow her chastisement of the enemy. Isabel had always been one of the keenest shots in the Celestians, an elite among the elite. As if in acknowledgement of this, there came a death cry from one of the grey robes as a careful bolt shell stove in a tender's ribcage. The Sister Superior stepped past Portia, firing again and again at the marching servitors.

'Ah,' Portia cried in desperation. 'If only I had a storm bolter!'

Despite the onrushing threat, a peculiar amusement rippled out among the women, the charged emotions so close to death turning to black humour. 'Offer it to the servitors,' retorted Cassandra. 'It would kill them quicker than any gunshot.'

Miriya's face split in a fierce grin. If this were to be the end of them, then in the name of Katherine, Celestine and the Thousand-Numbered Saints, the Sisters of Battle would make the end a costly one for LaHayn's lackeys.

Something in the walls shifted and banged against flat plates of metal, and without warning the floor lurched to one side. Iron clasps as big as her head snapped open on the walls and ceiling. The gun servitors shrank back as the women lost their footing.

'What in the saint's name...?' cried Cassandra, grabbing at an iron pillar.

Suddenly the corridor down which they had been forced was drifting away from them, a gap widening with each passing second. Miriya's perception was confused for a moment before she realised that the dead-end corridor was nothing of the kind – it was a trap, an open-ended box at the end of a conduit, suspended on chains like the cells they had seen from the maintenance gantries. There was little to gain purchase on and the Sororitas skidded on the sheer metal deck as a crane arm pulled the captive chamber away, swinging it over the wide open void between the keep's inner tiers.

Portia teetered close to the edge and her boot slipped out from under her. Isabel was near and she tried to grab her, but habit made her offer her bloody, numbed arm and the limb refused to obey. Portia fell backwards out of the lurching box and plummeted down. Isabel turned away as a sickening crack of bone and shattered ceramite briefly joined the tide of clamour inside the keep.

Another Sister lost. Miriya allowed herself one tiny moment of anguish at Portia's ending and then sealed it away inside her heart. There would be time to mourn later, when candles could be lit and canticles to the fallen recited. 'On your guard,' she snapped. 'Be ready!'

With a swift jerk, the motion of the container was arrested and the box hung for long seconds in midair. The women could see nothing outside except the glitter of lights on the far tier and coils of dark vapour, then the chains above squealed and the metal box went into freefall. Miriya was slammed against the side of the container and clung to it, watching the levels of the keep flash by, watching the flat expanse of the lowermost tier rise up to meet them at a frightening speed. She screwed her eyes shut and called the God-Emperor's name.

When the impact came, she feared her neck would be snapped. Instead she was thrown into Cassandra and the women collapsed in a heap, tossed around inside the box like gambler's dice in a cup. The headlong fall of the container had been halted a metre or so from the ground, deliberately to shock and disorient them. Blood gummed her right eye shut as Miriya struggled to get to her feet and failed. Every joint in her body sang with pain. She made out the blurry forms of robed men advancing on the box, shock-staves in their hands. Like the power mauls of the enforcers, the weapons delivered punishing electrostatic discharges that could cripple and maim. Miriya managed only to croak out a denial before the tenders swarmed into the container and beat the Sisters into senselessness.

Consciousness, when it returned, did not come in a slow trickle or gentle awakening. It forced itself into Verity's perception like a violent intruder, hammering jagged chunks of painful wakefulness into her. She felt sick and gasped as she failed to prevent her stomach from ejecting thin, watery bile. There was the coppery metallic taste of blood in her mouth, and the acrid taste of raw ozone. The stink of air ripped open by electricity filled Verity's nostrils and she suppressed another gag reflex. The action made her head loll, her neck rubbery and loose. The Hospitaller blinked, and tried to take stock. The cool, clinical portion of her mind ran through a checklist of injuries, finding contusions and cuts, but thankfully nothing that would indicate broken bones or internal bleeding.

How long? How long was I unconscious? Labouring, she drew in a breath of tainted air and attempted to look about her. There were iron manacles circling her wrists and ankles, linked by chains to a strange pulley device above. More chains and more pulleys were connected to the slumped forms of Sister Miriya and the other Sororitas.

'Miriya?' she managed, pushing the slurred word out of her mouth, her tongue like a lump of old leather. 'Cassandra? Do you hear me?'

When no reply came, she tried to turn in place, but the exertion was like shifting a sack of wet sand. Verity let herself sink to the chilly black flagstones beneath her feet and massaged the painful places in her arms and legs. Looking about, she could see that the chamber they had been placed in was not a holding cell, but a large workshop. Banks of benches with quiet tech-adepts and servitors surrounded them, hard at work on unfathomable tasks beneath the sickly light of ancient biolumes. There were tall, indistinct objects at the edge of her perception, but the Hospitaller couldn't begin to grasp their purpose.

A groan drew her attention back to Sister Miriya. The Battle Sister righted herself. 'My weapons… equipment. Taken?'

'It appears so,' said Verity, her voice croaky. 'My medicus ministorum has been removed from my person, even my holy tome.'

'Mine as well,' replied the Sororitas, searching the pockets in her robes. The Hospitaller had heard it said that the copies of the sacred texts carried by Sisters of Battle held kill-needles and memory-metal knives concealed in their pages along with the God-Emperor's wisdom. The women glanced up as footsteps approached.

Verity followed Miriya's gaze and felt ice form in the pit of her stomach as Lord LaHayn emerged from the shadows. A group of tenders followed him in tight escort, and one marched with his hood back, a device in his hand trailing cables behind it. The deacon wore a peculiar aspect. He seemed distressed, in the manner of a parent disappointed with a misbehaving child.

'Sister Verity, Sister Miriya. You cannot know how unhappy it makes me to find you here.'

The furious Sister Superior was suddenly on her feet. 'What in Holy Terra's name are you doing in this foul place, cleric?'

LaHayn threw a nod to priest at his side, and the man turned a dial on his control unit. The pulley over Miriya's head ground its cogs and she was hauled upward with a jerk, just enough to take her a couple of centimetres off her feet. She hung there like a puppet painted in black enamel, cursing the deacon.

'Show some respect for my rank, Sister. Now, tell me, how did you get here?' he asked calmly, his voice carrying. 'Tell me how you found the Null Keep.'

'Go to hell, traitor,' barked Cassandra, and for daring to speak she too was hoisted upward with a painful wrench.

'Traitor...' LaHayn rolled the word around his mouth, as if it were some rare delicacy to be sampled. 'Perhaps in the eyes of a fool. A true servant of the God-Emperor would understand I am anything but seditious.' He studied Verity. 'Will you answer me, Hospitaller? I know I could put these Sororitas to the question for days and nights before they broke – but you? I think you would not be so strong.'

'T-test me, if you will,' Verity managed, fighting down her fear.

LaHayn nodded. 'Perhaps another query then, something easier. Torris Vaun. Where is my errant witch?'

'Don't answer him,' snapped Cassandra. 'He knows where his lackey is. He's playing games with you.'

Cold amusement bubbled up in a frosty chuckle. 'My lackey? Ah, perhaps Vaun was that once upon a time, but those days are long gone, more's the pity. Perhaps if I had not allowed my attention to wander...' LaHayn snapped his fingers, putting an end to his reverie. 'No matter. What's done is done.' He watched Verity's face, thinking. 'Yes. I think I can answer my own questions. He brought you here, didn't he? Vaun found his way back and he used you to get here.' Another nod. 'Cunning. He's lost nothing of his skill.'

The unhooded tender spoke for the first time. 'There was no sign of the pyrokene on the upper tiers, ecclesiarch. If he is indeed within the perimeter of the keep–'

LaHayn snapped out orders. 'Triple the guards at the engine hall. Draw weapons for all adherents. Vaun is to be captured intact.'

The priest frowned. 'My lord, that will deplete numbers in the dungeon tiers.'

'I am well aware of that, Ojis,' retorted the deacon. 'Now do as I say. He'll try to breach the chamber. We'll take him there.' Ojis turned to relay the commands to the other tenders as LaHayn brought his attention back to the women. 'I suppose I should thank you. In your own muddling way, you have fulfilled the decree I set you: to bring me Torris Vaun alive.'

'That creature should have been terminated when the Argent Shroud found him on Groombridge,' snapped Isabel, nursing her injured arm.

LaHayn sneered. 'Do you know how rare he is? You can't begin to comprehend the investment he represents, the effort I have spent. His value is a thousand times that of your lives.' He looked away. 'I want him to live, woman. He is the last piece in a puzzle I have spent a lifetime assembling.'

'So it is you we should blame for Vaun's rampage, then?' Verity asked, finding a reserve of defiance inside her. 'All this leads back to you, lord deacon. You sent the killer to the librarium. You're the spider in the web, not that witch.'

'Your fortitude against my shadow was quite unexpected, I admit. As for Vaun, his time runs thin. I might say the same about you,' he frowned.

'You would spill the blood of the Daughters of the Emperor?' spat Cassandra. 'You would be dead at Vaun's hands if not for us. We saved your life at the Lunar Cathedral.'

'You did,' nodded LaHayn, 'and that is the only reason why I have not executed you out of hand. Sisters, you present me with a conundrum: what am I to do with you? I do so object to the waste of material with such promise.'

'If you will end us, then do it now,' demanded Miriya. 'The stink of the witch about you fills me with repugnance.'

He approached her. 'You are mistaken if you believe that this is a matter of collaboration, Sister Miriya. No, this is about *control*. My Great Work is dedicated to the harnessing of the psyker gene, just as the magos biologis craft germs for a virus bomb or the Mechanicus construct a cogitator.' Verity could see the deacon warming to his subject, the same arrogant poise he showed when he addressed the people during the Games of Penance moulding his manner. All he lacked was a pulpit from which to hold forth.

LaHayn gestured to Ojis and the tenders. 'Many have been brought into my fold, Sisters. Dedicated adherents to the God-Emperor, one and all. If only you understood my vision, you would see the perfection of it.'

Verity saw the opportunity and seized it before the others could take a breath to decry him. 'Then tell us, lord deacon. Explain what possible prospect could compel you to craft a secret opus, hidden from the eyes of the Imperium.'

He laughed. 'Oh, how arch. Do you think me so venal that an ill-worded taunt would make me spill my secrets to you?'

'But you will,' growled Miriya, 'because you crave an audience. You and Vaun are alike in many ways, deacon. Your egos drive you, you're compelled by the belief in your own rightness. You both live to prove that those who deny you are wrong.' Miriya's eyes narrowed. 'So do it. Attest to us how right you are.'

* * *

The ancient man-made halls of the Null Keep were just as he remembered them. The floors of old black basalt slid past and recollections crowded in on him. Sense-memory of his youth came forth, still dull at the edges with the lingering effect of the neuropathic philtre. The feeling of the cold stone against the slaps of his bare feet, the tenders watching the young prospects as they made them play hunt-and-seek in the service tunnels.

He halted in the half-dark, licking his dry lips, working the wire binding off his wrists. The psyker felt a peculiar sense of elation, perhaps even a little fear. He let himself toy with it for a few moments, before purging it from his mind. This place – it had been the site of his awakening, but also of his greatest betrayal.

Vaun's face twisted in anger. He hated himself for the way that he had admired LaHayn in the early days, the way that he had been only too happy to do the priest's bidding. But then, he had been immature and unschooled. Now he knew far better, and so he nurtured his hate of the man who had betrayed him.

He wondered how he could have missed something in his former mentor that seemed so obvious to him now. Like all the others LaHayn had covertly recruited from the tithes destined for the Black Ships, Vaun had only been a means to an end – a wager against the deacon's grand plan for glory. He reflected on this, and sensed there in the stone around him the faint traces of despair. So much had been done, so many horrors turned upon the minds and bodies of psykers in this place. Their collective misery stained the walls, it leaked like glutinous oil into the mentality of any who had the preternatural sense to feel it. Vaun shored up the opaque thought-walls inside him and blotted it out. It took much of his will to bring silence once more.

Gingerly, for the first time in months, the psyker allowed himself to think of the engine. He saw the device in vague, ghostly sketches, half-glimpsed, and faintly remembered flashes. The thought of the machine and its impossible geometries threatened pain. Conjuring it in his head was like probing a newly scabbed wound, and yet, it was the end goal for everything that transpired here. As much as Vaun feared it, he wanted it, but to lay his hands upon the device would not be an easy task. He drew himself into an inky pool of shadow as two tenders raced past him. To get what he wanted, Vaun thought, he would need to do that which he did best: engender anarchy and disorder.

As Miriya spoke, Verity watched the deacon carefully. 'Vaun showed us evidence of your experimentation on the witch-kin. Tell us why you are marshalling an army of freaks!'

LaHayn's face darkened with anger. 'Not freaks, you insolent woman. Enhancements. Improvements. My subjects are stepping stones on the road to the Emperor's destiny!'

'You dare to speak his name in this temple of horrors?' spat Isabel.

'Be quiet, girl,' he sneered. 'Your dogmatic order understands nothing of the Lord of Mankind's machinations.' LaHayn took a breath. 'I will indulge you, because it will amuse me to see your minds struggle to comprehend the awesome reality.' He dragged Verity to her feet. 'You know the story of the Heresy, of how the God-Emperor was felled by the archtraitor Horus and confined forever to the stasis of the Golden Throne.'

Reflexively, Verity made the sign of the aquila, the still-loose chains on her manacles clanking as she did so. 'And from there, the God-Emperor watches over us.'

'Yes…' LaHayn looked away. He seemed genuinely moved by the scale of the sacrifice made by the Master of Mankind. 'But what you do not know, what is recorded only in the most secret and arcane places, is the nature of the Great Work that He was about when Horus's perfidy drew him away.' The deacon's voice dropped to a low, reverent whisper. 'I have dedicated my life to that knowledge. I have found scraps of datum from across the galaxy, collated and sifted them, and drawn together a piecemeal vision of what

I believe to be the Emperor's lost labour. That is what I continue here, His works.'

'By cutting up psykers and stuffing them in bottles?' mocked Cassandra through gritted teeth. 'You'll have to do better than that.'

The deacon stalked away in annoyance, his voice rising to echo about the stone chamber. 'With each passing century, more and more psykers are born within the Imperium, far more than the Adeptus Ministorum will admit to. These are not mutant throwbacks, they are the hand of human evolution struggling to exert itself. The fools of the Ordo Malleus try to stem the tide but they are blind to the truth: the progression of mankind's psychic potential is inevitable, that it was the will of the Emperor to shepherd it, not destroy it.'

'Madness,' retorted Miriya. 'How can you claim to know the God-Emperor's mind? His intentions are beyond those of normal men. You've made some patchwork ideal from half-truths and rumour, then trumpeted it as fact. This is delusion, priest, *delusion*.'

He shook his head fiercely. 'Don't you see?' LaHayn hissed. 'He knew that one day all mankind would develop the power of the mind. It is our destiny. Think of it, imagine a time when every man is a god himself, a subject in an Imperium that spans the universe. Can you even begin to comprehend the glory of it?' The deacon's eyes glittered. 'Had He not been wounded so grievously by Horus, that destiny is where we would be now. He would have led us there. Instead He lies trapped on the Golden Throne, hobbled and frozen.'

Cassandra went pale. 'All humans, to become psykers? It sickens me to contemplate such a thing.'

'Bah!' roared LaHayn. 'If the psyker is such a canker, then why do we rely on them to light the way for our starships, to carry our communications, to fight on our battlefields? Where is your answer to that dichotomy? The Empire of Man would be in ruins without their kind, and if we could become them, we would know no boundaries.'

'The witch opens the gates to the Ruinous Powers–' began Verity.

'Only those who are weak,' insisted the deacon. 'The Ruinous Powers would be shattered if every human being could match them on their own ground.' He let out a sigh, suddenly spent with the effort of his argument.

Verity broke the silence that followed, her mind still whirling with the echo of the ecclesiarch's tirade. 'There are no words to contain the scale of heresy that you have uttered, lord deacon. This is… It is madness beyond all reason.'

'The colour of Chaos is on him,' spat Isabel. 'He must be tainted to believe such lies.'

LaHayn looked at her sadly. 'So limited in vision. So afraid to go beyond your rigid canon. If it is not written in your books of rules, then you cannot comprehend it happening, can you? You are afraid of anything that challenges your narrow views. It is easier for you to call me a heretic and claim I am loyal to the warp gods, than to accept I might be right.' He sneered at her. 'I pity you.' The priest-lord beckoned Ojis forward. 'I see now my breath has been wasted. I had hoped to offer you a place at my side, but none of you have the scope of vision I require.'

'If you kill us, more Battle Sisters will come,' blurted Verity. 'If we found the Null Keep, then so will Galatea.'

'If you are thinking of your little Mechanicus friend and that battered aeronef of Sherring's, don't waste your time,' said Ojis. 'Both were obliterated by our pyrokenes but an hour ago.'

'I will not kill you out of hand,' LaHayn turned away. 'The tenders are always short of fresh test subjects, psychic and latent. You'll serve them.'

Ojis worked the control in his hands and each of the chained women was hoisted up, a train of pulleys dragging them towards a cable lift.

'Even if you are right,' cried Verity, 'even if you are following the work of the Emperor, what can you possibly do? He lies in state on the Golden Throne, millions of light years from here. Will you make a militia of witches and have them tear His body from the heart of the Imperial Palace?'

'Terra was not the only place where He performed His experiments, child.' The deacon's voice faded as he wandered into the shadows of the workshop. 'Neva's connection to the warp was no happenstance. It was His doing. This planet is an experiment, and before He fell, the Emperor left something here.' LaHayn looked up to watch them vanish through a slit in the chamber wall. 'I'm close to unlocking the last secrets, and when I do, I will remake mankind in His image.'

The rough conduits of the mountain's lava tubes pre-dated the arcane constructions within the confines of the Null Keep. Many of the tubes still connected to the murmuring, quiescent core of the volcano, funnelling hot air and steam throughout the ashen cone. There were others, like this one, choked with collapsed stone and forgotten. Vaun used his hands and feet to ease himself down the angled tunnel, pressing his weight to the walls to drop metre by metre. It pleased him to see that the map he kept in his head had changed little. There was a kind of secret amusement that came to wandering freely within the very heart of LaHayn's castle.

Alone, the psyker could admit to himself that his scheme had not unfolded in the manner he had expected, but then his greatest skill had always been his ability to improvise. That was why LaHayn had selected him as his personal pyrokene assassin, it was the reason why Vaun had only ever been sent on the most dangerous, most problematic missions for his teacher. The irony that this was also the factor that had led to Vaun's ultimate rebellion was not lost on the psyker.

He dropped onto a shallow ledge. In the stone wall nearby there was a shuttered grille and beyond it – if his memory served him correctly – the uppermost tiers of the place the tenders called 'the sty'. Heavy bolts held the vent in place, but they were nothing more than simple steel. With care, Vaun applied his fingers to the first of them and concentrated. In moments, the metal was glowing cherry red. Gradually, the bolts began to sag and distend.

They were not cells, not in the sense that Miriya would have described them. Rather, the confinement that the gun servitors had forced them into were square pits sliced out of the volcanic rock, sheer-walled with iron grates closing off any means of escape. The Battle Sister peered up and made out the shape of a monorail line crossing the ceiling far above. No doubt sustenance was lowered in and cradles were used to hoist out the luckless when the tenders had need of them.

They had been kicked into a pit two at a time, Cassandra and Isabel in one, and Miriya here with the Hospitaller in another. After the machine-slaves had retreated, the Sister Superior called out to her comrades and was rewarded by a faint reply. Cassandra seemed angry and determined by the sound of her voice. Her strength by example would bolster poor injured Isabel.

Miriya completed a circuit of the chamber, probing each corner for anything of use, and at last sat heavily upon a rusted bedstead. Bruises were already forming in the places where her flesh had been slammed against the inside of her armour, first in the fall of the trap container, and now again from being tossed into this room.

'Any bones broken?' ventured Verity. Her face was dim in the gloom. 'Are you in pain?'

'Constantly,' frowned the Battle Sister. 'My trigger finger aches from lack of use.' She probed gingerly at her neck where the flesh was visible. 'Curious. I expected them to strip us naked.'

Verity coughed. 'Thank the God-Emperor for small mercies.'

Miriya shrugged. 'Merely an oversight on the part of that priest, Ojis. You know servitors, they will do only what they are told to do. He bade them bring us to the dungeons, and so…'. She gestured around at the black walls.

The Hospitaller came a little closer. When she spoke again, her voice was low, so as not to carry to the next cell. 'I am concerned for Sister Isabel's welfare. The wound upon her was quite severe. She may not last more than a day, perhaps two.'

'The Sisters of Katherine are resilient,' said Miriya. 'Isabel has known far worse than that. Mark me, she once took a glancing blow from the plague knife of a Death Guard and lived to tell of it. A week of fevers and delirium, but still she returned to the battle and gained honours.'

'I will pray for her, then. It is all I can do if I cannot minister to her injury.'

'I am sure she will thank you for that.'

Verity gave her a sideways glance. 'Truly? I am not so sure. In these days past in the company of you and your Battle Sisters, I have felt like an impediment. I fear Isabel, Cassandra and their like measure piety by martial prowess alone.'

'Then you are mistaken,' insisted the other woman. 'None of us doubt your dedication to the church, not after the strength of character you have shown, Sister. We are blessed to have you in our company. You may bear no weapon, but you have the soul of a Celestian.'

'Thank you.' Verity looked away. 'You have my sorrows on the passing of Portia. First Lethe, then Iona…'

'Each died in Terra's service,' said Miriya. 'We should all pray for an end so noble.'

'You have fought many battles together?'

A nod. 'On countless worlds. Insurrections and Wars of Faith. Witch hunts and castigations. We have spent much blood and ammunition together since our novitiate days at the Convent Sanctorum.'

Memory clouded Verity's eyes. 'My order also draws from the schola on Ophelia VII.' She gave a wan smile. 'I recall the day that Lethe was chosen for the Order of Our Martyred Lady. She was alight with joy.'

'Lethe was a good friend and a steadfast sister-in-arms. Know that I do not exaggerate when I say the squad felt her loss as keenly as you did.'

Verity nodded. 'I understand that now. To be Adepta

Sororitas... No matter which order we give fealty to, we are all defenders of the faith in our own way.'

'And your Sister, and Portia, and Iona are worthy to be named among them.' Miriya leaned close and placed a hand on Verity's shoulder. 'You understand that after what we have heard, we cannot suffer LaHayn to live a moment longer?'

Verity nodded again, the cold truth of the words lying heavy upon her. 'What must we do?'

'Purge him, Sister, or perish in the attempt.'

CHAPTER FIFTEEN

It was a dungeon, and the designs of such places had not changed in tens of millennia, since the very first days that men caged men and tortured them to gain secrets and superiority. Robbing their prisoners of even the dignity of that name, the tenders considered the tiers of cells in the Null Keep as a paddock for things they thought to be less than human. The clerics who had pledged loyalty to LaHayn's project kept his secret well. One glimpse at the men with eyes sewn shut and lips fused together in the test chambers was enough to instil that kind of devotion. There was always a need for more experimental subjects, whether it was for the psyker-slaves to practise on or for LaHayn's pet biologis adepts to doctor. The tech-priests liked to toy with the brains of the operant and the latent, trying to enhance the powers of the former and engender spontaneous psychic phenomena in the latter. These experiments were designed to induce 'breakouts' – artificially generated telepaths and psychokinetics – but more often than not, their end results were corpses or things that had to immediately be put down. Vaun stole past the testing rooms, the humming psychic landscape of silent screams prickling at the edges of his mind. His quarry lay elsewhere, deeper inside the prison levels.

There were only a few tenders in the main chamber, busying themselves with hushed discussion at a cogitator pulpit or ministering to the gaggle of gun servitors ambling about the perimeter of the room. The machine-helots were constantly in motion, never tiring of their endless patrols of the lava tube corridors.

Vaun recalled from his youth the way the once-men clanked about the stone floors, the mouths of their guns forever questing for something out of place, so that they might kill it. He had heard that the blanked minds of the servitors were festooned with implanted triggers, devices that would stir pleasure impulses in them whenever a runaway was brought down. The psyker used a maintenance ladder to convey him to the ceiling where the overhead cargo rail was fixed. Light did not reach up here, but his abhuman senses were more than enough to let him navigate his way, metre by careful metre.

Presently he came to a pulley and chain arrangement, dangling close to the guard station in the middle of the elliptical chamber. Vaun turned himself so that his feet were flat against the ceiling and his body pointed downward along the line of the chain. Below him, he could see the tenders in conversation, utterly unaware of the killer that hung silently above them.

'I've secured the new intake as you requested,' said the first, 'but there are not enough guards for the chamber.'

A nod from the second priest in grey. 'Ojis had them transferred to the engine room. The orders came directly from the deacon himself.'

'Is he here? Did you actually *see* Lord LaHayn?'

'I was not so blessed.'

Vaun sneered at the sanctimonious tone and gathered his power, cupping it in his mind like a hand shielding a candle flame. With a sudden shove, he pushed off and the heavy chain unravelled with a clanking rush.

The two tenders looked up in surprise, and their upturned faces met a rain of fire coming down. Streaks of unnaturally heated air ripped into them like laser bolts. Vaun spun about on the chain, letting the action whip him around. He spread the fingers of his free hand and let witchfire streak out from it in a wide red fan. The psionic flames lashed the priests who tried to flee and the slow-reacting servitor drones.

He dropped from the chain into a ready stance and moved to a tender who was beating madly at his burning robes. Ignoring the fire and the man's cries, Vaun hoisted the cleric off the floor and ripped a ring of heavy keys from his belt. The tender tried to say something, but Vaun threw him hard against the wall and he fell away. Flame licked about the ebon stonework, pooling in runnels of molten liquid.

Stubber rounds cracked past the killer and Vaun ignored them. At the back of his mind, he could feel the gaze of other psykers upon him, and in the half-dark it was possible to glimpse dulled eyes peering out from barred slots in cell doors. *Be ready, cousins.* He broadcast the thought to all of them. *Freedom is close at hand.*

The slow gun-slaves were gathering themselves and formulating plans of engagement. Vaun could hear them clicking orders to one another in the metallic prattle of machine code. He had to be quick. Stepping over a smoking body he found the second tender on his hands and knees, feeling his way towards an escape tunnel. Vaun took a handful of his robes and spun him over. Grotesque burns covered the pink-black mass of the priest's face and his hands were swollen claws. This one also had a hoop of keys, which went into Vaun's grip with the others. The tender tried to say something, but his heat-ravaged throat could manage nothing more than a mew. Vaun broke his neck with a savage kick and left him to choke.

Gun servitors advanced on him as he reached the wide cogitator pulpit. Vaun rammed the keys home in twin slots. Normally, two tenders would have been needed to perform the action at either end of the long console, but Vaun's psychic reach had none of the limits of his flesh and blood limbs. The keys turned, one by hand and the other by telekinesis, and a hooting tocsin warned of the opening of the cell doors. The servitors hesitated, weapons deflecting from the single target at the pulpit to the dozens of new ones boiling out of their confinement. Vaun tipped back his head and laughed as the ponderous machine-slaves were beaten down and torn apart by angry psykers.

He watched his erstwhile brethren fight like beasts. These were a poor lot, he realised, and barely one of them with the skills or brains of those he had recruited before Groombridge. The late, dull-witted Rink and disagreeable Abb had been the model of genius in comparison. These ones had no discipline, not an iota of the self-control that Vaun demanded from his men, and in such low numbers they would not last long against a concerted effort by the deacon's forces. The poor fools all bore scarring where the phase-iron of their cells had burnt them time and time again, but they would do. Even an army of rats would be better than no army at all.

'Cousins,' he called, the word cutting through the acrid, smoky air. 'There's more of those tinplate clockworks down here, and plenty of tender tenders to boot.' The escapees replied with lusty cheers. 'The time has come to pay back that old whoreson LaHayn in kind. Who among you would join me in handing out some reprisal?'

'*Aye*,' they called, tearing guns from flesh-mounts and surging into the tunnels. Vaun laughed again, his amusement lost in the clamour.

Thin drools of meat smoke dropped into the prison pit, pooling around the ankles of the women. With quick gestures, Miriya directed Verity back against the black stone walls, concealing her in the shadows. Gunfire, the crackling of flames and shouts of pain filtered down to them. The metal grille over the cell was sent clanging with noise as a troop of gun servitors stamped across it, weapons letting out chugs of stubber fire.

'It's him, all right,' growled Miriya. 'I know that voice. The witch clings to life like some kind of parasite.'

'I don't understand,' replied the Hospitaller. 'What could he want down here in the dungeons?'

The Sororitas kept her eyes fixed on the bars above, coiling the beads of her chaplet ecclesiasticus in her hand. From one end of the rosary of black pearls dangled a silver insignum in the shape of the letter 'I', dressed with a stern skull imprint: the sigil of the Witch Hunters. 'You heard his words. He is rallying them, inciting them. Like a lit torch to a drum of promethium.'

As if to give weight to her words, a flash of flames licked over the ceiling above, and a tender ran past, his robes burning.

Verity blanched at the strangled sounds of the priest's death screams.

'It appears we may not have the luxury of a considered escape,' added the Sister Superior dryly.

The popping of weapons died off and soon they heard the scramble of footsteps overhead. Faces, dirty with soot and grime peered down at the women with mixtures of avarice and hatred. A familiar, insouciant aspect soon joined them. 'Well, well. What an interesting reversal of fortunes this is,' said Vaun, savouring his amusement. 'How does it feel to be the prisoner now, Sisters?'

Miriya seemed to lack the words to convey her cold, hard anger at that moment, and so she simply turned her head and spat into the darkness.

Vaun's smile waned. 'I had thought Viktor would have killed you for me. I see that he couldn't even get that right.' The psyker sighed, and some of the other escapees about him giggled in amusement. 'Enjoy your new accommodations, ladies. I'm sure you'll find them just as disgusting as I once did.'

'You can't leave us here,' Verity blurted.

'Of course I can. You let me live when you had the chance to kill me, Sister Miriya. Now I have the opportunity to return the favour!' Vaun mocked, and he turned to go. 'While I go on to lay waste to this planet, you'll still be here, trapped and helpless, waiting for a rescue that will never come. Perhaps you'll die from starvation or infection. You might find a trickle of water from the upper tiers, which will sustain you for a time. Eventually, though, you'll need to find food.' He leered at the Hospitaller. 'But with nobody to feed you, there's only one source of meat down there.' With a callous laugh, he moved off, his new cohorts trickling away after him.

'Bastard.' The word slipped from Verity's lips before she realised it, and her cheeks reddened. 'Sister, forgive my profanity. It was unseemly of me...'

Miriya watched the grille carefully to be sure that Vaun had gone. 'On the contrary, Sister, I concur. He *is* a bastard, of the most loathsome order.' The Celestian turned her attention back to her chaplet. For a moment, Verity thought the woman was going to commence a prayer, but instead she gripped the skull icon adorning the insignum and turned it counter-clockwise. Workings inside the chaplet clicked and whirred, and with an oiled hiss a shaft of razored metal emerged from the device. Miriya saw her watching. 'Case-hardened argentium-carbide steel,' she explained, 'so that a Battle Sister may grant herself the Emperor's Peace if she is captured.'

Verity's face blanched. 'You don't intend to...?'

Miriya shook her head. 'It is not yet time for either of us to kneel before the Golden Throne. Not while there is work to be done.' The Battle Sister wrapped her fingers around the silver fleur-de-lys on her breastplate and twisted it, yanking the metal decoration off its rivet. She turned it in her other hand and held it like a push-dagger.

The Hospitaller's eyes widened as she began to understand the other woman's goal. 'How can I help?'

Miriya shrugged off her battle cloak and tensed. 'Pray for divine intervention.' The Battle Sister drew back and then ran at the wall. At the last second she used the rusted bedstead like a springboard and threw herself at the stone facia. Sparks flew as the chaplet blade and the steel flower bit into black rock. Impossibly, Miriya hung there, clinging to her improvised pitons. With slow, unbending will, Verity watched her push upward, grinding the knifepoints against the sheer basalt for leverage.

The younger woman did as she was asked, and began a whispered litany.

The priest Ojis bowed so low that LaHayn thought the man's hooked nose would touch the stone tiles. 'Your grace, there has been an incident on the dungeon tiers…'

'Elucidate.'

'A failure of containment in the cell blocks.' The deacon thought for a moment he detected a measure of reproach in the priest's voice, but he let it go. 'It appears the locking mechanisms were released. Several test subjects and aberrants scheduled for exploratory execution have escaped. There are not enough gun servitors to police the entire level…'

'How did this happen?' he snapped. 'Whose failure is this, Ojis? Answer me.'

'My lord, I did warn you about depleting the numbers of–'

LaHayn advanced on the man. 'You dare lay the blame at *my* feet?'

Ojis paled. 'No, no, my lord.' He backed away a step. 'I was merely making an observation.'

The deacon snarled and looked away. 'This is not coincidence, Confessor Ojis. The witch Vaun is at work here. I know his methods. This is a smokescreen.' He tapped his lips. 'You are to take direct control of the frateris militia inside the keep. Get below into the dungeon tiers and bottle up those freaks. Terminate them all.' LaHayn began to walk away.

'But, your holiness,' piped Ojis. 'I am not a warrior.'

'We are all soldiers in the Emperor's war,' the deacon replied. 'Never forget that.' He threw Ojis a last look. 'I am relocating to the engine chamber. I do not want any more disruptions.'

'But what about Vaun?'

LaHayn grimaced. 'He'll come to me of his own accord, mark my words.'

* * *

'Emperor, hear me, give me strength,' the Celestian prayed, her arms tight with tension and effort. 'Grant this mortal shell a grain of wisdom, a teardrop of Your might...' With the last word, she pushed herself up to the very lip of the prison pit. Miriya did not look down. If she fell now, it could break bones or worse, snap her neck. As she had told the Hospitaller, she did not have the luxury of death while the witchkin was still loose. 'Channel Thyself to me, make Your will known through this vessel.'

Grasping the metal grate over the pit, the Battle Sister turned herself about and found the place where a throw-bolt secured it in place. She ground her boots into the walls, pressed the ceramite curve of her armour's spine to the iron grille and steadied herself. 'I am Your wrath,' intoned Miriya, completing the catechism. 'Your fury and resolve. Give me strength, I am the Hand of the Emperor.' The words released a flush of adrenaline into her body and the Celestian threw her full weight against the bolt. The metal clanged and bent, but did not give way.

She let out a snarl of anger and effort. Her boots slipped on the stone, then found purchase again; she would not get another chance at this. 'Give me strength,' spat Miriya, drawing concentration from the acts of faith performed by the living saints. *'I am the Hand of the Emperor!'* New energy coursed through her, fuelled by her devotion, and she slammed herself against the metal. With a screech of breaking steel, the bolt snapped in two. Suddenly she was on the floor of the dungeon, the iron grille hanging open behind her.

A ragged figure – shorn of all hair it was impossible to know it if were male or female – gawped at the sight of the Sororitas, and ran away down the stone corridors, calling out in strangled yelps. Miriya ignored it and set to work dragging a pulley cradle into place on the overhead rail. Within a few minutes, Verity had joined her and soon they were hoisting Cassandra and Isabel out of the other pit. The Hospitaller went to the injured woman's side and began to minister to her. Broken slats of wood discarded in the melee went into a makeshift splint.

Miriya surveyed the corridor. All along the walls, cell doors lay hanging open, some discoloured by flames or pocked with bullet impacts. There were dead servitors in heaps, some distinguishable only because their brass and steel bionics were visible among the blackened meat and bones of their corpses. The bodies of tenders lay about in corners, and in some places the remains of what were likely the prisoners of the Null Keep, malnourished and shabby humans still fresh with operation scars.

Cassandra approached her squad commander and gave her a hollow-eyed, determined look. 'What say you, Sister Superior?'

'This indignity will not stand, Cassandra. We must see this place wiped from existence, as quickly as His spirit will let us.'

'Aye,' nodded the veteran Battle Sister. 'My thoughts still reel with the enormity of this madness. It beggars my belief to comprehend it all... To think that at the start of this we were chagrined at such an assignment.' She looked away. 'With each step we take on Neva, we spiral closer to insanity!'

Verity broke in with a sharp cry. 'Someone's coming.'

The ragged figure had returned, and this time with company. There were six of them, all in the shapeless coveralls of the keep's inmates. Miriya raised an eyebrow as she realised that some of them were carrying Godwyn-De'az pattern bolters. The largest of them, a scarred female, had the Sister Superior's plasma pistol tucked in her waistband. The psyker prisoners were wary: they knew that these women would be far more difficult prey than the slow-brained servitors.

Cassandra broke the watchful silence. 'Those weapons are icons of the Imperial Church, and they do not belong to you. Put them down, now.'

The large woman grunted like an animal. 'These toys not yours no more. Mine.' She prodded herself in the chest.

'Where is Vaun?' demanded Miriya. 'Where is your leader?'

The woman spat. 'Ain't my leader, ya painted chapel harlot. He's taken those who'd follow and gone.'

From the corner of her eye, Miriya saw Cassandra fingering her rosary. 'You are in charge here, then?'

The woman nodded. 'Got something to say 'bout it?'

Cassandra frowned. 'I find myself wondering. How could your mother have given birth to an ork with pink skin?'

It took a second for the insult to register, but then the hulking female was swearing and grabbing at the gun. The Battle Sisters moved as one. Miriya tossed the broken fleur-de-lys like a throwing star and used it to open the neck of a witch balling ticks of lightning around his fingers. Cassandra's chaplet, with its hidden blade revealed, crossed the space between the Sororitas and the prisoners, burying itself between the beady eyes of the ringleader. The other four were still reacting as the Battle Sisters engaged them hand-to-hand, breaking necks and snapping bones with deft motions and kicks from their boots. The last of them skittered away, pressing fingertips to his head. A wall of hard air rolled forward and battered the two of them back. Miriya felt a rush of panic as she was shoved towards the dark maw of the open prison-pit.

A gunshot rang out and the last errant psyker fell screaming, clutching his stomach, the invisible force dissipating instantly. The Celestian turned to see Isabel with her recovered bolter wobbling in an unsteady, off-hand grip.

'A fine shot,' she managed.

Isabel's face was sallow and clammy. 'Not so much. I was aiming for his head.'

Cassandra handed Miriya her plasma pistol. 'They must have found our wargear.'

'Perhaps it was in a storage cell nearby?' opined Verity. 'I should search for my medicus case. I doubt these commoners would have known what to do with it.'

'Be quick,' ordered Miriya. 'Vaun has sown havoc here for his own reasons, and we should take advantage of it while we can. We must contact the Canoness.'

Above the gloom of the dungeon tiers, the Null Keep's inner chambers spread open into honeycombs of interlocking voids. In the past these spaces had been formed around great reservoirs of magma flowing from the core of Neva, but in the thousands of years since they had become cool and dank, turned over to the works of man.

Like all the spaces within the volcano-citadel, the air was forever heavy with a dry, stone-baked heat that took the moisture from a man's lungs. Vaun moved up one of the broad spiral ramps that led to the upper levels, patting sweat off his brow. The arid, claustrophobic air welled up unpleasant memories of his youth, and he damped them down with a determined snarl. At his heels, the loose gang of escapees followed. Their initial bellicose manner had softened somewhat as they left the dungeons behind. The smarter ones among them were starting to think beyond the next five minutes, wondering what good the breakout would do them if they had no plan, no escape route, and no direction. Predictably, they looked to their rescuer for guidance.

Vaun hesitated in the shadow of an ascent ramp and held up his hand, halting the others. The open chamber ranged above them was a maintenance bay for the landing pads high on the peak of the volcanic mount. Cranes as tall as watchtowers cradled a handful of coleopters and the pregnant shapes of cargo blimps.

'Skyships,' said a lisping voice behind him. 'We should take one and fly for it.'

Vaun looked back at them, not bothering to single out the speaker. 'Are any of you pilots?' Silence greeted him. 'Do any of you know where the deacon hides his bolter turrets on the outside of the keep? No? Then by all means, be my guest.'

'We might be able to do it...' ventured another, a gangly female. She pointed upward. 'Skinny up the cranes, maybe.'

'You'd be dead before you tasted sky,' growled the psyker. 'Stick with me and you might live to see daylight.' He pointed towards the cable-car train lying unattended at a nearby dock platform. 'We'll take that to the upper tiers. If we do it quietly, they'll never know it until we're knocking at the door.'

'The upside?' hissed the bucktoothed lisper. 'You wanna go

deeper into the keep?' He rolled his eyes. 'The tenders keep us outta those decks for a reason, mate. It's runnin' alive with warp-poison up yonder!'

'Perhaps,' admitted Vaun, 'but not in the way that you can understand it.' He gave them a cold smile. 'Trust me, cousins, the only way out is to go through the deacon.'

'So you say,' retorted the man. 'We're grateful for you throwing the switches an' all, but I reckon from here on in, we'll take our chances.'

The psyker took a threatening step closer to the escapee. 'I didn't bust you out as a kindness, little fellow. You're all in my debt now. You can repay it by doing what I tell you.'

The lisping man twitched. Vaun sensed the twinkle in his aura as the escapee coiled up whatever witch-mark power he had in preparation to strike. 'You're not the boss o' me–'

Vaun did it so quickly that the prisoner had no time to scream, there was just a flash of yellow across everyone's retinas as the fireball flew from his hand and burnt its way into the lisping man's chest. Flames sizzled and popped, the corpse turning about in a wild pirouette before collapsing in a heap. The other ex-prisoners staggered backwards, the brutality of the quick murder had taken every one of them off-guard. The psyker gave his charges a level look, reeling in the enjoyment he felt. 'LaHayn's up there,' he said, jerking a thumb at the roof, 'and he's holding on to a prize bigger than anything you wastrels have dreamed of. I'm going to take it, and you're going to help me.'

'The train, right?' said the gangly woman, nervously. 'What're we dallyin' for, then?'

Within moments the cable carriages had cast off and began their slow ascent of the funicular rails. A warm anticipation buzzed in Vaun's hindbrain. He couldn't be sure if it was some side-effect of proximity to LaHayn's engine chamber or the rush of his own excitement, but the further they climbed, the more he failed to hold back a predatory grin on his face.

There were fumes everywhere, and the air tasted like sour meat on Ojis's tongue. His trembling fingers searched forward over the metal grid of the elevator cage's floor, tracing through expanding puddles of oily fluid and wet spongy masses of what could only have been spilled brain matter. The confessor's legs did not appear to be working, and so with the dignity of his exalted station left far behind, he did his best to haul himself out of the lift. His mind reeled, the chaos that had erupted around him fuzzing his recollection of events.

He had been in the cage, descending into the dungeon tiers with his adjutants and the handful of servitors he had been able to divert away from the deacon's blockade. The chimes sounded as the elevator arrived in the staging atrium, and then...

Then there had been gunfire and screaming, the detonation of something large and pulpy spattering all over his hood and robes. Black-clad shapes, glittering like sword beetles, brandishing weapons. *An ambush*.

'This one is still alive,' the voice rattled in his ears, as if something had been knocked loose and broken inside his skull.

Strong, gaunt fingers took him by the arms and hoisted him up. The priest's vision swam with pain as his legs turned uselessly beneath him. Bone was poking wetly from his right knee joint. He managed a gasp as his mask was pulled off.

A face gained definition before him. A woman, after a fashion, sun-toned skin marred with grime and lines of blood. She had eyes like blue diamonds and the set of her jaw was cruel. With a start, Ojis recognised her. She saw it too.

'I am Sister Miriya, of the Order of Our Martyred Lady, and you are my captive. Answer my questions and you will be granted mercy.'

Ojis blinked. His eyes were gummed with gluey fluids. He managed to nod woodenly.

'He has the sigils of a confessor on his rosary,' said the first voice again, from somewhere behind him. 'This one was with LaHayn before.'

'Yes,' said Miriya, studying him carefully. 'Ojis, wasn't it?'

The priest paled. She knew his name as well! This was going very badly. 'Please...'

'What are you doing here?' she demanded. 'Where's the deacon?'

'I was sent to suppress... escape.' His cranium ached as he tried to look around. Ojis could make out more dead bodies in the corridor. Whatever had happened down here, they had arrived to late to do anything about it. 'His holiness... in the engine chamber, at the central deep.'

'Engine chamber?' repeated a new voice. He saw another woman, clad in white robes, her golden hair in distress. 'The Null Keep has an engine? But this place is a building, not some kind of vessel.'

Ojis felt woozy as he shook his head. 'Not... Not that kind of engine.' He licked his lips. 'Please... Help me.'

Miriya drew him closer. 'Where is the keep's communicatory? Speak, heretic!'

'Above,' he wheezed out the word. 'Can't get there without me.' He raised a hand. A fat gold ring glittered on one finger. 'I... I have the command signet.'

'Confirmed,' said the other Battle Sister. 'There is a governance mechanism preventing access to the uppermost levels of the citadel.'

Miriya's face soured and she let the cleric drop in a heap. He cried out in pain, but she ignored him. 'There is nothing so low as a false priest, Confessor Ojis. The God-Emperor keeps a singular hell reserved for your kind.'

Ojis looked up at her. 'But... the ecclesiarch is enlightened. He knows the way...' He broke off, coughing.

'The way to damnation,' Miriya replied, pressing a plasma pistol to his forehead. The gun hummed to life.

'No... No. Please. I recant!' burbled Ojis. 'Please, Sister Miriya. You and I, we are both the kindred of the cloth. I beg you!'

Miriya paused. 'You have betrayed the Imperial Church and the God-Emperor of Mankind. What could you possibly hope to beg from me, heretic?'

In a small voice he said: 'Forgiveness?'

The chilling look in her eyes was all the answer he received. Her finger tightened on the trigger.

'Sister, wait,' called one of the other women. 'You cannot shoot him.'

Ojis sagged, relief flooding him. *I'm saved!*

'Why?' demanded Miriya.

The other Battle Sister indicated the lock panel on the elevator controls. 'This device not only requires the key of his signet ring, but also an optic scan.' She pointed at the confessor's face with a combat blade. 'Had you shot him with a plasmatic burst, his eyes would have been destroyed.' She offered the knife to Miriya. 'You should use this instead.'

Miriya accepted the weapon with a gracious nod. 'Thank you, Cassandra. Please, hold him down for me.'

The confessor's body performed one last service for the church: as the lift cage arrived at the top of the ascent channel, she threw it into the elevator bay. The still-warm mass of corpse-flesh set off the servo-skulls in the guardian niches at the door to the communicatory, drawing their laser fire. Cassandra and Isabel used the distraction to shoot down the machines and move in. Inside the cramped chambers, blinded vox-adepts cowered in corners, too terrified to react against the intruders, constantly mumbling the message hymns burned into their neural tissues. Thin slivers of watery daylight peered in through observation ports, showing the Nevan sun as it climbed over the rocky crags beyond.

Miriya made the sign of the aquila and addressed the central vox terminal, speaking directly into a bronze mask that turned to present a mouth grille to her. In a clear but fatigued voice, she said a string of hallowed code phrases, prayer lines seemingly chosen at random from the Books of Alicia. The machine knew the cipher, as every communications device in the Imperium did: an emergency Sororitas contact protocol, known only to those of high Celestian rank and above.

'Hear me,' she began, 'I seek audience with the honoured Canoness Galatea of the Order of Our–'

'Miriya.' Galatea's voice crackled back at them through the mask-speaker. She turned the Battle Sister's name into a curse.

'If you wish to confess, the time for that has passed. You should consider yourself deserter extremis.'

Isabel choked back a rebuke. 'How... How could she answer so quickly? Such a message should take hours–'

'Silence your Sister, Miriya,' retorted the Canoness. 'Look to the west. Your censure comes on swift wings, errant one.'

Verity pressed her face to one of the window slits. 'I think I see something. Bright glitters in the dawn sky.' She looked back at Miriya. 'Aircraft?'

'A reprisal force is inbound to your position, Sister Superior,' continued Galatea. 'Once I understood your wilful denial of my orders, I had the captain of the *Mercutio* scry the area about Metis City from orbit. His sense servitors tracked that aeronef you stole all the way to the wastelands.'

'There is an explanation for my every action,' insisted Miriya. 'I initiated this very communication to inform you of my location–'

'*You disobeyed me,*' raged the Canoness. 'You took this world's most wanted man into your own custody. What possible explanation could you have for that?'

'I have uncovered a conspiracy of which Torris Vaun is only one facet, my lady,' Miriya said cautiously. 'Within this fortress, the lord deacon is engaged in a dire plan of the highest heresy. I shall willingly give myself to any punishment you will ask of me, but I must insist you first hear this!'

The vox channel crackled for a moment, then Galatea's voice returned, resigned and grim. 'The transports will be within strike range in less than five minutes, Miriya. You have until then to convince me not to kill you.'

The Battle Sister began to speak, explaining all that had transpired since the assault on Baron Sherring's mansion.

CHAPTER SIXTEEN

Each time he entered the chamber, there was a moment when Viktor LaHayn recalled the very first time he had done so. He remembered the rough hessian blindfold being pulled from his eyes, the strange, directionless green-blue light impinging on his vision. He remembered the hand of the Gethsemenite abbot on his wrist, tight with anticipation, but it was the giddy rush of vertigo that came when he laid eyes on the engine that had always stuck with him.

The abbot was dead now, murdered along with the rest of his sect by Vaun, but the great device rumbled on unchanged, the two great spinning rings of black steel forever turning about the construct's central axis like spun coins. LaHayn had to stop to look at the thing. The motion of the rings, the slow orbit of the metallic rods within them; their movement made him light-headed. It was a marvel of ancient and lost technology, the way that the disparate components worked without touching one another or apparently connecting in any way. The engine was as large as a house, yet it floated above the floor of the chamber effortlessly, steady as a rock. Nothing held it up but the azure glow. The tech-adepts had once tried to explain the method of the sciences behind it, but LaHayn had dismissed them. It was enough for him to know that the engine was the creation of the God-Emperor.

He approached it. A low fence of brass bars kept the unwary from getting too close, but the deacon ignored it, scattering a couple of cowering Mechanicus engineers as he stepped into the nimbus of the machine's energy field. The adepts clicked and whirred at one another in urgent data streams. Like his tenders, they too were garbed in featureless grey robes.

Once, as with every other tech-priest in his service, they had been loyal members of the Cult of the Machine God, sworn servants of Mars. But that had been before LaHayn's agents had recruited them, by kidnapping, subornment or by acts of piracy. To a man, they had all protested and struggled against the demands he had made on them – *until* he showed them the engine. It was pitiful, in a way. Every single Mechanicus he took had willingly broken their oath and pledged themselves to his service the moment they laid eyes on the device. They knew it for what it was: a physical connection to the great works of the Emperor. They had many names for it: the Psymagnus Apparat, Anulus Rex, the GodHand... But LaHayn preferred the designation the Gethsemenites had given the device. They simply called it the engine, a fitting name for a device that held the power to remake the stars.

The last days of the God-Emperor were a mystery to many. His actions in the dark time before the betrayal of the Warmaster Horus were shrouded in mythology and layers of obfuscation ten thousand years thick, but in all the holy tomes that spoke of His final actions before the enshrinement on the Golden Throne, there were mentions of His Works, of the secret machinations He was about in the laboratoria beneath the Holy Palace on Earth.

In forbidden tomes, LaHayn had discovered scraps of old creed that the current generation of the Ministorum had declared apocryphal. He collected references to things that flew in the face of the current beliefs, names that none dared to speak, talk of star-children and the births of new gods.

The deacon courted death a hundred times over just for daring to possess such knowledge.

Through all his gathered secrets, he traced one thread, unravelling it from the tapestry of the God-Emperor's clouded legacy. That strand of causality spanned the light years that stretched from Terra to Neva, undeniable proof that this distant world was touched by His hand, just as it was coloured by the passage of the warp. It was plain to see once the pieces were assembled, and the priest-lord saw it with shining eyes. The engine was the Emperor's bequest to humanity, to Viktor LaHayn himself. Like a sentinel, it had waited here beneath the stone walls of the Null Keep, waiting for one with the breadth of vision to know its purpose and awaken it. There was absolutely no doubt in Viktor's mind that he was that man.

The deacon came as close as he dared to the spinning rings and held out a hand, letting his fingertips enter their aurora. Trickles of force shifted through him, and he became a prism for their light. It was a gentle caress, the merest fraction of the true energy inside. He could feel the primitive matter of his brain struggling to comprehend the power of it, and always, the same fleeting sense of something magnificent just beyond his reach. *If only...*

Not for the first time, LaHayn let himself drift and dream about what it would be like to know such capability. *To have the power to become one with the machine... To touch the distant mind of my god...* The enormity of that idea struck the breath from him.

'Soon.' The words fell from his lips. 'It will come to pass.'

He retreated beyond the cordon and found a tender on his knees, the cleric's face flat against the floor so he would not lay eyes upon the holy workings of the engine. 'My lord deacon,' said the priest, 'word from the high crags. A force of strike craft approach in skirmish formation. The sensor servitors read them as bearing the mark of the Sororitas.'

His lips thinned. 'How many?'

'Ten, perhaps more. Their silhouettes match the configurations of troop transports and armour carriers.'

LaHayn swore an oath so base that the tender flinched. 'My hand has been forced. The Sisters of Battle are too narrow-minded to accept any explanations of our mission here.' He sighed. 'They cannot be allowed to interfere. You are to decant the pyrokenes. Deploy them in defence of the keep.'

The tender dared to look up. 'How many, my lord?'

'All of them. The time for half-measures is over.'

Orders were relayed; commands became deeds. In the primary chambers where the ebon basalt vaults held ranges of glass cubicles, the hanging cable guides and open crane claws turned to the work of unlocking the psyker pods from their mountings. Ferrying them in the same steady, patient manner as burrowing insects would convey precious eggs within a colony mound, the machines took the huge fluid-filled beakers to exit chambers and tipped the contents upon the dark rock floor. One by one, LaHayn's slumbering army of witches was being rudely awakened, and in the depths of their doctored minds, anger lit fires that the tenders directed towards the oncoming enemy.

Within the motion of this activity, in among all the moving carriages and turning cogs of the keep's cableways, a single train of cargo trailers moved against the flow, passing upward unseen towards the closed tiers.

The pilots brought their craft through the treacherous rocky straits surrounding the Null Keep, keeping low to avoid the desultory puffballs of anti-aircraft fire from bolter emplacements on the upper battlements. Canoness Galatea had not considered opening a channel to the citadel with any request for surrender, those within could clearly see the black and silver livery of the transport flyers and they knew who it was that approached. If the denizens in the keep had wanted to sue for peace, they had ample opportunity to ask for it – not that it would have been granted.

The razor-cliffed valleys leading to the tower of black stone were narrow and forbidding. Galatea had consulted with the Seraphim commander Sister Chloe during the flight from the staging area, and via hololithic conference with the sensors officer aboard the *Mercutio*, a rough and ready plan of assault had been drawn up for the attack on the keep. Stealth, it seemed, was the key strength of the location – but once that advantage had been squandered, it was no more or less defensible than the dozen other castles and strongpoints that her order had broken in the past. She hid it well, but there was a small fraction of the Canoness that was thrilled by the prospect of battle. Too long in the high realms of Neva's moneyed society classes had made her feel distant and removed from the true purpose of the Sisterhood, and the glory that was to be taken in punishing the disloyal.

Her intention was not to lay waste to the tower, but to break the lines of defence and take those within as prisoners of the church. She numbered the lord deacon and the errant Sisters of Miriya's unit among her quarry – it would be easier for her troops to gather everyone and return them to Noroc for a full Inquisitorial inquest rather than attempt to sort through the web of accusations here. Whatever the outcome today, it would mean that Neva's church and state would be forever changed in the aftermath.

It was difficult for the Canoness to countenance the idea of a senior ecclesiarch in league with psykers, but worse treacheries had been known to happen.

The flyers split from formation and began a rapid deployment, dropping to skate their landing gear across the black sand without slowing to a hover. Drop ramps yawned open and Battle Sisters threw themselves out, trailing descent tethers that would slow them and prevent the women from breaking their necks on landing. Other ships disgorged the flat ingots of tanks. Galatea saw the bulldozer blades of Repressors grinding forwards and the black shapes of Immolators bearing down on the keep's outer perimeter. Units of Sister Retributors and Sister Seraphim went with them, the lightening sky making their armour glitter.

Chloe's voice crackled in her ear. 'My lady, we are about to deploy. Engagement commences on your mark.'

'Begin,' she said into her vox pick-up. At that word of command, her flyer dipped towards the ground and the Celestians in her personal guard made ready to disembark. It happened quickly: the ship scraped dirt with a hollow howl and Galatea threw herself out of the gaping hatchway. Then in a flood of hot downwash from the thrusters, the angular shape was powering away and the Canoness came to her feet surrounded by walls of black stone and women hungry for battle. 'Press forward,' she began, but a thunderous salvo of fireballs cut into the air ahead of the tanks, drowning out her voice with their passage.

'Flamers?' said one of the Celestians. 'Inferno guns, perhaps?'

There was a familiar taint in the air, a greasy thickness that made her gut coil. 'Not flamers,' she growled, 'witchfire.'

Close to the keep, hidden gates were rolling open and out of them streamed figures in mad, violent disorder. To a man, they were all ablaze, pulling streams and spheres of unnatural flame from their bodies to hurl at the Sisters.

Galatea crossed herself with the sign of the aquila and began firing.

The way down from the communicatory was nowhere near as swift or as simple as their ascent had been. The elevator cradle steadfastly refused to operate at Verity's increasingly frustrated commands, and finally the Sisters were forced to descend to the lower tiers of the keep by the zigzags of steel staircase that ran alongside the lift shaft. They moved in near-silence, never speaking, with only the occasional grunt of pain from Isabel to punctuate their passage. They went down and down for what seemed like uncountable numbers of steps. At random, clatters of moving metal or distant explosions would find their way into the shaft and filter to their ears. The sounds seemed vague and second-hand, the dim echoes of a battle being fought by others.

Eventually, the stairs spread out to a shallow deck of

corrugated metal and bare, open grids. Verity made the mistake of glancing down at her feet and her stomach knotted tight inside her belly. In the ruddy gloom, it appeared as if she were standing on thin air, the access shaft dropping away into abyssal depths below her boots. She looked away, taking care from that moment to keep her gaze steady at head height.

There was a balcony at the edge of the deck; sawtooth bays along one side allowed small cable cars festooned with guide-lines and metallic cogs to dock there. They resembled smaller versions of the omnibus-carriages from Noroc, even down to the protruding runner board at the rear and the handle-operated switching gear. Other docks were empty, home only to gently twitching bunches of cable.

Cassandra studied the bronze dials set into the nearest of the cable cars. 'The tenders must utilise these carts to travel around the keep's interior.' She plucked at a row of rocker switches, each labelled with a string of text in High Gothic. 'Destinations within the tower are listed here. Some are locked off.'

'Show me,' Verity watched Miriya drift closer. Cassandra pointed out switches with fine brass cages over them and lock-imprints where a signet was to be placed. The Battle Sister fished Ojis's severed finger from a compartment at her belt and tested it in the locks – the switches obediently opened.

'This one...' said the Celestian, picking a cable car. 'The late confessor has kindly provided us with passage to the restricted tiers of the citadel.'

Isabel's voice wavered with suppressed pain and reflexively Verity went to her to check her dressings. 'Were not the Canoness's directives clear, Sister Superior? Forgive me, but did she not say we should attempt to link up with the landing force outside?'

Miriya nodded. 'That is fully my intention.' With a clicking of oiled gears, the concertina-mesh gate on the cable car opened. 'But only after we have completed our immediate mission.'

'To find Vaun?' asked Verity, absently dabbing a counter-infective philtre on Isabel's bandages.

The Celestian shook her head. 'To kill him.'

The pyrokenes moved forward against the Sororitas skirmish lines in a tidal wave of unholy fire, the coiling stink of rotten, burning meat advancing ahead of them on the dry wind. Jets of orange promethium from heavy flamers on the front ranks arced outward to meet them, but the burning liquid splashed harmlessly about the witch-soldiers, lapping at their heels like breaking surf.

From her vantage point, Canoness Galatea saw the failure of the guns and barked an order into her vox. 'Bolters, forward! Projectile and energy weapons only.' With unerring precision, the Battle Sisters with flamer weapons dropped back to let their comrades with boltguns and meltaguns take their places. The oncoming pyrokenes met a spread of heavy shells and microwave beams as they boiled over the pass.

To Galatea's fury, the fusillade did not break their advance. Those hit by the incoming fire stumbled, some fell, but barely enough to make a difference. The swarming, burning figures overwhelmed a troop of Retributors and scorched the earth about them, then the fire-psykers ran over a silver and black Repressor tank, attacking it with their bare hands.

Abhuman fingers, clawed and shrouded by a nimbus of flames, dug into the metal of the armoured vehicle's flanks and bulldozer blade. The psychic heat softened the plating, riddling the Repressor with gouges where the pyrokenes dug into its surface like hot pokers pressing into wax. The tank crew were firing in all directions, but the creatures seemed oblivious to the shredding barks of the guns. Galatea saw one of the burning men rip the hatch from the tank and throw it away, then seconds later a shriek of sound came from inside the vehicle as witchfire flooded into it.

The Canoness shouted a battle prayer at the top of her lungs and urged her troops into the melee. Overhead, she heard the throaty roar of jet packs as Sister Chloe led the

Seraphim, each woman borne up on streaks of white, each with a gun in either hand stitching tracer fire across the advancing foe.

The speed of the witch-fiends was frightening: they moved like an insect swarm, tumbling and scrambling over obstacles and each other, setting alight to everything around them that could combust. Galatea's bolter howled on full automatic, the sickle magazine clip emptying into the closest pyrokenes she could target. The psykers danced and twitched beneath her fire but failed to fall. She saw great fat chunks of flaming meat being ripped from them and blown away, and still they came on. Whatever devilish force of will drove them, it was incredible.

At her side, a Battle Sister with hair the colour of granite joined the Canoness with her storm bolter. It was enough: the psykers exploded in concussive bursts of noise, detonating hot, fleshy fragments and needles of bone.

'Emperor's blood, these creatures take a lot of killing...' growled the Battle Sister.

Galatea shot her a look. 'Fortunate, then, that we have much of that art to provide.'

'Aye,' snapped the woman, pivoting in place to engage more of the enemy line. Her gun flashed orange-red and more death screams filled the smoke-clogged air.

The cable car continued to rise through the deck of the keep, passing through levels where tenders ran back and forth like frightened birds or darkened tiers that showed flashes of workings as old as the heavens. They moved too quickly to determine much, passing into narrow channels wide enough that only two cars could fit within them, then suddenly back out again into open voids strewn with curves of decking. The thin glow of aged biolumes gave the Battle Sisters little chance to see much more of their surroundings than glimpses, but they could hear the distant thrum of great machinery, and the faraway noise of gunfire.

Verity stayed close to Sister Isabel. The woman steadfastly

refused to allow the Hospitaller to give her wounded arm anything more than the most cursory of examinations, or even to let her change the bandages that had become rust-brown with clotted blood. She had accepted nothing from Verity but a few dermal pads, small adhesive discs impregnated with pain nullifying agents. A trio of the white gauze circles ringed the neck of the injured Sororitas like a collar of dull jewels. Isabel's face was tight with denied agony, her skin pale and sallow.

Verity drew an injector carousel from the scentwood box at her hip and dialled a dose of powerful restorative from the glass tubes inside it.

Isabel eyed her warily. 'What are you doing?'

'You require medication,' replied Verity. 'It is my duty to give it to you.'

'I refuse,' the Battle Sister responded. 'My wits must be sharp, now more than ever.'

'Do as the Hospitaller says,' Sister Miriya said gruffly. 'Pain is a distraction. I need you focused.'

Isabel grumbled under her breath, but let Verity give her the dosage. The woman glanced up as she withdrew the injector. A high-pitched humming tickled the edge of her hearing. 'That noise...'

There was little room inside the cable car, and the iron box rocked on its guide wires as Miriya came up with her plasma pistol in her hand. She had heard it too.

'Look sharp–'

Lasers, thread-thin and red as hate, lanced out of the darkness and cut across the carriage. Verity yelped as a beam took a finger's length of hair from the end of her hair, but nobody was injured.

Miriya and Cassandra fired back into the black void and something exploded with a shattering crash, but the humming did not cease.

'Servo-skulls,' explained Isabel, using Verity's shoulder to prop herself up. 'Guardians. We're getting close to the sealed levels.' Two more of the grinning silver orbs dogged the cable car as they ascended, moving between support stanchions as they kept pace.

Isabel fired, missed, and cursed. Cassandra's aim was true, and she clipped one of the skulls squarely in its anti-gravity drive mechanism. The automaton spun out of control and collided with its partner, destroying both of them.

Verity tried to peer out of the open cradle, but without warning Isabel dragged her down with a handful of her robes. There was a fleeting impression of something huge and metallic dropping from the upper levels, and the cable car rang like a bell as a brass-clad gun servitor landed amid the Sororitas. The quarters were too close for the armed women to shoot at the machine-slave, and Verity choked in fear as the thing swung a multi-barrelled stubber gun at her head. Something clicked and whined inside the gun mechanism but it failed to engage. This close to the servitor, Verity could see its one human eye glaring down at her and the ropes of spittle coating the helot's lips. It moved, trying to crush her against Isabel.

She struck out at the hybrid with the only weapon she had to hand – the injector – burying the needle in the wet jelly of its organic eye. The device discharged a massive quantity of stimulant potion, and the gun servitor went rigid with shock. It gave a rattling gasp and sagged against its own leg pistons.

'Did you kill it?' ventured Isabel.

Verity swallowed hard to rid her mouth of the taste of bile. 'A heart attack.' She glanced at the empty injector in her hand.

Cassandra frowned, examining the dead mechanism's casing. 'See here. It was already damaged. Looks like a glancing hit from a flamer.'

Miriya cradled her pistol, peering into the dark as they ascended through it. 'There should be more of them out there. Why aren't there more?'

'Thank the Throne for small mercies,' said Verity, as the cradle bounced over a set of points and began to slow. They turned, the carriage lurching from side to side, as a flat docking platform hove into view. The console ticking off the distance markers clicked to zero and without further surprises, they arrived at the secure deck.

The women disembarked in quick order. It was Cassandra who found the corpses of two more dead gun servitors and with them, a dark-skinned man in the grimy coverall of a prisoner. There was no flesh on the man's hands, just the burnt sticks of his fingers. His clothes were crosshatched with lines of scorching.

'What does this portend?' demanded Isabel, irritably.

Miriya glanced at a train of cargo carriages locked to one of the other docking rigs, her expression grim. 'It means we are not the first to arrive.'

The loud hailers bellowed out the words of Katherine's Lament, and Galatea felt the passion swell in her veins. Unbidden, a savage grin broke out on her face. Yes, there was death and destruction about her, yes, her Sisters were fighting and dying in conflict with a mass of the most dire witches, but by the eyes of the Emperor, she felt alive with divine strength.

The Canoness waded into the sea of flames and dispatched any tainted souls that dared to stand against her. At her back, her bodyguard of elite Celestians marched with the battle hymn on their lips and bloody vengeance falling wherever they turned their guns.

A pyrokene freak scrambled from the basalt rocks, howling murder. The witch had been shredded by the near-hit of a frag grenade detonation, ripping the psyker's legs from his waist, and yet still the mutant came on, shouting through the aura of gold fire surrounding it, projecting itself forward on the spindly pins of its arms. It threw itself at Galatea, mouth yawning to present a throat full of fiery bile.

The Canoness reacted with preternatural speed, the adrenaline racing through her veins in a flood of holy quickening. Her bolter's breech clacked open, the gun empty, and she took a chain at her belt and whipped it upward. At the end of the pewter links was a golden ball the size of a man's fist:

a censer, still fuming with a potion of consecrated oils and sacred herbs. Galatea brought it up and used the device as a mace, batting the pyrokene away with a single stroke. The solution within the censer spilled across the pathetic creature's face and sent it screaming into the dirt. There it lay, clawing and dying as the potent oils ate into it like acid.

Galatea reloaded and moved on, her Celestians shooting in controlled hurricanes of bolt fire. There had been a moment when the pyrokene attack had begun, when the momentum of the Adepta Sororitas advance reeled, but the Canoness had turned them through it and now the psykers were in disarray. Broken from their wall of murderous fire, they were easier to kill in isolated clumps.

The constant rattle of heavy bolters and the ear-splitting hiss of meltas overwhelmed the rumble of unchained witchfire. Brute, ungoverned power was no match for the ruthless, unstoppable fervour of the Battle Sisters. To a woman, they felt the hand of the Emperor at their backs, the spirit of the martyr swelling in their hearts. There was no such crime as the dark horror of the witch in the eyes of an Adepta Sororitas, nothing so base and so vile as a mind that had eschewed the warmth of His light and turned their face away – towards avarice, towards godlessness and the anarchy of Chaos. Their unbreakable faith shielded them against the malice of these foes, such forces of inner will that the weaker of the witch-kin would find their foul cantrips ineffectual, but what they faced today was of a very different order. If Sister Miriya were to be believed, these were mutants fashioned by the hand of man, and worse, the hand of one who wore the garb of the High Church.

The tanks had been staggered by the enemy, but now they rode high and with steady pace, crushing the blackened bones of fallen witches into the volcanic sands that coated the narrow valley approach. Hot tongues of energy from multi-meltas flashed, ripping into the battlements of the towering Null Keep.

Sister Chloe's voice called on the general vox channel, her

words taut and urgent. 'Hear me below. The witches are drawing back. Be wary!'

'It's a trap.' The words came from her lips before Galatea was even aware she had spoken them, some deep-rooted battle sense drawing the conclusion before her conscious mind was even aware of it. 'All tanks, converge fire upon the entrance cavern to the keep. Ignore all other targets.'

'What other targets?' began the grey-haired Battle Sister with the storm bolter, again at her side. Her words died in her throat as the last few witches came together and began to hurl fire in their direction.

At the same instant, pockets of black sand about their feet bubbled and churned. Sooty pyrokenes, aglow with hate, dragged themselves from burrows beneath the ground, emerging behind the advancing Sisters. Galatea whirled and cut them down before they could get free of the basalt dirt. The Celestians fell into a combat wheel and released bolt fire to all points of the compass.

'Too little, too late,' snarled Galatea to her enemies. 'Tactics first, force second,' she lectured. 'Whoever commands these wastrels is no soldier.'

The tanks drowned out the sound of the rout of the psykers as they fired in one destructive salvo. Beyond the thinning ranks of the witches, the guns of the Immolators found their mark. Dark obsidian stone and heavy iron split asunder as spheres of explosive force tore their way into the Null Keep. The holdfast was breached, and the Sororitas onslaught came on.

'The door's locked,' said the gangly woman, throwing Vaun a look over her shoulder. 'The old creep ain't gonna open it just 'cos you ask nicely...' She flicked at her fingers where streaks of greenish fire clung across the rows of her knuckles, and spat at the black gates of phase-iron.

Vaun glanced around at the scattered corpses of the gun servitors, the broken pieces of the machine-slave force that the tenders had left to perish defending the engine chamber.

He frowned, unable to find something suitable. The psyker turned his attention to the escapees. At last his eyes fell on a fat male, balding and sweating hard in the humid caverns. A line of acid drool lapped from his flabby lips, spattering at his feet.

'Flame-spitter, aren't you?' Vaun approached him, measuring the man's size. He seemed close enough for what was needed.

The fat man nodded once and more drool left his mouth as he spoke. 'Sometimes, I just can't keep it in.' He had a highborn accent, proof that it wasn't just Nevan commoners that LaHayn preyed upon. The other prisoners backed away, sensing danger. 'What's wrong?'

Vaun smiled warmly. 'Nothing. You'll do fine.' The psyker closed his eyes and turned a hammer of psychic force inside his mind which released itself in a thud of displaced air. The fat man went squealing away and slammed into the heavy doors.

'What...?' The shock robbed the drooling witch of any other words. He tried to get up, but the force of the push had broken both his legs.

Vaun pictured the churning roil of psionic ectoplasm simmering in the fat man's ample gut. His kind of pyrokene was a peculiar breed, manifesting their ability like mythic dragons spewing fire from an endless reservoir of incendiary bile. The fat man and his sort were walking flamethrowers.

The psyker let his mind create the reality. He projected a boiling heat inside the wailing man, watching him twitch and moan. Chemical reactions made his body expand, the grey fleshy wattles on his neck stretching tight. Vaun's errant minions went for cover just as the fat man exploded. The wet concussion hammered at the phase-iron doors, chewing a ragged hole in them. The gates tilted and sagged off their huge hinges.

Vaun strode into the engine chamber with his head held high, and rough laughter in his chest.

* * *

The stinking wave of putrid concussion knocked LaHayn against the ornate gold control podium, and he reflexively snatched at the argentium pepperbox gun connected to his wrist by an onyx rosary. Lasers keened at the far end of the chamber as tenders and servitors alike fired on the new arrivals; but through the noise, the grating, hateful sound of one man's amusement told him immediately who had dared to breach the sanctified hall.

The tech-adepts in the sub-pulpit beneath him tried to disengage themselves from their cogitators and flee, but the priest-lord struck out at them with savage blows. 'Cowardly fools. This is no time to abandon the work. Proceed as I command you and begin the commencement!'

They reluctantly followed his orders, and while the firefight raged on, a crackle of ancient cogs echoed about the chamber. LaHayn watched as one vast wall of the engine room grew a vertical fissure along its length, opening with ponderous speed to emit a cherry-red glow. The metres-thick doors drew back to allow a heavy tide of dry heat to roll in; beyond them was the open throat of the volcanic chimney at the Null Keep's heart, and just in sight the slow tides of the mountain's magma core.

The rings of the ancient device basked in the ruddy glow, picking up speed as the power from the geothermal tap increased. For a moment, LaHayn forgot the battle raging nearby and felt a childlike excitement blossom inside him. 'Dear God-Emperor, it is working!' Eyes shining, the deacon made the sign of the aquila and anointed the controls at his podium with a vial of sacred unguent. He looked up, barely able to hold back the tears of joy, as the shifting metal planes inside the spinning rings shifted and merged. They turned about and coalesced into something that could only have been a throne. LaHayn worked the controls, moving his fingers over them in complex patterns that he had made into personal rituals. 'Yes,' he cried, 'at last, the conjunction of events comes to pass. As it was foretold, *as it should be!*'

The iron throne extended out of the spinning glow on a

rod of brilliant white, cracking the black stone with the wash of its energy. The priest threw himself down and bounded towards it, the blessed radiation engulfing him in warm, soft clouds.

He was only an arm's length away when the firestreak lashed into him. The burning thread of psy-force entered LaHayn's body from behind, just below his ribcage. It cut straight through him in a fountain of bloody steam, melting bone and organ meat. The deacon crashed to the basalt floor, the dull reflection of his agonised face staring back up at him.

Vaun made a tutting noise as he approached. 'Your problem has always been that you leave everything to the last moment, Viktor.' The psyker waved his hand and let another salvo of flame lines hiss from his fingertips, savaging the closest tech-adept. He paused over the priest as LaHayn struggled to drag himself across the stone. 'No, no. Too late now. You had your chance.'

'Not... ready...' the deacon groaned. 'Until... now...'

'That's just what I wanted to know,' grinned Vaun. He glanced up, licking his lips. 'This is it, then? The Psi-Engine of Neva? The machine that will make me a god?'

'No...'

'Oh yes,' retorted Vaun, 'and because I'm feeling so generous, I'm going to let you live long enough to see it happen.' He left LaHayn behind and marched into the glowing aurora. 'Goodbye, Viktor. And thank you.' He settled into the steel throne, shuddering with power.

The priest rolled on to his side and propped himself up. 'Ah. No, dear boy. It... It is I who should thank *you*.'

For the first time, uncertainty formed on the psyker's face. He opened his mouth to say something, but the throne folded about him, wrapping him in flat planes of burning metal.

Vaun cried out, but it was Viktor LaHayn's laughter that filled his ears.

CHAPTER SEVENTEEN

The sound of gunfire drew them in, the last pointless defences of the engine chamber echoing down the hellish corridor to the cable car dock. Grim-faced, Miriya led her Sisters over the ugly wreckage of the iron doors. It was only then, when they were inside the cavernous hall itself, that they saw where the blood-coloured illumination was coming from. Rising above the torn remains of the dead tenders, of the butchered prisoner pyrokenes and the golden stump of the command pulpit, the great circling rings of the engine hurtled around one another in defiance of gravity. Miriya and the other women were struck silent by the sight of the machine. The thunderous roars of white energy crackling about it were mesmerising. In coils of actinic blue, strings of text in High Gothic emerged along the faces of the rings, detaching themselves to float in the air like windblown leaves. A rumbling pulse throbbed from the shifting planes of metal at the core of the impossible construction, and with every falling beat the Sororitas could hear the wailing, plaintive cries of a man.

Vaun. The sound of his voice chilled her to the bone. It was not the arrogant, brutal confidence she had come to expect from the psyker, but a horrific cry of terror, as if his very soul were being stripped from his body.

The open flue of the volcano seared the air with great wavering sheets of heat, beating at their bare skin and sluicing sweat from their bodies. Miriya shook her head to break the spell of the fantastic machine and shouted commands to her Sisters. They reacted unhurriedly, blinking with lizard slowness.

'Verity, Isabel, remain here. Cassandra, you and I will approach the... the device...' Miriya checked the charge of her plasma pistol and frowned. The weapon was close to exhaustion.

'With respect,' ventured Cassandra, 'we need every able hand.' She gestured at the dead strewn about them. 'In smaller numbers, we guarantee we will share their fate.'

'Aye,' Isabel added. 'I'll not stand back and watch. The Hospitaller can see to me if I falter.'

Miriya glanced at Verity. 'What say you, Hospitaller?'

But the sight of the machine entranced the golden-haired woman. 'Look,' she said, raising her hand to point. 'The deacon...'

The Sister Superior heard the resonance of LaHayn's voice carry to her and her face paled. 'God-Emperor, no... Please, no. He has already begun.' She was ashen. '*We are too late!*'

'Release me!' screamed the psyker, every cell in his body alive with crackling energy that poured into him from the warp. 'The power...'

'Power?' mocked LaHayn, dragging himself to the top of his podium. 'But that's what you wanted, isn't it, Torris? Power beyond all avarice, power to rape, murder and pillage across the galaxy? Now you can taste it all.'

Vaun cried out in agony, slamming himself against the seamless cowl of metal holding him inside the spinning rings.

'Tell me how it feels, little man,' demanded the deacon, his eyes locked on the pain-wracked face of his former apprentice. 'What is it like to be a vessel too small to hold the magnificent potential of the empyrean?' He laughed. 'The suffering must be unspeakable.' He moved levers and dials that had not been touched in over ten millennia, shifting the huge mass of the engine in place. In turn, the throbbing hum of power drawn from the raging magma lake below them increased, feeding the ancient mechanism's needs.

'You are such a fool, Torris,' said the priest-lord. 'I am almost saddened by the way I was able to draw you to me. How strange to think that on some level, I actually hoped you might be able to best me. I suppose that is the forlorn hope of every teacher, is it not? That their prize student will one day exceed them?'

'Hate you,' spat Vaun. 'Heartless.' He tried to muster the fire in his mind, but every ounce of raw flame he could call upon was instantly sucked away into the raging white discharges about him.

'Oh, you wound me,' retorted LaHayn, clutching at the very real injury in his gut. 'But never again. Like the errant son you are, you came back to have your revenge on the father figure in your pathetic, wasted life. Blinded by your greed, your mindless desire for anarchy. Never once did you suspect that it was because I wished it!' He shouted the words. 'You are here because I let you come, boy. I stayed the hand of the Sororitas on Groombridge, I allowed you to come here and play your foolish games with Sherring!'

Vaun shook his head. 'Liar.' His fists balled in helpless anger.

'Hard to accept, isn't it?' LaHayn coughed and dabbed blood from his lips. 'But it is the truth. I knew I would never bring you home by capture or coercion. I had to make you think it was all *your* idea!' He propped himself up on the lip of the podium. 'Who do you think it was that ensured Sherring discovered the location of the keep? Who was it that let him get away with his corruption of the *Mercutio*'s crew and the secret arming of his forces in Metis? I did, you dupe. You gave me the excuse to destroy my most troublesome rival into the bargain!' The priest smiled, showing blood-flecked teeth. 'I want you to understand this, my boy. Every freedom you have ever enjoyed, every liberty and choice you think you had, all of it has been by my permission. Each day of your pathetic life, from the moment you took my hand outside that burning church, you have travelled only as far as my leash about your neck would permit–' LaHayn's words cascaded into a hacking, painful cough. When he looked up again, a steely hate coiled in his eyes. 'You were my greatest triumph, Torris. The strongest, the most powerful psychic killer I had ever fostered – but you are *nothing* compared to what I will become. You have outgrown your usefulness, and it is time for the tool to perform its final task.' He threw open his hands. 'The engine is ready, after a hundred thousand lifetimes – and you are the spark that will ignite it.'

'Never,' screamed Vaun, reaching into himself to pull every last iota of destructive energy from within. 'Never, *never*, NEVER!'

The engine howled with sympathetic feedback, and to the deacon's shock, the rings released immense hammers of flaming psy-fire to the four corners of the black stone chamber.

Each planet has its legends of the apocalypse, the roots of superstition stretching back through time to the cradle of mankind. Some speak of murderous solar explosions, others of eternal winters or heavenly raptures that would scour worlds clean; on Neva the myth of destruction was one of fire and brimstone. The parables left behind by the long-dead first colonists foretold of a horrific day when the magma core of the planet would rage out of control and shatter continents with eruptions of molten rock.

Torris Vaun's mind held onto those visions of catastrophe as his towering rage boiled inside him. The tight confines of the machine throne coiled about his body, tightening around his skin and pressing invisible forces into his brain – but at the same time, the resonating engine was filling him with impossible power, charging his crude flesh with reserves of psychic potential beyond anything he could comprehend.

His mind was drowning in a screaming sea of churning, raw emotion, the spinning rings slowly forming a conduit through him into the soul-shattering madness of warp space. Vaun's thoughts were slipping away from him, the matter of his skin and bone becoming less and less defined as the machine absorbed him. In moments, he would become a shade, a ghost of the man he was. With sudden, blinding clarity he understood what was happening to him, what it was that LaHayn had conspired to do. In the crudest, most basic sense the ancient psionic device was no different from any other engine. To fully bring itself to optimal capacity, it required a spark of ignition – a scrap of human kindling to set it running to full power.

You are the spark. The priest-lord's words echoed in the blazing halls of his mind. It was inconceivable for Vaun to contemplate that the energy surging about him was only the primer for the engine's true millionfold capacity. He tried in vain to hold the thought in his mind but the conception of it slipped away, leaking out. The psyker was drowning in sunfire, dying by degrees as the killing light subsumed him. The fear and terror at his predicament were burning out of Vaun, leaving nothing in their place but raging anger, at LaHayn, at himself, at the Battle Sisters and at his hated homeworld. The murderous loathing rose up like a black tide as he accepted the brutal truth – he had been used, played like an instrument by that unspeakable old monster, turned to do the deacon's mad bidding even when he believed that his life was his own. And now he was going to die for his mentor, he would vanish and disintegrate into pure psychic energy so that LaHayn could take the power of the engine for himself.

Vaun allowed himself one last moment of regret: he had forged such great plans from the day he had learned of the psi-engine's existence. The psyker pirate wanted to turn it to his own cause, to make himself unstoppable against the Inquisition or any other foe that would stand against him. He did not care about the wars between LaHayn's precious Emperor and the mad beasts of the Chaos Gods – all he wanted was to aggrandise himself, to plunder any world he cared to and shatter those that displeased him. All that was ashes now, and in moments he would be too.

He thought of the boy Ignis, dead now, his face lit with callous glee at the thought of a planet's death. *I'll give you that, lad,* he told the ghost-memory. *We'll have revenge yet.*

Below on the pulpit, LaHayn wheezed and shouted something angry and incoherent. The damnable priest could see Vaun's refusal to go quietly reflected in the flashing dials of his arcane console. The psyker forced a laugh out of the necrotic flesh of his throat and drew inward, gathering in the very last mental embers of his own violent identity. The spinning rings clattered against each other with showers of sparks; the engine was not designed to hold an unwilling sacrifice.

Vaun let the memories of those ancient death-myths fill him and with one final effort, he plunged his raging spirit into the thundering magma core and let it loose.

Without warning, the black earth around them rang like a struck gong. The Canoness stumbled and barely regained her footing, one of her Celestians snapping out a hand to steady her. In annoyance she shook off the woman's grip and barked out a command. 'Report.'

Her words barely carried over the sullen, grinding rumble of rock on rock, and high over their heads loose basalt pebbles flickered and shifted.

'Seismic activity,' came the voice from the command vehicle. 'Auspex detects energy surges inside the keep.'

The cracking of stone broke around them and Galatea threw herself aside as fissures cleaved the ground around her. She watched in mute horror as a shallow pinnacle of black rock detached itself from the sheer valley wall and dropped into the midst of a Dominion squad. The Battle Sisters were not given enough time to scream. Others threw themselves from the path of tumbling boulders and avalanches of dark sand. Those too slow to react paid with their lives.

Ahead of them, the open maw where the keep's broad iron

portcullis had been breached ground against itself, shedding a rain of dusty particles. For a moment it seemed as if the tremors were falling, but then they rose again, twice as powerful.

'It's getting worse,' said the Celestian at her side, voicing the Canoness's thoughts for her.

Galatea tabbed the control stud that changed the vox channel and broke into the frequency used by the transport flyers. They were still close by, orbiting on station. 'Heed me,' she snapped, 'pilots report, what do you see up there?' She turned her face to the sallow sky and frowned. Something seemed wrong about the clouds around the citadel. They were moving even though there was little wind, spinning into odd, ring-like formations.

'Eruptions in all quadrants.' The flat voice of a flight servitor informed her without emotion or inflection. 'Pyroclastic flows sighted in several areas. Volcanic disturbance increasing exponentially.'

'Impossible,' snarled the Sororitas. 'This zone is seeded with magma stabilisers. There hasn't been an eruption on Neva for a thousand years.'

'It appears we are overdue, then,' Galatea's eyes narrowed. She could see it now, hazy gossamer waves in the air as plumes of heat might rise from a campfire. They radiated out from the tower to all points, and with each new pulse the rasping earth twitched again. A distant crash of noise reached them in the black arroyo as another peak some kilometres distant blew itself apart, the upper quarter of the jagged stone tooth disappearing into a vast blot of grey ash. Sulphurous fumes turned her, coughing, from the fractures in the ground. Within them she saw the dim glow of lava marching inexorably upward.

'What is happening in there?' She asked the question aloud, not just of herself but also of the shuddering mass of the stony fortress.

'Your grace?' The Celestian gave her a searching look. 'Shall we go on?'

Galatea's order was on the tip of her tongue when a fresh shudder ran through the stone and earth. With a sound that drove nails of pressure into their ears, the rock beneath the treads of a fully loaded Rhino troop carrier gave way. The slab-like armoured vehicle skidded against the tilting plane of ground it lay upon, jets of smoke blasting from the exhaust pipes as the driver tried to fight the sudden incline. Women threw themselves off the roof and leapt as best they could from open hatches, but in grotesque slow motion the tank sank backward into the crevice with a howl of tortured steel. Half a dozen Battle Sisters, dead in the blink of an eye.

The earth's torment did not lessen. Now it moved like something alive, trembling and shaking. Galatea staggered again as she shouted into the general command channel. 'All who hear, heed me. Fall back from the keep. All Sisters are to withdraw in skirmish lines, no delays, fleet of foot!' She threw a nod to her guardians and the Celestians drew close to her. 'Pilots, execute recovery operation immediately!'

There was a dull reply from one of the coleopters. 'Landing zone is unstable. We may not be able to make a touch-down–'

'You'll do it, or by Katherine's eyes I'll see you whipped.' The retort ripped at her throat with each breath of tainted, hellish air. 'I'll sacrifice no more Sisters to this blighted place.' Galatea panted and coughed. Her troops were already donning their helmets and she did the same, sealing out the foul atmosphere. Inside her armour, a blessed draught of recycled air came to her and she swallowed it with a wheeze. Her optics caught sight of a flyer dropping low, thrusters flaring through the spreading drab haze. She waved a squad bearing injured women past her, once again shifting her vox frequency to the select channel used by the Imperial Navy. '*Mercutio*, respond. This is Canoness Galatea, notae gravis.'

'*Mercutio*,' came the cool tones of the warship's commander. 'We are monitoring your situation from our orbit at high anchor, milady. Is there business for us?'

'Aye,' she replied. 'The church has need of you.'

* * *

'What are you doing?' bellowed the deacon. 'You cannot defy me. This is the will of your god!' He spat with bilious anger, blood flecking his lips, pain knifing him in the stomach. The gold and brass frame of the pulpit shuddered with every humming pulse of misdirected power that flashed from the clashing rings. Furious with frustration, LaHayn slammed his fists against the ornate panel before him. This was not supposed to happen. The subject was supposed to die quietly, willingly, giving up his mind-essence to set the engine to speed!

'Curse you, Vaun, you arrogant insect!' About the chamber, stone pillars fell into rubble and elaborate obsidian statues ten millennia old were dashed to pieces. Through the open gates to the keep's volcanic core, the leaden lake of magma was alive with crashes of escaping gas and heavy, torpid waves.

'No,' the psyker's words were distorted and lengthened, pulled like tallow into a dull drone. 'Curse *you.*'

LaHayn could make him out in the depths of the energy nimbus, a pale and paper-thin shade of the insolent rebel that had faced him in the Lunar Cathedral, and yet still Vaun resisted him. From the corner of his eye, the priest-lord saw movement on the floor of the engine chamber, but disregarded it. The last of Vaun's pathetic band of escapees or some surviving member of his own servant cadre? It mattered nothing to him now. He pulled at a nest of bronze levers and the pulpit lurched forward, a coiled armature unfolding beneath it. The golden podium came up and into the edge of the aura field, setting showers of sparks glowing in the air.

'Destroy it all,' moaned Vaun. 'Revenge. *Beaten you.*'

'Never,' snarled the deacon, coiling the line of an onyx rosary in his hand. It was difficult: his blood slicked his fingers and made the links slippery. 'Not by a wastrel… witch like you. You're just the ember to prime the pump!' At last he pulled the box-shaped holdout gun into his grip, clasping the ornate surface. With infinite care, he aimed the ornamental weapon at his old pupil's face. 'No escape this time.'

LaHayn's thumb pressed down on a bejewelled trigger button and the little gun released a hollow thunderclap.

LaHayn heard the crackle as Vaun desperately tried to thicken the air between the muzzle and his skull. He saw the recognition of failure dawn on those pallid features, and with a grating shout of victory, he basked in the glorious moment of the kill. The psycannon bolt lanced through Vaun's fading mental shields as if they were nothing more than cloth. It entered his skull through the nasal cavity and travelled into the meat of his brain, shedding needles as it did. The penetration core ruptured inside him, imploding. With nothing to animate his flesh any more, Torris Vaun, the corsair of Neva, hated criminal and witchkin lawbreaker, died with a feeble gasp. His final release of mental energy melted into the psi-engine and the machine glowed white.

The deacon let the spent gun and rosary drop from his fingers, clattering away to the floor below him. He rocked with shallow, pained laughter, clutching at the edges of the pulpit. He had left ruddy fingerprints everywhere his hands touched the shining metal. 'It is done,' he told himself. 'Every great endeavour requires a sacrifice.' Taking a shaky step, LaHayn moved towards the edge of the podium. The spinning rings were within arm's reach, throwing rays of warmth across him each time they passed. He was smiling, tears shining on his face even though every movement was like fire in his belly. But no, he had come too far, struggled too long to die on the very cusp of his destiny. He felt the hand of the God-Emperor upon him, beckoning him forward.

'I will do it, master,' he said aloud. 'I will do it for your glory.'

Something heavy and dangerous thrummed past his head and set him off-balance. The priest-lord cried out and grabbed at the ivory relief carving of the Imperial eagle on the crest of the pulpit, a single heartbeat away from falling short. He turned his gaze downward and saw, like ants crawling around the foot of a giant, the figures of Sister Miriya and her damnable companions. The woman raised a pistol and he knew that she had drawn a bead between his eyes.

'Viktor LaHayn,' she intoned. 'You are bound by the law of the Imperial Church. Stand down and submit to chastisement or you will be executed for your heresy against our God.'

He could do nothing else but laugh at her.

Miriya ignored Cassandra's muttered cursing. She could see how easy it had been to miss with her bolter shot – the air danced around the high metal pulpit in shimmering waves and cascades of glowing blue symbols tumbled silently about them like falling snow. For the moment, the rolling havoc of the volcano had subsided, but the lava flow still rumbled at their backs, ready to turn violent again at a moment's notice. All of them had witnessed Vaun's murder. The peculiar disintegration of his body set them aghast, but Miriya ordered them closer. The witch was dead, and that was one less deed for them to fulfil. Just LaHayn remained, mad and wounded and commanding this insane mechanism that only the Emperor Himself could master – if the heretic was to be believed.

He looked down at them, a bloody horror in ruined robes. The Celestian had seen men and women live far longer than they should have with stomach wounds such as his, weeping and praying that death would take them and spare them the agony. LaHayn's face was a mass of conflicts: rapture, pain, hate and elation. 'B-bear witness,' he croaked. 'Think yourselves as lucky as Alicia and the Brides of the Emperor when they were brought before Him after the Apostasy... You will see. *You will see!*'

'Kill him,' hissed Isabel. 'Before it is too late, kill the damned heretic!'

But there was something, some tiny fragment of Miriya's soul that could not break the awe she felt before the spinning rings of the engine. She could not give voice to the manner in which she knew, but with a certainty that was as solid as the stars in the sky, she *knew* that LaHayn was correct about one thing. This machine was not the creation of man, but of her God-Emperor. The truth of that froze her blood in her veins.

LaHayn stabbed a finger at her. 'You see it. You know it is real. Understand me, girl, once I embrace the engine I will be remade. That is its ultimate purpose, to rewrite the book of life. I want this gift, I am destined for it!'

Verity shook her head, desperate to deny him. 'You cannot interfere with the work of our Master...'

The cleric tipped back his head and revealed the base of his skull. The familiar bolus of the silver sphere implant was visible beneath his skin. 'Oh, but I can.'

'You are no psyker,' retorted Cassandra.

'In moments, I *will* be. The greatest of them.'

'No...' murmured Miriya. The concept of such a thing was too much for her to take in.

'*Yes!*' he roared, spitting blood. 'Oh yes! I shall fulfil our god's will. I shall travel to Terra and awaken Him, and we will transform mankind in His image...' His voice cracked. 'Listen to me. All the pieces are in place. The keys found, the codes broken, the assumption is upon me. Consecrate it with your faith, dear sisters. Watch me take up the mantle lost by blessed Malcador and become the Second Sigillite!'

Miriya's breath caught in her throat and her hand wavered. LaHayn invoked the name of the Emperor's first-chosen adjutant, the secretive administrator-priest selected in the days of the Great Crusade, the man who – so the legends said – had been the first human being to bear the mark of the soul-binding ritual that forever connected him to the Father of Mankind.

Malcador had perished thousands of years ago and no man had ever dared to try and take his title. It was written that the Sigillite was one of the most powerful psykers in creation, second only to the mental might of the Emperor. That the deacon believed he might stand in Malcador's place was either blasphemy of the highest order or the folly of lunacy.

Her aim steadied and her finger tightened on the plasma pistol's trigger. 'Viktor LaHayn, in the name of Holy Terra, consider your life forfeit.'

The priest-lord threw his body from the podium as she fired. There was the shriek of clashing energies and then the chamber turned white with pain.

The burning light sent Verity to the floor, pressing her face to the stone to stop her from being blinded. Isabel was not as swift and she fell to her knees with an animal howl on her lips. The white flash rolled away and Verity resisted the urge to claw at her eyes, blinking furiously. Every glowing ember in the chamber felt like a needle through her skull. She staggered, off-balance, almost falling over the prone Battle Sister. Her gaze travelled upwards even though some inner voice screamed not to do so.

The motion of the spinning rings had changed. Slower now, more languid, they turned and dropped close to the ground, coming about one another, crossing and re-crossing. As they moved, their orbit was tethered by lines of invisible force to a glittering shape at the hub of motion. Suspended there in a rack of red-gold light, the Lord High Deacon Viktor LaHayn was screaming in silence. His face reflected a merging of two polar opposites – utter, inchoate fear and rapturous joy. By turns his aspect showed one and then the other, waxing and waning through each emotion. White particles gathered about the places in his stomach and torso where he had been injured – Miriya's shot having hit its mark, for all the good it had done – and gradually tapes of flesh and new muscle were gathered out of the air to repair him.

Verity sensed the Sister Superior stumbling to her feet. A flash of plasma from her gun darted into the nimbus of the engine, but once within it slowed to a crawl, the white fury of the sun-hot gas dissipating. Cassandra fired too, her bolt shells puffing into powder where they struck. The Hospitaller sniffed. The air was growing colder by the second, patches of frost blossoming on the stone floor in defiance of the fact that a live volcano rumbled only a few metres distant. Icicles crackled as they formed on the walls and the podiums about the chamber. Her breath emerged in pops of vapour, and the chill crept into their bones.

Miriya grimaced. 'Hard to kill, this priest…'

'He's drawing energy from the air itself!' Verity suddenly understood. 'Preparing…'

'That shall not come to pass,' growled the Sororitas. 'Sisters. Curb the witch!'

Cassandra drew the gunmetal ingot of a snub bolter pistol from a holster in the folds of her robes and pressed it into Verity's hand. 'Take this, and use it. No oaths or excuses now.'

Verity swallowed a gulp of frosty air and nodded, holding up the weapon. At her side, Isabel aimed through bloodshot, blurry eyes. All of them opened fire at once, shells and plasma bolts flaring darkly against the nimbus of the rings.

LaHayn's head jerked, as if he noticed them for the first time. The Hospitaller could see where his thin mane of silver hair was leaving him, the shape of the implant clearly visible as it pulsed beneath his skin. Her stomach knotted in pure loathing. The man had done it, with deliberate intent he had turned himself from a pure-strain human being into a psychic aberration. Just like the crawling wisps of frost vapour about their ankles, Verity sensed the deacon's burgeoning powers reaching out, tracing tendrils of insubstantial mind-stuff. There was a pressure behind the bridge of her nose, as if an iron rod was being forced into her brain. She kept firing, the bolt pistol making her bones jar with every discharge.

Insects.

The word tolled through the four women and made each of them cry out in pain. Verity's eyes flooded with tears and she blinked as they chilled upon her icy cheeks.

'Don't falter,' shouted Miriya, her throat catching. 'For the God-Emperor–'

I Am Your God Now. The impact of the voice was a physical blow, cracking the newly formed ice sheets. *You Will Be The Last To Defy Me.*

'Have faith!' The Sister Superior was weeping brokenly as she said it.

There were still shots in the gun, but for all the effort Verity put into squeezing the trigger, nothing happened. Hopelessness, sharp as a razor, cut across her soul.

From the rings came a hoop of perfect gold light, crackling with dark spheres of exotic radiation. The ephemeral circle radiated out across the engine chamber and struck the four Sisters, violating their minds with terrifying ease. It was the manifestation of the priest-lord's will to break them.

Verity felt as if her bones had turned to water. She sagged, struggling just to stay on her feet, abruptly weighted down with a dreadful, heartbreaking despair. Suddenly everything seemed meaningless, her every thought and deed for nothing, her life a waste of breath and blood. She was dimly aware of Isabel behind her, crying like a child and lamenting. Cassandra, always tall and strong, as hard as steel, she too slipped to her knees on the rimes of hoarfrost and folded in on herself, becoming small and pathetic inside the hollows of her armour.

'Throne, no.' The Hospitaller couldn't be sure who it was that cried out, but she saw Miriya blurring, coming closer. She felt like she was drowning in misery, every pore of her body clogged with grey desolation, each breath hollow and leaden. *It was him*, she raged inside, *LaHayn is doing this to us, turning our dark fears upon us!*

'We must resist,' wept Miriya, shaking Verity by her shoulders. 'We cannot let him stop us.'

Try as she might, the Hospitaller only saw a blurry dark shape in Sororitas battle armour, and the face of her poor, dead sibling looking back at her.

'Lethe, Lethe,' she sobbed. 'Don't leave me. Please. I'm lost without you.'

Inside her heart, the cavern of sorrows she had held at bay after her sister's death yawned wide and swallowed her whole.

* * *

Miriya shook her head, struggling to break the priest-lord's telepathic hex, but the force of his mind clung on and coiled about her psyche. Everywhere she turned she saw the faces of the dead, the marching regretful corpses whose lives had been entwined with hers on the field of duty. Lethe and Iona, Portia and Reiko, they stalked her with mournful aspects and empty souls, crying her name, accusing her with sorrowful whispers. And there were more beyond them, ranks of those she had fought alongside in the past and survived: Sister Rachel in the bombed out ruins at Starleaf, killed by a Traitor Guard sniper, Nikita and Madeline lost in the catacombs of Pars Unus, and more and more. Her Battle Sisters and her victims surrounding her, beating her down with each deathly wail. Her mind reeled, on the verge of shattering.

She fell to the icy floor and cried out in pain as something sharp lanced into her palm. The agony snapped her thoughts into clear focus for a second. There, buried in the heel of her hand was a golden aquila charm on a broken onyx chain. *A sign!*

She whirled about, pulling on her last reserves of devotion, brandishing her pistol and snarling. 'I deny you. You are false, priest. I name thee traitor!'

So Be It. LaHayn's dark eyes flashed as he gathered up a coil of killing psychic power. Miriya found Verity at her side. The Hospitaller gripped the careworn sliver of her votive rosary in one hand and pressed it into the Battle Sister's grip.

'Must not... suffer the witch... to live...' she managed, every word a monumental effort.

'Aye,' said Miriya, drawing her Sister to her. 'In the God-Emperor's name, we shall not bow before you, LaHayn!'

Die, Then, he said, unleashing unhallowed flames upon the two of them, witchfire shrieking across the chamber.

'Faith,' cried the women in one voice. 'Faith unfailing!'

CHAPTER EIGHTEEN

A spiritu dominatus, *Domine, libra nos.*

The sacred words of the Fede Imperialis, the hallowed battle-prayer of the Adepta Sororitas, formed in the minds and hearts of Verity and Miriya. *From the lightning and the tempest, Our Emperor, deliver us. From plague, deceit, temptation and war, Our Emperor, deliver us. From the scourge of the Kraken, Our Emperor, deliver us.* The two women clung to one another, eyes averted from the hell unfolding about them, each clasping the silver rosary chain. The tiny thread of beads was a mere token, such a small thing, an icon of personal devotion with none of the pomp and glory of the church's great artefacts, and yet it was no less a key to the faith of Sister Verity, no less a symbol of fidelity to Sister Miriya. The witchfire thundered across the icy stone and engulfed them in blue lightning, but still they prayed. *From the blasphemy of the Fallen, Our Emperor, deliver us. From the begetting of daemons, Our Emperor, deliver us. From the curse of the mutant, Our Emperor, deliver us.*

Legend had it that the faith of the Adepta Sororitas was so strong that no psyker could ever break their conviction, that only the most monstrous of the witchkin could threaten their purity. It was said that when a Sister was at her most pious, when she was at the moment of most virtuous sacrifice to the God-Emperor's spirit, the shield of faith that surrounded her could turn any blow from the mind of the aberrant and unholy. Only when her faith was tested to the breaking point could a Sororitas truly know the power of her own zeal.

Miriya gripped the silver rosary and shouted the words of the invocation to the skies. 'A morte perpetua!'

Verity's voice carried the final line over the crash of psychic flames. 'Domine, libra nos.'

As suddenly as it came, the searing, murderous heat faded away, back into the bone-chilling cold. Verity's eyes snapped open and she saw Miriya before her, holding on to her rosary for dear life. 'We... We are unharmed... By the Throne, we turned the killing blow. By faith alone we set our souls as armour!'

Miriya's eyes shone and she turned, raising her plasma pistol in her mailed grip. 'Yes... Katherine preserve us, dear Sister, yes. We resisted!'

NO! LaHayn's rage made the chamber shake. *This cannot be. You should be dead, you pestilent whores!*

The Battle Sister released her grip on the rosary and faced their enemy. 'I will die when the God-Emperor calls me to His side, not at the whim of a crooked, insane freak.' She sent a salvo of plasma bolts hissing into the priest-lord's aura. 'You failed to break us, LaHayn. Now the turn is yours!'

To Verity's shock, the Celestian threw herself into the glowing nimbus of energy, her black ceramite gauntlets sparking as they took purchase on the surface of one of the spinning rings. She called her name, but it was too late to stop her. With a sudden hot flash of bright lightning, Miriya was drawn into the deacon's psi-sphere by the motion of the loop. Inside the orbit of the halo, the woman seemed to shimmer, as if time moved at a different speed within the radius of the engine.

There was an abrupt and terrible awareness of dislocation. It was at once alien and familiar, bringing back the memory of an unnatural sensation each time she had been aboard a starship plunging into the miasma of warp space. Miriya's senses rebelled for a split-second and she forced bile down from her throat as the world about her *shifted*.

Inside the corona of the ancient device, she drifted as if in zero gravity, held fast only where she could cling to the turning hoops of phase-iron. It was like looking out through a sphere of frosted glass, the shapes and colours of the chamber beyond visible but clouded into distorted blurs. There were strident, strange sounds in here with her, drawn-out shrieks and muttering cries, thoughts bleeding over from the minds of every other living being within the keep. For a moment, she thought she heard Torris Vaun, yelling in agony, but then the echo faded.

LaHayn drifted above her, eyes aglow with hate as he stared down at her. 'How dare you approach me. You soil this holy construct with your presence!'

'Heretic,' she retorted. 'You have no right to speak of what is holy. You sacrificed the privilege of the church and your own humanity, the day you decided to revive this artefact!'

The priest threw up his hands and his anger fluttered in red sparks. 'How can you be so wilfully blind, you arrogant wench? It is you who seeks to block the path of the Emperor, not I. You who cannot see the glory of this device!' He drifted closer to her, radiating power. 'I will *know* Him. I will peel back the veil of time and grasp the mind of the God-Emperor as no human has for ten thousand years!' LaHayn smiled. 'And when I do, when He shakes off the dust of eons and opens His eyes, it will be my face before Him. It will be my reward that is granted!'

Miriya levelled her gun. 'There are no words to plumb the depths to which you disgust me, priest. This madness ends here.' She fired.

The deacon scrambled to throw up planes of force, dragging sheets of flickering radiation from the inner surfaces of the rings to block each shimmering plasma bolt. The Sororitas saw blinks of panic in his eyes. With her outside the spinning rings he had been able to marshal his power more easily, but with an adversary this close to him, he was finding it a challenge to maintain the upper hand. That this newborn witch had power beyond any she had encountered before was not in question, but LaHayn was new to the command of such abilities and he wielded them with clumsy application. He was on the defensive, reacting to her instead of fighting back. She moved and fired, moved and fired, harrying him.

LaHayn spat with fury and did something with his free hand. Miriya felt another vertiginous shift in the depths of her gut as the entire engine began to move across the chamber, the walls passing slowly by beyond the glassy aura field.

'More,' he growled beneath his breath, 'more power to me...'

Inexorably, the engine drifted out across the throat of the volcanic chimney, ascending to where geothermal power conduits snaked up the inside of the basalt flue. The thick adamantium channels extended into the fluid core of Neva, to energy-exchange mechanisms of such advancement and age that their science was unknown to all but the most learned Mechanicus adepts on Mars. LaHayn hissed and exercised his new strengths, drawing raw energy straight from the grids.

Miriya's shots pealed harmlessly off the shields he placed in their way, every bolt melting. The Celestian felt the pressure within the engine sphere as the priest-lord engorged himself, his body resonating with potential. LaHayn's wiry, whipcord frame was changing, gaining mass and presence by the moment. He was taking on the aspect of the god that he believed himself to be.

She kept firing, the plasma pistol growing hotter and hotter in her hands as the red rage of boiling magma churned beneath their feet. The emitter coils atop the breech of the weapon were glowing blue-white with discharge and the heat of the labouring gun touched her flesh through the flexsteel and ceramic plates of her gauntlet. Overload warning glyphs were blinking on the grip. But still she kept firing.

'Why do you reject me?' shouted LaHayn. 'Don't you understand what I am doing? Do you want our Master to exist forever in stasis, frozen in eternal death, starved of life, the chance to complete His greatest work denied?'

'You are only a man,' she shot back, 'and no man can dare to command the destiny of the Emperor!'

He leered at her through the haze of spent plasmatic gases. 'Put aside the weapon, Miriya. Your heart is pure, you have proven that. The God-Emperor will need souls as pious as yours when He awakens, you can become part of this new beginning... Think of it,' cried the deacon. 'You will be the new Alicia Dominica, greater than any of the living saints!'

His invocation staggered her; the name of the greatest Sister of Battle, the hallowed Mother of Every Order, echoed in her mind. To be spoken of in the same breath as she... It was an incredible thing to consider.

'You can be that woman,' LaHayn pressed, sensing her hesitation, 'all your errors undone, all your failures reversed, every death made a life – if only you stop resisting the truth.'

Lethe and Iona. Portia and Reiko. She saw them all and more in her mind's eye, the imploring looks on their faces, and she had her answer. To give any other would have been to deny them the creed for which they had died, and to deny the truth that lay within her heart. 'In Katherine's name,' she screamed. 'Death to the witch!'

Sparks stung her as the gun's delicate mechanisms began to boil, the heat radiating off it in waves and melting the ceramite on her fingertips. The plasma bolts, usually collimated and regular in form, spat from the pistol now in screeching ejections of fury, lengths of heat lightning crackling off the weapon. LaHayn snarled and fought away the attacks, enraged at her refusal to capitulate. The gun was seconds from a critical failure, and with a hissing snap the casing cracked along its length. The warning glyphs were a virulent red. At the last moment, Miriya let her muscles take over and she hurled the weapon at the priest-lord as hard as she could.

LaHayn's mistake was that he reacted as a man, not as a psyker. His nascent powers could have deflected the thrown gun in an eye blink, but he was too new to them for it to be a reflex. The deacon caught the weapon in his hands and howled as the scorching heat of it burned him, and in that instant the overloaded plasma pistol detonated in a fireball.

The blast ripped great strips of molten flesh from Viktor LaHayn, flashing the soft tissues of his eyes to cinders, carving him open with daggers of flame as hot as a sun. His bone and marrow turned to molten slag, the opulent ministerial robes and golden icons he wore becoming blackened ashes in less than a second. Miriya's armour went slick and flowed like oil as she turned away. The ignition threw a bow wave of air compressed into a hazy white ring, slamming her out of the dying energy nimbus and against the sheer walls of the volcano's flue. She fell, clawing at black stone and adamantium decking.

With their organic component abruptly immolated, the spinning rings lost all synchronisation and clashed with an ear-shattering cacophony. Metals that had been forged in the hearts of long-dead neutron stars and etched with the blood of artisans from a thousand planets came apart. The rings fractured, dashed against one another, and lost all coherence. The aura field popped like a bubble and the machinery of the Emperor's lost engine fell the rest of the distance to the waiting deeps of the magma core. Somewhere down there, what remained of the High Ecclesiarch Lord Viktor LaHayn of Noroc boiled away into greasy vapours.

There was very, very much pain. The invisible knife rattling between her ribs was quite likely a broken bone piercing her lungs. The blood that bubbled out of her mouth with each exhalation virtually confirmed that. Her right eye was gummed shut with fluid weeping from a gash on her scalp and when Miriya attempted to run a hand through her hair it came away daubed with crimson. The power pack on her back had shut down, forcing her to move the weight of her battle armour without assistance from the synthetic myomer muscles beneath the ceramite sheath. In turn, some joints in the armour had become fused together by the brief, intense heat.

She took a ragged breath laced with sulphur fumes and looked down from the metal ledge where her headlong fall had finally ended. Her vision swam, but she swallowed the moment of disorientation. Far below she could see the vast doors that opened on to the engine chamber, where Verity and the others Sisters still remained, but the fall of the machine had torn the conduits away; she had no way to descend to them. Miriya tapped her vox, but her reward was an earful of static. Reluctantly, she began to push her way upwards, towards the beckoning oval of sky above. Each movement was like torture, but she was resolute.

The clattering ruin of the falling machine brought silence in its wake among the three Sisters. Verity, Isabel and Cassandra knew that the destruction of the engine marked the execution of the heretic deacon, but with it a dark fate for Miriya. Ash falls and coils of volcanic haze were thick about them, and rumbling tremors did their best to knock them off their feet.

Cassandra spat and threw a grimace at the entrance to the chamber. 'Rockfall,' she said in a weary voice. 'The way is not clear to us.'

Isabel was on her haunches, her eyes lost beneath a makeshift bandage. 'Sister, speak plainly. Is there any way out of this lightforsaken cavern?'

'Not for us,' came the reply. She glanced at the Hospitaller. 'Sister? What say you?'

Verity's attention was elsewhere. At the far corners of the chamber there seemed to be constellations of light gathering, small soundless flickers of colour that moved and flowed like mercury. 'Do you see that?' she asked.

As she spoke, a large cluster of the light-wisps fused and crackled. The sound sent a shiver through the air, splintering the walls with its passage. 'What was that?' demanded Isabel, instinctively grabbing her gun.

Cassandra paled. 'Oh, Throne.' She pointed. There were more pinpricks appearing by the moment, some of them hanging in the air like hovering insects. 'It's the warp. It's leaking through.'

Verity found herself nodding. She had once been on a transport ship bound for a relief effort on behalf of the Ministorum where the vessel's Geller Field had suffered a dangerous fluctuation on entering the empyrean. On the lower decks, where the field had been at its thinnest, similar phenomena had occurred. Ghost lights, dancing dots of colour that were the tiniest pinpricks of warp matter impinging on the real world. They were the probes of the intelligences that swarmed in warp space, hungry to taste souls. 'The engine,' she said. 'LaHayn's machine... It must have softened the barrier with the immaterium. Things... will break in.'

'There!' Cassandra aimed and fired. For a split second Verity had the impression of something disc-shaped and trailing filaments emerging from a coruscating shadow, then the bolter ripped it apart. The Battle Sister quickly reloaded, frowning. 'Back to back, quickly. There will be more of them.'

The climb took agonising hours, or so it seemed. With blood pooling in her boots, Miriya pushed herself over the lip of the volcanic vent and staggered down the sharp incline. A few hundred metres away she saw the artificial rock shelf where the oval landing pads sat. An aeronef laboured into the air as she approached, dangerously overloaded. It began to sink almost as soon as it took off. She estimated it would get no more than a kilometre away before it fell back into the wasteland.

An insistent droning circled her head and the Celestian tried to swat away whatever insect was causing it. She concentrated for a moment and realised that what she was hearing was the feed from her vox. Fumbling at her ear bead, she listened again. The citadel's arcane jamming systems did not operate beyond the inside of the keep. It was a chorus of overlapping channels and commands – her vox had obviously been damaged in the fall – but she recognised the orders being flashed back and forth.

'Retreat?' she said aloud. To hear it said after all they had fought through clouded her expression with annoyance. She spoke into her pickup. 'Say again,' Miriya demanded. 'Whose gutless orders are these?'

The reply buzzed in her ear. 'Miriya. For Katherine's sake, where are you?' The Canoness was furious.

'Atop the keep,' she replied. 'Who gave that order?'

'I did. The target zone is clear. You should be long gone!' Miriya could almost see the snarl on Galatea's face. 'You were ordered to rendezvous with the attack force. You were told to leave the keep!'

'I... intended to carry out that command in due time–'

'You have contravened orders once more,' shouted the distant voice, 'and now you'll pay the price for it.'

'I chose to... chose to interpret your orders differently, Canoness. I beg your forgiveness...' Miriya was close to the landing pads now. She saw two robed men working with frantic pace at an idling coleopter.

'Do you hear me?' spat Galatea. 'Let there be absolutely no room in your mind to interpret *this* command. Sister Superior Miriya, you are to desist in all combat activities immediately and evacuate the Null Keep to our rally point in the southern valley, where you will submit yourself for arrest. You have less than eleven standard minutes to comply!'

'Eleven minutes?' she repeated. 'Until what?'

'Until the orbital bombardment from the *Mercutio* reaches your co-ordinates. Pray tell, Sister, do I have your full and undivided attention now?'

Miriya choked on the words. 'A lance strike will reduce the entire citadel to rubble.'

'And whatever remains of LaHayn and his heretic army,' replied her commander. 'Unless you wish to join them, I advise you to find transport, and quickly. Ten minutes and twenty-two seconds.'

'My squad is still down there,' she snapped.

She heard a sigh. 'Regrettable. They will be honoured for their service to the church.'

Miriya cut off the vox link and swore a gutter oath. 'I'll not throw any more lives away for nothing,' she told herself. 'Never again.'

With care, she approached the coleopter, letting the whine of the engine cover her footsteps. The tender didn't know she was there until he took a fist-sized lump of volcanic rock in the temple. He went sprawling and she used the motion to divest him of the long-barrelled lasgun he carried. The second man reacted with shock as he walked into view around the curve of the fuselage.

'You,' she snapped. 'Can you fly this aircraft?'

He gave a wary nod.

'Good.' She aimed the lasgun and took the prone man's head off with one shot. 'You'll be next unless you do exactly, precisely what I tell you. Understand?'

Another nod, this time wooden and nervous.

She followed him into the cockpit pod and pressed the still-warm muzzle to the back of his head. 'Take us down the throat of the mountain, quickly.'

The man jerked in the chair and started to speak, but Miriya swatted him with the gun barrel. 'Remember your associate? Remember what I told you? Now do as I say!'

The coleopter's motors chattered up to full speed, and with a bump they left the landing pad, the blunt nose turning towards the steaming maw of the volcano.

The things that came through the holes in the air were horrors the like of which Verity had never dreamed: skinless things with hundreds of yellow-toothed mouths, screeching furies and spidery forms with too many clacking legs. These were the common predators of the warp, the mindless monstrosities that infested the immaterium beyond human consciousness. The sounds they made as they died were terrible, the liquids spilling from them in garish colours that matched nothing in creation. The gun Cassandra gave her spent the last of its bolt rounds all too quickly, and half in fright, half in fury, the Hospitaller threw it at the creatures.

Step by step, the encroaching fiends pushed the Sisters back to the very edge of the chamber, where the steep drop-off plunged hundreds of metres to the lava lake below. Torturous heat at their backs, and a massing wall of Chaos beasts at their front. Verity, Cassandra and Isabel measured their lives by each breath of air.

The injured Sororitas snarled in despair as her bolter's breech snapped open, the last of her ammunition expended. 'I'm spent,' she told them.

The hordes hesitated. They seemed to understand that the prey was at the point of no return, and they giggled and snapped at one another in anticipation.

Cassandra glanced at the sickle magazine in her bolter and blew out a breath. 'I have three rounds remaining,' she said carefully. Her eyes tracked to Isabel and the wounded Battle Sister returned a weary nod. Then Cassandra looked at Verity with a hollow sadness on her face that the Hospitaller had never seen before. 'Sister? Do not fear. I'll make it quick.'

'No,' Verity shook her head, realising that tears were on her face. 'It is not us I feel sorry for, but our Sisters. They are the ones who will have to shoulder the pain of our loss.'

Cassandra nodded. 'You are brave, girl. I would not have thought it of you. I am glad you proved me wrong.'

'And I,' said Isabel. 'Lethe was proud of you. Now I understand why.'

'The honour was mine.' Verity bowed her head and whispered a prayer, waiting for the Emperor's Peace, but in a roar of downwash, an entirely different saviour arrived.

Encouraged by a series of colourful threats and a shot through the canopy, Miriya forced the pilot to bring the coleopter into a hover by the open gates into the engine room. The situation imprinted on her refined tactical mind in an instant, the Sisters against the edge, the line of shapeless, hooting forms. There was a control board at her right hand and she stabbed the glyphs to activate the stubber guns in the flyer's nose. Rigged with cogitator sense engines, the weapon cupolas saw where she aimed them and busied themselves by automatically opening fire on anything that moved. The pilot dutifully turned the coleopter to present its flank to the women below, and Miriya felt the aircraft pitch as they scrambled aboard.

'Here,' she heard Verity call from the cramped rear compartment.

'Go,' Miriya prodded the pilot with the lasgun, but he needed no more goading. More things were leaking through the expanding warp rifts and these new ones had wings and claws. At maximum thrust, the spindly flyer rose through the ash-fogged air and out into clear sky, turning southwards.

Cassandra came into the cockpit and started to speak but Miriya held up a hand to silence her and pointed at the sky. Dozens of quick, twinkling stars were falling down towards the Null Keep.

By the time the shockwave of the first impacts reached them, they were safe in the canyons, and leaving LaHayn's mad dream further behind with every passing second.

Through the chapel window, Verity could see the tower of the Lunar Cathedral, clad in flapping tarpaulins where the work crews were busy putting the hallowed church back to the state it had been in before the attack. On the streets, the newly appointed governor, Baron Preed, had softened the news of his predecessor's death by declaring a national holiday, and a bloodless one at that, lacking in any enforced tithes. In part this was due to the hasty installation of a new deacon at Noroc's church, the moderate cleric-teacher Lord Kidsley. In the days that followed the obliteration of the Null Keep, news spread quickly about the perfidy of Lord LaHayn. His name was anathema now, icons of his face taken down and torched by the hundreds.

Privately, Verity held the opinion that only one death would never be enough to pay back such a base and self-serving man. Sister Miriya's thoughts on the subject had been predictably harsh, involving more profanity than was mannerly for a woman of the cloth.

As if the thought of her brought her into existence, the door opened to admit the Battle Sister. She was without armour, still limping from her recent injuries, and yet she seemed no less imposing than the day Verity had first met her. They exchanged nods.

'I was not aware that Galatea had summoned you as well.'

'She did not,' said Verity. 'I came of my own volition.'

Miriya frowned. 'Why?'

'I could do nothing less.'

The Celestian was about to say more, but the chapel door opened once more to admit the Canoness, and with her Sister Chloe, her acting adjutant.

Galatea threw Verity a hard look. 'I had thought you would be off-world by now, Hospitaller.'

'Soon, Canoness. However, before I left, I felt my expertise might be needed here.'

'No one is sick here, girl.'

'I speak of matters of truth, not illness. I am well versed in both.'

Galatea took up a place at the altar. 'Neva rebuilds,' she said at length. 'I have begun a series of purges among the ruling cadres to expunge any lingering traces of LaHayn's sacrilege. This sorry episode will resonate through this world's history for centuries to come... if indeed the planet survives that long.' She gave Miriya a steady, unflinching stare. 'You proved me right, Sister. You brought me trouble... So much trouble.'

'That was never my intention.'

She snorted. 'It never is.' The Canoness pointed to the distant cathedral. 'The Synod want you executed, Miriya. Despite the part you played in terminating the heretic and the witch, your wayward disobedience colours everything!' She banged her fist on the altar. 'Twice you openly defied me, and by extension, the Imperial Church!'

'I did what I thought was right,' said the Celestian.

'Right?' snarled Galatea. 'You invite a death sentence. You place me in a very difficult position, Sister. What am I to do with a woman who blatantly flouted the orders of her superiors?'

'Let her live,' said Verity. 'Let her serve the church with the same honour and courage she showed at the keep.'

'Those things are meaningless without order,' Chloe broke in. 'Each Sister serves as part of a whole. None of us are a law unto ourselves.'

'I will accept whatever outcome the church decrees.' Miriya murmured.

'You would die?' snapped the Hospitaller. 'Even though you did what any loyal Sister would have done?' Verity faced Galatea. 'This is how our faith tests us. Not by rigidly adhering to books of ancient canon without care or thought, but by placing us in harm's way and trying our resolve with challenges beyond our experience. If we are forever rigid and unbending, if we never dare to take a chance against our enemies, then what good are we to our Emperor?' Her passion was sudden and heartfelt. 'We become nothing but mindless zealots locked on a course, blinkered and bound... like Viktor LaHayn.'

There was a long silence before the Canoness addressed Chloe. 'She's quite eloquent, this Hospitaller.'

'Yes, I thought so,' agreed the Sister Seraphim.

She sighed. 'I do not wish to see you perish, Sister. But nevertheless, insubordination cannot go unpunished.' Galatea's gaze rested on Miriya, and in a moment of cold familiarity, she repeated the words of LaHayn. 'There must be reciprocity.'

The woman nodded. 'I understand.'

The Canoness approached her. 'Sister Miriya, it is my judgement that you be stripped of all your honours within the order and your status as a Celestian elite, henceforth reduced to the line rank of Battle Sister.' She took the chaplet ecclesiasticus from Miriya's belt loop and broke it, tearing off a handful of beads from the length before handing the mutilated rosary back to her. 'You will continue to serve the

God-Emperor in the church's mission. Perhaps in time, if you temper your bouts of non-compliance, He may grant you the chance to regain these privileges. If not, then at least you may fight and die in His name.'

Miriya bowed. 'Thank you for your mercy, honoured Canoness.'

Galatea turned away. 'The *Mercutio* breaks orbit at ten-bell, Miriya. I want you aboard it when it does. I will have enough to deal with in the coming days without you to concern me. Go now.'

Verity could see the rejection wounded her, but she hid it well. 'As you wish. Ave Imperator.'

'Ave Imperator,' chorussed the other women, as Miriya hobbled from the chapel.

Mercutio detached from the commerce station with elephantine slowness, the broad prow of the frigate turning away from the orbital complex to the open seas of space. In the observatorium, Miriya was alone with her thoughts.

She felt conflicted: part of her was relieved that at last the debt she owed to Lethe and the others was paid in full, just as part of her felt isolated and morose at her dismissal and censure. The Sororitas was to take the *Mercutio*'s journey to the port on Paramar and there submit herself to the local convent for a new tasking.

Something in the ebon sky caught her eye. There were shapes moving out there, dark as the volcanic glass of the Null Keep. She crossed to the transparent dome to get a better view.

Black Ships. There were two of them, approaching Neva in a silent formation. The sight made her shudder, it was almost unheard of for more than one of them to be seen at a single time.

'They have come to pore over the materials and research left behind by LaHayn,' said a voice. Miriya turned to see Verity, clad once more in her travelling robes, as she entered. 'They will take what they want and sanitise the rest.'

The Sororitas did not question the Hospitaller's presence;

she felt comforted by it. 'I find myself wondering, Sister. What if LaHayn did have some flawed insight into the Emperor's works?'

'Perhaps he did,' admitted Verity, 'perhaps not. It is not our place to know such things. At least, not yet. One day, when He rises from the Golden Throne, all questions will be answered.'

'Yes.' Miriya made the sign of the aquila, watching the dark vessels pass them by.

'You have other questions,' noted the younger woman.

'My destiny is clouded, Sister. For the first time in my life, I know not what my destination will be.' She closed her eyes for a moment. 'I am unsettled.'

Verity drew closer. 'Then, if you wish, I might offer a path to you. My duties in this system are at an end, just as yours are. I have already been given orders to join the mission of Canoness Sepherina, who journeys from Terra to perform a rite of reconsecration on the planet Sanctuary. You would be welcome to join me.'

'I would appreciate that.' She extended her hand. 'Thank you, Verity.'

'I owe you my life, Miriya. I do it gladly.' The Hospitaller took her hand and smiled.

Mercutio sailed on, amid stars as constant as their faith.

HAMMER & ANVIL

CHAPTER ONE

The howling sand found its way into everything.

Every crevice in her breastplate, every tiny void in her battledress, every moving part of her wargear. It was almost a ritual on this wasteland world, the daily regimen of cleaning a new sacrament to be performed alongside the usual rites of the convent laid down by the High Canoness. In corridors and rooms, in spaces large and small, the sand would accrete in drifts if not properly dealt with. It seemed that no amount of baffles or electromagnetic fields could keep it entirely at bay.

Sister Elspeth had once joked that perhaps the sand was alive, that it might be some sort of mite-sized swarming animal that craved warmth and shadowed corners. Elspeth was dead now, killed just after matins when the attack came. The sand had been her grave, her life leaking into it from her ragged wounds. Decima held her hand at the end, as the sand drank in all she gave it, the pale orange dust shading slowly into crimson mud.

Decima thought about Elspeth as she struggled across the dunes, hunched forward against the force of the endless winds, the dust dragging at her heels and the gusts jerking the shemagh wrapped around her face. Clever Elspeth, who was good at regicide and games of tall card, pious Elspeth who sometimes mumbled the catechisms in her sleep. But dead now. And killed by something the like of which no Sister had ever seen.

She shivered, despite the sullen, intimate heat of the day. The burden pulled against her arm, the cord around it twisting, and Decima threw a glance back at the container. The metal drum was grey and grimy, and it left a trail vanishing into the sandstorm, a line leading back towards the convent. Decima squinted along the path she had left behind her.

How far was it now? Not for the first time, she cursed herself for leaving in such a hurry, without first securing the helmet twinned with her Sabbat-pattern power armour; the infra-red sensing lenses and preysight mechanisms within the helm would have been of great use at this moment.

But there had been no time. The order came with the demand for instant obedience. *Go now*, the canoness had said, her voice hard and sharp. *Take it and go*.

Decima wanted to believe that it was some spark of courage the senior Sister saw in her that had rewarded the young woman with so important a task, but in her heart she knew it was not so. The role of custodian had fallen to Decima simply because she was there when no other was at hand. She had no high rank, no great sigils of courage to her name, barely a few beads upon her chaplet. Her status might have been far elevated over the ordinary masses of the Imperium, but still Decima was only a line Sister Militant, just a foot soldier in the Wars of Faith.

She dared to wonder; might this moment be the calling of her to greatness? She pushed the thought away. To consider such things was to aggrandise one's self, and that was a sin.

Her lot was to be at the command of He Upon the Golden Throne, the God-Emperor of Mankind whose light illuminated the stars. Decima had been inducted into her order while still a child, recruited like a myriad of other orphans from the schola progenium for the varied organs of the Imperial machine, and like them she knew no life but one of service. Decima and a legion of her kindred were the Sisters of the Adepta Sororitas, the army of right in the employ of humanity's great church.

What her church needed in so distant and desolate a world as this had never been made clear to Decima, but it was not her place to ask such questions. She was to do as she had been commanded to, and be grateful that she had so clearly defined a purpose in the universe. Others – commoners – were cursed with the need to search for meaning in their lives. Not so for Decima; the church was there to give significance to her as it saw fit. That burden, at least, was lifted from her.

At this moment, her purpose dragged behind her, forming a bolus of sand at its blunt prow, resolutely digging itself in and doubling the effort needed to move it. Decima muttered a sanctioned curse through the cloth covering her mouth and turned back to the metal drum. Her bolter, mag-locked to her backpack, caught on the red cloak over her shoulder, clattering against her black armour. She didn't like the idea of not having a hand free to grab the weapon if she needed to, but the sluggish pace of her encumbrance overcame her concern.

In a moment, Decima had the metal container in her arms, cradling it as one might hold a fat child in swaddling clothes. She tried not to think about what it contained. The emotional weight of her burden dwarfed its physical mass, and it pulled at Decima's heart. It made her fearful, an emotion she seldom experienced on the battlefield. She had never expected to bear such responsibility, but she had been chosen because she was alive, and because Sisters far better trained in the arts of warfare than she – Celestians and Retributors among them – even now gave themselves up to ensure her escape.

Cowed by this thought, the enormity of her duty fully asserted itself, and Decima pressed on with renewed pace. With each footfall she spoke a word from the Prayer of the Released, pacing herself through the sands.

The storm robbed her of all but the most basic senses. A digicompass in the vambrace of her armour was the only thing she was willing to trust. In her time on this world, Decima had learned that the sands and the strange rocky towers they shaped could confuse and disorient the unwary traveller. On the old galactic maps, this ball of stone and dust had been christened after the star it orbited – Kavir – but in the ninth century of the forty-first millennium it went by the unremarkable name Decima's Order had given it. To the Sisterhood of the Order of Our Martyred Lady, this world was known as Sanctuary 101.

It was difficult to reckon the passage of time. Little of the weak light of the yellow-white Kavir sun penetrated through the swirling clouds, so charting the advance of the hours proved fruitless. Instead Decima went on, one foot in front of the other, watching the sand shift beneath her boots. More than once she fell, losing her step as she crested one of the dunes, tumbling, then scrambling after the container when it rolled away, afraid it might split open. But it remained intact; the metal pod was crafted using lost techniques from the Dark Age of Technology, and would have survived a fall from orbit unharmed.

The desert played other tricks on her. At times, Decima thought she saw shapes at the very edge of her perception, ghostly forms close by, but not so close that she could define them. Humanoid shapes? Or was it just the dance of the dust in the wind and her tired mind making patterns where none existed?

She remembered the glimpses she had caught of the things that had come to kill them, the forms that ended Elspeth and the others. In the gloomy corridors of the convent, the attackers had first shut down the fusion reactor and plunged the outpost into darkness as the storm took hold. Decima did not know how, as the power core was locked away behind thick shield doors and protected by gun-servitors. Still, it had been done.

So, in the dark, then. She only had impressions of them, blink-fast moments captured by the cruciform flare of muzzle flashes. Emaciated things that reflected any illumination, like torchlight off tarnished brass or the muddy rainbow of oil on water. A sickly green glow following them wherever they went. Silver cutting blades. Those things, and the screaming. Inhuman sounds of tortured air molecules being torn apart before lances of searing light. Decima remembered the purple after-images burned into her retinas, even as she tried to forget the smell of ancient soil and warm blood.

The sounds of the conflict, the skirl of beam fire and the chattering of bolters, these had followed her out onto the sands as she fled with the burden in tow. The noises were soon swallowed up by the clouds, along with any sight of the convent's central tower, the keep and outer guardian walls. It seemed like a lifetime ago.

She passed beyond the outer markers, skirting the narrow buttes that surrounded the valley where the outpost lay, and went on into the open erg. Decima had never ventured so far from the convent alone and without a vehicle.

As she began to wonder if she was far enough away, the digicompass transmitted a vibrating pulse down to the palm of her glove. Decima hesitated, studying it. Yes. She had entered the canyon at the base of the wind-sculpted towers far to the west, a point of relative calm among the more horrific of the planet's storm zones. The worst could sandblast flesh and strip an unprotected woman to the bone, or bury a stalled transport so it might never be found again. Lives had been lost from the convent's population through both manners of death over the years.

Decima fell into the lee of a tall, spindly finger of ruddy marble and shook dust from where it pooled in the clefts of her wargear, her combat cloak snapping as the wind ran over it. The ground became rocky here, islands of stone protruding from the sand, but in turn the airborne dust was harsher. Fines of powder became specks of flint, and Decima narrowed her eyes, pulling the shemagh tighter.

Working as quickly as she dared, the Battle Sister found a spot out of the weak sunlight and twisted a single grenade into the sand, turning it until it was almost hidden in the dust. She yanked the primer pin and sprinted away to a safe distance. Like the sounds of death and conflict from the outpost, the muffled grunt of the detonation was flattened and consumed by the sandstorm.

Decima brought the container back to the hollow her makeshift demolition had cut and climbed in with it. The grenade had excavated a space large enough to serve as a foxhole, but the woman had other plans. With great care, she laid the metal container at the bottom of the hollow and took a precise reading from the compass; then, using the butt of her bolter as a makeshift shovel, Decima started to bury the pod.

She had only made two or three passes when she paused, her heart tight in her chest. The Sororitas thought about what she was doing, about the priceless value of the object she was consigning to the embrace of the desert, and it stopped her dead. Decima imagined herself like a mother interring the corpse of an infant, suddenly afraid to turn another spade of earth over its face for fear it might suddenly awaken in terror. Was it right to do this? To bury such a treasure in this wilderness where it might never be found again?

The artefact must never fall to the xenos. The voice of Canoness Agnes echoed in her thoughts. *This is my last command to you, Sister Decima.*

Her last command. By now, the canoness had to be dead. The battle had been lost even before Decima had fled. She had known it was inevitable when the order had been given. All human life at the outpost colony on Sanctuary 101 was in the process of being exterminated, and Decima's deed was the final action to be taken.

But what will happen to me? The thought crystallised for the first time in Decima's mind, and she trembled. She allowed herself to think beyond her mission, beyond the collective of the Order's will and to her own survival. She would bury the capsule and then... Return to the convent? Sit atop these rocks and wait to starve? The nearest Imperial colony was months away across the savage currents of the warp. Rescue, if it were ever to come, would mean a long, long wait–

There was motion in the sand near her boots. Something was in the hollow with her, lurking in the gravel. Something like silver or tarnished brass.

Decima exploded from the pit and rolled away, bringing up her boltgun, working the slide to clear it of any fouling by force of habit. Clumps of oily sand puffed out from the weapon as half-glimpsed shapes moved through the veil of the dust cloud, closing in. She saw gelid emerald light burning within iron skulls and limbs made of dead metal.

The bolter spoke, and she made every shot count, blowing open frames that mocked the bone-forms of human ribcages. Others mantled their fallen in silence, drawing a closing ring around her, advancing, inexorable.

Decima killed them – or so it seemed – and they melted into the sand, crackling green fire dissembling them, fading the things from her sight. They resembled machines, but on some level the Battle Sister knew that they were nothing so simple. There was an ephemeral quality about their manner and motion, an unquantifiable something that hinted at a deeper truth. Whatever these things were, a living mind animated them. No machine could ever radiate such malice. This understanding came to Decima like a blow, even as she knew it would count for nothing.

The bolter ran dry, the slide locking open as the clip was spent, and Sister Decima, last survivor of Sanctuary 101, regretted that she had not saved the final round for herself.

CHAPTER TWO

The noise from the vox was like rainfall.

Imogen remembered the sound from her years as a novice on Ophelia VII, walking the halls of the Convent Sanctorum as grey skies emptied themselves over the panes of stained-glass windows five hundred metres tall. The rain, she remembered, would sluice down the faces of saints as if they were weeping.

None wept now, so it seemed. None shed tears for the mottled orange sphere hanging out there in the distance before her, all surface detail upon it hazed by cloud and distortion.

The Sister Superior stood in silence before the speaker grille, which protruded from the observer's desk in the guise of a cherub's face; in turn, the desk itself lay across the watch gallery below the starship *Tybalt*'s keel sail. At this station, a crew serf could stand to take readings with a laser sextant should the whiskered sensor barbs at the cruiser's prow ever malfunction, but most often it stood unattended. The vox-unit was typically inactive, but Sister Imogen's hand had strayed to it when she entered, tracing the sigil of the holy aquila as invocation before switching it on.

Her eyes narrowed, pulling her face tight beneath its frame of rich henna-red hair. She couldn't quite frame the impulse that had made her do it. Imogen had come here to take a look at their destination, just a passing notion to fix it in her mind, and reached for the vox control without conscious thought. The communications system was self-tuning, automatically skipping across standard Imperial frequencies as its simple machine-spirit looked for a signal to lock on to.

The planet gave no purchase. The rain-sound of the static from the brass child-face of the cherub went on and on like a mournful, whispering dirge. If there had ever been any cries into the void from the desert world, then they had long since passed into the blackness. More than a decade on from the day the attack had come, and there remained nothing but the endless hiss of cosmic background radiation, the strange kind of anti-silence that was more solemn than the tranquillity of any sepulchre.

Imogen switched off the vox and frowned. Soon the *Tybalt* would fire its manoeuvring drives for a close planetary approach and the naval cruiser would settle into low orbit. Even now, the helots and servitors on the warship's command deck were poring over their scry-screens, analysing the returns from the vessel's sensors. Would they find anything that differed from the second-hand readings the Ordo Xenos had given them, she wondered? It was hard to be sure; all the Sister Superior knew was that the Inquisition's data had been heavily censored before the Sororitas had received it. Not for the first time, she asked herself what truths had been edited from those documents before they were passed to the Order of Our Martyred Lady.

She turned her back on Kavir – on Sanctuary 101 – and left the observation gallery. Imogen would see it at close hand soon enough.

The Sister Superior let a conveyor take her up the vertical spine of the *Tybalt*, past the gunnery tiers to the egress decks where the materiel for the mission was being assembled. The last few checks were being made, the final chances for any mistakes to be corrected. Once they nestled into orbit, the next phase of the operation would begin, and with all the sharp precision that the Sisters Militant were known for. Imogen entered the cavernous bay where ranks of Arvus- and Aquila-class shuttles were being attended by workgangs in leather oversuits and powerframes. The labourers were busy loading cargo pods, and prefabricated Phaeton-pattern construction units that could be assembled into any one of a hundred different modular buildings. They hummed and sang in low tones that resonated off the decks, around them the smell of promethium fuel mingling with sweat and coolants. Some of the helots were commissioned men in service to the Imperial Navy, but the majority were tithed workers bound by oath or deed of penance to the Sororitas. Some were minor criminals working off their debt to society through hard labour, others ordinary citizens who had willingly given up their rights in order to show their devotion to the church. They would be the army of restoration once planetfall had been made, and above them, marching back and forth along a suspended gantry, was the man who they called master.

Imogen inclined her gaze as Deacon Uriahi Zeyn caught her eye and bobbed his head. The priest spared her only a cursory glance, quickly returning to his business of motivation and command. This he accomplished over the workgangers by use of a lengthy electro-whip and an implanted vocoder module in his throat. Zeyn's machine-augmented voice blasted hymnals across the egress bay, punctuated with harsh snarls of oratory drawn from the *Book of Atticus*, *The Rebuke* or other devotional tomes. The whip he used now and then to underline his points, or to give a little discipline to those who tarried. The flashes of blue sparks it left behind illuminated his face.

The deacon was a large, rangy man of pale face and small, deep-set eyes. He had a fierce beard of carroty-red and a halo of wild hair to match. Imogen found him quite coarse, uncouth for an anointed member of the cloth, but she could not deny that he drew great results from his charges. Without pausing to engage him, the Sister Superior walked on, her boots snapping across the iron decks in time to the rise and fall of the songs of the workers.

Canoness Sepherina, Imogen's commander and the mistress of this mission, would want a full and clear-eyed report on the delegation's readiness before vespers, and so as she walked, the Sororitas became watchful. She looked for anything that hinted at a concern, intent that none would be found. The long journey from Holy Terra to the Eastern Galactic Rim was almost at an end, and at this late stage it would not serve Him Upon The Throne to falter.

This would be Imogen's first experience of a re-consecration, and like all her sisters, she understood the great import of such an event. In the Wars of Faith and the Great Service, it was a fact of life that many Adepta Sororitas would be called to the God-Emperor's side as death claimed them. But once in a while, those deaths were of such magnitude and horror that the very ground on which they took place became... *unholy*. In the name of Imperial Truth, it was thus important to sift such earth of its darker resonances and return it by blessing to right and good. Zeyn's workers would rebuild what physical damage had been done down on the planet, but it would be the canoness who would repair the spiritual wounds of the place. Together, the members of the mission would make it whole again.

This was the deed that would be done at Sanctuary 101; but it was not the only one, nor was it the most important task of Sepherina's sacred undertaking. In time, and if circumstances required it, then the full scope of things would be made clear to the rest of the Battle Sisters. For now, it was necessary to keep the secret for the good of the duty. Imogen understood this, and as with so many things in her service, she did not think to question it.

So long a journey to get here; and yet she recalled the day when her orders were cut by the High Mistress of her Order as if it had only been a moment ago.

* * *

Imogen had stood to arms in the role of adjutant and guardian to Sepherina at a meeting on Apophis, a repurposed asteroid in high orbit around Holy Terra. The site belonged to the Ordo Xenos, and what glimpses the Sisters had been granted of the complex's interior were fleeting, giving rise to worrisome questions as to exactly what the Inquisition's alien hunters did there. The thought of being in close proximity to anything connected to heathen non-human life made the woman's skin crawl. Sister Imogen had fought the xenos many times, killing ork and eldar, and any number of other nameless things that aped the intellect and perfection of mankind. As they walked through the snaking lava-tube corridors inside Apophis, she had kept one hand close to her bolter, and the other on the chaplet that hung around her neck.

Finally, Sepherina and her party had been shown into a meeting room laser-cut from the dense meteoric stone, and left to wait until the man who summoned them finally graced the Sisterhood with his presence.

Inquisitor Hoth, a male of stocky build beneath a wide-brimmed preacher hat, entered with his own retinue: a pair of gunmen who showed the manner of mercenaries more than virtuous servants of the Golden Throne. The men surveyed the Sisters with eyes that were wary and predatory in equal measure. Imogen had let them look at her, concealing nothing. Better that they see the steel and plate of her power armour, better they know the presence of her gun and blade. She recognised men like them. They understood only crude vectors of approach, force and violence. Eventually, they looked away, and for the rest of the meeting kept their gazes turned elsewhere.

Hoth, on the other hand, radiated a singular air of unconcern that bordered on condescension. He took a seat and busied himself with a data-slate, picking at icons on the screen, moving them back and forth like beads on an ancient abacus. Imogen was uncertain if he were actually working on something, or if he were toying with the device to amuse himself. The man behaved as if he was barely aware of them in the room with him.

Hoth had granted them audience after a long silence. The deposition from the Sisterhood had come in person to ask again upon a request, which had been circling through the vast machine of Imperial bureaucracy for almost seven solar years. Such a period of time was little more than the blink of an eye, when measured against the monumental epochs of officialdom that weighed down most decisions made by the Adeptus Terra and the great organisations of the Imperium. But for the Order of Our Martyred Lady, it had been as if a century passed for each wasted day. Seven years before they met in that stone chamber, the convent at Sanctuary 101 had gone dark, the last communication from it an agonised scream.

As ever, the engine of empire moved slowly, but the Sisters had made ready to set sail for the Kavir system, preparing ships and warriors, only to be prevented from departing by the Ministorum itself. It came to pass that on the advice of the Ordo Xenos and the personal diktat of Inquisitor Hoth, the Sisterhood were denied permission to return to Sanctuary 101 and determine what had happened there.

Of all the Canoness Minoris in the Order, Sister Sepherina had been the most vocal over this insult to the authority of the Sororitas. The Ordo Xenos had no power over the Sisterhood, and yet Hoth had drawn on his own vast web of influence to convince those who did that he, not the Sisters, should be first to Sanctuary 101 in the wake of this mysterious event. The matter had created great enmity between the two organisations, and much in the way of politicking and sharp words, all of them for nothing. The inquisitor was known to Imogen's Order, and his interest – some said *his obsession* – with certain strains of alien life was not a secret. But despite all the entreaties, the requests and veiled threats, Hoth had made sure the order remained in place.

Until that day.

Without explanation, without apology or acknowledgement

of the Sisterhood's great pain, he told them they now had leave to return to the planet and lay the ghosts of their dead to rest. *'My interest,'* he said, *'has shifted to other matters.'*

Sepherina exploded with questions and demands as Hoth stood up after making his pronouncement. *What happened at the convent? Did anyone survive? Did you go there?* The inquisitor ignored them all, and finally the canoness was railing at nothing as Hoth crossed back towards the door. It was the first time, in years of duty alongside the other woman, that Imogen had ever seen Sepherina lose her temper.

Seven years of being banned from setting foot upon their own outpost world, with only the vaguest of justifications, seven years of rumours about the invasion of a new kind of alien form, all cast aside in a moment.

And so, in the nine hundred and third year of the forty-first millennium of the Imperium of Man, Canoness Sepherina was empowered to command a mission back to the silent outpost. Even with good warp currents, six more years Terran standard time had elapsed as the starship *Tybalt* travelled first to Paramar to equip, and then on to the distant Kavir system.

At Paramar they had taken on the last of what would be needed on Sanctuary 101, the hardware, the building supplies, the workgangers. During their voyage, this need had been communicated to the Sororitas by the Ordo Xenos through the sketchy reports the alien hunters had decided to give up. They supplied recordings of destruction across the entire keep and complex on the outpost planet but with no word of what had caused them or why. Images of fallen buildings that seemed to have been brought down by beam fire or in some cases, earthquake. The only direct question that the Ordo Xenos deigned to answer was on the issue of the planet's safety. According to them, the so-called 'threat vector' to Kavir was gone, like a passing storm. There was nothing there now, they said.

These words had come to the Sisterhood, and along with them, a new edict.

Inwardly, Sister Imogen chafed at the thought of it. It was not enough that Hoth and his kind had trampled the death site of hundreds of loyal Sisters, doubtless indulging his sickening interest in all things inhuman; no, now the Lords of Terra, in some mercurial wisdom, had granted passage to a party of technologists from the Adeptus Mechanicus. They were led by Tegas, a wiry being of questor rank – Imogen hesitated to call him a 'man', for there seemed to be little of the flesh about him – and like Hoth, he too seemed to be more set on things outside the remit of the mission to reconsecrate the convent.

The Sister Superior had a detail of women she trusted implicitly, each of them appointed to secretly observe Tegas and his small group. They had done this since Paramar, and so far the questor had shown no sign of being aware of the... secondary objective.

Tegas's orders were that he and his team assist the workgangs in the reconstruction on Sanctuary, but such a task was rarely given to an adept of his rank. She knew there was more to the cyborg's company here, and she wondered if the canoness had been told the true reason. That was doubtful. Sepherina was as pragmatic as she was pious, and it was highly unlikely she would not choose to share this information with her trusted combat commander. Some of the other Sororitas wondered if Tegas might be on this voyage because of some misdeed he had committed, that he was joining them in sufferance and penance. It was as good a hypothesis as any, but Imogen did not hold to it. The oily questor walked like a rat on its hind legs, all snout, spindle and points, and the Sister's instinctive dislike of Tegas made everything he did appear to be untrustworthy.

Imogen dismissed the cyborg from her thoughts as she approached a squad of Battle Sisters of the line, the women drilling in loose formation with deactivated chainswords and bayonet-equipped bolters. They snapped to attention as she came closer, standing ramrod straight and proud, the rich crimson of their combat cloaks and war tabards framing the ebony shimmer of their battle armour. Imogen was not afraid to admit that her heart swelled in her breast each time she laid her gaze on her Sisters. If she ever needed a reminder as to what was right and purposeful, she had only to turn her face to look at these women and know that those qualities were embodied in them. In the ocean of uncertainty that was this dark universe, the Sisters of Battle were the unbreakable bulwark of humanity's faith.

It mattered little to Imogen if men like Hoth or Tegas looked upon them and muttered the word 'fanatic' behind their hands. They did not understand the divine truth that the Sisters of Battle knew in their souls, and they would never know the joy of true betrothal to the greatest creed in human history. The God-Emperor, in all his divine majesty, had made the Imperium to vouchsafe mankind and keep it protected from all threats. The heathen alien, the witch-psyker, the abhuman and the foulness of the mutant, even the sickening monstrosities of the Ruinous Powers – all these forces beat at the walls of humanity's salvation and tried again and again to drag it screaming into impiety and damnation.

None saw this as clearly as the Sisters of Battle. Oh, it was true that they did not fight this tide of enemies alone, but one could not expect the common soldiery of the Imperial Guard to weather such threats. The Inquisition, while companionable in some forms to the work of the Sororitas, often dallied too closely with the very things they set out to expunge. And the Adeptus Astartes, the Emperor's Space Marines... They were a melange of conflicted, tribal warrior bands that embraced undependable psychics and the tenets of transhumanism. A few of their number were perhaps more tolerable than the others, and all were faithful to the Throne in their own crude conduct... But they were never to be trusted.

In a way, Imogen pitied them. They would never understand the *glory* of pure faith, the freedom from doubt it gave.

The Sister closest to her bowed her head slightly and

saluted with the aquila, hands folding open over her chest. 'Milady,' she began. 'If I may ask, when will we be ordered to embark?' The woman nodded towards the waiting shuttles.

Imogen studied her and said nothing. There had been other things brought aboard at Paramar, and among them came a contingent of additional Battle Sisters tasked to join the mission after the fact. This one was a member of that group, one of the latecomers who boarded with hospitallers and medicae support staff from the non-combatant Order of Serenity.

Sister Miriya. Imogen remembered the woman's name. The Sister Superior made it her business to maintain a watchful eye on Miriya. She had heard the barrack-hall rumours about the woman, the tales of a Sister with a wide independent streak and an overly forthright manner. Imogen's gaze dropped to the chaplet around Miriya's neck, and she reached out for it, running her thumb over the golden sigil and the line of adamantine beads it hung from. Miriya did not move.

Each bead represented an act of great devotion to the church, be it the burning of a witch or a victory won. Miriya's line was scuffed and damaged in a manner that could not be traced back to battle wear. It had been quite clearly and deliberately broken, cut short and then re-set. Imogen released the chaplet and let it fall free. Sister Miriya had once been a Celestian, serving as commander of her own squad at the rank of Eloheim, but now that honour was lost to her. Imogen did not know the full details of the incident, but she was aware that the woman had disobeyed a direct order given by Canoness Galatea of the Neva convent. The end result left Miriya reduced in rank to that of an ordinary Sister Militant.

Imogen's lips thinned as she considered her. Surely a Sister who broke the chain of command deserved far more punishing censure than this? Excommunication or even castigation into the ranks of the Repentia, there to self-flagellate and pray each day to redeem herself. Galatea's mercy seemed... *soft*.

'You will be told when it is time, and not before,' Imogen

snapped. She did not like Miriya, the way she held herself or the way she presumed to speak without first asking leave to do so. The Sister Superior studied her dark shock of ink-black hair, the scars that marred her face and the blood-red fleur-de-lys tattoo upon her cheek, searching the other woman for the air of defiance she knew hid beneath them. Had the choice been hers, Imogen would have refused the Sister's petition to join the *Tybalt*'s mission, but Sepherina had ideas about *leading by example*. The canoness spoke of offering Miriya a place where she could touch upon her fealty to the God-Emperor, a role where she might find renewed purpose. Imogen had little time for such things. She believed in firm acts of piety and a constant, unchanging devotion. There was no place for the uncertain or the free-thinker here.

The matter was not helped by the arrival of two other Sisters from Miriya's former squad, who had also accepted reduced rank – the tall and muscular Cassandra, and the younger one, Isabel. The latter bore scars that were still new, and sported a pewter augmetic eye that had yet to lose its sheen. Whatever injuries these two had suffered, it had apparently hardened their bond with Miriya rather than weakened it; and even though their former commander was now their equal in rank, they still showed her an undue degree of respect, deferring to Miriya almost by force of habit.

Imogen had watched them perform fight drills and it could not be denied that Sister Miriya and her cohorts had ample combat skills. But it was becoming increasingly clear that she would need to break them of their past patterns of behaviour, if they were to be of proper service during the mission.

The former Celestian did not reply to Imogen's words, but she did not look away either. The air of subtle defiance in the other woman was not undimmed. Miriya would never seek to challenge her openly, Imogen knew that. She was not a fool. But if the Battle Sister believed she would be able to erode Imogen's command status in any fashion at all, there would be a reckoning.

'Canoness Sepherina will address the ship's company

personally,' continued the Sister Superior. 'There will be a sermon and a hymnal of dedication before we set off for Sanctuary 101.'

'We will be ready,' Miriya replied, even though Imogen had not asked the question.

She leaned closer to her subordinate so that when she spoke again her voice remained unheard to all the others around them. 'The last word here is always mine, Sister Miriya. I would remind you never to forget that.'

By reflex, Miriya opened her mouth to say something, but then she thought better of it, and at last lowered her head with a shallow nod. *A start*, Imogen told herself. *Perhaps this one can be properly disciplined after all.*

It was then she noticed the slim, winsome woman in duty robes of earthy brown, watching her from across the bay with something bordering on an accusatory gaze. The girl was one of the hospitallers, and she had a streak of annoyance in her expression. She clearly objected to Imogen's mordant manner towards Miriya.

With that realisation, the Sister Superior placed the pretty young girl's face. Verity Catena, of the Order of Serenity. Her name and her details were known to Imogen from the same records that had spoken of Miriya's misdeeds on Neva. Verity had been involved in that situation as well, the non-combatant swept up in the melee of a secessionist rebellion that ended in the burning of a city, and purges on every level of a planet's hierarchy. As she understood it, the woman had been kindred to a Battle Sister who died in service to the Throne while under Miriya's command.

Did Verity blame the other woman? Imogen considered the question for a brief moment. Was the death of her sibling the reason why she had chosen to join this mission, to find a way to renew her faith? There were rumours that the Neva incident had been rife with all kinds of witchery and unbelief, enough to be deeply troubling to one not hardened to the extremes of the God-Emperor's great duty.

Still, Imogen recalled a complimentary letter appended to

Verity's records from one of the senior Battle Sisters involved in that brief conflict, according her respect for her courage under fire. The Sororitas of the non-militant orders, the hospitallers, dialogous and famulous, had some education in use of weapons and the like, but they were not fully trained in the ways of war like their combatant Sisters. It was rare to see someone from an Order outside the sphere of conflict given such a citation.

But that did not mean, therefore, that Verity had tacit permission to show disrespect to one of her betters. Imogen turned the full chill of her icy gaze on the hospitaller. 'You are restless,' she began, staring directly at Verity but speaking to Miriya and the rest of the assembled Battle Sisters within earshot. 'This journey has been lengthy and it has tested your patience. There is only so long a Sororitas can sharpen her wits and her blades before they begin to dull from inaction. Only in the rigid application of our martial faith can we do what were born to.' Imogen walked slowly through the ranks of the women, approaching Verity with every step. The hospitaller paled slightly. 'Each of you believe you are worthy in the Light of the God-Emperor. Each of you believes that you are ready, that you have been *tested*.' She gave the last word hard emphasis, and broke Verity's gaze.

The Sister Superior gave a solemn nod. 'The women who stood beneath the Kavir sun on Sanctuary 101 believed that as well. But now they are dead, their lives crushed beneath the heel of an uncaring and hateful universe. They have gone to His side at the foot of the Golden Throne, blessed be their memories–'

'*Blessed be their memories,*' chorused the Battle Sisters, their voices like the rush of waves on a shore.

'And now we come to take their places.' Imogen nodded again. 'We must be ready, kindred. For even if the fate that destroyed them is truly passed, know that behind it lie a thousand more aching to end us. We are like a candle blazing against the vacuum, struggling to remain alight in the airless void, fighting for what we know to be right. For our faith.' She glanced around at their faces, ending with Miriya. 'So we must remember our duty, our place in the scheme of things. None of us can presume to know what lies before us. We can only hold fast to our belief.'

In the silence that followed her words, a stocky Battle Sister with skin like weathered teak and tight curls of black hair dared to raise her hand in question. Imogen decided to grace her with her attention. 'You have something to say, Sister Ananke?'

'We were told this world is bereft of life, Sister Superior.' Ananke's manner was clipped and brisk. 'Is that not so? Will we meet an enemy at the gates of the convent? Will there be a battle to retake what belongs to our Order?'

Imogen detected the faintest traces of hope in the other woman's words. Ananke wanted her to answer in the affirmative, voicing the same sentiment that others on the mission shared. They wanted to exact revenge on whoever had dared to attack Sanctuary 101.

Such impulses were useful, but if not controlled they could become self-destructive. The Sister Superior was not ready to let the rule of the women fall to their baser instincts. 'There will be duty, Ananke,' Imogen said firmly. 'That should be your only concern, whatever your task, be it soldier or otherwise.' She glanced back to Miriya and then to Verity once again.

When the hospitaller retreated into the shadows of the landing gantries, the Sister Superior smiled thinly.

The insect was an arthropod as large as a man's arm, its jointed body shiny and a shade of green so dark as to almost be black. Minute hairs coated its legs and torso, evolved to trap moisture from the dry atmosphere of the desert planet and serve as sensory addenda to the large palps that moved about its head. Long, multiple-jointed legs slid carefully over the side of the powdery dune, the body of the creature slung between them. The insect sampled the cold night air, and felt the perturbations of it for signs of other life. It was a predator, feeding on smaller varieties of its own phylum and the flying mites that bred in the lee of rocks or other wind-traps.

It hesitated on a patch of sand, considering as best the cluster of nerves that were its brain would let it. It sensed a level of warmth above that which should have existed here. This was enough to make it pause.

The top of the dune burst beneath it. In the fractional moment before the insect's skull case was crushed by rough, malnourished fingers, it flailed and tried to bring up its stinger; but another hand was already ripping the barb out with manic, fearless strength.

The displaced sand went away on the constant wind, and the human figure clad in rags it revealed pulled wildly at the corpse of its prey. Dust trailed off in lines, returning to the desert underfoot, as fingers twisted off the insect's legs. These morsels were first sucked dry of fluid and then crunched down through cracked, blackened teeth, the dark chitin splintering and cutting greyed gums. Careful not to lose too much of the arthropod's thin blood to the ever-thirsting sands, the ragged figure dropped into a settle, and proceeded to dismantle it with ichor-stained hands. This was a female, a large one, and it was fat with unlaid eggs. They were easy to swallow, soft and salty. The memory of any gag reflex at the foul taste was long gone.

++*You are revolting*++ said the Watcher. ++*Everything about you is foul*++

The figure had been listening to the voice in the air for so long that it considered itself to be the Watched, although it did all it could to make sure the Watcher never really knew where to find it. Instead, it concentrated on savouring the kill. It was a good one, tasty with it. Something to be enjoyed.

Eventually, though, as always, the Watched responded. Wiping greasy matter from a dirty face, a question emerged. 'Why observe me, then? Why keep looking at me through my eyes? Go. Go away. I don't like you. Don't need you.'

++*Perhaps I already have*++ said the Watcher. ++*Perhaps I stopped speaking to you a very long time ago, and what you hear inside that ruined meat you call a brain is your madness leaking out++*

The Watched did not like it when the ghost-speaker played clever word games like this, and screamed in annoyance. The ragged figure picked up the discarded stinger and ran the barb over the bare skin of one arm, following the healed lines of scars where this had been done dozens of times over. The insect poison burned against the sunburned flesh and the agony was sweet and powerful. It made the hateful, callous voice from the air go silent for a while.

But only for a while.

++You should not stop next time. Dig the venom head in. Then you will die and this will be done++

'I refuse to die.' The reply was supposed to be strong and defiant, but it came out sorrowful and broken. It was difficult to speak sometimes, as if the ability to form words and release them into the air was somehow degrading with the passage of time. Perhaps it was the metals and the stones embedded beneath the flesh of the Watched that did that. It was hard to be certain. 'I am waiting.'

++You are dying. Your mind is like a broken tool. Useless++

The Watcher was going to say more, the ragged figure knew it. But then something among the bowl of stars overhead made all voices go silent. There was a new sight to see beneath the dull reflected glow of the mismatched asteroidal moons.

Looking, peering, daring to hope, the Watched saw new dots of diamond-hard light moving against the path of the turning of the world, passing close to the dull glow of the Obsidian Moon. It could only be a starship.

'It could only be.' The words crumbled like ancient paper and at first the Watcher did not respond. 'No more waiting.'

Down on the surface of the desert world, the revenant in torn pennants of blackened cloth stood atop the dunes and let out a wordless cry, empowered by an emotion that had no shape or name.

But eventually, like the turning of seasons to winter or

the fouling of meat not eaten soon enough, the Watcher decided to speak.

++*Waiting for what?*++ it asked, knowing full well that the Watched had long ago forgotten the answer to that question.

CHAPTER THREE

Harsh dawn light refracted through the atmosphere, drawn into streaks through the high clouds. Like rods of dusty gold, the rays of the Kavir sun warred with the ceaseless churn of sand. As the heat of the day began its slow approach, the land would warm and the storms would begin anew. The cycle of hot and cold, of wind and abrasive dust, had carved the landscape of the colony in exotic, unearthly ways. Towering buttes of rust-coloured rock rose from the sands here and there, uncapped mountains with flat, cracked plateaus atop them. Twisting arroyos once cut by running water were now howling passages where the dry winds played. Stone sculpted by forces of nature loomed in spheroid or wave-like forms, resembling great off-cuts from the workbench of some mythic artisan deity.

With the dawn came a flock of landers, metal birds and winged tugs bearing the first of the missionary parties. Screaming through the air on plumes of fuming exhaust, the flight circled the wide misty plain of the great erg before angling in towards the narrow valley to the east. Signals sent to autonomic defence batteries were not replied to, but the pilots were still not so foolish as to fly in high and visible. Despite the assurances of the Ordo Xenos that this site was not dangerous, the Adepta Sororitas were unwilling to take that fact on bare trust; it was all too possible that the machine-spirits of the convent's weapons were still active, perhaps damaged or even corrupted. It would not do for the Order of Our Martyred Lady to have their shuttles shot down by their own guns.

They went in as low as they dared, the heavy Arvus-class transports disappearing into puffs of powder thrown up by ground-effect, lagging behind the swifter Aquila shuttles. One of the bird-like ships blasted over the top of the convent's central donjon at zero height, but there was no answering blaze of laser fire. The defence cannons were as dead as everything else.

Sister Verity heard the command as it was relayed back through the chain of landers, and the Arvus lurched as it turned sharply. She and a handful of her fellow hospitallers were crammed in the back of the cargo shuttle among storage pods filled with emergency supplies, portable field wall emitters and other hardware. At first Canoness Sepherina had been reticent to let them travel with the initial landing party, her military adjutant Sister Imogen citing the need to place combatants on-planet as higher than that of other Orders. Verity had not allowed the wintry Sister Superior to sway her, however; instead she stressed the importance of having medicae staff to hand in this uncertain environment.

Imogen had a harsh, brittle laugh that was as cold as she was, and Verity recalled it. Imogen mocked the hospitaller, suggesting she was foolish to think that anyone might have survived down here to be in need of an apothecary's attention. All thermographic and scry-scanning passes over Sanctuary 101 had shown no evidence of life among the stony ruins. But in turn, Verity's reply gave her pause. There was no telling what hazards lay down on the surface. Was it not better to have a nurse immediately to hand if some danger were to waylay a Battle Sister?

Sepherina accepted her logic and gave the Order of Serenity

leave to join the landers. In irritation, Imogen had ensured they rode in this, the least comfortable of the cargo transporters.

Supporting herself on a dangling tether, Verity crossed to one of the small portholes in the hull and peered out through the armoured glassaic. The other Sisters were content to stay where they were, strapped to the deck, engaged in a litany round as they prayed for a safe landing. Verity mouthed the words as well, touching a finger to her lips and the Imperial sigil engraved into her duty armour. Like the rest of the hospitallers, Verity had changed into a stripped-down version of a Battle Sister's combat rig. It wasn't the Sabbat-pattern power armour the militants took into war, more like carapace kit of the common Imperial Guard, but it was protection enough for auxiliaries like them. Verity had been told it could absorb the power of stubber bullets or an indirect las-bolt, but she had no wish to test the veracity of that claim.

Peering through the portal, she saw the endless sand and then caught her first glimpse of the place they had come to rebuild.

Ahead, the dark walls of the outpost emerged from the haze. The outermost embattlements were intact in some places, in others nothing more than broken rockcrete, and beyond the inner wall and the great keep were visible. Both still stood, but like the outer ramparts, they were dead, silent and in disarray.

Their shuttle was the last in the line of ships to touch down, joining the other craft in a semi-circle inside the main compound. Verity glimpsed the beetle-black of armoured Battle Sisters moving to take up a perimeter as the Arvus landed, the undercarriage grunting as it kissed the ground. She bowed her head and gave a breath of thanks to the transport's machine-spirit just as the aft drop ramp cracked open and fell away. Heat and airborne fines of powder assailed her, blowing into the compartment on a ragged gust of wind. Verity scowled and fumbled for the goggles in a pouch on her hip and settled them into place, but the corners of her eyes already felt itchy.

She lowered her head to exit the cargo shuttle, and her first step onto Sanctuary's soil was not an elegant one, but a half-stumble. The gravity here was slightly less than Terran standard. Verity recovered, pausing to adjust her eye-shields. All around her, servitors were moving back and forth, swift and purposeful with their work. Sepherina wanted the craft unloaded immediately so they could climb back into orbit and recover the next supply load from the *Tybalt*. The engines of the shuttles keened as they idled, blowing the harsh scents of ozone and promethium across the massive courtyard.

The convent appeared as if it had been derelict for centuries. Sand of differing hues along the red end of the spectrum was heaped in drifts, collected at the feet of the watchtowers and in the shadows of support braces. In places, she saw airlock doors yawning open and blackness beyond them. Verity walked away from the Arvus, taking it in.

Sanctuary 101 was a moderate-sized outpost, and built from the same kind of Standard Template Construct design that characterised a million other edifices used by the Sororitas. She spied pre-fabricated bulwarks stamped out of steel from some world a thousand light years away, alongside laser-cut walls made out of the local rock. This was no transient base designed to last a few months; the Sisters had wanted this place to be a permanent site, to stand proud against the sand and the wind for hundreds of years to come. To see it like this, untended and deserted, was saddening.

Verity crossed close to a metallic bollard protruding from the dust-covered floor. It resembled a stubby tree made from junkyard pieces, all cables and ceramite discs instead of leaf and branch. There were dozens of them circling the edge of the keep.

'Etheric coils,' said a voice behind her, and she turned. A Battle Sister cradling a bolter walked past her, tossing her head to push tails of stone-grey hair over her shoulder. 'Keeps the sand out when it works. Gives off a hum that'll make your teeth itch, though.'

The woman was Sister Helena, one of Imogen's Celestians,

an imposing warrior with laughing eyes in a face tattooed with a rain of silvered teardrops. 'It doesn't seem right,' Verity offered, the thought forming into words before she could consider its meaning. 'All this.' She gestured around.

Helena glanced at her. 'You've seen battlefields before.'

Verity nodded. 'Aye, Sister. But not like this desolate place. It is like a picture-puzzle with a missing piece. It feels... *incorrect* here.'

The other woman frowned. 'It's the dead,' she told Verity. 'That's what is wrong.'

'What do you mean?'

Helena walked on, her expression grim. 'Do you see any bodies?'

The servitors marshalled the off-loaded gear in the middle of the courtyard, building a rectangle of containers on a mound of dark earth. Judging by the surround of a low ornamental wall around it, this had once been some sort of devotional garden, but flames had come and burned it black. The Sisters Militant stood sentry in a wide combat wheel, holding station as the emptied shuttles began to rise back into the air. Verity watched the ships go, the low clouds enveloping them as they raced away towards orbit. They would be back within the hour and the unloading cycle would begin anew.

There were just three of the other hospitallers with Verity, and they did their best to stay out of the way of the Battle Sisters as they moved around, setting up perimeter sensors, fixing devotional wards to the low walls and the plinths that marked out a grid in the middle of the open space. Boots crunched on drifts of sand, and as she studied the surroundings, Verity realised that whatever statues had once stood on those pedestals were missing like the corpses of the dead. She saw untidy heaps of rubble scattered around, and was briefly startled to see eyes looking back at her from one of them; the face was made of sun-bleached marble.

'They smashed all the statues,' said Zara, one of the hospitallers. 'Who would do that? *Why* would they do that?'

'Hate takes many shapes.' The answer came from the frost-white lips of an imposing woman who resembled the marble more than she did true flesh and blood. Verity and Zara bowed slightly as Canoness Sepherina walked past them, the woman's heavy Aspiriate cloak leaving a trail through the drift-sand behind her.

Sepherina had no hair upon her head, but her scalp was heavy with lines of detail and electoos that spelt out lines from the Litany of Saint Katherine, just visible beneath the ballistic-cloth coif she habitually wore. The gold-rimmed gorget of her battle armour framed a face that was lined with age and war-scars. The canoness radiated a stony kind of authority that was effortlessly intimidating, even towards veterans with decades of experience in the Order. She was poles apart from the acid, often waspish nature of her second-in-command, Sister Imogen.

A party of armed Sororitas were moving with the canoness, wary and prepared for anything. Among their number, Verity spotted Sister Miriya and the two of them shared a brief nod of acknowledgement.

Almost three years had passed since the day they had crossed paths, at the funeral of her blood sibling Lethe on the planet Neva – and in that time much had happened. Verity considered the Battle Sister to be a trusted friend, having long since absolved her – as Lethe's former commander – of any responsibility for her sister's death. Their shared trials on Neva had forged a bond of comradeship, but Miriya had made it difficult to maintain over the last few months of the *Tybalt*'s voyage. It was as if the closer they came to Sanctuary 101, the more withdrawn the Battle Sister had become. Even her compatriots Cassandra and Isabel had seen it, but there seemed little they could do to draw her out. Perhaps now the mission had truly begun, Miriya would find her purpose refreshed... And yet, as Verity considered this desolate place, she felt her own spirits diminish. There was something ephemeral in these ruins, like a radiation of despair. The dead convent seemed to reek of human anguish.

Sepherina appeared to sense the same thing, and the canoness turned. 'This place...' she began. 'This place was once full of life and faith and the Emperor's Light, and it will be again.' The woman's voice carried across the courtyard. 'We will see to it. I shall not delay in that responsibility.'

Her hand disappeared into the folds of her cloak and returned with an iron torch-rod, at the widest end bearing a brass basket shaped like a crown. Sepherina touched a control on the side of the rod and a puff of bright fire ignited among the brass splines. Verity had seen such firebrands before, carried by preachers as symbols of human faith.

'His Light has returned to Sanctuary 101,' she told them, emotions warring across her expression. 'Come see it with me.'

'Milady.' Sister Imogen was approaching. 'We should wait, the scouts have yet to be certain that this place is safe–'

Sepherina cut her off with a gesture. 'No. We will not tarry, Imogen. The Sororitas have been made to wait long enough, do you not agree?'

Imogen was chastened, but she continued on. 'The questor and his party will be aboard the next flight of shuttles. He will expect to be met.'

Sepherina gave a sharp nod. 'He will be, then. By *you*.' The canoness turned. 'Sister Miriya. You and your squad will accompany me.'

Miriya nodded. 'Aye, mistress.' She glanced at the women standing with her and they stood to attention.

Verity looked back to find the canoness studying her. 'And the hospitaller shall come along as well.' Without waiting a moment longer, Sepherina led the way across the quad, towards the oval doors that passed through the inner walls to the keep proper.

Verity fell in behind the lines of Miriya's unit, keeping pace with Sister Ananke at the rear. She chanced a look back over her shoulder and saw Imogen watching them, an unreadable expression on her alabaster face.

* * *

Inside, the oppressive sense of gloom was stronger, but the canoness braved it with the torch in her hand, casting it this way and that as they moved deeper into the building. The jumping flames cast their glow across walls coated with a layer of powdery mineral dust that glittered like sunlight off snow. Emergency illuminators powered by chemical reactions were still active, but after a decade they were little more than waypoint markers that gave some measure of the distance the Sisters travelled.

Miriya kept her focus clear and steady, holding her Godwyn-De'az pattern bolter across her chest in a combat-ready carry, her finger resting on the trigger-guard. Despite her personal feelings towards the Sister Superior, Miriya found herself agreeing with Imogen. Sepherina was the highest ranking woman of the mission, and it was flirting with danger to allow her into a zone where the nature of any threats was still to be confirmed. It bordered on recklessness, and it seemed uncharacteristic of the canoness.

Or was it? Miriya had to admit that in the older woman's place, she would have done the same thing. In a way, this gesture on her part, this defiance of the fates and ready danger, was the impulse lying at the core of this entire mission. Others might have allowed Sanctuary 101 to return to dust after it was attacked, perhaps written it off as a sad loss and moved on to other, easier places to find purchase.

That was not the way of the Sisterhood, however. Some might mock them for it. Miriya knew that many common soldiers considered the Adepta Sororitas to be the living model for the trait of dogged bloody-mindedness, and there was truth in that. But this was what they did.

If a Sister is knocked to the ground, yea, will she not gain her footing again, stand and fall and stand again? Die upon her feet for her Emperor? The words were from Alicia Dominica herself, the first Sororitas. Thousands of years after they had been uttered, they still rang true.

Sepherina's defiance went beyond simple reason. She was leading by example, daring an uncaring universe to come again and strike at their faith.

Miriya remained silent as they went on, passing from the entry cloister and through into one of the wide radial corridors that led into the central keep. The building was modelled after the great Convent Sanctorum but on a far smaller scale. The sand was here too, years of it blown in through open doors, making the air dry and cloying. In the light from the torch she saw the way ahead. The sand lay in uniform ripples where it had been deposited by waves of wind, and there were no visible footprints like those the Sisters left behind them. If anything did live in this place – be it an enemy or just some example of local wildlife – then it had not passed this way for some time.

The convent was a shambles. It was not the broken and destroyed remnants of a battle fought and lost, but rather the aftermath of some great act of nature. It did not look like vandalism, more as if a hurricane had been let loose in the corridors and allowed to tear down the tapestries and devotional works hung upon the walls. Through open doors into rooms they passed, Miriya glimpsed collapsed bookcases, their texts spilled out across the floor. More than once, Canoness Sepherina hesitated at these sights before moving on.

She heard Ananke speak in a low, guarded voice as they passed a choke-point where the corridor narrowed. 'This is the fifth defensive post we have passed since entering the building. None of them show signs of having been manned.'

Cassandra answered. 'I have yet to see a single corpse.'

'Look sharp,' Miriya muttered, and from then on no one spoke again. But she knew that all the Sisters were thinking the same thing. *Where are the dead?* Miriya had not been privy to the documents given to the Sororitas by the Ordo Xenos and she wondered what they said about the bodies of her comrades. Had the enemy taken those who were killed, or was it the work of some other agency?

They skirted the chambers of the central keep and followed the mistress towards the core of the massive donjon. Even as they approached the tall steel doors to the central chapel,

Miriya felt a curious tingle of anticipation run through her. It was not quite fear.

Sepherina slammed the doors with the heel of her hand, and on groaning hydraulic pistons, they slowly inched open. Air, cold like a tomb's breath, issued out and made the torch flame crackle and writhe.

The Great Chapel of Sanctuary 101 was a hexagonal space, each of the six walls rising several stories high to support a dome of dark stone. Light fell into the massive chamber from glassaic discs set in the roof. There was one for each of the Orders Militant Majoris, each inlaid with stained panels that formed the shape of their sigils: a heart upon a *crux maltese*, roses in white and blood red, a death's-head, a chalice. These five lay around the largest in the centre of the dome, and it should have exhibited a crimson inverted cross topped by a white skull – but the glassaic had been brutally shattered and only a shaft of weak, dusty light was visible. The fragments of the Order's symbol lay in pieces across the broad, ornate altar in the middle of the space.

The group moved in, past lines of tipped-over pews cut from red woods shipped in from some far distant forest world. Six marble pillars supported the roof and the Battle Sister saw impact points in the dimness where stray gunfire had kissed their surfaces. Low dunes of sand deposited through the broken windows slowed their progress. Relicals full of prayer-books and minor devotional shrines were half-buried in the drifts, emerging from the mounds of dust like the wheelhouses of sunken ships at low tide.

Here, more than any other sight that had greeted them at the outpost, was desolation and emptiness. The chapel of an Adepta Sororitas convent was meant to be a place of safety and contemplative piety, warmed by the constant glow of electrocandles, tended by servitors. There, a Sister of any Order could come and kneel at prayer, and know with absolute certainty that she was a part of something far greater than herself, far greater than individual human life. It was meant to be a place of transcendent unity.

This was a shadow of that ideal. It was as if the very heart had been ripped out of the convent. The faces of the Saints and Honoured Palatines on the friezes around the pillars and the walls seemed infinitely sorrowful, and for a moment Miriya shuddered at the thought of what horrors they might have witnessed in this place.

If only there was some sign, she thought, *some idea of it.* Even that would be better than the not knowing.

In the very centre of the Great Chapel a circular dais made of white marble glowed in the faint light, and atop the altar there were the statues. The smaller of the two, at a scale twice human size, was a rendering of Saint Katherine. She was depicted as she had been in the days when their sect was known as the Order of the Fiery Heart, as the hand of the church's vengeance. It was her murder at the blades of the long-destroyed Witch-Cult of Mnestteus that had led Miriya's sisterhood to rename itself the Order of Our Martyred Lady, and even now as she looked upon the stone face of the statue, the Sororitas veteran felt a familiar sensation of ingrained sorrow.

Towering over Saint Katherine was a giant bent down upon one knee, one hand reaching out to her like that of a parent protecting a child. Made of the same white marble as the altar, the statue of the God-Emperor of Mankind was shot through with platinum and gold detail that even a thick patina of dust could not completely dull. Like the friezes, in this dark place the image of the statues appeared to convey a very different message than the one they were meant to instil. It almost seemed as if the statue of the Emperor had been frozen in mid-motion, as He tried to protect Katherine from some unseen force come to destroy her.

The squad were, for a moment, distracted from their duty as they shared the same thoughts, and only Canoness Sepherina moved, approaching the foot of the dais. Miriya saw her run her hands over a missing stone in the altar.

Then Sepherina bowed her head and began, very gently, to weep.

Miriya frowned and turned to Cassandra and the others, gesturing with quick flicks of her hand, sending the women off to make a circuit of the chamber. They did as the veteran commanded, using the pin-lamps beneath the barrels of their bolters to peer into the shadowed corners of the chapel nave. Verity remained, hesitating, then stepped forwards. Miriya came in step with the slight, auburn-haired hospitaller as she approached the canoness.

'Milady,' Verity began. 'I fear there are none in this place who need me.'

'I was once a novice here.' Sepherina turned to face them and the older woman's aspect had changed. 'Sanctuary 101 was where the God-Emperor first spoke to my spirit.' The distant, steady aspect Miriya had come to know during the journey from Terra had slipped away. In its place, the canoness seemed suddenly more human as the tears lined her cheeks. Miriya was surprised by the surge of empathy she felt for her superior officer. 'I feel as if this is my failure.' She gestured around, her voice quiet and fluid. 'I was meant to return to this outpost. Circumstances prevented it. Otherwise I, not Sister Agnes, would have been canoness here on that day twelve years ago.'

'What could you have done differently, mistress?' Miriya asked. 'You would have suffered the same fate as our lost Sisters.'

Sepherina looked away, back at the strange gap in the altar's surface. Closer to it now, Miriya could see it was a compartment of some kind, concealed in the structure of the carved stone. It was quite empty. 'I do not know. I only wish I could have stood here at that moment and had the opportunity.' She sighed, and to Miriya it seemed as if the woman was bearing a great weight upon her.

Verity saw it too; the hospitaller was as perceptive to the nature of wounds on the soul as she was to those on the flesh. 'But there is more that troubles you.'

The canoness nodded. 'Aye, Sister.' She nodded towards the drifts of sand. 'I know many things that have yet to be said. I know why there are no bodies here.'

'The enemy...' Miriya began, but fell silent as Sepherina shook her head.

'They were not taken by the aliens that defiled this place,' she retorted, some measure of her former manner returning. 'The Ordo Xenos... Inquisitor Hoth himself... He removed the corpses of our kinswomen.'

Verity could not mask her shock. '*Why?*' she demanded, aghast. 'Why would the Inquisition do such a thing? Why would you *let* them?'

Sepherina's expression returned to its stony neutrality at the accusation in the hospitaller's voice. 'Consider your tone, Sister,' she warned. 'I know you think of the dead here and remember the loss of your own sibling, but that does not give you the right to speak out of turn.'

The other woman nodded woodenly, her cheeks burning. Miriya, however, was not so easily silenced. 'Verity's point is valid, mistress.'

'Aye,' repeated the canoness, wearily. 'And it is one that has tormented me throughout this journey. But it was the price the Order had to pay. Hoth played his games and made certain that we would not be granted permission to return here by the High Lords of Terra.' Her lips thinned. 'I was on the verge of launching a mission to this planet, sanctioned or not, when he relented. The bodies of our dead were the fee, curse Hoth for his avarice.' She sighed. 'The inquisitor has promised that those we have lost will be returned to us in due course... After he has completed his study.'

'Our war dead are not playthings for the Ordo Xenos,' Miriya grated. 'What can a man like Hoth hope to learn from them?'

'A greater insight into the alien threat that swept across this world,' said Sepherina, clearly repeating the poor explanation she had been given. 'For the good of the Imperium of Man. And by the word of the Ecclesiarchy, we are bound to honour his agreement.'

'We have come all this way,' said Verity, finding her voice once more. 'And still no one has voiced the name of whatever malice overcame this outpost–'

'I know its name,' Sepherina told them.

She would have spoken again, but Sister Ananke's shout echoed across the chapel. '*Milady*! Your attendance, please! There is something here!'

Miriya heard the danger in the other woman's tone and brought up her bolter to the ready.

They found Ananke standing near a cluster of fallen support struts brought down by a blast shock. Helena and Isabel were already there, weapons at their shoulders, aiming into a pile of rubble.

'What is it?' demanded Sepherina, any trace of her moment of emotion now vanished.

'Keep back,' warned Ananke. 'It may be a trap designed to draw in responders.'

Miriya looked in the direction that the dark-skinned woman was pointing her gun and saw the cloudy glint of something metallic among the broken stones. She looked at the fallen struts again, casting a soldier's eye over them. 'This looks like damage from a krak grenade detonation.' She shook her head and indicated one of the big marble pillars nearby. 'Poor weapons discipline. They could have brought one of the columns down with it.'

'They were desperate,' offered Verity, her gaze momentarily losing focus as she imagined the moment of terrible concussion inside the chapel's confines. 'Fighting with all they had…'

The Sororitas hoisted her boltgun over her shoulder and snapped it to the mag-plates on her backpack. Miriya was about to advance across the rubble pile when she paused; taking the initiative was something a Sister Celestian was allowed to do, but she wasn't that any more. *You are only a Sister Militant now*, she chided herself, *remember that. You are a line soldier in the church's wars*. Taking a breath, she turned to the canoness. 'Milady, with your permission?'

'Proceed, Miriya.' Sepherina gave her a nod in return.

She was aware of the other women drawing back a few metres as she slowly and carefully picked her way over the debris towards the object Ananke had sighted. The other Battle Sister remained were she was, her weapon trained and rock-steady.

At first Miriya though it was some variety of prayer box, for such things were commonplace in the chapels of the Sororitas. Perhaps it had been caught in the grenade explosion, landing amid the rubble. Then she saw how very mistaken she was.

The object was angular and clearly machined. It appeared to be steel, but the surface was heavily tarnished and pitted with tiny dents. Intricate etching, too fine to be seen at anything beyond arm's length, covered the surface of it. Miriya saw an infinity of symbols all made from the same collection of lines and circles, engraved into the metal in ordered rows; they made her think of mathematical formulae she had studied as a girl in her classes at the schola.

There were two large pits in the surface of the artefact, and Miriya gingerly inserted her fingers into them. The object moved in her grip and she pulled. The rubble and the sand resisted for a moment, unwilling to give up the prize; then it shifted and came away.

It was twice the mass she had expected it to be, more than half of it hiding under the broken stones. The Battle Sister turned it over in her hands and went cold with a shock of sudden recognition.

The object wasn't a realistic rendition, not with human proportions – indeed without those of ork, tau or any other alien she recognised – but it was very definitely a skull made of heavy, silvered metal. It had a drawn, long chin, a slit of a mouth and dead sockets where Miriya had put her fingers. Wisps of hair-fine cable dangled from where a neck would have been, and there were clear signs of heavy damage on the obverse surfaces. This was no strange piece of artwork or abstract statuary, it was a factory-built thing, and old with it. She looked at it and a shadow settled over her thoughts, a monstrous antipathy that was as difficult to place as it was powerful. Fragments of recall, things from vague mission briefings and half-remembered rumours, accreted in her thoughts. *This is a xenos thing.*

She looked up to see Sepherina coming closer. 'Is this what killed our Sisters, mistress? Is this the face of it?'

The other woman nodded. 'I know its name,' the canoness repeated, 'and now, so do you all.'

'*Necron*,' whispered Verity, her voice carrying through the sudden silence.

In the next second, the snarl of thrusters sounded overhead and shadows crossed the jagged rent in the dome, as the second flight of shuttles and landers dropped towards the courtyard.

With a sudden sneer on her lips, Sepherina reached out and snatched the machine-thing's skull from Miriya's hands and turned on her heel, her cloak snapping.

Tegas descended from the Aquila shuttle as if he were on rails, travelling without moving, the train of his rich brick-red robes pooling around him. To an outside observer, he would appear to drift to and fro without the crude piston-like actions of organic locomotion, but the keen-eyed might spot the momentary flicker of tiny spidery limbs along the line of the ground, forever concealed beneath the hem of his robes. If one could get close enough to look, they would have seen a vast legion of insectile mechanisms propelling him forwards. Tegas had been made of metal from the waist down for the last one hundred and eight years, and he was working on the upper part of himself all the time. He had used his voyage to Sanctuary 101 on the *Tybalt* for just such a thing, replacing some fleshy elements in the pieces that remained of his intestinal tract and painstakingly refurbishing an eyeborg module.

He let his mechadendrites wander a little, sampling the aura of the planet. He drank in the air and the temperature level, let his digital senses taste the gravity index and parse the radiation count. He looked with thermographic and etheric-trace vision clusters, taking in gigaquads of raw data on the physical make-up of the world.

The Adeptus Mechanicus had arrived, and now things would get done. He teased himself with a program that synthesized the effect of excitement, then dumped it and returned to his standard operating mode. The mundanes all around him, the women in armour and the lackey workers of either gender, they talked and he recorded it all. Tegas heard them saying things about the deadness of the planet and he mocked them in binary. They saw little with the crude jelly of blood vessels and nerves in their heads, crude in comparison to the questor's superlative multi-sight. This world was alive on the microwave, ultraviolet and phototropic level in ways they would never be able to know.

Tegas sent burst-transmission orders to his retinue. There were eight in the party, five of them minor adepts the questor had chosen for their combination of pliancy and intelligence, the others carefully disguised combat skitarii that would pass as non-military Mechanicus helots to all but the most invasive of scans. They formed a cyberconcert and began to create a communal data pool for all the party members. Tegas left them to that chore and continued to glide around the landing pad. He used an encrypted vox-feed to tap into the virus program he had injected into the *Tybalt*'s machine-spirit back at Paramar, and sifted through the vessel's orbital scans of the local continent.

As such, he was partly distracted when a mid-frequency noise sounded close at hand, and Tegas had to pause to remember it was the sound of his name being uttered at volume. He turned to the source of the voice, attempting to calculate its stressors and emotive index.

The canoness Sepherina approached him, her face locked in an expression of irritation. It was not the first time Tegas had seen it. Others from the Sororitas party were with her, skirting the unloading in progress all across the makeshift landing field. Tegas added identifier flags to his visual field so he could remember which of the females was which with a glance.

'Esteemed canoness,' he began, pre-empting her words with

his own, each digitally modulated to project an air of concern and a non-threatening manner. 'It is rewarding to be here at long last, is it not? I–'

'What else have you kept from us?' she demanded, cold fury in her gaze. 'It goes without question that you conceal. It is what your kind do, questor, with your infinite assurance in the perfection of your machine intellects!' Sepherina shook her head. 'But this goes too far.'

Tegas decided to continue as before, and consider the woman's discontinuous statement as he did so. 'I am eager to begin our survey of this planet, praise be to the Omnissiah for guidance protocols.' He was aware of the adepts in his party watching intently. 'I have not kept that wish a secret, milady.'

'What is it you told us you were looking for?' The question came from the female-designate Sister Imogen, and it was like the bark of a canine to him. A moment of emotion-analogue came and went. The name of it was *exasperation*, he seemed to recall. 'Relics from before the fall of Old Night?'

'Enough subterfuge,' Sepherina snapped, drawing something up from the folds of her battle-cloak. 'You're here for this, aren't you?' The woman's hand blurred and she threw something in Tegas's direction. The closest skitarii moved like lightning, racing to intercept on autonomic protection principles, but the questor belayed the order with a beam code pulse and snatched the object from the air with his serpentine manipulators.

He felt the thrill-program activate by its own volition and run swift. The relic held before him was a piece of xenos technology, of pure necrontyr origin, rad-scanned to an age of several million years, quite badly damaged but still relatively intact.

Tegas had to make an effort to stop himself from locking into a work-loop and losing himself in this glittering prize. He looked away, carefully ensuring that the metal skull was handed off to one of his subordinates. 'How interesting. Thank you for this fascinating artefact, canoness.'

'Necrons,' said Sepherina, with open loathing. 'What the Abbess and the Prioress council suspected is true, then. They destroyed this place.' She stabbed a finger at him. 'And the Adeptus Mechanicus knew all along!'

He allowed his shoulders to slump in an approximation of a human gesture of defeat. 'We suspected,' he admitted, altering the tone of his voice-synth to something less arch, more regretful. 'Inquisitor Hoth gave little information about what might be found in the Kavir system... To both of our organisations.'

'We should have been told.' The female advanced on him. 'You should have spoken of this. It changes everything.'

'Does it?' He asked the question innocently. 'The dead are still dead, the convent still in need of our cooperation to rebuild it. And this world may hold relics of a more human nature, ones that may have incalculable value.' He cocked his head. 'More than some piece of alien scrap.'

The lie was delicious; in truth he would have blithely sold the life of any one of the Sisters for such a thing.

Sepherina made a disgusted noise and folded her arms across her chest. 'It becomes clear to me that you and your party will require more supervision on planet than I first expected. Until I say otherwise, you will do nothing and go nowhere without a Sororitas escort.'

'That is unacceptable!' In his affront, Tegas suddenly forgot his voice-modulation protocols. 'The Adeptus Mechanicus is not under your authority! You have no right to give such an order.'

'The Adepta Sororitas serves as the martial contingent in this mission,' she replied. 'And as military commander, it is my estimation that you will not be... *safe*... unless you are closely escorted.'

Was that a threat? Tegas could not be certain. He had lost the ability to measure the subtle tones of emotions in unmodified humans years ago. It was part of the reason why he disliked being forced to associate with them. 'Canoness, I must insist that you–'

But once more she was speaking over him. Sepherina addressed the rest of her troops and the members of the workgangs. 'Before all other requirements, before even our food and water and shelter, there is a deed that must be done in this place. A duty that has lain incomplete for over a decade. This night we will see to it.' She shot an acid glare back at the questor. 'No one leaves the convent. That is my decree, and it will be obeyed.'

A dozen different phrase-strings and sentence constructs presented themselves to Tegas, but he nulled them all. There was no point in talking; that was clear even to him. Better to humour the female for the moment and continue on as planned beyond her sight and her histrionics.

'Of course.' He bowed low, his hydraulics whining. 'By your command, milady.'

CHAPTER FOUR

The preparations had been completed just before the planet's short, eighteen-hour day concluded, and the canoness made demand to the captain of the *Tybalt* that the flights of the last few cargo shuttles be halted for the duration. She made it clear she would brook no interruption of the service.

Miriya stood at attention as Sepherina used her firebrand to light a ceremonial brazier, and in a steady, careful voice, the older woman read a passage from the *Dominican Tracts* on the importance of sacrifice and fealty.

All the Battle Sisters, the non-militants, the workgangers, even Tegas and his party, had been gathered to witness the moment, although the Sororitas had no doubt that the questor was disinterested in the event at hand. Tegas and his serviles became like statues, staring blankly at the stone walls behind the canoness, each of them ignoring this moment of human remembrance for some other kind of bland mechanical communion.

Are they inside their own heads, talking without speaking, mocking us? She imagined it was so. It was said that many of the Adeptus Mechanicus possessed the ability to communicate via wireless speech, as a telepath could voice from mind to mind. Miriya wondered what she might hear if she allowed the vox-module in her armour to seek their frequency.

She dismissed the thought and looked away. As Sepherina reached the end of her reading, Sister Imogen took up a place at her side, a data-slate in her hand. In the gloom, Miriya saw the glow of lettering across the face of the slate: lines of names. It was the roll-call of the dead, the missing.

Once again Miriya considered the actions of the Ordo Xenos. It sickened her to wonder what men like Inquisitor Hoth would want with the corpses of their departed Sisters. Did he have a pact with Tegas, using agents of the Magis Biologis to pick over the dead women's remains, even now? Probing old wounds and pallid corpse-flesh for some vague inkling as to the function of the weapons that had killed them? The thought left a foul, ashen taste in her mouth.

Sepherina made the sign of the Imperial aquila, and then raised a hand to point into the sky. 'There,' she said, her voice husky with controlled emotion. 'That distant light is Holy Terra.'

The assembled Sisters glanced up to see, but there were a million stars in the night overhead, and they showed nothing to distinguish one from another. Miriya did not question, however. She took it as an article of faith that the canoness' indication was true.

'For all the darkness that has touched this world, the God-Emperor's Light has never left it. The breath of His divinity has not ceased, even in the blackest of times. We are the manifestation of that truth.' She took a breath. '*A spiritu dominatus. Domine, libra nos.*'

The words in old High Gothic were the opening phrase of the Fede Imperialis, the great battle hymn of the Sisterhood. Normally sung with full voice and to greater glory, this night they joined to speak it like a litany.

'From the lightning and the tempest, Our Emperor, deliver us.' Miriya knew the words by heart, and closed her eyes as she became a part of the refrain. 'From plague, deceit, temptation and war, Our Emperor, deliver us. From the scourge of the Kraken, Our Emperor, deliver us. From the blasphemy of the Fallen, Our Emperor, deliver us. From the begetting of daemons, Our Emperor, deliver us. From the curse of the mutant, Our Emperor, deliver us.'

On they went, their utterances in unity, the poetry of it echoing off the walls and out into the windblown night. Miriya picked out Isabel's steady tones, the hard edges of Ananke's declarations and, nearby, Verity's gentle voice.

'*A morte perpetua. Domine, libra nos*. That thou wouldst bring them only death, that thou shouldst spare none, that thou shouldst pardon none.' She opened her eyes to say the final line, an ember of vengeance as yet unfulfilled stirring deep in her chest. 'We beseech thee. *Destroy them.*'

Only Sister Imogen had not joined in the chorus; instead, as they had spoken the words of the hymnal, the canoness' second had begun a litany of her own, reading out the names of the dead in a low monotone.

'We will remember them all,' said Sepherina, stepping towards a metallic cargo crate. 'The Emperor knows their names.'

The canoness worked a latch on the box and it fell open, revealing rack upon rack of identical porcelain statuettes as long as a woman's arm. Each was a machine-carved image of the Saint Katherine, knelt in a memorial pose. Sepherina bowed before the container, picked up the first of the statuettes, and carried it away to an area near the storm wall. The servitors had cleared the space before sunset, baring the ground in preparation for the ceremony.

Miriya watched her walk reverently to a point tagged on the dirt with a dye marker and erect the little cenotaph with quick, careful motions. As it settled in the dirt, an illuminator within the carving activated, giving off a soft, yellow glow. Sepherina bowed once again and walked away.

One by one, in orderly fashion, by rank and by squad, the Sisters went to the container and each took a stone icon, carried it to the open space and duplicated the actions of the canoness. Slowly and surely, the memorial garden began to grow, as line upon line of the figures spread across the ground. There was one statuette for every life lost on

Sanctuary 101, and with the light from within, the etching of their names upon the face of the stones could be seen.

Miriya took her carving, and placed it as she was bid to. The name on the stone glittered briefly before her eyes.

Decima.

The Sororitas bowed her head and gave a silent prayer to the God-Emperor, hoping that the soul of her lost sister was now safe and eternal at His right hand.

When she rose and turned back to rejoin the others, she saw Tegas staring impassively back at her, his jewel-like eyes glowing red in the shadows of his hood.

The questor was elsewhere. His husk, the proud machine and slow meat of him, stood silently in the vast quad, but his consciousness was in another place, a stream of flexing data in the shared information pool that writhed invisibly between the other members of his party.

All of them were here, all engaged in the connectivity of it. They shared the responsibility of processing the pool-data between them, utilising a variant form of swarm logic to bounce the cloud of information back and forth. Through machine-code and binary lingua, they communed by use of laser beams, each tuned to be beyond human sight into the far ultraviolet ranges.

The data they shared had many overlaps. The basic factual information about the planet, the environment, the numbers of the mundanes and the materials they had brought down with them, all that was affirmed and filed away. Other matters, like snatches of overheard conversation, were being parsed and edited together to provide a full surveillance of the day's proceedings. These things occurred on a secondary, almost autonomic level of processing that to the adepts was as unthinking as breathing in and out.

What floated at the top of their data stacks was the discourse about what was to happen next. In strings of ones and zeroes, sometimes with hexadecimal epithets and complex octal-layer nuances, Tegas conversed with his operatives.

They shared questions and dismissals of the need for such activities as the memorial service. Of course they understood the call for such societal constructs, the sense of closure these rituals brought and so on – but they had no empathy for it. The funeral was a pointless thing, celebrating nothing, meaning nothing. It could not be compared to the importance of, say, a rite of activation upon a sacred device or the anointing of holy mech-oils upon an augmentation. What the Sisterhood engaged in was little more than the flailing of uneducated children, an attempt by the inept to catch the attention of beings far greater than themselves. The Adeptus Mechanicus, on the other hand, knew exactly how their rituals affected the matrix of the universe, down to the last piconeper. They measured and collated their prayers to the Omnissiah, encoded them on punch-cards and magnotape. Each entreaty to the Machine-God was precise and controlled, laid out to a flawless standard.

What Canoness Sepherina was doing here was little more than *noise*, like trying to liberate hydrogen and oxygen from water by singing to it. Tegas shared with the others a complicated logic train in an old programming language, which when run revealed a mocking comment on the Battle Sisters. The adepts devoted a single clock cycle to an amusement simulation and then deleted it.

The matter at hand occupied them now. All of them felt the same emotive analogue that Tegas had originated. They chafed under Sepherina's overly strict dictates, her commands that the group remain within the walls of the convent and effectively under guard by the Sororitas. Even now, they were kept from their own resources; up on the *Tybalt* was a self-contained portable laboratorium unit, a rare example of an STC construct built for the Mechanicus's use. Normally, it would be one of the first pieces of hardware deployed to a planet's surface, but the canoness had ensured it would not arrive until the last flight of cargo shuttles. It was the latest in a long line of indignities the questor's party had been forced to suffer.

This was not a tenable state and Tegas's group could not be expected to remain so corralled. Every moment that the Mechanicus team remained at the site, they squandered the most valuable of resources – *time*.

The questor wanted to be gone from this place and his analysis of the canoness' behaviour – backed up by referent studies from his cohorts – made it clear that the woman would not alter her orders any time soon. Thus, logic dictated the consideration and implementation of an alternative process. One that risked censure and perhaps even open violence.

The cargo shuttles had brought down a number of small ground vehicles, including Rhino transports for the Battle Sisters and more general all-terrain rovers for use where the heavy APCs could not venture. One of the skitarii had already observed and marked the location of an unarmed Venator-pattern scout car that would serve their needs. Tegas would have preferred a contra-gravity craft like a land speeder instead, but there was no other choice.

In the space of a few seconds, they assembled what data they had on the probable patterns for the guard patrols, the weather forecast for the next few hours and a rudimentary route map for their exit route.

Comparing the typical sleep patterns of the Sororitas with the biorhythms of females of their body mass provided intelligence on the optimal moment for the group to move. Unaugmented humans were prey to fatigue and distraction in a way a cyborg could never be. It was simply a matter of predicting a moment of inattention and exploiting it. The plan accreted in the data pool and became solid.

Tegas saw the program of it unfold in his enhanced mind, rendered like a thought-experiment simulacra. At a time index exactly four-point-two-six hours Terran from now, they would assemble at the Venator, where the vehicle's engine spirit would be lulled into temporary quietus; then, in silence, the skitarii would manually propel the scout beyond the fallen quadrant of the southern wall and into the lee of the prevailing winds. Once into the haze of the storm front, the Venator could be driven at speed and the Sisters would never hear it. Probability percentage of successful egress without detection eighty-seven point six-six recurring. *Adequate odds*.

Across the courtyard, Sister Imogen continued to drone on and on. Used to processing communications at great speed, to the questor the vocalisations of the Battle Sister seemed infinitely slow and tedious in the extreme. In that way, she resembled much about the unimproved mass of humanity that Tegas found so tiresome.

Somewhere in the data pool, an errant voice floated the question of the legality of what was being done. After all, Canoness Sepherina had not lied when she spoke of her Sisterhood's military authority here.

The dissenting voice was noiselessly shouted down. To underline the point, Tegas briefly switched back from millisecond-fast machine code to the laborious configurations of actual human language. Using the archaic dot-dash forms of orskode he broadcast to his assembled group. *'The Order of Our Martyred Lady have been allowed to believe that they are in control of Sanctuary 101 because it is expedient to do so. But that mistaken belief will not be allowed to prevent our mission from being fulfilled.'*

There were no other arguments. Instead, Tegas opened up the sealed info-philes buried in his cortex processor for just this moment, and shared them. The data within revealed advanced topographic reports and an understanding of the planet's geography, details rendered so finely that they could only have come from observers who had spend months – if not years – on the surface of Sanctuary 101.

The maps were just one piece of the knowledge Tegas had that the Sisters did not, and he had no intention of revealing any of it to them.

++Why are you here?++ asked the Watcher.

The revenant did not answer, instead remaining motionless against the curvature of the tall pillar of red rock. Pressed flat into a cleft in the dark-coloured stone, it was possible to remain hidden and still observe most of the keep and the walls down in the shallow valley. Soft droplets of yellow light were appearing inside the broken walls, breathed into being by the motion of figures in dark cloaks. The lights slowly formed a grid, dots making lines.

There was meaning in them, but it escaped comprehension. The ragged figure peered out of the darkness, owlish and frustrated. Understanding refused to surrender itself.

++*Answer me*++ demanded the Watcher. ++*Answer me*++ ++*Answer me*++

The reply fell away into the night. 'I am doing what you do. I am watching.'

++*Why?*++

'Stop asking me questions you know I cannot answer.' The Watched slapped at the skin of a dirty, malnourished face. 'You are in my head, so you see the holes in it. Stop trying to make me fill them with your lies.'

The Watcher went quiet. Perhaps it was ruminating on that thought, or perhaps it had merely become bored. This sometimes happened. There were times when the voice went away for a long time, a long time indeed. Even moments when it seemed like the revenant would be free of it.

It came back each time, though. In a way, it was like one of the parasite ticks that dug themselves into the fur of the burrower rodents that lived to the north. It was in too deep to ever fully be excised. And cutting it out would likely kill the host.

Eyes that were exhausted and hollow turned back to observe the motions of the ritual being performed inside the tumbledown ruins. Figures clad in shining black armour moved back and forth, red cloaks glittering under the cold stars. Every few moments, when the breath of the winds shifted and dropped, sound carried over the dunes and the rocks to the hiding place. Voices, but not harsh and judgemental like the one that came from the air. Soft and gentle tones, resembling things buried deep in old memory. Things that swam disconnected from the here and now, searching for meaning, finding ritual shapes.

Ritual...

The word carried weight for a reason that did not seem immediately clear. What did it mean? Probing at the thoughts it brought with it was like pulling at the tap-roots of a complex cactus bed. They came away in clumps, tugging on one another, ripping and tearing, spilling precious moisture, wasting it.

But instead of water, there was a swelling of something else. *Emotion.* A gasp escaped into the night air, dragging up a horrible dark tide of sorrow with it. Fingers clenched and limbs trembled, a shockwave of feeling resonating through them. Shifting like a collapsing dune-front, the Watched experienced particles of what could only be memory, but they shimmered so fast that they were gone before they could be focussed upon. Torn away. Disintegrating.

++*You do not understand what you are doing*++ said the Watcher, the discordant words melting out of the gloom.

The Watched tried not to listen, tried to focus on the figures in the ruins. This was important. It meant something special, something that could be understood if only the right words were found to explain it, the right sense to frame the emotion.

Those things were missing, however. Those things had fallen into the holes in the revenant's head, vanished into black and distant voids.

++*You disgust me*++

The trembling hands, cracked by age and the tribulations of survival in the arid desert, rose up and touched the dirty flesh about those fatigued eyes. They came away moist; streaks of wetness flowed over cheeks, cutting lines down through years of ingrained grime.

The Watched blinked and vision blurred. 'What does this mean?'

The voice was cruel. ++*It means you are weak and you should die*++

* * *

Verity arose with the dawn to find her fellow hospitallers already at work in the temporary pergolas set up in the courtyard, preparing a field medicae clinic for the members of the mission. She gave morning prayers; her internal body clock was having difficulty synchronising with the Kaviran day-night cycle, and months living in shift-patterns aboard the *Tybalt* had not helped smooth the transition.

A pair of workgangers were the clinic's first visitors. Both men were marked with whip-wounds from Deacon Zeyn's flail, having been beaten hard for some minor infraction. They were edgy and eager to return to their detail, fear riding high in them that Zeyn would be less forgiving the next time.

The hospitaller had fallen asleep to the sounds of the deacon's exhortations to his serviles. He seemed tireless, burning with a zealous frenzy that made itself known through barked hymns or the snapping tip of his electro-whip. Verity made her excuses and left the pergola, crossing the quad to observe.

Zeyn was there, shouldering away a massive piece of fallen masonry, singing harshly as he did so. All around him, vacant-eyed servitors and sweating, red-faced workgangers toiled in the growing heat. They were in the process of clearing the rubble from the foot of the southern wall, in preparation for repairs to the fallen section of battlements.

In other circumstances, the chants Zeyn led – The Emperor's Prayer, Holy Terra We Beseech Thee, Praise For The Throne, and all the others – they would have given Verity a swell of pious love. But somehow, when the words were spat from the deacon's mouth like a spray of bullets, they became hard upon her ears and her heart. The duality of the thought made her uncomfortable; and then it became of no consequence as the noise of the singing was lost in the shriek of thruster noise as the last sortie of Arvus lighters and Aquila shuttles dropped into the valley.

She looked up, shielding her eyes. Two of the boxy lighters carried a complicated rig of cables between them, and caught in its cradle was a long, slender capsule made of dull steel. It resembled the fuselage of an aircraft or a vast shell casing, and Verity saw ports in the hull where armoured windows nestled next to thick airlock doors. The construct bore code symbols that did not quite resemble numbers. The only recognisable sigil was a disc that bore the cyborg skull and cogwheel device of the Adeptus Mechanicus.

The lighter pilots brought the module down towards the courtyard, and the pod extruded a series of skeletal support legs as the ground approached. But the moment the steel feet touched the surface, there came a great howling thunder from the earth beneath the hospitaller's feet.

Verity stumbled against the sudden earthquake, falling against a stand of cargo drums. She saw the ground under the pod crack and give way. The stones there, already weakened by whatever battle had swept through the convent in the past, were stressed past their limits by the weight of the module.

The engines of the Arvus transports keened, the support cables twanging as they were pulled tight. The Mechanicus's laboratorium module swung wide like a massive demolition ball, clipping a tall plinth and shattering it. Verity ducked by reflex as it thrummed over her head, the wind of its passage pulling at her wimple.

Where the pilots had tried to put it down, a sudden sinkhole appeared, and through it could briefly be glimpsed the structures of the convent's myriad underground crypts and passageways. Verity heard screams over the roar of the engines as hapless workgangers too slow on their feet were knocked aside and to their deaths in the spaces below.

The courtyard resonated as the laboratorium was finally deposited on the stones a few metres distant, and by the Emperor's grace the ground there was firm and unmoving. Gathering herself, Verity ventured forwards from behind the cargo drums, gingerly peering into the cracks. She heard Zeyn exhorting the workgangers to leave those of their fallen number to their fate.

'Hospitaller.' She turned to see Sister Imogen crossing the quad. 'Stay back. This area is unsafe.'

'There could be wounded–'

The Sororitas spoke over her. 'This may be deliberate sabotage.' Imogen stabbed a finger at the laboratorium, where a group of Battle Sisters were taking up positions around it, boltguns at the ready. 'Stay back,' she repeated.

'I do not understand,' said Verity. 'This is an accident, nothing more. The convent grounds are known to be unstable. How can–'

Once more Imogen ignored her words. 'Questor Tegas and his retinue have vanished. Something is afoot, nursemaid.'

Verity went cold. Vanished? Did she mean abducted, or killed?

The other woman must have seen the question in her eyes. 'We have been played for fools,' she snarled, marching onwards.

The chamber had formerly served the convent as a tertiary mess hall for the novices of Sanctuary 101, but for the moment it had been repurposed for Canoness Sepherina to use as her interim command post. The electrocandles hanging by votive chains from the walls were still twitching from the aftershock of the collapse in the courtyard, throwing shifting shadows in the places where the daylight did not reach.

'The casualty report is still being collated, mistress,' said Miriya, with a bow. 'But Sister Xanthe reports we have lost several of the workers.'

Sepherina accepted her account with a vague gesture of her hand, without turning away from the vox-unit on the stone table before her. 'You heard that, captain?'

'*Aye, milady*,' came a tinny reply from the vox's speaker grille. '*I think this may just have been an unlucky coincidence.*' The voice of the *Tybalt*'s commander was riddled with feedback and static, his words becoming echoes as the starship continued to move further out of planetary orbit.

'I do not believe in such things,' Sepherina insisted. 'This happens now, at the very hour when your obligation to the Order is at an end? I suspect cunning in it.'

'With all due respect,' said the captain, 'these issues are now yours to deal with, canoness. The Imperial Navy has its own timetable to keep to and the Emperor's summons waits for no man. My ship is urgently needed in the Cynnamal system to reinforce the line against an ork incursion. Tybalt's shuttles are in recovery, and we are preparing for warp translation.'

Miriya saw Sepherina's mailed fist tighten. 'Tegas did this deliberately,' she went on. 'He knew your schedule. The questor has defied me and stolen away into the night. A rover was taken, and we do not know as to where.'

At first, when the discovery had been made just before dawn, Sister Imogen had aired the thought that the Mechanicus party might have fallen victim to an outside force. However, it had soon become clear that Tegas had absconded with the vehicle for reasons known only to the adept. The Battle Sisters on guard duty had already been chastised and given over to Deacon Zeyn for reprimand, but the damage was done.

'If you cannot remain to assist me in this matter, then I ask you to grant me one request before you depart,' said the canoness. 'Your vessel's scry-sensors. Make a cast over the surface in the sector surrounding the convent. Tell me what you detect.'

'I anticipated your request, milady, and this was done,' buzzed the captain. 'A datum transit of the scan is now in progress, although I warn you it will not be pleasing.' Miriya heard the chatter of a typehead as a slot on the bulky vox mechanism began to spew out a thin streamer of paper. 'I put it to you that Questor Tegas has allowed his enthusiasm for this mission to outstrip his good sense. If I were you, I would allow him to exercise it and let the man be damned for any hardships it brings to his party. Ave Imperator, canoness.'

'Ave Imperator, captain.' The vox-speaker bubbled static and finally went silent. Sepherina snatched at the paper strip and threaded it through her fingers, her expression stony.

Miriya glanced over her shoulder as Sister Imogen entered the chamber. The Celestian gave her a dismissive glance.

'Report,' said Sepherina, without looking up.

'I sent out a squad of scouts and they tracked the Venator's path to the edge of the valley, but there the sands become unreadable. We could follow no more.'

The canoness nodded once. 'Tegas appears to have masked the rover's locator beacon. According to the *Tybalt*'s sensors, the vehicle was moving southwards when it was consumed by a magnitude seven sandstorm. Energetic interference prevented any further tracking.' She let the paper strip fall from her slender fingers. 'He knew that would happen.'

Miriya swallowed. 'If I may,' she began. 'A small party in another of the rovers might be able to pick up some traces after the storm passes.'

Sepherina and Imogen shared a look that Miriya could not read, and then the Celestian answered for her commander. 'No. Let Tegas go. He has cost us one Venator already, more than likely got himself buried under ten metres of sand by the drifts out there.'

The canoness nodded again. 'If the adept wishes to perish in the desert, I see no reason why we should not allow him to do so. I will take the advice of the good captain. We have far more important deeds to do here in the convent. The reconsecration has begun. I shall not see it abandoned because of one foolish man's recklessness.' She brought her hands together. 'We complete our sacred deeds first, and perhaps then we will consider sending out a search party.'

Imogen turned to Miriya. 'Gather a tactical squad and assemble at the gates of the central keep.'

'If it pleases the Celestian, may I ask why?'

The other Battle Sister eyed her. 'We do as the canoness ordered. We go to secure the lower levels of the convent.'

'Be careful down there,' added Sepherina. Miriya sensed the caution carried more meaning that she could see, but the fullness of it escaped her.

They gave Sister Verity an illuminator rod and a portable narthecium pack, and ordered her to assemble with the

Battle Sisters. She shared a wary greeting with Ananke and Cassandra, both of whom were armed for combat. Without explanation, Sister Imogen arrived with Miriya at her side and they entered the great donjon once again.

This time their route took them around the circumference of the keep, presently to a chamber where the floor had collapsed into the lower level, becoming a series of broken ramps. Verity thought about the catastrophic moment of subsidence she had seen in the courtyard and tensed. The motion of earth and rock like the waves of an ocean brought back memories she wanted to forget, of the planet Neva and the close press of danger.

They descended carefully into the crypt levels, where the convent's honoured dead were interred, past murky storage spaces packed one atop the other. Up above, the damaged rooms of the keep seemed strange and ghostly. Down here, it was an altogether different shade of gloom.

Verity had seen the plans of the convent before they arrived on the planet, and she recalled the shape of the underspaces; they were radial arms extending out from beneath the keep, corridors fanning off into clusters of cell-like antechambers.

Several of the passageways were impassable, clogged by stone and sand. They encountered three of these, and at each occasion Verity observed a flicker of distress on the face of Sister Imogen. Each time, the Celestian gathered up the data-slate she carried and made a series of notations. Her grim features were reflected in the glow of the device's screen.

They divided into smaller parties of three and swept all points of the compass. Verity went with Miriya and Cassandra, keeping out of the way of the two warriors as they picked their way up the length of a dusty corridor. And at last, she could hold in the question no longer.

'What are we looking for?'

Miriya halted, her boltgun's muzzle dropping, the beam from the lamp slung beneath the barrel hanging like a solid spar in the mote-filled air. 'That has not been made clear by the honoured Celestian.'

'I imagine we'll know it when we see it,' Cassandra added, sarcasm colouring her tone. 'As if there are not enough uncertainties about this mission as it already stands.'

Miriya opened her mouth to speak, then thought better of it and said nothing. Verity saw her do so and touched her arm. 'You have more to say on this.'

They exchanged a loaded look. The two women, as disparate as their disciplines were, had been through much together. The bond of shared past hardships overcame what reticence there was in the Battle Sister. 'Sepherina is keeping something from us.' The reply was low, almost a whisper. 'Imogen knows. There is more to this mission than just the return of Sanctuary 101 to the God-Emperor's Light.'

'You believe Tegas's unscheduled excursion is part of it?' said Cassandra.

'No.' She frowned. 'I saw the canoness' face when she heard of that. Whatever the questor is doing, he has his own agenda.'

Cassandra sighed. 'You make the waters muddier, Sister. Clarity fades even more.'

'Aye,' agreed Miriya. 'And I dislike it. This smacks of subterfuge, and that is not the way of our church.'

'I am sure the canoness has her reasons,' offered Verity, but the conviction of the words was absent.

Then without warning, the corridor was suddenly echoing with the flat concussion of gunfire.

Miriya did not think; she only *reacted*.

Her combat cloak crackled as she spun and raced back down the stone corridor, back towards the junction where they had broken off from the rest of the group. She did not need to look over her shoulder to know that Cassandra was on her heels, and Verity a few steps behind. The hospitaller was sensible and would remain out of harm's way, but Miriya knew her well enough that she wouldn't run and hide at the first sound of battle. The winsome young woman was strong that way, in a manner that many did not see on first meeting her.

She ran into the cries of her Sisters. The crash of low-gauge bolt-rounds rumbled around the stone walls and muzzle flashes blasted staccato shadows across her sightline. Miriya heard the hiss and whine of heavy ballistic rounds coming up the tunnels from the far shadows.

She glimpsed a crumpled figure lying in the dust, shrouded by a snarl of crimson cloak and tabard. The face was turned away from her, but the woman's chest still moved; alive then, for the moment.

Miriya dropped into cover behind a pillar and found Helena reloading her weapon. 'What is it?'

'Automata,' snapped the other woman. 'We came across a pair of them further down one of the radials. They failed to respond to voice commands, then opened up on us.'

Chancing a look, Miriya bobbed her head out of cover and got shot at for her trouble. 'Those are Sororitas issue gun-servitors. Our own machinery, trying to kill us?' Even a glimpse had been enough to spot the familiar fleur-de-lys on the torsos of the war machines.

'Malfunctioning,' Helena corrected. 'Their machine-spirits are unhinged.'

'Return fire!' Miriya turned at the sound of the shout and saw Imogen and a few of the other Sisters laying down an arc of shots, but the rounds did little but chip away at the layers of armour-plate of the mobile gun-slaves. Sat atop heavy tracks like miniature tanks, they were mobile turrets controlled by the remnants of human helots wired into metal bodies. But something had gone wrong here, and whatever defensive program they had been fed was still spooling through their broken minds. She wondered how long they had been down here, waiting since the convent's fall for something new to shoot at. They were the first sign of life any of the Battle Sisters had seen on Sanctuary 101, and they were trying to kill them.

'Rot these things,' spat Imogen, her fire team pausing to reload. 'We need a heavy cannon down here!' She muttered something into the vox pick-up at her neck.

Miriya's lips thinned as she weighed their tactical options. The gun-servitors were making a slow but steady advance, and the women would be forced to fall back long before a Sister Retributor could reach them with a heavy bolter or a multi-melta; by then it would be too late for the injured Sororitas lying across the stone floor. The corridor was too enclosed to trust a flamer to do its work, and after seeing first-hand how fragile the stone walls here really were, grenades were out of the question. A close-in attack was the only option.

'Hold this.' Miriya glanced at Verity and thrust her bolter into the other woman's hands.

'Sister, what are you doing?' asked Helena.

Miriya reached over her shoulder and pulled at the grip of her combat blade. The long, blocky shape of her chainsword fell easily into her hands. The power rune on the hilt showed ready and she gave the throttle bar a quick squeeze. The tungsten-carbide teeth of the blade whirred, drawing Imogen's attention from across the corridor.

'Mistress,' she told the Celestian, 'if you will draw their fire...' Miriya ended the sentence by hefting the sword.

Sister Imogen was going to deny her request, she saw the emotion immediately in the other woman's eyes. But then the Celestian paused, and nodded. 'Show me,' she told her.

Miriya saluted with the chainsword and burst from her cover.

Imogen's orders were a cry of anger far behind her, and she was dimly aware of a hail of bolter-rounds shrieking through the dusty air as the Sisters opened fire. The closest of the automatons reacted sluggishly, soaking up the salvo as it dithered between targets, unsure if it should aim at her or at the ones pouring shots into its armour. Miriya ignored it and charged on towards the second gun-slave, which had no such doubts. Instead of human arms, it had gimballed frames that housed a pair of autocannons, each crested with an ornately machined drum magazine. The maws of the guns traversed to find her, stuttering as they went. The servitors stank of rust and decay. They had not been properly maintained in more than a decade, left to rot down here in the dry air, lubricants and unguents cooking off in their artificial veins.

The guns discharged at full power; one of them locked up almost immediately, a brass cartridge lodging to cause a stove-pipe jam. The dead cannon gave off a whining, grinding sound, and it made the gun-servitor shudder as if it were about to retch and vomit. The other gun worked flawlessly, however. It punched holes in the air where Miriya moved, lashing at the tips of her combat cloak as it tried to rebalance and strike the centre of her mass.

The Battle Sister fell into a kick slide and rolled, faster than the helot could traverse. Putting her free hand at the guard along the backside of her chainsword, she rose back up and slammed the bare teeth of the weapon across the armoured plate of the fleshy thing inside the gun-servitor. Pulling the trigger bar, the chainsword's throttle brayed and it bit deep. Miriya leaned in, pressing her full weight into the attack, and felt the sword cut into the ablative sheets, throwing out great streamers of sparks.

Then there was blood and organic matter, and the chugging fire from the active cannon became more sporadic. Acting quickly, she hurdled the dying machine and shoved it across the corridor with all her might, spinning it as it went. The autocannon blew fist-sized holes across the stone walls in a line of peaks and troughs. Miriya brought it to rest on the torso of its armour-plated companion and watched the dying helot blow the other gun-slave off its treads. The Battle Sister drew back her chainsword and drove it point-first into the entry wound she had made. A mixture of gore and oil bubbled up and frothed. The servitor fell dead.

Across the corridor, Sister Imogen strode to the fallen machine and placed her boltgun to its braincase, executing the slave with a single point-blank shot. Cordite smoke wreathed the air, the acrid smell souring.

'They were protecting something,' said Helena, stepping up as Imogen advanced past the destroyed cyborgs.

Miriya went to the fallen Sororitas and found her still breathing, although her torso was a red ruin. 'Sister Thalassa, do you hear me?' That earned her a weak nod. 'Emperor's Blood, she lives still. Verity! We have need of you!'

The hospitaller raced to the injured woman's side and set to work without hesitation. Miriya looked up and watched Imogen ignore the moment, proceeding instead to the mouth of the radial corridor that the gun-servitors had been guarding.

She rose to her feet, a grimace etching her features. 'Is this what you brought us down here to find, Celestian?'

Cassandra pointed her torch-light at the doorway; like the others, it was filled with fallen stone. 'There is evidence of explosives use there.'

'They sealed the corridor deliberately,' said Imogen, but the words were more her thoughts voiced aloud than an answer to any question. 'This was the entrance to an egress tunnel. They didn't want anyone to follow.'

'Follow what?' Miriya demanded.

When the Battle Sister turned back to face her, her gaze was icy. 'Gather up the casualty and fall back. There's nothing here.'

CHAPTER FIVE

Human eyes would have seen nothing.

The tide of the sands, endlessly roaring across the ranges of the landscape, reduced visibility down to less than an arm's length. Crude organic optics would only have perceived the wall of razored dust, filling everything, and if an unprotected human had dared to stand here, their skin would be scoured from their bones, their lungs clogged with gales of particle matter forced down their throats.

To be in this storm and to be of flesh was death, but Tegas and his party were not so weak. Even the least mechanoid of them possessed little more than forty percent crude organic content, and all that lay beneath thick lamellar hoods or metal implants. To the servants of the Mechanicus, the lowing maelstrom of dust did not stop them from viewing the contours of the landscape in terms of thermal change, magnetic texture and radiation level. These modes of sight made the journey across the desert as clear to them as if it were a cloudless day. Electrostatic discharges presented the only real hazard of note, the frequent flashes of stuttering micro-lightning arcing through the haze or buzzing against the hull of the Venator scout. At one point, Adept Lumik had taken a discharge to the skull and zeroed out for a few seconds; an issue that would have been easily manageable if not for the fact that Lumik had been driving the vehicle at the time. Fortunately for Tegas and the others, the sand had slowed them to a halt before they could veer off the dune-tops and into the ravine below. Lumik seemed to be functioning adequately now, but the questor had already filed a notation in the communal data pool to have her placed at the head of the next maintenance rotation.

The Venator bounced over a rocky rise and began to descend a shallow ramp of orange sandstone. Tegas gave a portion of his thoughts to the digital map, drawn from the sealed data-files implanted in his brain back on Paramar. They were close now, and even as the realisation formed, a long, slow pulse of ultraviolet laser light flashed across his vision quadrant. Judging by the attenuation and frequency shift, the beam had been fired from an emitter less than a kilometre distant. The questor snaked one of his mechadendrites – the one with a lasing diode in the tip – up through the scout car's canopy and flashed back a response pulse. If Tegas had still possessed a mouth, he would have smiled.

They dropped into the sheer-sided vault of an arroyo cut from dark, streaked basalt. The wind and the ceaseless storm faded a little, becoming irregular twisters of dust dotted here and there instead of constant humming sandblasts. Shapes made themselves better defined as the rover closed in on its target waypoint. Among the wind-carved rock that reached out with sharp-edged, blade-like layers, there were other things that seemed foreign among the smooth, rounded surfaces. Nothing in the rocks of this planet appeared with straight lines, all of it was turned or curved. One could think of it as chaotic and unchangeably natural, if one were so inclined. Thus, when shapes made of harsh geometric angles appeared, it was almost shocking.

Stone, or something like it, of a viridian hue so deep it was almost black. It resembled slate or some variety of great metallic crystal, huge vaults of it growing storeys high. In a way, Tegas mused, it seemed invasive, almost like a cancer that had metastasized inside the planet's crust. What was most curious was the manner in which the sandstone seemed to have grown around it, as if attempting to absorb a foreign object.

He glimpsed flickers of dull light and adjusted the range of his optics. There were figures up on one of the flat surfaces, a trio of worker helots in the red tunics of the Adeptus Mechanicus, scrambling about a platform that appeared to be affixed to the dark stone face by blobs of thick adhesive. He measured the radiant index from the muzzle of a meson cutter. They were taking samples of the material, or at least making the attempt. Tegas looked away. He knew from experience that the helots were wasting their time. Nothing could cut that stone; Omnissiah knows, he had tried to do the same at other times, on other worlds.

Presently the rocky ramp flattened out and they approached the encampment. Fences made of cutwire ringed a perfect formation of laboratoria modules, generator units and habitat pods. The camp backed onto a sheer wall of dun-coloured rock that went up to the desert surface, and picked out across its face were vents cut into the plane of it. Strings of lamps were visible, disappearing into the tunnels beyond.

The fence rolled back to give the Venator entrance and Lumik brought the scout car to a juddering halt.

On the ultrasonic, Tegas heard a scalar tensor of greeting codes being broadcast as he stepped from the rover and let his robes flutter in the breeze. He bowed slightly to announce his arrival.

The camp looked busy, and that pleased him. He had half expected to find it as dead as the Sororitas outpost, but instead the place seemed the model of efficient Adeptus Mechanicus operations. He turned in place, a slow three-hundred-sixty degree rotation, making a recording of all he could see. As he turned back to his starting place, he heard a familiar series of interrogative codes.

'Tech-priest Ferren.' There was something impressively formal about using words to make the greeting, and Tegas saw no reason to do otherwise.

Ferren bowed, the hisses of his leg-pistons breathy and wet. 'Lord questor. When we detected the ship in orbit, we knew you had come at last. It has been too long.' Like Tegas, the priest was a near-humanoid shape beneath red robes, although he lacked the runic trimming of his superior's garb and the signifier plates bearing the sacred equations of rank. Beneath the robes, Ferren resembled a collection of cables and thin piping that had been tied together to form the shape of a man, in the manner of a rustic corn-dolly. Multiple eye-clusters moved back and forth across his head, circling the equator of his scalp at different scan rates. He had once been a trusted adjutant to the questor like Lumik and the others, but Ferren's cleverness had made it clear he could better serve the Lords of Mars elsewhere. Tegas felt a moment of pride in the fact that his protégé had flourished in what others might have thought was a makeweight assignment.

'This site hides you well,' Tegas replied. 'Even the *Tybalt* could not detect you from orbit.'

'We went dark,' Ferren demurred. 'And the composition of the stone and the... the artefacts here do much to cloak us. It is quite remarkable.'

'I have no doubt.' Tegas sensed Lumik approaching; she had developed a limp, doubtless from the shock-effect.

'There are... many here...' she clicked.

'Fifty-two servants to the Omnissiah's glory,' Ferren replied.

Tegas cocked his head. His records showed that sixty-four souls had set out on this clandestine endeavour. Ferren anticipated his question and transmitted a tight-beam data packet to him, within which was an updated crew complement document. Those listed as missing or deceased had only the most cursory of loss reports. Tegas filed this away for later address.

'We have made much progress since our last communiqué,' continued the tech-priest, allowing marker-echoes of satisfaction to filter into his vocoder's speech patterns. 'You will be pleased, my lord.'

'I expect no less,' said the questor. 'After twenty months

of sifting through the sands here, I will be most dismayed if our agreement with Hoth has rewarded you with nothing of merit.'

Ferren had a group of demi-adepts come and escort Lumik and the others to a refurbishment post in the habitat cluster, where they could see to the sand clogging their gears, while the questor went with him directly to the primary laboratorium station.

Once they were alone, it was only nine point four minutes before the tech-priest asked the question Tegas knew he was desperate to voice. 'What of the Ordo Xenos's involvement in our endeavour? We have heard nothing since our arrival. Have they kept their side of the bargain?'

Tegas glanced at him. 'You are here. I am here. For now that seems as we agreed it to be.'

'But the Adepta Sororitas have come with you.' Ferren's metallic hands knitted in a nervous, human gesture. 'How many Battle Sisters did they bring?'

'A sizeable military force. Enough to kill us all, if they wished it.' Tegas said the words without weight, leaving the stark declaration hanging as a test of Ferren's courage.

'Our tech-guards are formidable. They would find it a hard-fought battle.'

'It will not come to that.'

'It may come to *something*.' Ferren offered him a capsule of libation, which the questor accepted and injected into a port in his cheek. 'What we have unearthed here in the shifting sands... If the Mechanicus wishes to fully exploit it, we will need Sanctuary 101 turned over to us.'

'The Sisterhood have prior claim. Don't you think that if we could have taken this world so easily, we would have? But voices in the court of the High Lords of Terra speak strongly about the sanctity of the Sororitas colony...' Tegas made a negative noise. 'And for now we must show at least the pretence of concord with them.' He helped himself to another capsule, enjoying the pleasing rush of the chemical's effect.

'Hoth is working to the same endgame as we are. And he has the ears of men of power on Terra and Mars.'

'The Sisters of Battle will not go quietly,' insisted Ferren. 'Not when they learn what we have learned.'

'And what is that, my student?' Tegas slid across the floor towards him. 'Would it be something to do with this?' The questor produced a cloth bag from within the folds of his cloak and tossed it onto a nearby workbench.

Ferren's mechadendrites picked at the sack like snakes striking at a prey animal, and removed the object within. Light glittered off the necron skull and the tech-priest emitted a sound that resembled a gasp of pleasure. 'Where did you find this?'

'Canoness Sepherina discovered it inside the convent. Apparently the inquisitor's sweep teams were not as diligent as he claimed.'

'And she just... *gave* it to you?'

Tegas chuckled. 'The woman was desperate to be rid of it. I think she was unsettled by the presence of the thing.'

The adept turned the metal form over and over. 'I am detecting major internal damage within this module. Breakage of core hyperdynamic spatial linkage arrays, phase-effect nulls... That would explain why this piece did not deresolve with the rest of the corpse-metal when the unit was destroyed.' He carried the skull reverently to another bench, where the torso and helmeted head of a helot was surgically implanted into the workstation there. The servitor awoke with a jerk and took the alien item from him.

Ferren hesitated, and Tegas sensed he was not yet willing to let his concerns be so easily distracted by this new gift. 'The women in the convent...' He made a gesture in the air with his clawed hands. 'In truth, my lord, it is not their discovery of this dig site, or indeed how long we have been in secret violation of their colony that concerns me. It is the Ordo Xenos that I fear. We are very far from home out here, and their reach is long. Since we have been on the surface, there have been anomalous sensings of objects at the edge of the system. I suspect they are probes.'

Tegas gave a nod. 'Sent by Hoth or his agents, no doubt. I don't blame him. He wants to keep an eye on his investment. I imagine that he already has a covert operative embedded among your personnel.'

The tech-priest reacted with a shocked twitch. 'I hand-picked my party for this mission! There are no–'

The questor waved him into silence. 'Don't be naïve, Ferren. I believe his spies were aboard the *Tybalt*, and it is very likely that at least one of the workgangers brought here by the Sisterhood is also in his employ.' He looked away, gliding around the room, peering into stasis jars and microgravity pods. 'It matters little. If Hoth could have secured this world by force, he would have done so. And then the Ordo Xenos and the Adeptus Mechanicus would be at guns drawn over this dust ball, even if the galaxy at large knew nothing of it.'

'If that happens…' ventured Ferren, his vocoder module crackling.

Tegas shook his head again. 'No. This is a matter in which we all are treading carefully.' He studied some fragments of silver inside one of the preservation capsules, losing himself in the eerie glitter of the alien metal. 'Do not allow yourself to be distracted by issues beyond your control. Instead, tell me what you have learned. This world once belonged to the necrontyr. *Say it.* I want to hear you say it to me.' There was almost a measure of pleading in his voice. The questor had ventured across half the Imperium to get here, and he wanted it to be true above all else.

Ferren's machine-face bobbed once, twice. 'It is so. There is no doubt. The necron species came to this planet several million years ago… Or at least, one faction of them did.'

'A *faction*?' Tegas echoed the word, the data-rod implants in his hindbrain glowing with life at the suggestion and the connections it made in his thoughts.

'Oh, indeed, my lord. At first it seemed like an error in data processing… My dig party compared the scans of materials recovered here at the main site with those given to us by Hoth and his people. There were discrepancies.'

'Human error,' Tegas said automatically. To a man, the members of the Adeptus Mechanicus had little respect for the methods and record-keeping of any of the Imperium's other august institutions, the Ordo Xenos included. If there was a discrepancy, it was typically a mistake made by someone outside the axis of the Mechanicus.

'My initial hypothesis,' agreed Ferren. 'Until we recovered samples of our own to mount a comparative analysis.'

The questor emulated a thrill of excitement. 'What did you discover?'

'Data that lends weight to a theory of differential sects within the alien society. It appears that the commonly-held opinion of the necrons as a monolithic culture, with little in the nature of divisive internal power blocs, is short-sighted at best.' Ferren pointed a mechadendrite at the servitor working on the skull. 'I believe that the necrons which attacked the convent and killed the Sororitas are not the same as the ones we have found evidence of here.' He indicated the scraps of metal inside the stasis pods. 'Construction, detail, cosmetic presentation, internal structure. All show numerous points of differentiation. Many of which are external and largely decorative, lending credence to the concept of tribal structures within the alien civilisation. Time-dating indicates that both groups of necrons are contemporaries.'

Tegas could no longer contain his anticipation at this idea and turned in small circles as he played with Ferren's discovery in his mind. 'This theory has been aired before... It has been less than popular... But if we have proof...'

'I am convinced of it,' Ferren insisted. 'For all we know, Kavir could have been the location of some sort of conflict, perhaps the result of a schism between two tribes of these alien machines. It would explain much... The patterns of damage in the crypts beneath the rock. The wreckage we have unearthed.'

'Then perhaps... Perhaps the Sisterhood were only collateral damage.' Tegas simulated a guttural chuckle. 'That would dent their pride somewhat. To know their sainted

Battle Sisters died merely because they happened to be *in the way*.' He gave an oily sigh. 'I would see more of your works here, Ferren. Show me all that you have done.'

'It would be my honour,' said the tech-priest, beckoning him to follow.

'Milady, you will be displeased.' Imogen said the words with a bow and looked up to give the canoness her full attention.

Sepherina stood on the other side of the desk she had taken to using as her place of work inside the temporary command post, and glared at the Celestian. 'It is not for you to decide what will or will not please me, Sister. *Speak*! You return from the catacombs beneath the donjon with wounded and weapons spent... Explain yourself to me.'

The woman frowned, before outlining in frank and unembellished manner what the scouting party had discovered in the crypt-levels. Sepherina's grim expression hardened as she went on.

'The gun-servitors,' she broke in, 'where were they hiding? We detected no sign of them, they did not respond to any machine-call summons.'

'I can only suspect that they were hidden from scrying by the thickness of the rock.' Imogen nodded towards the stone walls. 'From what I can determine from the remains, they were set to work autonomously and left to their own devices.'

'For twelve years?' Sepherina demanded.

'Aye.'

'To what end?'

Imogen came closer, her voice dropping. 'They were guarding the mouth of a sealed tunnel. The passageway does not appear on any of the official documents or architectural drawings of the convent buildings.'

The canoness glanced down and found a pict-slate on her desk, containing those self-same files. She paged through them, eyes narrowing. 'You are certain of this?'

'I am,' Imogen replied. 'Consider it, milady. The passage from the great chapel to that chamber below...'

Sepherina did so, viewing the maps, tracing a line along the route from the main hall, down along the ramps to the lower levels and around the circular corridors. 'If one were to go to ground, this is the path they would have taken.'

The Celestian nodded her head. 'A secret egress. We both know such things are a matter of course in our holdfasts across the galaxy, and it answers many questions. The enemy never made it down there, they never encroached that far. Perhaps they were stopped, driven back, or perhaps–'

'Perhaps the last Sister was already dead by then,' Sepherina broke in.

Imogen nodded once more. 'It is likely. I would warrant that if we examine the final command strings given to the servitors, we would find they were ordered to bring down the tunnel entrance and then guard the blockade until they were unable to do so any longer.'

'Without Tegas and his people, that is beyond us,' muttered the other woman.

Imogen went on. 'It was only the passing of time and the action of it upon their elderly and ill-maintained systems that turned the helots against us. They did not recognise us as humans, as their masters.'

'And Sister Thalassa paid for that with her blood.' Sepherina's lips thinned. 'Our first casualty and it comes from a bullet made by Imperial hands. Curse this place!' She banged her fist on the table. 'Every brick and stone here is a punishment to me!' When the older woman looked up once more and met Imogen's gaze, cold fire burned in her eyes. 'Say the words, then, Sister Imogen. For the letter of the record, tell me of your... of *our* failure once more.'

She released a long, slow breath. The Celestian had wanted so much to give the canoness the reply she truly wanted, the answer that both of them had devoted themselves to, but instead she was forced to speak a different and damning truth. 'The relic that we seek is not in the catacombs. Nor within the central donjon and the outer wards, even the greater span of the convent grounds. It is gone, mistress, and I cannot tell you as to where.'

Sepherina allowed a weak nod and she settled heavily into a chair. 'And so it goes. Our long voyage has been for nothing.'

'I have not given up hope,' Imogen insisted. 'If we can track the path of the egress tunnel, then we may be able to find the opposite end. If the relic was evacuated that way...' She trailed off. Even as she spoke, her words seemed vague.

'The God-Emperor and Saint Katherine themselves will damn me if I fall short in this, Sister.' Sepherina spoke quietly. 'It will be the greatest failure of my life.'

Imogen shook her head. 'The burden is shared equally.'

'No,' said the senior Sororitas. 'It lies upon me. I should have been here! For years I have carried this remorse about my neck like a millstone, and today it weighs more than it ever has. I have come so close only to have my hopes dashed at the last instant... I swear that if I fail, I will surrender myself to the Repentia and give up my name, and even that will never be enough.'

For a moment, Sister Imogen tried to imagine her canoness, masked in rags of blood-crimson, fighting under the whip as a member of the Sisterhood's penitent brigade. Women who had wronged the Order or who voluntarily accepted reprimand filled the ranks of the Repentia, and it was written that they would fight the enemies of Imperial Truth until they were redeemed through death. She rejected the image. 'Do not say such a thing,' said Imogen. It troubled her to see the iron-willed Sister so distressed and sorrowful over something she had little control over. 'All things are the God-Emperor's will. If it was His wish that you not be in this place, then you served Him by being elsewhere. And now you will serve the Golden Throne by bringing His Light back to this forgotten world.'

'It is not enough,' Sepherina said softly. 'Dear Sister, it is not nearly enough.'

A gauntlet rapped on the door to the chamber and a figure

entered, bowing as she came into the pool of light cast by the electrocandles. Imogen recognised the hospitaller Verity.

'Forgive my intrusion, milady,' began the younger woman, 'but I was ordered to report to you immediately with word of Sister Thalassa's condition.'

'Give me something to be thankful for,' Sepherina snapped at her. 'Tell me you worked your own miracle with our Battle Sister's life.'

Verity coloured slightly. 'I would not claim to work miracles, mistress. But by the God-Emperor's Grace, Thalassa lives. Her torso armour took the brunt of the barrage from the autocannons, protecting her vitals from a fatal level of damage. However, it saddens me to tell you that she will not walk again under her own locomotion. Our facilities here are crude and those remaining intact in the convent's valetudinarium do not include tissue regeneration devices. I would recommend augmetic surgery upon her person after she has had time to recover.'

Sepherina gestured at the hospitaller. 'So authorised. See to it, Sister.'

The comment was clearly a dismissal, but the nursemaid did not move from where she stood; rather, Verity remained in place, her amber eyes steady on the canoness.

'Is there something more, girl?' Imogen demanded.

Verity shot her a look. 'Those broken machine-slaves robbed a woman of her legs. I cannot help but wonder why she was forced to surrender her future to a mission that goes unexplained.'

Imogen's eyes widened at the hospitaller's challenging tone. *Who does she think she is to speak in such a fashion?* 'It may be so within the Order of Serenity for a Sororitas to talk out of turn as you have, Sister Verity, but this mission is under the auspices of the Order of Our Martyred Lady – and your insolent manner courts censure and castigation!'

'Is it disrespectful to seek the truth of something?' Verity replied. Her voice trembled, but she fought to keep it steady. 'Every Sister here will give her body, their life in the

God-Emperor's name, but with cause. Is it too much to ask to know why poor Thalassa will now end her days walking on iron legs instead of those she was born with? The question is asked, Sister Imogen, and not only by me. The question echoes about the halls of this place.'

Sepherina rose and her cloak fell open behind her. She rounded the desk, advancing on the hospitaller. 'What question?'

'We…' Verity could not help herself, and she shrank back a step. 'We were brought here to reconsecrate this sacred place. But that is not all, I believe.' The young woman steeled herself and met Sepherina's eyes. 'What are you looking for, mistress? Can we not be told, so that no more blood is wasted and shed?'

For a long moment, Imogen thought that the canoness would strike the hospitaller across the face for her temerity, but then the tension in Sepherina shifted slightly, and her stiff pose eased a little. 'I could ask you the same thing, Sister Verity.'

The reply caught the other woman off-guard. 'I-I do not understand.'

'I know what happened to you on Neva. The mad plans of that deluded traitor LaHayn, but before that the death of your sibling Lethe. You put that to the earth and gave her to the God-Emperor's will. You signed upon the charter for this mission – my mission – to Sanctuary 101 because you are looking for something. What is it?'

'I don't–'

'Do not lie to me,' Sepherina warned. 'Answer.'

Verity swallowed a breath. 'Avowal. I seek a way to reaffirm my dedication to Holy Terra and my oath as a Sororitas.'

'And here you will,' Sepherina told her, 'as long as you remember who you are. As long as you remember *your place*.' She turned away. 'Sister Miriya. She came upon this endeavour because you encouraged her to join us. And like you, she is seeking something. Do you know what it is?'

Verity's reply took a long moment to form. 'Peace?' she offered, at length.

The canoness allowed a thin smile. 'That remains to be seen. Miriya has been a dangerous and unpredictable soul among the regimented choir of the Adepta Sororitas. She has stood out when she had no need to, and drawn discord to herself. Think of her now, a promising career set back decades because of hubris.' Imogen saw Verity open her mouth to leap to the other woman's defence, but Sepherina continued on. 'Those who stray too close to such behaviour can be coloured by it.' She glared at the hospitaller. 'Don't allow her mistakes to let you feel you may make them also. Unless you too wish to be considered as outspoken and troublesome?'

'It is not that,' Verity managed, but Sepherina silenced her with a look.

'You are dismissed,' said Imogen, taking her cue.

Verity frowned, and she bowed and walked away.

When they were alone again, Imogen glanced across at the canoness. 'Milady,' she began. 'I hesitate to say so, but the girl is right. There will come a time when we need to inform our Sisters.'

Sepherina looked away. 'Yes. But I'll not allow a nursemaid to tell me when that moment has come.'

The Watched knew where the interlopers were going, the men with their clanking metal limbs and their ever-present stink of machine oil. It wasn't a difficult assumption to make. There was only one destination, and it was a place visited before. Many times, in fact.

The ragged figure scrambled down the sheer face of the rock into the arroyo, knowing instinctively where the handholds and foot wells were. There were places to hide from the red-robed men when they drifted past on impellor platforms, places where the Watched had sat and observed. A memory of the day they had arrived resurfaced. The revenant thought of the solid, unflinching certainty from that moment. A knowledge that these visitors were here to do ill, and in secrecy. A sense of *wrongness*.

Towards the bottom of the steep-sided canyon, it always

seemed as if the ghost-soul voice of the Watcher inside the revenant's head was dimmer, as if it were attenuated. But never quite gone, though. There was nowhere on the planet where it could be silenced.

The Watched took care to descend into the encampment without being seen by the guards patrolling the site, drawing close its ragged cloak to remain nothing but a shadow. And inside that ruined mind, thoughts ground against each other like flints, throwing sparks of emotion that were hard to parse. The Watched sifted through the wreckage of a shattered self, trying to understand.

Only one thing was clear; something had changed now that the convent had been reoccupied, and these intruders were a part of it. If only one could understand what these things meant to one another. If only these pieces of disparate jigsaw images could be remade.

The machine did not lay dead upon the iron slab. Rather, it twitched and clicked and hummed in desultory, shuddering motions that seemed pathetic. On its back, the construct's six hinge-like legs wavered in the air, and Tegas could see where the null-grav coils along its thorax had been forcibly removed. The stumps of metal limbs were tied down with steel hawsers, the lengths of them cut in half.

Ferren saw where the questor was looking and nodded sagely. 'I had the manipulator claws severed after we captured it. It killed two helots with them.'

'A sensible precaution,' Tegas muttered, although something in him was offended by the careless and brutal manner in which the cutting had been done. The machine's sensor head tilted up in an attempt to peer at him as he approached, but it too was strapped down. He glimpsed a cluster of milky emerald eyes and broken visi-lenses between the figures in Mechanicus red, who surrounded the alien robot like carrion eaters plucking at a corpse. Servo-arms and serpentine actuators worked in the guts of the construct, causing spits of sparking discharge as they delved into the machine's body.

'I believe we will have it fully dismantled in the next few days.' Ferren was proud of his work here. 'A nigh-intact tomb spyder, broken down and collated in every detail.'

Tegas watched his former student's men working and was not impressed. They lacked the finesse he would have demanded, and he lamented at the thought of how much data was being lost through their crude experimentation. 'How is it that you have this automaton to begin with?'

'A survey party disturbed it,' Ferren replied, something in his manner making it clear there were details he didn't want to dwell upon. 'It was only just emerging from a dormant state... One of my tech-guard managed to englobe it with a stasis sphere before it could fully awaken.'

'You were favoured by random probability, then.' Tegas watched the machine-autopsy continue, the stink of hot metal and strange lubricants thick in his olfactory sensors. 'This is your great prize?'

Ferren shook his head, his body language showing dismay. 'No. No, my lord. But I thought you would be pleased... It is rare that such a find–'

'Yes,' Tegas broke in, becoming impatient. 'I am aware. But your communiqué made many vague promises, adept. I wish to see something new, something that I have never encountered before.' He gestured towards the tomb spyder. 'This is not even a true necron, it is one of their tools. Your findings show potential... So please, tell me you have more to show me than just stone towers and broken automata? I want more than theories to take back to Utopia Planatia, Ferren. I want knowledge that will change the galaxy.'

The tech-priest hesitated, then shot a burst of machine-code at one of the lesser adepts working at the dismantling. 'Get the artefact,' he commanded.

The tomb spyder's head twitched as it tried to follow them about the room, and from somewhere deep within its casing the alien device issued out a thin humming that echoed like a cry of animal pain.

Tegas glanced back. 'You are tormenting it,' he noted dispassionately.

'I do hope so,' Ferren replied.

The Watched had been here before. It knew the layout of the place, having stalked across the rooftops of the lab modules and dormitoria in the deep of night, spying on the red-robes without really understanding the reason why. Once or twice, the ragged figure had even entered the stone hallways inside the rock face, there where the men had cut away the rubble to reveal the alien geometry within. But the Watched did not like to tarry there. Inside that echoing place, it felt as if a million eyes were turned inwards, and the weight of something vast, black and nameless drifted just out of sight. Waiting for the moment to emerge and consume everything.

Listening now, the revenant clung to the top of an equipment shed. The mutter and buzz of the red-robes passed by. They were agitated about something, but the cause was unclear. Hidden in the folds of the torn, filthy hood, a scarred face twisted in a grimace, fighting with itself for any small scrap of knowledge. *It was such torment!* To see a thing clearly and not to be able to name it, even though the word danced on the edge of understanding. The Watched suffered this pain every day, but at this moment it felt so much worse. The new arrivals had made this happen; they had shone a bright light into the voids in memory, and the revelation was shocking. So much lost. *So much lost.*

'What is this?' The words fell away in a breathy whisper.

Then there was the crunch of sand beneath a boot, and one of the red-robe soldiers was suddenly there, a face spindly and sharp like that of a snake sculpted from iron. A lasgun in one clamp-fist grip. A mouth full of lenses and blue-glowing eyespots.

The Watched surrendered to animal impetus and attacked. Hood flapping, the ragged figure threw itself from the top of the shed and collided with the soldier, knocking it to the ground. Hands that ended in broken gauntlets dressed with crude claws of scrap metal lashed out and cut gouges in the pasty, grey skin of the red-robe soldier.

They struggled with the lasgun, then lost it between them in the sands. Reinforced cyborg limbs went against wiry bone and muscle, one powered by energetic battery cells, the other by sheer force of madness. Floodgates of emotion opened up inside the mind of The Watched and tears came again even as anger boiled beneath them. The cyborg staggered, losing ground, clawed feet slipping in the drifts of dust.

The ragged figure's free hand vanished into the stained, dirty robes and came back with a black blade, a shortsword made of a material that only barely existed in the real world. It went into the soldier's biogenerator implants, through the solar plexus with a sound like whispers. Oily blood spattered on the sand from the exit wound as the two combatants embraced.

The cyborg's last act was to tip back its head and emit a silent scream in the ultrasonic ranges beyond normal human hearing.

'Tell me about the deaths,' said Tegas, drawing up the crew complement data that Ferren had sent him on his arrival. 'The information you provided is incomplete.'

'It is basic, I admit,' said the tech-priest, shifting on his splay-toed iron feet. 'But I felt it expedient not to waste time with extraneous data. Suffice to say that an expedition like ours is not without its hazards. I have lost operatives and skitarii to cave-ins and traps left by the xenos to secure their tombs.'

Tegas's tolerance for Ferren's manner was thinning. 'What are you trying to conceal? What is it that you were afraid to admit on an open channel?' He drifted closer to his subordinate. 'The necrons... Your reports to Mars said you had found only sub-level forms, nothing humanoid or demi-intelligent. Did you lie?'

Ferren reverted back to a blink-code of panicked denials transmitted in the infra-red wavebands. 'No. Nothing like that. I am certain.'

Tegas scanned the stress levels in the reply and discarded it. 'You are not.'

'I am!' Ferren retorted. 'We have echo-mapped the entire interior space of the underspaces beneath the alien towers! We have encountered nothing there beyond the complexity of insect-machines! Whatever was here is gone!'

'Gone?' The questor turned on Ferren, a moment of pure, almost forgotten humanity rippling through him; the emotion of anger. 'I have travelled light-years to this ball of worthless rock on your word, adept, on the promise of something incredible! But now you suggest that all you have is another empty tomb and a theory I have heard before?'

'No,' Ferren repeated. 'I have more.' The lesser adept trundled back, proffering an object in outstretched hands to the questor. 'Look. See for yourself.'

Tegas took the artefact. It was a scroll, like those used in ancient days upon Terra to store knowledge before the advent of bookbinding. But it was not made of anything resembling paper. The sensing modules in his fingertips registered an incredibly ordered level of atomic structure in it, and attempts to identify the nature of the scroll's make-up classed it as some form of metallic crystal. It was thin, flexible and light.

He drew it open, and the action of light falling on the scroll's surface brought it to life. A silent waterfall of images and complex mathematical structures fell across the revealed page. Infinitely long lines of text revealed themselves, resembling the circle-spar iconography of the necrontyr. The scroll showed orb-like panes of data growing out of each other, and when Tegas tilted it, the images changed to reveal even more script layered atop them. It moved past with incredible speed, a library's weight in texts passing by in a second, more following, more and never ending. The questor saw glimpses of known necron constructs – the dark pyramidal Monoliths, the skeletal forms of their warriors, the glowing emerald spears of gauss weapons and the scimitar curves of vast interstellar ships – but there were other things there as well, forms made out of arcs of grey steel that clawed at the ground, elongated skulls with cyclopean eyes and tripedal walking machines that could only be war engines. He was looking through a tiny window into the heart of the necron machine, and what he saw there was beyond the scope of his imaginings.

'I theorise that the iron scroll is some form of information storage apparatus,' said Ferren, 'and possibly more besides. It may even be a remote, portable terminal for a larger expert system.'

Another human emotion pushed to the fore of Tegas's thoughts; the one he liked the most, the one he found it the hardest to part with. 'I take back my doubts,' he said, greed colouring his every utterance. 'This is impressive, Ferren.'

The tech-priest said something in reply, but Tegas was no longer paying attention to him. All that occupied him now was the desire to take this object to his own laboratorium unit back at the convent. It would be important to move swiftly so as to secure credit for this discovery for himself, he mused. Someone of adept's rank could not be allowed to deal with a find of this magnitude, this thing that could be the Rosetta Stone for all understanding of the necrontyr race. It had to be contained, managed... And properly exploited. In the right hands, the alien artefact could carry a man from the rank and file up to the giddy heights of High Adept of Mars, and Questor Tegas had entered into many bargains and accords in his life in the attempt to make that ascent.

More importantly, Tegas would have to consider how to handle the Ordo Xenos, who would throw aside any pretence at a slow and steady partnership and wade in with weapons and warships to secure the iron scroll, once they learned of its existence. *If they learned of it.*

Tegas folded the scroll closed, saddened to stop the rich flow of information, but it would be easy to become seduced by its potency. He watched Ferren wilt a little when it became clear he was not going to hand the object back to him. 'I will deal with this,' he said. 'You understand the need for that.'

Ferren's reply was lost in the sudden ultrasonic shriek of the camp's alert siren.

They scrambled out into the dusty gloom and into a chorus of laser fire. Tegas saw streaks of bright yellow flashing up at the wall of stone above them, blasting divots out of the red rock in crackling concussions.

'What is it?' he brayed. 'What are you shooting at?' Even as the demand was made, the questor spotted a blink of movement up on the sheer stone mass. A figure, humanoid in form, scaling the towering side of the arroyo in leaps and jerks, vanishing in and out of shadow as it moved. He immediately scanned in a dozen variant vision modes to pinpoint the intruder, but it was difficult to achieve. Something about the hooded cloak that hid the creature caused his sensor returns to simply slide off it. Already it was getting beyond the range of the tech-guard's laser weapons, and they were reluctant to open up with anything heavier than shoulder arms for fear of bringing the rocks down on the encampment.

Tegas turned on Ferren. The adept was doing his best to show a neutral aspect, but the questor knew him well enough to see straight through it. 'What is that?' He pointed towards the diminishing figure. He saw lifter platforms rising up in pursuit, but they were too slow to catch the fast-moving intruder.

'The deaths,' Ferren bleated. 'Some were murders.'

Tegas looked away and found the crumpled corpse of a skitarii. The biosynthetic innards of the soldier-cyborg formed a pool around it as the body twitched, mech-agumented nerve clusters still firing after meat-death. 'You were going to keep this from me...' He spun and whipped at Ferren with two of his mechadendrites, swatting the tech-priest into the wall of a gear shed. 'Explain now!'

'It has been plaguing us for months,' he admitted. Ferren began to spill it all out, as if relieved to be able to divest himself of a burden. 'I suspect it may be some kind of guardian left behind after the xenos left the planet.'

'*Necron?*' Tegas spat the word, broadcasting a stream of binary curses with it. 'There is a live alien on this planet, and you simply *omitted* that fact from your reports?'

'You would never have come if you thought there was danger!' Ferren became shrill. 'The Ordo Xenos would have arrived instead and all this would be lost to us! Hoth monitors all our signals! He would know!'

Tegas's fury built, and partly at the realisation that Ferren was correct. He spat oil into the dirt, reverting back to a human action in this moment of high anger. 'Why is it still alive?'

'We can't catch it,' admitted the tech-priest. 'We need help. Perhaps you could influence the Sororitas to–'

Tegas whipped at him once more to make Ferren fall silent. '*Imbecile*! Has living out in this wilderness clogged your processors with sand? The Sisterhood cannot know of this! That thing must be killed by the Adeptus Mechanicus. Do you not understand? *It knows the existence of this camp*!' He pointed into the air. 'I am very disappointed in you, Ferren. It seems I have arrived just in time.'

'I. I. I–' The tech-priest was making stuttering noises.

'I am taking full command of this expeditionary force,' snapped Tegas. 'This is so ordered.' He looked inwards, encoded the directive into machine-code and transmitted it on wide-band.

All of Ferren's men stopped what they were doing and bowed to the questor.

CHAPTER SIX

It was night, and Sister Miriya found herself in the memorial garden once more.

The Sororitas on Sanctuary 101 had taken to calling it that – *the garden* – despite the fact that nothing grew from the sand-clogged ground except the stone markers bearing the names of the dead. She walked with reverence between the ordered rows of little statues, her path illuminated by the glow of the eternal lamps inside each sculpture of Saint Katherine. Ghost-light flickered like candles in the shadow of the shield wall looming above, the saw-toothed battlements cutting a jagged line across a clear, dark sky. Miriya saw a figure move up there; it was Sister Pandora, her bolter in her hands, walking her circuit of the perimeter. The other woman glanced down, her face hidden behind her Sabbat-pattern helmet. By rights, it was against orders for anyone to be outside after curfew had been called, but Pandora said nothing. She merely gave the other woman a solemn, understanding nod and moved on.

Miriya looked away, her gaze drawn back to the rows of statuettes. She felt churlish, betrayed by her own venality. Unable to find sleep in the makeshift barracks that had been set up in the convent's exercise halls, the Battle Sister had stolen away in her duty robes and walked out into the cool night, in search of... *What?*

'Why am I here?' she asked softly, to the air, to the dead, to the image of the Saint. None gave her an answer.

If one wanted only a factual, colourless reply to that question, there was ample explanation. Miriya was here because of her mistakes.

First, her errors in allowing her second-in-command, Sister Lethe Catena, to be killed during the escape of a dangerous psyker captive; then her inability to widen her focus and the near-obsession with which she pursued her former prisoner. These things had caused her to fall into the orbit of the Lord Deacon Viktor LaHayn, a man of such hubris that his plans dared to shake the pillars of the Golden Throne itself. In the end, LaHayn and his sacrilege were obliterated and Miriya found some measure of reprisal, but there had been a high price to pay.

She glanced down, her fingertips finding the beads of her chaplet, caressing the places where the chain had been broken and then repaired. Each tiny orb represented an act of devotion in the name of the Imperial Church. Once there had been many more adamantine beads on the chain, sufficient to signify officer rank as a Celestian Eloheim, but now there were barely enough to compare with that of a Novice Constantia newly raised to the status of a Sister Militant.

Miriya had committed a crime against her Order. She had disobeyed the direct orders of her Sister Superiors and risked life and limb in order to follow her own agenda to the bitter end. At the time, it had seemed like it was the only choice, but the passage of weeks into months made that certainty appear less solid – and on the voyage aboard the *Tybalt*, Miriya had found herself with much time to reflect on the way things might have played out differently. She was fortunate to be alive, she reflected, but frequently that mercy felt like just another kind of punishment. The sentiment was not lessened by the manner in which women like Sister Imogen treated her.

In the aftermath of her demotion back to the line rank of Battle Sister, Miriya felt lost and without purpose, and it had been the hospitaller Verity who offered her a path. The young woman impressed the warrior with her keen intellect and an inner reserve of strength that belied her gentle aspect, and so Miriya accepted her Sister's suggestion – and her forgiveness. Lethe had been Verity's blood kindred, and with her friendship, Miriya could at least believe that one of her mistakes had been absolved.

But it was not enough. She looked around, taking a deep breath of the dry air. Miriya signed on to Canoness Sepherina's mission because she believed that she would find some kind of renewed purpose in it. She believed this pilgrimage to the rim of the Imperium would let her make peace with herself. It had not done so. Rather, it had shone a light upon harsh truths that Miriya had never wished to dwell upon.

She tried to lose herself in the endless rounds of prayer and practice, drilling and singing and fighting. But she had never been one for introspection or the layered games of interaction between rank and file, church and state. Miriya was a warrior first and foremost, and she craved the pure focus of combat.

Battle was her true chapel. Here, on this distant outpost that lay nigh-forgotten by the rest of the galaxy, she was far away from the Order's great Wars of Faith, far from the places where her sword arm and her boltgun could serve the God-Emperor in dispatching the infidel. It troubled her to admit that without the clash of gunfire and the screams of the unworthy in her ears, all Miriya could hear were the sounds of her own shortcomings. The thought seemed seditious. Could it be true that she was so enraptured by the spilling of blood that without it she would crumble?

Her soul was turning inwards, and she did not like what she saw there. Sister Miriya's absolute faith to Holy Terra was not in question – that had never, *it would never* leave her – but now she felt as if she were a blunted blade. She was broken and rusting, and might never again be called to the heights of martial glory she had once reached for.

She would do her duty to the letter, because she was an Adepta Sororitas and even the death of every star in the sky would not change that. But Miriya was deeply troubled by the yawning hollow in her spirit, as it seemed to grow ever wider with each passing day.

The Battle Sister looked down at the memorial markers and wondered if that would be her fate – to live and die here, and be recalled only by those who had not known her.

I followed Verity out to the middle of nowhere because I thought that distance would bring me clarity… And for my sins, I have found it. Miriya's aspect became grim.

Turning from the lines of memorial markers, her line of sight crossed the courtyard, where the workgangers had erected their temporary bivouacs and wind shelters for the reconstruction gear.

Miriya glimpsed a motion between a stand of rockcrete panels and a tethered habitat module. She froze, old battle senses stiffening her muscles. This late, only Miriya and the guards were at large. She wondered if one of the workers might have been foolish enough to venture outside of their cabins after the last shift. Or perhaps it was a trick of the eye, the motion of the wind casting a moving shadow from the edge of an untethered tent-flap.

Then she saw it again, certain this time, and Miriya knew her instincts had been on the mark. Staying low so as not to stray into the pools of light cast by the windows of the hab modules, a cloaked figure moved in jerky starts towards the central keep. The umbra was human in scale, but the Battle Sister could not pick out anything visible beneath the hood or in the depths of the wide sleeves. Her first thought was that it was one of Questor Tegas's errant tech-priests sneaking back into the convent, but then the figure moved slowly past the struts supporting the Mechanicus laboratorium module and kept on going.

Intruder. It could be nothing else. Taking steady, careful steps, Miriya advanced, never taking her eyes off the cloaked form. She cursed her circumstances; she had no vox on her, nor any weapon better than the combat knife in her boot. She was afraid to call out in hopes that Sister Pandora might still be within earshot. This one could be a scout for all she knew, there could be others of them in the deeper shadows where Miriya could not see. If she sounded an alarm without being certain, the workgangers would panic at it and doubtless break into disorder.

Her feet crunched on a broken stone and the figure spun in the direction of the sound. Miriya dropped to her knees behind the cover of a cargo drum, and took the opportunity to draw her blade.

Her mind raced. Whoever – or *whatever* – this interloper was, Miriya had only spotted them by pure chance, and the thought of that set her blood running cold. It had to mean that the cloaked intruder had not only made it past the perimeter line of sensing rods deployed by Imogen's scouts, but then across open sand to the walls of the convent, through them and into the courtyard without ever drawing the attention of Pandora or the other Sisters on guard duty.

She chanced a look over the top of the drum and saw nothing. Even that brief moment of losing direct visual contact had been enough. Miriya snarled a sanctioned curse under her breath and sprinted back towards the wall. Gathering up a loose pebble, she pitched it at the battlements and it cracked off the stonework. After a moment Pandora's helmet emerged over the ledge, leading with the muzzle of her bolter.

'Spread the word,' Miriya hissed, low and quick. 'But quietly! Something is inside the perimeter! One intruder, humanoid.' She pointed. 'I saw it heading towards the central donjon!'

Pandora hesitated. Technically, she outranked the other Battle Sister even though they both had veteran's laurels, but Miriya's manner was still that of a unit commander; she had to remind herself to show fealty. 'Please, Sister Militant,' she added, appending the title to pay due deference.

Sister Pandora nodded and cocked her head. Miriya knew the motion. The guard was sending a subvocalised message via her vox-bead. Without waiting for a reply, Miriya broke into a jog, skirting the piles of rubble arranged by the worker helots, and made for the great keep as quickly as she could.

She reached the steel doors to the primus atrium and found they were already hanging open.

For a little while, Verity allowed herself to think she was back on Ophelia VII, in one of the Yabarantine Naves that dotted the landscape of the great Cardinal World. She imagined turning her face to the west in order to catch a glimpse of the moonlight off the towers of the Synod Ministra, the city-sized complex where some of the Imperium's most notable religious texts had been authored. The thought warmed her.

But then she opened her eyes and she was half a galaxy away from that sainted place, still here in the Kavir system, kneeling before a damaged altar and tending to a cluster of votives that seemed small, lost in the murk and the debris of the place. Deacon Zeyn's workers had done a passable job of clearing away the worst of the wreckage in the Great Chapel, but the sting of rock dust was still in the air and thick in the hospitaller's nostrils. The dust... The damnable dust coated everything, seeming to materialise out of nowhere to re-cover any surface a millisecond after it was wiped clean.

She listened to the soft crackle of the candle flames, and caught the scent of rose-oil wafting up from them. Each candle had a prayer machine-printed about the body of it, open and bland missives to the God-Emperor full of generalities and receptive hopes. They were a common sight in cathedrals across the Imperium of Man, cheap enough that a single Throne coin would buy you a box of them to place in your own domicile shrine, should one so wish. Here, this night, Verity had gathered up a few of them to light in the name of Sister Thalassa, and bound them with entreaty to Holy Terra. Perhaps a miracle might be visited on the injured woman and the shard of autocannon round that had lodged in her spinal column would yet be expunged; certainly, Verity and Zara and the other hospitallers had exhausted every earthly manner of doing so.

Verity's head was leaden with fatigue and she craved sleep, but still she had come to the chapel at this late hour to light the candles and say the words. She saw it as much a part of her duty as she did the healing of the flesh of her Sisters.

A dolorous moan echoed out behind her, and the noise made the woman go tense with surprise. She turned and saw a vertical crack of lamplight across the chapel, wavering in the gloom. The steel doors had opened, the groan of the mechanism sounding like a solemn lament. Verity came up from her knees and took two steps away from the altar, her brow furrowed. She had expected no other company in this place at this hour. Belatedly, a breath of wind came across the chamber and made the candle flames mutter.

Unbidden, fear prickled Verity's flesh, and she was suddenly very aware that she stood in a haunted, desolate place.

Then there was the whispering. It seemed to come from very far away, and it was difficult for her to place its location. A woman's voice, that was all she could be certain of. *And coming closer.*

Emotion, something base and animal in Sister Verity, uncoiled inside her chest, something abruptly afraid and very human. She backed away, shrinking into the lee of a towering marble column, her heart thudding in her chest. Her need for sleep was banished by a powerful kick of adrenaline. Verity let the shadows swallow her and pressed herself to the far side of the stone pillar, not daring to breathe. The whispering voice made its approach, carried by loping footfalls, and by turns it defined itself until she could hear the words that were being spoken.

'You know nothing,' said the voice. It came through cracked lips and a parched throat. 'Get out. You have no right to speak.'

Verity heard the shuffle and drag of boots, the murmur of a heavy cloak being pulled across the flagstones. Part of her cursed this moment of weakness. She was a Sister of the Adepta, not some child who ran and cowered at every shadow. She had faced great horrors in her service to the Golden Throne, seen terrible things as she tended to the wounded upon the battlegrounds of piety, sights that would have sent lesser souls running for the hills.

And yet at the same moment she felt an icy fear gripping her chest like claws made of frost. There was something out there in the gloom that she did not want to lay her eyes upon, and she could not answer as to why.

'I hate you,' said the voice, dripping with venom and old revulsion. 'You cannot...' There was a moment of silence, as if the speaker was listening to an interjection that could not be perceived by Verity's ears. '*Silence!*' The voice returned with an angry snarl, and boots scraped on the stones.

The hospitaller set her teeth and at last dared to peer around the column, listening to the thump of her blood in her ears.

She saw a human figure in a shabby cloak the colour of rust, turn and lash out at the cluster of candles atop the altar. With a single sweep of a clawed hand, an arm clothed in ragged strips of cloth emerging from the folds of the cloak, the husk-voiced woman dashed the votives to the floor, breaking the glass cups, snuffing out the flames and spilling fluid wax where they fell. She spat and ground them to powder beneath her heel. In the flashes of motion, Verity glimpsed slivers of the body hidden under the cloak as she moved: an emaciated form swaddled in tatters, flesh covered in scars, matted locks of dark hair. It seemed to be a human. *Seemed to be*. She could not be certain of anything.

'You can't stop me,' came the hissing words. 'No. No no.'

Verity realised then it was the voice that lit the fear inside her. There was a gallows manner in it, a tone that resonated as harshly as the slamming of a sepulchre's gate. Hearing the hooded one speak was like hearing the voice of death itself.

With a strange gentleness, the figure gathered up one of the untouched candles left to one side by the hospitaller, and put it in pride of place on the altar. Head bowed, she struck a tinder-rod and lit the wick. The whispers returned as the cloaked head bobbed, muttering a litany that Verity could not define.

The hospitaller retreated into the gloom, not daring to take her eyes off the intruder, feeling her way back towards the main doors. Her hand flailed in the air and was suddenly arrested in the grip of another. Verity swallowed a yelp of surprise and spun to find Sister Miriya close by. The Battle Sister carried a wicked combat knife in one hand, and in the other a thick rod of steel rebar recovered from one of the rubble piles.

'I followed it,' Miriya said quietly, nodding towards the altar. 'It came in over the walls.'

'*She*,' gasped Verity. 'It is a human being. I think.'

Miriya accepted this without comment. 'The other exits from this chapel – they are secured?'

'Aye,' said the hospitaller.

'Then we have it– We have *her* trapped.'

Verity glanced back at the altar. There was only the candle there now, burning steadily. 'Miriya–'

The warning had barely left her lips when a clattering noise and the snap of a cloak sounded out across the chapel. The hooded woman was moving, disappearing into thick stands of shadow, reappearing, moving in and out of cover.

The Battle Sister strode forwards, throwing Verity a last nod towards the chapel doors. The hospitaller understood, and raced across the stone floor towards the entrance.

'Show your face!' Miriya demanded, hefting the steel rod like a sword. 'Surrender now and there will be no bloodshed. Resist and you will be killed!'

Verity skidded to a halt at the doors, hearing the rattle of loose stones out in the shadows. The chapel's internal lighting system had not been repaired, and only a string of free-standing work lamps cast a corridor of illumination across the nave to the altar. Beyond its reach, the occasional shaft of moonlight cut through the dark ranges of the wide chamber.

'Show yourself, intruder!' shouted the Battle Sister, her temper flaring. Verity sensed movement out in the corridor as Cassandra emerged into the chapel, clad in full wargear and carrying her bolter. Isabel was a few steps behind her, and armed in a similar fashion.

'There!' Verity pointed in the direction of the sound.

Cassandra gave a nod. 'The alert is being passed to all sentries. Stand back. Let us deal with this.'

Rubble shifted out in the shadows and the armed Sisters advanced at a run, closing in to join Miriya.

'We need preysight to find this thing,' she heard Isabel say.

'No need,' responded Cassandra, and plucked a small orb from her belt and tossed it into the air. The silver sphere described an arc that took it up into the rafters of the Great Chapel's dome, and at the apex it burst into a glaring white clump of fire. The flare-pod began a slow drift back to the ground, but the stark illumination it threw out cast sharply defined shadows that shifted and wheeled.

Verity saw motion over on the west wall and called out; the ink-blot shape of a ragged cloak flickering as it dragged itself up the length of a dust-caked tapestry.

Isabel fired warning shots that chewed great divots of masonry from the walls, but Miriya was already cautioning her not to seek a kill. 'We take her alive!' she shouted.

The Battle Sister's hopes seemed unlikely, though. Verity marvelled as the intruder scaled the sheer stone facia where there seemed little purchase, before leaping across yawning gaps to swing around support beams and stanchions. Isabel ignored her former commander's call to stand down and tried to bracket the fleeing figure with shots. Each round was far past true, however, and the cloaked figure launched itself into space. She made a powerful, hurtling push and darted through the broken fingers of glassaic ringing the shattered portal in the roof dome. Dislodged fragments fell in a chiming rain against the altar as the intruder vanished into the darkness.

Other Battle Sisters pushed through the doors behind

Verity, and she saw Helena there, bearing a drawn power sword, with Pandora at her side.

'Did you see it?' Pandora snapped.

Verity nodded. 'I saw it.'

Miriya sprinted back towards them. 'She's outside, on the top of the dome! We can still catch her!'

Helena nodded. 'Tactical squad, with me!' She stormed back out into the corridor, with Isabel and Cassandra on her heels.

'You won't catch her.' It was a moment before Verity realised that she had said the words.

Miriya halted and shot her a look. 'We will try.'

Sister Pandora placed a heavy, gauntleted hand on the hospitaller's shoulder. 'Girl, what did you see? Tell us.'

Verity looked towards the altar, where a lone candle still burned, and she gave an involuntary shiver. 'I saw the walking dead,' she replied, speaking from the heart. 'Not a resurrected, not something animated by the Ruinous Powers. Worse than that. A woman like a living ghost. Flesh and rags. Scars and tears... And that voice...'

'Verity,' said the Battle Sister. 'Your words make no sense.'

'Tears,' repeated the hospitaller. 'I saw tears on a broken face. She was weeping as she lit the votive.'

Dawn light was creeping over the walls of the convent by the time the canoness had called the gathering in the courtyard, fingers of orange-pink colour changing the shade of the sky. A low cloud of dust disturbed by the warming of the desert drifted down in the valley, and it seemed as if the outpost was some manner of island floating amid a sea of rolling haze.

Sepherina stood atop one of the cracked plinths and glared down with undisguised fury at the Battle Sisters Imogen had assembled. 'This shall not stand!' she snarled, searching their faces in turn. Miriya didn't look away when she met her gaze. At her side, she felt the hospitaller Verity stiffen.

Isabel, Cassandra, Pandora and a dozen other women stood in a precise line in front of the canoness, while the

Sister Superior Imogen watched from one side. None of them dared to speak, each fully aware of their failure in allowing the intruder to escape.

'In Katherine's name, I am sorely disappointed in each of you.' Sepherina shook her head. 'Did the length of our journey here make us slow and lax? Have the edges of our wits dulled through inaction?' She swept a hand over the group. 'I expected better, Sisters. First we suffer the indignity of that fool Tegas fleeing in the night like an errant child, and then the very sanctity of this hallowed place is violated!' She smacked her fist into her palm. 'And by what? You cannot even concur on the nature of this freakish trespasser!'

Miriya shared a glance with Verity. The young woman had been the best witness to the true nature of the hooded figure, but Sister Imogen seemed disinterested in the opinions of the 'nursemaid', preferring to cull a series of half-formed impressions from Pandora and the other women who had been on guard.

'How did this happen?' demanded the canoness. 'Imogen, answer me!'

The Battle Sister gave a contrite nod. 'The outer perimeter... There are still gaps in our security coverage, and despite our best efforts, we cannot cover every inch of the outer walls. The damage is in the process of repair, but–'

'I will hear no more excuses!' thundered Sepherina, her eyes flashing. 'Rouse Deacon Zeyn and the worker helots, have it done now! From this moment onwards, they will work around the clock until the walls are fully sealed and this convent is no longer open to attack! Work them until they drop, if needs must!'

Imogen nodded again and spoke into the vox-bead at her throat, relaying the new orders.

'Until further notice, Sanctuary 101 is now on combat alert status,' continued the canoness. 'All tactical squad leaders will make ready and weapons will be drawn. No more mistakes. *Vigilance*, Sisters.'

'*Vigilance*,' chorused the women, bowing their heads as they spoke the word like a benediction.

When Miriya looked up again she found Sepherina's cold eyes turned on her once more. 'Sister. You raised the alarm. You were the first to see this... person.'

'Miriya broke curfew,' Imogen added, without preamble. 'An action that will earn her even more demerits.'

The canoness silenced the Sister Superior with a raised hand. 'Why were you outside?'

The truth seemed a weak explanation, but it was the truth nonetheless. 'Sleep eluded me, mistress. I decided to take the night air. I have no excuse for my actions.'

'Tell me what you saw.'

She did so, recounting the moment in the garden, the warning she passed to Pandora – and then her desperate room-to-room search through the halls of the central keep that ended in the chapel. 'Sister Verity was there,' Miriya concluded. 'She saw better than I.'

'Is this so?' Sepherina measured Verity with a long look. 'You were in the chapel.'

'I was, milady,' said Verity. In turn, the hospitaller spoke of what she had seen before the altar, the maddened, terrible voice of the intruder and her strange actions.

Imogen offered the canoness the votive candle that had been left behind. Sepherina examined it, turning it in her gloved fingers, frowning. Finally, she looked away. 'Did the intruder speak to you?'

Miriya saw Verity give an involuntary shudder. 'She did not.'

'What kind of invasion sends a scout into a chapel to pray?' Imogen asked, her low opinion of Verity's account clear in her tone.

Sepherina shot her second-in-command a sharp look that silenced her once again. 'If this... person... dares to show themselves again within the bounds of our sight, I want her captured and interrogated, is that clear?'

'*Aye*,' came the reply.

'I will personally chastise any Sister who fails in her duty to protect the purity of this site!' she spat, her anger rising once more. 'I will–'

'*Target-sign!*' The shout went up from the walls, and Miriya recognised Sister Ananke's cry. The dark-skinned woman was high on the battlements, her bolter at her shoulder. 'Dust plume, to the east. Approaching at speed!'

'To arms!' cried Imogen, and the group surged into motion, gathering up their weapons, racing to find cover and sight-lines.

'Get inside,' Miriya told Verity. 'You'll be safer there.'

'Will I?' asked the hospitaller, and the question was heavy with import.

'Just go,' said the Battle Sister, as Pandora came to her side and thrust a loaded bolter into Miriya's hands.

The dust clouds churned beyond the East Gate, or what was left of it. There had been a portcullis and gantry there when the convent was built, but in the process of the first attack that had left the outpost empty, that entrance had been demolished. Evidence of heavy energy weapon fire and the sheer brute-force power of a ramming apparatus showed that this had been the main point of attack when the necrons had come to cull the Sisters a decade ago.

Miriya fell in with Pandora and Cassandra, taking up positions behind the stub of a collapsed pillar. She checked her ammunition clip and brought her weapon to her shoulder, sighting down the optical scope.

A curtain of billowing sand filled the sight's vision block and she panned the gun slowly across the zone beyond the fallen gate. Miriya found the plume of trail dust immediately, and for a brief second she thought she caught sight of a slab-sided shape moving inside the ruddy cloud.

'Do you hear that?' asked Helena. 'Beneath the wind, a regular noise. An engine.'

'A vehicle,' Pandora agreed, listening to the chatter on the primary vox-channel. 'Ananke reports a detection from the thermographic scanners. Four hundred metres now and closing.'

Miriya's finger tensed on the bolter's trigger. 'Are we to fire?' Sepherina had said the words and ordered them to combat alert – and the letter of that standing order included directives to shoot anything that refused to identify itself. The sound of the engine reached her, a steady, rolling thrum.

Helena recognised it immediately. 'A Venator. It's one of ours.'

As the Battle Sister named it, the vehicle emerged from the low mist of windborne sand and started up the incline to the ruined gate, but in the next second the rover decelerated sharply and fishtailed in the dust, juddering to an ungraceful halt.

A dozen Sororitas guns were trained on the Venator, across from cover or down from the battlements. Any sudden motion, any threatening action, and the vehicle would be torn apart by bolter fire.

A hatch angled open and a hooded figure emerged. Unlike the intruder, this one wore the distinctive crimson of the Adeptus Mechanicus, and one by one, its fellows dismounted the rover, nervously clustering behind their leader.

'I calculate that you will demand an explanation,' called Questor Tegas, his voice rebounding off the broken walls. He appeared supremely unconcerned by countless guns aiming at him.

Miriya put her sights on the questor's head, observing the motion of his manifold eye implants, trying to measure his intentions.

Sepherina appeared beneath the broken arch of the East Gate, directly in the path the Venator had been following. She had twinned bolter pistols on her belt, and her hands strayed dangerously close to the weapons. Sister Imogen and two of her Celestians followed on behind her.

The breeze carried their voices so that all the assembled Sororitas could hear their exchange. 'In respect for your title and your exalted position,' began the canoness, 'I will grant you a moment to explain your actions.'

Tegas tilted his head. 'Milady...'

'If I do not find your words satisfactory, there will be consequences,' she concluded.

The questor stiffened at Sepherina's tone, and when he spoke again the obsequious manner he had shown before was wholly absent. 'I do not answer to you, Sororitas. You have no right to compel answers from me if I do not wish to give them.'

'You dare to play games of rank with me?' the canoness retorted. 'You vanish in the night by stealth, ignore my commands, steal one of our vehicles? I am within my remit to shoot you where you stand!'

'Your *commands*?' Tegas echoed. 'I think you overstep your bounds, milady. For all the authority you may think you claim, you have no power over the Adeptus Mechanicus. I do not need to justify my actions to you.' His augmetic arms folded closed over his chest with a hiss of pistons. 'You ought to give praise to the God-Emperor for the fact that you and your women are even standing on this planet. Had we wished to do so, the Forge Masters of Mars could have annexed this world and evicted your Sisterhood from it for all time, honoured dead or none!'

Sepherina's hand blurred and suddenly she had an ornate bolt pistol drawn and levelled at Tegas's head. His skitarii and adepts jerked and twitched, each bringing up their own weapons in a defensive arc. For their part, the rest of the Battle Sisters maintained their unwavering aim. If the word was given, they would reduce the servants of the Mechanicus to oily smears on the sand, and never hesitate.

'You vanish,' the canoness growled. 'then we are invaded by an unknown interloper, hooded and robed as you are.'

For a fraction of a second, Tegas's body language changed. He lost the tension of the moment, shifting. Then a heartbeat later he was stiff and rigid. Still, Miriya glimpsed the faint blink of laser light off the tip of one of his mechadendrites as he sent a silent communication to one of his adepts. 'I know nothing of that,' he said, at length.

'You are lying to me. And I believe we have been told

many lies along the path of this journey, questor. Yours are only the most recent.' She advanced a step. 'You will tell me where you have been and why you defied my orders to remain inside the compound.'

Tegas sighed. It was a feigned motion, as he had no need to breathe in a conventional fashion. 'Your draconian edicts irritated me,' he replied. 'I decided to ignore them. To teach you a lesson.'

'Arrogant cog–' muttered Imogen.

Sepherina shook her head and the other woman's invective ended before it could go further. 'And so you committed a crime of theft and conspiracy against the Imperial Church?'

'It is within my remit as a questor to appropriate military vehicles, should I wish to,' Tegas sniffed. 'As to your guards failing to observe our departure... I suggest you take that up with them, and review the Sister Superior's tactical deployment.' He paused, glancing around. 'We were eager, canoness. Eager to sift the dirt of this world through our manipulators, to see it at first hand... Not to wait inside the walls of this convent until you deigned to let us off your leash.'

Sepherina slowly lowered the bolt pistol. 'And what did all your eagerness get you, Tegas? Tell me, out in the wilds, what great sights did you see? Was it worth incurring our anger?'

'Our expedition found nothing of import,' he replied. Watching through the targeting scope, Miriya could not shake a sudden, sharp certainty. *Once more, he lies.*

If the canoness thought the same, she did not show it. 'Your impatience could have seen you killed. You acted recklessly!'

'Perhaps I did,' Tegas allowed. 'But your recalcitrant manner forced my hand. And if indeed there is another...' He paused, framing his words. 'If there is some unknown agent at large on this world, would it not better suit us both to put aside our differences and address that concern instead?' Tegas asked Sepherina to relay the events in the chapel before the rise of the dawn, and he listened intently as she did so, offering nothing in return. She showed him the votive candle and he took it, scanning it with a fan of photons before passing it back to another of his minions.

Finally, he spoke again. 'With your permission, then, I will retire to our laboratorium to conduct a deep analysis on this matter.'

Sepherina seemed as if she were about to launch into another tirade, but then she turned and beckoned to Helena and Pandora. 'Sisters. Come.' They did as they were ordered, and the canoness gave Tegas a level stare. 'From this moment on, no member of the Adeptus Mechanicus will be allowed to venture outside of your laboratorium without a Sororitas escort.'

'For our own safety?'

She ignored his comment. 'Any who fail to adhere to this order will be classed as intruders and shot. Do I make myself clear?'

The questor bowed slightly. 'Absolutely.'

'Then get out of my sight, before I reconsider.' She turned her back on him.

Tegas blinked another beam-signal at his entourage and they filed in behind him, past the Celestians and into the convent proper. Miriya lowered her boltgun, and watched them go, the questor drifting as if floating over the courtyard flagstones. The last of the adepts passed close to her, carrying a cylinder the colour of iron in its grippers. She caught the damp cave odour of sandstone, and the tang of machine oil.

'Imogen.' Miriya turned as she heard Sepherina call the Sister Superior's name. The canoness waited a moment, until Tegas's troupe were distant, and spoke again. 'I will not have the cyborg's motives remain a mystery to me, is that clear? I want to know what he was doing out there.'

'I could take a team,' Imogen offered. 'Attempt to retrace the course of the Venator. We may be able to find out where he went.'

Sepherina nodded, and Miriya saw an opportunity. She came forwards and bowed. 'Milady, if I may?' She pointed at the rover. 'The vehicle's machine-spirit – if we could interpret its datum, we might be able to narrow down the area of transit. We know how long Tegas was gone for. If we can reckon the charge remaining in the power core.'

'None of us are tech-adepts, Miriya,' Imogen's reply was brisk. 'The workings of such things are known to Tegas's people, and I doubt he would give an honest estimate.'

'Untrue,' Miriya corrected. 'I believe Sister Verity has some experience with technological devices. On Neva, her skills proved very useful.'

'The nursemaid?' Imogen made it clear she was unconvinced.

The canoness frowned. 'Bring her. I want this matter dealt with.'

'And what of our intruder?' said the Sister Superior. 'What if she returns?'

Sepherina looked up at the warriors on the battlements. 'She will not find so easy a path this time.'

CHAPTER SEVEN

The rover crested the top of the sand dune and skidded, the six knobbled tyres spinning as they failed to find purchase in the red dust. At last the Venator lurched to a halt and the gull-wing hatches rose. In quick order, the squad of Battle Sisters deployed from the vehicle and formed a combat wheel. Exiting from the driver's compartment, Sister Cassandra bit back a curse about the lineage of the machine and paused to take a sighting from the Kaviran sun, almost obscured from the ground by the dust clouds. She muttered darkly, her words lost behind the breather mask that covered her mouth and nose.

Imogen dropped from the rear crew bay as if she were a queen stepping from a royal chariot and stalked around the vehicle. 'Another halt?' Her face was hidden behind the helmet of her power armour. 'I thought we had this zone fully charted.'

'Not well enough, Sister Superior,' said Cassandra. 'The digi-compass continues to drift off true. Something in the rocks, a magnetic ore perhaps… It is interfering with the automap.' She showed the display of the auspex unit in her hand. 'It will take me only a few moments to sight and recalibrate.'

Sister Miriya stood at the open hatch at the rear and

watched the exchange silently, leaning into the desiccating wind, listening to the rush of sand particles across her black wargear. They had been searching for several hours now, working through a grid pattern, and the armour of each of the Sororitas was slowly turning a dull mud-red as the dust coated the ceramite surfaces of vambrace, breastplate and cuissart. She had secured her combat cloak, but still it pulled at her shoulders with each new gust. Close by, the other Battle Sisters crouched and peered out into the haze. Like Imogen, they wore their helmets sealed. Sister Danae carried the steel-grey bulk of a meltagun, while Sisters Kora and Xanthe were armed with standard-pattern bolters.

The Venator rocked on its fat all-terrain wheels. A Masakari-pattern variant of the smaller standard scout car, this vehicle differed from those used by the units of the Imperial Guard or the Adeptus Arbites. It had a longer wheelbase, an enclosed space for a driver, and instead of mounted lascannons, an aft compartment where six women could be carried in supremely uncomfortable proximity. But even a unit specially-adapted for use on desert worlds like Sanctuary 101 was finding this sortie hard going. Still, it was better suited than a heavy armoured vehicle, like a Rhino or an Immolator tank, which would have sunk to its deck in the powdery metallic sands.

Miriya glanced up and caught sight of spires, spindly fingers of rock that rose up from the shallow canyon walls around them, carved by the action of the winds. The breeze moaned through eyes in the stone, rippling over the tips of the dunes. She looked away and bent to duck inside the rear of the Venator.

Verity was in there, whispering a prayer over a keyboard of brass buttons and a flickering pict-screen. She was pale and sweaty, and her face was set in a frown.

'Sister,' Miriya began. 'I fear I was too hasty to enlist your help on this excursion.'

The hospitaller looked up. 'Oh. Miriya, no... I am glad I could help. I only wish I could do more.' She absently fingered the hem of her robes, earth-brown with green-gold trim in the signature colours of the Order of Serenity.

'You said you had worked with the Sisters Dialogus and their thought-engines... I believed you would have some measure of understanding about the scout's systems. If I was wrong, if I overstepped my bounds...'

Verity shook her head and gave a wan smile. 'No. It is not that. It is merely that the vehicle's machine-spirit is of a different order to the devices I am familiar with. And I am no expert.'

'We cannot ask the *experts*,' Miriya noted. 'The adepts are not to be trusted.'

'Yes.' Verity pecked at the keyboard with her fingers. 'We must be close. From what I have been able to glean, Questor Tegas proceeded to this zone and here the vehicle remained stationary for several hours. We need only find the exact locale to be certain.'

'We will find it.' Miriya caught a glimpse of Sister Imogen through one of the gun-slots in the hull of the Venator, as she snapped an order at the other Sororitas. Verity followed her line of sight.

'I think the Sister Superior does not share your belief,' said the hospitaller wearily. 'The longer we are out here, the shorter her temper seems to grow.'

'Imogen dislikes anything she cannot see down the barrel of a bolter,' Miriya replied.

'A narrow mind is a pious mind,' Verity replied, reciting an axiom from the pages of *The Rebuke*.

'I am certain she believes that,' said Miriya. Her words trailed off. There was more she wanted to say, but she could not find the right way to phrase it.

Verity saw the furrowing of her brow. 'What is it, Sister?'

'Why are we here?' The question spilled out of her. 'Why did we come to this desolate place, Verity?' The weight of uncertainty that she had felt before, in the memorial garden, returned to her.

'For the duty.'

She shook her head. 'No. More than that.' Miriya met her gaze. 'I know what you wanted from Sepherina's mission. After the death of Lethe and... And what we saw on Neva...'

Lethe.

The moment Miriya said her name, Verity saw her sister as clear as day, her dark hair framing a hawkish, elegant face, eyes that were old before their time. Her blood sibling, hardy and strong, always there to protect her. But no longer. Lethe was gone, and Verity remained.

Each time she thought she had made her peace with that truth, there came a moment when she realised that she had not, that she never would. Even though they had gone to separate orders of the Sisterhood on ascension from their schola – Lethe into battle with the warriors of Saint Katherine, Verity to the medicae savants – she had still felt as if her kinswoman was keeping her safe. But Lethe's death had brought home a terrible reality to her; the harshness of this universe, something that before she had been able to keep at a distance, came in and struck her in the heart.

Verity believed that it was the duty of every servant of the Imperial Church to improve humanity's lot in the galaxy, to beat back the night and the dangers of the alien, the mutant, the witch and the traitor. And for a time it had seemed possible, knowing that Lethe was out there, fighting for the same ideal.

Her murder shook Verity to the core. It threatened to shatter her faith. It brought her fury and sorrow of a kind she had never experienced. Miriya had stood with her and helped Verity find her way back, but the journey had changed her.

What she had *done* had changed her. Verity remembered the weight of a boltgun in her hands, the shock of the report as it fired. She remembered the first man she had killed in cold blood. It had been to save a life, Miriya's life... But in that act she had lost a piece of herself, and it seemed as if she would never find it again.

'I came on the mission to find... *peace*.' She looked away

from the other woman. 'Sanctuary 101 is so far from the Wars of Faith, I thought that... I *hoped* that there would be a kind of stillness here. No distractions. No reminders. Just a chance to engage in the pure work of reconsecration. And perhaps renew my union to my God-Emperor into the bargain.'

'That peace... It is not here.' Miriya offered.

Verity shook her head, sorrow settling on her. 'I have not yet found it.'

Miriya's hand reached out and touched her friend's; and for a moment, Verity saw a terrible vulnerability beneath the hard, armoured soul of her Sister. 'We'll keep searching, you and I,' she said. 'He will show us the way.' Miriya nodded to the bulkhead, where a small brass icon of the Golden Throne lay bolted to the Venator's roll cage.

Verity wanted to say more, but then the vehicle shifted on its chassis as Imogen climbed inside the crew bay. 'Correct the maps by four and one-third increments,' she ordered, and Verity nodded, immediately obeying the command. For the moment, her conversation with Miriya was at an end.

The display on the pict-screen shifted by degrees, turning to compensate for the magnetic effects as the other Battle Sisters boarded. Verity heard Cassandra grunt as she dropped into the driver's seat and gunned the sluggish engine. The Venator jerked forwards in fits and starts before the tyre treads finally bit and the vehicle lurched into motion.

'And where now?' Imogen demanded, twisting off her helmet as the hatch locked shut.

Verity peered at the map and indicated the mouth of a narrow defile half a kilometre from their position. 'This way, I think.'

'You think?' echoed Sister Kora, doffing her own helm to reveal an olive-skinned face shining with sweat. 'How long do we have to keep turning circles out here?'

'Until we find what Tegas was looking for,' Imogen told her, ending any further debate on the matter. She called out to the forward cabin. 'Cassandra! Follow the ridge towards the arroyo.'

'That will take us downwards,' came the reply through the grille between the compartments. 'The trail drops away, into a network of narrow canyons.'

'At least we'll be out of the wind, then,' said the Sister Superior, nodding to herself. 'Proceed.'

'They are humans,' insisted the revenant. 'I won't listen to your lies about them any longer. I saw it with my own eyes.'

++*What you see is only the product of a broken mind, weak and pathetic*++

The voice of the Watcher was like an earthquake inside, a thundering echo through bones and meat. The hooded figure dug clawed, bony fingers into the shredded rags at the edges of the dirty robe and pulled at them in anger.

Far below, glimpsed only as a ghost-image, the vehicle picked its way across the desert, the women on board ignorant of the fact they were being observed all the while from atop one of the rock spires.

'You said they were phantoms. Aspects of myself walking and talking in mimicry of the real, falling from the sky...' The words dissolved into a wild chuckle. 'Not true. Not true not true not true not true...'

++*And if they are real, what of it?*++

'It means I am not insane.'

++*It means nothing. They will die like all the rest, screaming and boiling away into vapour*++

The head inside the hood shook back and forth. 'No. No. I won't be alone again. I will not allow it.'

Something like laughter bubbled up from the darkness within. ++*You have no say in the matter*++

The revenant stumbled and stood up. There, fresh in memory, was the recall of the moment in the chapel. The first time daring to return to the ruins. The candle. The precious votive. The prayer spoken, known so bone-deep it could not be remembered now, only spoken through pure flesh-recall. 'Liar.'

++*What do you think will happen to them?*++ The Watcher's

whispers were made of pure poison. ++*It all depends on how foolish they are. If they leave soon, they might live. But it they keep prying, keep digging*++

'Keep strutting and playing as if this world belongs to them...' The words formed in a husky, breathy staccato, spoken before the ghost-voice could form them.

++*If they make a nuisance of themselves, they will wake the storm*++

New tears began to fall, splashing on the red stone, drawing out the colour of the rocks like blood. 'That must not be.'

++*They will perish in agony just like those who came before them*++

Down in the canyons, the heat-form of the rover began to cool and fade as it passed into the lee of the sheer rock face.

++*You cannot prevent that*++ said the constant voice. ++*You can only bear witness*++

'Not again,' she said, and jumped from the high ledge, scrambling down the fast, familiar path.

Disquiet settled in Sister Miriya's gut as the Venator descended from the desert landscape and into the shadowed netherworld of the canyons. The rust-coloured rock and the endless dust gave way to rectilinear shapes that rose up either side of the narrowing gorge, planes of alien stone that unsettled her with their unnatural, almost machined geometry. 'What is this place?' she whispered.

'Give your arming prayers, Sisters,' Imogen ordered, looking around the crew compartment. 'Be prepared for anything.'

'What do you think those forms are?' asked Xanthe, staring through a viewport. Without her helmet to hide them, the sallow-faced woman's elfin eyes were wide with trepidation. 'I've not seen such structures before.'

'I have,' muttered Danae. The taciturn warrior offered nothing else to the conversation, instead running her fingers over the frame of her meltagun, whispering to it.

A dull chime sounded from the panel before Verity, loud as the peal of a cathedral bell in the sullen quiet of the vehicle.

The hospitaller peered at the pict-screen and frowned. 'A detection,' she began. 'A lasing beam, it appears. There was a brief moment of contact from a kilometre distant. Gone now.'

'A targeting sweep?' said Kora, clutching her bolter.

'No,' Verity went on. 'The beam was too weak.'

Miriya remembered what she had seen in the courtyard of the convent, the blink of laser diodes between Tegas and his adepts. 'A communications signal,' she said. 'Something just sent an interrogative to us.'

'And if we do not reply in kind?' Imogen frowned. The Sister Superior leaned forwards. 'Cassandra, what do you see out there?'

'The canyon narrows,' began the Battle Sister. 'I...' She trailed off. 'I see structures! A fence... A gate!'

'Slow your approach!' Imogen stood up and shouldered open a hatch in the roof, daring to peek out. The Venator's engine grumbled and the vehicle decelerated. Miriya did not wait for an order; she came up beside the other woman, her gun at the ready.

There, ahead where the arroyo came to a dead end, grids of machine-stamped metal had been used to wall off the passage, and behind them a cluster of workshacks and habitat modules were visible, arranged in a precise radial formation.

'Another outpost...' said Imogen, disbelief in her words.

'Movement,' warned Miriya. At their approach, the gates were rolling back, clanking as they retreated away.

Cassandra called up from the driver's compartment. 'Eloheim? Your orders?'

'Take us inside.'

Miriya shot her a look. 'Are you sure?'

'Do not second-guess me, Sister,' replied Imogen, dropping back into the cabin.

Once inside the perimeter fence, the Venator rumbled to a halt before the hab modules, the engine still growling as it ticked over. Miriya chanced a cautious look through one of the gun slits and quickly took the measure of what she saw.

Judging by the amount of dust and silt that had collected around the stilt-leg pylons supporting the habitat capsules, this encampment had been in place for some time. Not in the measure of years like the convent, she estimated, but months at the very least. In some places the glassaic windows were still unblemished by the abrasive scouring of the winds, and the anechoic coating on the module exteriors was largely intact. She spied autonomic weapon turrets raised up on spindly towers, each aiming outwards down the canyon, and with a cold twinge of certainty she realised that the launchers up there could easily have obliterated them before the Venator had come within sight of the outpost.

'Contact, to the right!' hissed Sister Kora, at the aiming slits.

'More here, to the left,' added Verity.

Miriya looked and saw a group of figures in red robes, flanked by plodding gun-servitors and skitarii. 'The Mechanicus.'

Imogen's face twisted in an ugly scowl. 'Falsehoods and damned subterfuge... That whoreson Tegas lied to our faces!'

'I do not understand,' said Xanthe. 'What is this place? What are they doing here?'

'Fine questions, all of which I will have answers to,' snarled Imogen. 'Sister Miriya, with me. The rest of you, weapons to the ready.'

Leaving her helm locked to the mag-plates on her hip, the Sister Superior threw open the gull-wing hatch and jumped down to the sand. Miriya came after her, her thumb snapping off the safety catch on her bolter. The wind pulled at her dark hair, whipping it back off her face. Miriya's earlier misgivings were now a thunder in her chest.

'In the God-Emperor's name, who is in charge here?' Imogen shouted, daring the Mechanicus adepts and their minions to remain silent. 'What is the meaning of this? Answer me now!'

One of them shifted and took a step forwards. Miriya saw the rank medallion of a sanctified tech-priest about his neck. The adept's face – such as it was – did not seem familiar to her. In fact, she quickly became certain that none of the assembled group had been on board the *Tybalt* with them on the journey from Paramar. And there were far more of them than Tegas had brought with him.

They were already here. Miriya felt a sickening feeling in the pit of her stomach.

'I am Ferren.' The tech-priest made a conciliatory gesture. 'Honoured Sisters, welcome. Your arrival is unexpected. That is inopportune.'

'Sister Superior.' Cassandra's voice buzzed in their ears, thick with static, her words carried to them by vox-bead. 'Long-range communications are inoperative. We cannot reach the convent by machine-call from this location.'

'Look sharp,' said Imogen, biting out the words.

Miriya said nothing. Was that some deliberate ploy on the part of these interlopers, or just an effect of the planet's turbulent magnetosphere? Whatever the cause, the squad were on their own in this. No warning of their discovery could be sent.

Slowly, the weapon-arms of the gun-slaves and the laser carbines of the skitarii rose to a guard position. Miriya studied the adepts and wondered if they were using their unvoiced speech to coordinate their actions. She moved to draw up her gun in return, but the instant she moved, a trio of actinic blue sighting beams threaded through the air to dance across her breastplate. She lowered the bolter again and they winked out.

'I must ask you to lay down your armaments and step away from the vehicle,' continued the tech-priest. 'Have the five others inside the scout car disembark one at a time.' His shifting crimson eyes scanned the Venator, doubtless picking out those within via thermographic vision cues, like the preysight of the Sabbat helmets. 'You are trespassing. This matter must be addressed.' He sighed, a grating wheeze that echoed the grind of old gears. 'I would prefer not to resort to violence.'

'You have the arrogance to accuse *us* of trespass?' spat Imogen. 'Tegas came here to find you, didn't he? Because of all this!' She gestured around angrily at the hab modules and the obvious signs of work on the stone walls, the cuttings and the laser-burned cavern entrance. 'Mark me, you will answer for your deceit!'

Miriya caught her gaze for an instant and saw something there; a look, an intention she couldn't properly interpret. She decided to construe it as she saw fit.

The tech-priest tilted his head in a quizzical gesture. 'I see that it is unlikely I will find a dispassionate response here.' The circle of weapons moved to take aim, directed by silent command.

'He's going to fire...' Cassandra's garbled whisper sounded distant.

'Your curiosity has brought you to this, Sister. I am disappointed that there is no other way to resolve our situation. If only you had turned back, returned to the convent, ignorant of what you have seen. Now I am required to take steps that–'

The Battle Sister did not let the tech-priest continue any further. Miriya squeezed the trigger of her bolter and fired it into the ground on full automatic discharge, allowing the slamming recoil to drag the muzzle upwards. The mass-reactive bolt shells ripped into the sandstone before her, kicking up a sudden torrent of dust and rock fragments.

With the first shot, Imogen was moving, firing her own weapon from the hip, shooting at the gun-servitors, aiming to kill the bearers of the heavier weapons. 'Cassandra, *drive*!' she bellowed, and Miriya heard the throaty roar of the Venator's motor as it lurched forwards, skidding.

Danae emerged from the scout's upper hatch with her melta weapon, and fired shrieking lances of heat in a fan of flame that scattered the skitarii. The vehicle ground through the sand and surged away, wheels spinning.

Fire flashed and Miriya broke into a duck-and-run, feeling the dry air crackle around her as crimson beams stabbed towards her. Laser strikes fused sand into clumps of dirty silica at her heels as she ran towards the rear of the Venator. She bit back a scream of pain as one shot found its mark and melted into the ceramite and flexsteel of her shoulder pauldron. Smoky flame puffed and guttered out on the trim of her cloak, but she did not slow.

The Venator was racing in turning circles across the camp's central area, absorbing glancing shots and dodging others, trying to avoid a direct hit. Miriya saw Cassandra put the scout vehicle into a controlled drift, and the rear quarter swung out, smacking a gun-servitor into a broad support spar. The knobbled wheels spat dirt, and she waded through it, reaching for the grab rails along the flank of the vehicle.

She caught hold with her free hand and felt others pulling her in. Miriya put her foot on the running board and discharged her bolter one-handed, firing blind into the broken lines of the Mechanicus soldiers.

'Run for the gate,' Imogen shouted over the vox. 'Don't wait for me, go!' Miriya saw her moving and firing, trying to avoid salvoes of beam fire from a quad of skitarii.

'Not without her,' she snapped. 'Cassandra, swing us around.'

The other woman didn't reply, but the Venator wallowed into a snarling turn and bounded back across the uneven ground, the tonnage of the rover bouncing to such an extent that the right-side wheels caught air under them before slamming back down on the axles.

Even as they came towards her, Miriya saw the scowl on Imogen's face at the disregarding of her orders. The Sister Superior broke into a sprint, tossing a krak grenade over her shoulder as she ran. The explosive bounced off the top of a workshack and detonated with a flat concussion that echoed down the box canyon.

As the Venator passed her, Imogen threw herself at the open hatch and landed on the deck, las-bolts cutting crimson pits in the hull of the vehicle. 'The gate!' she roared. 'Hurry!'

'Too late,' Xanthe replied. 'Look!'

Up ahead, the tech-priest's minions were closing the metal barrier, the gap narrowing by the second. Even with its mass, the scout car would be wrecked if it attempted to ram the gates. And now, without Miriya or Imogen loose on the ground to draw their attention away, all the gun-servitors and skitarii were training their aim on the Venator.

Miriya ducked in beneath the gull-wing hatch and tried to pull it closed behind her, but the mechanism had taken a hit and it was stuck solid.

'You've trapped us,' Imogen glared at her. 'We needed to get out of here, raise the alarm!'

'We are not dead yet,' Miriya retorted.

'The cavern!' Cassandra gave a shout from the forward compartment. 'There may be a way through, or–'

'Do it,' Imogen ordered, holding Miriya's gaze a moment longer. She turned away. 'The rest of you, firing positions. Beat them back!'

Ferren sent furious streams of machine-code across the local network between himself and his adepts, trying to correlate and forecast the motions of the Sororitas, but like so many things commanded by the drives of organics, they were difficult to predict.

At first, the unforeseen arrival of the females had sent him lurching towards a panic spiral. It was not enough that the questor had come here and overturned the careful order of things the tech-priest had set up within the compound. Now, through some process that Ferren could not know but did not doubt was Tegas's fault, the Sisters of Battle had come searching the deserts and traced his superior's route back to this place.

Ferren calculated his options within a microsecond, evaluating and considering all possibilities he could see, and discarding those that did not suit him. He had considered obliterating the rover on the approach, killing it and everything within using a barrage of missiles from the launchers in the towers. He rejected it, instead intending to engage in a more subtle approach.

If the vehicle could be taken intact... If the Sororitas squad could be terminated quickly and carefully... Ferren had assembled a plan to murder them and deposit their corpses out in the deep desert, where the local predators could pick the meat from them and the sands could rid him of everything else. And if they were located after the fact, they would be considered victims of misfortune, fools who had become lost in the dust clouds. The dig site would remain unknown, and his precious work would be protected. It was a good plan, a complex one, but a valid one.

Now ashes, though. Ruined by the unpredictable actions of meat-brains who could not even show the logic to understand when they were beaten.

A memory engram resurfaced in Ferren's mind, brought up to the fore by the incident. It was of Tegas, in a time before the tech-priest had gained his current rank and stepped out from under the shadow of his teacher. The questor had mocked him for making every schema he created too elaborate, too clever by half. *'Simplicity is the true measure of an intelligent mind,'* he had said. Now Ferren wondered if he should have listened. The missiles would have worked just as well.

'End them,' he cried, his annoyance expressing itself in human lingua.

The Venator was damaged and trailing smoke, but like a wild beast it trampled on, unwilling to die, maddened by pain. He tried to touch its machine-spirit and recoiled in horror.

Then the rover turned in his direction and put on a burst of new speed.

Cassandra thrust the accelerator bar all the way forwards to full military power and the Venator bucked, indicator needles twitching into the red. The holy rosary hanging from the canopy snapped and clattered against the windscreen as the vehicle bore down on the treacherous adepts.

At the last second, the tech-priest seemed to blur, his mechanoid legs coiling to project him out of the rover's path. Instead, the bull-bars across the prow of the vehicle met the torso of a slow-moving gun-servitor and the helot crumpled across the hood of the engine compartment. Doggedly, it still tried to follow its task programming, arms ending in stubber muzzles scrapping across the bonnet, hammering at the windscreen; but without claws or manipulators, it could not find purchase. Metal squealing on metal, the blank-eyed servitor slipped off and under the wheels of the Venator. The vehicle's tonnage crushed it into the dirt, bursting wire-implanted meat in a spatter of blood and processing fluids.

Fighting through a skid, Cassandra pointed the front of the rover at the tunnel mouth cut into the sheer stone wall. The buzzing impact of laser hits became a steady cascade across the aft of the vehicle. A dull bang sounded and alert icons showed critical damage to the rearmost axle. The Venator began to drift, and Cassandra tried to resist it.

In the crew compartment, the lurching passage of the rover threw the Sisters around like stones in a can, and it was difficult for any of them to maintain good firing discipline.

'Reloading!' grated Danae, dropping back from the open roof hatch to eject a spent fuel cartridge from her meltagun. Hot gases escaped from the breech, stinging Verity's eyes. The hospitaller held on for dear life, pressing herself into the corner of the cabin.

Xanthe bolted forwards, rising up to take the other woman's place and Miriya was moving with her. The sounds of the battle were near-deafening, the roaring of the engine mingling with the howl of bolters and the air-splitting skirl of laser beams.

'Almost there,' Cassandra was shouting, 'Hold on...'

Verity's attention was pulled away by the Battle Sister's words. She turned back just in time to see Xanthe die.

The younger Sororitas, her shoulders and head poking out of the roof hatch, gave a sudden, savage jerk before her knees gave way and she fell into the compartment. Xanthe came back trailing a mist of hot, pink vapour and the stink of burnt iron. Her face was a ruin of blackened meat, cored straight through by a las-bolt.

Then darkness rolled over the vehicle as they crashed through barrier panels and into the cavern mouth.

The rear axle finally snapped, sending fragments of itself into the fuel lines and pneumo-veins webbing the underside of the Venator. The wheels locked and the scout car juddered sideways to a halt.

Crimson warning symbols filled the dashboard display. Cassandra kicked open the driver's hatch and pulled herself free of the restraint web, pausing only to wrench her bolter from the magnetic mount at her side.

She turned to see fingers of orange flame reaching up around the rear of the rover. Imogen and the other Sisters fled the stricken vehicle. The last was Danae, who shoved the hospitaller out before her, her teeth gritted.

Cassandra counted them one short. 'Xanthe...'

'Dead,' replied Miriya. 'We need to move.'

'Aye...' Cassandra bit down on her sorrow. She was fond of Xanthe; her voice during the hymnals was something incredible to hear.

Imogen had the dead woman's weapon in her hand and she forced it on Verity. 'Take this. Make yourself useful.' Without waiting to hear her response, she glared at Cassandra. 'The vehicle–'

'Too much damage. We'll have to go deeper on foot.'

Untended, the fire reached into the crew compartment and took hold. Black smoke belched from the open hatches, building in the confines of the cavern mouth. More laser bolts whickered past as the Mechanicus skitarii came running.

'So be it, then.' Imogen nodded. 'With haste, go!'

'Go where?' Verity asked, kneading the grip of Xanthe's bloodstained boltgun. 'We have no map, no means of knowing where this tunnel leads.' Her voice gave a hollow echo off the dark stony walls.

'We stay, we die,' said the Sister Superior, ill-tempered at the interruption. 'Out there we are only targets. In here… We can better choose the circumstance of our fight. *Move!*'

Danae had already advanced, leading with her meltagun. 'This way,' she called, her words resonating. The Battle Sister pointed the way into a black, fathomless passage that curved off, lit by bio-lume pods every hundred metres or so.

Retreating, the squad drew away and down into the throat of the cave, the directionless, hazy glow of the daylight quickly fading to be replaced by the dimness of the rock tunnels. Cassandra heard their armoured boots crunching on crystalline sand as they ventured on, and smelled the tart odour of ozone. The temperature dropped sharply, the stone walls radiating a hard chill.

She looked up and crossed glances with Sister Miriya. 'This place feels like a tomb,' she muttered.

'If we tarry, it will be ours,' replied the other Sororitas.

'Are they still outside?' Tegas asked the question even though he knew the answer.

'Yes, questor,' said Lumik. Since the static-flare, she had picked up an odd clicking reverberation in her vocoder unit.

He ignored her and sent a command to the remote optics on the exterior of the laboratorium module. A slaved visual feed entered his cortex, and he saw the two Sisters of Battle at guard ready outside the main hatch, where he had left them hours earlier. They remained impassive, their faces set in identical masks of dour focus. Tegas ran a cycle of amusement at the expense of their pomposity, and shared it with his entourage as they worked on the metal scroll from the dig. It lay there on a glowing sensor bed, surrounded by scanner arms and manipulator tentacles.

He orbited the workspace, considering. The Sororitas were fools. Outside, they believed they were in charge of this situation because of their guns and their stoic manner, as if somehow their blind faith made them superior to the Mechanicus. He did not doubt that if they had the means, the Battle Sisters assigned to be these so-called escorts to his staff would stand guard until the Kavir sun fell from the sky. They were single-minded that way, but what some called tenacity Tegas saw as evidence of limited intellects.

The Sisters of Battle ascribed all things to the will of the God-Emperor. They did not question the structure of the universe or the order of things, as those highest among the Adeptus Mechanicus were born to do. Where the sons and daughters of the great thinkers of Mars sought union with the Omnissiah and pushed back the boundaries of knowledge, the Sisters... The Sisters were the very exemplar of the *status quo*. They were blunt instruments, the bludgeons of the Imperial Church. They were artless beings, lacking in vision.

To say such things aloud would be to court suggestions of sedition, perhaps even heresy; and among some of his staff, Tegas knew there were those who would shy away from such daring thinking. But not one of these things was actually *spoken*, using crude flesh and air pushed through tubes of cartilage. Instead, they existed as vague thought-patterns rendered in binaric lingua, currents of concept floating through the shared data pool.

Let the Sisters think they had the measure of this place. Let them strut about and rebuild their precious convent. None would dare venture into the laboratorium, for the law of the Ministorum classed the module as de facto territory of Mars, a tiny embassy of the Mechanicus light years from the solar system. Tegas would be within his rights to class any invasion of that space as an act of war.

The edict granted him the isolation he needed to complete his own examination of Ferren's relic. He drifted closer to the scroll, peering at it. Tegas had already absorbed every teraquad of data his errant protégé had gathered about the device, but he had ordered his own retinue to perform the same suite of tests again. He needed to be sure of what he was looking at.

If Ferren's data was correct, if his interpretations were sound, it seemed to suggest that the scroll-device was operating in discontinuous phase with the rest of space-time.

It was acting through quantum linkages to gain access to instrumentality at levels undreamed of in Imperial computational devices. Information, stored in the very structure of subatomic particles. An infinity of facts, entire histories encoded within it; and most amazingly, all this on something that might be a trivial gewgaw to the beings who had manufactured it.

Tegas was excited and agitated in equal measure. The thrilling possibility of the device's library was compelling, but he chafed at the thought of how hard it would be to interpret it. It would not be just a life's work, but several lives.

He gave in to the impulse to touch it again, and pushed away the sensors, brushing his augmented fingers over the softly-glowing lines of glyphs. Understanding of it seemed so close, like something just out of reach, tantalising, daring him to make the connection.

He lost himself in it. Time passed – hours or seconds? He disengaged his internal chronometer; and when the correlation at last snapped into focus in his mind, Tegas felt a rush that was orgiastic.

The questor's hands opened and subdivided into spider-leg shapes, moving and tracing over the symbols. The scroll's unusual metal reformed itself, becoming a triangular section, almost the image of some great fan used by barony dowagers at the courts of the High Lords of Terra.

Hololiths blossomed from the steel-grey surface in mad profusion, far more than he had seen beneath Ferren's hesitant touch. Rings of virtual controls and what could only be command interfaces layered themselves atop one another, daring him to reach out and touch them. An invisible churn of electromagnetic radiation was building all about them, doubtless some side-effect of the device's activation. Tegas ignored a twinge of vertigo and felt a wave of panic-analogue push through the data pool. Lumik and the other adepts were shocked and afraid by the reaction. They were counselling calm and care, suggesting that he back off, and progress no further. Data had to be gathered. Considered. Evaluated.

All those things were true.

'But no discovery is ever made without boldness,' Tegas said aloud, reaching into the emerald glow.

CHAPTER EIGHT

Miriya heard the change in the structure of the caverns before she saw it, the hollow beat in the way the echo of their footfalls abruptly shifted. She glanced over her shoulder to where Sister Kora was taking the last place in the overwatch line, and then back.

Ahead of her, Verity gasped and Cassandra muttered a quiet oath. The tunnel disgorged them into a cavern bigger than a Titan hangar, the vast space lit by shafts of sunlight that fell at steep angles through jagged rents in the rock. Bridges made of the strange greenish-black stone they had seen elsewhere joined the far sides of the open void, and there were tiers of a sort, plates of harder sandstone that protruded from the walls like fungal discs. Patches of the dark stone were more frequent in here, and when Miriya chanced to run her hand over them all the warmth from her fingers was stolen away, even through the ceramite of her gauntlets. In places it seemed as if the alien material had grown out of the Kaviran sandstone, as if one had been remade from the atoms of the other. She found the strange fusion unsettling.

Avoiding the puddles of daylight, Imogen led the squad on a looping course around the perimeter of the chamber. Miriya looked back once more, and saw the faint glow of spot lamps bobbing along the walls of the tunnel behind them. She could hear the rat-scramble skittering of the Mechanicus's soldiery following them, inexorably tracking the fleeing women with thermal scopes, pheremonic scans and other sensing technologies that the Battle Sisters could only guess at.

Miriya's gaze ranged around the chamber. It would be a good place to make a stand, to ambush the skitarii and discourage their pursuit. But there was little cover, and the sightlines between the mounds of dusty rubble were cluttered.

Sister Danae halted and peered at something. Imogen saw and turned. 'What is it?'

'I am uncertain,' said the other Sister, pointing.

Like the black stone, out of place among the irregular shapes of the natural rock formations, there stood a thick pane of vitreous glass. Miriya estimated it was some eight metres tall, half as wide, and as thick as her fist. It was without doubt an artificially manufactured thing, the top and the sides of it cut sharply and perfectly level. It was like some strange free-standing window, anchored in the dirt.

'Another one,' called Verity, gesturing with Xanthe's boltgun. 'In the shadows.'

'More over there,' called Cassandra, casting around with her pin-light. 'Throne... There's dozens of them.'

The glass panels were arranged in a loose circle, broad faces aimed outwards towards the walls. Miriya had a sudden flash of memory, recalling the hololithic paintings in the Museum of the Holy Synod, which were set out in a similar pattern for the troupes of pilgrims who came to pay homage. But this place was no gallery, and these were no works of art. Something in the brutal, geometric shape of them rang a wrong note with Miriya.

'It is xenos,' said Danae, giving voice to the suspicion they all shared. She looked away and spat. 'We should leave this place. It was a mistake to come here.'

Imogen shot her a hard look. 'The choice was hardly open

to us.' The sounds of the skitarii approach were growing louder with each passing moment. 'Look sharp, find cover. We'll make our stand in here.'

The Sororitas all nodded their agreement, but Verity's attention was elsewhere. Miriya grabbed her arm. 'Sister...'

'Do you feel that?' said the hospitaller, pulling up an auspex unit from where it hung at her belt. 'In the air? Like a... An electric charge...'

Miriya opened her mouth to say no; but then she *did* feel something. A faint tingling on her bare skin, a fresh scent of acrid ozone.

'It's like the air after a storm passes,' muttered Kora.

Danae was raising her meltagun. 'We should not be here!' she grated

A flicker of light caught Miriya's eye and she saw a glimmer in the depths of the nearest glass pane. Faint green sparks, like fireworks bursting in the sky observed from a great distance.

Verity's auspex gave off a sudden clicking sound and the tingling over Miriya's face became a crawling, itching sensation. Loose votive chains clicked and moved of their own accord, pulled gently towards the nearest of the shimmering panels.

Then a sudden throbbing pulse of viridian light bloomed in the cavern, each pane glowing bright like slow sheet lightning.

Ferren moved with his troops, a laser carbine modified for his personal use mounted on the largest of his servo-arms. He kept in the middle of the pack, surrounded by his best skitarii. The tech-priest wasn't about to deny himself the chance to engage some of the Battle Sisters first hand, but he was no fool. He had only middling combat prowess beyond the reams of match-move data he had downloaded from the central processing matrix of his warrior squads, but it was likely that he might be able to step in at the final moment and deliver a coup de grace to one of the intruders before she died. Ferren wanted to see how that event train would feel, to examine if it would stir any extant emotions in him. It would make an interesting experiment, and a fine way to show Tegas that he was not the null unit the questor considered him to be.

He wondered if he should feel remorse for such thoughts; after all, the Sisters were servants of the Imperium just as he was. They were not the arch-enemy.

Ferren dismissed the thought. The logic process here was clear. The women had discovered something they should have not. They could not be allowed to relay that information to their kindred. Murder was the most effective means of silencing them. A simple and effective process.

They were close now. The scouts leading the search party down the tunnels were beaming back their targeting data to the rest of the group. Sound sensors cut a picture out of the gloom, listening for the motion of boots on stone, the whine of power armour, even the thudding of human hearts. The Sororitas had entered the main chamber, the area that one of Ferren's adepts had named 'the hall of windows' in a moment of uncharacteristic whimsy.

The panes of glassy material, as much as they resembled fused silica, were actually some kind of extruded metallic crystal with a tensile strength greater than steel. In months of examination, none of Ferren's explorator team had been able to uproot them or gain insight into their functionality. And while they were proof against all but the most powerful ballistic rounds, the Mechanicus expedition had learned early on that they were transparent to las-bolts. If the Sisters were going to use them as cover, they would have an unpleasant surprise to face–

Ferren's train of thought was halted by a sudden surge of new inputs from the sensing palps at the tips of his mechadendrite cluster. A spike in exotic radiation came from nothing, spent neutrinos and quark-flux particles creating an invisible mist that could only be perceived by one with the eyes of a machine.

The tech-priest beamed an interrogative to the communal data pool and found he was not the only one detecting the same variance. Even as he communicated with his minions in microsecond-swift binaric pulses, comparing readings and building a theory, he began to register another effect. The local background level of electromagnetic radiation was rising exponentially, decay rates and backscatter patterns indicating the epicentre of the anomaly was out there, in the chamber.

Specifically, it appeared to be emitting from the windows themselves.

The electromagnetic force did not diminish; it became uncomfortable for the skitarii and the other adepts, causing misfires in their neural implants and stutters across the interface of their brain-augmentation connections. Ferren took an involuntary step backwards, his accelerated thoughts cycling, becoming glitchy as the energy discharge grew stronger. He tried to engage his tempest shields, but the force was strong, overwhelming them. His deep logic cores began to auto-deactivate in order to protect vital data such as his persona matrix and his primary memories.

It was hard to concentrate. The pulse was like blades being drawn across the cords of the tech-priest's cerebral implants. But one element did seem clear. The pattern of the energy resembled something similar, a configuration that Ferren had detected emitting from the iron scroll during his examinations, but on a far more diminished level.

He had just enough time to wonder about the connection between these two things before the discharge topped out and sent every one of the Mechanicus reeling. The cyborgs gave off static-laced screams that resonated down the stone tunnels as they went blind, toppled over, and fell into stuttering restart cycles.

Green fire filled every one of the glass panes to their brim, sparks of photonic discharge glittering for brief moments around their blade-sharp edges. The depths of colour and hard light twitched, and in defiance of what seemed real, they extended into themselves. Like a mirror looking into a mirror, corridors made of infinity spiralled away. Energy flowing in watery puddles sent out ripples; and then, as if they were doors cut into the air itself, from within the spaces metal claws reached for the edges and drew outwards.

Some of the panes were broken, by rock falls or the destructive actions of Ferren's explorators, others were blocked by drifts of sand that trickled away, sucked into some nowhere space. Those that were open and clear became doorways spilling sickly light.

Shapes moved in that light, lensing it around them. Skeletal shapes, things stamped out of ancient machine-shops on worlds long since consumed by dead suns. They walked with solemn purpose, stirring from aeons of sleep. Pitiless and with perfect focus, summoned by the unwary, the spindly forms of necron warrior-mechs stepped back onto the sands of Sanctuary 101.

Verity's heart hammered in her chest as the glassy portals poured out more and more of the machine-xenos, ranks of the bony steel figures striding silently from out of nothingness. One after another, they formed into precise cohorts, groups of five taking up wedge-shaped patterns as if they were soldiers engaged in a parade ground drill.

She had never seen a necron with her own eyes before. What the hospitaller knew of them came from vague rumours and half-heard stories that were more supposition than truth. To look upon them now drew up powerful emotions in her: fear and terror, indeed, but also a kind of revulsion that sickened Verity to her stomach. The machine-things seemed to radiate an ephemeral sense of something ancient and callous. They were utterly inhuman in a way she could not find the words to describe.

Each of the necron warriors mimicked the structure of a humanoid skeleton, spun from dull chromium, spindly limbs ending in clawed hands that clasped weapons made of pipes and glowing emerald rods. Elongated death's-head skulls were animated by cold fire, casting this way and that as they entered the cavern. Most chilling of all was the way they moved without noise.

Verity's hands were frozen around poor Xanthe's bolter, her breath caught in her throat as if to utter a single sound would be to shatter this horrible moment.

Miriya, Danae and the others were ready, poised to fire. 'Eloheim?' Verity heard Kora hiss at the Sister Superior, the question in the word. But Imogen said nothing, her face pale with the same shock, petrified in the moment and unable to speak.

In the next second the necrons were advancing. They marched forwards, out of the circle of glowing panels and on towards the assembly of Mechanicus skitarii dithering at the entrance to the great cavern. The red-robes seemed to be in some disarray, but there were dozens of them, with many weapons in their grasp. *The greater threat?* Verity wondered. *Is that what these things see in them?*

The question became moot as some of the tech-guard gathered enough of their wits to fire on the warriors. Crimson light flashed, las-bolts threading from the barrels of beam carbines and into the arrowhead formations of the necrons.

A few of the machines stumbled and faltered, ignored by their companions. The others raised their weapons in perfect concert and returned fire.

Emerald flame, eldritch and crackling, engulfed the closest group of skitarii and began the work of disintegrating them. Verity's mouth dropped open in shock. Where the tech-guard troopers had organic flesh, their skin and nerves, their meat and bone were flensed apart and flashed instantly to puffs of ash. The pure cyborg parts of them, the implants and the biomodules, became blackened pieces of slag, spilling onto the dusty floor as they collapsed and perished.

The necrons advanced to the sound of their killing, feeding into the mouth of the tunnel.

For one long, giddy second, Verity held on to the hope that

somehow the xenos machines had missed the presence of the Sisters, that perhaps they would ignore the women seeking cover behind the rocks; but then the last two squads of the warrior mechanoids came to a smart, point-perfect halt. They turned on their heels and reversed their march.

Verity saw the chilling glow in their eye slits as the metal faces turned to glare down on the Sisters.

The moment broke Imogen's hesitation, and she screamed. *'Fire!'*

Ferren cannoned his way down the twisting tunnel, the ululating sound of the alien gauss flayer beams rebounding all around him. Green lightning flashed off the dark stone walls, reflections of kill-fire preceding the execution of his precious skitarii.

His mind was in a chaotic state, on the verge of a cascade breakdown. Memory stacks full of data carefully stored and collated over the last few months had been broken open by the electromagnetic burst and the shock of this sudden invasion. The tech-priest tried desperately to understand what was going on, to reason out the course of events as they transpired.

The explorator team had been inside the caverns for so long, they had done so much, and yet Ferren and his cohorts had been unable to find anything more complex than a dormant tomb spyder in a stasis cowl. All the time they had been here, and he had come to be convinced that whatever Sanctuary 101 had represented to the necrontyr before, its value had become nothing. For whatever reason, the execution of the original Sororitas colony had marked the end of necron interest in this world – and who was there who could disagree with that hypothesis? The ways of aliens were, well, they were *alien*! Unfathomable by even the sharpest of human minds!

The necrons had swept over this planet more than ten years earlier, made their kills, and then moved on. *This was fact.* Ferren was certain of it. *This was fact.* There was nothing here but the relics, a rich seam of remains to be mined and information to be gleaned.

The necrons had moved on. In the months he had been in command of this secret expedition that certainty had become almost like a mantra for Ferren. But now he realised that the truth was not as he had wanted it to be. What the tech-priest could not face, the grotesque emotional reality he kept denying, was that he was *afraid*.

Afraid that the Mechanicus had sent him to this place to die. Afraid he would never be able to advance beyond his present rank. And more than anything, afraid that the pitiless machines were still hiding beneath the sands, waiting for the moment to come and kill again.

His fear was real now, and Ferren cursed it as he listened to the dying screams and frenzied cries for aid from his tech-guard.

He emerged into the main passage, the open area in the throat of the caves where the smouldering wreck of the Venator still sat, wreathed in grey smoke. Gun-servitors, cut off from command-and-control inputs by the electromagnetic surge, had reverted back to base programming and were taking up defensive positions, drawn to the sound of the alien attackers. Ferren pushed past them and staggered towards the mouth of the cave, fighting down the sickeningly human sensation of panic that threatened to overwhelm him. He concentrated on the terms of the sacred equations, part of his braincore chanting them in order as a calmative, while another level of his intelligence was weighing his combat options.

His last command had been to fall back, and the skitarii were attempting to follow it. The necron foot soldiers were unwilling to let them go, however, matching the pace of their escape and cutting down anyone foolish enough to show their back to the maws of their gauss guns. A dozen more life-sign indicators winked out in the shared data pool, their connections severed by the sudden termination of all cerebral function.

Ferren calculated how many troops he had already lost and the figure was deeply troubling. In a matter of a few minutes, the necrons had emerged – *from where?* he wondered – and cut a swath through the tech-priest's elite. The punishing, inexorable numbers made the situation clear to him.

Raw information streamed through the communal pool in painful jags. The explorator team were totally outmatched. Conservative estimates reckoned that the xenos machines would complete full extermination of everyone in the encampment within less than ten solar minutes, should they exit the cavern.

Should they exit the cavern. The qualifier sounded in his thoughts, and Ferren cast around, even as the skeletal constructs emerged behind him, wading into the teeth of the gun-servitor lines. Heavy cannons crackled and chugged, and necrons fell; but there were more in the ranks behind, each stepping up to seamlessly fill every vacated space.

Ferren dove through the layers of information in the data pool and found something he could use, buried in the memory of a minor adept involved in the geophysical survey works. His piston-legs spitting as he ran, the tech-priest dodged through glancing flickers of green fire and found a workshack module nestled close to the cavern wall. It was a hardened capsule protected by secure hatches, but its primitive machine-spirit recognised Ferren immediately and opened all locks to him.

The odour of harsh chemicals, of hexogene rings and complex nitrotoluene clusters, assailed his sensing pallet. Inside, there were racks of metal cylinders, each marked with warning trefoils and warding runes; geo-mag charges of various explosive potentials, used to crack the recalcitrant rock during excavations and deep digs.

Had there been time for finesse, Ferren would have downloaded a stream of datum to a functionary like the surveyor adept and had them carry out his wishes, but the moment was now, and the tech-priest understood that he would need to do this himself. Before it was too late.

More icons faded from the communal network as he found and encoded a detonator spike. Ferren ignored the screaming and activated the charge. As the timer bar began to shrink, he dropped the unit and fled. In his thoughts, he ran a simulation of the detonation effect. It was a crude and poorly-placed alternative, but it would be enough to bring down the cavern mouth and seal it off from the rest of the encampment. The necrons would be contained, and while that meant a sizeable number of sacrifices among his skitarii – the ones still fighting back there, ignorant of what the tech-priest was doing – it also meant that the expedition proper would survive.

More importantly, it meant that Ferren would survive. He applied maximum motive energy to his augmetic limbs and sprinted across the stone floor towards the yawning entrance.

The glancing energy bolt swept over him and severed the tech-priest's right leg at the hip, throwing Ferren into a headlong tumble that was arrested only by a collision with the stub of a half-buried boulder. He doused all pain receptors the moment he was struck, but it was too late to stop the initial surge of agony. Ferren scrambled, a mess of torn, dirty robes and spindly iron-black limbs, flailing around like a swatted insect unable to right itself.

The shot had been random, a miss that had taken him instead of its intended target, but it mattered little. Ferren's mechadendrites and arms splayed out, stabbing at the dusty ground, trying desperately to pull him away towards the cave entrance.

But it would not be enough. Not nearly enough.

Ferren released a furious roar of scrap-code, putting all his sudden and very human anger into a last eruption of noise.

The explosion drowned him out.

The necron warriors attacked the Battle Sisters with a precision and a focus that was beyond any enemy Miriya had faced on the field of conflict. No motion they made was wasted, every footstep and aimed shot was perfectly calculated and deftly laid.

Gauss fire shattered the rocks they had chosen as their cover, driving them out to duck and run among the glittering panes of glass. Miriya was wary of the strange portal-panels. No more warriors had emerged from the doorways beyond them after the initial invasion group had come through, but there was no way to know if more were on their way.

Danae moved and fired with the meltagun, shooting from her hip, panning it about in a sharp arc that engulfed the glass panes and the machine-forms alike. The panes she hit slagged and misted, the fires within dying, but they did not shatter. Miriya could not help but wonder what kind of exotic matter could resist the sun-hot power of a melta blast.

The necrons returned fire with their own weapons, laying down fields of coruscating green energy that soured the air and sounded shrieks across the echoing chamber. Miriya executed a shot from half-cover and placed a three-round burst of mass-reactive bolts in the chest of an advancing warrior. The steel skeleton was blown back off its clawed feet and it crashed to the ground in a ruined heap. It gave no cry of pain, no utterance or curse against her as she cut it down. The silence, the eerie cohort of stillness that surrounded the necron attack, was as chilling as the blank horror of their skull-faces.

And then, to her shock, the thing Miriya thought she had killed rose again. The grievous wound across its torso was shrinking, the metal plates there flowing like mercury, what could only be splines and wires beneath knitting back together to undo the injury. The necron strode towards her, raising its flayer high to present the curved axe-blade across the bottom of the muzzle, an executioner stepping up towards the killing block.

'Throne and Blood!' spat Kora. 'What must we do to end these things?' She ducked as she ejected a spent clip from her bolter, slamming a fresh magazine into its place.

'If in doubt,' said Miriya, recalling the words of a venerable abbess who had once been her weapons instructor, 'aim for the head.' She thumbed her bolter's fire-select switch to its fully automatic setting and squeezed the trigger. Rounds thundered from the gun and punctured the skull of the advancing mechanoid, this time splintering the steel into shimmering fragments, decapitating it. Even though it was robbed of a mouth with which to scream, the necron finally emitted a death-howl. It was a grating, static-laced skirl of noise, a synthetic parody of a shriek that vibrated out from its entire body. Like the xenos machines themselves, the sound was a mockery of something born of flesh.

And it was just a single kill among a force of attackers that outnumbered the Battle Sisters two to one. The warriors had shifted into a skirmish line and now they advanced inexorably, drawing in to block any path of escape, forcing the humans towards the circle of glassy panels and the sheer rock walls.

Somewhere down in the tunnels, a massive concussion sounded, swiftly followed by the long, drawn-out rumble of collapsing rock. The ground beneath their feet trembled, but the necrons did not stumble.

'What was that?' called Verity. 'An earthquake?'

Clouds of heavy dust billowed from the tunnel mouth, but no one answered the hospitaller's question.

'Concentrate your fire!' called Imogen, stabbing a finger towards the machines. 'Knock them out of the line, one at a time!'

'They shrug off bolt shells like rain,' snarled Cassandra.

Miriya saw Verity trying her best to engage with the attackers, the hospitaller's aim true but her skills lacking. 'Stay close to me,' she called.

'The tech-guard...' began the other woman. 'That noise...'

'They fled and paid for it,' Miriya broke in. 'So we fight or die alone in this.'

As she said the words, something moved in the gloom above their head, and a shape unfurled like a raptor's wings. A figure was falling into the alien light cast by the undamaged panes. A hooded shape carrying a black sword that reflected nothing.

* * *

The woman Verity had glimpsed inside the Great Chapel was transformed. The hesitant, stuttering figure who had wept and prayed before the broken altar was a killer now. For the first time since they had arrived, the necrons showed something akin to confusion, disrupted by the sudden appearance of a new enemy that had come as if from nothing.

Two of them pivoted to fire and the black sword spun. Viridian sparks flared as the muzzles of gauss flayers were cut away by the passage of the blade. The dark edge slashed at the machines, opening them to the air. Verity saw bisected parts of a necron warrior fall away, the cut ends polished and mirror-bright. The mechanoids collapsed to their knees, shuddering. She watched them grasping for severed limbs, trying to reconnect them to fresh stumps.

'The intruder...' said Miriya, the same flash of recognition on her face. 'From the convent.' The Battle Sister shot Verity a questioning look and found her confirmation.

'Keep firing!' yelled Imogen, for the moment unwilling to question the actions of this new arrival.

Every gun the Sisters had poured bolt-rounds and sun-fire into the enemy line, and like a cable stressed to breaking point, their unit coherence abruptly snapped. The necrons dispersed, regrouping. Those with heavy damage dropped back, protected by their comrades as they entered regeneration cycles.

The hooded woman dodged the slicing claws of a warrior and made it to the middle of the cover where the Sisters were gathered, protected by the lee of the rock in the glow of the glass panes.

'No time,' she spat, her voice thick with venom. Verity could see some of her damaged face, she could smell the stale human odours of her. 'No time no time no time.'

'In the name of the God-Emperor,' said Imogen, 'who are you?'

'No time!' she screamed back, grabbing the Sister Superior's arm. 'More are coming. Coming back!' She jabbed the sword in the direction of the tunnel. The steady clattering steps of necron footfalls were echoing ever closer. If the earlier noise had been a cave-in, then the machines sent after the skitarii would be doubling back, soon to bolster the numbers they had left to deal with the Sisters.

With strength that belied her form, the ragged-clothed revenant shoved Imogen towards the nearest portal-pane. 'Go now,' she shouted, her words slurred. 'We all go now, or die here!'

'Through that... gateway?' cried Sister Kora. 'To where? This is insanity!'

Verity looked away. In the gloom of the tunnel mouth, countless dots of green light were growing distinct. The damaged necrons in the chamber were reforming into attack groups, and they were waiting. Waiting for their brethren.

'That is where *they* came from!' Imogen retorted, pointing at the machines. 'You would have us venture deeper into danger?'

'Go now,' said the hooded woman, slow and deliberate, 'or die.' She raised the black sword and held it threateningly at the Sister Superior. The blade did not resemble any kind of metal; it was like a river of ink, a shadow made solid.

'What choice do we have?' Miriya insisted. 'Anywhere is safer ground than here! You said it yourself, Eloheim. We must choose the circumstances of our fight.'

Imogen's eyes flashed. 'Don't twist my words against me, Sister Militant!' She put hard emphasis on Miriya's rank. 'This circumstance is accorded to you! I should have left you behind at the convent.' The Battle Sister glared at the hooded figure. 'And you. Why should we listen to you?'

'*A spiritu dominatus.*' The scarred woman uttered the words like a curse, guttural and harsh. '*Domine, libra nos.*' The utterance sent a shock through the assembled Sororitas, but then the revenant was moving, shouldering Imogen aside at the last moment. 'Stay and die.'

'It is the only way we can survive,' Miriya pleaded. Behind her, the necrons began to advance across the chamber once more. There were dozens of them now.

Imogen very deliberately spat on the dirt. 'The Saint will curse you for this,' she growled, and turned towards the woman with the blade.

The cloaked figure did not look back, and stepped across the glowing glass threshold.

One by one, they followed her.

The passage was terrifying. The transition could only have lasted for a fraction of a second, but from Sister Miriya's point of view it felt like an eternity. The watery green light engulfed her, seeming to lap over her flesh like a slow tide of oil, and then everything became distorted.

Her perception was twisted and useless. She saw dreamy shapes, colours and synesthesic effects that her mind could not interpret, giddy vivid impressions that could have been motion, heat, terror or some mixture of all. Miriya screwed her eyes shut and repeated The Emperor's Prayer over and over, clinging to the rote words and her unshakable – so she still hoped – faith.

This portal, this alien gateway, was not meant for unprotected humans, and she could sense it trying to reject her. Miriya felt as if the power of the thing was actively repelling her flesh and blood, acting on it like the disparate poles of a magnet. Her skin crawled with sickening sensations that threatened to crack the Battle Sister's iron resolve. This tunnel through nothingness skirted close to the psychic maelstrom of warp space, and she could feel the incredible pressure of the immaterium just beyond the walls of her own mind. *It was so close.*

And then, just when it seemed as if she could stand it no more, she was staggering, her boots ringing on a metal deck. Miriya tried to open her eyes, and found her skin layered with a coating of frost that crackled as she moved. Patches of steaming ice covered her wargear, sloughing off in sheets as she stumbled.

Miriya beat off the shock and took a deep, shuddering breath. The air was tinny and thin, harsh in her throat. Her blurred vision cleared and the first face she saw was a jigsaw of shadows and scarification. The hooded woman turned away and Miriya moved, finding Danae, who was rising from where she had fallen to one knee.

'The Emperor protects,' gasped the other woman, making the sign of the holy aquila. 'He delivered us...'

'To where?' Miriya wondered aloud, echoing Sister Kora's earlier question.

Jade light flowed over everything before them, rendering a landscape made of tarnished steel into something even more alien. They stood upon a square iron platform as big as one of the *Tybalt*'s loading bays, and it was suspended in the air by no visible means. Along one end were a line of glass panes identical to the ones in the cavern, most of them dark and unlit, but a handful – including the portal they had just passed through – throbbing with power. Some distance away there was a crescent-shaped section where the deck rose up as it had been pressed out of giant mould. It sported what had to be controls of some kind.

'This is some sort of staging area,' Danae muttered, her thoughts following Miriya's.

The Battle Sister cast around, for a brief moment feeling a flash of gratitude to her Emperor as she counted Verity and the rest of the squad all safely there with her; but then she realised what she was seeing beyond the edges of the floating platform.

The open space inside the rock chamber had been massive enough, but this void dwarfed that by a magnitude of several thousand times.

An iron sky ranged above her head from horizon to horizon: a great metal dome broken into clean geometric sectors by lines of that familiar dark stone, cut in perfect, mathematically precise segments. Off in the distance, a massive obsidian spike emerged from the inside of the dome. It reached out across the open air towards them like a mountain placed on its side, and rods of brilliant light stabbed out from it at what seemed to be random intervals. Pools of white glow fell on rectilinear shapes, pyramids and ziggurats crested with gold filigree and emerald crystals. Others found silver monoliths discoloured by time that glittered dully.

These beams were what provided most of the illumination inside the vast chamber, although it seemed as if every shadowed structure had a soft glow of its own. Miriya tried to estimate distances and scale, but it was hard to reckon without something familiar to compare it to, and the deep shadows and stark illumination conspired to trick the eye.

'Step back,' said the revenant, appearing at her side. She was crack-throated and hoarse. 'This must be done.'

Before the Sororitas could react, the hooded figure had the black sword drawn. Miriya retreated, realising that she had ventured close to the raised console. At the far end of the platform where the other Sisters were gathered, she heard Kora call out in alarm. Something had followed them back through the gateway.

A necron warrior was emerging from the closest of the glassy portals, backlit by the flow of powers that deformed space-time. Even as it placed its leading foot on the metal deck, it already had its gauss flayer aimed directly at Sister Cassandra.

The black sword fell in silence, describing a shallow curve that sliced cleanly through the metal panel. All power in the device vented with a crackling shout and the alien console went dead; at the same moment, all energy fled from the active portals and they became panes of flat, seamless glass once again.

Pieces of the necron warrior remained fused in place, half out of the gateway as it returned to its solid state. The light in the warrior's dead eyes winked out.

Miriya turned back to the revenant. 'You closed the passage.' The hood bobbed once. 'Then how will we be able to leave this place?'

'I did it once before,' came the distant reply. There was a strange sense of old pain and sorrow beneath the words. 'I will do it again.'

'We're moving!' called Cassandra. Perhaps it was because of the damage to the console, but now the platform was in motion, dropping slowly, descending towards a wide ring of steel that resembled a great cog wheel laid flat.

Miriya chanced a look over the side of the platform and saw a near-identical reflection below of what existed above. She had a sudden flash of understanding; they were inside a colossal iron sphere, as if the alien architects of this monstrosity had built themselves a small world and then turned it inside out. The Battle Sister struggled to hold on to the idea and she felt a giddy echo of the portal transit shiver through her. It was difficult to grasp the concept that something so alien, so contrary to the true order of things, could actually exist.

'Do you see those?' Cassandra asked as she came closer. She pointed with her bolter. 'There.'

At first, Miriya could not grasp what the other woman was showing her, but then one of the light beams caught something nearby, and in the overspill from the blinding glow Cassandra's subject became illuminated.

In the half-dark, what the Sororitas had first thought to be shadows cast by support columns and stanchions was revealed as a great open cradle of metal claws and sinuous cables. There, hanging like a player's puppets at rest, were countless numbers of identical humanoid shapes, silver-sheened, eyeless and dormant. She saw the skeletal forms of warriors like the ones they had fought in the cavern, but there were dozens of other variants that stood taller and more muscular than their spindly cohorts. Her breath tight in her chest, Miriya brought up her bolter and peered down the optical sight to gain a closer look.

She saw hulks that aped human shapes, seamless heads with single cyclopean eyes, and gleaming, beetle-like things. There were strange craft cut from arcs of black steel and carbon, great constructs that resembled open ribcages made of metal, drifting at anchor in the thin air next to huge tetrahedral carvings like giant tombstones.

'Ghost Arks,' hissed the hooded woman, naming the necron monstrosities. 'Monoliths and Night Scythes. Wraiths, immortals, scarabs…' She trailed off. 'Sleeping now. Waiting to come again.'

'How many can there be?' whispered Cassandra, awed and horrified in equal measure. 'This is not just one army. There could be legions of these machines in here.'

'You must see,' said the revenant, in a dead voice.

'We will,' Imogen insisted, striding towards them with fire in her eyes. 'We will see who brought us this madness!'

Before anyone could stop her, the Sister Superior's hand shot out and tore at the hood concealing the other woman's face. She gave it a savage jerk and pulled it back. The scarred woman let out a low moan, as if the action of light upon her pallid flesh caused her physical pain.

Imogen recoiled at what she saw beneath the hood, and Miriya could not stop a gasp from escaping her own lips.

They each saw a human aspect, but one that had been dismantled like a jigsaw puzzle, pieces of it opened and then reattached with thick lines of purple scarring and melt-burns. The face was a page across which cruelty had been written, over and over again. She had no hair, and her skin was translucent, taut across bone; but most shocking was the arc of dull steel – *necrontyr steel* – that crossed her cheek and covered the orbit of her right eye, the metal a setting for a bloodshot orb.

'*You must see,*' she repeated blankly, as the platform thudded to a halt above the great dock.

CHAPTER NINE

++*They are going to kill you*++ said the Watcher.

'No,' she muttered. 'No.'

The red-haired one, the one with the strident voice and hard eyes, glared at her. 'What are you?' Disgust oozed from her words.

++*You have saved them for nothing*++

The Watched shook her head back and forth, pulling at her hood. 'There is something you must see,' she told the Sororitas, ignoring the voice in her head.

But her words fell on deaf ears. The other women were threatened and distrustful, their circumstances pushing them to seek violent options before any that required deeper thought. She could not blame them, suddenly finding themselves here in the belly of the alien enemy. But that could not be allowed to change the course of things. They had to see. *They had to*.

'Sister Imogen,' said the one with the dark hair, the scarred face and the serious gaze. 'Perhaps we should–'

The one called Imogen did not listen. Instead she aimed her bolter squarely at the Watched. 'You serve them. Is that why you enticed us here, so you could give us to your xenos masters? You are one of them!'

++*They are going to kill you*++ repeated the voice.

Fury flashed into life behind her eyes. 'No!' she roared, hard and loud. 'You do not understand! Look! Look!' She brought up the dark edge of the voidblade in her hand, slow and careful. 'See!' she spat.

The periphery of the sword's cutting field, existing a microsecond out of phase with the rest of the weapon, buzzed as she lay it across the palm of her other hand. The entropic aura disintegrated the rags wrapped around her skin and made a perfect line along her dirty flesh. Bright crimson blood welled up and ran in streaks down her fingers.

'I took this weapon from them.' She stepped forwards and ran her hand over the chest-plate of the other woman, smearing her vitae over Imogen's armour. 'I am human.' It had been an eternity since she had dared to voice those words. 'Like you.'

'Not like us,' muttered another of the Sororitas, cradling a heavy meltagun.

She forged on, driven by some emotion welling up from deep inside, something she could not quantify. 'You must trust me. *You must see!*'

++*They will not follow you*++ the voice mocked. ++*You cannot make them understand*++

'See what?' demanded the Battle Sister; but the Watched was already leaping off the lip of the floater platform, down to the cog-shaped docking ring.

The hooded woman dropped and for a moment Verity was afraid she had stepped into the empty air and to her death. Then she heard the clank of boots on the metal decking and saw her running, a loping sprint across the dock, weaving between the metal spars and gleaming stone plinths.

Danae hesitated at the edge. 'Do we follow?' She shot a look at Imogen. 'Sister Superior, your orders?'

'Whatever that one is,' said Kora, 'human or xenos, she is of a broken mind. One look in those eyes makes that clear as daybreak.'

Imogen made a terse gesture, leading with her hand. The Sisters followed the hooded woman off the platform and onto the dock.

Verity gave an involuntary shiver. All around machines moved slowly, great turning armatures and floating modules going this way and that. It gave the impression of a massive engine of some sort, turning at a steady idle. She could not shake the sense that an intelligence was at work in this place, intent on alien schemes that would only bode ill for the Sisterhood.

Imogen drew herself up. The hesitation, the moment of fear she had shown in the sandstone caverns, that was gone now, and she seemed determined to expunge the echo of it with decisive action. 'I will not have our path determined by the whim of an unhinged stranger! We are the daughters of Saint Katherine, honour to her glory–'

'*Honour to her glory*,' repeated the Battle Sisters, in immediate rote chorus.

'And we are not here to die!' Imogen went on. 'This day unfolds to our will.' She glanced at Danae. 'Take two Sisters... Miriya and the nursemaid...'

The woman with the meltagun didn't even attempt to hide her displeasure as she shot a look at Verity. 'Aye, mistress.'

The Sister Superior pointed to the horizontal spike tower. 'Scout that construct. Look for something that resembles a command centre or a control nexus. Report in by vox, standard interval.' She looked back at Cassandra and Kora. 'You are with me.'

'And the... The interloper?' Cassandra asked, nodding in the direction the hooded woman had gone.

'We track her,' Imogen said. 'She wants to show us something. We'll find out what that is.'

The group broke into two elements and Verity fell in step following Miriya as the Battle Sister took point in their formation. In turn, Danae walked a few metres behind her, panning her heavy gun back and forth, searching for a target. Within moments, Imogen and the other Sisters were gone, vanishing behind a forest of towering metal tubes and iron-stone supports.

The hum and crackle of energy fizzed above their heads where power conduits channelled lazy streams of green lightning back and forth. Platforms like the one they had ridden on moved silently, impelled by invisible ribbons of force. Verity took each step carefully, measuring her path and trying to watch every angle of approach at once. She had no illusions that her rudimentary military training would be of any great use if an attack came, but she would not allow herself to be the one to falter in her vigilance. This was alien ground, there was no doubt about that. On Sanctuary 101, even though it was a desolate outpost world, Verity had always felt that the God-Emperor's sight could reach her.

But this place... Whatever or wherever it was... She had never known something so *alien*.

'What is it all for?' She asked the question preying on her mind.

'Perhaps it is their home,' offered Miriya, without looking back. 'Perhaps the conduit we passed through has taken us to their point of origin.'

Such a thought made Verity's blood run cold, and she made the sign of the aquila. 'I pray that is not so.'

'Wherever we are,' Miriya went on, 'this is not a place for the likes of us.' She nodded towards towering ramps and other crescent-consoles like the one they had seen destroyed earlier. The constructs were strangely out-of-scale to human dimensions. They were made for something taller, a breed of life form that would tower over Verity, and one with a radically different set of aesthetic senses. The repetition of dull chrome and black stone went on forever, broken only by glassy crystals sculpted into coffin-like geometries, or golden iconography made of circles and radial lines.

The hospitaller cast her eye over the icons as they passed beneath arches detailed with them. It was a language, she decided. The configuration of it could mean nothing else.

She could not help but wonder what it might have said if she could translate it into Imperial Gothic. Verity touched the auspex unit hanging at her belt. In a moment of clarity she had turned the device's memory spools to an automatic recording state; there was no telling what they might find in here, and if they should make it back to safety, a log of what they encountered might prove invaluable as intelligence.

If they made it back.

The deck beneath them slowly became a ramp that curved up around a thick circular pillar, and with a nod from Danae, they ventured on. The underside of the spike-tower was above them now, throwing out dazzling shocks of white light. This close to it, Verity could see what appeared to be window slits in the flanks of the construction.

'We'll get as near as we can,' said Sister Danae. 'Search for a path inside. In the meantime, be wary.'

But as they rose, they saw nothing, and the tension began to settle on Verity like a cloak of heavy mail. Finally, she voiced her concern. 'Why have the xenos not come after us? They passed through the portals to attack the Mechanicus outpost, but now we are in the heart of their lair, they ignore our presence?'

'A good question,' grumbled Danae, clearly occupied by the same disquiet.

'The ones in the caves,' said Miriya. 'Something must have summoned them.'

Danae gave a sniff. 'How can you know that?'

'There was an energy effect before the portals opened. I think it was that tech-priest's doing. We have no idea how long he and his explorators were down in the arroyo. The God-Emperor alone knows what they were doing there, and what they may have meddled with.'

'Poking swords into a hornet's nest, aye,' said the other Battle Sister. 'You have the truth there. If we return to the convent, there will be a hard reckoning for the works of the questor and his brethren.'

'But the…' Verity swallowed. 'The necrons.' Just saying the

name made her stiffen. 'They must know we are here, now. Why do they not come to kill us?'

Miriya halted and glanced up. Above them, a wide frame of metal girders drifted along an inverted rail spur. A battalion's worth of silent warrior mechanicals dangled from the frames like corpses on meat hooks. 'They are quiescent,' she said, her voice low as if she were afraid she might wake them. 'We speak of them like hornets in a hive. So they are hibernating, as the hornets would be after a hard winter. They do not stir in number because nothing threatens them.'

'Or perhaps it is because they are watching,' said Danae grimly. 'Perhaps our predicament amuses them.'

'They have no soul, no mind as we know it,' said Verity. 'They are only automata.'

Miriya shot her a look. 'Are they? What does the Imperium really know of these things? What truths?' She grimaced. 'This is the root of the very reason the Ordo Xenos were so loathe to let us return to Sanctuary 101. They must have known we would find something here!'

'You have it about-face, Sister,' said Danae. 'We did not find them. They found us.'

'The hooded one?' said Verity.

Danae gave a nod. 'We should have killed that creature when we had the chance.'

Miriya's lips thinned, but she said nothing more. Verity refused to remain silent, however. 'It... *She* is not a thing.'

'You saw the face!' scoffed the Sororitas. 'A mess of flesh and metal. Like one of those Mechanicus cogs, or worse! Pretending at being a woman.'

'I saw her,' Verity went on, her conviction growing. 'But with different eyes to you, Sister Danae. I saw a lost soul. I saw...' *A kindred spirit.* She could not bring herself to say the words. She frowned. 'I know this,' Verity began again. 'If we survive to flee this nest of darkness, then she must come with us. In Saint Katherine's name, I will not see the lost left to wander without the God-Emperor's light.'

'Have you forgotten your own words already, girl? You

cannot save the soul of a thing that does not possess one to begin with,' Danae replied, her tone hardening. 'Put such thoughts from your mind. That is an order.'

Verity glanced at Miriya, but the Battle Sister said nothing.

The black stone pyramids formed a long corridor, a grid of them arranged perfectly with each arrow-sharp corner a hand's span from the construct to its side. The Sororitas moved in single file, casting wary glances up at the barrels of inert flux arc projectors that lay pointing into the darkness. Silent as they were now, the lines of Monoliths resembled arcane sculptures from the hand of some obsessive geometer, sinister and threatening even while at rest.

'It is a manufactory,' whispered Kora. 'It must be so. We have found our way to some xenos equivalent of a forge-world.'

Sister Imogen looked at the younger woman. 'If that is so, then where are the workers, the helots? Where are the foundries and weapon shops?' She shook her head. 'This is more a reliquary than a place of creation.' The Sororitas paused and ran her hand over the flank of a Monolith, making a mark in the thick patina of dust that coated it. 'These devices have not seen power in thousands of years, I would warrant.'

'Perhaps more than that,' offered Cassandra.

Imogen gave a grim nod and moved on. Presently, the floor dropped into a ramp that opened out to a long, low chamber dominated by rows of circular display screens.

The hooded woman stood at the far end, kneading her hand, dressing the wound she had given herself. She glanced up as they approached.

'Is this what you want to show us?' asked Imogen.

'You have not witnessed enough,' came the husky reply. 'Not yet.'

Kora peered at one of the displays. It was filled with alien iconography, trailing down its span in cascades of unreadable text. 'Not enough? An army of thousands, and you say it is not enough?'

The revenant shook her head slowly, the hood exaggerating

the motion. She pointed at one of the circle-screens. 'Each of these represents a single cohort of combat forces. One group, like the Monolith brigade above.'

Cassandra's eyes widened as she took in the count of the screens. 'But there are... There must be hundreds of displays here.'

'And this is but one monitoring bay. There are many more.'

Imogen's jaw hardened. 'I tire of your games, creature. You make your object lesson clear. Say it, then. The number, if you will. Tell us how many of these Light-Forsaken machines are sleeping here. A legion's worth? *More*?' She advanced, brandishing her boltgun. 'Do you mean to terrify us?'

'I mean to illuminate you,' came the reply. The revenant backed away as Imogen approached. She opened her arms to take in the screens with the gesture. 'The enemy waits out the march of time in this place.'

'It *is* a tomb,' said Kora.

'No,' Cassandra corrected. 'It is an *armoury*.'

The hood bobbed in agreement. 'That one sees the truth of it. This complex is a staging area for invasion on a cosmic scale. A hub at the centre of the wheel, only one of many seeded in the deep past, left to wait out the aeons. Here they sleep, and they are maintained and prepared for eventual revivication. An army that numbers in the *billions*.'

Silence fell as the weight of the words settled in on the women. Imogen's face grew pale as she processed the import of what the revenant had said, her bravado slipping for a moment. 'If what you say is so... With those portals, they could strike en masse in an instant. No force sent by lander or teleporatrium could hope to match such numbers...'

'Is that what they did on Sanctuary?' said Kora.

'Aye,' whispered the hooded woman, the word almost a sob.

'We have seen enough xenos here to invade a dozen worlds.' Cassandra shouldered her weapon. 'And you tell us there are *more*? Where is this place? What cold hell have you dragged us to?'

The revenant moved to a panel and raked a bony hand over it. The display changed, rippling as it did so. 'I did not take you so far,' she said. 'Not so far at all. *See.*' She pointed.

Cassandra and Imogen studied the altered display. The rain of glyphs became a tactical display, orbital paths and system dynamics similar to something one might find on the bridge of a warship.

'How did you do that?' Kora demanded, but her question went unanswered.

'You recognise this.' The voice from deep inside the hood seemed distant.

Imogen gave a slow nod. 'I do. This is a visual of the planet... Of Sanctuary 101 and its lunar satellites.'

'We came here,' she went on, as the display centred on a dark orb of black rock spinning in a high orbit over the desert world, one of the planet's captured asteroidal orbitals. 'For what is stone is a lie, a falsehood hidden by alien guile.'

'The Obsidian Moon.' Cassandra gasped. 'This complex exists... *inside* the Obsidian Moon?'

'Impossible,' snorted Imogen. 'The *Tybalt* passed within a hundred kilometres of the surface of that satellite. A base of this magnitude would have been detected!'

'Would it?' came the question. 'The machines alter space-time with their arcane technologies, they twist dimension and void. You felt that in the gateways. They do the same here, coring out the moon as their hibernaculum, building something of impossible aspect where it should not exist.'

'And yet it does,' added Cassandra. She shuddered. 'It stretches the mind to contemplate such terrible science in the hands of aliens.'

Imogen glared at the revenant, emotions warring across her face. Finally, inevitably, anger won through. 'We have seen enough. We must return to the planet. A warning must be given!'

But the hooded woman shook her head. 'This is not what you must see.' She beckoned with her bloodied hand. 'Come with me.'

* * *

They entered the tower and found it made almost entirely of the black stone. Every face of it was polished to a sheen, and sculpted in sharp angles harsh enough to cut flesh if one were to press upon them. Miriya cast an eye over the walls in passing. Only a beam, a laser device of some impressive power, would have been able to forge such mathematically intricate designs. There were no blemishes, nothing to mar the cold perfection of the architecture; only a repeating shield-shaped motif etched into the walls. The design resembled an oval buckler, or the carapace of a beetle.

'The dust...' Verity said it before either Miriya or Danae had formed the thought. 'On the lower levels, the dust of ages was everywhere. But here... Nothing.' She looked at the Battle Sister. 'What does that mean?'

'It means that this place may be...' Miriya struggled to find the right word. '*Active*.'

'Weapons,' reminded Danae, as she progressed down the black corridor. 'If the enemy is revealed, we must be ready.' The command was more for the hospitaller's sake than Miriya's, but still she dutifully re-checked her bolter's fire select switch once again.

The beams from the underbarrel torches on their boltguns probed the darkness, finding a hexagonal metal door. A soft green glow emitted from a circular panel in the wall nearby.

'An operational system there,' noted Verity.

Danae nodded, and using silent battlesign gestures, ordered Miriya to take up a ready position on the far side of the hatch. When she was ready, the veteran slapped at the control and the hex-hatch opened, splitting apart into triangles that retreated into the stone. A draught of stale air wafted out, and Miriya caught the cloying taste of old decay upon it. The sensation collected at the back of her throat, but she resisted the reflex to cough and spit.

Leading with her meltagun, Danae entered the chamber beyond and Miriya fell in with her, aware of Verity taking nervous, careful steps behind her.

'Do you smell that?' said the hospitaller, grim-faced.

'Something... rotting?' Danae ventured.

The chamber was dark, and the light following them in through the doorway was weak. The torches picked out only pockets of imagery – a steel platform there, a cluster of viridian tubes here – and nothing that made sense to Miriya.

'On Tsan Domus,' Verity continued. 'I came to know that smell.' She spoke in a dead, distant voice. 'The air reeked of it.'

Danae halted, half turning. 'That world was a war grave,' she began. 'It–'

Miriya saw the other woman's boot cross a line of dark metal in the floor, and some invisible switch was tripped. Rippling out around them like a cascade of silent lightning, illuminators snapped into life and enveloped the chamber in a stark, antiseptic glow.

Danae spun back on her heel and what she saw made her recoil. She made a small noise of alarm, a faint cry, something she was probably not even aware of. Miriya's reaction had no voice, but she felt it in the blood draining from her face and the sudden chilly sweat beading her neck. For her part, Verity seemed only sorrowful. If the hospitaller had walked the fields of Tsan Domus – the site of Ultima Segmentum's worst witch-cult uprising in four hundred years, where an entire Order Militant Minoris had been murdered and defiled – then what they saw now was the echo of that horror.

In orbs made of cloudy, metallic glass there were corpses opened with all the detail of an anatomist's textbook. Miriya's knowledge of flesh and blood, human or otherwise, was limited to the knowledge of how to do harm to it and the most basic field medicine. About her, she saw layers of skin and bone, nerve and sinew flayed away, and suspended by unseen means. Museum-perfect displays that were part art-work, part experiment. The Battle Sister was reminded of the exploded technical diagrams of gun components she had memorised as a Novice Cantus. But instead of frame, coil and lever, these things were aorta, marrow and organ meat.

There were dozens of the spheres, many of them containing

exhibits so finely dismantled that it was impossible to know what species they might have originally come from. She saw what could have been parts of a greenskin, the dull blue hue of a tau, or perhaps they were all human remains, the last of the women who had died defending Sanctuary 101.

That last thought rose slowly in Miriya's mind, making her sickened and angry, becoming firm as she saw other objects in among the meat-diagrams. Here, a scrap of red combat cloak stained with dried blood, a Sabbat-pattern helmet stove in by a mammoth blow; there, a shattered plasma pistol lying near a grey, dust-caked metal drum etched with a fleur-de-lys. These things seemed like discards, trinkets to whatever mind had arranged the shape of this obscene gallery.

'Is it…' Danae swallowed, grimacing. 'A trophy room?'

Verity shook her head solemnly. 'This is an arcade dedicated to cruelty, ordered by something that sees no horror in what has been done. No more than a child might pluck wildflowers and press them into the pages of a notebook.'

'Why?' Miriya asked, the question escaping her. She crossed to the nearest orb-pod and peered at a circular display floating near it. Alien text filled the disc, and she wondered what it might say. Was it the record of the agonies of a long-dead Battle Sister, captured after the invasion? Or coldly harvested genetic data, preserved for future iterations of necrontyr to study, so they might better destroy any humans they encountered?

'I thought the machines were only killers,' she went on. 'All records speak of them as turning their victims to ash. What purpose does a… *harvest* like this serve?'

Miriya looked back when neither Danae nor Verity gave reply, and she saw that they had other concerns to occupy them.

From the far end of the gallery, a black mist whirled silently in the air, moving as ink would flow through water. Tendrils of it looped out and back, some reaching to touch the orbs it passed, like the brief caress of an owner upon the brow of a pet. The accumulation of darkness was asymmetrical, seeming to emerge from a single solid point in the middle of the mass. Miriya's mind suggested the shape of a cloak, swelling with a ghostly breeze.

Each of the women took aim, and as if it was obliging them in some mocking fashion, the gloom reformed, retreating and solidifying into an obsidian staff that drank in the light all around it.

The staff was clasped in the taloned hand of a creation that resembled the warrior machines only as much as a deck serf might be said to resemble a Space Marine. Lean of limb and sculpted gaunt, the necron was a thing made of steel planes and ribbed iron. Gold accents and bright rings of platinum decorated every inch that was not polished chrome-bright. Unlike the tarnished metal of the mechanicals they had fought on the planet, this construct looked old-new, like a well cared-for antique.

It studied them with unblinking emerald eyes, and when it spoke, the voice was the sound of knife-edges drawn across one another.

'You have come so very far,' it said.

'Now,' said the revenant, kneeling at the edge of the high platform. 'You will see.'

Imogen, Kora and Cassandra dropped into a crouch and came as close as they dared to the sheer drop. After the end of the platform, there was nothing but empty air for a good thousand metres until the top of...

Of something...

The architecture of the construction was like everything else inside the Obsidian Moon, all time-soiled metals surrounding carved rectilinear ribs of heavy stone – but where those shapes seemed to at least adhere to some rational, if alien, design ethos, this thing was an impossibility.

The Sister Superior tried to take it all in with a single glance, but it would not come to her. Like an optical illusion, lines seemed to begin and end on themselves, hard-cut corners forming into angles that collapsed upon one another.

It made her head swim to try and hold the shape of the thing in her mind's eye. An inverted tetrahedral surround of old iron, it stood bigger than the central donjon of the Sanctuary convent, glinting with flickers of power. Dull, unearthly light gathered in the open framework of the thing, the same brilliant green hue they had witnessed elsewhere.

Cassandra was the first to make the leap of concept. 'It is another portal.' She glanced at the hooded woman and the revenant nodded once.

'Very different to the simple doorways we passed through,' she intoned. 'This is an engine of transmission far more powerful, capable of instantaneous conduction across vast tracts of interstellar space. A Dolmen Gate.'

Imogen sucked in a breath of dry air and forced herself to look upon it once more. Where the glow emanated, she saw something like a scrap of gossamer net, dancing as if borne by winds. It seemed to be pulling from the dust itself, formed out of nothingness. 'Where does it lead?' She dreaded the answer to the question.

'Everywhere,' said the revenant, retreating into the shadows. 'The dolmen bores down into the matrix of the universe, the grid of line and power that underpins all things.' She cocked her head. 'The eldar have a name for that network. They call it "the webway".'

Cassandra uttered a curse. 'I have seen the Harlequins use that magick,' she grated. 'Tunnels through space, big enough to bring tanks and war machines from worlds away. You say the machines know this lore as well? How is that possible?'

'I have no answer for you.' The hooded woman was sorrowful. 'It operates by no means I can understand. The necrons are slicing into the ethereal realm with this device, but the mere act corrodes the stone it is made from.' She pointed towards the edges of the massive gate mechanism; parts of it were laced with cracks and fragments drifted about it in pockets of null gravity.

Insectoid machines continually scrambled over the length of the dolmen, mandibles flashing as they worked to cut and sculpt and mend the stonework. Imogen knew repair effort when she saw it. 'They are preparing the device,' she said.

'A long task,' said the revenant. 'It is the reason for this entire construct. The layers of space run thin here. The barriers between our realm and the conduits of the webway lie close to the surface in the Kavir system.' She pointed upwards, to where complex arrays of wide metal tubes ranged over their heads. 'They draw power from a vast energy core to keep it open a crack.'

'Is this why the Sisters in the convent were killed? To protect the existence of this?' Kora wondered aloud. 'The necrons were defending a strategic asset...'

'Perhaps,' Imogen allowed, never taking her eyes off the face beneath the torn, ragged hood. 'If this... gate is opened, then it will not just be Sanctuary 101 that will feel the lash of these aliens. Countless worlds could fall beneath their shadow.'

'Attacks would come without warning,' said Cassandra. 'Legions of these war machines phasing in out of nowhere...' She paused, considering the scale of it. 'God-Emperor... The Imperium would be defenceless.'

'Simultaneous mass invasion, from here to the shores of Holy Terra herself,' said the revenant. 'The xenos would slake the thirst of their warlords with human dead.'

Imogen rose with a sudden jerk and in a single step she was glaring into the depths of the dark hood. 'You know so very much about this place, about the necrontyr!' she snapped. 'Tell me why that is, creature! You are not one of them, I will accept that. But you cannot be human! All humans on Sanctuary were murdered!'

'Yes,' she agreed, her words thick with emotion, 'that is so.'

'Where did you come from?' asked Cassandra.

'From my own hell,' whispered the ragged figure. 'Damned to serve as witness to all this. But I escaped. Traded one prison for another.' She tapped at her head. 'Now returned here for you. So you can–'

'So we can *see*,' Imogen broke in. 'But what good does that do us if we all remain trapped here in this iron mausoleum?'

'We are all witnesses now,' the revenant said, shuddering. 'We are all the Watched, if we live long enough to be so.'

'Cease your riddles–'

But the woman was no longer listening to her. She pointed outwards at the dolmen. Metallic forms were darting up towards them, shimmering in and out of vision like flickering images from a damaged picter. Twisting, serpentine spines grew from legless, manta-like torsos made of black metal. Arms ending in bouquets of blades reached out in silence.

'We are seen,' said the hooded woman. 'The wraiths come for us.'

'Know me,' the necron began, showing no move to make an attack. 'I am Ossuar, Great Cryptek of the Sautekh Dynasty, citizen of Mandragora the Golden and Woken of the Great Sleep.' The words had a ritualistic quality to them, and Verity sensed a peculiarly theatrical manner in their delivery. She would not have been surprised if the machine had taken a courtly bow at the end of its utterance. Such declarations of self and intent were commonplace in the courts of the Imperium, but to hear an alien using such a mannered form of address was unusual. It was likely only the shared shock at this statement that had stopped the immediate release of a salvo of fire from the Battle Sisters.

The machines she had seen in the caverns had appeared as puppet things, clockworks that aped human form but with no more intellect to them than an animal predator. She had never expected that a necron might be able to communicate with them, or indeed, that one would ever wish to.

'It speaks,' muttered Miriya, scarcely able to believe her ears. 'Like automata playing at being alive.'

'It is your kind that imitate true life,' came the reply. There was almost a masculine tonality to it, and without thinking Verity immediately classified the creature as a *he*. 'Strange organics, lost in your limited meat without the glory of biotransference.' The machine-xenos spoke as if they were meant to understand the meaning and import of his words.

'You come so far to be here. So eager to interfere with us. To embrace death.'

Miriya answered it with questions. 'Why did you do this, alien?' She indicated the glassy orbs. 'What do you hope to learn from such acts of spite?'

'To feed well the food stock must be tasted. And there was also the puzzle to be solved.'

'What puzzle?' Verity was unable to stay silent.

The creature Ossuar made a noise that might have been a sigh of pleasure. 'How it was you came to evolve. The answer still eludes.' He raised the abyssal rod in his claw, and the extraordinary non-glow of fluid dark moved around the tip. When he spoke again, Verity was convinced she heard amusement in his tone. 'But you return, offering me more material to explore. Gratitude to you.' The staff shimmered, coming up in a threatening rise. 'Your offer will not be wasted.'

'Kill it!' spat Danae, finding her voice; and suddenly the moment of brief peace was shattered.

The wraiths came in fast, their spine-tails lashing at the air. Imogen fired first, and to her horror the shells from her bolter passed harmlessly through the closest of the machine-things as it went intangible.

Broad-shouldered and possessed of blank skull masks, they danced around the Sororitas, hovering on pillars of etherium energy, cocking their heads as they examined the humans. Hands that were little more than blade-sharp manipulators clenched and unclenched as they considered the intruders.

'I can see through them…' said Cassandra, tracking one of the wraiths with her gun muzzle. 'They must be decoys… Holographs!'

The hooded woman had her black sword in her hand. 'They are very real. They exist out of synchrony, moving back and forth between phantasm and corporeal to strike and fade.' She shot a look at the Sister Superior. 'We must fall back, now.'

'You are not in command here,' Imogen retorted.

Kora gave a yell as the wraiths moved. The Battle Sister's hand tightened on her trigger and she fired into the closest attacker, shell casings clattering around her. The wraiths broke apart and passed through stone pillars as if they were made of smoke, diving silently on the young woman.

'No!' Cassandra called out the warning just as the machine-ghosts crowded around Sister Kora. Ethereal claws and tail-barbs passed harmlessly through her torso – and then suddenly became real, manifesting *inside* her flesh.

Kora's death-scream was smothered by an expulsion of blood from her mouth, and her bolter fired wide.

The revenant swept in, her tattered cloak whirling, her dark blade a sweep of shadow. The alien sword took the head from one of the machines while it was still at the business of killing Sister Kora, avenging her. The weapon swept on and slashed at another wraith, damaging it severely.

Following her lead, Cassandra and Imogen unloaded their guns into the wraiths that dithered around Kora's body, briefly catching them as they were manifest in phase with this plane of existence. But in an eye-blink, they were turning ephemeral once again, ducking, weaving, preparing another attack.

This time Imogen did not hesitate. 'Retreat!' she barked. She tore an incendiary grenade from her belt and tossed it towards the Battle Sister's corpse.

Cassandra swallowed a prayer in Kora's memory and did as she was commanded, the hooded woman moving at her side.

The explosion hammered at their backs as they ran.

In the confines of the gallery, the fight became a storm of fire and darkness. Danae's meltagun forged lines of solar flame that lashed at the necron creature, and in return he unleashed black beams of negative energy that froze air molecules to snow in their wake. Verity dashed into cover as Miriya fired true, marching rounds up the chest of the machine to beat at its near-featureless face.

This Ossuar, this creature that called itself 'the cryptek', swatted the rounds away as if they were nagging insects and rolled the staff in his talons. A sinister shroud of oily smoke emerged from the rod and flowed towards them in a towering wave.

Miriya yanked on the breather mask stowed in her gorget, fearful that the alien had deployed some kind of gaseous weapon – but the shroud behaved like a living thing, rising up in curtains of rippling gloom.

Incredibly, she felt it plucking at her mind, prickling her skin. A sudden sense of despair loomed over her, so strong it almost forced a sob from her mouth. She felt a snake of dread uncoiling inside her chest, slithering across her will. The nightmares of an orphan child that she had banished from her mind in adulthood, burst through the walls she had built over them and gathered around her.

'Curse you!' Miriya spat, reaching deep within herself for the wellspring of defiance that she knew was there. The Sororitas had no concept of how Ossuar's weapon was working its assault on her senses. Through science or arcane magick? It was impossible to know. But she was sure of one thing – she would resist it.

The litany came easily to her, and Miriya invoked the Light of the Emperor, saying the words in a breathy rush. The effect was immediate, it was electric; she felt renewed as she looked within and touched her love and faith for her god.

Yes, she told herself. *Still strong.*

Miriya was elated; before, at prayer and at peace, she had searched for this moment and been found wanting. But now, in the teeth of battle, it came ready and real, as if it had always been there.

With her free hand she drew her chainsword and swept it up to beat at Ossuar's staff. The nightmare shroud parted before her savage attack and the necron actually staggered, as if he were surprised by the vigour of her counter strike.

Blade met staff with a clash of sparks and the force of it shoved the two combatants apart once again.

A hooting, braying tocsin was sounding through the gallery,

broadcast from some hidden speaker. Ossuar made an angry sound and dodged a beam-blast from Danae, weaving, gathering himself.

The circular screens shifted, each showing the same series of bright white icons; Miriya knew an alert when she saw it.

The necron drew a dark veil across the chamber, shifting behind it so they could not draw a bead on him. 'More of you elsewhere,' he grated, seeming to pluck the datum from the ether. 'What clever animals you are.'

That fragmentary moment of distraction was enough for Danae to take her shot. A blast of energy shattered one of the orbs close to where Ossuar moved, and the detonation blew the machine-creature off its feet. The cryptek scrambled, trying to right himself.

'This way!' cried Verity, retreating towards the hexagonal hatch while the necron was still in disarray. Miriya broke cover and ran to her.

'We are not animals!' Danae shouted, and as she fell back she immolated the rest of the glassy capsules with wildfire.

As they staggered into the corridor, a piercing whistle sounded from their vox-beads. Unknown to them, inside the gallery the thick iron walls had dampened their comm signals almost to nothing. Miriya wondered if it was some other consequence of the strange veil-effect Ossuar had generated.

Cassandra's voice was barely discernable through a rush of crackling static. *'If you read us,'* she was saying, *'we are regrouping. Home in on our location.'*

'I have it,' Verity noted, fumbling at her auspex unit. 'Below us. Not far.'

Danae fired again into the hatchway and glared at them both. 'I am done with this place,' she spat. 'Find me our Sisters and let us be gone!'

Behind them, a tinny rattle sounded across the stone walls, and Miriya looked up. 'The... the cryptek...' She said the alien word and scowled with it. 'He won't be done with us yet.'

She saw one of the etch-shapes in the stone *move*. Emerald light blinked on within it, a single eye emerging along with six needle legs. The ovals shifted against rock and fell to the floor. One, then two. Then dozens. The beetle-like machines twitched, shaking off dormancy, taking in their circumstances. They found the humans.

'Scarabs!' hissed Danae. 'Run!'

++What can you do?++ demanded the Watcher.

'Save us,' she told it, furious at the words. 'Watch me do so.'

++*You will fail*++ came the reply. ++*They will die and you will be trapped here. Again*++

'Shut up!' shouted the revenant, skidding out of her run to a halt.

++*You should not have come back*++

The one called Imogen grabbed her shoulder and spun her about. 'In Terra's name!' She snarled at the revenant. 'If you lose your mind now and strand us here, I swear I will slit your throat before they come for us!'

She pushed the Sister Superior away. 'I am sane,' she muttered, pretending that was true. 'I brought you this far.' The hooded woman tugged at her cloak and sprinted into the corridor of inert Monoliths, moving from one to another, brushing her bony fingers over them.

Behind her, the thunder of bolters sounded as the Battle Sisters duelled with the wraiths. The ghost-machines dogged them at every step, dancing in and out of reality. She had seen them use that tactic before, forcing their enemy to waste their ammunition, wearing them down.

In the brief moments they did become solid, the baleful light of their exile beamers flashed. Anything caught in the rays cast by the devices vanished, dimension-shifted into some random otherwhere.

++*You wonder how you know these things*++ said the Watcher. ++*Surrender and you will understand*++

This time she did not give any reply. Her hands crossed the surface of another silent Monolith and at last she felt the touch of what she had been searching for. 'Here!' she cried. 'To me, quickly.'

More footfalls sounded from along the corridor, and she glimpsed three more of the armoured women approaching from the other direction. Far behind them, the floor undulated and shifted, a metallic carpet of hissing, chittering forms moving in a slow wave. The scarabs were coming to dissemble them and carry their corpses to the reclamators.

++*If you are fortunate*++

'We are trapped,' said the one called Cassandra. 'What escape is this?'

'I have a way,' she told them, and she meant it. 'It will cost me much…'

'More than your life?' asked the dark-haired one with the scar on her face. Miriya, that was her name. The one who had stalked her through the halls of the convent.

'Yes,' she told her, with brutal honesty.

She let herself fall into the fugue state and touch the horrors inside her own mind. There she found the geometric shapes and the patterns she needed, the equations that would activate the mechanisms and find a pathway from this place. *Back to the planet. Back to the ruins and the dust.*

They reached out to her, these fragments of alien knowledge. They tried to grab her, drag her down into the dark of herself. It was hard to fight back, and they took a toll, breaking pieces of her off, hoarding them.

But it was done. The dull pane of polished stone across the face of the Monolith ran like a vertical puddle, eldritch light pooling upon it. The necron craft hummed and rose off the ground, impelled by internal powers she had awakened.

'Another portal…' said Cassandra. 'And where will this one take us, witchling?'

She answered the question by stepping through.

The scarabs and the wraiths were all around them, and the Sisters had nowhere else to go. Miriya heard Verity cry out as one of the insectoid machines bit her and she shook it off.

The flash of light from the portal gate in the front of the

Monolith bathed them all in an eerie glow. The woman in the hood didn't hesitate; she vanished into it.

'We seem to be making a habit of this,' growled Danae, and she propelled the hospitaller before her, firing at the wraiths. 'Do we even have a choice but to follow?'

Imogen's pale face darkened with chained fury, but she said nothing as she followed the revenant once more into the unknown.

The cryptek arrived to see the dimensional interface cycle ending, the conduit phase collapsing back into the structure of the Monolith. The pyramid settled back to the deck, inert once more, and the serviles milled around, waiting for a new command. He dismissed the scarabs and had the wraiths scan the chamber for damage estimates. The organics were careless with their weapons; the ruination these humans had caused in the gallery alone would take many of their man-years to mend.

Ossuar traced the activation runes on the Monolith and entertained a concern. No organic should have been able to operate this mechanism. It was simply impossible to comprehend.

Yet it had been done. He drew a recall of the instant from the groupmind memory bank of the scarabs and examined it.

A distant sensation awoke in Ossuar. It had been so long since he had experienced such a thing it took a while to process and identify it. At last, he found a name for it: *an emotion*.

The cryptek filed it away for later consideration and studied the dead portal.

It was clear that the situation on the planet was moving beyond his capacity to control. Here, inside the Hub, Ossuar had a perfect understanding of his capabilities and the powers he had to draw upon. But there? Outside in that realm, beyond these hallowed corridors... He reluctantly conceded that it required the talents of a different entity.

The time had come to awaken the nemesor.

CHAPTER TEN

There had been a time – so many centuries gone now that it was almost a dream and less than a memory – when Tegas had been fully human.

Then, barely a youth, he had been recruited out of the schola progenium where the evaluators of the Adeptus Mechanicus had found him. Recruited, if one were to use that word as a synonym for *taken*.

Young Tegas had been foolish, stupid. It embarrassed the questor to consider him now, regarding that frightened boy as little better than an infant, fouling itself and incapable of feeding without assistance.

On the way to Mars he had tried to take his own life, utterly ignorant of what glories the Machine-God would open to him upon his arrival. He had eaten poison aboard the transport ship, and almost succumbed to the potency of it. In the end, the toxins had only hastened the need for the excision of many of his internal organs and the implantation of newer, better replacements.

The only sense-memory he still carried from that moment was how the poison felt as it ran through him. The sickening disconnection it brought between his thought and his action, the sense of a body dying outside of his control. The fear.

He remembered that clearly, all these years later, as Adept Lumik fretted over him, plucking at him to help him rise from where he had fallen.

Gathering his wits, Questor Tegas swatted her away and got up, shaking off the ill-effects of... *What?*

He reviewed his internal program loops. He had made this happen. In his eagerness to probe the secret of the iron scroll, something Tegas had done had released a surge of electro-magnetic energy unlike any he recognised. The alien radiation swamped the interior of the laboratorium, and the efficient ray-shields that so cleverly protected the module from outside surveillance or imaging had trapped the force of it inside.

The questor's timebase was so corrupted he could not immediately ascertain how long he had been inert. Parts of his internals were still off-line, cycling through reboot phases. He grunted and staggered to the workstation.

The scroll was still there, sheathed in an emerald glow, mocking him with its complexity. I did do something, he told himself. The back-shock had not been some kind of security measure, but the side-effect of a larger event. Tegas knew what he had seen in the holograph glow of the scroll's interface. *Control.* The virtual switches he had tripped, they had sent signals along quantum filaments, the electromagnetic surge spilling out around them. *I did something.* He smiled. *I summoned something.*

A fear reaction would have been more logical at this juncture, he reasoned, but strangely, even the smallest glimmer of that emotion escaped him. This was experimentation, he told himself. It was not without risk, even to one's self, and whatever data or effect was generated from the result, he was confident he could address it. Tegas did not consider this arrogance.

What is that ancient axiom I have heard soldiers spout at moments of extreme crisis? Tegas cocked his head, thinking aloud. 'That which does not kill me makes me stronger.' Or in my case, smarter.

'L-lord?' stuttered Lumik, hanging on his words. Her tics were becoming more pronounced. 'I d-do not understand–'

He rounded on her. 'Are we secure? The Sororitas, outside... Are they aware of anything amiss? Have we suffered damage?'

'Yes. Apparently n-not. One death.' She answered his questions in quick succession.

'Good.' He gestured at the iron scroll. 'We will make it inert, examine our recorded data and then proceed from there.'

'Lord,' Lumik went on. 'We cannot. We have been trying to revive you for fifty-seven minutes.' She pointed a mecha-tentacle at the alien artefact. 'The device is drawing on power from an unknown source. Speculation: extra-dimensional. It resists all attempts to enquiet it.'

'What?' He pushed her aside, listing as he stomped across the lab chamber's metal decking. This was not right. The device had never shown any sign of being self-sustaining in its actions, not in Tegas's examinations or any of the tedious studies run on it by Tech-priest Ferren.

'W-what did you do?' she asked him, unable to keep accusation from her tone. 'We were supposed to observe, evaluate, collate. Nothing more. Those w-were the orders.'

'Orders?' Tegas said in harsh echo. 'Ah yes, the so-called "suggestions" of Inquisitor Hoth and the Ordo Xenos.' He turned an eye-cluster to glare at her. 'We are the children of the Omnissiah and all knowledge belongs to us. For Mars's sake, we do not adhere to the demands of the Inquisition! If that were so, then those stunted minds would have shackled every last creative thought from our species long ago!'

He crossed to the scroll, ignoring the other adepts who seemed afraid to venture too close to it. The alien holograms were flooded with glyphs that moved so fast even his enhanced cognition subroutines could not interpret them. The sight of the icons made him feel pleasantly giddy, as a flesh-and-blood man might react to a potent glass of amasec.

'What are you doing, you lovely thing?' he asked it, his smile widening.

The device chose to answer him.

* * *

The iron scroll had shown many interesting characteristics, including a capacity to alter itself on an atomic level by moving sheets of molecules back and forth. At first it was a roll of metallic paper, then a fan of thin, feather-like blades. And now, it changed once again.

It *opened*.

Radiance, a rippling emerald shimmer like captured lightning, emerged from the edges of the scroll as it unfolded along its length. The device deconstructed itself, a sculpture formed of metal paper unmaking its shape. As Tegas and his adepts watched in stunned awe, organo-metalloid materials deformed as new molecular patterns stored deep in particle waveforms imposed themselves.

The scroll became the fan, the fan became a pennant, the pennant bending into a thin spline, curving up and growing. Chains of molecules reordered and knitted in new configurations, mimicking an accelerated biological growth cycle.

The questor watched it with a mixture of anticipation and anxiety. Lumik stuttered and jerked as she pulled at the hem of his robes, begging Tegas to stop it, but even if he had been capable, he would not have done so. He was enrapt by the dance of reconstruction, the living metal cresting to make itself into a ring of chrome a little over two metres in diameter.

Across the disc of the ring a net of crackling green sparks formed, merging, reforming. A liquid effect, the visual component of exotic radiations interacting with air molecules, appeared. It was like a child's toy, the membrane of a giant bubble held tense in the hoop.

Tegas and the others studied the effect with senses that perceived realms beyond human sight, sound, smell. The questor's probes danced in the air around him, sampling and tasting. Unusual particulates that resembled ozone, calcites and other elements were being generated by the membrane, wafting invisibly into the laboratorium. Waves of radiant, invisible energy spilled out with them, and Tegas felt the passage of air on the few pieces of skin that formed his face.

On an impulse he could not fully quantify, he reached up his hand towards the glowing, filmy light. Tegas wanted to touch it. He knew that it would give under his steel digits. He wanted to sift the energy in his fingers, like sand.

The membrane quivered and burst before he could reach it.

Displaced air screamed and crashed in tiny thunderclaps, and the ring vomited shapes wreathed in clouds of icy vapour. Human figures exploded into the room. A hooded form, then others in flashing black armour and crimson capes crusted with rimes of frost. They crashed across the workstation and landed in disarray, colliding with examination gimbals and servitors too slow to get out of their way.

Battle Sisters. The surreality of their arrival caused a brief computational error cluster in the questor's thoughts before his mind caught up to what he was seeing. The adept had been right – extradimensional energy was the key. The scroll had been the information repository, the fan, the control matrix and the ring...

The ring was a portal...

Tegas's train of thought was broken as Lumik generated a droning scream of alarm, and he flinched backwards as the disorder ensued.

A green bolt of energy emerged from the shuddering membrane and flashed out across the chamber, destroying a cogitator console in a pulse of black smoke. The questor saw other things emerging at the foot of the ring, slower than the first arrivals: beetle-sculptures made of steel and emerald glass, venturing forth – no, coming *through* – with slow machine cunning. Tegas remembered the construct Ferren had been tormenting, the tomb spyder; these were the smaller cousins of the same automata, the so-called scarabs.

'Get back!' shouted one of the Sororitas, a woman with dark hair and a fierce aspect, directing her command at Lumik. Without waiting for the adept to obey, she opened fire with a bolter and destroyed the first of the mechanoids with pinpoint shots.

The woman who had come through first – the one in

a stained and torn robe that stank of old, soiled matter – lurched back towards the ring and snatched at it. Reflexively, afraid that she would destroy this incredible piece of technology, Tegas tried to stop her.

Without pause, she batted him away and he crumpled to the deck. In that instant, he got a scan of her and the data returned was a confused mix that was hard to interpret. Hot and cold thermal patches, low-yield radiation, organic resonances, evidence of biomech implantation. She did not make sense. The scan was closer to a Mechanicus cyborg than a Sister of Battle.

The question was pushed away when the woman snatched at one of the threads of silver fibre making up the lines of the ring. Impossibly, it broke, and like the tension in a bow string failing, the perfect hoop of alien steel came apart with a blinding crackle of spent power. Lashing across the room, the metal cut a line of orange sparks over ceiling and deck, bisecting illuminator strips and severing the arm of a gun-servitor that had wandered too close. Tegas watched in amazement as the metal did its trick once again, retreating into itself. Within seconds, it was weaving back into the shape of the scroll, as if nothing had happened.

He marvelled at what he had seen. If these modes of function were available to this necron construct, then the questor could not help but wonder what other shapes it could take. *Poor Ferren*, he mused, *he has no understanding of what he discovered*. He was a child grubbing in the dirt for lost coins, who found a God's ransom instead.

He would have laughed if not for the circumstances he was now forced to face.

Tegas turned and found Sister Superior Imogen's gun pointing at his head. He gave the very smallest of bows. 'Milady,' he offered, as if greeting her at evening prayers. 'Welcome.'

'The laboratorium...' Among the Sororitas, a hospitaller with a drawn, pale face, peered at her surroundings. 'We have been returned to the surface.' Her comrades were swiftly getting their bearings, and they did not like what they saw.

Lumik and the other adepts were cross-communicating silently, and the shared data pool was in danger of brimming over with questions. Where did the Sororitas come from? How does the device work? Who is the hooded one? Has the dig site been compromised?

The answer to the last of those he saw in Imogen's eyes. She didn't need to say it and he felt no need to conceal the lie any longer. Now was the time to exercise damage control, before things could spiral into violence. The Adepta Sororitas were a pious lot and largely narrow of mind, but once roused to anger they would carry their rancour until the death of time itself. Tegas did not wish to find himself at the sharp end of their wrath.

Not now he had something so perfect within his grasp.

'This object,' rasped the hooded one, tracing a bony finger around the closing scroll. 'I sought the closest way back to the convent and the Monolith interpreted that wish literally. It repurposed this device to form a temporary endpoint to the conduit.'

'Where did you find it?' Imogen demanded of him. 'Speak, questor!'

'It is good fortune that I did so,' Tegas deflected. 'It came from the desert... I was able to fathom some of its functions.' That was almost a truth, and he pressed on. 'If I had not, perhaps you would have never made it back from...' He let the words hang, and predictably, one of the other Sisters filled the silence with the answer.

'We found the caverns,' said the one carrying the meltagun. 'Your secret outpost!'

The unaugmented were so easy to manipulate, he reflected, unable to avoid giving voice when caught in the highest of emotional states. 'I can explain.' Tegas modulated his tone to appear contrite. 'I fear we have all been misled–'

'More lies will only bury you deeper, you boneless clockwork!' Imogen growled. 'Your men tried to kill us.'

Tegas silently cursed Ferren's lack of restraint, but said nothing.

'Their actions summoned the xenos,' Imogen went on, 'and for that we may all perish!'

There were so many things he wanted to know, but the questor realised that his next utterance would be his final one unless he acquiesced. Beaming an order to the other adepts to give no resistance, he bowed to the Sororitas in surrender. 'I am sure there is an explanation for all of this.'

'We will see.' Imogen beckoned her second in command. 'Bring him!' spat the Sister Superior. 'And his toy as well. The canoness must know what we have seen.' Imogen glared back at Tegas. 'You will have a steep price to pay for what you concealed from us, maggot.'

'Sister,' said one of the others. 'What about... her?' She pointed at the woman in the hooded robe.

'She comes too,' said Imogen, cutting at the air with her weapon. 'It is time to reveal all the damned truths hiding in this place.'

The entrance corridor to the stasis-tomb sloped away, and the steady tread of Ossuar's iron-clawed feet echoed in the heavy air. A single pair of lychguards stood sentinel at the entrance to the nemesor's vault, warscythes crossed over their chest-plates, the tall fans of their ornate skulls raised as dead eyes stared into nothing. They had not even acknowledged the presence of the cryptek. Instead, after a moment of sampling the intelligence stream via mnemonic probe from the complex's knowledge nexus, they silently interpreted his intentions and let him pass. Ossuar scanned them as he passed, making a vague attempt to glean an understanding of their thought processes. But the works of the mind of the battle-forms were always hard for him to grasp. It was a cryptek's way to see the universe in a different manner from those of the warfighting castes, after all.

Ossuar and his kindred were harbingers, and that had been their singular purpose since biotransference, unchanged despite the passed aeons of the Great Sleep. Psychomancers like he were the ones who knew the hearts of the unenlightened child-races the best, and he had often fought with his gift-powers at the fore. Ossuar's brethren, be they geomancer or plasmancer, the time-weavers or the storm-callers, were the intellectual elite of the necrontyr, echoing in eternity what they had been before the C'tan had come to uplift them. But he and his kind were not soldiers. They were ultimately thinkers, the learned of the dynastic houses. It was not their place to engage in the petty actions of killing the meatbound en masse.

Although... On some level, Ossuar had to process the truth that engaging the human females in direct armed conflict had been briefly... *exciting*.

He followed the inclined corridor down towards the antechamber, led by a vee of wayfinder scarabs etched with the sigil of the Sautekh clan. The cryptek bore the same mark himself, etched by laser on his steel sternum. Data traps in the walls registered him and let him pass, deactivating lethal gauss emitters hidden inside ornamental carvings.

The nemesor's sleeping chamber opened to him, and the scarabs bowed on their six legs before retreating into their wall-slots. Ossuar paused to examine the latest status update in the Somnus Codex and saw that the revival process was well into the final stage. Beyond, to the right, the annex chamber brimmed with weapons of all kinds, a personal armoury that contained flayers and etherium projectors, gauntlet-mounded voidblades and null spears, tachyon arrows and hyperphasic swords. Ossuar found such an overt display of these killing tools to be without purpose. In his existence, the cryptek had never found the need to use anything other than the abyssal staff he carried with him at all times. But then warfighters did so fetishise their weapons, a truism that appeared to be valid across all species, even the most inferior ones.

Ossuar made the sacrosanct signs of Activation and Eternity for the monitor eyes observing the interior of the tomb, partly as it was expected of him to pay such ritual obeisance to the Stormlord, but largely to operate the gestural control interface that would lower the force wall between him and the inner chamber. The glittering field dissipated and the cryptek entered the sleeping room proper.

The nemesor's sarcophagus had already risen from its holding claw and was in the process of moving from the horizontal plane to the vertical. A thin trickle of dust rained down from the intricately-machined surface of the iron coffin. Although the slumber in this outpost had been only an infinitesimal fraction of the millions of cycles their kind had spent in the Great Sleep, Ossuar still experienced a moment of trepidation. Awakenings were always difficult things, he recalled, and trauma of mind was sometimes the result. The cryptek recalled his own rise from the Timeless Dream and how helpless it had made him feel at the start, in those vulnerable moments before his machine body re-engaged with his essence. It was not an experience he would ever wish to repeat. Ossuar had privately vowed he would never go dormant again, and that had been in great part why he had taken the role of woken custodian of this place.

The lid of the sarcophagus broke in a line across its centre, and then its length. The four quadrants of metallized stone folded up and away, and the nemesor was revealed.

The warlord, like Ossuar, displayed the same skeletal form as all humanoid necrontyr did, the shape a deliberate echo of the frail bones they had left behind when they embraced the majesty of biotransference. But where the cryptek was spindly and long of finger, the warrior-general was almost muscular. Layers of redundant lamellar armour made of living alloy plated his torso and limbs, and a splayed head-crest framed a gaunt steel face that was bright with copper accents. The Sautekh symbol was brazen upon the general's forehead, as sharp this day as it had been when the master of their dynasty, the undying Imotekh, had burned it there with his fire gauntlet. The Royarch of Mandragora had favoured the nemesor, and the mark made it certain that all who gazed upon the warlord would know so.

A green flash signalled the return of awareness to the figure in the coffin, and his eye slits glowed with renewed life.

Ossuar bowed his head. 'My Lord Khaygis, dream no more. You are needed.' The nemesor's name had not echoed in the halls of the outpost for many cycles.

The general's vocoder favoured a vocalisation like stones grinding across one another. 'Cryptek...' said Khaygis, weighing the title. 'How long?'

'A breath of wind, little more.'

The general rose, slowly and carefully, testing his limbs as he stepped free of the casket. Tiny phylacter arachnids scuttled across him before flinging themselves back into their container, now that their tasks of repair and maintenance were done. 'It must be an issue of import, then.' Khaygis's intonation had a hollow quality, a resemblance to something echoing down a long stone tunnel. 'It must be so, for the great Ossuar to admit he faces something he cannot overcome with intellect alone.'

The cryptek cocked his head. 'I would say that I require... your unique insight.'

'Of course you would,' Khaygis replied, folding knife-blade hands into a fist and back again. 'Show me now.'

'Very well,' began Ossuar. 'But first it might be necessary for me to explain certain facts.'

The nemesor gathered up his robe of command and settled it over his steel shoulders. 'You misunderstand, cryptek.' He closed on the other necron, his leering metal face straightening. 'I have no wish to listen to you give me the interpretation of things you think I should know. I told you to show me.' He reached up and folded his talons around Ossuar's jaw. 'So show me.'

The cryptek felt Khaygis's intrusive mnemonic probe as it beamed from the antennae hidden in his crest, the dataphiltre touching Ossuar's outer consciousness. Hastily, he re-ordered his internal firewalls to protect his deep secrets as the nemesor looked into his recent memory stores.

It might have been possible for Ossuar to fully resist the

violation of his mindframe, but to offer even token resistance to the nemesor would have been seen as disobedience. Khaygis was cementing his place in the hierarchy from the very start, reminding the cryptek that although he had exalted rank as one of the Stormlord's greatest harbingers, he would never be beyond the general's command.

The two of them shared nothing but suspicion of each other's motivations. The cryptek considered the nemesor to be little more than a violent braggart, while in return the general saw the harbinger as ill-focussed and obsessive.

Reluctantly, Ossuar accepted the situation and allowed Khaygis to duplicate a full memory feed of everything that had transpired during his dormancy.

As she had been commanded, Sister Miriya leaned forwards and rested the barrel of her bolter against the back of Questor Tegas's skull, her finger upon the trigger.

'At my word of command,' said the canoness, biting out every syllable, 'you will kill this mendacious wretch, is that understood?'

'Aye, mistress,' she replied, holding the weapon steady.

The veteran glanced across to where the ragged, hooded woman stood watching, with Sister Verity at her side. Sepherina frowned, weighing her options.

'She helped us,' Miriya volunteered. 'We all would be dead now if not for her, and this perfidy would have gone unchecked.'

From his position on his knees in the Great Chapel, the Mechanicus adept made a clicking, sighing noise. 'If I can be allowed to explain? All will be made clear.'

At the corner of her sight, Miriya could see where the rest of Tegas's group were surrounded by a ring of similarly-armed Battle Sisters led by Pandora, who cradled a storm bolter in her grip. All of them were experienced in the duties expected of an Adepta Sororitas execution detail.

Sepherina looked to Sister Imogen. 'The device,' she began. 'Where is it now?'

'Secure,' Imogen replied tightly. 'Sister Danae and a group of Retributors hold it in one of the deep prayer cells as we speak. Wards have been placed around the object and explosive charges made ready. If it so much as twitches, it will be destroyed.'

'You cannot do that,' said Tegas.

'You have no right to demand otherwise,' Sepherina snapped.

'You misunderstand,' Tegas replied, his head still bowed. 'I make no demand of you. I simply tell you the facts. You cannot destroy it. You *will not* be able to. The material it is composed of is a living alloy.'

The canoness' eyes narrowed. 'You know so much, questor. How many things have you kept from me since Paramar?' She advanced on him, her fury building. 'Lies standing upon lies! There is nothing you have said to me that I cannot doubt, your every word and gesture subterfuge and artifice!'

Miriya had watched the silent tide of anger rise in the veteran's face as Imogen brought the Mechanicus adepts before her and explained what had taken place. She could not miss the way that Tegas hung on the Sister Superior's every word when she described the portals that took them to the Obsidian Moon, and the tale of what they had encountered there. Miriya suppressed a shudder as Imogen described the echoing metal corridors of the necron complex, the thought of being there crawling at the base of her neck.

It was only now that she had returned to the convent that Miriya was able to parse the sensations she had felt in the lair of the machine-xenos. In all the time they had up there, it was like something in the Battle Sister's spirit had come loose and disconnected. Now that feeling was gone, and she found a moment of understanding.

There was a numbness about the necrons and their machines that leaked into the air around them. A sense of dead space, of decay. Not like the rot of a plague zombie or the charnel stench of a battlefield, worse than that. It was a complete and total absence of the force of life.

Miriya had walked in a place and encountered beings that

could only be described as *soulless*. For one whose existence orbited around the light of faith and the power of the human spirit, to experience that chilled the Sororitas to her marrow. The necrons were antithesis, raw and real and made manifest.

She fought down the cold in the core of her soul and snapped back to the moment at hand.

'A concealed dig site, staffed by explorators from your ministry,' Sepherina was saying. 'It is not enough that Inquisitor Hoth and his lackeys disrespected our dead and engineered the exile of the Sisterhood from their own outpost! Now I learn that the Adeptus Mechanicus has been here, perhaps for years, grubbing in the dirt in secret!'

'I admit,' Tegas said carefully, 'that some omissions of data have been made.' The canoness made a growling noise and spat; the questor pressed on before she could order him shot. 'I was aware of Adept Ferren's presence on the planet. I did not know how large his party was, or what they were doing.'

'Liar,' snarled Imogen, and Miriya was forced to agree.

Tegas kept speaking. 'I came here to deal with him. *Quietly*. Ferren was acting on his own initiative, without oversight. His actions jeopardised the Mechanicus's relationship with the Ecclesiarchy!' The questor shook his head. 'I knew, yes. But how could I have told you? How would the Order of Our Martyred Lady have reacted to such information?'

'With burning censure,' Imogen replied.

'Exactly.' Tegas nodded sharply. 'I came to order Ferren to cease his work here, to remove himself from this world. Please, milady, you must believe me.'

Sepherina moved back and forth in front of the questor, shaking her head. 'That is your explanation? I break through the shell of your untruth and find another nested beneath. Will there be another beneath this one, and another and another?' She pointed a finger at him. 'I submit to you, adept, that you have abused the trust of the Adepta Sororitas to bring you to Sanctuary 101. Once before you warned me that you and your masters might annex this planet for your own needs. I believe that you have attempted that very thing, you and Hoth together in alliance for whatever spoils lie beneath these sands!'

'But why involve us?' Miriya let the question slip.

The canoness looked across at her. 'To cover their lie. Because even they cannot be seen to defy the Imperial Church so blatantly. They pretended to share this duty with us, but all along we are seen as nought but an impediment.' Sepherina looked back at Tegas. 'Tell me, questor. Is Hoth coming here? Have you drawn plans to destroy my Sisters, bury us in the dust on this distant world where no eyes will see?'

'You do not understand,' said Tegas, his tone turning flat and cold. 'This is more important than the corpses of a few dead women.'

Sepherina drew her chaplet and a thin blade emerged from its length with an oiled click. 'I'll slit your throat for your betrayal!'

'Be sure to take the life of your Sister Superior and this one with the gun at my head into the bargain,' Tegas retorted. 'If your blade seeks traitors, they are deserving.'

'A pathetic ploy!' snorted Imogen.

'Is it?' Tegas spat back. 'I have analysed all sensor data on that… female.' He nodded at the revenant. 'You have allied yourself with a monstrosity! A xenos hybrid! You have willingly consorted with something that is inhuman! That is a grave sin against Saint Katherine's name, is it not so?'

'More lies…' said Miriya.

But the canoness hesitated and pointed her chaplet blade at the revenant. 'You,' she said. 'Lower your hood. Show yourself to me.'

Recollection flowed like icy waters.

Time was an abstract for a necron. Once, when they had been organics, the passing of the eras seemed like such a terrible burden, a great cosmic weight upon the back of their species. But when the C'tan came with their gifts of understanding, all that had changed. The passage of the Stargods through the lives of the necrontyr race had left them forever changed, and with the ending of the great war with the Old Ones, they had found a new purpose. Led by the Silent King, the necrons revolted against the powers that had remade them from meat-matter unto the immortal perfection of steel – and finally, trapped in a history mortally wounded by war, they went to the Great Sleep to wait out the millennia.

Time… So much time had passed in the null-state. Both the cryptek and the nemesor shared the same sensation from their past, the same sense of affront they had experienced on awakening. The galaxy they had left behind sixty million years ago had been broken wreckage, a warzone torn open by battles that had erased entire star systems from existence as easily as insects were swatted from the air. The one they awoke to was whole and healed… But it was infested. Not just by the accursed eldar, the lackeys of the old enemy, but by new things that pretended at intellect, that swarmed in the dirt of worlds and believed themselves superior.

The throneworld Mandragora the Golden had awoken to changed fortunes, newly rich in this strange, pestilent present. Its master, the Stormlord Imotekh, had grasped the reality of things far quicker than any of the other Royarchs who had survived the Timeless Dream. Served by a legion of dynasts that counted Ossuar and Khaygis in their number, Imotekh's crusade for dominance began in emerald fire.

It was this fire that swept to the star the humans called Kavir.

Imotekh's steady march across the galactic plane wove its course even now, out in the depthless tracts of interstellar space where necron tomb ships and harvester cruisers travelled at near-light velocities. The Royarch's grand schema, embedded in the mindframes of every necron in his service from warlord to drone, was to reunite the scattered, sleeping remnants of their species under his sigil. They had come to the Kavir system in search of the Obsidian Moon, and the Dolmen Gate that lay hidden beneath its surface. The Atun, the dynasty that had built it, was weak and scattered, and the Sautekh had claimed it for themselves.

It was almost as an afterthought that the pocket of organics on the surface of the nearby planet were exterminated. Worthless things in the eyes of the Stormlord, impediments to the cause, the human outpost died and the moon was annexed. It was victory.

Or to be accurate, it was a victory of a kind.

Hidden inside the moon, a treasure trove of Atun soldiery and weapons inert but undamaged, ready to be reprogrammed and turned to Sautekh allegiance. Great value to any Royarch, even one as powerful as mighty Imotekh, whose war fleet already brimmed with death-dealers. And there, the Gate itself, rare and precious. Capable of penetrating the immaterial walls of the subspatial network existing in the bones of the void itself.

Rare and precious, indeed. And *broken*, much to the Stormlord's annoyance. Perhaps by the ravages of time, perhaps in the final spasms of the war with the Old Ones... It mattered not. Without the Dolmen Gate in full order, the weapons stored inside the Obsidian Moon could not be deployed, their function stunted.

Ossuar remembered this moment well. He remembered Imotekh's irritation at cracking open this prize only to find it useless to him.

The cryptek saw opportunity and took it. Every member of the Stormlord's hierarchy knew their master was driven by his fire, his eternal desire to press on and never again be tethered to just one single world. Despite the counsel of his trusted warlords – generals like Khaygis – Imotekh refused to remain and dig in at Kavir. There was too much out there, too many other Tomb Worlds yet to be found and awakened, too many dangerous and savage child-races to be left unculled.

It had been Ossuar's manoeuvrings in the Royarch's court that provided the solution. The cryptek used his influence to ensure that the suggestion did not appear to come from him, but in the end it was only he who could direct it.

The Stormlord could gather his fleet and depart; but someone would need to remain behind, to stand as custodian to the Obsidian Moon while the repairs progressed. Ossuar nobly offered himself in service to that role, to watch over the reconstruction of the Dolmen Gate and the slumbering army, freeing the war fleet to move on and seek new objectives. When the work was done, the fleet would return,

And if, in the performance of this duty, Ossuar was allowed to indulge his own interests in the dissection of organics and experimentation upon them, then so much the better. Alone, unburdened by the drive to battle, he would have his time.

But trust did not come easily to the Stormlord, and indeed it would be a foolish Royarch who allowed a cryptek to stand as de facto master of such an important – if still inert – resource. Rebellions had emerged from such mistakes, and it was the nature of harbingers like Ossuar to seek ways to aggrandise themselves.

Khaygis was the watchman left to oversee Ossuar, placed in suspension while his soldier-mechs followed the cryptek's every move. Should he go against his master's wishes, Ossuar would be nullified, his biopattern engrams deleted and his machine-frame repurposed as a warrior drone.

'All this I know,' said the nemesor. 'I was there. Show me what happened while I slept.'

'As you wish.' Ossuar opened more of his memories, and braced himself for the inevitable torrent of invective he knew would come.

After the fleet departed, Khaygis had soon grown weary of watching the cryptek study the dusty halls of the lunar complex, and tormenting the handful of survivors from the human colony to their death-state. Eventually he chose to embrace the Sleep until such times as the Dolmen Gate was ready. That had been nine solar cycles ago, by the local reckoning.

And now Khaygis saw what had gone on beneath his slumber. Ossuar's experimentation and the agonies he had inflicted upon the survivors. The arrival of more organic ships, drawn by the death-cries of their colony. Humans from those vessels, allowed to grub in the dirt and touch the relics of necrontyr greatness.

The nemesor's claw slipped around the Cryptek's iron neck. 'What have you done, fool?' he demanded. 'You allowed the organic vermin to return to the planet and you did not exterminate them?' Something like confusion entered his tone as Khaygis scanned the rest of the data. 'More of them? Why, Ossuar? What reason could you possibly compute to let these parasites run free?' The ephemeral, invisible data stream between them abruptly ceased as the general cut himself off.

'They fascinate me,' admitted the cryptek. There was little point in denying it. 'I saw no harm. They were ignorant of us.' He cocked his head. 'We were once like them. The recursion of evolutionary patterns is most compelling. I learn so much from deconstructing them.'

Khaygis emitted an angry buzz and shoved Ossuar away, stalking towards the annex. 'I see now I should never have taken the Sleep, even for a moment. You have treated this duty like your own private science experiment.' He glared at him. 'You harbingers always think you are subject to no rules but your own!'

'It is only my boundless curiosity that–'

The nemesor gathered up an ornate fire gauntlet and silenced Ossuar with a flicker of green flame though his fingers. 'Curiosity?' he echoed. Khaygis reached for a tachyon arrow launcher and secured it around his other wrist. 'That is nothing but the cloak about your desires for power above your station.' He pointed a talon-finger. 'You have put us at risk. What if more of these organics are coming here? With a fleet of ships? Enough to destroy us?'

'They are only humans.' Ossuar could not keep the mocking tone from his vocoder. 'Parasites, as you said. What threat are they?'

'If they are no threat, then why did you wake me?' Khaygis boomed. 'You are in error and you know it full well! And now you have created this mess you panic and come to me to repair the damage for you!'

'Panic is an unproductive emotional state that I do not emulate,' Ossuar insisted. 'The need for it has long since been edited from my consciousness.' He turned as heavy footfalls signalled the arrival of the two lychguards. The cryptek realised that Khaygis must have summoned them via beam-signal.

The dark blades of the warscythes in the hands of the towering guardians turned towards him, directed by the nemesor's silent commands. 'I should have you decompiled,' said Khaygis.

'And when the Stormlord's fleet returns, what would you tell him?' Ossuar retorted. 'That I suffered a damaged actuator and accidentally fell upon an upturned blade?' He pointed at the warscythes. 'The Royarch expects much. The repairs to the dolmen will never be complete without my stewardship!'

At length, Khaygis nodded. 'Know that you remain intact only because of that truth.'

Ossuar allowed himself to bow slightly. 'I beg forgiveness for my presumption. I see the error, indeed. I ask you for your aid in terminating the organics.'

'At last, a directive I can compute.' Khaygis waved the lychguards away and came close to the cryptek. 'How it must sear you to be forced to emulate submission to me. What analogues of resentment do you process at this moment, Ossuar?'

'I exist only to serve the will of the Royarch,' replied the cryptek.

'Then do so by following my every command as if it were that of the Stormlord himself,' Khaygis grated. 'And curb your own petty obsessions until the work is done. Once the Gate is repaired and the army here wakes, you will have enough humans to cut upon and dissect to sate your curiosity.'

The hood fell, and Verity heard the collective gasp as the Sisters in the chapel looked upon the revenant's face and beheld the damage there.

Slowly and carefully, the woman shrugged off the tattered, ragged robe and picked at streamers of cloth, so old and dirt-stained that they tore like strips of sloughed epidermis as she peeled them from her arms and her throat. She mumbled to herself, so low and hollow that Verity could not make out the words.

A human female, indeed, but mutilated by callous intention. Implants of alien design, some of steel, others green crystal or metallic stone, emerged from pockets of sunburnt flesh or pressed up from beneath translucent skin. The works that had been done to her lacked the ritual nature of bio-organ embedding used by the Adeptus Astartes, or even the embrace of machine parts practised by Tegas's precious Mechanicus. She was a tormented woman who carried her tortures with her, *inside* her.

'Throne and Blood,' whispered Sister Pandora. 'How can she still be alive?'

'How indeed,' accused Tegas. 'The scars, canoness. Do you see the scars on her?'

Verity looked, and she saw. Self-inflicted marks along malnourished limbs and bare skin, lines and circles that mimicked the arrangement of the necron glyphs she had seen inside the alien complex.

'An agent of the xenos, after all...' Imogen was saying. 'I was right to suspect.' She raised her boltgun.

Suddenly, the hospitaller was stepping forwards, putting herself between the revenant and the muzzle of Imogen's gun. 'No!' she cried. 'No, you will not do this!'

'Step aside, nursemaid,' said the Sister Superior. 'Truth must out, and force will see to it. First the hybrid and then the adept.'

'*No!*' Verity shouted the denial again, her voice booming across the chapel. 'You are so quick to hate you do not take a second to think! Do you not question how she came to be here, or who she is?' The young woman pointed at the sorrowful, emaciated figure behind her. The revenant's cheeks were wet with tears. 'You must look with better eyes than that!'

'They did that to her,' said Miriya. 'The necrons... *The cryptek.*'

Verity crossed to the great altar, careful to keep herself in Imogen's sightline, and found what she was looking for among the fresh votives and prayer tapers; a data-slate. She gathered it up and crossed back.

'From the moment I glimpsed her face two nights ago,' she began, paging through the slate's contents, 'I knew. When I saw her within this chamber, I knew this woman was a kindred spirit.'

'I...' The revenant bowed her head. 'I don't know why I came here.'

'I do,' Verity replied. 'This slate contains the memorial record of every Sister who perished at Sanctuary 101, all the faces and names of the dead we honoured outside.' She halted, a gasp escaping her lips as she found what she was looking for. 'I was uncertain before... But no longer.'

The hospitaller pressed the slate into the cracked, dirt-smeared hands of the other woman. 'What... is this?' she asked, looking down at the device. Teardrops splashed across the glowing screen.

'This is you,' Verity told her, her heart hammering behind her ribs. She turned back to face the canoness. 'Her name is—'

'*Decima*,' said the revenant, the word catching in a sob. 'My name is Decima.'

On the slate, an unblemished mirror of her ruined face stared back from a decade past.

CHAPTER ELEVEN

For a moment, Miriya's attention was stolen away from the task before her and she stared at the living dead. The woman – *her Sister in arms?* – wept openly, gentle sobs echoing across the Great Chapel.

No one seemed able to speak. It was as if the revelation was so powerful that it silenced them all, robbing them of the power to challenge it.

But then Imogen finally gave voice and the moment shattered like glass. 'Sister Decima is dead. Perished along with all our kindred. There were no survivors of Sanctuary 101.' She made the statement a command.

'I beg to differ,' Verity replied. With deft, practised motions, the hospitaller opened the narthecium pack on her belt and produced a needle, with which she pricked the revenant's bare skin. She ran the needle into a slot on the auspex she carried and let its internal cogitator work, whispering a litany of operation to it. The device gave a chime and she held it up for all to see. 'A blood match. I swear on the Golden Throne, she is Decima.'

'I... am Decima,' mumbled the ragged woman.

'What she was is irrelevant,' Tegas insisted. 'What she is... is a necron plaything.' He glared at the canoness. 'Ask her something, milady. Go on. Ask her a question that only an Adepta Sororitas of this convent could answer.'

Sepherina's glower shifted and she eyed the weeping woman. 'Calm yourself,' she told her, 'and tell me the name of the abbess who commanded here.'

Miriya saw Decima's face tighten in pain as she tried to dredge up the fragment of recollection. It seemed to wound her just to make the attempt.

'That...' She paused, panting for breath. 'I don't...' Abruptly, she gave a savage jerk as if swatting away an invisible insect. '*Shut up!*' she hissed.

'Who do you speak to?' Verity asked gently.

'I don't know!' shouted the woman. Then she looked to Sepherina and repeated the words with deep sorrow. 'I don't know. Her name... is lost to me. So much is lost to me. I am all that is left.'

'Convenient,' Tegas muttered.

'They cut it from her,' Verity interposed. She pointed up, at scarred skin over the revenant's skull. 'We cannot know what they took.'

'Or what they left behind,' said the questor darkly.

Miriya's patience for the adept was running thin and she shoved him with the muzzle of her bolter. 'Run your mouth some more. I dare you.'

Sepherina stepped forwards, ignoring a warning look from Sister Imogen, and ran her hand over the woman's face. 'Is it possible?' she wondered aloud. 'A single survivor? Alive after all this time?'

'He did not want to kill us all at once, milady,' came the reply.

'Who?'

'The cryptek. Ossuar. The one who tormented me.'

Nearby, Sister Pandora ventured a nod. 'Human experimentation. The xenos abused her flesh so it could better learn how to kill us.'

'I am... so sorry...' said the woman, trembling beneath Sepherina's touch. She was barely holding herself together, and Miriya could see Verity's eyes were wet with sympathetic emotion.

'Decima.' At last the canoness said the name. 'How can we know she is you? The adept, curse him, speaks the truth.' Sepherina held up her chaplet-dagger. 'It would be safer to kill you.'

'It matters little now,' came the reply, thick with emotion. 'I weep for us all. We are all dead.'

'Her mind is broken,' said Imogen. 'Let me end her, mistress. I will make it quick. A kindness.'

Sepherina raised her hand to the Sister Superior, but did not break eye contact with the revenant woman. 'Do you mean to threaten us?'

She gave a slow shake of the head, her gaze dropping until she was glaring at Questor Tegas. 'I mean to tell you,' she began. 'His kind are to blame. I watched them come, watched them cut open the desert and the rock as if it were theirs to toy with as they pleased. Before... Before, the machines were sleeping. Once before they had awoken and fought one another, and we died in the crossfire.'

Tegas said nothing, his synthetic face impassive.

'His kind have disturbed the machines.' She pointed a skeletal finger at the questor. 'The ones in the canyon, his servants... I studied them, tried to stop them. Killed one or two... But I could not prevent it. They have drawn the attention of the necrontyr, stirred them from stupor and indifference... Just as the Sisterhood did before. ' She shuddered. 'We paid with blood then. The cost will be the same now.'

'If that is so,' Tegas said, refusing to remain silent. 'Then why now, hybrid? What have you done to stir up the hornet's nest?'

'Not I,' she insisted. '*You* did this. You should have stayed away. The cryptek... He ignored all the clumsy digging in the sands, as long as it was of no consequence. But no longer.' She looked back at the canoness. 'Heed my warning. The machines will rise from their stasis-tombs. Many more of them. They will not return to their sleep until this world is devoid of all alien life.'

'They are the aliens!' Imogen snarled. 'Not us!'

'Not so,' said the woman, shaking her head. 'Not *here*.'

Her words brought the chapel back to the long silence once more. At length, Sepherina turned away, retracting the blade into her chaplet. The canoness glanced at Sister Imogen. 'Send a message to the *Tybalt*. Tell the captain to return here immediately.'

'The ship has been gone for several days,' noted the Sister Superior. 'They may have already entered warp space.'

'Even if they are still within the Kavir system, a vox-signal may not reach them in time,' added Pandora. The party dispatched to reconsecrate the convent had no astropath among them. The Sisterhood were well-known for their abhorrence of even the sanctioned slave-psychics used by the Adeptus Terra, and it had been a point of honour that no such being would be among them on this hallowed duty.

'Send it anyway,' Sepherina told them. 'The Imperium must be warned. Inquisitor Hoth was gravely mistaken. The necrons are at large on Sanctuary 101.'

'They never left,' mumbled Decima.

Imogen eyed her. 'If this one is to live for the moment, then we need to know all we can about the threats we face here. She must tell us what she knows.' The Sister Superior shared a look with the canoness that only Miriya seemed to notice. A silent communication passed between them, and the Sororitas wondered once more what they had yet to speak of to the rest of the Sisterhood.

'Her mind is damaged, anyone can see that,' said Pandora. 'How can we know truth from illusion?'

'There is a way,' Verity replied.

The great machine moved about the business of warfare, gantries and rails interlocking so that carrier frames could approach the great cog-shaped embarkation deck and deposit their loads.

Ossuar tuned his expressionless iron face up to watch as an Annihilation Barge detached from a magnetic clamp and floated on humming impellors to the metal decking. The nemesor rode down with it, and he was dressed in his opulent battle robes and chain-tresses. The gold and silver of his matched battle gauntlets glittered in the half-light.

Khaygis's hooded gaze found the cryptek and the warlord graced him with a nod. 'Come to watch, harbinger?' Before he could reply, the general continued. 'Stay out of my way. You have interfered enough.'

Ossuar bowed slightly, spending his irritation in the tight grip he kept on his abyssal staff. The black rod whispered with power, but he kept it in check. Even the smallest exhibition of defiance here and now could have dangerous consequences. It was better to let the braggart strut about and have his posturing. At the end of the matter, when the humans had been exterminated, Khaygis would grow bored again and drift back to slumber... And Ossuar would be in charge once more.

When the first warning had come – when it had been made clear that the idiot organics were playing with the scroll they had happened upon, ignorant of the great powers it contained – the cryptek had sent out a phalanx of warrior drones with simple kill orders and assumed that would be enough. His error had been to underestimate the ingenuity of the humans, specifically the females who against all odds had turned his attack back upon itself, and infiltrated the complex.

Ossuar would never admit the blame for that rested with him. He knew it, but he would never voice it where Khaygis could hear. Any admission of error would be taken by the general and used as a knife to carve him with. He could not afford to weaken his position, so it was with cloaked resentment that he allowed the nemesor to strut and snarl.

It was the survivor that troubled him more than anything else. He had done so very much to take the female to the ragged edges of her body's endurance, cut her and modified her and made her his great experiment. When she escaped from confinement all those cycles ago, he had almost been able to process something akin to disappointment.

He felt – if it was possible for Ossuar to actually *feel* anything – betrayed by her. The cryptek had let her live after all her fellow humans had been culled, and all he had asked was to observe her pain and catalogue it. He had learned much about the manner in which organics operated, recovering vast quantities of data that had been considered irrelevant during The Uplifting. Then, the Stargods had promised the necrontyr they would never again need to consider organiform matters... But that had been one lie among all the others.

Ossuar's work was important. He and his fellow psychomancers were the harbingers of despair, and to fulfil that title they needed to understand pain in all its forms. The female had been of great help in that regard.

But she had fled, and the cryptek had reluctantly closed the book on that research. He had never computed the possibility she might have still been *alive* down there on the desert world, and certainly not after all this time. The odds were too great.

The humans seemed to have a knack for defying probability. Ossuar idly wondered if he could set up an experiment to test that theory; he would need a lot of disposable organics for it to work.

Another carrier halted and disgorged a fresh cohort of drones, ready to board a waiting Ghost Ark. There were now two battle-strength phalanxes of warriors armed with charged gauss flayers, several of them still bearing the command mark of the Atun dynasty. This great complex and the Dolmen Gate at its heart had once been an important base for the Atun, before the war broke up their dominions and left them fragmented. It had been easy for the Sautekh to take the Obsidian Moon for themselves sixty million years later. In time, every necron bearing the mark of the Atun would be re-branded as Sautekh. Inwardly that was already so, as insidious abjuration programs crafted by the

Stormlord's cybermagii had already reset their allegiance to the great Imotekh.

The warriors were joined by a unit of immortals. These were necrons of a more powerful build, with greater battle-zone survivability, shock troopers armed with twin-chamber gauss blasters or the crackling power of tesla carbines. The nemesor's own lychguard were also there, including the pair that had menaced Ossuar in Khaygis's crypt. There was more than enough for the task at hand, he estimated, much more. And yet, the general's army was still not yet complete. Other transport frames were coming closer, some bearing heavy autonomous weapons and even a Monolith.

'Do you think the humans will be so great a threat as to require this much firepower?' He asked the question as Khaygis strode past him. 'The organics have a term – *overkill*.'

The general halted and his emerald eye band took the cryptek's measure. 'I have heard of it,' he admitted. 'I should like to observe it first-hand.' Khaygis advanced on the other necron. 'This deed will fulfil more than one purpose, Ossuar. Perhaps, if your consciousness existed outside of the abstract of your theorems and experiments, you would be able to process that fact.' He gestured at the assembled ranks of drone-soldiers. 'This time, I will wipe out every organic on the planet.'

'Events repeat themselves,' offered the cryptek.

'Negative,' replied the warlord. 'This time there will be none of them left for you to keep as a plaything, no pets left for you to let run wild and unchecked. Nothing but ashes. Not even a trace, a fragment, a splinter.'

Ossuar raised a taloned hand. 'With respect,' he began, 'it remains important that I be allowed to research the organics. The Stormlord himself ordered that I do so.'

'The Stormlord ordered that to be rid of you from his war fleet,' Khaygis shot back. 'How else could Imotekh divest himself of your peculiar obsessions?'

'It is not an obsession,' Ossuar insisted. 'It is science!'

The general turned and sent a summons towards one of

the new arrivals. 'Justify it to yourself as you will. But the humans will die, and the termination of that broken little toy of yours will be foremost among them.'

'I would prefer otherwise,' said the cryptek, trailing after the nemesor as he walked away. 'I have invested much in her... At least, allow me to recover the implants inside the female for repurposing–'

Khaygis did not answer him. Instead, the warlord waited as the soldier he had called upon approached and bowed. Ossuar recognised the configuration of the new arrival's wargear; the hyperspatial waveguides etched into the dull steel armour, the airstream lines of the metallic skull and the dark gaze of the solemn optics within. All these things were characteristic of a deathmark, the marksmen assassins of the great dynasties.

The sniper bowed to his commander. Across his back was the slender, lethal shape of a synaptic disintegrator rifle, the signature weapon of the necrontyr's most deadly killers. Khaygis offered the deathmark a glassy bead, a data-jewel containing information on the sniper's assigned target. The bead activated, displaying a DNA trace and energy signature that the cryptek identified as belonging to his test subject.

'With respect,' Ossuar ventured, 'would it not make a more efficient use of forces to assign the deathmark to eliminate the human commander instead?'

The sniper silently absorbed the data and returned the bead to Khaygis. 'No,' said the general. 'The hybrid you made offends me. And there is another reason.'

'Which is?'

The nemesor gave him a cursory glance. 'Because you wish it.' Khaygis nodded to the assassin. 'Go now.'

The deathmark bowed once more, and the dimensional matrix in its armour glowed brightly. The sniper became insubstantial, ephemeral, before vanishing entirely. Unstuck in space-time, the assassin now existed in a hyperspace oubliette, a micro-dimension out of synch with this universe. From there, the deathmark would track the woman and be drawn to her, waiting in nothingness until he was ready to execute his sanction.

Khaygis looked back at him. 'A lesson must be learned. Not just by the humans, but by you, harbinger. You will be reminded of your place.' His grim visage loomed. 'We are necron. We ascended above these meat-things when the fleshtime was forgotten. But you still dally with them, and it repulses me. I will break you of this addiction.'

'You do not understand,' Ossuar replied. 'The human organics are not a real threat. They present no danger to the great works to repair the Dolmen Gate.'

The general's manner shifted, and his eyes flashed. Khaygis stiffened. He was not one to have his edicts questioned. Resolute ire built behind his words as he spoke again. 'Arrogance brought you to this place, psychomancer. If your skills were not so rare, I would have dissipated your consciousness on the Stormlord's command even before the Timeless Dream! Had you adhered to the letter of Imotekh's commands instead of nurturing desires for power above your station, these other humans would have never been allowed to set foot on the planet! Your pitiful attempts to conceal the depth of your illicit works have been fruitless. I know the full scope of what you have done. There will be censure for your acts, Ossuar. Know that.' He turned away, signalling the activation of the portals. 'But first I will correct your mistakes.'

Zara brought what was needed from the medicae tents set up in the convent courtyard, and as the Sisters Militant looked on with their doubts clear upon their aspect, Verity and the other hospitaller set up the monitorium units.

Imogen had found them a room inside the central donjon, what had once been a chamber for storing prayer books. The space had only high, unreachable slit-windows thick with silt and a single doorway. Outside, Sisters Helena and Danae stood in the corridor with weapons drawn and ready; within, the canoness stood with Miriya and Cassandra as her guardians, watching like a hawk.

Decima sat in a reading chair of old, distressed oak, unmoving, barely breathing. The business of disarming her, of persuading the woman to give up the weapons concealed beneath her cloak, had not been easy. It was only Verity's steady, careful entreaty to her that had finally convinced the revenant survivor to agree – that, and Sister Imogen's departure.

Typically, Imogen's blunt manner had been at the forefront, and finally Canoness Sepherina had ordered her to stand down and convey Tegas and his party away, to a place where they could be put under house arrest. If she remained close by, it was clear that Decima would never relax. She feared the Sister Superior's intentions towards her, and rightly so. Verity did not doubt that Decima would have joined her long-dead comrades already, had Imogen been in command here. For now, the Sister Superior had been charged with imprisoning the questor and preparing the convent's defences for the threat of attack.

'What kind of blade is this?' Sepherina asked the question as she turned Decima's night-black sword over in her hands. 'The metal of the grip and the pommel is unlike anything I have ever seen.'

'The edge cuts through steel as if it were smoke,' Cassandra told the veteran. 'I saw her use it on the necrons. It is some product of alien science.'

'Yet it weighs next to nothing.' The canoness made a slow practice swing with the weapon, and the air crackled quietly in its wake. 'Where did it come from?' she asked.

Decima blinked. 'I don't remember. I think I took it from them. It was a long time ago. When I escaped.'

Sepherina handed the sword off to Cassandra, who took it as if it were coated in poison. 'It is important that you remember,' she told the ragged woman. 'Your life depends on it.'

'Ours too, I think,' noted Miriya.

'Don't be afraid,' Verity told her, as she connected a thin wire to an auspex, then the far end to a probe disc she placed on Decima's throat. 'You're safe here.'

'No,' Decima told her, with chilling firmness. 'None of us are safe here. They came once, they will come again. There will be no errors this time. They learn.'

The canoness found another reading chair where it had fallen, and righted it, dragging it to set herself down at arm's length from the other woman. 'Decima,' she began, 'if that is who and what you are… You will remember for us.' Sepherina gestured at the walls. 'Our records of what transpired here are full of blank spaces and voids, half-facts and missing time.'

'Yes,' breathed the revenant. 'I know.'

'I need to understand,' the canoness went on. 'I need to be sure of what you are, beyond all shadow of a doubt. Are you the woman Sister Verity believes you to be, or some cleverly constructed proxy that speaks with her voice and apes her manner?'

'I have no answer to give you,' came the reply.

'For your sake,' said Sepherina, signalling Miriya and Cassandra, 'I hope that is not so.' The two Battle Sisters raised their bolters and took aim. Miriya felt reluctance drag on her a moment, but she pushed it away. *Orders were orders*. If the proof Verity was looking for could not be found, then Miriya would put a bolt-shell through Decima's heart, and Cassandra another through her skull.

'Rest now,' Verity was saying, as she held an injector bulb at Decima's throat. 'This will ease you into the memory.'

The injector touched her flesh and Decima went rigid, her bony limbs stiffening. 'Don't speak to me,' she hissed, glaring past the Sister into the middle distance. 'I won't stay silent for you! I won't!'

'She talks to ghosts,' Zara said, with trepidation. 'To voices only she can hear.'

'Perhaps we need to listen to them as well,' Verity shot back, gently soothing the other woman's distress.

Decima slumped as the drug from the injector passed through her. The revenant's eyes lost focus, and her arms slackened, hands falling into her lap.

'Is it done?' said the canoness.

Verity nodded. 'She is on the edges of a trance-state, lulled by the philtre. She won't harm herself.'

Sepherina leaned closer. 'Hear me. You will tell the tale of what happened here. Spare no detail. How did you survive the attack on Sanctuary 101? How have you managed to live in the wilderness for more than ten years? What did the xenos do to you? Answer me.'

++Confess to them++ said the Watcher. ++*Tell them the truth of how you failed so utterly. And when you are done, they will execute you*++

The voice seemed to boom off the confined walls all around her. She blinked, peering at the faces of the Battle Sisters. Couldn't they hear it? It was so loud, so strident. It was impossible to ignore. How could they be deaf to it?

++*You failed. You know how they punish failure*++

'I failed...' The words left her lips.

The canoness eyed her. 'Explain.'

++*Tell them and you will die for it*++ screamed the voice. ++*You can still escape, kill these ones and flee, back to the desert where it is safe*++

Her hand gave a reflexive twitch, and she felt betrayed by the impulse.

The Watcher seized on the moment. ++*Out there you cannot die, out there you will be free to hide and watch these ones perish when the attack comes, you alone will survive again*++

A dark emotion took hold in her chest. 'I survived,' she went on, sickened at the horrible, inescapable truth of that statement.

With care, the woman called Decima pressed her torn nails into the palms of her hands until they pierced the skin and drew thin rivulets of blood. The pain provided a focus, and it made the voice turn distant.

At first, the words came with hesitation and care. She cautioned herself and edited her speech before uttering it, but from moment to moment that began to change. The pain, the buzzing burn from the small cuts on her hands, was magnified through the echo chamber of her memory. She remembered *hard*, the terrors of capture and confinement, of escape and evasion, all of them returning to her as little by little Decima allowed the floodgates to open.

The other women fell silent as she told them of the first attack. 'There was no warning. They came just before the dawn, destroying the power plant. In the gloom, they hunted the Sisterhood down every corridor and passage.'

'The necrons,' prompted the canoness.

She nodded. 'Skeletons of steel... I saw a...'

++*A sickly green glow following them wherever they went. Silver cutting blades*++

Decima heard the words and could not be certain if she had said them. And suddenly she remembered a face that had been lost to her for years. Elspeth. Her dear Sister, her confidante and close friend.

++*Clever Elspeth, who was good at regicide and games of tall card*++ The Watcher was very far away, but not enough to go unheard. ++*Pious Elspeth who sometimes mumbled the catechisms in her sleep*++

She shook her head, bringing up one blood-marked hand to grind the heel of her palm into her eye-socket. 'Iron skulls,' she managed. 'A baleful gaze like burning emeralds. We had never seen anything like them.'

The others were hanging on her every word. The canoness studied her, and for an instant, her face flowed like wax and she took on the aspect of Decima's own commander, a decade now dead and gone. She heard her words rise up from the depths of memory, and for a blessed moment the Watcher was blotted out.

'The artefact must never fall to the xenos.' She repeated the order that had been given to her on that final day.

Sepherina reacted as if she had be struck, jerking back so much that the reading chair she sat upon scraped across the stone floor. 'What did you say?'

'This is my last command to you,' said the revenant, a faraway look in her eyes, her tone thick with emotion. 'Go now. Take it and go.'

'Take what?' whispered Cassandra, from the side of her mouth. 'What artefact?'

Miriya could only guess; but then she caught Verity's eye and saw a measure of understanding in the hospitaller.

The canoness held up the blade of her hand to silence them before anyone else could speak. 'Who said that to you?' she demanded.

'You did,' said the ragged woman. 'She did. Agnes. The canoness.' Her bloodied hands came up and she held them in the position one might adopt if they were holding a newborn child. 'I cradled it,' she went on. 'Against the storm and the fire, I was mother to it. Protector.' The hands began to tremble and they dropped away.

Colour darkened the woman's face. She slumped forwards, and her manner shifted as Miriya watched a great shame overcome her.

'Where…' Sepherina stopped, and glanced around at the others. She was hesitating, afraid to complete her question within their earshot. Finally, the canoness' gaze crossed that of Verity, and her tone grew firm again. 'Where is it now?'

It was a long time before the revenant answered, in a small, sorrowful voice. 'My disgrace is eternal. He Upon The Throne sees it still. I can never escape it.'

Sepherina shook her head in frustration. 'Where?' she insisted, heedless of the other woman's distress.

'I was unable to complete my mission. They came and took us both. I expected to die…' A shudder passed through her thin frame. 'The cryptek had other intentions for my flesh.' Suddenly she was shivering, even though the air in the store room was close and warm. She began to whimper and mutter in low, almost inaudible tones.

'The alien broke her mind,' said Verity. She glanced at Zara, who looked up from the auspex and returned a grave nod. 'But did not destroy it.'

'The power of faith can endure much,' said Miriya. 'The Emperor protected something in her.'

The canoness' brow furrowed. 'How did you escape?'

'The Watcher told me how,' she admitted. The name meant nothing to any of them. 'I fled into the desert, and I survived. Alone with only the voice.' She tapped a torn finger on her temple.

'She hears voices we cannot,' Cassandra repeated quietly.

'Is it any wonder?' said Verity. 'Surviving alone out in the desert wilderness, recovering from torture and experimentation.' The hospitaller gently took the revenant's hands and dressed the self-inflicted wounds there. 'Her persona must have fragmented and crumbled as she struggled to stay alive and search…' Verity looked at the canoness. 'For that which she lost?'

'Take care, nursemaid,' said Sepherina, ice forming on the words.

'But she's right, isn't she?' Miriya let her bolter drop from her shoulder-ready stance. 'Ever since we landed on this dust ball, you and Sister Imogen have been looking for something. This is not about the necrons, or the dead, or Hoth and Tegas and whatever secret pacts they may have made. You have hidden something from us, milady. And since the very start of the pilgrimage, I would warrant.'

Verity nodded at her Sister's statement. 'What could be so important?' she asked. She did not demand, or insist that Sepherina answer her – and yet, the compulsion to reply crackled in the air.

Slowly, the canoness got to her feet and studied their faces in turn. Her hand twitched close to the butt of her holstered pistol, and her stony, unreadable expression returned.

But only for a moment. By degrees, the hard, unchanging aspect she showed them disintegrated, and Sepherina showed them truth. She looked stricken, like the lost orphan girl she once had been, like they *all* had once been.

Verity felt a jag of sorrow as, for the first time, she gained some sense of the great burden that the canoness had been silently shouldering.

'A lie has been told,' Sepherina began. 'A great gift was stolen from us in this place, twelve years ago. An artefact of exalted significance, something priceless and irreplaceable. Lost by pure chance in the xenos attack.' She looked down at Decima, who hung her head low, mouthing a prayer.

'A relic?' asked Cassandra.

'Aye,' The canoness nodded. 'This secret is known only to a few of the highest-ranked abbesses and certain members of the Sisterhood. I have borne this burden ever since Hoth first told us of the loss of Sanctuary 101. It has been my singular onus since then, and now you will all be sworn into the same oath, on pain of death.' Sepherina waited for them to nod their wary agreement before she went on. 'It was deemed that it would travel the galaxy, making a pilgrimage to every convent, holdfast and citadel of the Order of Our Martyred Lady. No matter how remote or how far from the axis of the Core Worlds. It was ordered so, to bring a moment of light to all places we called ours.'

Verity had heard of such things; while most pilgrimages of Imperial artefacts and saintly relics required that devotees cross space to come to them, there were some shrines that were constantly in motion, aboard ships or with cadres of preachers and missionaria soldiers to protect them.

But what had happened on Sanctuary 101? What had been within these walls when the necrons had struck?

'*The Hammer and Anvil*,' said Sepherina, and she spoke the name as if it were agony to do so.

Miriya, Cassandra, and the other Battle Sisters went white with shock, and Decima let out a faint sob. Their shock was palpable.

Zara frowned. 'I... do not know that name,' she admitted.

'It is an object sacred to the daughters of Saint Katherine, the founder of their sect,' Verity told her, nodding at Sepherina and the others. 'The nature of it will never be revealed to us, or to anyone else outside their Order. But I have heard the name, and I know that it is of great value to them.' Verity recalled the stories about *The Hammer and Anvil*. Some said it was a weapon of great power created by the Emperor himself during the time of the Horus Heresy, capable of blinding suns; perhaps a great storehouse of cosmic knowledge without rival among any species, human or xenos; or a device capable of shifting the flow of time itself, built by a rogue caste of technologians employed by the apostate lord Goge Vandire.

Cassandra turned on the canoness, her eyes flashing. 'How can this be?' she spat. 'The relic is on Ophelia VII, in our shrinehold!'

'No,' Sepherina told her. 'That is the fiction told to the galaxy at large. In reality, it has been in motion for the last four hundred years, secretly crossing and re-crossing the space lanes as it visited every place we hold sacred...' She trailed off. 'Until it came here.'

'And this was done without the knowledge of the wider Sisterhood?' Miriya asked.

Sepherina nodded. 'Private ceremonies were held in each place, as blessings were made. It was done in secret so that the relic would not be threatened.' She frowned. 'There are many who would wish to possess it.' The canoness reached into a pocket concealed in her robe and returned with a small, oval pict-slate. 'This image is all that remains.'

The display showed a container made of heavy, starship-grade metals, inscribed with runes and wards, carved symbols of the Sororitas spread across the surface. Decima's hand went to her mouth when she saw it, harsh recognition etched across her features.

'It is lost,' she moaned. 'I failed...'

'It is *not*,' said Verity, snatching the pict-slate from Sepherina's hand. 'It is not lost. I saw this object.' The closer she looked, the more she became certain.

Miriya saw it too and gave a silent nod of agreement.

'Where?' Sepherina demanded. 'Speak, for Throne's sake!'

A grey, dust-caked metal drum etched with a fleur-de-lys. The memory of it snapped into hard focus in Verity's thoughts. 'Ossuar... The necron tormentor. I saw that container in his laboratorium. What you seek is up there inside the Obsidian Moon.'

Sister Imogen placed them in the cell-crypts, one member of the questor's team in a compartment, each of them separated by one empty cell, with a local-range countermeasures transmitter set up in the corridor to make it difficult for them to engage in wireless communication. Similarly, the acerbic woman had left Battle Sisters patrolling the corridor outside, watching for any of the Mechanicus adepts who might have dared to use a mechadendrite or laser beam to connect to one of their fellows.

Tegas had weighed the options, judging if an attack against their captors would work, and the probabilities returned to him were less than favourable. He elected to offer no resistance for the moment, and Lumik and the others followed his example.

Instead, he decided to play a longer game. For all the things that had been done to offend the Sisterhood, it was only acts of heresy that they would kill for without hesitation, and Tegas would never betray the Throne. Sepherina and Imogen, for all their stern snarls and righteous anger, would not murder him out of hand. He was alive because they wanted him to face what they considered his misdeeds before the High Lords of Terra. It would never occur to them that perhaps some of those self-same High Lords were complicit in what was going on in the Kavir System.

He decided he would wait and look for an opportunity; but Tegas didn't expect to see it so very soon.

'A great gift was stolen from us in this place, twelve years ago. An artefact of great significance, something priceless and irreplaceable. Lost by pure chance in the xenos attack.' Sepherina's voice came to him on a narrow bandwidth that the crude Sororitas jammer had no hopes of blocking. It was being transmitted from a microscopic surveillance probe no bigger

than a sand-fly. In the moments before Imogen had turned her guns on him, Tegas had released the miniscule robot from a pod in his arm. Currently, it was hiding in a crevice on Sister Cassandra's power armour, the crackle of static over the transmission indicating to the questor that it was close to the Battle Sister's backpack microfusion generator. He ordered the probe to crawl into a position where its sensors could better relay the ongoing conversation.

Now Sepherina was talking about secrets and clandestine pilgrimages, and Tegas's interest was piqued.

Then she said the name of the relic, and unbidden, the questor's emotive emulator gave him a kick of adrenal reaction. *The Hammer and Anvil*. He knew of it; like a million other relics and legendary items from the deep past, the Adeptus Mechanicus had a file on the object. It was inconclusive, little more than a list of possibilities, but it was undeniably tempting.

The revelation made immediate sense to him. All this time, and he had been labouring under the impression that the Sororitas wanted nothing more than to bury their dead and make melancholy speeches about the victims of necron aggression... But they were here for the same reason he was, in search of a glittering prize.

If the Sororitas relic was in the Kavir System, then Tegas's quest had just gained a new and exciting objective. There was still time to salvage this mission, still time to turn it to his advantage and return home not only with Inquisitor Hoth's gratitude but also an artefact that would lead him straight to exalted rank and high office on Mars.

Necron weapons and a fabled, sacred item of lost-tech. It was a bounty worth risking everything for... And if the Sisters perished in the winning of it, then that would be a tragedy he would have to endure.

Tegas granted himself leave to do something human, and smiled as he listened on.

CHAPTER TWELVE

Uriahi Zeyn ran a thick-fingered hand through his unruly hair and pulled it back into a tight, high ponytail, binding it up with a brass wire as he climbed the spiral staircase inside the watchtower.

Each stone of the steps was engraved with words from one of the verses from *The Book of Atticus*, and he whispered them to himself from memory as he rose into the dimness. There was scant light inside the tower other than the faint pre-dawn glow that ventured in through the gun slits in the stone walls. The deacon emerged on the battlement tier and took a moment to pause, drinking in the sound of the work-gangers going about their duties below him, at the foot of the shield wall.

They did not sing, because the canoness had ordered them to maintain a sense of order and quietude. Zeyn disagreed with that – the work was a sacred task, and being unable to raise voice in the duty of it seemed somehow negligent. He loved the hymnals and a day without them was like being denied water or air. The only sounds were the occasional mutter of the men and the steady clink of metal on stone as they cut and placed the blocks that would rebuild the collapsed segment of the wall. Floating lume-globes drifting over the heads of the workers offered weak illumination, but enough that Zeyn could see them all and measure the pace of their efforts.

He wanted to sing with them, but Sepherina forbade it. The thought brought a grimace to his lips. The God-Emperor had so much to watch over, he mused. How was He supposed to turn His gaze this way, if not by hearing the songs of His most devoted?

The workgangers saw Zeyn and they all put on a spurt of fresh exertion, and made sure not to meet his gaze. The deacon's electro-whip hummed in its holster, and there was not a single man or woman among them who had not felt the lash of it. Zeyn folded his thick arms and scanned the group, searching for any infraction he could punish.

He counted the shift a man short.

The whip came out and uncoiled, a neon-bright streamer twitching in his grip. 'You.' The preacher pointed at the nearest man to him. 'The work party is shy a soul. Tell me where he is–'

He had no need to say the words *or face the whip*. The man pointed up at the higher tiers of the guard tower.

'Went there, he did,' came the nervous reply. 'Went for water, padre.'

Zeyn nodded down to the flagstones below, to where one of the Sister Hospitallers was moving among the labourers with a jug. 'There's enough here.' The deacon gave the worried workganger a threatening look that promised censure if this proved to be a falsehood, then he turned on his heel and returned to the spiral stairs. Careful to walk as silently as his bulk would carry him, Zeyn climbed to the very top of the minaret.

The slender tower was designed with a gun post at the apex, where a heavy weapon could be emplaced and give a full sweep of the outlands beyond the convent's walls, but the damage suffered in the xenos attack had collapsed part of the structure, opening the tower to the air and ripping away its easterly battlements.

The deacon had been a soldier in the Imperial Guard before he had gone to his holy calling, and he had lost none of the military training the instructors had beaten into him a good thirty years earlier. It was these skills that spotted the makeshift tripwire arranged by the roof hatch. An oil can dangled from a cord, a handful of pebbles inside it. The crude device would have been enough to warn anyone on the roof they were about to be discovered.

With care, Zeyn made safe the alarm line and slowly went the rest of the way. He emerged on the roof to find a workganger in a leather vest bent down over what appeared to be a pict-slate. A stylus in one hand moved in swift little jerks of motion, as lines of ideograms were entered into the device's memory.

The deacon let the lash out once again, and cleared his throat.

The man started and jerked to his feet, grimly holding on to the slate, his other hand fumbling at the catches on his vest. 'Beg... Beg pardon,' he began. The glow of the whip made his face pale and ghostly.

'Sloth,' Zeyn began, measuring out the word. 'Sloth is one of the aspects of a man of low character. He lets his fellows do their share and shirks his. Thinks he's better than the rest...' The deacon had given this lecture and the accompanying discipline a hundred times, and was about to again – but something in the worker's manner stopped him.

The pict-slate. The slight man gripped it like it was his lifeline.

Zeyn was adroit with the use of the electro-whip, enough that he could strip a single leaf from a tree branch. He flicked his wrist and the tip snapped up, cutting a line of blue fire over the workganger's hand. The man screamed and the slate went flying, spinning away cross the flagstones.

The deacon bent to recover it. The device's display was covered with symbols that he couldn't read, coded numeric runes in long, meaningless strings. 'What is this?' he demanded, searching his memory for the worker's face, his story.

It came to him: Jonah Sijue, an indentured citizen working

a six-solar contract with the Imperial Church, as payment for a feast day infraction. He was a stonecutter, and he should have been hard at work, lasing rock into perfect cubes for the new wall.

What Jonah Sijue certainly was *not* was a man who had the wealth to own a device of such fine manufacture as this slate, nor was he a man of such learning who would be able to parse a complex text-code like this one.

Sijue's face lost its dull, cow-like blankness and grew an expression of cold, steady focus. 'Turn it over,' he told the deacon, without fear.

Zeyn did so, and there on the back of the device was a symbol stamped into the metal. A capital letter ringed by wards in High Gothic; an 'I' bracketed by crossed spears.

'You know what that means,' said Sijue, rubbing at the wound on the back of his hand. 'Now return it to me.' Gone was the obedient, servile nature the man had shown on their previous encounters.

'The Inquisition,' Zeyn had to say it aloud just to be certain of it. 'You... You are not of the ordos! You are a helot, a drudge doing the Church's work!'

Sijue drew a disc of dark metal from inside the lining of his vest, and it unfolded into the shape of a holdout pistol. A silencer baffle shrouded the muzzle. 'Clever toy, isn't it?' remarked the man. 'Like a logica game. Something too clever for you to meddle with, priest.' He gestured at the slate. 'Give it back, now. Give it back and we'll forget all of this. I'll go back to work. And so will you.'

Zeyn wasn't a fool. Oh, the Sisterhood had kept their motivations close and spoken little of what happened on Sanctuary 101 before this reconsecration – but he had heard the stories, the rumours. The workgangers spoke freely when they thought he was not listening. They talked of many things, some ideals fanciful and unlikely, others less so. Some said the Ordo Xenos were enamoured of this planet and wanted it for themselves. Some said they were being watched by the Inquisition at every turn here.

He hadn't done anything to disabuse the workgangers of these beliefs. Paranoid men tended to work harder than those at ease with their lot. But Zeyn had found it hard to imagine that the exalted guardians of Imperial integrity would be drawn to somewhere so remote and so desolate as this world.

He thought differently now, however.

'Put away the whip and give me the slate,' said Sijue. 'I won't ask you a third time.'

Sudden heat boiled at the back of Zeyn's thoughts. 'You will kill me to keep this secret? Whatever master you serve, you do so in darkness!' He took a warning step forwards, and the tiny gun muzzle rose with it. 'In the name of the God-Emperor, I refuse!'

'I serve Him as much as you do,' Sijue replied coldly. 'As much as any of these fools or those sanctimonious nuns. But there are some things more important than prayers or–'

He never finished the sentence. From below, down on the broken wall, a man cried out and the voice broke the pre-dawn hush with such abruptness that they were both distracted for a split-second. Sijue reflexively glanced away, and Zeyn reacted without thought, snapping the whip once again.

He caught Sijue across the chest and face, and the smaller man spun back in a cluster of sparks, howling. The deacon ran to him and batted him down, one heavy punch from his ham-sized fist enough to disarm and put him on the floor. The gun clattered away, as the wind began to pick up. Particles of loose sand hissed across the stones.

Warily, Zeyn peered over the lip of the tower and looked down, careful to keep the injured man at the edge of his vision. He saw the workers breaking rank and scrambling to climb back over the half-repaired wall, some of them in such haste they were shoving one another aside in panic.

What was putting them to flight? His grip stiffened on the whip's handle as he glared out past them, to the open, rock-strewn sands beyond the convent walls.

Out there, in the half-dark and the low clouds of dust, he saw what looked like fireflies, lines of them bobbing and dancing as their phosphors glowed; but then they began to resolve into other shapes, the green glimmering moving in steady, careful motions, radiating out from eye-sockets in metal skulls.

The swarm of lights broke apart and changed, the trick of it as clever and dangerous as Sijue's secret gun.

He heard the man curse under his breath and speak a prayer to Holy Terra as he caught sight of the same thing. 'They c-come,' he blurted, his manner shifting once more, this time into raw fear. 'If we see them, they are already surrounding us!'

Zeyn rounded on him. 'Did your ordos masters do this?' he demanded. 'Are they here because you brought it on us?'

When Sijue looked up at him, his eyes were blank with absolute terror. 'I have no wish to learn the answer.' Something made a bony crunch inside the man's mouth and Sijue lolled back, his eyes rolling to whites, a toxic pink froth gathering on his lips. His chest stuttered and was still.

The deacon looked away and saw lines of metal soldiers moving inexorably into the glow of the work-lamps, silent and purposeful.

Khaygis was disappointed.

He had yet to be challenged by the meat, on whatever worlds he faced them, in whatever form they opposed the might of his armies. Each time he awoke from the sarcophagus-sleep, he hoped that the next battle would be the one to truly test him – but that day had not yet come.

And even now, as he watched the phalanxes of his warriors and immortals advancing on the human outpost, he doubted that the organics who fled before their march would prove to be a worthwhile foe. He wondered if he ever would meet an enemy he could consider worthy, and thought it unlikely. After all, he was a soldier who had fought in the War in Heaven, once of those who had seen the Old Ones defeated in the time before the slumber. Millions of years later, and the galaxy saddened him with its inability to produce an opponent to match those he had killed so long ago.

He had been here before. It was the nemesor who had commanded the first assault on this compound, a dozen solar cycles ago. Then, fresh from the Atun pacification, it had seemed like a new test of his skills and his soldiers. The necrontyr had never faced this particular tribe of meat-being before, these females that called themselves *'Soh-ror-it-az'*, who emitted strange choral melodies as they fought, and refused to surrender.

But they died as easily as the rest. In the end, the assault on the outpost had been more an execution than a military strike. The females had been unprepared and poorly commanded. Khaygis, linked into the slave-minds of every last warrior under his authority, had flowed through their defences like liquid mercury, arriving by portal and Monolith. He had killed many with his own talons, and never been truly threatened along the way.

The humans died in their droves, not knowing what had destroyed them, unable to name it. He would ensure they would do so again, and this time he would be thorough.

Gauss flayer beams erupted in a wall of flames as the leading rank crested the broken wall, blazing into the backs of the organics who attempted to flee. Defensive gunfire from the towers and the unbroken stretches of wall answered back, and the nemesor sensed the first few shutdowns as warriors were knocked off-line by the massive kinetic impacts of ballistic rocket-shells. Even as they fell, they entered regeneration cycles, the living metal of their bodies knitting back together over their bloodless wounds. Khaygis stroked the resurrection orb at his side, hastening their return to battle with a small measure of the device's powerful essence.

The immortals, true to their name, marched undying into the teeth of the human guns and let fly with their tesla carbines. Blue-white fire reflected off their morose skull-faces as chains of living lightning leapt into the human cohort, ripping from one organic to another, gathering power from the life-force they liberated with each screaming kill.

Alarm bells tolled inside the walled outpost, and with the

great acuity of his vision band, the nemesor could pick out the arrival of more of the combatant females, a blaze of green reflecting off their space-dark battle armour. They did not rush to meet his first advance, but instead fell into defensive stances, setting up fire corridors and chokepoints.

He cocked his head. These ones were better prepared than the others had been; they had been waiting for an attack, not caught unawares by it. Perhaps they would be more of a challenge.

But that was unlikely. Khaygis turned away and transmitted a new order-meme to his forces. The constant, dusty wind picked up its tempo, and from high overhead, a new sound joined the melee.

The Tomb Blades came in fast, the scream of their repulsor drives resonating off the hillside. Resembling some strange combination of a cargo-crane's claw and a metallic throne, the flyers shone dully in the wan light. A flight of three craft, each armed with a particle beam cannon, tore down over the walls and stitched lines of crackling red-orange light across the flagstones. The beams cut black lashes into the rock, and the workgangers who did not get to cover in time were flashed to wet clouds of cinders when the fire-light touched them.

Sweeping ahead of the advancing lines of the necron warriors, the flyers hammered at the defensive positions manned by the Battle Sisters, looping in the pre-dawn air and slicing into their barricades. The warrior mechanoids wired into the command trains of the Tomb Blades were less pilots than they were components in the killing machine, there only to process the complicated strings of attack data and combat patterns. They piloted their craft dispassionately, focussed blankly on the business of breaking the morale of the defenders so that the ground forces could progress more easily.

But the God-Emperor's Sororitas were not ones to break. Years of duty, of unflinching discipline, of battle against all the foes humanity had to face made them ready to weather alien attack without hesitation.

The women who had died in Sanctuary 101 twelve years earlier perished because they had believed this world to be benign. They had allowed the desolation and the emptiness of the planet to lull them into a false sense of security – and they had paid for that with their blood, ending their lives in desperate defence of this remote outpost.

The women here now knew full well the dangers their Sisters had not seen, and they were ready for them.

As the Tomb Blades wheeled in the air and came back for another pass, a squad of Sister Danae's Retributors took position and made ready. Experienced Battle Sisters to a woman, they were specially trained in the use of heavy weapons. They considered themselves to be the hammer of the Sororitas forces.

Danae gave the command for weapons free and the Retributors cut the sky. Heavy bolters thundered, dense mass-reactive rounds blasting the necron flyers. The searing bright discharges of meltaguns joined them, throwing brief flares of stark, juddering illumination over the courtyard.

They found their target, and the first true enemy casualty was struck as a Tomb Blade erupted in fire. The pilot within was so heavily damaged that not even its inbuilt reanimation protocols could overcome the storm of shot and shell, and the flyer disintegrated into a metallic rain, clattering down over the open quad.

Particle fire answered back and claimed the lives of Battle Sisters, the kills coming so fast that they were robbed of the chance to scream. The Retributors fought harder, avenging their kindred with defiant retaliation. A second Tomb Blade was hit, colliding with the third as it struggled to maintain airspeed. Both flyers, oozing thick and acrid smoke, broke off the attack and flipped over, rolling away towards the hills and into the embrace of the echo of engine noise. Their attack blunted for the moment, they retreated to repair and regenerate.

The Sororitas regrouped and gathered up their injured while the ranks of necron warriors, steady and unhurried, continued to approach.

Her red combat cloak flaring, Sister Isabel sprinted across the courtyard as flayer beams probed towards her, blind-firing bursts of bolter shells in the direction of the alien advance.

In a strange way, she felt *relieved*. Ever since the Sisterhood had returned to Sanctuary 101, an ominous air of foreboding had hung over everything. Isabel was not the only one who had felt it; the eerie graveyard emptiness of the desert planet had weighed heavily on the minds of many of her Sisters. Every day that passed on the surface tightened the rack of tension. Each of them held the secret fear that the xenos who wiped out the first colony would return – and now they had, the terrible waiting was over. The threatened storm was breaking at last.

Silence and tedium dragged on Isabel's nerves like razors on her skin, but battle she could embrace as if it were an old friend.

Her bolter's slide snapped back as she expended the last shell in the clip, and she vaulted a low wall to drop down into cover behind the rubble of one of the destroyed statues.

Sister Ananke was close by, methodically aiming, firing, aiming, firing. She ignored the streaks of eldritch green flame that lashed at the stone around her. The pungent stink of burnt rock and fused sand soured the air. Isabel ducked and busied herself loading a fresh magazine.

'How many of them have fallen?' Isabel asked, without preamble. She scanned the enemy approach with her single cybernetic eye, drawing in target data. She counted many.

'Hard to tell,' Ananke replied, between shots. 'We put them down and they resurrect, they rise again.' She fired again. 'I swear I have killed the same ones a dozen times now.'

Isabel executed a pop-up attack and blasted an immortal back into the dust. 'Aye,' she admitted, 'they all look the same.'

With exaggerated, spindly motions, the necron machine dragged itself back to a standing position, and then walked on as if nothing had happened. Each of the immortals raked energy fire across the courtyard with each step nearer they took

Ananke followed Isabel's lead and joined her as she attacked the same target again. This time, it dropped and disappeared behind the advancing line, but it was not clear to either of them if it was down and out, or if the necron would once more rise to plague them.

'We need reinforcements,' Ananke grated into her vox-bead. 'Cutting and sniping at them won't be enough.'

Isabel said nothing. She had come from the central keep, where the raising of the alarm had sent the Battle Sisters to combat ready, each standing a post to repel the invasion. From the crackles of weapons fire coming from the battlements to the west and the south, it seemed that the wall breach before her was not the only place where the xenos were making their assault. She had no idea if there was anyone who could come to their aid; but it was clear that they did not have enough guns to hold the line for long.

'Steady your will,' came a strident voice, so loud that both Battle Sisters heard it through the vox and the air. 'Sing with me!'

A deep, bass voice bellowed out the first line of the hymn Holy Terra We Beseech Thee, and Isabel's augmetic eye caught the movement of a figure bounding over the fallen statuary.

Lit by surges of green fire, Deacon Zeyn came running like a wild man, his hair streaming out behind him, his eyes lit with fervour. In one hand he gripped an industrial laser cutter liberated from the wall rebuild, and in the other his electro-whip spun and flashed. 'Against the alien, we prevail!' he shouted, burning white light across the line of the necron advance.

Isabel saw the immortals actually slow for a moment, as if they were startled by the sudden appearance of a lone human, coming in to fight them hand-to-hand. But then, they were only machines, were they not? The unpredictable ways of men were not known fully to them.

'To the deacon!' shouted Ananke, seeing the same opportunity. 'Go!' The dark-skinned Sororitas leapt from her cover, firing and running. Other Battle Sisters nearby heard her cry and followed suit.

Isabel grinned and mantled the plinth before her, leading with her gun. 'We prevail!'

Zeyn's whip lashed out and struck the leading elements of the necron line, discharging its full power into the machine-skeletons. They performed a mad dance as the electro-discharge misfired their motor controls, and one of the immortals jerked, sweeping up its gauss blaster while still firing, turning its gun over the torsos of its brethren.

Isabel used her cyber-eye to target and shoot without needing to raise her bolter to her shoulder, sprinting into the dithering necron skirmish line. The machines had been caught off-guard, but they were quick and they would adapt to the new circumstance in moments.

'Sing!' shouted Zeyn, and Isabel did, joining the Sororitas in the hymnal, letting the martial rhythm of the tune carry her forwards, shield her from doubt and hesitance. She killed an immortal with a salvo that took off its head, and the machine crumpled, disintegrating into a bright flash of light. Zeyn's lash rose and fell, his makeshift laser weapon bisecting limbs and burning through steely skulls.

Other emerald flashes sparked along the assault line as the necrons staggered and finally broke formation. The bodies that did not fall to later rise seemed to melt into the energy flares, as if swept away by teleportation or some alien manner of techno-sorcery.

The immortals and their warrior cohorts tried to reform but the Sisters had the taste of blood in their mouths now, and they were closing the gate, forcing the machines back towards their breach. Zeyn's mad, reckless charge had been all that was needed to rally the Sororitas.

All at once, a silent signal seemed to pass down the line of the necrons, and they fell back en masse, retreating towards the breach in the shield wall.

Something rang a wrong note with Isabel, and she skidded to a halt. 'Wait…'

'Follow them!' roared Zeyn, scrambling up a low hill of rubble and fallen masonry. He raised his whip high, spinning it like a glittering rotor, daring the necrons to find him with their shots. 'Our faith is our armour! In the God-Emperor's name!'

Whatever instinct it was, either a trained warrior's intuition or something of divine providence, Isabel's attention was seized by a motion behind the mass of the defenders. She spun to see a group of spindly humanoid shapes loping across the courtyard from the western wall. *They were inside! Behind us! How could they be inside?*

The necron warriors raised their guns and fired as one, burning light lancing over her head as she dodged away.

The shots converged on Deacon Uriahi Zeyn and tore him out of existence. The last verse of the song from his lips extended into a blood-chilling shriek, as the gauss flayers did their work. His mane of hair and the ruddy skin of his face became ashes, the bones beneath briefly blackening before they too were made powder in the nimbus of jade fire.

'It's a feint! They are inside the walls!' Isabel shouted into the general vox-channel. 'The enemy is within!'

The moment the gunfire began to sound, Questor Tegas went to the barred door of the cell-crypt and called out to the Sororitas on guard. One of them, a woman with a hard face and narrow eyes, hove closer and glared at him.

Before she could speak he banged a metal fist on the inside of the door. 'It is the xenos,' he told her. 'You cannot leave us in here while they attack the convent. We can be of assistance to the canoness!'

'I have my orders,' the Battle Sister replied. 'And you are not to be trusted.'

Tegas's mechadendrites trailed over the dusty floor of the

cell, hissing trails through the dirt in unconscious reflection of his mood. Armed with the information gleaned by his surveillance probe, he was unwilling to sit out the conflict and allow Sepherina's troops to engage the necrons alone. He was not prepared to place his life and that of his party in the hands of the Sororitas. 'Honoured Sister,' he began, biting down on his irritation and modulating his voice into something that would make her manner more pliant.

She shut him down with a crash of noise, slamming the butt of her bolter into the door. 'Do not speak to me again!' said the woman, spitting at him. 'It is your lies–'

Tegas never learned what it was that *his lies* were responsible for. At that moment, the corridor outside the cells was filled with sound and light.

A shrieking sound of air molecules being slashed apart. A blazing viridian light that caused his optics to shunt to counter-glare settings.

The Battle Sister was caught in the nimbus of a necron flayer blast and her death-cry was lost in the howling discharge of the alien guns. The last of her Tegas saw was the woman's flesh puffing into scraps that resembled burnt paper.

Bands of colour searing the receptors of his artificial retinas, Tegas recoiled from the barred window in the cell-crypt door and pressed himself flat against the nearest wall, where any observer peering inside would be unable to see him.

He heard crashes of noise and more skirls of particle beam energy, registering reflected flickers of light off the stone that matched the albedo of the necron guns. Metal claws tore open cell doors and burned the interiors with millisecond bursts of kill-fire, advancing down the corridors towards his hiding place.

Tegas wondered how the aliens had managed to push so quickly into the outpost's underground levels. Had they teleported in through those infernal gateways of theirs, or dug out through hidden tunnels? Were there paths into the convent that Imogen and her dogged Celestians had been too ignorant to see? It did not matter; all that mattered was that he was going to die in here, and the monumental unfairness of that struck Tegas like a bullet.

He found old hate and let it rise. Why had the Omnissiah cursed him so? How did it serve the grand design of the Machine-God to place the questor so close to such riches and then end him before he could reach them?

His hands found the sacred symbol of the Great Cog where it hung about his neck, and he traced the shape of it, hoping that his deity would be watching him.

Sister Isabel's warning was redundant to the Sister Superior, having come too late for her to save the lives of the Sororitas at her sides. Within the central keep, from either side of the corridor, necron warriors had advanced seemingly from out of nowhere, and the Battle Sisters had died in the initial exchange of fire.

Imogen spent her last grenades to avoid the same fate, and dived into a stairwell as the machines fired towards her. The only escape route was upwards, and Imogen scrambled up the narrow spiral staircase, cursing her luck. Behind her, she could hear the inexorable scrape and crunch of iron feet. They were almost at her back, less than a turn or two behind her.

At the next landing she came to a halt and lifted her gun, aiming back the way she had come. *How dare they make me run*, she told herself. *The faithless have no rule over the faithful.*

The first two that emerged she put down with shots to the head, but there had to be a whole platoon of them marching up after her, and Imogen did not have enough shells for them all.

'Aside!' Strong hands shoved her to the wall and a figure in armour lurched past, emerging from a doorway across the landing. Imogen saw the other Battle Sister hurl a cluster of fragmentation grenades down the mouth of the stairwell and then dive for cover. She dropped to the stone floor as the grenades detonated almost immediately, the fuses dialled down to their shortest setting.

The concussion deafened her and blasted the necrons into pieces, choking the spiral staircase with broken rock and broken machines.

Then Imogen realised who had come to her aid and her expression soured. 'Sister Miriya. Where is the canoness? You left her side in the midst of an attack, in the company of that hybrid?'

The other woman's voice was woolly and difficult to understand, but Imogen could read lips well enough. 'No need to thank me, Sister,' Miriya replied, coughing at the thick dust in the air. 'Sepherina is safe. And Decima is not our enemy. She sensed the necron approach...'

'But not soon enough to make a difference!' She pushed the other woman aside and strode out onto the upper level of the keep. 'Begone. Get to your post.'

'The canoness bid me to ensure you were safe–'

Imogen rounded on her with sudden fury. 'I do not need your help, *Sister Militant*!' She turned Miriya's low rank into an insult.

She expected an angry reaction, but Miriya's manner was sombre. 'Why do you challenge me at every turn?' asked the other woman. 'Why do you make everything between us a contest that only you can win? I obey your orders and you show me nothing but contempt!'

'Now is not the time for this.' Imogen turned to walk away, but Miriya grabbed her arm.

'We may perish at the enemy's hand at any moment,' said the Battle Sister, 'and I would rather go to the God-Emperor's side knowing what insult I have done to you, for I can see no other explanation!'

Imogen shrugged off her hand. 'You dare give me commands? But of course you do! You swan about as if you are of high rank and noble status. You are Sister Miriya, the woman who defied the orders of her canoness on Neva, and was allowed to escape chastisement for it!'

Miriya held up her broken chaplet. 'I *was* punished for that. And you punish me still, for something you know nothing of!'

'I know you disobeyed your commander!' Imogen shot back. 'We are an Order, Sister! And Order means we obey, without question. I am the instrument of the Imperial Church! But you are an unprincipled opportunist, forgiven by a mistress too weak to see you executed!'

The other woman stepped back, her expression one of shock. 'Is... is that what you think of me? That I would put myself before my Sisters?' Miriya's manner hardened once more. 'You have no idea what happened on Neva. I was ordered to leave my squad behind to die, when I still had the chance to save them! I chose otherwise!' Distant gunfire cracked, echoing down the long corridor.

Imogen hesitated. Something in the other woman's tone made her moderate her own. 'That is not what is said in the convent, and among the Sisterhood. It is said that you allowed women under your command to die.'

'I *allowed* nothing,' Miriya replied, a note of pain in her words. 'But I was responsible for lives lost... And I did not wish to see more die for nothing.' She glared at the Sister Superior. 'The words of those who do not know the truth mean nothing to me. But would *you* have done otherwise, Imogen? Let your Sisters die, even if there was the slimmest chance you could prevent it?'

I would obey my orders. Imogen wanted that to be her answer, but she knew it could not be. Finally, her lip curled in a sneer and she turned away. 'I will not argue with you. Come. I'll not allow the canoness to fight without my arm at her side.'

Miriya's expression remained unchanged as she followed the Sister Superior down the corridor at a run.

Out in the tunnel beyond the cell-crypts the sounds of conflict were deafening, the noise of the necrons now joined by cries of pain from human mouths and the dull drumming growl of heavy autoguns. One of the surviving Mechanicus weapon-slaves must have been freed and shrugged off its concealment, reverting back to battle mode to engage the aliens.

Finally, Tegas heard the clash of xenos blade on forged steel as the axe-head upon a gauss flayer barrel met the door to his cell-crypt. The metal around the hinges deformed and bent, before the axe bit and sliced, the monomolecular edge cutting it cleanly.

With a thunderous crash, the cell door fell inwards and kicked up puffs of rust and dirt. The questor saw the glitter of the necron axe-blade, and his limbs, his servo-arm, his serpentine mechadendrites, all came up to defend him in a flurry of claws and talons.

Adept Lumik entered the cell with the gauss flayer in her hands, holding it like a child given a las-rifle to toy with. She found him where he cowered and spoke without any judgement or emotion. 'The necrons killed the g-guards,' she told him, anticipating his first question. 'The gun-servitor k-killed the necrons.'

He peered past her and saw a mess of death. The ashen remains of the murdered Battle Sisters and some of Lumik's fellow adepts, pieces of molten slag surrounding a mortally wounded servitor lying on its side, legs kicking pathetically. 'We should not have been able to defeat them,' he said quietly.

'They broke their attack pattern unexpectedly,' the adept explained. 'We t-took advantage of it.'

Tegas looked back at Lumik, and on an impulse he couldn't identify, he snatched the alien gun from her. It was surprisingly light, almost as if it were hollow inside, and it felt *wrong* somehow in his grip. The questor was immediately overcome with a desire to be away from the weapon, a physical repulsion that shocked him with its potency.

It wasn't time for him to be playing with these things. Not now. *Not yet.*

He threw the flayer gun into the corner of the cell and pushed past Lumik. 'Strip the autoguns from the helot, take what the Sororitas carried. Then follow me.' He lurched into the smoke-filled stone corridor, his lung filters wheezing.

'Where are we going?' Lumik asked.

Tegas kept walking and didn't answer her.

For one moment, it seemed as if the necron assault would close around the throat of the convent's defenders like a steel hawser pulled tight. They came in from three points of the compass, some emerging as if from nowhere directly among the blockade points manned by Sepherina's best fighters. Weapons blazed on both sides, but it was human casualties that escalated fastest. The Battle Sisters were spread too widely, covering every angle of attack, redundant or not. They reconfigured quickly, squad by squad responding to the enemy sortie, but the necrons were precise with their kills, carving into the convent's defences with a scalpel's precision.

The Sisters met them with massed firepower. They weathered their blows and some died, but those who lived, wounded mortally or not, mocked the machines by rising on sheer force of will to fight on. With prayers and acts of faith upon their souls, the Adepta Sororitas let the love of their God-Emperor drive them into the fight, and let their hatred of the alien propel them beyond reason and mere endurance.

The necron line cracked in places as it had before Deacon Zeyn's impassioned rally. It cracked and it broke, and the wave of steel marching forth suddenly fell into retreat.

Warriors and immortals began to phase out by the dozen, squad after squad dissipating into crackling sheets of energetic expulsion as space-time warped about them. The ripple effect echoed down their lines and it was only a matter of moments before no xenos soldiers stood within the walls of the Sanctuary 101 outpost.

Silence fell upon the Battle Sisters; silence and the slow, sullen rise of the Kavir dawn.

'The enemy have fully disengaged,' Cassandra told the canoness. 'Danae and Helena report in from the primary and secondary contact points. The necrons gave up and retreated.'

Her voice was caught in the wind. Up here on the gently sloped roof of the main donjon, they could see the full spread of the stronghold and the valley beyond the walls. She searched for the glitter of sunlight off silver and did not find it.

'No,' muttered Decima, standing to one side, next to the hospitaller. Verity had remained with them while Sister Zara had left to aid the wounded.

Sepherina did not acknowledge the other woman's utterance. 'This is certain?'

'Aye,' said Cassandra, unable to keep a measure of incredulity from her voice. 'If fate blesses us, I think we may have bloodied their noses and sent them reeling.' She glanced at the revenant. 'They expected the rout they faced last time they came here, but this time we were ready for them.' For a moment, the Battle Sister dared to hope that she might be right; but then that hope faded and died as Cassandra met Decima's cold, empty eyes and remembered the endless army she had witnessed inside the necron orbital complex.

'I have never believed in fate,' Sepherina replied, glancing around as Sister Miriya and Sister Imogen emerged from inside the keep. 'Report,' she demanded.

Imogen shared a wary look with Miriya and bowed briefly. 'Multiple vectors of attack. Casualties were high, but we held the line. The fight was in the balance until…'

'Until they left.'

'You mean, they retreated,' Verity corrected.

Miriya shook her head. '*Retreat* suggests they were giving ground. This was nothing of the like. They made a tactical withdrawal. They are regrouping.'

'Why would they do so?' Cassandra asked. 'They could have kept up the pressure.' She did not want to say the rest. *We would have lost, eventually.*

'A probe,' Sepherina told them. 'The xenos were testing us.'

'Khaygis is their nemesor. Their commander,' Decima offered. She ran a bony finger over one of the implants in her face. 'I think I heard him.'

'Is this… nemesor… still out there?' Imogen strode boldly to the edge of the roof and glared out into the desert.

'They never left,' whispered the ragged woman, her gaze turning inwards, weighed down by brutal memory. 'They never, never left…'

'That much appears clear now,' said a new voice. Guns were raised as Questor Tegas and a few of his Mechanicus adepts stepped up onto the windswept roof.

Imogen scowled. 'How did you get free?'

'Your Sisters fought bravely,' Tegas said, with solemnity. 'They saved my life.'

Sepherina took a warning step towards the adepts. 'Or perhaps you killed them in the confusion.'

'Then why would I be here, now?' he shot back at her. 'You are wilfully blind to my knowledge in all of this, canoness. You do not want to associate with me because you cannot see past your prejudice for all that is not of the Sororitas.'

'You dare?' Imogen went for the haft of her power maul, but Sepherina stopped her with a gesture. Cassandra watched as the canoness gave Tegas permission to continue with a terse incline of her head.

'Speak on,' she said. 'I will let you talk yourself into an execution.'

Tegas sniffed. 'I know more about the necrontyr than any other human on this blighted rock, more even than this broken toy.' He pointed his servo-arm at Decima. 'The deaths here, among your Sisters in the year eight-nine-seven? Those were not the first of our species to be executed by these xenos monstrosities. They were merely the first to be *widely known*. Human eyes laid gaze on the necrontyr more than two centuries before that day.'

'Impossible,' said Verity, although she spoke as if she were trying to convince herself. 'A threat so grave… The Adeptus Terra would not have remained silent over such a danger to the Imperium.'

The questor snorted at her. 'Are you all so naïve?' He paused, and Cassandra realised he was accessing some internal reservoir of memory. 'Solemnace. Morrigor. Lazar and Bellicas. Have any of you heard of those worlds?' When none of them answered, he nodded and went on. 'And you never will. The Imperium faces so many threats from within and without. The common people need not know how close the necron claw is to their throats.'

'How many attacks have there been like this one?' Sepherina demanded. 'Tell me what other knowledge Inquisitor Hoth imparted to you!'

'I will tell you this.' Tegas nodded again. 'This is a false dawn. A probe, as you yourself said, canoness. It is a pattern repeated by the necrons on dozens of battlefields. The xenos have fallen back to repair and rearm. And when they return, it will be in numbers so great they will shake the earth with their passage.'

CHAPTER THIRTEEN

There was a moment when Miriya thought that the canoness would give the kill-command, then and there atop the roof of the central keep.

The Battle Sister saw the moment unfold in her mind: Sepherina snarling the order, the other Sororitas bringing up their guns. A howl of shots. Tegas, his arms wheeling as the impacts blew him over the lip of the roof.

It was all he deserved, after all. He had lied to the Order of Our Martyred Lady, perhaps for years, first about the secret Mechanicus explorator base in the canyons, and then about the deadly threat of the necrontyr themselves.

'You should die for what you have done,' said the canoness, giving voice to Miriya's thoughts. 'I would be remiss to let you draw breath a moment longer.'

'That would be a grave mistake,' Tegas replied. His voice was level and lacked any note of fear, but Miriya imagined that too was just one more trick in his arsenal of subterfuge. Inwardly, the questor had to be terrified. One misstep now and he would be executed where he stood. 'I have no reason to keep anything from you any more, milady. Events on the ground have exceeded the remit I was given. We now all find ourselves on the horns of the same dilemma.'

Sepherina looked away, disgusted with him. Her gaze ranged up into the pale dawn, and she found the hazy ghost-shape of the Obsidian Moon, still visible high in the sky.

Finally, she spoke again. 'If what you say is so, we need to reformulate our defensive strategy.' The canoness glanced at Cassandra. 'Pass orders to the defence squads to move the force wall generators surrounding the convent's genatorium chamber. Shift them out to the edges of the keep.'

'That will leave our power systems unprotected,' said Verity.

'If the xenos get that far inside again, it won't matter,' Imogen offered grimly, as Cassandra spoke quietly into her vox-bead.

'And him?' Miriya pointed at Tegas with the muzzle of her bolter.

'I will allow the questor to live, for the moment,' said Sepherina, and Tegas visibly relaxed. 'His skills and insight may provide use to me.' She stepped closer to him. 'Do you understand that, *cog*?' Tegas flinched at the pejorative. 'The second you fail to be of any tactical value, you are deadweight.'

Miriya shouldered her weapon and glared at the questor. 'So this is what we will do?' She turned to the canoness. 'Stand and die?'

'Sister Miriya!' Imogen snapped harshly. 'You forget yourself! You will speak with deference to the mistress!'

She bit her lip and bowed. 'Of course... I meant no disrespect...' Miriya looked up. 'But my question stands. We must find a new strategy, my lady. If we do not take the fight to the xenos, they will overwhelm us!'

'It is not your place to question the orders of your superiors,' Imogen went on. 'I would think that lesson would have been made abundantly clear to you since Neva!'

Miriya ignored her, concentrating on holding Sepherina's gaze. 'We must deal with this threat at its source. We must go back to the Obsidian Moon...' She trailed off. 'We all understand the reasons why.'

'I do not disagree,' said the canoness, 'but such a raid would be suicidal, given the countless numbers of enemy troops you reported in the alien stronghold.' She glanced up again. 'We have no vessels to make the trip, no way of entering the chamber you spoke of in the canyons...'

'There is always another path,' Tegas spoke up, pulling his cloak closer about him as the wind rose. 'I can offer a solution.'

'The iron scroll,' said Decima, breaking her silence at last. 'It turns to many functions.' She glanced away, muttering at nothing, her voice low and harsh.

The questor pressed on, suddenly animated by the challenge. 'Now I have seen it in operation, I believe it is possible for me to conjure the portal configuration from the device's matrix. All that would be needed is an active necron gateway within the Obsidian Moon to connect to. I could open a pathway into the complex.'

'But can we destroy it?' Cassandra asked, cutting to the heart of the matter.

'He lies still,' murmured Decima. '*Shut up!*' she spat, whispering at voices only she could hear.

Tegas paid no attention to the revenant. 'As we have a reactor core inside this outpost, so the xenos have a dimensional-phase device to provide power to their largest facilities. Yes, Sisters, I can deactivate it if you take me there.'

Imogen heard the avarice as it finally bled into his voice and raised her gun again. 'The hybrid is right! He lies again, and even now I do not doubt he is scheming, to find the ends of this that will most benefit him!'

'The ends?' Tegas echoed. 'Even my most favourable probability equations give us a success ratio of one in five thousand iterations! At this moment, what benefits me most, Sister Superior, is not dying!'

The winds carried the questor's angry words away, and for a time there was only the low howl of the sand over the stone.

'We will stand and fight,' Sepherina said, at length. 'It is our way. We are the unbreakable bulwark ranged against the enemies of mankind. It has ever been so.' She glanced at Miriya. 'Our Sisters perished here and in their memory we will stand their posts. We will fight to the last bolt-shell if the God-Emperor decrees it.' She took a step towards the edge of the roof. 'And while we fight, Sisters, you will go into the catacombs of the alien machine and cut its throat.'

'You are certain of this course of action?' said Imogen.

Sepherina nodded. 'If we do nothing, Sanctuary 101 will fall silent once more. History will repeat itself.'

The ghost of a smile twisted Tegas's not-quite-face and faded as fast as it had appeared, perhaps an emotive artefact of the questor's true feelings. He was behaving as if he had won a victory, Miriya realised.

She decided to challenge him. 'Why do we need to put our trust in the Adeptus Mechanicus? We have among our ranks a Sister of Battle whose knowledge of the necrons outstrips that of Lord Tegas.' She inclined her head towards Decima.

The other woman reacted, wringing her hands. 'No,' she slurred, 'No, no. Don't go. *Be silent*! I don't want to go back again.'

'You would trust this...' Tegas paused, struggling to find the right word. 'This damaged, broken soul over me?' He approached her, and Decima shied away. 'Do you have any idea what she really is?'

'The necrons did that to her. The cryptek, the one that called itself Ossuar.' Decima flinched as Verity said the name. It was strange; inside the caverns and the alien complex, the lost Battle Sister had been strong and defiant, but here and now she was cowed and fretful.

'*We lose if we wait,*' she whispered, eyes set on some unknowable, distant point. 'Yes. Yes.'

Tegas opened his cloak with a theatrical gesture. 'It seems that the only way I can cement my trustworthiness to you is by example. So, I will give it. I will show you what this poor, pathetic wretch really is.'

'She is a human being!' Verity insisted.

'Like a Space Marine is a human being?' said Tegas. 'Like a psyker? Or a ratling, or an ogryn? Like *I* am?' He flared his manipulators before Decima and she stood her ground, chewing on her scarred lip.

The tip of one of Tegas's mechadendrites snapped open like a metal bloom. A fan of glassy triangles emerged from it and spun into a circle, clicking into place. The pieces created a device that resembled an outsized magnifier. The lens misted and grew definition as Tegas ran it over Decima's limbs, a few centimetres from the surface of her flesh. Terahertz waves bombarded her harmlessly, reflecting through the meat and bone of her to display a three-dimensional image. The myriad of metal implants forced into her flesh became starkly visible.

'A test bed, I think,' Tegas said, becoming distant and clinical. 'This necron scientist you named... He was experimenting on the human form. But I would need a full dissection to be certain as to what he was trying to prove.'

'You won't touch her,' Miriya said firmly.

'No?' Tegas moved the lens up towards Decima's head and she tried to back away, making small, whimpering noises. 'When you see this, you will change your mind.'

The lens framed a model of the revenant's skull, rendered in layers of colour and photic density. Visible clearly, clasped to the occipital region, was a device that Miriya had seen before, inside the halls of the Obsidian Moon.

It was a variant design of a necron scarab mechanoid; smaller than the others, the malevolent beetle-form buried in the meat of her neck, its needle-like legs embedded in her spinal column. As she watched, the Battle Sister could see it moving slightly, as if it were alive.

'I'm sorry,' Decima began to weep. 'I'm sorry I'm sorry I'm sorry...'

'We don't know what name the xenos have for them,' Tegas said, in a hectoring tone. 'Inquisitor Hoth called them "mind-shackles", although I find the term overly fanciful myself.'

Cassandra's bolter was raised. 'A mind-control device?'

'Aye,' nodded Tegas. 'But this one appears to be damaged.' He indicated places in the scan where the machine's carapace was darkened. 'I'd warrant that the malfunction of the shackle scarab was what allowed her to flee the necrons all those years ago. It let her have some free will back.'

Verity looked ill. She placed a hand on Decima's arm and the other woman shrank back as if she had been burned. 'She hears voices in her head. Is it the cryptek, tormenting her?'

'Perhaps,' said Tegas. 'But it could just be the damage to her mind expressing itself. The effects of trauma on the human psyche have such unpredictable effects.'

Imogen frowned. 'It does not matter. Either way, she cannot be trusted.'

'I could say the same for him,' Miriya retorted, pointing at the questor.

'No,' came a quiet voice. The revenant's gaze crossed over them. 'What the cog says is true. I am flawed. I am dangerous to you. If you bring me too close, Ossuar will see... He might see through my eyes.'

'You don't know that,' insisted Verity.

'You cannot take the risk, Sisters,' Decima said, with grave finality.

From the throne atop his personal command Monolith, Nemesor Khaygis surveyed the ranks of his troops. Lines of warriors stood ready, some freshly advanced through portals from the orbital complex, others returned and regenerated after the initial attack wave. Immortals and lychguard waited motionless for his word to strike. His army was frozen in time, waiting to reanimate, waiting to kill.

The nemesor gazed over the Monolith's battlements, the contra-gravity motors beneath him emitting a steady, resonant thrumming that beat at the air. Khaygis paused to take a moment of communion; he connected his intellect to the broad control matrix that spread out among all his lesser soldiers, sampling their recent memories and collating the data there.

The warriors were barely sentient in the true sense of the word. Before the Great Uplifting and the sweet release of biotransference, they had been the lowest of the necrontyr castes, the workers, the menials and the poor. The Stargods had freed them from the tyranny of conscious thought, stripping away all emotion and character until only the very core of being remained. The smallest possible spark of animate life, rendered soulless and servile.

How content they must be, Khaygis mused, *for never having the need to think for themselves again.*

Their superiors, the immortals, had been the soldiers of the dynasts in the fleshtime, and their reborn forms reflected that fact. The immortals were better armed, better armoured, and they retained a tiny fraction more of what they had once been. Not enough to give them a name or a persona, of course, but enough that their martial training remained intact. It was an efficiency, after all, not to waste the time and effort that had been put into training them. But they too did not have the intellect to exist anywhere beyond the moment. Both were walking weapons, tools of killing, and they performed those functions admirably.

Khaygis did not remember his biotransference. All he recalled was awakening in this machine body, rippling with power and lethal potential. His overriding recollection of that glorious moment was a sense of incredible freedom – freedom from petty things, like the decay of his organic form and the worthless moral codes of mortal beings.

The nemesor did not remember who he had been before the Uplifting. That part of him had been edited out and discarded. He must have been a man of great rank to be allowed to retain any elements of self, and that was explanation enough for him. The first act Khaygis had performed in his new machine-form was to kneel before his master, the Stormlord Imotekh.

Others were not so lucky, of course. Some did not pass through the eye of the transformation without suffering damage, and some were warped by distortions of self in ways that took millennia to manifest themselves. There were the destroyers, the berserker kin of the necrontyr who sought only to obliterate all that lay before them. Their minds were stripped down to the killing urge and nothing more, broken by engram decay and consumed by nihilism. But they were nothing compared to the loathsome horror of the flayed ones, who flocked to the shedding of organic blood like carrion eaters. Driven by a compulsion that the harbingers called a 'curse', the flayed ones garbed themselves in the skins of dead flesh-forms and plundered battlefields for the meat of corpses. Some said that they were possessed by a madness that drove them to an obsession with the flesh they had lost – as if they were trying to rebuild it from the bodies of those who died opposing the necrons. Others spoke of one of the murdered Stargods, his last act before perishing in the War in Heaven the release of a virus that would one day turn them all to the same path.

Khaygis detested both these aberrant kind, and would never allow his forces to enter battle with either counted among them. Perhaps it was an element of self he retained from the being he had once been, but the nemesor saw combat as a sacrosanct thing, a place where all truths could be put to the test, where will and might would answer all questions. If he had still been capable of such an emotional state, it might have been true to say that Khaygis cherished warfare in the way a parent would love their offspring.

He completed his collation of the data, and the nemesor sifted through it. At once he saw it all, every single sporadic contact, every engagement, every melee kill, flayer strike, tesla blast. A map of death drew itself in his mind as the necron general experienced a hundred little wars from the perspectives of his soldiers, all in unison, laid atop one another. He saw where the fallen had been defeated, he saw where the victorious were mighty. For those brief moments, Khaygis sat at the heart of the network and *absorbed*.

When he was ready, the nemesor disengaged and the emerald light of his eyes glowed brightly. He had his plan, gathered from the aftermath and replay of the first assault. He had his soldiers, outnumbering the females inside the outpost by a very significant factor.

In his mind, Khaygis already had his victory. It was inevitable that the necrons would overwhelm the human invaders. All that remained now was the tedious business of the actual killings. The theorem of death he had posited needed to be proven.

Behind him, harsh jade-coloured light spilled out from the power crystal atop the Monolith, framing the nemesor with shifting aurorae as he pointed with his fire gauntlet. Khaygis aimed the glowing glove out across the desert wastes, towards the near-distant valley where the organics were marking out their last moments of mortality.

He transmitted the battle plan to his assemblage, every detail of it perfect in their minds, with no space for misinterpretation or alteration. He told them all where to go and what to kill.

Then Khaygis spoke a single word, and vocoder relays in his machine-frame relayed the sound out through the Monolith's onboard resonator arrays. It was not required for him to do so, but the ritual of it, the finality of the gesture, appealed to him.

The word was '*Execute*', and without battle-cries or elation, without fear or hesitation, the necron army began its march towards Sanctuary 101.

'This could be a ploy,' Verity said quietly, pitching her words so that only Miriya could hear them.

The Battle Sister glanced up at her from where she crouched, in the middle of checking her combat gear before she set off on her mission. 'You think that I have not considered that?'

Verity looked around at the walls of the Great Chapel and grimaced. 'It is not enough that you must do this, but that the xenos machine must be activated *here*, in this holy place…'

'Is is the best-protected part of the convent, Sister,' Miriya reminded her.

'Indeed,' Verity replied, 'but it still feels like sacrilege.'

'I do not disagree,' said the other woman gravely. She paused. 'I am well aware of Tegas's intentions. I have a bolt-round put aside just for him, when the moment comes.'

'The Adeptus Mechanicus are not faithful, not like us,' Verity insisted.

'Don't tar them all with his brush,' came the reply. 'I have fought alongside adepts who acquitted themselves with honour in service to the Golden Throne. Tegas is not the best of them, by any measure.'

'They serve an adulterated deity,' the hospitaller continued. 'They worship a Machine-God, only an aspect of the God-Emperor... How can any of them ever see His true glory as we do?'

'We can debate theology if you wish, Sister Verity,' Tegas called out from across the cavernous room as he approached, flanked by Cassandra and Danae. 'But forgive me if I suggest that this is neither the place nor the time for such things.'

'He hears me...' Verity whispered.

Miriya made a motion near her ear. 'With all the augmetics crammed inside his bones, I imagine he could hear the tread of every sand-fly within these walls, if he wished it.'

'And more besides,' said the questor, a cold and avaricious smile in the words.

'Enough,' said the canoness, standing nearby. She beckoned to Sister Ananke, who approached holding a storage pod. At Sepherina's direction, she warily opened the container and removed the grey shape of the iron scroll. Ananke seemed physically revolted by her proximity to the device. Decima lurked in the shadows of the pillars behind her, watching the events unfold from beneath her hood.

'Give it to him,' ordered the canoness.

Ananke did so, only too pleased to be rid of the xenos artefact. Tegas took it eagerly, and she backed away, unlimbering her bolter. Nearby, Sister Imogen and a trio of other Sororitas were already at weapons drawn, taking aim at Tegas's head.

He feigned a disappointed sigh. 'Is this really necessary? I have given my word that I will cooperate with you.'

Sepherina made no move to have the other Battle Sisters lower their weapons. 'Make it work,' she told him, 'and know that if you betray us in any way, you will not live to see the fruits of it.'

'Perish the thought,' the questor replied. 'After all, my dear canoness, we both want the same thing.'

'Do it!' Imogen barked, her patience wearing thin. 'Now!'

'As you wish.' Tegas turned his manipulators in towards the scroll and moved them over the surface of the device, tracing circles and lines, making alien symbols.

Verity's attention was caught as she heard Decima give voice to a soft whimper, and then in the next second the necron artefact went from a piece of inert metal to a glowing, writhing cord of green fire.

Tegas reacted with shock, his cyber-limbs going rigid, but he held on tightly to the device. The living alien metal shivered in his grip, changing its forms with a disturbing fluidity that made Verity's skin crawl. First it opened into the scroll, alive with symbols and texts, then it became the fan of angled panes, emitting light and colour. It was briefly a cube, then a rod, before finally unravelling into thin wires that wafted in the air like grass stalks in a breeze.

'Yes!' The questor was elated. 'I have it now!' The human emotion seemed ill-fitting and out of place coming from the Mechanicus adept.

The spline-threads grew in length and diameter, Tegas releasing the reforming device to be free to find its ultimate expression of form. It began to re-knit itself, making curves that turned slowly to bring their sparkling tips towards one another. The alien metal came together with a ringing sound to form a hoop large enough for a human to step through. A haze of energy wove across the span of it, glistening with exotic radiation. Verity was drawn in by the play of light and colour, mesmerising, almost seductive...

And alien. She shook her head and forced herself to break eye-contact. The portal's membrane quivered, seeming harmless as it stood there – but Verity had seen with her own eyes what lay on the other side of that threshold, the infinite armies and their incomprehensible machines waiting for the moment to wake.

The very thought of being asked to go back there filled her with an ice-cold dread. She chanced a sideways look at the canoness. Would Sepherina order her to do so? Verity felt ashamed by her fear, but could not stop herself from silently praying that the command would not come.

She had never been in a place like the necron complex, a place where the absence of spirit was almost a tangible thing that could be touched and tasted. The hospitaller struggled to frame her thoughts, to find the right words to describe the sensation she had felt up there. It was simply... *emptiness*. A void like no other, a place where faith itself could hold no purchase.

She shuddered at the thought, as Decima ventured to speak.

'You have little time,' said the ragged woman. 'Extended use of the device will draw their attention. You must hurry.'

Sepherina closed on Tegas. 'It is done?'

'Indeed,' he nodded twice.

The canoness looked away, towards the Sister Superior. 'Imogen. Assemble a squad and proceed to the alien stronghold. Your orders are to destroy it or die in the attempt.'

The other woman gave a crisp salute. 'Understood.' Imogen searched the faces of the other Battle Sisters surrounding her. 'I need five women whose souls are strong, who are ready to meet the God-Emperor this day. We may never return from this mission. We may die on alien soil. Who will join me?'

'I will.' Miriya was the first to step up, the last question barely out of the Sister Superior's lips. Verity had expected no less of her friend.

'And I.' Danae hefted her meltagun. At her side, Sister Ananke gave a solemn nod of agreement.

'Here or there,' said Cassandra, coming to the ready. 'Where we end matters little, as long as it is in His name.'

Sister Pandora was the last, mirroring Imogen's salute. 'Aye.'

'Noble,' offered Tegas primly. He took a breath. 'I should think it would be best to send a proxy first...' He looked towards his junior adepts, and Verity saw them shrink back in fear. None of them wanted to pass through the portal, to be the one who might set foot in a necron trap.

'You said it was done,' Sepherina said, coming close to Tegas. 'The passage is open, yes?'

'Yes, but prudence–'

She never let him finish. In a swift flourish of motion, the canoness grabbed fistfuls of the questor's cloak, and with the enhanced strength borne of her power armour's artificial musculature, she lifted Tegas off his feet and threw him bodily into the shimmering membrane.

The formation of a cry left his lips, but it was abruptly cut off as he touched the event horizon of the portal and vanished into nothing, an emission of bright energy marking his passage.

A callous grin formed on Imogen's face for a moment, then faded. 'Squad ready, milady.'

'Make certain he keeps his word.' Sepherina bowed her head. 'Blessings of the Golden Throne be upon you, my Sisters. *Ave Imperator.*'

'*Ave Imperator*,' chorused the Battle Sisters.

'Good luck,' said Verity, a forbidding tightness clasping at her chest.

Miriya paused at the threshold and threw her a nod; then she was stepping into the portal and light-flashes filled the chamber.

Decima watched the women go, one after another, her hooded eyes distant and unreadable.

The first assault had been a slow, steady approach. The necron commander had programmed it so, spending the attrition of his lesser troops to gauge the placing and the potency of the human defence forces inside the outpost.

The second attack was fast and fluid. In the cover of the low clouds of sand kicked up by the heat of the sunrise, the enemy approached the convent and broke into a swift march as they came within visual range of the defenders. Lychguards, immortals and warriors went in formation, flowing around rock outcroppings and rises in the dunes. They moved like a horde of locusts.

Leading them was an iron monster.

The Triarch Stalker was a towering, three-legged machine that walked on limbs that resembled great scything blades, the arrow-sharp tips planting pits in the sand where they fell. A cluster of sensor discs gave the impression of a spider-face across the mechanism's central body, accentuated by manipulator talons that drooped like open mandibles. A triarch praetorian rode high in the control nexus above, all function from the necrontyr soldier subsumed into the greater body of the war machine. The first few shots – beams fired from long las-rifles wielded by the remnants of Tegas's personal tech-guard – were absorbed harmlessly by the invisible panes of dispersal shields that hung around the stalker.

The maw of a glowing crimson cannon swept back and forth, searching for a suitable target, and then with a howl of flash-burnt dust, a rod of punishing fire leapt forth. The heat ray angled upwards and brushed the battlements over the main gate, where Tegas's shooters had made their gun-nests. Rock turned dull crimson and flowed to lava, and the tech-guard were reduced to screaming torches.

It was the signal that the final clash had commenced. Every Battle Sister on the line went weapons free and opened fire on the necrons. Warriors and immortals returned their hate with the precise threads of flayer-beam, denaturing stone or ashing flesh wherever they found their marks. The lychguard led the way, blocking killing shots with the dispersion fields surrounding their long kite shields. With their warscythes, they sliced cleanly through lines of hastily-laid razor-web and anti-infantry spike traps. The stalker crabbed sideways across the approaches, dodging throbbing pulses of plasma as it tuned the heat ray to a wide dispersal and sprayed fire into the places where the wall had already been partly breached.

Up on the battlements, Sister Helena dropped as a shrieking hail of green lightning sliced the air where she had been standing. She cursed and scrambled forwards, pulling her bolter tight to her breastplate.

'Report!' she called out, as she spotted Sister Isabel. 'My vox is down.'

'All vox is down,' Isabel corrected. 'Don't ask me how, but the machines have neutered all the frequencies.' She had to shout to be heard over the sound of the other Battle Sisters around her, all of them firing down into the enemy advance in a cacophony of snarling bolters.

'I feared as much. It is the Monolith,' Helena said grimly. 'Did you see it out there? Like a castle set adrift, in the distance at the rear of their lines... They broadcast electromagnetic fields, disrupt our comms. They're trying to make us fight in isolation.'

'They outnumber us,' said Isabel. 'Five-, perhaps ten-fold. Runners from the south and west walls say there are more coming in from across the sands.'

'Bah!' Helena spat and executed a pop-up shot, finding and beheading an immortal marching below them with a pinpoint bolt-round to the throat. 'The God-Emperor damn us all if we let these clockwork toys repeat their desecration of this place!'

A woman's scream sounded from behind her, and Helena turned in time to see a Sororitas tip over the edge of the wall and fall to the rocks below. The upper half of the Sister's torso was a blackened ruin, trailing meat-smoke and embers. Seconds later, another heat beam slammed at the air, and the halo of it thundered over them both.

Isabel hissed like an angry cat and Helena swallowed a jolt of pain as the train of her hair crisped and caught aflame. She beat out the fire with the palm of her gauntlet and grimaced. 'That bloody walker,' growled the veteran. 'We have to kill it.'

'With what, song and sermons? It is shielded.'

Helena nodded bitterly. 'The *Tybalt* is long gone, and with it our hopes of reinforcement or evacuation...' She trailed off.

'The latter would never be set to pass,' said Isabel. 'The Adepta Sororitas gave ground here once. We would dishonour those who died to do so again.'

'Aye, that's truth. But there's another way,' Helena replied. 'How many grenades do you have?'

'Four remaining.'

The veteran thrust hers into Isabel's hands. 'Take mine too, bind them, synchronise the fuses.' She chanced a look over the battlement; the stalker was shifting in place, planting its feet and making ready to fire on the wall. If it widened the breach, the line would collapse. Helena watched the jerky motions of the crested necron wired into the machine's core, visible behind the shield panes.

'What are you planning, Sister?'

'A daring and foolish thing, for an old crone like me. When the moment is right, pitch the grenades at the shield. I'll do the rest.' She didn't wait for Isabel to reply. Instead, Helena broke into a sprint along the line of the battlements to the next tower, a burnt stump that had been torn open by sustained streaks of enemy fire.

The necrons bracketed the air around her with green flame and Helena felt it tear the air molecules from her lungs, filling her nostrils with acrid ozone. She made it to blackened nub of rock that was still searing hot to the touch and rolled to a ready position. Her marksmanship was unparalleled within the Order, or so the veteran liked to believe. Now she was going to prove it.

Isabel did exactly as she was meant to. A spinning cluster of tethered krak grenades described a narrow arc down towards the dorsal panels of the Triarch Stalker, and at the perfect moment, they detonated. The force of the blast was enough to weaken the quantum shields for an instant – long enough for Helena to lay a lethal three-round burst on the praetorian pilot.

The necron war machine lowed like an animal and stumbled off its axis, treading on a dozen of its own kind as it lost balance. Helena heard Isabel and some of the other women on the firing line give voice to a cry of triumph, but even as they did so, she knew they were premature.

The stalker was wounded, gravely indeed – but despite

their desperate plot they had not killed it outright. Instead the mechanoid blundered straight into the wall and accomplished with sheer brute velocity what it had wanted all along.

With a noise like slow, tortuous thunder, the battlements cracked, sagged, and gave way. Helena saw black-armoured figures falling as the stone blocks lost cohesion and came apart from one another. The stalker collapsed to its knees and lay twitching, but like a brood spider engulfed by its hatchlings, the lines of necron soldiers swarmed over the carapace of their fallen battle engine and poured into the cracks in the convent wall.

Helena felt ice in the pit of her stomach and she dragged herself up, reloading as she went; and for the first time in what seemed like hours she looked back into the outpost proper.

The middle ward and the courtyard were a mass of smoke and gunfire, and this breach point was only the newest of several others. There were silver skeletons in droves, green lightning shrieking back and forth, screams and dust and death everywhere she laid her gaze.

The second fall of Sanctuary 101 had begun.

CHAPTER FOURTEEN

She steeled herself for the sensation once again, but nothing Miriya could do was enough to prepare her for the experience.

The giddy, sickening rush of motion-without-motion, the lurching twist that set her perceptions reeling, they engulfed her as she fell headlong into the portal. In that timeless non-space, she was no longer entering a doorway, but tumbling down an impossibly infinite well of light and sound, a void through which it seemed she would fall forever. Miriya was twisted inside out, exposed to dimensions that were unnatural to the human animal. She held on to her faith as she had before, and prayed until it was over.

The strange translucent ice left behind upon her by the force of the transit crackled as she took the next step. Metal rang under her boots and she angrily brushed at the thin rime of frost over her flesh, spitting out flecks of it. Her bare skin felt raw and wind-burnt.

'Katherine's Eyes...' muttered Ananke, crouching close to the ground. 'What in Hades was that?'

'Just the opening of the door, Sister.' Miriya offered the dour woman a hand up, and she took it.

'When we are done here, I will walk back,' came the reply,

and the blank stubbornness of her words made Miriya's lips split in a harsh grin.

All around them, the other Battle Sisters were recovering, gathering their wits and probing the gloom for enemy contact. Miriya blinked droplets of melt water off her eyelashes and cast around, taking in their point of arrival.

Behind them, a perfect square cut into the side of a small, black pyramid was rippling like a pool of water, but in defiance of gravity it stood upright. The glow it cast showed pyramids ranged away in a line before them, and Miriya had a jolt of recognition.

'The Monolith yard, where we fled before,' she began. 'We've returned there.'

'No,' Imogen said, panning around with the beamlight beneath the barrel of her bolter. 'Not the same place. This is another storehouse for their infernal machines, near-identical in form and function.'

As Miriya considered, she realised Imogen was right. There was far less ambient light here, the shadows deep and brooding, and the dormant Monoliths were of a different livery. She picked out rich lines of gold detailing lost under thick layers of dust.

'Do you see that?' said Pandora, pointing. 'A glyph, there. It repeats on all of these craft.' She indicated a shape that resembled a broken arrowhead, the tip blunted, the shaft barbed, with a circle cut into the blade.

'I saw that before,' said Miriya. 'The creature we encountered, the cryptek... It bore that mark upon it.' She tapped her chest-plate to indicate the location, her voice trailing off as she realised something was amiss. 'Where is Tegas?'

The questor was nowhere to be seen. Each of the Battle Sisters activated their lamps, throwing stark white beams out through the dusty air. Behind them, the portal in the Monolith was fading, losing its power. Within a few seconds, it had reverted back to solidity, resembling little more than a pane of vitreous glass.

'The damned cog was only a moment ahead of us...' said Danae, scowling. 'Did the machines take him?'

'Do you hear that?' Pandora had walked ahead of the group a few steps. She held up her hand for silence.

Miriya caught a sound in the dead air of the vast chamber: a peculiar, hollow tone, like a rattle. She pointed. 'It came from over there.'

The Sister Superior hefted her gun and gestured for the squad to move forwards. 'Tactical stance,' ordered Imogen. 'No weapons fire unless I give the word.'

Miriya fell into step behind Pandora and followed the slender woman through a narrow gap between two of the dormant necron craft.

Pandora glanced back at her, her pale brow furrowing. 'What is that sound?' she whispered.

The peculiar echo gave the noise a machine-like quality. It reminded Miriya of a running motor or the working of gears. They emerged into the next row of Monoliths and she realised that it was the rhythm of laughter.

Tegas was walking slowly down the line of the silent pyramids, his hands, his servo-arm, his mechadendrites extended to their full span, tracing lightly across the angled surfaces of each Monolith he passed, stroking them. Faint green sparks showed here and there, flicking between the alien machines and the questor. He tipped back his hooded head and made the stuttering motor-laugh again. The moment disquieted Miriya. It seemed improper to witness the Mechanicus lord expressing joy for such alien stimulus.

'Tegas!' she hissed. 'Step away!'

He halted, turned and faced them, as Imogen and the others filed out through the gaps between the pyramids. 'This…' he began, shaking his head. 'This is incredible.' The questor looked up towards the high, iron-dome sky above them, where emerald lights moved back and forth in silence. 'Oh, my dear Sister Miriya, if you could see with my eyes…' He waved at the air, as if he were clutching as things only he could perceive. 'Layers of data etched into the atmosphere itself. Quantum shift matrices, electromagnetically-encoded mnemonics, gardens of exotic particles singing in symphony…'

Tegas described a slow pirouette, folding in his limbs to prayer poses. 'Is this what they perceive all the time, I wonder? It is like swimming in an ocean of data, one within another within another within another within another–'

'*Questor!*' Imogen snarled at him, and he fell silent. 'Whatever machine-sorcery you are toying with, cease it! If we alert the xenos to our presence, we will be lost before we can begin!'

Tegas gave her a mocking look. 'Sister Superior, think for a moment. We have just arrived inside this complex through a direct dimensional shunt corridor, forced into connection by brute means. If the necrons were awake down here, they would have sensed that immediately and come in their droves!' He opened his hands, taking in the silent stone craft. 'Anything? No. I have already intuited that this entire quadrant is in enforced dormancy, perhaps awaiting a greater battle to be fought. We have nothing to fear.'

'All the same,' Imogen went on, 'I gave you an order. You will obey it.'

Tegas stiffened. 'The Sisterhood have always looked down on my kind. You are happy to have us maintain your guns, forge your power armour, build your tanks and your starships... But you baulk at the idea of seeing us as equals. Your canoness' treatment of me, disgracing my rank as if I were a slave to be cast about without a care! That is intolerable!' His vocoder crackled, almost as if it had difficulty processing something like real emotion, real anger. But then his tone changed again. 'But I forgive it. I am glad she sent me through first. The riches here are a thousand times the reward for that indignity.' He wandered back towards the closest Monolith, reaching out to touch it once more. 'So many riches,' he cooed. 'I want to take everything in this place to pieces, see how it works...'

'I never thought his kind were capable of greed,' Ananke said, out of the side of her mouth. 'Isn't that too human for them?'

Miriya stepped up and grabbed Tegas's hand. The motors

in the cybernetic arm whirred as they struggled against the Battle Sister's enhanced strength. 'Remember why we are here,' she told him. 'This sortie is not for your amusement. Your life rests in our hands.' She raised her bolter.

Tegas relented and stepped away. 'I remember,' he said, after a moment. 'Forgive me. The shock of the unusual... But you're quite right, of course. We have a mission to complete.'

'The power core,' said Imogen. 'Lead us to it.'

He bowed and set off, Pandora following close behind.

As Imogen drew level with Miriya, she leaned close to speak to her. 'We have a mission to complete,' she said, mirroring the questor's words. 'The relic. The hospitaller saw it in the laboratorium space you described. Can you find it again?'

Miriya looked up, studying the gantries and giant moving components of the complex. 'Perhaps. If I can orient myself, find one of the shifting platforms to the upper tiers.'

'It is a... *secondary* objective.' Miriya could see it cost Imogen to say that. 'The Saint burn my eyes from me for speaking these words, but the destruction of the Obsidian Moon must take precedence. It is better we deny the relic to the future than save it only to allow these machines to blacken the stars.'

She knew the Sister Superior was right, but still Miriya could not stop the pulse of shock in her heart as the meaning of the order sank in. *The Hammer and Anvil*, truly lost, truly destroyed? Miriya wondered if even a lifetime among the Repentia would be enough to repay the guilt for allowing that to happen. 'It won't come to that,' she managed.

Imogen's hard manner returned. 'Don't be naïve,' she said, marching on.

The noise of the war came down the corridors and it sounded like the ending of the world. Over the moans of the injured and the whisper and buzz of medicae tools, the crackle of near-distant bolt fire and alien energy weapons was constant. Every once in a while a massive explosion would make the walls tremble and quake, sending streamers of dust down upon the heads of the hospitallers and their charges.

The Sisters of the Order of Serenity had moved their temporary infirmary out of the exposure of the courtyard and into this chamber, a long, curved room with a vaulted roof, studded with pillars. It had been a garrison hall when the convent had first been built, and a handful of the sleeping pallets that remained in disarray had been repurposed for the injured among the Battle Sisters.

Verity, Zara and the others worked diligently. This was combat-zone protocol, where the wounded were stitched back together as swiftly as possible and sent back into the fray; but in truth there were very few who needed their skills. Most of those who took a hit from the necron guns died of it almost immediately, and those that did not were lying in shallow comas, their bodies shocked almost to the point of total physical shutdown by the raw trauma of a near-hit. She used a valetudinarian gauntlet to run over the flesh of a flash-burnt workganger whimpering in his drug-induced sleep. Scalpel blades, auto-sutures and remedial probes clicked out from mountings on the fingers of the metal glove, tracking over his skin. Using the gauntlet was like second nature to Verity, the device as much a part of her as a boltgun was to a Sister Militant.

She glanced at Thalassa, who lay half-awake, the bandages across her gut dark with blood from a wound yet to heal. The Battle Sister was grim-faced, staring at the stone roof and listening hard, as if she could piece together the course of the fight from the sounds it left behind.

Verity turned away, in time to see Zara look up from the unmoving form of a Sister Dominion brought in from the west wall. Their gazes met across the infirmary and the other hospitaller gave a slight shake of the head, before pulling a death-shroud up over the Dominion's face.

'They keep coming,' said a voice through gritted teeth. Decima stood in the lee of a broken pillar, watching. 'Even now, they are forcing us back from barricade to barricade, drawing us closer to the central donjon. The tide is inescapable.'

Verity wondered for a moment if Decima was reliving a

memory of the past, or if she was describing the battle at hand. 'Why are you here?' she said.

'The canoness took my weapon,' she said. 'Forbade me to fight. Told me to *stay out of the way*.' Decima shook her head. 'I cannot be trusted.'

A familiar sharp stab of compassion cut into Verity once more. She felt such empathy for the broken-minded woman, a deep sorrow that Decima herself seemed unable to express. 'I don't believe that. You came here, to stand guard over us.'

'I did?' The question whispered from her lips. 'I did,' she repeated. Then with a sudden jerk of motion, Decima lashed out and grabbed Verity's hand. 'You are a medicae. Can you excise it? You know how to cut and stitch meat, yes?'

'Yes,' Verity's reply was wary. 'Decima, what do you mean?'

'*Decima*,' she repeated. 'I want to be her. I can't be sure.' She balled a fist and screwed it into her eye. 'There are memories, but they are locked away. I see them like picts on a screen, but they connect to nothing. I can't know who they belong to. You tell me I am this woman. The Watcher tells me I am not... I am...' She turned and shouted at her invisible tormentor. 'Stop it! *Stop talking*!' Verity was startled as Decima brutally slapped her own face. A trickle of thick, oily blood began to weep from the woman's cracked lip. She stabbed violently at the meat of her neck with her bony fingers, at the place where Tegas had shown the damaged mindshackle implant lying beneath the skin. 'This thing! This thing makes me ill! I can't make it stop!'

'How can I help you?' Verity asked at length. She felt a cold hollow open up inside her, fearing the most final of options would be requested. It would not be the first time the hospitaller had been forced to grant someone the Emperor's Peace, and with every occasion of it, it was as if she had lost a piece of her soul along with them.

At last she looked up at the survivor, and saw something inexplicable. Like the glow of plasmatic discharge around the masts of a starship in the warp, a strange halo of eldritch light – faint but distinct – twinkled around Decima's head.

'Wh-what is that?' Thalassa had seen it too, and was dragging herself up from her sickbed.

Decima's answer never came. Something caught her attention and suddenly she was screaming, howling like a furious animal. The revenant threw her weight into Verity and the two of them went tumbling across the garrison hall floor as a bright light flashed in the confines of the chamber, dazzling her.

At first, Tegas thought he might need them.

The danger inside the necron complex was, of course, incredible. If they so much as tripped a single alert, a phalanx of warriors would be dispatched to their location and they would be terminated. The questor had thought he would need the Battle Sisters for that eventuality. Not because he believed that they could win through by force of arms – no, that was idiotic – but because they would occupy any necron reaction force for a while by fighting and dying, giving him the time he needed to slip away.

But now he was here, now Tegas had seen and swum through the invisible miasma of raw data filling this place like rich fog... He changed his mind.

Already he was beginning to understand the first principles of how the necron network operated. With the correct quantum transmitter, it could be accessed from anywhere in the universe, instantaneously communicating through the entanglement phenomena of controlled quanta. Modification protocols inside Tegas's internal systems were working on adapting one of his many communicator arrays to perform just that function. Already, he had gently sampled a few benign subroutines and chanced a low-level intrusion into the dormant sectors of the complex's invisible grid. Soon, he would be ready to try something more pro-active.

One of the subroutines was generously filling his redundant data-stacks with mapping data that showed the scope and design of the Obsidian Moon facility. He found it odd that the necrontyr did not keep all information under walls of heavy data-security, but then they were not like the Imperium. In the nation of the Emperor of Mankind, ignorance and fear were the core tools of rulership; and the best way for the Adeptus Terra to keep the people ignorant and fearful was to keep them unaware of even the most basic of truths. In many sectors of the Imperium, it was a capital crime for a common man to possess a star map without official sanction to do so. On some worlds, it was illegal even to *read* without a licence.

But the necrontyr had no reason to keep their lower orders afraid and unaware. The roots of those things – of fear and the need to know – did not exist within their greater ranks. What the Imperium hoarded like gold was freely available among the necron species. Information abounded within their networks, uncountable near-infinite amounts of it there for the taking. Millions of years of data, and Tegas's first impulse was to want it all.

But that was impossible. Here he was, his memory stores colossal and robust by any definition, but even he was a cup attempting to hold an ocean.

An emulation of frustration turned to pragmatism after a nanosecond or two. He could not encompass the whole of the alien matrix, nor should he try. Even with the new reams of data he had now, Tegas would be able to count himself the most knowledgeable authority on the necrontyr in human space. *If* he was able to survive and escape the conflict.

He considered that. It pleased him, the idea of returning to Mars, swollen with gigaquads of information on the alien machines. Not only would it erase all question of any past errors of judgement in his service, not only would it see him raised into the ranks of the Lords of the Red Planet, but this gift would allow him to shift the balance of his relationship against Inquisitor Hoth and the Ordo Xenos from subordinate to superior. *They* would come to *him* on bended knee. The Adeptus Mechanicus would be shown the respect it was due.

But he needed more. Sub-brain sectors of Tegas's mind

were formulating a plan for how he would be able to weather the storm of this little war, and had been for several days. He needed only to allow the necrons to wipe out the Sororitas again and ensure he did not draw their attention. Eventually, the machines would revert back to their dormant state, and a window of opportunity to flee would open.

He would take a prize with him, though. Something that would be a bargaining chip to anyone who came to the rescue, be it Hoth's agents or more of the Sisterhood. The relic; he would take *The Hammer and Anvil*.

Tegas listened to everything. He heard Imogen and Miriya talking. On the planet, his probes had heard the hospitaller wench spill out her story about the necron laboratorium where the Sororitas artefact had been seen, and the maps the aliens did not guard told him where that was.

The questor began to prepare a script in his mind. It would begin with his return to the convent, alone. He would be sorrowful at the deaths of Imogen's entire unit. He would present Sepherina with the relic as a token of that – but there would be no time to be thankful. The necrons would be coming – he could broadcast on their communications lines and ensure they were alerted – and he would slip away in the fighting, keeping the artefact for himself.

He looked up at the towering metal walls and intricate, crystalline machinery far overhead and simulated regret. Yes, it would be necessary to destroy this magnificent place as well, but perhaps one day they would come back and sift the remains for something of use. Hard choices needed to be made, if he were to live through this. After all, if he perished, this would all have been for nothing.

In a battle, it would be easy for one intelligent being to hide in the cracks while the women and the machines annihilated one another. Tegas would need to play the long game, but it would be worth it.

They halted at a four-way junction and he paused, sampling the air with the sensors on his servo-arm.

He felt Sister Pandora's presence behind him. 'Which way now?' she asked, the alien immensity of the place lost on her.

Tegas eyed her. She was like all the others, too blinded by dogma to appreciate the strange geometries and incredible artistry of the complex's design. The Sisters only hated, he told himself. It was foolish to expect anything else of them.

The questor pointed with his servo-arm. 'That way. The corridor will lead us closer to the main power core.'

'You seem certain,' Imogen sniped. 'How can you be so sure?'

'I am detecting the largest outflow of energy in this entire complex above us, in that direction. It can be nothing else.'

'Go on, then,' said the woman.

He nodded obediently, and looked away, waiting for the right moment as he walked onwards.

The moment had come.

For the deathmark, the passing of time was something that registered in only a distant fashion, a set of numerals that shifted and changed from one optimal to another. Waypoints, in effect, marking the path of the weapon from activation to execution to re-tasking. The cycle endless, the progression constant.

In silence, phase potentiality altered and softened a sector of space-time inside the human complex, and allowed the necron marksman to slip out of the hyperspatial oubliette where it had observed and prepared. The alien killer emerged from the dimensional blind and activated the hunter's mark. The datum-jewel on the target provided by Nemesor Khaygis was rich with information and perfect for the sniper's needs. The designator transmitter inside the deathmark's armour-hood embedded the neutrino-boson template upon the target, tuning it so the marker glow would fluoresce across five-dimensional space. Wherever the objective went, if she made it to the immaterium or into a teleportation chamber, passed through chronometric barriers or the heart of a star, it would not matter. Until the decay-pattern fell below the receptor threshold – little more than an hour by human reckoning – the energy halo would denote the inescapable eye of the assassin upon her.

It was unheard of for a target to outlast the mark upon them. This deathmark's own records showed only one objective of note, an eldar exarch who managed to avoid termination for a full five minutes before the kill-shot claimed him. It anticipated no such challenge from this mind-damaged human.

The deathmark raised its synaptic disintegrator rifle and fired, unleashing a streak of compressed lepton particles across the chamber.

Decima's answer never came.

She slammed Verity into the flagstones as the burning streak of energy went wide of them, claiming poor Thalassa as its victim instead.

The wounded Battle Sister released a bloodcurdling scream as the weapon ripped through her neural tissue, destroying all synaptic activity within her brain. She crumpled, her body a nerveless sack of meat, eyes open and turned to ruby. Blood trickled from her nostrils, her ears, pooling around her head. Horribly, she seemed to be still alive, dying slowly, her legs twitching as her ruined neural matter misfired and dissolved.

Panic erupted in the infirmary as Verity and Decima scrambled to find cover.

'Deathmark!' said the revenant. 'necrontyr assassin-cadre!' She scowled at the strange glow shrouding her. 'He's here for me. I am targeted for termination. It must be the scarab implant... It has locked on to it.'

Verity chanced a look around the side of the fallen pillar where they hid and saw Zara and the others leading a frantic evacuation of the infirmary. Further out along the length of the garrison hall, she glimpsed a shift of black mist and dull steel. A thread-thin laser beam, bright and green, swept the room.

'Zara?' Verity called into her vox. 'Get them out, warn the Battle Sisters! We will keep it occupied!'

'No!' Decima shouted. 'You must go! It only wants me! The deathmark will kill its target and then fade away. Let me die!'

'Was that what you were going to ask of me? A moment ago, when you said you were not sure?' She leaned closer, her voice trembling. 'Did you want me to... release you?'

'Yes.' The reply was instant. 'No. *Yes*. No. No. Yes.' Decima ground her teeth together and bit out the word. '*No*.'

Another streak of energy lashed over their heads, crackling into the stonework.

'But the choice is not mine to make,' said the survivor, with sudden clarity. 'It has been taken from me.'

Verity's fear transformed inside her, becoming a fire, becoming power. 'I refuse to accept that,' she told her. She raised the gauntlet on her hand, the construct of brass filigree and complicated clockwork unfolding like a flower of blades and needles. 'If you are willing to die, then are you willing to risk? Do you trust me?'

Decima screwed her eyes tightly closed and Verity knew she was enduring the silent persecution of the voice in her head. 'I trust you,' she said, in a small voice.

'There will be a lot of pain,' Verity told her, reaching for Decima's neck.

They were somewhere above the Dolmen Gate, by Miriya's reckoning, close to the same tier where they had arrived through the first set of portals. She looked around, trying to make sense of the repetitive, identical chambers. The laboratorium is nearby, the Sororitas told herself. I am certain of it.

It was difficult to be certain, however. The structures of the necron complex were modular in design, thousands or even millions of identical components slotting together in harmony to build the vertiginous walls and endless corridors that ranged away into the gloom. There was none of the artistry or the elegance of a craftsman's work that characterised the way things were made in the Imperium. No artisan had designed and constructed this place; the cavernous inner spaces of the Obsidian Moon had been built with all the cold and inhuman precision of a cogitator program.

Through vents in the steel walls she glimpsed regular flashes of light dazzlingly bright, and her skin prickled with static electricity. On the far side of that barrier, vast amounts energy had been chained and put to work powering this place. She could only guess at what kind of science could create such a thing.

'Access way, here!' called Pandora, ahead at the point of the squad. With her gun she indicated a hexagonal tunnel at right angles to the passage they were in.

'Show me,' said Sister Imogen, stepping up to take a closer look.

Miriya turned to Tegas, who had slowed to a halt. 'Is this the way?' she asked him. The questor didn't answer at once, and she repeated her question more sternly.

At last Tegas gave a slow nod. 'Yes,' he said at length.

A crawling, nagging sense of disquiet pulled at Miriya's thoughts. Tegas seemed distracted, his attention somewhere far away. He exhibited the same behaviour pattern he had days earlier, in the convent. Then, he had been silently communicating with his cohorts – but now? What was he doing *now*?

'Those markings,' said Danae. She nodded at the walls of the tunnel. 'The etchings in the black stone...'

Miriya looked and she went cold. She had seen the shapes carved into the dark walls before. *Perfectly laser-cut ovals, shield-shaped designs with a single dull ruby at the top of the circumference.* She heard the faint crunch of metal on rock.

'No...' She spun back towards Tegas. 'Do not–'

The ovals buckled in and inverted, and Imogen and Pandora were directly below them. Danae cried out, but it was too late. The walls of the tunnel – not an access way at all, but some sort of storage gallery – came alive as iron insects boiled out of the stonework where they had been quiescent.

A tide of chattering scarabs surged forwards at waist eight and Pandora spun away, knocked out of the path by the Sister Superior. Imogen's gun cracked once as she got off a single shot, and then she was swallowed up by the writhing mass of insect-forms.

Tegas battered Miriya with the heavy grasping pincer at the head of the servo-arm growing out of his back, and the blow knocked her off-balance. Suddenly the questor was fleeing, claw-feet flashing across the tiles as he raced away. She hesitated for a heartbeat, unsure of what target to prosecute.

The other Battle Sisters engaged the massive scarab swarm, the horde that somehow Tegas had been able to summon. The wave of writhing metallic beetles came on and on, and did not slow. In the middle of the mass a shape moved, and to her horror Miriya saw Imogen stagger back to her feet through sheer force of will.

The scarabs covered her like a coat of whispering chainmail. Blood ran in rivers from her bare flesh, and her power armour sparked and jerked where the machines were biting into the myomer muscle bunches and drive-trains. She beat at herself, clawing at the things as they ripped her with a hundred sets of razor-sharp mandibles.

Imogen's right eye had already been gouged out, but the other glared forth and found Miriya, angry and accusing. Over the buzz and whine and wet bone-crunch of the scarabs feasting on her, the Sister Superior managed to give voice to one final command.

'Don't fail!' she choked, gurgling as a bright froth of blood fountained from her lips; then in the next second she was falling back into the mass of the swarm, the machines eager to take her to pieces.

Miriya turned her back on the engagement and broke into a sprint, her boots clanking on the steel floor as she went after the questor.

The deathmark ignored the other humans as they fled the area of engagement. None of them appeared to possess anything approaching a weapon, nothing that the assassin's external sensors registered as capable of penetrating its armour-hood.

Unhurried, it marched across the vaulted hall with the disintegrator long-rifle raised to the shoulder, the discharger array in the muzzle humming with power. The target designator glowed in the virtual field of the necron soldier's vision, shifting back and forth behind a low barricade of fallen masonry. The energy dispersal was unusual, outside standard parameters, and the assassin consulted the datum the nemesor had provided on the target organic once again for clarification.

It was an atypical humanoid, heavily modified with necrontyr technology. The hunter's mark flickered around a key element of the modifications, a mindshackle scarab module. Khaygis had supplied all data on that device as well, and it had made tracking the target a simple matter of homing in on the unit's emissions.

But now the reading was attenuating, becoming irregular. The marker glow was bisecting, behaving as if it were in two places at once.

The deathmark halted and lowered the rifle. This was unusual, unprecedented. Two minutes had elapsed since designation. Time was passing now, out here in the universe, and the target was not yet terminated. These factors were converging. The kill needed to be made sooner rather than later.

A sound split the air; a brutal scream of pain. The assassin noted it and continued onwards. A slit in reality opened briefly and the deathmark sealed its disintegrator back in the dimensional oubliette. It returned with a secondary weapon – a silver hyperphasic sword capable of cutting through all but the densest matter. The works of the dynasty's assassin cadres were not always conducted at extreme range; sometimes the close-in kill was the better method. The necron marched towards the fallen pillar, raising the sword.

The glow of the hunter's mark split in two and went in opposite directions.

The brass gauntlet on her hand wet with blood, Verity bolted from cover and ran for the door. The broken, twitching scarab device was still clutched in her fist, the needle-like legs kicking and pressing against her grip. It glowed with the same ethereal light that had framed Decima's head, and she was very much aware that holding it made her as much a target.

Then she made her mistake, the kind of error that a Battle Sister would not have indulged. She looked back.

She had to. Removing the scarab like this, on the spur of the moment without any adequate preparation, with only the most basic of tools and a prayer to the God-Emperor for success... It was more than likely that doing so had given Decima the very mercy death Verity had argued against.

She saw no sign of the injured, bleeding woman. The hospitaller thought of the raw, open wound on Decima's neck, where she had peeled back the meat and scarred skin down to the bone...

There was a chance, she had thought, that the deathmark would be confused by the forcible removal of the marked implant, perhaps even enough to defeat its targeting logic. That seemed foolish now.

The necron was right behind her, and she stumbled as it slashed at her with a glittering sword.

She lost the scarab in her fright. It clattered to the ground, where it began to wander in a circle, leaving a trail of Decima's blood behind it. The deathmark gave it a dispassionate glance and stamped on it, destroying it outright, killing the glow.

For a moment she thought it would kill her too, but the blank skull-face of the necron, polished to a mirror-bright sheen, only showed disinterest. It turned away, looking for Decima once again.

The deathmark found her. The woman came screaming out of the shadows, her scarred face and neck wet with newly-shed blood. With the hunter's mark on her, the glow made Decima into a terrifying sight; she was a spectre of vengeance, the unquiet spirit of her dead Sisters sent to exact payment on those who had killed them.

* * *

In her hand, Decima had a piece of rockcrete larger than her head, and she slammed it into the deathmark with such wild violence that the xenos assassin staggered under the blow.

++*You cannot win*++ howled the Watcher. ++*You can never silence me*++

She rained down attack after attack upon it with the might and the pace of the feral, breaking the stone on its shiny metal ribcage as the alloy caved in and broke.

'I will not fall to you,' Decima shouted. 'You are gone! I have killed you! *Leave me!*' She was screaming, insane with her emotions. All of it had been bottled up inside, unable to find release; but no more.

++*Never*++ came the reply. ++*I am in your head. I am in your psyche*++

The alien fought back, swiping with the sword, cutting air as it tried to slice the revenant in two. Decima feinted and came close, inside the deathmark's guard. Before it could react, she grabbed the ball-joint of the necron's arm and pivoted, forcing it against itself. The weight of the assassin-mechanoid shifted and it was unable to arrest the fall.

'She tore out the machine,' hissed the woman. 'I don't have to hear you any more. I take back my soul! I take it back!'

Decima made sure the deathmark fell slowly, inescapably, onto the upturned tip of its own blade. With a scratching hiss, the hyperphasic sword entered its metal skull beneath the chin, and gently worked its way up to pierce the armour-hood.

++*No*++

She glared at her own blood-stained reflection in the deathmark's polished face, listening to the voice in her head die into silence.

++*no*++

'I am not you!' she spat venomously at it. 'I was never you! Never!'

The necron did not respond, the emerald light in its eye sockets fading to nothing.

CHAPTER FIFTEEN

The sandstorm was drawn to the valley by the static flashing into the air, as the blue-white flickers of tiny lightning charged the atmosphere. The clouds of oxide dust swirled and mingled with plumes of black smoke from untended fires, the hellish gloom they cast ignored by the invaders as they marched ever onwards. Around them, burning vehicles, shredded pergolas and the blackened husk of the mobile explorator module stood mute witness to the thoroughness of the alien assault. Human dead lay where they had fallen, ignored by their killers and abandoned by their comrades in the rush to fall back to safety.

A bright hail of gauss-beams, tesla blasts and accelerated particle streams cascaded across the open courtyard, the angles of attack slowly shifting as the necrons advanced. The howling bolts of fire impacted the sheer, rounded sides of the last untouched structure inside the convent proper – the keep.

The dark red stone of the towering donjon glittered with a heat-haze effect thrown up by a void shield generator. The energy barrier deflected the torrent of death, great ripples shuddering in the air all around it as the device laboured to protect the last stronghold on Sanctuary 101. Once, the force wall had been part of the arsenal of a great Battle Titan, and in the aftermath of the War of Faith in which it was lost, this component of it had been bequeathed to the Order of Our Martyred Lady. It had served them well for three hundred and eleven years, but now it teetered on the edge of a catastrophic overload, stressed beyond all limits.

With each wall breached, the Sisters had fought until they were about to be overrun, using every weapon at their disposal. They set mines and flame pits, they used converging fire and counter-siege tactics that had been ancient before the days of Holy Terra's Old Night. The necrons were destroyed, but the advance did not cease. The ranks that followed marched over their crippled fallen, and those that were obliterated simply vanished in crackles of green fire. For every one that was destroyed, another was there to step into the breach.

The canoness ordered the Battle Sisters back, and back, and back, until at last there was nowhere else to go. Now they waited inside the keep, the Sororitas and a tiny handful of terrified survivors from the workgang party and Questor Tegas's Mechanicus contingent.

From inside the transparent, purple-hued barrier, wounded and weary Sororitas looked out through gun slits as the inner ward of the convent became a mass of silver alloy skeletons. The necron numbers seemed endless, and their cold desire for battle relentless.

Then, somewhere up on the third tier, a Battle Sister began to sing. The unmistakable refrain of the Fede Imperialis echoed down the corridors, and with each woman who heard it, a new voice was added to the choir. Soon, every Adepta Sororitas within the walls of the keep was at one with the words, the harmony of them swelling in a prayer. Above the crash of beam fire, the battle-hymn rose high.

On the other side of the void shield, warriors and immortals in massed ranks concentrated their firepower on specific points of the energy barrier, loci that the Canoptek wraiths had scanned and determined as the ideal points of overload for the attack. A ring of steel remains ringed the edge of the crackling force wall, shredded pieces of attackers and a single ill-fated deathmark that had attempted to penetrate the barrier through hyperspatial transition. The humans had been careful, raising the power that coursed through the void shield until it was dimensionally impregnable. But the intensity required to do so was monstrously high, and it would exact a grave cost in time.

The nemesor observed from his war-throne as his command Monolith cruised over the rubble that was all that remained of the outer walls. He sampled the data returns from tomb spyders scuttling around the perimeter of the void shield, reading their scans. Khaygis raised a taloned finger and at once all gunfire within the courtyard ceased. The only sounds were the crackle of static discharge, the thrum of contra-gravity motors, and faintly, of human voices in one of their peculiar tonal harmonies.

He needed only to linger. Even if the massed necron army stood here, silent and waiting, there would come a point when the human barrier would reach the end of its operational lifespan and fall. The nemesor did not need to expend any more energy. The march of entropy would do the job for him. He made a quick calculation – in a few solar rotations, he estimated, no more.

Of course, that time could be reduced to a single Kaviran day with sustained bombardment, perhaps even hours if he placed his Monolith's particle whip and flux arc cannons to the deed.

Or it could be dealt with *now*, at this very second.

Khaygis raised his hand and made a motion, a gesture like beckoning. A new sound rose to join the others – grav-motors, but of a different calibre, faster and higher pitched. A flight of Tomb Blades droned out of the dust clouds at the edge of the valley, flanking a third craft that drifted slowly across the sands, its arched prow turning towards the central keep.

The ground troops parted, creating a path for the barge to follow. Made of blackened carbon and bright alloy, the craft resembled an inverted steel ribcage, and at the stern a triarch praetorian sat wired into a battle chair, surrounded by glowing planes of systemry and function. Slung beneath the barge, running almost the entire length of it, was a cylindrical mechanism that held spirals of lethal radiation inside a maw crested with collimator vanes. Its designation was etched in glyphs along the rise of the scorpion-tail sail above the central deck. There were many names for the craft, honours and dedications presented by the Sautekh dynasty for all the battles it had won them. If its description could be translated into the poorly-nuanced tongue of the humans, they would have named it a Doomsday Ark.

The barge halted and as the Tomb Blades made a cursory strafing run against the force wall, the great cannon along its spine moaned with power. Bright spears of discharge flashed from heat vanes, fusing sand to glass beneath it.

When it was time, the nemesor closed his open claw into a fist, and the Doomsday Ark fired. Such was the power of the blast, it momentarily drained the potential of the barge, sending it dropping to the earth as it recovered; but the searing bolt of actinic plasma it unleashed roared across the courtyard like a spear made from the flesh of a star.

Those Battle Sisters not behind their helmets or quick enough to seek cover were instantly and permanently blinded. They did not see the writhing charge of energy meet the haze of the void shield, did not see the massive release of contrary power as one overwhelmed the other.

The barrier protecting the keep was shattered with a single blow, and monumental back-shock resonated through the generator's beam-vanes. Down in the basement levels, the generator exploded, killing the operator crew and its guards. Fire caught and bedded in there.

Silent but for the crunch of their metal feet on the sand and the rubble, the necron army began to advance on the naked, unprotected citadel, raising their guns to the ready. From every weapon slit and barred window, the Battle Sisters opened fire, lines of tracer, flame and plasma sleeting down at the wall of alien steel.

Khaygis watched. In a few moments, the Doomsday Ark would be returning to active power levels, and soon after that it would have enough energy for a second blast from the main cannon. The nemesor plotted the best points of attack. The weapon would be able to bite chunks out of the thick stone walls of the central donjon, perhaps even undermine it enough to force a total collapse of the structure. He could hold back his troops, let the long guns do all the work. The humans would eventually perish.

Except...

Except that did not seem like it was *enough*. Khaygis reached deep to find the root of his thought and could not place it. He could only be certain that it was *not enough* to stand off and assail the human stronghold until it was ruins. These fleshthings needed to die with terror in their hearts, seeing the faces of the necrontyr as they perished.

The nemesor would not compute the same errors that Cryptek Ossuar had allowed to progress. The humans had to perish, with a zero degree of survival. He would see to it personally, through the eyes of his soldiers. Through his own claws, if need be.

Khaygis transmitted the kill command, and the walls of the keep were breached. He watched his troops swarm inside, re-enacting the massacre from twelve years ago with swift and perfect efficiency.

How long have *I been a traitor?* The question rolled around Questor Tegas's mind as he ran, letting the autonomic pathing processors in his scuttle-claw feet follow the route he had programmed for them.

Treason is merely a matter of dates. The words rose up from some deep memory store, something that Tegas had absorbed from a data stack centuries ago, the origin and context of the truism lost to him.

He didn't truly consider himself a turncoat. To be that, he

would need to go against the Adeptus Mechanicus of Mars and the Omnissiah, and there would never be a moment in the questor's life when that would occur. All weakness in that regard had long ago been burned from him.

No, what he did now was the *opposite* of treason. He was committing a supreme act of total allegiance, freeing himself from the burdens that surrounded him so that he could return to the Mechanicus as a herald... And as a hero.

Of course, some distasteful acts were required. The women, for example. He had to divest himself of the Battle Sisters for his plan to reach its conclusion. It surprised him how easily he was able to remotely interfere with the lowest levels of the necron hierarchy, beaming signals into the ambient network all around him. He was elated that it had actually worked, and already redundant subsections of his thought-process unit were busy evaluating the import of what had happened. Tegas had alerted the scarab-mechs, raised them up from dormancy to active attack mode. *Could that possibly mean... By the Machine-God, what if I could command them?*

The possibility was delicious. For a brief second, Tegas imagined himself entering the Hall of Forges in Olympus Mons with a phalanx of necrons as his slaves.

He pushed the thought away. This was no time to become distracted. He was deep within alien territory, undefended, on borrowed time. Tegas steeled himself, marshalling his thoughts towards the search for the prize – the Sororitas relic. With it in his possession, he would have all the coin he needed to pay his way to glory.

The laboratorium was exactly as he had heard the hospitaller describe it to Canoness Sepherina. The questor slowed and moved as stealthily as he was capable, extending antennae and probes from his body through sewn holes in his robes. He broadcast a low-level electromagnetic signature to mimic the same outputs he had detected from a necron warrior, mouthing a prayer that the alien sensors inside the complex would not be intelligent enough to see through his digital masquerade.

He approached a hexagonal door and it broke open in segments. Tegas pointed an eye-cluster back over his shoulder to ensure he was not being followed, and then advanced. At one moment, one of the females – Sister Miriya, he recalled – had been on him, but she had been waylaid by a warrior patrol Tegas had managed to avoid.

Dead now, he decided, and entered the chamber.

The dark stone and the sharp-cut walls stood out in shades of white and pale green to Tegas's enhanced eyesight. He found the sensor strip on the floor, and with a burst of anticipation-analogue, he let the chamber illuminate around him.

Tegas set himself to data-gathering mode and drank it all in. He looked through hundreds of eyes at the glassy globes and the organic remains they held in stasis, the holographic panes of alien data accompanying them. Some of the containers showed signs of recent damage and he made a negative noise. Doubtless that was the work of the Battle Sisters, blundering around like clumsy, ignorant children.

He found a display of broken armour pieces and dead firearms, and there among them, discarded and ignored, was a grey, dust-caked metal drum etched with a fleur-de-lys.

Tegas ran his hands over the container, scanning it for micro-fractures, energy bleed, booby traps, anything untoward. The sensors in the tips of his fingers registered nothing, and gingerly he gathered up the capsule, turning it over.

It was undoubtedly the correct item. He found the bloodlock and the personal sigil of the previous canoness of Sanctuary 101, embedded in the seal that had remained undisturbed for over a decade. Tegas measured the weight of the object, and could not escape wondering what he would find if he opened it.

He reviewed his files on the artefact known as *The Hammer and Anvil*. Data was scarce. The Sisters of Battle guarded their secrets with great care and vehemence, and this was one of their most precious. It was unquestioned that the relic dated back to the thirty-sixth millennium, to the Age of Apostasy when the mad High Lord Goge Vandire had plunged the Imperium into his so-called Reign of Blood. Some said it pre-dated the creation of the Adepta Sororitas, having been gifted to the progenitors of the Battle Sisters when they were still known as the Daughters of the Emperor. Others said it was a tool, a powerful weapon granted to the Sororitas by the High Lords of Terra during the great Reformation, when the remnants of Vandire's cults were mercilessly purged from the galaxy. Many records of that era were sketchy, but the Adeptus Mechanicus had reports of entire worlds being 'burned at the touch of the Hammer' and 'broken upon the Anvil' of the Sisterhood's fury. If those words were more than just figurative... The thought hung in Tegas's mind.

And yet the identity of the relic was unknown to the galaxy at large, and had remained so to all but the most highly ranked Sororitas for thousands of years.

Tegas looked at the capsule and felt *hungry*. He had no need to eat, his internal systems fed by a microfusion generator and monthly ingestions of a polymer nutrient gel dense in metals and proteins, but he remembered the sensation from when he had been fully human. Even as he set the pod down on the stone floor, he knew what he was doing was folly. Logic screamed at the questor to take the capsule and flee with it, to find some safe location far from prying eyes before he even contemplated what he was doing now.

And yet, he did not stop himself. The need to know was just too great. It swamped his reason. *I will just take a look*, he told himself, *just enough to lay my eyes upon it and know*. He could not conscience the thought that he might perish in his escape from here – and the chances of that were substantial – without ever having uncovered the secret the Sororitas had kept. Information was meant to be known, known by those with the intellect to use it. That was Tegas, that was the Adeptus Mechanicus. It was his right. More than that, it was his *duty* to know.

With a cutting laser in the tip of his servo-arm, he delicately excised the security lock-out on the capsule and worked to open it. The task would have tested anyone else, but not the questor. The Sisterhood had failed to remember that their security devices and their strongboxes were made by the Mechanicus. Every lock could be defeated, if one understood it.

Time passed. The lid came off and clanked to the floor, a whiff of old air curling in the cold of the necron laboratorium. Tegas detected the flicker of a stasis field disengaging. Whatever had been inside had been kept in a timeless condition of suspension by the field effect.

His manipulators trembled slightly as he reached inside and grasped the object within. *A thick, heavy rectangle.* He detected metals and plastics, combinations of chemical surfactants and cured organic matter. *Leather. The relic is covered with a sheath of cured leather.*

Tegas had expected a pistol, a skull, an orb of gold, a crown made of crystal. He had expected something xenos and inhuman, or daemon-made and unholy. A hundred possibilities. But nothing like this.

In his hands he held a book. Thick, secured by dense bindings and a latch that held it shut. There, on the hide cover, etched in gold, the title: *The Hammer and Anvil.*

His driving curiosity, the one human emotion he had never been able to fully purge from his persona, faded away and was replaced by something else, something rare. *Confusion.*

The questor carefully opened the book at its first page and coiled his mechadendrites around it, scanning the tome across every possible perceptive range. The form could be illusory, he told himself. There were files on Mars that described things that resembled books, such as the *Malus Codicium*, the *Ravonicum Rex* or the *Epistles of Lorgar*, things that were so much more. Pages encoded with telepathic matrices, subspace memes, even possessed by daemonic energy from the warp. There could be nanoforms within the ink itself, the paper could be psychoactive, even the spine might hide data needles that led to other riches.

He detected nothing, only the great age of the pages. The

book was old, on the scale of hundreds of centuries. Tegas blink-transcribed the text into his personal data pool, dragging it through counter-encryption programs, layering it one image atop another, sifting for patterns. He created a disarray of meaningless information, the rational words on the paper rendered into recurring gibberish by his attempts to read something into them.

In his hands he held a book, pages of verses and observations on faith and duty, penned in pious manner but with no sense of focus or aim. It was not a disguise for something else, it was not imbued with preternatural power on any scale that Tegas could detect.

As he scanned it, and scanned it again, the questor's confusion deepened. There was no secret message lurking in these words, no code embedded in the patterns of the text. No blueprints for a weapon so powerful that it could burn a world of heretics. No ethereal powers lying dormant, no binding made of daemon's skin or ink drained from the blood of aliens.

All he held in his hands was *a book*. Ink and paper and binding.

'This is... nothing else!' Tegas bit out the words, trembling. He shook the container, but only particles of dust fell from it. The questor brandished the tome in his claw grip. 'What is this? *What is this?*'

'Read the name.' Tegas spun in place and found the woman Miriya standing in the entrance to the chamber. He had been so invested in the relic he had not heard her approaching. She was panting, her face bloody, but her manner was reverent. 'The author's name,' she demanded. In her hand she held a smoke-blackened bolter.

Tegas looked down at the title page and read aloud what was written there, scratched in a careful and deliberate hand. *'These words and thoughts are mine. Know me. I am Sister Katherine Elysius, Daughter of the God-Emperor.'*

'Blessed be her name, mother of my Order and first among the companions of Alicia Dominica.' Miriya completed the ritual phrase and bobbed her head. She hoped that Saint Katherine could forgive her for failing to make the sign of the aquila, but under the circumstances she did not trust Tegas enough to take her eyes off him. 'You opened it. You have no right to touch it, cog! You dirty the words of my mistress with your presence!'

'Words...' The questor shook his hooded head. 'In the name of Terra, tell me that there is more to this than just words on a page!'

He waved the ancient tome at her and Miriya felt a jolt of fright. She was furious at him for his desecration of the relic, but at the same moment terrified he might damage it. 'Give it to me, or I will kill you where you stand.'

Tegas didn't seem to hear her. 'There is nothing in this, is there? No secret but the one you have invented to surround it!' he shouted. 'How can this worthless text be so highly valued? There is no new knowledge here, no insight that unlocks the universe! *It is just a book*! I risked everything for the doggerel of a dead nun!'

'You blaspheme my Saint.' Miriya took aim at his head. 'It is *her* book, you maggot! Written in her own hand, her own words laid down for her Sisters to come. For me! It is faith, in its purest form!'

'I know faith!' Tegas shot back at her. 'I have conviction enough for the Imperial Cult and the Omnissiah!'

'Your only faith is in your own arrogance,' Miriya said coldly. 'You have no understanding of what it is to believe in something bigger than yourself.' The words seemed to come from somewhere far away, as if they were being spoken by a part of the Battle Sister that had been silent for many months. '*The Hammer and Anvil* is Katherine's soul poured out onto paper. You hold the only copy still in existence. The physical matter of it, the pages, the binding... Those things have no value at all. But the inscriptions within, questor... The Martyred Lady herself wrote them. In this, that book is beyond any material worth to the Adepta Sororitas. It is our secret prize, carried from convent to convent to bless each outpost of our Order with Katherine's memory. I wondered why Sepherina fought so hard to return to Sanctuary 101… I did not fully understand until she told me of the book.' Miriya glared at him. 'Do you understand now, Tegas? The coin with which you measure the value of the world does not carry to all of us! What you think worthless I see as priceless.'

He was silent for a long moment. When he spoke again, the questor's voice was loaded with venom. 'I should destroy it out of spite. You and your Sisterhood have been nothing but impediments to my designs from the very beginning!' Then with a jerk of motion, he threw it down. 'Take your precious book, then, and read aloud all your dead Saint's homilies and sermons on the nature of faith. We will see how far that gets you.'

Miriya reached for the book, and a cold breath of air passed over her face. It brought with it the heavy aroma of old dust and heated metals.

She knew that odour. The Battle Sister spun, bringing up her bolter to aim down the length of the chamber. Her blood chilled as she glimpsed a curl of inky mist creeping along the walls of the laboratorium, sliding over the glassy spheres and the lines of steel supports.

'Faith,' said a sepulchral voice. 'Once, I had so much of that. But now it is forgotten to me. I struggle to remember how it was to process that concept.'

'There!' Tegas stabbed a finger into the gloom. 'I cannot read the nature of that mass… It is radiation-opaque–'

'Be silent!' Miriya snarled at him.

The veil of black melted into the walls like a tide retreating across a shoreline, revealing the arched, decorated form of the cryptek. Ossuar tilted his head to study the Battle Sister. 'You came back,' he offered. 'Good. Things were left unfinished at our last meeting.'

'It speaks…' Tegas managed, bringing up his mechadendrites to wave in the air around him. 'Analysing.'

'You may make the attempt, human,' said the necron. 'You will understand nothing.'

'I understand enough,' the questor retorted. 'You are not superior to us.'

'No?' The machine eyed him. 'Do you actually believe that you gained access to our information network on your own? You are here only because I allowed it.' It approached, studying the questor with open curiosity. 'Fascinating. You have attempted biotransference through an organic replacement progression. Flawed. Your theory is based on a faulty base concept.' The cryptek eyed the Sororitas. 'Is this part of your "faith"? These false beliefs, the insistence you show on defying us?' He gestured with the black staff in his claw, pointing it towards them both. 'I wonder how it will be of use to you when I dismantle your living forms.'

Miriya's expression darkened. 'I am Adepta Sororitas,' she told the xenos, 'and we do not suffer the alien to live.'

She pulled the trigger on the boltgun, and unloaded the rest of the mass-reactive rounds in the clip into the cryptek's torso.

On the other side of the towering stained glass windows, a hell-storm was raging. The tiles of the Great Chapel's ornate floor trembled beneath Verity's feet with the deep impacts of heavy weapons fire, dislodging stones and rains of dust from the high dome over her head.

She helped Zara move the last of the wounded into the lee of the granite altar, wrapping the injured woman in a combat cloak. The Battle Sister's breathing was shallow and she was in delirium. The woman lay unaware of where she was or what was taking place around her.

'Perhaps it is for the best,' said Zara in a low voice, her thoughts paralleling those of the other hospitaller. 'When the end comes, she will not be troubled by it.'

Verity rounded on the other woman. 'We are not dead yet!'

Zara looked away, to the tall steel doors where Battle Sisters were arriving in twos and threes, their guns smoking hot from firing. 'I beg to differ,' she replied.

Verity shook her head and walked away, her hands finding

one another as another lengthy barrage of enemy shots shook the pillars around her. Zara's morose manner was infectious, and she could feel the same creeping sense of desolation welling up inside her. She spoke a litany under her breath to stave off the sensation, but it was hard to focus. The roar and shriek of alien weapons were so close, they sounded as if they were on the far side of the chapel's curved walls.

As if in response to her thoughts, a metal stay broke from the constant vibrations and the tall tapestry it supported crackled as it fell to the ground, pooling in a heap. The others ignored it, the Battle Sisters busy as they secured great wooden pews across the only other means of egress from the chapel, the door to the transept. And there, strangely calm among it all, she came across the canoness.

Sepherina was lighting votive candles, one after another, arranging them in rows along the front of the curved altar. She seemed oblivious to the dissonance of the encroaching battle.

It had been on her orders that they had drawn back to the chapel. When the force walls faded and died, the command had come over all the vox-channels. Sepherina did not tell them to retreat. She did not use words like 'withdraw' or 'surrender'. Instead, the canoness told them that the hour was upon them.

'*Come to the chapel,*' she had said, '*it is time for matins.*'

Verity looked up as green light flashed in the windows. It did not seem like any morning prayers she had ever experienced. They were in the eye of a hurricane, the pitiless advance of the necrons and their constant guns drawing closer with every passing second.

The chapel was the closest thing to an impregnable space in the convent, but then those who had made those claims had also promised that the walls would never fall, that the wards would never be breached. Verity considered this as she watched the trickle of survivors slow to almost nothing.

Now Sepherina was speaking into an auspex activated in recording mode, moving her hands in a benediction. Verity came closer as the gun-thunder sounded again, and caught some of her words.

'It is my hope,' she was saying, 'that those who come to find this will also find forgiveness for us. We did not fulfil this mission, and for that I will pay penance in eternity. Look to us at the God-Emperor's side, Sisters, and know that we did our best.'

'Last rites?' Verity challenged, as Sepherina placed the device on the altar. 'Is that all we have left now?'

'That and our devotion.' The canoness made the sign of the aquila before the statues towering over her. 'I only wish it had been enough. But I was foolish to think so.' Her hand fell to the sheathed sword at her waist. 'I believed our tenacity and fortitude would be enough to cut through all the lies and lost truths in this place.' She glanced around. 'But arrogance has doomed us all. Hoth's, Tegas's... and mine.'

'I don't want to die here.' Verity said the words without thinking.

Sepherina gestured at the statues. 'Under the eyes of Saint and God-Emperor? What better place is there?' She paused. 'Do you have a weapon? You should have a weapon.'

'You already consider us dead,' she shot back. 'What is the point, what would I be defending?'

The canoness looked at her with surprise. 'Your Sisters,' she said, with mild reproach. Sepherina drew one of her own bolt pistols and pressed the master-crafted gun into the hospitaller's hand. 'There. I give this as a gift to you. Its name is *Ithaca*. I was awarded it on Gamma Solar for victory in the pogroms there.'

She cradled the pistol in her hands. 'I am not a Sister Militant.'

'You are today.' Sepherina walked on, down the aisle towards the doors. 'Close the way, my Sisters,' she called, her voice carrying over the din. 'Come to the altar and draw near.' She pulled the coif from her head and discarded it, running a gloved hand over her bald, tattooed scalp.

'Wait!' Zara cried out. 'Someone comes!'

Wisps of grey smoke curled around the open door as the Battle Sisters standing guard there hesitated on the threshold. Guns growled in the corridor beyond, and then a figure stumbled through the gap, bloody but still walking tall, the muzzle of the storm bolter in her hands glowing dull red.

'Sister Isabel…' Sepherina accepted a weary salute from the other woman.

'Not the last,' coughed the Sororitas, jerking a thumb over her shoulder.

Verity holstered the pistol and gathered up her narthecia pack, following Sepherina as another shape came through the smoke. The last arrival resolved itself into a ragged figure supporting another.

Decima, her torn hood pulled back from her scarred face, gently set Sister Helena down. The veteran had cruel burns all down one side of her body, and she was barely conscious.

'Tesla carbine,' explained Decima. 'The blast was attenuated but she caught enough for it to wound her deeply.'

Verity nodded, drawing counter-infectives and pain-killers for the injectors in her medicae gauntlet. She worked on bandaging Helena's wounds, and the other woman stirred. The hospitaller stole a glance at Decima's troubled expression. The last she had seen of the revenant had been when the attack began in full force. In the disorder following the first breaches of the wall, Decima had vanished. Verity thought she might have gone searching for a death in battle, but now here she was, a life saved in her hands.

A life saved, for all that it mattered. With a heavy crunch of gears, the chapel doors were sealed. Outside, the rattle and howl of the attack began to lessen, but still there was a steady drum resonating through the floor beneath them.

'They're marching out there,' said Isabel, with a wheeze. She halted, bitterly wiping smoke-dirt from the lens of her artificial eye. 'Nothing to stop them now.'

'Thank you… child…' Helena's eyes fluttered open as the medicines began to take effect, and she righted herself. She gave Decima a terse, respectful nod, and limped away, looking for a place to make ready for the last attack.

The revenant walked the length of the aisle back to the altar and Verity trailed after her. At the foot of the statue, Decima went to one knee and adopted the position of a supplicant. The hospitaller could not help but see the mess of raw, dried blood across the back of her neck where she had forcibly removed the mindshackle. Crude dressings, wet with fluid, covered the worst of the wound.

'You must be in such pain,' said Verity. 'Your body and your spirit.'

Decima shook her head. 'It is a benediction,' she told her. 'All is silence.' She raised a hand to her temple, touched the skin there. 'I thought they had cut out my soul, but it was only veiled. The Watcher concealed it from me. You restored it.'

Verity said nothing. In the aftermath of the deathmark's assault on the infirmary, she had found herself occupied by the question of the device she had found implanted in Decima's flesh. There was no way to be certain at what level it had still functioned, and she wondered if it ever really had.

What if the voice that tormented Decima had been something other? What if, instead of this so-called Watcher's words issuing from her necron tormentors, they had originated elsewhere? Verity was chilled by the thought that poor Decima's ordeal might have come not from without but from within her own agonised psyche.

Like Sepherina, Decima tortured herself over her survival of the massacre at Sanctuary 101, and together both women had endured their torments in different ways – but perhaps in the end, both equally destructive. Both believed themselves to have failed their Order. It troubled Verity deeply to consider that it might take death itself before either of them could find their peace.

A shadow fell over her, cast by the shifting light from the fires burning outside. Verity stepped aside as the canoness came nearer. 'I misjudged you,' Sepherina told the kneeling woman. 'Rise now. The God-Emperor knows your name. Saint Katherine sees you.' She gave a wan smile. 'And so do I.'

Decima did as she was commanded. 'Milady?' Puzzlement coloured her expression. 'I do not understand.'

'You faced the enemy alone to save your Sisters in the garrison hall. Isabel tells me you did the same for Helena, braving necron fire to recover her. If I doubted your devotion, it was wrong of me.' She reached out a hand and touched Decima's face. 'You have endured so much. I cannot take one more thing from you.'

Sepherina reached inside her robes and produced the voidblade she had confiscated from Decima hours before. 'This is yours. A spoil of your war, I believe.'

The revenant glanced at Verity, almost as if she were asking for guidance, and the hospitaller gave a nod in return.

Decima took back the alien weapon and weighed it in her hand. 'I have punished many of them with this, a sword of their own creation. It was fitting.'

Outside, there was silence now, no marching, no gunfire. When the canoness spoke again, she did so with full voice, enough to carry across the room. 'Mark my words. I grant my blessing and the blessing of the Order to this woman. Know her name, kindred. We welcome Sister Decima back into our fold. I know now she has never left it.'

A brittle smile came to the survivor's lips. 'I have waited a lifetime to hear that.'

Verity met Sepherina's gaze, and it was unreadable. Did she mean what she said, or was this some final act of kindness for the ragged woman, in the moments before the necrons came to end them all?

The questions went unanswered as a heavy fist of iron slammed once-twice-three times into the sealed doors of the chapel. Then another rang on the metal, swiftly joined by another and another, more and more crashing impacts. The Battle Sisters scrambled to their fighting positions as the sound of steel on steel grew louder and louder. The doors began to flex against the steady concussion, the makeshift blockades before them trembling.

'Give them nothing,' said Sepherina, raising her gun and drawing her sword.

Verity pulled the bolt pistol into her hands, as the hinges broke and the doors collapsed like a falling drawbridge.

Beyond, she saw nothing but steel and emerald.

CHAPTER SIXTEEN

The impacts punched into the flawless metal of the xenos machine-form, and Sister Miriya felt a momentary surge of triumph as the cryptek staggered backwards, caught by surprise at the sudden violence of her attack.

The moment did not last. What she had thought was nothing more than some kind of ornate talisman around Ossuar's neck cracked open. It was a phylactic charm, and from within it a horde of gel-like spiders emerged, swarming over the necron's chest and burying themselves in the wounds she had just inflicted. Even as she watched, the living metal began to flow and scab over, in a parody of organic healing.

Miriya ejected the clip in her bolter and reloaded. Tegas scrambled across her sightline, and she hesitated on the trigger. But the questor was not exhibiting some sudden instance of bravery.

'Stop! Stop!' he cried, his vocoder amplifying the words, making them crackle. 'We have no need for further violence! We can find common ground, a peace!'

Miriya's expression soured at the thought of such a thing, and she scrambled to gather up the holy relic they had come here for, while the moment was open to her. Her hand clasped the leather cover and the Sororitas fought down a shudder of fear as she bound the sacred book to the votive chains on her belt. She vowed to stain the pages of Saint Katherine's great work with her dying blood rather than see it stolen once again.

Tegas was still talking, almost babbling as he tried to get all the words out. 'There is much we could learn from one another, your technology, our insight–'

'If you believe there could ever be a unity, even for a moment, between our species, you are ignorant in the extreme.' Ossuar's voice was acid. 'You organiforms are below us, and ever will be.' The necron cocked his head, examining Tegas with a pitiless stare. 'Once I thought there might be value in you as experimental stock…' He glanced at Miriya. 'But no. Khaygis was right. You are not worthy of our attention. A diversion, nothing more. And now one to be swept away.'

Some part of Tegas's innate arrogance reasserted itself at the cryptek's dismissive manner, and he rose up, his servo-arm swinging high. 'No! I will not allow it!'

Ossuar made a sound that might have been laughter, a million years ago. 'You have no say in the matter.' The necron's abyssal staff rose and from the tip jetted a stream of black, inky matter that resembled smoke but moved like fluid. Miriya instinctively went to cover, but Tegas's scuttling feet were too slow over the metal deck.

The smoke-wreath hit him and enveloped the questor like a claw made of living mist, wrapping itself around his body, pouring into the hood of his cloak. He let out an inhuman scream, a sound like a recording of a man's cry run back and forth through fields of distortion. Quivering, he fell, the synthetic shriek becoming a long, drawn-out moan.

Then Ossuar was calling more blackness from the rod, letting it spread out around him like a cloak. Miriya grimaced. She had seen the cryptek use this trick before, and no sensors or preysight would be enough to penetrate the rippling wall of dark the necron bent to his will.

Still, she had to try. Miriya thumbed the fire-select catch on her boltgun from full-automatic to single-shot setting, and began a quick dance of move-and-fire, putting rounds into the gloom as she saw flashes of metal in among the mist. Random shots blasted into the walls or exploded the orb-like containers ranged in lines along the laboratorium gallery. Storage fluids that stank sickly-sweet frothed and gushed into hidden gutters beneath the deck plates, and shards of glass-like material crunched underfoot. The unrecognisable gobs of meat and flesh-matter pooling on the tiles blackened and decayed in the open air.

The veil of black swept towards her, and Miriya vaulted away from it, but the churn of inky colour was too swift for her to avoid. In the close confines of Ossuar's gallery of horrors, there was little room to manoeuvre. She was aware of the book pressing into her beneath the folds of her combat cloak, anchoring her to the moment with its presence.

Green light glittered and faded at the corner of her vision. The Battle Sister spun and fired into the smoke, but the instant the round left the muzzle of the bolter she realised she had been duped. A fast, spindly presence faded in behind Miriya.

Ossuar was suddenly there, the iron skeleton looming over her. The abyssal staff flashed, dark on darkness, and the heavy, smoking tip slammed into her like a club. Even through her power armour, Miriya felt the strike in the marrow of her bones. It seemed to penetrate her wargear effortlessly, a shocking flash of cold that deadened her arm. She lost the boltgun to her nerveless fingers, heard it clang against the deck and slip away.

For a split-second Miriya was terrified to glance down at her limb, her mind telling her that there would be nothing there but a withered stick of elderly bone and paper-thin skin. But still she looked; her hand was bloodless and twitching with nerve-shock, but whole. Retreating, she shook off the illusion and kneaded her fingers. It was like touching the hand of a corpse.

Ossuar did not come after her. He raised the staff until it

was horizontal across the plane of his now-repaired torso. The liquid gloom emerged from the shimmering rod, but instead of a flow, this time it was a deluge. Smoke-black haze exploded from the cryptek's weapon and flew at her.

Reflexively, Miriya threw up her hands to protect herself as the shroud swathed her body. She knew what to expect after her earlier confrontation with the alien, but this time the attack was a hundred times more powerful.

Darkness fell and she was suddenly in the heart of a depthless void. Nothing seemed real or substantial. She flailed, trying to find the walls and support pillars she knew were there, but there was *nothing*.

The dark was in her mind. The weapon was not just something that could confuse vision. The necron technology was projecting a nightmarish mantle that cut her off from everything. It was not like the poison of a psy-witch, oily and insidious, toxic to thought; no, Miriya had faced psykers before and it did not feel like this.

Ossuar's weapon was very different. It was touching some primitive level of her animal brain, buried under the rational and logical. It awakened the most base of primal fears – of the dark, of isolation, of death. Even as she understood it, she felt the shroud drawing tighter, starving her mind of reason as a strangling hand would choke air from her throat.

The void filled with emotion, and that emotion was every shade of despair. It was raw and bloody, inescapable. Suddenly, Miriya was drowning in regrets and misery. She saw the faces of the dead from days past, heard their cries pealing against the walls of darkness. Her Sister in arms and trusted friend Lethe, sad Portia whose potential had never been realised, Iona and her milk-pale face beneath the crimson cowl of a Repentia… And beyond them, a hundred, a thousand others, the whole mass of the women who had died at Sanctuary 101, rising up to blame her for failing them. The dreadful phantasms drew closer, mirrored everywhere she turned her gaze. She could not close her eyes. She could not shut them out, trying and failing to find the words of faith that had saved her before. The ghosts were drowning her, smothering her in desolation, killing all hope...

Hope...

Forcing the nerve-deadened hand to work, Miriya reached beneath her cloak and her trembling fingers found old leather and iron latches. She forced herself to think of what was written on the pages of *The Hammer and Anvil*.

'Fear is the enemy of hope. Hope is the foundation of faith. Faith is the weapon to kill fear.' The axiom came to her as if Katherine herself had breathed the words into her ear.

Illumination came from within, streaming from a place in her heart that could never be extinguished, never be doused. It could only be hidden, concealed by the subterfuge of the enemy. The foe would fight to convince you that it was gone, the fire of the soul doused and ashes, that hope was dead... *But it was a lie.*

It was eternal, and so clear to her now that it amazed Miriya she could ever have been uncertain. She spoke a litany to invoke the Spirit of the Martyr and burned her doubts, steeling herself. In one hand she clutched the sacred book; the other reached for the grip of the chain-sword sheathed upon her back.

The darkness died, and the moment shattered. It had only been the briefest of instants, and yet in the grip of the nightmare shroud it had seemed like hours.

Ossuar reared up and emitted a sour, hissing sound. 'Still you defy,' he intoned.

'All acts of faith are acts of defiance,' she shot back. Miriya attacked with a battle-cry, sweeping down with the snarling chainblade. The cryptek blocked the blow and fat yellow sparks gushed from the point where the tungsten-alloy teeth met the alien material of the abyssal staff.

Vehemence propelled Miriya's attack, that and her righteous fury. She executed a sweep and parry that opened Ossuar's guard for a moment too long and the blade fell across the plane of the necron's skull. The Battle Sister put her weight behind the weapon and there was a horrible screeching clatter as the spinning teeth ripped open the cryptek's chromium face. Optical lenses and sensing elements were crushed instantly, and the alien gave an atonal howl.

He struck out blindly with the abyssal staff, beating Miriya back with a random blow. 'My vision is impaired... I cannot see...' Ossuar swung out again as the phylactery medallion irised open, spider-menders teeming as they boiled across his silver skin towards the wound. 'Foolish. I will self-repair. And you will pay for daring to strike a harbinger of the Sautekh dynasty!'

Black mist emerged from nothing, curtains of dark falling. Miriya swung again at the necron, but the cryptek was gone. He appeared, stepping in and out of the churning veils, moving from one side of the laboratorium to another without seeming to cross the physical space in between. Nearby, Tegas groaned, dragging himself into a corner out of the fray.

Tucking away the holy book, Miriya stooped and swept up her bolter from where it had fallen. She turned in a single motion to fire at the retreating alien. But each shot was late, an instant after Ossuar passed into the veil and escaped her. He was trying to wear her down, buying time to heal himself as she expended her ammunition on illusions.

'I will not fight with ghosts,' spat Miriya, and threw herself into a rapid spin, dropping low to one knee to let the boltgun describe an arc across the room. She did not fire towards where Ossuar was; instead she filled the air with bolt-rounds, firing towards where he *would* be.

Half a clip of shells exploded against nothing, but then she found her phantom in the space between manifest and immaterial – and blasted it back into corporeality. Ossuar took a cluster of rounds in the torso and crashed into a stasis orb.

Ruined, broken sounds spilled from the necron's damaged skull. The angular metal mask was broken and fractured, and Miriya saw complex crystalline workings behind the façade. The cryptek lunged wildly with the abyssal rod, savage and random.

Did it feel fear? she wondered. Did it feel that, now she had blinded it? Was the machine capable of emulating that state? Miriya wanted it to be so. It did not seem right that Ossuar should be able to cause such terror and yet go untouched by it.

With a brutal axe-blow strike of her chainsword, Miriya took off the cryptek's arm at the elbow joint and it lost the staff. The necron's self-repair systems were going into overload, frantically trying to fix the critical damage. But the Sororitas could inflict it faster than Ossuar could heal it.

She cut and chopped at the machine-form, taking little victories in the guttural, haphazard noises that spilled from the cryptek. The necron rallied, raising a clawed finger to point towards her.

'You think you can win?' The words were laced with static. 'There are more of my kind than stars in your night. We owned this galaxy before your species was born. We killed the first gods and we will kill yours.'

Slowly, deliberately, Miriya knocked the machine down once more and sheathed her chainsword. She raised her bolter and rested it on Ossuar's damaged skullcase. 'My God cannot die,' said the Battle Sister. 'He lives in faith, and faith lives in us.'

Miriya blasted the harbinger's head into fragments of steel scrap, and watched the green fire of disintegration crawl over the remains of the torso, crackling with the last ergs of energy inside the alien machine.

Questor Tegas was where he had hidden, still trembling from the after-effects of the nightmare shroud. His neural implants were stuck in a restart loop that made him twitch like a victim of palsy. The Sororitas dragged him to his feet and backhanded the adept across his synthetic face.

'You are considering how to kill me,' he grated, regaining his composure. 'But circumstances have changed.'

'Not really.' Miriya glared at him. He could see her raw need to cut him down where he stood, burning hard in the woman's eyes. 'We still have a mission to complete.' She grabbed a fist of his robes and shoved him towards the corridor. 'Move.'

'Why should I?' he shot back. 'I abandoned you... You want revenge for that. It is what you are. The daughters of Saint Katherine. It is what you are known for!'

She ignored his words. 'Sister Superior Imogen is dead. That means that I am the most senior Battle Sister, so command of this mission is mine.' She showed him her bolter, menacing him with the weapon. 'You life belongs to me now. The duration of it will depend on how you obey me from this point onwards.'

'What I did...' He tried to frame the words. 'I was forced to make unpalatable choices.'

'Unpalatable,' she repeated, in a dead voice. 'You left us to be killed.'

'It was for a higher purpose! For the good of the Imperium and Holy Terra. Your sacrifice would not have been forgotten!'

Miriya halted. 'Do you believe that, Tegas. Honestly, and truthfully?'

He nodded, without thinking. 'Of course. I am the Omnissiah's loyal servant.'

There was a long silence before the Sororitas spoke again. 'If that is so, then you have only one chance to redeem yourself, questor. Do you understand?'

'You want me to do as I first promised. Deactivate the necron power core.' He had intended to do that all along, but there was no point in revealing so to the Battle Sister. 'I will.'

'Do it,' she said solemnly, 'and I promise you salvation.'

'I will,' he repeated, moderating his voice-synth, imitating the tones that would best convince her he was not lying.

She did not respond; finally Tegas gave a nervous bow and set off back the way they had come. His tertiary sensors registered a flash of leather-bound pages and iron chain, there beneath the woman's combat cloak.

* * *

The machines came in through the yawning doorway and met a cascade of bolter fire with viridian counterblasts. The atmosphere inside the Great Chapel became a humming, crackling thing that vibrated with sundered air molecules. Flayer beams, tesla gun discharges and bright particle streams washed out in murderous waves. The heavy scents of ozone, cordite and promethium coiled in wisps of white vapour, the effluent of the gun-chorus that screamed defiance against the alien invaders.

Verity had never witnessed such savage combat in so confined a space. Even though the chapel proper was big enough to hangar a dozen bulk landers, it was still too small for the battle that raged within it. A war had been bottled up inside this chamber, poured in and left to rage against itself.

She heard the death-cries of Battle Sisters as they were reduced to cinders by the concentrated fire of the xenos. Necron soldiers widened the entrance with heavy beam blasts and they surged forwards. The fallen of their number vanished in snarling crackles of energy – although she could not be sure if they were self-destructing at the final moment, or being swept away by some form of teleporter. When they died – if one could call it that – the necrons emitted a piercing howl that seemed deliberately pitched to grate on the spirit and chill the blood. At all other times, they were voiceless, silent in the face of the Battle Sisters as Canoness Sepherina exhorted her troops to heights of pious fury.

Verity was behind a heavy oaken pew, with both hands holding the bolt pistol Sepherina had given her. So far, the hospitaller had missed more times than she had hit with the shots she had taken. Verity silently vowed that if she lived to survive this horror, she would work to improve her skill with a weapon.

Her training with firearms was only the most basic. As a medicae in the Imperial Church's service she was often in harm's way, but always in the company of true warriors, never expecting to be called on to fight the enemy face to face. Verity was not squeamish about the weapon, but she lacked the cold ability to kill that women like Sepherina had. Her calling was to life, not to death; but the necrons were something between those two extremes. They were hollow and soulless – one look into those glowing eyes and that could not be denied.

Not for the first time, Verity turned inwards and called on her own faith to steel herself... And by the God-Emperor's grace, she found it.

The great wooden bench in front of her upended and spun away, as if it had been reeled in by an invisible line. A metal statue rose up and threw a shadow over the kneeling woman.

It was a lychguard. Stocky and heavy-set where necron warriors and immortals were thin of line and skeletal, the machine was plated with silver armour accented in platinum and copper. A fanned crest of intricate design emerged from the back of its metal skull, and it advanced with a tall kite shield sheathed in sparks of energy. In its other hand, the alien held an axe-like weapon made from dark blue metals, the cutting edge mirror-bright.

On impulse, Verity jerked the trigger of the bolt pistol and spent the rounds in the clip harmlessly against the spatial dispersion effect surrounding the shield. As the breech snapped open on the empty magazine, she fell backwards, desperately trying to put distance between them. All around, the chaos of the battle continued, ignorant of this small drama among the greater conflict.

The axe – a warscythe – moved, falling towards her face. She jerked away, and felt the wind of the blade's passing brush her lips. The very end of the curved axe-head met the chest-plate of her duty armour and sliced through it as if it were smoke. Panic flooded Verity as she stumbled, expecting a gusher of blood to emerge from the cut; but only desultory impact fibres bled through from within. She had out-stepped the blow by a tiny fraction. A centimetre less and it would have cut her open through the breastbone.

The lychguard shifted its stance, taking its time. The pitiless gaze of the machine-form glared down on her. The next blow would not be in error.

The axe rose, just as a blur of motion came from the shadows nearby. With a grunt of very human effort, Decima came racing into the fray, her black-bladed sword flashing. The necron turned to meet her attack, bringing up the kite shield, but she was already leaning into the blow.

Verity watched Decima force the voidblade into the crackling field around the shield with all her might – and *through* it. Decima carried the strike all the way, ripping across the long guard. The shield broke in two, necron technology cut cleanly by necron technology.

Verity wondered if she saw a moment of anger as the lychguard discarded its now useless wargear. It swung the warscythe at the other woman, and the two alien blades met with a discordant clang. The necron was a head taller than the gangly survivor, and at least twice Decima's mass. She did not let that halt her attack, however, and sword and axe met again and again.

Verity dragged her attention from the wild melee and fumbled a fresh ammunition clip into the bolt pistol, before bringing it up to take aim. She hesitated, her finger tight on the trigger. Decima and the lychguard were in a lethal dance, in close, blade leading blade, searching for a breach in the other's defence. Verity was suddenly afraid to take the shot. One mistake and Decima would die.

Then the choice was made for her. The necron found the opening it needed and slammed Decima in the head with the butt of its warscythe. She rocked and fell back, losing her footing. The lychguard seemed to pause, as if it were calculating the perfect plane of the blow it would make, the single, flawless killing strike that would end the life of the tattered Battle Sister.

Verity opened fire, shouting wordlessly as she pumped the pistol's trigger, letting the muzzle rise with the slamming recoil of the rounds leaving the barrel. The necron tried to protect its head with its armoured hand, distracted and off-balance for a brief instant.

Decima took the moment and made her riposte. With a piercing cry of anger, the woman spun in a lethal pirouette and leapt, coming back down with both hands on the hilt of the voidblade. The black sword entered the lychguard's torso where a human being would have its clavicle, and rotated with the force of the blow. Decima pushed all her might into it, and took the alien's crested skull from its shoulders. The headless necron sank slowly to its knees and trembled, sparks gushing from the neck stump.

Decima withdrew her stolen weapon and took a step towards Verity. 'Sister,' she began. 'I will keep you–'

Safe. The word died on her lips as the tip of the warscythe burst through her stomach, dark arterial blood splashing on the stones. At her back, the beheaded lychguard was still twitching, the last action communicated from its dying machine-mind to stab her in the spine.

Verity screamed as Decima's legs went dead and she fell forwards off the axe-head, crashing to the floor in a heap. Amid the raging gunfire, no one heard her.

'Sis-ter.' Decima managed the word through a mouthful of bloody spittle. She reached up with her bony, malnourished fingers and touched the tears on Verity's cheeks. 'I never heard…' she gasped. 'Before, I could always hear them. In my head. The Watched… I was always watched… But this time… I am free.'

'Decima, I am so sorry…' Verity wanted to reach in and seal the cut with her own hands, even as she knew that was impossible. The hospitaller recognised a mortal wound all too well.

'Will you forgive me?'

She felt a jolt of shock. 'For… what?'

'I could not protect the relic.' Each word was a labour for Decima. 'Katherine will hate me for that.'

'No. *No!*' Verity shook her head. 'She will *love* you for it, Sister. You gave up so much to survive. To warn us.' Bitter sorrow welled up inside the hospitaller. She felt powerless and broken as she watched the woman fall into the arms of death.

'Sister,' she gasped. 'I had forgotten that we are kindred. But I remember now.'

'I will not forget,' promised Verity; but Decima did not hear her.

Danae, Cassandra and the others stood among a drift of smashed necron scarabs, the charred and blasted remains of the machines carpeting the stone floor. Miriya heard the Sister Retributor speaking in low tones as she came closer.

'Imogen Nal, Sister Superior of the Order of Our Martyred Lady, honoured soldier of the Golden Throne, and daughter of Ophelia VII and the Convent Sanctorum. We remember your name and lay you to rest in this place. The sight of the God-Emperor finds you even here.' Imogen's ruined body lay in front of Danae, and she held her meltagun trained on the woman's corpse. '*Ave Imperator*,' she concluded.

'*Ave Imperator*,' repeated Miriya, drawing hard looks from the rest of the unit as she dragged Tegas along with her.

'You left us,' Pandora accused. 'Imogen died because of–'

'She was dead already, and she knew it,' Ananke spoke over her, silencing the other woman. 'But the girl is right. You fled in the middle of an ambush.'

'I did not flee.' Miriya looked to Danae. 'Finish the rite, Sister. We cannot leave Imogen's body to these creatures.'

The Retributor said nothing for a long moment, a silent challenge in her eyes. Then at last she looked away. Imogen's wargear had already been stripped of equipment, grenades and ammunition, leaving only her armour, her chaplet and personal votives. On the battlefield, the corpse would have been recovered for a proper burial, but here such attention was impossible. Instead, her funerary would be concluded by the most expedient means.

Danae bowed, and pulled the meltagun's trigger. Plasma-bright fire hummed from the weapon as she used it to immolate the Sister Superior's body, turning metal, bone, flesh and ceramite into an ashen mass.

'It's done,' said Cassandra, grimly dressing a fierce wound

at her neck. She nodded towards Tegas, who stood shifting his weight from foot to foot. 'An execution next?'

'He lives,' Miriya replied. 'We need him.'

'You decide this?' said Pandora. 'You abandon us in a fight to rescue a worthless cog, and now you give out orders?' Her face creased as the acrid smell of burnt human flesh reached them.

'That is her right,' Danae noted. 'She may take seniority if she wishes. She has the laurels.'

'I gave my oath to Imogen,' Pandora retorted, 'not to her.' He looked at Danae and Ananke in turn. 'So did you!'

'You gave your oath to the Order,' Miriya corrected. 'Imogen understood what was at stake here. This is not about anything else.'

'No?' Pandora stepped closer, glaring at her from under her thin tresses of red. 'She did not think you fit to be in command. We have all seen the broken links of your chaplet. What gives you the right to take the Sister Superior's place now?'

'You don't need to follow me,' Miriya told her, a weariness in her words. 'But you will follow this.' She reached into the folds of her crimson combat cloak and produced the book.

She dropped it into Pandora's stunned grasp. The young Battle Sister's expression transformed in a heartbeat. 'It... it is real.'

'Take it, if you think you are worthy,' Miriya told her. 'Guard it until it can be placed in the hands of the canoness.'

The others made the sign of the aquila over their armour. 'They told us the book was held in the Convent Sanctorum,' said Ananke, disbelief in her tone. 'How can it be here?'

'Saint Katherine's words have been in transit across the galaxy for decades, hidden behind a falsehood,' said Miriya. 'Going from outpost to convent, chapel to colony. Giving secret blessing.' She nodded to Pandora. 'Open it. Read.'

Her hands shaking, the Sororitas did so. Her eyes glistened with tears as she gave voice to the first words she saw. *'Our greatest strength is the steel that lines the heart of every woman. The mother, the daughter, the sister. Her love is eternal and unbreakable. It is the blade that cannot be blunted.'* Pandora's voice turned husky with emotion. 'Throne and Blood... These are the Saint's words.'

'This is why we came back to Sanctuary 101, this is the real reason we returned.' Miriya gave a grave nod. 'Not just to lay the ghosts of the dead to rest, not for the convent or in the name of the God-Emperor. We came for that.' She pointed at the holy tome.

'If we have the book,' began Ananke, 'then is not the mission ended? We should quit this alien mausoleum and abandon it to the xenos.' She gave Tegas a level look. 'And leave the questor for them to toy with.'

'We're not done here,' Danae said, before Miriya could speak the words. 'Book or no book, too much blood has been shed. The necrons have to pay the butcher's bill.'

'Aye,' Miriya agreed. 'We need ask ourselves only one question of how we are to proceed. *What would Katherine do?'*

With great care, Pandora closed the book and secured it beneath her cloak. 'The Saint would kill them all,' she replied.

Miriya nodded and turned to Tegas. 'The power chamber above the Dolmen Gate. You will lead us.'

The adept gave a jerky nod and moved off, the Battle Sisters falling into a skirmish line behind him.

The humming from beyond the trembling stone walls of the chapel grew into a roar, and Verity looked up from Decima's corpse to see a slab-sided shadow pass over the taller of the stained-glass windows. The shape moved with slow, deliberate menace, and for an instant she was reminded of an ancient battle galleon gliding across a calm ocean. She heard Sister Helena cry out a warning, but the words were lost to her in the din.

Then the fire came. A stream of purple-white flames burst through the wall high above her head, and lashed out in a shuddering line. The flaring rope of energy sliced horizontally through the supports, the windows it touched puffing into clouds of brittle shards. It moved from right to left in a single sweep, stonework losing all coherence and collapsing in its wake.

A great gust of wind and rock dust rolled in across the chapel proper as the eastern wall came apart in jagged chunks and the thunder of cracking stone. Verity shielded her eyes and saw the looming shadow framed in the breach it had just created. A great, hovering ziggurat made of black stone drifted closer on a haze of anti-gravity force, and it shouldered its way through the opening. With its presence in the chapel alone, the necron Monolith committed the worst blasphemy imaginable.

Gauss flayer arcs on each corner of the floating pyramid twitched and moved, seeking targets. They laid down pulses of energy that ripped up the intricate mosaics across the tiled floor, flash-blasting discarded prayer books and Battle Sisters alike into embers and ash. Verity went low, dropping into the lee of a fallen pillar, and she dared to look up once again.

Atop the Monolith, before the towering crystal emitter of a particle whip, there was a throne that appeared to be woven out of thick brass cables. A necron bedecked in a metal cloak rose from it, glaring out imperiously over the war his kind had brought to the convent. It raised its hands and pointed them into the battle. From one leapt pulses of green fire, boiling through the smoky air to set stone melting where they impacted; from the other, projectiles trailing lines of energetic particles hissed across the chamber. Verity saw one such arrowhead strike a Sister Dominion with such force that it picked her up and carried her off her feet, into the shadows.

The machine paused, scanning the chamber with its cold gaze.

'What is it?' she asked aloud. 'Looking for something?'

'Stay down, nursemaid!' A muscled hand grabbed at her and dragged her out of sight. Verity found herself next to Sister Isabel, who worked at the slide of a bolter jammed by a misfire. 'It's some kind of commander unit,' she added.

'In all the hells, what else could it be? He's come to end us personally.'

The idea that the robotic, artificial killers would even be capable of such a want or a need seemed jarring to the hospitaller. Even after the confrontation with the cryptek back on the Obsidian Moon, she found it hard to imagine the aliens as anything other than sophisticated automata. Verity could only see them as clockwork, bereft of anything like human sentience or emotion. They were like the uncommon minions of the Legio Cybernetica, things that mimicked the shape of life but bereft of the essence that animated a living thing. She said as much to the grim-faced Battle Sister.

Isabel shot her a look, made fierce by her augmetic eye implant. 'They have no soul, aye. But they live, that is certain. Just don't ask me how.' She hefted her bolter. 'Stay here,' said the Sororitas, as she made to rejoin the fight. Isabel turned back and glanced at the pistol in Verity's hand. 'Count your rounds, Sister,' she told her, 'and keep the last for yourself.'

The Battle Sister vaulted over the fallen pillar and vanished into the haze, firing as she went.

The Monolith's particle whip discharged, and in the confines of the breached chapel it was a sound like the end of the world. Huge pieces of the majestic dome overhead were sliced apart, and they crashed to the floor with earthshaking impacts, kicking up more dust to clog the thickening air. Verity reeled, and saw a glimpse of the pale blue sky overhead, framed in a ragged tear across the ceiling. Up there, pallid with the reflected light of the Kavir sun, she could make out the ghostly curve of the Obsidian Moon, still visible after the dawn.

She thought of Miriya, and felt afraid for her friend and Sister. There was no way to know if she was still alive up there, or if Imogen's strike team had failed in their mission to penetrate the heart of the necron complex. Verity's thoughts were touched by the horrible certainty of her own imminent death, and as the screaming and the firestorm rolled on, she worked the slide of the bolt pistol to eject a single round into her hand. Verity rolled it between her fingers, touching the shell to her forehead and then the fleur-de-lys on her duty armour. She pocketed it, and dashed from cover.

The necrons were everywhere she looked, fighting in hand-to-hand scrambles with Battle Sisters or engaging them in gun duels through the smoke and fire. She realised she was standing next to the grand altar, and lying at the base of the stone dais there were a dozen dead women who had perished at the foot of their Saint. Scattered among them were emptied weapons, ammunition boxes... And a silver-grey cylinder that resembled a scroll made of metal.

Thrumming a bass note so deep it seemed to shake Verity's ribcage inside her flesh, the Monolith progressed up the rubble-strewn aisle towards her, relentlessly closing the distance. She started towards the iron scroll as a fan of emerald laser light swept back and forth across the chamber. The beam crossed her and she gasped, expecting to be burned alive, but it was a harmless scanning ray, emitting from a device on the necron commander's throne.

The beam fell on the scroll and hesitated. The necron in the cloak raised his crackling gauntlet again and released a stream of green fire that reduced the device to molecular vapour.

Verity's stomach knotted with shock. The alien device was the portal to the Obsidian Moon, and although the manner in which it worked was beyond her understanding, the hospitaller knew that without it Miriya and the other Battle Sisters would be trapped. 'You have killed them!' she shouted, and fired on the alien commander. The mass-reactive rounds keened harmlessly off the fuselage of the Monolith, but still she pressed on. 'No more! In the God-Emperor's name, *no more!*'

'*No More! No More!*' From all around her, Verity's cry was taken up by Battle Sisters who emerged from the smoke to lend their arms to her impassioned attack, and salvoes of bolt-shells and melta blasts crashed into the Monolith's dense hull.

A woman with a brazen sword in one hand and a bolt pistol in the other charged headlong past the hospitaller, the rich blood-crimson of the sanctified Aspiriate cloak at her back flaring as she ran. Canoness Sepherina sprinted up a fallen section of the roof, canted at an angle like a ramp, bringing her level with the battlements of the rumbling Monolith.

As Verity looked on, blazing with righteous fury like the Saint she so revered, Sepherina threw herself into single combat with the necron commander.

CHAPTER SEVENTEEN

Tegas's internal chronometers, accelerometers and positioning sensors were finely-tuned pieces of archeotechnology, and operating in concert they were capable of telling him at any time, in any place, of his exact location against the greater skein of the universe.

But not here, and not now. Energies out of balance with the questor's understanding of space-time assailed him, and he was – for want of a better term – *giddy*. His claw-like hands found the safety rail running alongside the thin gantry where they had emerged, and he clung to it as if on the deck of a ship in a high gale. Tegas was tilting as his neural matrix tried to reorient itself against new fields of micro-gravitation. The Sisters of Battle, with their crude human sense organs, were barely affected by the shift in the invisible energy that webbed the air around them. They moved with stealth, silent and steady. The hard-faced one with the meltagun – Danae – glared at him accusingly, and motioned with the barrel of her weapon for him to keep moving.

They could not see what he could see, the threads of neutrinos and bosons liberated and roiling all around them, the streamers made of high-energy particles so rare and charmed that their existence was only theorised by the high thinkers of the Adeptus Mechanicus.

All this emitted from the perfect white cube some five hundred metres below them. Like the access gantries that criss-crossed the core chamber, it was suspended by nothing, hanging there in defiance of both logic and physics.

The chamber itself was a vast tetrahedron, four huge triangular slabs over three kilometres in length along each edge, assembled together into a pyramid-like structure. Walls of dull, mirrored metal rose up all around them, broken here and there by wide slots that opened out into the darkened service spaces of the Obsidian Moon. Each apex was an exposed cluster of crystals and metal rods, their purpose unknown. Beyond them, over their heads Tegas could see flat transport platforms bearing quiescent Monoliths and Ghost Arks, and far below, through to the space where the damaged Dolmen Gate was under repair.

The cube floating in the middle of the chamber resisted all attempts from his mechadendrite sensors to take a read of its surface. Crackles of blue light formed a shifting aurora around the object where the output of a powerful electromagnetic field prevented it from interacting with anything larger than an air molecule. He could see busy tomb spyders moving on the lower walkways, and the floating shapes of Canoptek wraiths drifting around monitor podiums. Occasionally they would pause and adjust something on one of the control panels. The questor guessed they were there to regulate the flow of energy to and from the cube.

'No defenders,' said one of the women, in a low voice. 'It may be a trap.'

'Aye,' said Danae. 'Pandora is right. This place should be crawling with the xenos.'

'They're not here,' Miriya told them. 'They sent their armies away.'

'Where?' said the one called Pandora. But as the question left her lips, she must have realised the answer.

Tegas had glimpsed the nemesor's order-memes floating

at the edges of the necron communications matrix when they first arrived. Almost every active combatant unit had been committed to the attack on Sanctuary 101, in an act of massive military excess. To do so was an almost human act of resentment and hubris, and Tegas found that to be most interesting. Perhaps the necrons were not as devoid of emotional response as they appeared to be. He noted the possibility for later consideration.

His gaze was drawn back to the core. *The cube*. He could not help but turn every optic cluster, every sense module he had, onto it. Behind that barrier was a power source as primordial and as lethal as the forces of creation – a singularity. Tegas heard the women wondering aloud as to the nature of it, and for a nanosecond he considered attempting to explain the phenomenon to them. But they were only soldiers, and their minds, however tactically capable, were simply too limited to understand the awesome power before them.

It was no surprise to Tegas that his sensors returned him only gibberish. The singularity was an elemental effect so uncommon that what mankind knew as the laws of physics simply ceased to apply within its influence. That the necrontyr could shackle such a power to their will was incredible, but then this was a species that apparently dated back millions of years, to an era when things half-recalled by race memory and distant myth walked the stars. The xenos had shown they had knowledge of forced spatial distortion, dimensional transit, teleportation, quantum gravity… The questor would have given much to plunder the mind of one of their scientists, if such a thing were possible.

The singularity was an artificially-created event in space-time, shrouded by some form of exotic material acting as its event horizon. The energy differential between this plane of reality and the one where the singularity existed as an orbifold was being siphoned off, becoming self-reinforcing, bleeding cosmic amounts of radiation into its shell – or so he theorised. The science of it was staggering, and again Tegas felt hungry looking at the object. Somehow, the necrons had manufactured this thing and turned it to power not only the altered dimensional spaces of the Obsidian Moon, but also to the activation of the Dolmen Gate. He did not wish to contemplate what might occur when the necrons finished their repairs on the Gate and opened it. A day, a year, a century; however long it took them, in the end the Imperium would suffer for it.

Tegas realised that he was being spoken to, and with effort, he disengaged himself and turned away. Sister Miriya was standing over him. 'Tell me how to destroy it,' she demanded, nodding towards the object.

He reacted as if he had been slapped. The brutality of her order repelled him. 'You do not understand,' Tegas told the woman carefully. 'To de-power this magnificent creation will take time.' He pointed down towards the lower levels, to the monitoring platforms where the wraiths were working in ignorance of being observed. 'We will need to isolate each control station, perform a staged shutdown...' He relished the idea of it, of getting into the heart of the necron machines and dismantling their code. 'You will have to protect me as I work. It may take several hours, but I believe I can deactivate it.'

The dark-skinned Battle Sister made a spitting sound and looked away.

'What if that is impossible?' said Miriya. 'What if we are forced to destroy these... platforms?'

Tegas shook his head. 'If the singularity core enters an uncontrolled collapse, it will annihilate...' He spread his hands. 'All of this.'

Miriya gave a slight nod, and peered over the edge of the rail. 'Thank you, questor. You may consider your obligation fulfilled.' She stepped away and called out 'Grenades!' as she snapped krak munitions from the clips where they hung at her belt. Tegas blinked as the rest of the Battle Sisters mirrored her actions. She set to work twisting a fusing dial near the trigger pin. 'Set timers for staggered detonations.'

'No! *No!*' Tegas's voice caught up with his panicked thoughts and he snarled, grabbing for Miriya's arm. 'No, you can't! You will doom us all!'

She shrugged him off. 'Have faith, questor,' Miriya said coldly. 'I've done this sort of thing before.' She glanced at the rest of the squad. 'Ready. Ready. *Release!*' A rain of grenades were dropped over the edge of the gantry and they fell towards the glowing, perfect cube.

This time Tegas shouted so loudly that the echo of his voice bounced off the metal walls and down far enough for the wraiths to detect the sound. They were already lifting, anti-gravs propelling them up to deal with the intruders, when the first of the krak grenades detonated. It destroyed part of a lower gantry, and the walkway buckled, dropping down to collide with the halo of the electromagnetic field.

The Battle Sisters were already firing, raking bolt-shells and melta blasts towards the monitor platforms that Tegas had indicated. He pounded his fists on his head in ferocity. 'What have you done? You stupid, ignorant animals! That is something rare and faultless, and you are–'

Ananke backhanded him and Tegas collapsed to the metal decking. His sensors went wild with random, contradictory readouts as the women methodically destroyed every governance system, every monitor and control unit they could reach from their high vantage point.

He crawled to the edge of the gantry and dared to peek over the edge. Monstrous discharges of unrestrained force lashed at the necrons below them, ripples of gravity waves tearing supports from the walls and twisting walkways like paper. The flawless white cube rippled and began to crumble. As Tegas watched, wide-eyed, a rain of precipitated non-matter began to fall upwards, peeling away. He glimpsed a burning flare of radiation emerging beneath, but he could not look away.

He reached out a hand towards the singularity, and the light radiating out from it shone through the metal of his cyberlimb; for a moment he saw through the steel and plastoid, glimpsing the intricate workings within. He struggled to understand.

That was all he had ever wanted to do, *to understand*. Everything on this road had been towards that end, in the name of Mars and to the glory of the Omnissiah.

Tegas was lost in the sight, barely aware of movement around him. The women were running, fleeing back the way they had come, out through the walls of the tetrahedron chamber. He watched the radiant glow shiver and brush against the walls as it cut loose, growing larger as it slipped its chains. Great gouges of metal simply vanished, reduced instantly to atomic particles.

'Questor,' Miriya had to shout to be heard over the sizzling crackles of energy. He looked up and found her standing before him.

'You... are a weapon,' he told her. 'I see it now. All of you, weapons, blunt instruments of a blind church. You care only for vengeance.' He tried and failed to stagger to his feet as the gantry rocked. 'There are so many riches here! The necrontyr hold the keys to a cosmos of understanding!' Tegas found his full voice and bellowed at the Battle Sister. 'But you would rather shatter it all, and for what? In the name of a few corpses and a zealot four thousand years dead?'

'I gave you a chance to redeem yourself,' she told him, her eyes never leaving his as fire lashed around them. 'Salvation.'

'I brought you here!' he spat. 'Gave you what you want! Is that not enough?' Tegas held out his hand. 'Are you satisfied now? Help me up. At least I may live to tell of this!'

'I promised you salvation,' Miriya replied. 'Not your life.'

The Battle Sister raised her bolter, and the last sound Tegas heard was the roar of the shot.

Locking her gun to the mag-plate on her armour, Miriya kicked the traitor's twitching corpse over the rail and watched it spin away into the frothing mass of energy below. Cassandra was screaming at her to run, and she took her Sister's advice, breaking into a sprint as shockwaves resonated across the chamber.

Katherine, show me the way, she said to herself, the gantry shaking beneath her boots. In truth, she hadn't expected to live this long. One look at the device in the core and she had known what would become of them. Perhaps the cog had been correct, perhaps if they had been granted the time it might have been possible to render the entirety of the necron complex power-dead and inert. But this was a war now, not a scientific experiment, and all the lies and the subterfuge were boiling over into battle. The only way now was to destroy, to attack whatever stood in their path and strive for victory.

Or death.

That was the nature of the Sisters of Our Martyred Lady. They were revenge made manifest. In this place, at this moment, Miriya and the others were the answering echo to the screams of the women who perished twelve years ago. The necrons had come to kill, but rather than punish them, men of weak character in the Imperial hierarchy had allowed their gaze to be turned by the prospect of alien knowledge. Decima's ruined face flashed through her thoughts and she pushed the image away. It sickened her to consider it; the lesson this place had taught her was that nothing with its roots in the ways of the xenos could be trusted. It could not be tamed, or appeased, or allied with. It could only be killed.

We cannot suffer the alien to live.

'Miriya!' Cassandra shouted her name in a warning, and she dared to look over her shoulder.

The wild overspill of energy had punched through the triangular walls and raked the upper tiers. As the Battle Sister watched, great slabs of decking were liberated into free molecules by lightning strikes as big as warships. Monoliths, still glowing with internal power, their dimension gates shimmering, fell into the chamber through cracks in the walls and came crashing down towards her, ricocheting off the dull metal.

She was almost at the hatchway when a black pyramid cut through the gantry she stood on, ripping her footing away from under her. Miriya grabbed at the rail as it twisted and bent, and suddenly she was dangling over an ocean of white as the cube came apart. The light threatened to burn her eyes from her head with its glare. She saw the Monolith touch the expanding bow-wave of the energy field and it cracked like glass.

A strong, slender hand enveloped hers and she saw Sister Pandora dangling above, held in train by Cassandra and Ananke. 'Come,' she shouted. 'The book! We must return with the book!'

She hadn't expected to live this long. Miriya had been ready, they all had been ready. The Battle Sister imagined a catastrophic and immediate liberation of energy from the necron core after she gave her command – a single moment of white light as precursor to awakening at the God-Emperor's side. Better to perish and deny the Saint's holy tome to the galaxy than risk its loss again. Katherine would understand. She would forgive her.

Would she?

'Sister! The mission is undone!' Pandora screamed. 'Take my hand!'

Miriya reached up and let them help her the rest of the way.

In the spaces beyond the wrecked gantry, the air was close and thick with ozone. The outermost layer of the power armour worn by the Battle Sisters was cracked with heat damage, and the crimson of their combat cloaks was marred with ugly scorch marks from the nuclear fires they had fled.

Danae led them to the spiral riser that threaded up through the decks, and they ran on in the hellish half-light, ignoring the rattle of the radiation detectors in their gauntlets and the inferno boiling beneath them. Ethereal fire rose like floodwaters, forever at their backs. Gravity itself began to malfunction, and they loped as they fled, desperate not to stumble, fall and be lost.

They passed tiers where entire legions of necron warriors stood in silent formation, their command trains broken, without even the sentience to seek an escape as the Obsidian Moon came apart around them. In other places, clusters of flyers swarmed like flies in a bottle, trapped inside vast staging areas that were sealed tight by emergency lockdown commands. Stasis tombs that dwarfed the size of the greatest cathedrals of the Convent Sanctorum were consumed by the rippling fires of the singularity as it grew towards a point of critical mass. The necrons slumbering within them had been there for millions of years, since the time of the War in Heaven. Now they would never wake again.

Up in the iron dome-sky far overhead, sections of the complex suspended by gravity shunts were suddenly cut loose to implode under their own impossible weight. Tesseract chambers holding isolated pocket dimensions exploded open and devoured themselves, unable to retain any stability in this reality.

The Battle Sisters crossed paths with a unit of triarch praetorians, and a brief, furious combat ensued as both sides engaged knowing that they were fighting in a burning house. Blasts of emerald light from the triarch rods of covenant cut the stale, smoke-choked air, but the Sororitas had the advantage of numbers and sheer fury. They left the machine-forms crippled or disintegrating, but the fight had cost them time.

The deck beneath their boots was trembling as the slow approach of the energy surge rose closer with each passing second; and at last Danae dared to ask the question none of them wanted to voice.

'Where do we run to now?' she asked. 'Or shall we kneel here and take a last prayer before the flames consume us?' The veteran looked around. 'We cannot outrun death.'

'You... *We* will die when the God-Emperor wills it, and not before.' Miriya replied, raising her voice to be heard by all of them.

'I think that moment may be here, Sister,' said Pandora, grim-faced.

She turned on the other woman. 'If that is so, then why did you pull me up from the gantry? I thought as you did, but what if... What if we are wrong!'

'There is no greater destiny for us!' Danae bellowed, with

sudden fury. 'We succeed but we fail! The alien complex will destroy itself, but the book will burn with us. This is our lot!'

Miriya shook her head. 'I refuse to accept that.' She glared at Danae. 'Do you remember what Sister Imogen said, when we arrived in this blighted place?'

'We are the daughters of Saint Katherine, honour to her glory,' repeated Danae.

'*Honour to her glory*,' said Miriya, with Pandora, Cassandra and Ananke mirroring her words.

'And what else?' Miriya went on.

'We are not here to die,' said Danae, recalling the moment.

Miriya pushed past her and moved towards a chamber along the line of the closest tier. 'The necrons we dispatched, they were guarding this area.'

She didn't look back as the other Sororitas, all of them battle-weary and fatigued, followed her one last time.

In the chamber stood hundreds of empty transport racks, the same sort of support frames that Miriya had seen the first time she came to the Obsidian Moon. They were the carriage for the necron warriors. The skeletal machines slept upon them, hung like slaughtered animals, released only when they went to war.

And before the racks stood thick, glassy panes, several of them glowing with ghostly light. *Mirror looking into mirrors. Corridors made of infinity, spiralling away.*

'Gateways,' said Danae. 'The same as the ones we found in the cavern on the planet...'

'This is the way,' said Miriya. 'The God-Emperor shows us the path.' With her boltgun and chainsword drawn, she chose the closest portal and walked towards it without hesitation.

There was no way to know where it would lead to. There was nothing but faith and prayer that could carry them now, into the non-space of the necron dimensional corridor and on to an uncertain fate.

Miriya marched with the words of a prayer on her lips, but

her thoughts rang with the words that Imogen had spoken an eternity earlier.

The Saint will curse you for this.

The audacity of the human commander was incredible. The organic actually believed that she was a match for the nemesor. She seemed to think that by force of fury and daring alone, she would be able to meet Khaygis in single combat and beat him. It was such folly.

The female dared to throw herself aboard his command Monolith and dirty the flawless hull with her flesh. Some distant, long-forgotten part of Khaygis was recalled, and with it the sense of repulsion.

The meat-things could not see themselves the way that a necron could. They could not detect the invisible cloud of crude chemical exhalations emitted by every pore and orifice on their body, they could not detect the oily matter and trails of sloughed hair and skin cells that were left behind them wherever they went. The microscopic effluent registered to the nemesor's enhanced machine senses in trails that clouded the atmosphere. Each lungful of air the female breathed out polluted the space around her. Khaygis was disgusted by her presence.

Braying a challenge in her crude human language, she went at him with an energy-enhanced sword, and the nemesor parried it away with his fire gauntlet in a puff of sparks. There was little room to manoeuvre atop the Monolith's battlements, and Khaygis feinted backwards past his command throne, gaining room. The burning brightness of the power crystal rising from the pyramid's peak cast everything with a stark light.

The human fired a shot from a hand weapon and the necron swept up the length of his iron cloak, allowing the metal shroud to deflect the kinetic impact of the bolt-round. The mass-reactive shot exploded and cost him a moment's balance.

The sword flashed, and swept down and across in a lethal

arc. Khaygis dodged the blow, but the blade carved into his throne and tore open the delicate mechanisms within it.

In return, Khaygis loosed a tachyon arrow, which keened from the launcher atop his other gauntlet and missed the human by a fraction. Sounds emerged from the female's lips – the nemesor probed his memory banks and found the recall of the same harmonics. They had been sung on the day the first humans had been terminated on this desolate world, and now they were echoing here.

Khaygis disliked the noise. He wanted it silenced.

The nemesor drew back his gauntlet and conjured a globe of green flame, moulding it with the care of an artisan, coiling it to maximise the kill power of the molecular inferno; but in the next instant his concentration was broken by a strident, noiseless warning that struck at him from out of nowhere. The fire guttered and ebbed.

An alarm cried in Khaygis's machine-mind. Resonating instantly down the quantum linkages of the necron communication network, a sudden cacophony of alerts were being broadcast to him from the automated systems up on the Obsidian Moon. He looked up on reflex, glaring out through the fallen roof of the chapel and into the sky. The satellite was visible up there, a pale ghost of visible light, but seen through necron eyes, in frequencies of radiation and energy, ripples of deadly invisible force shimmered all around it.

The core. The warnings screamed at him. *Something was amiss in the singularity core.*

He swung back towards the human female, for the first time deigning to grace her with words in her own tongue. 'What have you done?'

She answered by firing at him, laying two close-range bolt impacts in his torso. Khaygis howled at the pain-analogue feedback through his synthetic nerves and rushed at her. Before the woman could disengage, the nemesor was on her, and he closed the talons of the fire gauntlet around her bolt pistol and the fingers that held it.

Bright flame surged, enveloping the weapon and the human's

armoured hand. The ancient metals of the bolt pistol grew white-hot in an instant, and the woman grunted in pain, struggling to free herself.

Khaygis intensified the fire and the gun exploded, the last rounds in the near-empty magazine combusting with the heat of it. The human screamed and fell, her arm now ending at the bloody stump of an elbow, her chest and face peppered with fragmentation wounds. The nemesor's gauntlet was damaged, and it jerked as the motivators within it malfunctioned. He was unconcerned, however. All that mattered was making the human suffer.

Before she could recover, Khaygis found her fallen sword and broke it in two with a stamp of his foot. She managed to scramble to her feet, cursing him.

He gave her the grace of another arrow in the chest, the kinetic force of the dart impact throwing her over the battlements of the hovering Monolith. She clattered into the rubble below, leaving trails of blood across the broken stone.

Bolt-shells cracked off the black stone crenels around him, but he paid them no heed. The clarion of alarms in his thoughts was growing louder and more insistent by the second, and he struggled to maintain his focus. The nemesor's mind needed to be here in the battle-zone, not torn between this place and the unfolding situation in the orbital complex.

He leapt down from his vantage point and went after the human commander on foot. To kill her in brutal fashion would break the will of her troops to fight on, and the necrons would be able to complete their cull of this place swiftly. This time, it would be done correctly, and with thoroughness.

Khaygis sent a meme-signal back through the network as he advanced on the injured woman, a terse command to the cryptek to deal with any human infestation on the Obsidian Moon. A null response returned to him, and the nemesor immediately knew that Ossuar's functions had been terminally halted. *The fool had let them destroy him.* Had the moment not been so critical, Khaygis might have been amused by the irony of the event.

Command trains broadcast from the tomb complex inside the moon were breaking down, and the sensor relays from the central nexus were losing parity. The irritating, galling tenacity of the humans drew out what little emotion Khaygis still retained, and fury rose in his mind-frame.

With a silent summons, the nemesor sent a directive into the necron thought-web, ordering every active unit within the complex to disembark immediately. He sensed the dimensional corridor housed in the heart of his Monolith as it became active, opening a pathway between the shimmering gateway to the portals within the tombs. Sickly light splashed over the ruins and fallen pillars as Khaygis stalked forwards through a hail of weapons fire, finding his quarry slumped against the base of a wide stone altar. The alien glow framed him, casting a sharp-edged shadow over the woman.

Several of the great tapestries still hanging along the walls of the chapel had caught fire, and the thick cloth burned with a cloying smoke that churned about the chamber, mingling with the acrid tang of cordite discharges, the windblown sand and the ashes of the burnt dead.

Verity stood and fought with the Battle Sisters as best she could, in the shadow of Canoness Sepherina's single combat with the necron general. But to her untrained eyes, the fight seemed like anarchy and she had nowhere to focus her righteous anger. The smoke smothered her and robbed the hospitaller of her momentum. She became lost in the melee.

She met Sisters and necrons in equal measure, staying out of the way of the Sororitas, daring to engage marching warriors and scuttling scarabs where she could. A half-melted immortal tried to cut her open with the war-blades clustered around the barrel of its gauss blaster, and she shot back with the gun the canoness had gifted to her. Verity was keenly aware of her dwindling stock of shells, and she thought of the single loose round she had hidden in the pocket of her duty armour.

The immortal was sluggish, half its motivators damaged by melta blasts, but it retained the relentless manner of its kind, resolutely limping after her. Too late, the hospitaller realised the alien machine had been trying to herd her, backing her up towards the thrumming shape of the Monolith. Panic gripped Verity, and she expended all the rounds in the bolt pistol's magazine. By the grace of the God-Emperor, the necron tottered – and fell. Lightning crackled over its twitching form, and it gave out the now-familiar death shriek as a cowl of energy reclaimed it. The flash of light seared Verity's retinas and she spun away, eyes watering.

A shape trailing blood tumbled from above and crashed to the stones. She heard the crunch of cracked ceramite and broken bones at the point of impact.

Surprise hit Verity like an icy wave as she came to the fallen woman's side and saw Sepherina's face there, beneath a mask of blood. The hospitaller's training took over and she activated her medicae glove, injecting the canoness with a cocktail of drugs designed to keep the woman alive.

Sepherina gasped and her back arched as the medicine-load shocked her back to full awareness. 'Nursemaid…' she said thickly. 'It's not over yet.'

'I know,' Verity told her, and put her shoulder under the canoness' weight. It was a great effort to lift the woman and her heavy armour back to her feet, but the hospitaller managed it. Together, they staggered and stumbled away. Sepherina was dazed, her eyes unfocussed. Verity knew the signs; the woman had suffered severe loss of blood and concussion. She had to get her to safety.

But battle raged all around them. Nowhere on Sanctuary 101 was safe now.

'It comes,' Sepherina managed.

Verity heard the crunch of iron-clawed feet on broken stone, and she dared to glance over her shoulder. A gaunt, spindly figure was casting around, nothing but an angular shadow made of rods.

The canoness gave her a shove and pushed away. 'Stand

aside,' she growled, the effort hard on her. 'I will not meet my final enemy upon your shoulders.'

The necron commander stalked through the wreathes of smoke, its complete focus now on Sepherina. Behind it, other tall forms were gathering, making their last advance towards the altar. Verity backed away, fumbling at her pockets. She was suddenly very aware of the tempo of the battle; the gunfire and the cries of the wounded were tailing off, the air humming with the resonance of the Monolith's anti-gravs. At last, Verity found her bolt shell, and with trembling hands, she loaded it into the pistol.

The xenos heard the snap of the breech locking closed and turned its malignant gaze on her for a moment. She froze. Verity saw nothing in those soulless, glowing eyes that could connect to any human experience. It was not the blank gaze of an animal predator, not the madness of a witch or the ruined of mind. It was *alien*, in the ultimate sense of the word.

It twitched, as if in reaction to some distant sound only it could hear. Then, with cold dismissal, it turned away again, ignoring her in favour of its target.

'Come, then,' Sepherina called, pain threading through her voice. 'Bring your army to the foot of my Saint and my God. Do what you must, creature, but know their eternal wrath will find you!'

New, unearthly light blazed across the chamber, illuminating the necrons gathering around them. The watery glow spilled from the strange doorway in the Monolith's face, and Verity knew what it meant. More of them were coming. If an army had not been enough, there would soon be a swarm, a multitude of machine-life overwhelming everything human on this blighted world.

If someone comes to seek us, as we sought those who perished before, Verity thought, *they will find no trace. The xenos will leave nothing but dust.*

In the haze, new shapes formed out of the glowing portal, but they moved differently, in random and chaotic paths, running as if the Ruinous Powers themselves were at their heels. Cloaks trailed behind them, revealing night-black power armour and human faces.

'Miriya?' Her friend's name fell from Verity's lips in disbelief. She had counted the Battle Sister lost, and all her squad along with her.

And then, high in the sky, a new star was born and died in a blinding pulse of light.

The nemesor had barely processed the datum of the new transit when the collapse event entered its terminal phase. Even within a synthetic intellect capable of collating information at near light-velocity, he was unable to parse all the conflicting streams of sensor data at once.

The reinforcements he had called for did not arrive. Instead of triarch praetorians, more of the foul humans spilled through the dimension corridor he had opened to the tomb complex. In that instant, he understood the meaning of *hate* again. The organics were like the viral codes used by some of the more honourless necrontyr dynasts, endlessly replicating, hiding and striking, hitting and fading, seemingly impossible to eradicate. And now Khaygis understood what had transpired inside the Obsidian Moon. Ossuar's failings had been the doorway to let these parasites into their realm. His laxity had allowed them to steal the scroll-tool and turn it to their advantage.

If only he had killed them all this would not have come to be!

But the matter of the humans was dwarfed by the magnitude of what they had done to the Sautekh's prize, the complex taken by force of arms from the Atun Dynasty. Khaygis did not for one nanosecond consider the fact that his eagerness to hammer the humans into the sands had left the singularity core underprotected. He was incapable of conceiving of an error on his part. The nemesor was the perfect solider; his past had been erased and he had been built anew in gleaming steel form. A perfect reflection of his infallibility. He did not experience shock or surprise, but he kindled the newfound hate as he looked up into the Kaviran sky.

The shrieking alarms fed him the last few instants of the complex's existence, deluging him in reams of data that showed the moment in flawless detail. Every necron, from the lowliest of scarabs maintaining the tombs to the exalted lordship of Great Imotekh himself, carried in their braincase a communion link. The device allowed signalling over near-infinite distances, the ability to transmit data instantly through the arcane control of quantum entanglement phenomena.

Khaygis knew of some lesser species that spoke of ethereal cords connecting their physical forms in the real world with their spiritual ones in the phantasmal. That was idiocy, of course, but the Stargods had gifted the necrontyr with many technologies when they embraced biotransference, and this link was one of them, a near-literal expression of that mystical ideal. Each necron was connected in part or in whole to an invisible network that spanned the galaxy, broken only by lines of dynasty and fealty. When their physical structures suffered critical levels of damage, it was the quantum link that was the means by which their digital consciousness and their damaged forms were reeled back to the closest World Engine or Tomb Planet.

And through that link, the nemesor watched the Obsidian Moon die.

The singularity core, so dutifully maintained by the worker-drones of the Atun since the age of the Great Sleep, distorted and fractured. For one infinite second, the space-time event concealed within it was exposed as the electromagnetic barriers that surrounded it were broken. Mass from this reality was acted upon by gravitation akin to that at the event horizon of a black hole, and the orbiting complex was torn inside out by the collapsar in its heart.

But the effect could not sustain itself. It was unnatural, not the product of a sun's slow death and fall to darkness.

It had been forced into existence, the rules of nature twisted violently by the necrontyr who had built it with Stargod knowledge so many millennia ago. Now, reality wanted it expunged, and it crushed the anomaly. Massive sheets of radiation sloughed off the crumbling singularity, ripping into the exospheric layers of the colony world's atmosphere, dragging on the planet's heavy iron core with sudden gravitation. It did not die quietly, lashing out with such force that Sanctuary 101's orbit was shifted by several degrees.

Then the Moon was gone, falling into a pit of itself, imploding. Violent blasts of light marked the last expenditures of energy as the vast complex – with its billions of slumbering soldiers, its mammoth storehouses of weapons, battlecraft, its databanks packed with ancient knowledge – was utterly obliterated.

Khaygis felt a terrible emptiness open up in his thought-space as all the quantum filaments binding him back to the complex were suddenly severed. He saw it happening all around him, every necron losing their connection to their point of origin. In the web of the network, the phantom cords that bound them were flailing in the void, severed and bleeding.

Too late the nemesor realised what would come next. The torn dimensional links had nowhere to go, nothing to anchor themselves upon. With no terminus, the communion links entered a destructive feedback loop. The single driving impetus of the connection – to never be broken, to never allow a necron to truly *die* –overwhelmed all other functions of his army.

Like a wave of lightning, a cascade of green sparks advanced over the torsos of each necron on the planet's surface, every warrior and war machine suddenly caught in the wake. The dead-man's switch in their heads tripped, and the nemesor's horde began to phase out, sucked into a dimensional non-space that existed in the voids between realities.

As one, the necrons emitted the same piercing death cry, unable to stop themselves from being dragged into the undertow of the moon's destruction. Khaygis struck out, reeling from the effects. He was aware of other high-level warfighters trying to resist the compulsion of dissolution, the lychguards trying desperately to rewrite their own mind-code to ignore the recall order, failing and vanishing in flames.

Khaygis saw his command Monolith consumed by a shrieking bolus of jade fire, and watched his phalanx of immortals shudder into their own personal storms of self-destruction. He would not fall like this. *He could not.* He was chosen of the Stormlord, soldier of Eternity, the nemesor and meatkiller.

The necron general reached into his own digital matrix and found the compulsion-code dragging at him, begging him to submit to the recall command. An ordinary necron, one left after biotransference without the higher mental functions of a high born, would never have been able to hold it off – but Khaygis did. He perceived the communion links stretching away into the void, at last finding some unknown Tomb World hundreds of light years away. But he would not go, not yet. He could not. There was still a deed to be done.

'How does it taste, xenos?' spat the human commander, sensing his distress. His optic sensors penetrated her armour and her flesh. Her wounds were so grave she could not even rise to offer challenge to him. All that was left to her was to goad him with words, as useless as that was. The female nodded towards the halo of remains in the sky, the flecks of debris already catching fire as they entered the planet's atmosphere. 'My Sisters broke open your spider nest, shattered it! We have killed you! This is the God-Emperor's will!'

Khaygis set his emotive-emulation of anger into a repeat cycle and allowed it to shiver through him. He unshackled his logic blocks and let himself *feel* for the first time in aeons 'We are necrontyr,' buzzed the nemesor, 'We are undeath.' He raised up his damaged gauntlet and brought forth the fires. 'And this galaxy belongs to us, not the corpses that you worship.'

'*No!*' The scream distracted him from the moment of execution. The nemesor glimpsed the other female, the ineffectual one reeking of panic and fear-sweat, daring to raise a weapon towards him. A gunshot rang out and the bolt shell slammed into Khaygis's chest, shattering the chains of ornate rank and high office dangling about his metallic neck.

He edited the pain-sense out of his experience, deleting it along with the recall command string. All around him, his soldiers were disintegrating or falling useless, rendered broken by the destructive meddling of these human animals. Fire rose all around, casting a hellish glow over his gleaming steel epidermis.

It was then that Khaygis saw the organiforms had surrounded him. The pitiful remnants of the human defenders, the females in their crude powered battle armour with their primitive ballistic firearms. All of them had hate in their eyes, oceans of it drawn up from fathomless depths of fanaticism. The nemesor understood what that was, now he had allowed himself to experience the same thing. It only confirmed what he had always believed: that flesh was worthless, a lesser thing that infested space like a disease. They had cursed him with their malaise, just as they had the foolish, arrogant cryptek.

A moment before, and the war had been in the necrons' favour, but now his army were ghosts and it was Khaygis who found himself overmatched. Some distant part of his long-dead flesh-self wondered if this was the Stargods exacting their payment from him, reaching up from the grave for the betrayals of the necrontyr.

He recognised one of the organics, a female with a scarred face, black hair and a heavy, bladed weapon in her grip. 'I am undeath,' he told her, glaring as the woman and her cohorts drew into a ring around him.

'We will put that to the test,' said the Battle Sister, and without a word of command, all the humans came in to attack the nemesor at once. He gave them fire and arrows in return, but like his soldiers, they were ceaseless and fought as if they were beyond pain and injury. They were fuelled by madness, by faith, by something the xenos could never quantify.

With blades and war-axes, with clubs and stones torn up from the fallen masonry all around, they fell upon Khaygis and destroyed him.

EPILOGUE

'Once, a Novice Cantus came to me, troubled and uncertain. A slip of a girl, only a few strides down the eternal path leading her to the Golden Throne. She asked me a question. She asked me how we can ever truly understand what faith is.' The words carried in the cool night air. 'I told her that there is no coin to measure what we feel in our hearts. There are no scales upon which we might weigh the faith of one woman against another. There is only duty and blood. There are only deeds and words. There is–'

Lightning flashed in the clouded sky and deep thunder growled, as a spear of yellow sunfire lashed down from high above and struck a point far distant, out in the desert. A low rumble echoed over the landscape as the lance barrages fell from orbit.

As the echo faded, the reading continued. 'There is only the service to the God-Emperor, and the price that demands from each Sister can only be known by Him. But know that whatever fears must be faced, whatever hardships endured, that price is forever worth its full cost.'

With great reverence, Sister Miriya closed the cover of *The Hammer and Anvil*, and bowed to the book. She handed it to Pandora, who took it and wrapped the holy volume in a silk shroud. It was unusual that a woman of only a Sister

Militant's rank be allowed to speak in such a ceremony, but the memorial service had been at the express command of the canoness, and she had ordered it so.

Sepherina nodded from across the memorial garden, standing stiffly among the lines of tiny statues, cradling her ruined arm. She was still recovering from her fight with the necron general, and it would be many months before she was fully healed. Now that the starship *Tybalt* had returned with a support fleet from the Seltheaus system, there had been talk that she might be taken off-planet, to a world with a better valetudinarium, but Miriya knew better. Sepherina would never leave Sanctuary 101 again. She had sworn it so among the ruins of the Great Chapel on the day they had endured the necron invasion, sworn it on the names of all the dead.

Another streak of fire punched through the cloudbase and on the horizon there was a smoky flash as a far-off mesa was obliterated. The Imperial Navy had taken to the task of erasing all trace of the xenos from the outpost with lethal precision, bombarding every site in Adept Ferren's records from low orbit with lance cannons and megalaser salvoes. The pulverised rock kicked up into the atmosphere would forever alter the ecology of the planet, but it was a small price to pay to expunge the necron taint.

In the weeks that followed what the women were now calling 'the Second Battle of Sanctuary 101', survival had been difficult. Only a handful of them had remained, and some died from their wounds as they waited for rescue. But as their creed commanded, the Sororitas endured. *This was the full cost.*

Transports came with new cohorts of Battle Sisters, and the cycle began again. The daughters of Saint Katherine did not give up their ground. They had come to this world to rebuild, and they would do so. To conscience anything else was to admit weakness.

Others came, too. Delegations from the Adeptus Mechanicus in search of Tegas and Ferren, who feigned horror at the so-called 'unauthorised works' being undertaken by their adepts, as if they knew nothing of them. Miriya had been there when those men had arrived. Sepherina did not even allow them to step off the ramp of their shuttlecraft. She told them to turn around and return to Mars. She invoked ancient rules and declared Sanctuary 101 to be *Mausoleum Valorum* – a war grave world. She told them that nothing on this planet belonged to them, and if they ever dared to come grubbing in its sands again, the Order of Our Martyred Lady would see them all die for it.

The Mechanicus were not the only ones. It was rumoured that stealth craft from the Ordo Xenos – perhaps even the personal ship of Inquisitor Hoth himself – had passed close by and gone on their way, unwilling to test the patience of the Sisterhood any further.

A single, final lance beam flickered, casting white light over the faces of the assembled Battle Sisters, and the low rumble washed across the tumbledown walls of the convent. The replacement workgangs had been ordered to cease their reconstruction while the ceremony was taking place.

It was the last deed, the closing of the book on the horrors that had happened here. Nothing of the alien enemy was to remain. Every fragmentary scrap of necron metal that had been left behind, even the ink-black voidblade wielded by poor Decima, all had been loaded into a cargo pod and shot into the Kaviran sun under the eyes of the Sisters.

Sister Verity had been the one to pull the lever that sent that pod into the star. It was right and fitting for the task to fall to her, as the capsule contained something of far greater importance than alien debris. Decima's body, forever marred by the machine-implants that had been forced upon her, was buried in the solar fires. There, her flesh would find liberation to join her soul at the God-Emperor's side.

Miriya looked down at the votive statuette before her. Like many of the memorial stones, it had been damaged in the fighting, but the names etched upon each one were still clearly visible, and the eternal lights burning inside them glowed strong. Decima's name had been joined by others – Imogen, Thalassa, Xanthe and Kora, and many more. She looked up and searched the faces of the women around her. Ananke and Danae both gave her solemn nods in return; Pandora was silent in her role as warden of the book; her steadfast kindred Cassandra and Isabel inclining their heads in a semblance of salute to their former commander; and Verity, who stood unafraid to present her tears of sorrow, showed her friend a rueful smile. Miriya gave silent thanks to the Golden Throne for preserving their lives along with hers.

So many of her Sisters had fed the sands of this remote world with their blood, and why? For faith? Could such a prize be worth that sacrifice?

That price is forever worth its full cost. Saint Katherine's words echoed in her thoughts. 'Aye,' she whispered to herself. 'It is.'

Sepherina spoke. 'I told you all when we came to this place that the God-Emperor's Light has never left this world, that the breath of His divinity never ceased. I did not lie to you then.' She looked around, taking them all with the sweep of her remaining hand. 'That we are here is that truth made real. That we persist is proof.' The canoness bowed to the memorial stones, concluding the ceremony with the motion. 'We endure through our faith. We ever will.'

Miriya remained as the others filed away from the garden. They all had tasks to occupy them, but something made the Battle Sister dwell a little longer.

'We both came here for the same reason,' said a voice. She did not turn as Verity walked up to stand beside her, before the flickering lights. 'To seek peace.'

'The God-Emperor had other plans.'

A long moment passed before the hospitaller spoke again. 'I had doubts, Sister,' she said. 'After Neva, after my dearest Lethe's death and all that followed... I had hoped this mission of reconsecration would give me time to think.'

'And did it?'

Verity nodded. 'I began to wonder if my faith was still strong.'

Miriya sighed. 'You were not alone in that. For a time, I feared that I would never be able to serve the Church again, as I was meant to.'

'As a warrior?'

'As a soldier of faith. It is not the taste of blood that I need, Verity, though for a time I believed it might be so. It is the knowledge that I strive to fight the enemies of humanity and our creed.' She looked down at Decima's memorial. 'I was reminded of the price and the duty. The oath we give cannot be broken. Decima proved that.'

'*A Sister's faith never perishes*,' said Verity, quoting the Saint's words. She was silent again for a while. 'Do you think… that we have beaten them?'

'The necrontyr?' The Battle Sister's eyes narrowed. 'On this world, aye. But there will always be other worlds. And if need be, I will kill those enemies again.' Miriya turned away and looked up at the dark sky. 'We should have died here, Sister. All of us. Why do we live now? Because of a fluke of battle? The hubris of the alien enemy?'

'Because the God-Emperor wills it?' offered the hospitaller. 'That is what the preachers would say.' She took a breath. 'It fills me with sorrow that Decima did not live to see this day.'

The Sororitas watched as a break in the clouds revealed a scattering of evening stars beyond them. She found herself searching for the one that Sepherina had showed them on their arrival, the light of Sol and Holy Terra.

'She had faith,' Miriya told Verity. 'As do we. And that will always be enough.'

HEART & SOUL

The last day of the War of Faith on Meseda Quintus had finally come, but in the dawning of it the wounded world found no respite. Even as the orbital guns were silenced and the treads of the Sisterhood's Exorcist tanks ground to a halt, the planet moaned and wept and continued to die.

Meseda Quintus would never recover from the damage wrought across it in the War, its atmosphere polluted by radioactive fallout from the city-killing pogroms, its meagre seas fouled by toxins that had turned the once-emerald waters into brackish lakes of acid. Thousands of years from now, the ruined sphere would still be spinning, still webbed with scars large enough to be visible from far orbit. This was a just and right fate for such a place, for Meseda Quintus had broken that most sacred of human contracts with the Imperium of Mankind – it had turned its back on the God-Emperor.

Not all at once, of course. By the time the cleansing fire of the Adepta Sororitas reached it, this world's populace had lived through their fall from grace. It was a sorry narrative, replayed time and again on outlying colonies where arrogance and distance conspired to make the natives believe they were somehow *special*, in some manner no longer expected to obey the Throne and give Holy Terra its due fealty. Spread like a canker, the corruption found the weak and the venial, the ones who blamed all their ills on others, and it gave them the power to exact revenge. The wretched truth was that none resisted the taint that power brought with it, too blinded by the hate that boiled in their tiny, shuttered minds.

And so the forces of Chaos, may they forever be blighted, took them whole.

The rising of the Army of the Iconoclast happened on Meseda Quintus as it had on a hundred other worlds, and while the root cause they espoused and the masks its members wore differed each time, the result was the same. Mass graves for those of true faith, the rise of foul idolatry, shrines set afire... And *war*.

Amid the ruins of the last dissident city, Sister Miriya trudged through ankle-deep drifts of grey-black ash and glanced up at the bloody sky above, considering the destruction the Iconoclast had wrought here. She sucked in decontaminated, consecrated air through the metal half-mask breather that covered her mouth and nose, tasting the flavour of the sacramental oil in the mix that was said to hold the corruption of the Archenemy at bay. It did little to hide the flat, sour taste of burned paper and charred bone all around her.

At least now it is done, she told herself. *Finally, after years of tracking our quarry across the entire Segmentum, we have the heretic in our sights.* Miriya had expected to feel something uplifting – a furious martial joy, perhaps – at the knowledge that this particular crusade was nearing its end. But there was only fatigue in her. The pursuit of the Iconoclast had taken so much, not just in terms of worlds that had fallen and the deaths in its wake, but on a personal level. In chasing this hellish champion of disorder from world to world, Miriya had almost died twice, once during the escape from the voidship *Sedition's Bane* and again in the battle for Nexus Fifteen-Kappa. The war had given her new scars, without and within.

She remembered poor Pandora and the Sister's terrible,

agonising death at the Iconoclast's own hand, only one among many upon the scale of blood cost that the heretic would soon be called to pay.

The weight of it all threatened to crush her. It would have been easy to halt here, and sit upon one of the piles of rubble that were all that remained of the city around her. *To rest*, she thought. *For a while*.

Miriya's jaw hardened and she reached up to push loose threads of her dark sable hair back out of her eyes, briefly irritated by her own moment of vulnerability. Ignoring the steady burn of pain from the lasgun wound across her right thigh, she redoubled her pace and marched on, following the path cleared through the ruins by the advance of a massive Baneblade tank. Such weakness was how the Iconoclast's claws gained purchase, she reminded herself. The heretic picked at the places where a soul was fragile and pushed at it, promised to erase it... While all along widening the cracks.

'I have no need of that,' she said quietly. 'All that I am, my faith protects and nurtures. All that I will do, is in His name.' The rote catechism came to the Sororitas warrior without conscious recall, soothing her, strengthening her. She was bruised and bloodied, indeed, and she felt it deep in her bones – but she would not falter. Her duty here was not ended.

Miriya hefted her bolt pistol and ran her gauntleted hand over the sacraments carved in the frame and the holy sigil of the ancient *fleur de lys* upon its grip, the same symbol mirrored in the blood-red tattoo on her cheek and the hilt of the chainsword sheathed upon her back. Like the power armour she wore, the weapons were devotional tools and they cried out to fulfil their purpose.

Ahead of her, a thick wall of black smoke from the distant burning habitat blocks parted and she saw the staging area where her Order's forces were regrouping. The wind changed direction and brought her the gentle rush of women's voices raised in a hymn, and she resisted the urge to join with them.

The remains of the Vestal Task Forces that had been

deployed to Meseda Quintus were arranged in loose formation at the foot of a shallow hill that stood undamaged among the debris of the dead city. Armoured vehicles, penitent engines and gangs of twitching arco-flagellants lined up alongside combat squads of Retributors and Dominions, waiting for the end to come. All guns and missile batteries were aimed at the crest of the hill, upon which stood a cylindrical tower of glittering ruby light. It resembled a gigantic crystal drinking glass as if seen through a curtain of falling rain, shimmering and moving. Waves of purple lightning washed over the shape, crackling low like dull fire.

Inside the cylinder, through the peculiar light, Miriya could make out the ghostly edges of a building. It had once been a devotional shrine, the most ornate and holy of chapels in the Meseda star system, but that was before the Iconoclast had come. Now the distorted structure was a gruesome parody of its old self, a grotesque agglomeration of bone and meat laid over blood-soaked stone. It was a giant's gibbet, a cage for death and unleashed horrors. The powerful energy sheath around it contained the warped cathedral and everything within behind an impenetrable barrier of force, and if the adepts of the Mechanicus were to be believed, nothing could get out – but still Miriya felt her gut twist in disgust as she approached it, as if mere proximity to the place could somehow sicken her.

Her eyes raked over a barely visible symbol that burned black fire across the facing wall of the corrupted shrine – a stylised 'X' bisected by horizontal lines – and it repulsed her, making her turn away. *The Mark of Khorne*. She dared not say the words aloud, and made the sign of the Aquila as she whispered a litany of warding.

Miriya's gaze fell to a cohort of rust-robed Mechanicus adepts, their skitarii and servitors clustering protectively around them as they worked at a great device made of spinning brass rings and lenses of dark volcanic glass. Arcane streams of energy flowed from the machine and out into the cylinder of light, feeding its fires, keeping it alive. The wardens of Mars had made good on their promises to the Adepta Sororitas. Together, the Mechanicus' Array of the Sixth House of Phobos and the Battle Sisters of the Order of Our Martyred Lady had done what no others could. They had driven the heretic known as the Iconoclast back to their lair and imprisoned it within. Many lives had been spent to spring this trap, but it had been worth it.

At least, that was what Sister Miriya wanted to believe. *It won't be over until that creature is dead*, she thought. *I swear I will tear off the Iconoclast's mask and see the heretic's true face before I deliver the killing blow.* That brought a cold smile to her lips. *It will be fitting. No-one can hide from the God-Emperor's wrath.*

'Sister Miriya!' She turned as she heard the voice calling her name, and found a familiar figure rushing up towards her. 'You're safe,' said Sister Verity, her eyes expressive beneath the brow of the armoured coif that covered her head. 'When you became separated from the rest of the unit, I feared the worst…'

Miriya shook her head. 'The Emperor Protects.' Las-fire from some of the last heretic holdouts had caught the ground speeder she had been riding in, forcing it down in the ruins. Although her pilot had perished in the crash-landing, alone and wounded the Battle Sister had still been able to track down and make short work of the traitor gun crew.

'You are injured.' Verity was not a warrior, but a hospitaller of the Order of Serenity, and her duty was to maintain the wellbeing of her sisters. She came to Miriya's side and examined the dust-caked wound on her leg, clicking her tongue behind her breather mask. 'I'll see to this.'

'It's only a scratch,' Miriya replied. 'I've endured far worse.'

'Don't tell me my duty,' Verity said firmly, pulling a medicae auspex from her belt. 'And I will not tell you yours. You're far too stoic for your own good.' She ran the device's sensor head over the gouge in the Battle Sister's armour.

This was a dance the two of them had performed more than once. The warrior and the healer. At first glance, their friendship might have appeared at odds to their natures, but the Sisters had a bond forged by adversity, conviction and shared loss. There were few that Miriya would ever trust as much as the slight, winsome hospitaller, and an unspoken communication passed between them. Verity had been with Miriya's squad at the start of their mission against the Iconoclast and she knew full well the import of this day.

'You're eager to end this,' ventured the hospitaller. It was not a question.

'Not eager, Sister,' Miriya corrected gently. '*Dedicated*. I am beyond the point of calling this an act of glory. No, what we will do today is justice. The Iconoclast will finally learn the cost of betraying humankind for the hollow gifts of the Archenemy. The scales will be rebalanced... For a time, at least.'

Verity used an injector to apply a glutinous protective salve to the wound in Miriya's leg and gave a nod, accepting the other woman's words. She turned as a group of war-weary Battle Sisters approached, led by Miriya's squad-mate Cassandra.

'Eloheim,' called the warrior, using the honorific title to address her. 'What are your orders?'

It was a long time since Sister Miriya had gone by that rank, and if truth be told, Cassandra was violating protocol by referring to her in such a manner. But Miriya accepted the term for what it was – a gesture of respect from one Battle Sister to another.

'Nothing has changed,' she said, her gaze taking in the other members of her unit. Silent Isabel, whose pewter augmetic eye glowed like an ember in her scarred face; Ananke, her dark aspect forever locked in a scowl; Danae, peering at her through an unkempt torrent of red hair that was dirty with mud and war-smoke; and the others, Sisters Marcia, Rubria and Aemilia, the later additions who had joined them at the commencement of this mission.

All were waiting for her to give the word, and Miriya's hand strayed unconsciously to the pouch on her waist where she kept a cracked mnemonic gem in a bag of black velvet. The hololith recorded on that glassy stone was the personal warrant of their order's High Canoness Majoris, charging Miriya's strike team with their singular command: to terminate the Iconoclast in the name of the God-Emperor.

Over the years of the pursuit, she had watched the flickering holo-image again and again as it played through the short loop of its recording, and listened to the Canoness' severe, clipped tones as she delivered the heretic's death sentence. Now it was time to make good on the promise of that edict.

Miriya nodded, steeling herself for what would come next, but before she could speak, a figure in dark red robes came clattering across the cracked rubble towards them, servo-arms and serpentine mechadendrites flapping at the air. 'Honoured Sisters!' shouted a grating, oddly pitched voice. 'Something is coming!'

Questor Nohlan was a fussy, self-absorbed sort, but that in itself was no oddity among the ranks of the Adeptus Mechanicus. A devout follower of the Cult of the Machine-God, he was a loyal subject of Mars and Holy Terra, but his self-control could be lacking at times and at this moment he seemed to have wholly forgotten matters of decorum. His claw-like bionic feet clanked and scraped over the stonework as he virtually threw himself towards the assembled warriors. In the shadows of his hood, Miriya saw his glowing crimson eye implants were wide with near-panic.

'Calm yourself, adept,' she demanded. 'What is wrong?'

'Processing. Processing.' Nohlan skidded to a halt and made an attempt to marshal his thoughts. Miriya had served with the Questor on other missions, and she overlooked his sometimes erratic behaviour because she knew it masked a keen scientific mind. Indeed, had it not been for Nohlan's cadre and their force cage techno-relic, the victory that was within the Sisterhood's grasp would never have been possible. 'Ships, Sister Miriya. I have word from orbit that a wing of cruisers have emerged from behind the second moon of Meseda Quintus.' He pointed at the sky with the heavy manipulator claw that emerged from his spine. 'Shuttles are already on their way here!'

'Imperial ships?' asked Marcia, and Nohlan's head bobbed in confirmation.

'Reinforcements?' Ananke directed the question at Miriya. 'If so, then they have come too late to do any good.'

Miriya's brow furrowed. 'All craft are engaged on other pilgrimages and missions elsewhere. Our Order had no more ships to send us, Sister.' She glanced back to Nohlan. 'What pennants do these vessels show, Questor?'

The adept shifted uncomfortably. 'They are of the Adepta Sororitas, milady.'

He had more to say, but the sound of thrusters rose on the wind and all eyes turned towards the tormented sky overhead. Isabel's augmented vision was the first to spot the incoming Thunderhawks and she extended a hand to point. 'There!'

Two night-black shapes powered down through the clouds and executed a fast, low pass over the assembled task force units, before swinging around to make a raptor's landing in a clearing at the base of the besieged hill. The dropships were indeed Sororitas craft, with the sainted *fleur de lys* visible in bright bleached white on their wings – but they lacked the crimson trim characteristic to all war machines in service to the Order of Our Martyred Lady.

Still, Miriya knew their colours, for she had seen them many times and fought alongside those who bore them into battle. Shouldering her bolter on its strap, she strode down the incline to meet the craft as their drop ramps yawned open like howling mouths.

Matching her pace, Sister Cassandra spoke quietly so only Miriya would hear her. 'These are not of our fleet. Look there, the sigil upon the fuselage. The red heart cresting the white Byzant cross…'

'The Order of The Valorous Heart,' said Verity, overhearing and offering the name aloud. 'Why are they here?'

'We shall see.' Miriya halted and threw a look at her warriors, ordering them without a word to fall into honour guard formation. But despite their martial order, she could not help but note that all of her Order's Sisters looked war-weary and battle-tarnished against the flawless black-on-black of the new arrivals, who marched down the ramps in lockstep formation.

The ebon armour and robes of the Sisters of the Valorous Heart were in parade ground condition. Their Sabbat-pattern helmets gleamed in the fading light of the day, expressionless crimson eyes searching the battlefield as if they expected danger to arise at any moment. The only flashes of tint on their wargear came from the white and red of their holy sigil. Theirs were the original colours of the Convent Sanctorum to which Miriya's Order also belonged, from the days before the Age of Apostasy and the splitting of the ranks that had occurred in its aftermath. Although she could not see their faces, Miriya sensed the hauteur in the new arrivals as they took in the state of their kinswomen.

That thought made her lip curl behind her breather mask, and Miriya dismissed it before it could take hold. She stepped forward, finding the other Order's commanding officer by the golden honour-chains and ceremonial chaplet adorning her armour. 'Well met, Sisters. Your arrival was not expected…'

The Celestian's blank helm turned to study Miriya. 'Well met,' she repeated. 'In the name of Saint Lucia, I greet you, Daughters of Saint Katherine.' Her faceplate snapped open to reveal severe green eyes framed by a short fuzz of ash-blonde hair. 'You are in charge here?' There was a challenge in the words.

'By the Emperor's Grace, I am.' Something nagged at Miriya, and a sudden flash of recognition struck her. *I know this woman.* She looked closer and saw a familiar identifier in High Gothic, laser-etched into the skull sigil upon the Celestian's breastplate. 'Sister Oleande?'

Her utterance seemed to catch the other Sororitas off-guard. 'Aye. That is my name. You know of me?'

Miriya came closer. 'We have bled for the same ground, Sister. On the Icarus Front, against the predations of the xenos. A decade ago now, do you not recall?' She tapped her chest. 'I am Miriya. I commanded a force of Celestians then.'

'Ah.' Oleande gave a wan nod. 'Of course. Yes. Forgive me, Sister. Much has changed since then.' She seemed to refocus her gaze. 'But you are a Celestian no longer? I see no war-rosary upon you.'

Miriya nodded, not wanting to dwell on her own misfortunes. 'As you say, much has changed. But our duty remains the same.'

Oleande stepped down off the Thunderhawk's ramp and her troops followed suit. She gestured with her white-lined gauntlet towards the chapel sealed inside the force barrier. 'We came when we learned of your victory. You are to be commended… But I must demand an answer of you, Sister. Where is the Iconoclast?'

Miriya sensed an abrupt rise in tension among the assembled Sisters of the Valorous Heart as Oleande asked her question, and for a moment she was unsure how to react. 'Trapped,' she said at length. 'You have arrived as we regroup for the final act of our mission.' She nodded towards the imprisoned chapel. 'I intend to enter with a handpicked strike force and kill the heretic before the next dawn.'

'Have you come to affirm the execution?' asked Verity. The hospitaller knew as well as the Battle Sisters that the shrines of the Valorous Heart had suffered in the past from the actions of the Army of the Iconoclast, as much as those of Miriya's Order.

Oleande seemed visibly relieved, and she shook her head. '*Ave Imperator*. The Master of Mankind has heard our prayers and granted them.' She spoke the words to her cadre before turning back to face Miriya and the others. 'Sister, take joy in knowing that you have done what no others could. You have captured this traitor and ended a murderous reign of terror across the stars. And now you can rest.' Oleande cast an eye over their dented and laser-scarred wargear. 'Your fight is over. You may stand down. We will take things from here. We will do what must be done.'

Oleande's statement was so unexpected that it briefly robbed Miriya of the power to reply.

Not so with Ananke, however, who blurted out a fierce snarl of denial and shook her head. 'What say you?' she snapped. 'After we have spent years fighting this crusade, you come from out of nowhere when the killing blow is to be struck and ask us to *step aside*?'

'This is unacceptable,' Miriya said, finding her voice. 'Oleande, you must see that. How can you ask such a thing of us?'

The Celestian's eyes narrowed and her voice grew cold. 'I did not ask you for anything, Sister. I am telling you.'

Miriya bristled at the other woman's tone, and she sensed the same rush of anger wash over her cohorts. She was keenly aware of the difference in rank between herself and Oleande, even if the two of them were equal in veteran status and battlefield experience, but still it was hard to keep her tone level. 'You demand this?' She reached for the pouch on her belt. 'I have here a warrant from the High Canoness, supreme commander of my Order–'

'As do I.' Oleande cut her off, as one of her warriors stepped forward to show a sheet of photic parchment bearing the mark of the Ophelia VII convent and the sigil of the mistress of the Valorous Heart.

Without hesitation, Sister Verity imposed herself between the two groups of warriors, raising her hands in a gesture of conciliation. 'Can this act of justice not be… shared?'

'Never!' Oleande snapped. 'While the Valorous Heart has nothing but respect for the Sisterhood of the Martyred Lady and all they have given to expedite this mission, it must be affirmed that *our* Order has prior claim on the life of the heretic known as the Iconoclast. The heinous crimes of desecration committed against our most holy shrines by this criminal are monstrous in scope! Whole star systems burned in sacrifice to the Ruinous Powers. Sacred relics defiled and obliterated! Sisters and laypeople murdered in the most abhorrent of manners…' She lost momentum for a brief instant, her eyes briefly clouding with tears at the thought of such things. Then Oleande pushed on, snarling like a firebrand. 'All that matters is that this aberration dies screaming!

Do you not agree, that by the hand of my Order or yours, the end result is the same? The galaxy will be cleansed of the Iconoclast's existence and be better for it!'

'You cannot come here after all the blood that has been shed and all the battles we have fought are done.' Isabel's words were icy and hard. From the corner of her eye, Miriya saw that her Sister was gripping her bolt rifle tightly, in a battle-ready stance. 'After our Order has taken the burden of this mission for so long, we will not allow another to steal the glory of the final kill out from under us!'

A deathly silence fell across the hillside, broken only by the low hum of the force wall and the ticking of the Thunderhawk's cooling engines. The Sisters of the Martyred Lady were fatigued, that was undeniable – but they were still burning with rage enough to see their enemy ended. And if Oleande's warriors tried to stand in the way of that righteous vengeance, there would be violence.

Miriya's martial mind parsed the situation in a heartbeat. The remains of the Vestal Task Forces outnumbered the squads from the Thunderhawks, but if this became an open conflict, the death toll would be great, and there was no way to know how many more Valorous Hearts were on the ships up in orbit.

Then she caught up to her own thoughts and felt sick inside. *Sister fighting Sister*? It was unconscionable. They were not the Adeptus Astartes, whose fractious past had often set their Chapters into battle with one another; the Adepta Sororitas were supposed to be incorruptible and above such things, unified and forever whole through their true faith in the God-Emperor.

'This is not about glory!' Oleande admonished Isabel. 'The right to strike the executioner's blow is ours and ours alone!' She glared at Miriya. 'Will you force me to exercise my superiority over you, Sister? I shall make it a direct order if I must. Are you prepared to defy the will of the Covent Sanctorum?'

Miriya struggled to hold her tone in check. 'You ask too much.'

'I do not *ask*,' Oleande repeated.

A mechanical cough sounded behind her, and Miriya turned as Questor Nohlan stepped forward. 'If it pleases my Honoured Sisters, may I speak?' She nodded to him before Oleande could say otherwise and the adept went on. 'It would appear you both possess warrants of authority from your respective High Canoness, each of which is the mistress of an Order Majoris. By the letter of Imperial law and the edicts of the Ecclesiarchy, each warrant is equally valid. One cannot countermand the other, regardless of the rank of the Sister who holds it.'

'This is so,' added Verity. 'Only the Abbess Sanctorum of Ophelia can hold sway over such an impasse. Her word on the matter would be binding and final.'

Miriya put her hand on Isabel's forearm and the meaning of the gesture was clear. *Put up your weapons*. She met Oleande's gaze and held it. 'I will accept the edict of the Abbess on this matter, Sister. Will you do the same?' The rest of the sentence was unspoken, but everyone on the hillside heard the echo of it. *Or will we be forced to draw blood over this?*

'What do you propose?' spat the Celestian. 'That we send a message to Ophelia VII for the Abbess to rule on who has primacy here? That could take months to expedite!' She jutted her chin towards the force barrier. 'And while we sit here, the traitor has time to plan and prepare for us... Perhaps even escape that confinement!'

'Not so,' noted the Mechanicus adept. 'The ethereal envelope projected by the relic is not only a wall for mass and energy, but also a membrane against *time*. The enclosure was erected several hours ago, but for those trapped inside time will pass at a far slower rate.' A smug tone entered Nohlan's words. 'I can assure you all that the Iconoclast is going nowhere.'

'But we can move through the barrier from outside with the aid of the Cult Mechanicus whenever we wish,' said Verity, 'is that not so?'

Miriya nodded, still holding Oleande's gaze. 'So we hold

off entering the chapel until a higher authority decides which of us will have the honour of killing the Iconoclast. Unless you see another way to move forward, Sister Celestian?'

Oleande was silent for a long moment, then she reached up and slammed shut her visor. 'Send your message,' she snapped, and turned on her heel to march back up the ramp into her dropship. Her troops did the same, turning their back on Miriya and the others.

'How dare they!' Ananke could not hold her silence a moment more, and spat out the words as the Battle Sisters drew back from the clearing. 'Bad enough that they might demand to join us at the last moment, but to order us off a fight that is ours alone to prosecute–'

'It is no lie that they have fair cause to hate the Iconoclast as much as anyone,' said Verity. 'The heretic has cost them much.'

'No doubt,' said Marcia, 'but what coin have Oleande's Sisters spent in order to find the criminal? They did not fight with us, and we have paid with our dearest blood.'

Pandora's face, slack in death, rose and fell in Miriya's thoughts. *Truth*. Truth on all sides. But we must be clear-eyed on this. Our mission here is not just to take revenge for those we have lost. We were sent after the Iconoclast to serve the Emperor's will and enforce His edicts. *Suffer not the traitor to live.*'

'*Suffer not the traitor to live,*' intoned the others in unison.

Miriya glanced up at the sky. The crimson sun of Meseda Quintus was setting below the ruined horizon, and the constellation of bright stars revealed above were Sororitas warships in low orbit. 'Questor Nohlan. Contact the astropathic choir aboard our vessel and order them to commune with their kindred across the void. Have them reach out to the Ophelia system. You know what question must be asked.'

The adept bowed. '*Ave Imperator*. It will be done.'

'And what would you have us do, Eloheim?' said Cassandra.

'Be mindful,' Miriya admonished, striding away towards

their temporary encampment amid the rings of tanks. 'And be ready.'

As was usual with any battlefield mission of the Adepta Sororitas, one of the Rhino armoured carriers in the deployment had been designated as the operation's mobile chantry, and the tracked vehicle's interior had been adorned with candles made of Ophelian tallow and portable icons of Saint Katherine and the God-Emperor.

Estelle, one of the Novices Constantia whose duties were to maintain the sanctity of the shrineworks, bowed respectfully to Miriya as she entered. 'Milady. Do you desire solitude?'

'For the moment, aye.'

'As you wish.' The younger woman bowed and left her alone to pray for guidance.

The servos in her power armour stuttered as she knelt before the icons and made the sign of the holy Aquila. Miriya bowed her head and spoke the litany that had been the marker for every action she had taken in her life. '*A spiritu dominatus. Domine, libra nos. A morte perpetua. Domine, libra nos. Ave, Imperator. Domine, libra nos.*'

Only the wind answered her, a low moan through the Rhino's open hatch. Outside, the hymns she had heard before had ceased. Word had spread quickly through the encampment of Oleande's demands and Miriya's Sisters were ill at ease. None of them wanted to raise their voices in celebration, not if their prize was about to be stolen away from them.

She looked up into the eyes of her Order's founder. 'Holy Katherine, grant me wisdom this night. Give me strength.'

Does it matter whose hand is on the blade? A quiet voice in her thoughts dared the question. *As long as the traitor dies, does it matter?*

For a moment, Katherine's face blurred and briefly became that of Pandora – then Lethe, then Portia, Iona and Decima – and all the other lost Sisters Miriya had known, who fought and perished to uphold the ideals of the Order. What had they died for, if not for these victories?

How can it be anything but an insult to them if we are denied our retribution?

Someone entered the chapel-compartment behind her and Miriya turned to see Sister Verity make the stations of obeisance before the God-Emperor's icon. The hospitaller met her gaze with a nod. 'Forgive my intrusion. I thought I would find you here.'

'Have you come to convince me to let Oleande have her way?' Miriya eyed her. While Verity was trained to fight if the need arose, she was as much a woman of peace as the 41st millennium could allow one to be. She constantly sought that path through the thicket of dangers that the galaxy threw at her, and it was a testament to her strength of character that she remained resilient in her beliefs after all this time.

'I would never do such a thing,' Verity replied. 'She asks for that which she has not earned, even if the wounds of the Celestian's kindred make her deserving. If Oleande had only shown some humility in her words, made a request instead of a demand...'

Miriya gave a humourless chuckle. 'Ah, Sister. You show how little you know of the Valorous Heart. Humility is not their strongest suit. And Sister Celestian Oleande has never been one to court it.'

'You fought with her against the Eldar, yes?'

She nodded. 'Aye. The aliens were preying upon pilgrim ships and our Orders merged some of their forces for a time, in order to show the xenos the error of their ways.' Miriya remembered the bloody business clearly, and as the night drew on and the candles burned low, she told Verity a few stories of the battles that had been fought.

'Oleande is a warrior of great repute,' she concluded. 'But a woman of tempestuous temperament, not one of moderation. She has always shown the greatest, most ruthless zeal.'

'I've seen the like,' said the hospitaller grimly. 'Those who do not shy away from the taste of blood.'

Miriya nodded once again. 'Truth in that. Although I will say that she does not seem like the woman I remember from those days. Time has altered her... Made her harsher, if that could be possible.'

'Perhaps that is why she is so intractable,' offered Verity. 'We cannot know what trials she has faced since those days. But based on what you *do* know of her, answer me this... If the word of the Abbess Sanctorum goes against Oleande, what do you think she will do?'

'Obey,' said Miriya. But part of her was not as certain of that as she wished to be, and she felt compelled to illuminate her friend. 'You must understand, Verity, that the Sisters of the Valorous Heart carry a heavy burden. When the Reign of Blood was at its height, the apostate Goge Vandire duped our Blessed Katherine and the other mother-founders of our Orders into fighting *against* the Throne of Terra. It was only when they were brought to face the God-Emperor himself that they learned the truth and turned upon the heretic.'

Verity bowed her head. She, like Miriya and every other living Sister, knew this shameful chapter of their shared history only too well.

Miriya went on, recalling the lessons she had learned by rote as an orphan child in the Schola Progenum. 'In that act of redemption, the Adepta Sororitas was born. Saint Katherine created my Order, just as her cohort Saint Lucia created Oleande's.' Two of the original six Sisters of Battle, Katherine and Lucia were close confidantes and that strength was reflected in the names of their Orders – the Valorous Heart and the Fiery Heart. It was only much later, when Saint Katherine was betrayed and murdered by the Witch-Cult of Mnestteus, that her Order changed its name to reflect their terrible loss.

But while the Order of Our Martyred Lady embraced the edicts of righteous faith and cleansing fire that their mistress had embodied, Oleande's Order walked a different path.

'They believe they must atone for the mistakes of the past in all that they do. Their drive for penitence is unbounded, Sister, and they are inflexible in their crusade to redress a balance that can never be resolved.' Miriya tapped the Aquila symbol etched into the floor of the Rhino, in a gesture of fealty. 'This is why they press so hard to take the Iconoclast's punishment from us. To deny it to them will seem like a defeat. An insult.'

'I appreciate the clarity,' said the hospitaller. 'But knowing it does nothing to defuse the tension here. The other Sisters...' Verity paused, framing her words. 'Some of them speak of Oleande's cadre with far less charity than you do.'

'It has been a long campaign,' Miriya allowed. 'But we cannot allow lassitude to erode our correctness. And I–'

The distant, unmistakable crack of a bolt-round sounded outside the Rhino and both women froze. A heartbeat later, more shots rang out, and Miriya was already sprinting through the open hatch, pulling up her breather mask against the tainted air. Verity came scrambling after her, eyes wild as she cast around for the source of the sound.

Now that night had fallen, the hellish liquid light cast from the towering force wall gave everything around them a shifting, infernal cast. Other Battle Sisters were already climbing atop the hulls of parked tanks, scanning the landscape for threats.

Miriya could not stop herself from casting a look in the direction of the two silent Thunderhawks down in the clearing, a worrying possibility gnawing at her thoughts. Both craft were black shadows against the ground, silent and unmoving.

Bolter fire sounded again and this time she saw the twinkle of muzzle flashes up atop the crest of the hill, close to where the Mechanicus adepts had secured the giant tech-relic.

Miriya tapped a key on the side of her mask and snarled into her vox pickup. 'Report! Who is firing?'

Questor Nohlan's reply was instant, crackling through the audial bead in Miriya's ear. *'We are under attack! The Celestians are here–!'*

The signal suddenly cut out and Miriya saw another flurry of gun-flashes, the crackle of the shots reaching her an instant later.

'Did we miss some of the cultists?' Cassandra called out the question as she raced across the camp to Miriya's side. 'I swear we eradicated every last one! Those Throne-forsaken fools don't know when to lie down and die...'

'I fear it isn't our enemies,' said Verity, the thoughts mirroring those of Miriya, 'but our allies.'

'To arms!' shouted Miriya, and she broke into a run towards the crest of the hill.

Isabel was there before them, her face like thunder. Nearby, Rubria bent over the corpses of half a dozen skitarii and gun-servitors, examining them dispassionately. The impact marks on the chests of the Mechanicus soldier-servants were unmistakably the grisly entry wounds of bolt-rounds from a Godwyn-De'az pattern weapon, the standard long arm of the Adepta Sororitas.

Other adepts stood around in disarray, many of them keening to one another in binary cant as they clambered over the structure of the techno-relic, desperately checking its functions and the integrity of the force wall.

'Did you see it happen?' Miriya asked her Sister.

Isabel shook her head, anger and sorrow warring across her scarred face. 'I was close... But not close enough. I heard their voices, the gunfire... But by the time I got up here, they were through. *Gone.*'

Miriya's gaze shifted to a tall oval of brass that lay pressed against the undulating surface of the force barrier. It was the only place in the membrane of energy where an object could pass through from outside and back again, and the power field swirled and crackled within its bounds. Her jaw set as she tried to make sense of what had transpired.

Limping, dragging a damaged machine-leg behind him, Questor Nohlan came out of the shadows and gave her a weak, brittle smile. The expression seemed grotesque on his hybridised face of metal and flesh. 'It would seem that the Honoured Celestian Oleande did not wish to wait for a higher ruling.' Oil and watery processing fluids were dripping from beneath his cloak, but he paid them no mind. 'She was quite insistent.' He nodded towards the dead bodies. 'We were taken by surprise, you understand. Our protocols for such an attack are incomplete...'

'You did not expect an act of aggression from an ally,' concluded Cassandra. 'Curse them for this! What do they hope to achieve here?' She turned on Miriya, as if the other woman could give her the answer she could not find. 'Why in the Emperor's name would they do such a thing? Oleande must know she will be punished for it!'

'Perhaps she does not care,' said Verity without looking up, as she scanned the torn-open corpses with her auspex. 'She may believe she is atoning.'

'It is *impossible* for a Sister of Battle to turn against the Imperium,' said Rubria, rising to her feet, ignoring the hospitaller. 'Our faith is unbounded! There must be an explanation for this act!'

No one wanted to voice what lurked in everyone's thoughts, and so the words hung in the cold night unspoken and threatening. *Treachery. Betrayal. Disloyalty.* Miriya felt her heart shrink in her chest when she considered them.

No Sororitas has ever fallen. That was what a novice was taught from the very first days of training. In every convent, in every Order, it was the bedrock upon which their unbreakable conviction was built. To even dare to suggest otherwise was to court censure of the greatest severity.

And yet Miriya found she could not meet Rubria's searching, imploring gaze. Instead she cast around, taking in the rest of her squad. They stood around her in loose formation, their uncertainty clear in their manner. Slowly, her old, keen battle-rage began to rise. Familiar and empowering, the Sister let it fill her. There was only one thing that could be done.

'Questor.' She shot a look at Nohlan. 'Do you function well enough to stand with us?'

'Processing. Processing.' The adept made a clicking sound and reached under his robes, staunching the flow of fluids. 'I do, Honoured Sister. If you wish it.'

'I wish it.' She nodded and drew herself up before barking out an order 'Strike formation!' The call had the desired effect, and Isabel, Cassandra and the others snapped to attention, presenting their weapons ready. 'We go in after them.'

'Are you sure that is wise?' Verity said quietly. 'If Oleande and her troops are in there…' She faltered. 'We don't know what her intentions are.'

'Yes we do,' Miriya corrected. 'We know full well.'

At length, Verity gave a nod. 'I suppose so.' She gathered herself up and made a show of checking over her medicae gauntlet. 'I will attend you.'

Rubria looked askance at the slight hospitaller and it was clear that she considered Verity's offer to be foolish; but Miriya had served too long with the Sister of Serenity alongside her squad to doubt Verity's capability in even the harshest of war zones. To suggest she wait outside the force barrier would be a slur on her character, as marked as the affront Miriya had felt when Oleande demanded the same of her.

'Take your place, Sister,' she commanded.

Nohlan led the way to the brass gateway and pushed aside the fussing adepts minoris working at the humming power grids that surrounded it. 'The transition will be very unpleasant for unmodified humans,' he warned. 'Prepare yourselves.'

He stepped across, vanishing into the shimmering field matrix as if passing through a wall of captured lightning.

Miriya voiced an invocation under her breath and went after him.

The Questor's estimate was conservative at best.

Once, Sister Miriya had been hit by a witchkin's psychic shock-blast that lit up her nerves with white fire, searing her body with an agony that seemed to last an eternity. This was worse.

Although the energy membrane was as thin as a sheet of gossamer, it felt as if she had fallen into an inferno. The pain was unbelievable. Every atom of her seemed to be alight and burning, tearing itself apart with the murderous violence of the transition. For a moment, all she wanted was to die and have the agony end. But that flash of weakness was smothered even as it formed by something greater, something unbreakable. The knowledge that her duty was yet to be done.

This was but another trial, another moment of pain and hardship along the path that was destiny to every Adepta Sororitas that had ever lived.

Adversity is a test, her mentors had taught her. *Never fail it.*

And then she was through, pulling down her breather and fighting the urge to heave and bring up bile. Nohlan stood before her, twitching and giving off a peculiar ululation as he bled away the static charge that had built up in his cyborg body through the crossover.

The stale air inside the force wall cordon was still and rich with the metallic tang of spilled blood. Miriya looked behind her, for the first time seeing the world outside the force wall from the perspective of those trapped inside it. Frozen, smoky shapes that might have been human figures hovered out there. They looked like wraiths.

The other Sisters came through one at a time, each of them sweaty and twitching from the experience. Ananke and Isabel first, then Danae and Verity before Cassandra brought up the rear with Marcia, Rubria and Aemilia. Each of them shook off the effect of the transition in their own way. All of the Sisters knew it was only the precursor to the horrors that awaited them.

With quick, cutting gestures she silently ordered them into a staggered battle formation and shot Nohlan a look. By now he had gathered himself, and one of the mechadendrites emerging from beneath his cloak rose up to eye level like an angry serpent.

The tip snapped open to reveal a detector fan, and it moved this way and that, tasting the air. After a moment, he pointed. 'Processing. Readings are in conflict and... Unsettling. Processing.'

Miriya drew her bolt pistol and chainsword. 'Our mandate is a simple one,' she told the others. 'If you lay your gaze upon anything that is not loyal... Kill it.'

They advanced on what had become of the chapel. Miriya had seen picts of the building on mission briefing slates, images of the holy site in days before the agents of Chaos had come to Meseda Quintus. Once, it had been a monument to the glory of the Imperium, a series of towering spires arranged like the Emperor's crown rising up on the highest point of the city surrounding it.

Now those pinnacles were covered in blasphemous banners sewn together from human skins, tanned flesh branded with sigil of the Blood God, endlessly dripping with ichor. Heaps of skulls lay in drifts around the sides of the stone walls, and the pathways towards the holes blown through the shrine's sides were uneven roads of broken bone fragments ground into the dirt.

At her side, Sister Aemilia smothered a noise in her throat – half-choke, half-sob – as they approached a line of X-shaped crucifixes. Each of the frames were made of girders, and hung upon them were the brutalised bodies of their Battle Sisters, lost months before in earlier attacks on the city. Their armour punctured by sword blows and shots, their lifeblood staining the sanctified ceramite and the ground beneath them, they were a tragic sight to behold. It was no death for one as noble as a Sororitas.

Verity detached herself from the group, openly weeping but still standing tall, and from her belt she pulled a small, jewelled bottle filled with water from the Font of Memory on Ophelia. She whispered a prayer for the souls of the lost and flicked a measure of the sacred fluid at the feet of each of the dead.

They paid their respects with a final bow, and moved on towards the ruined chapel. 'The Emperor knows their names,' said Cassandra, throwing a final, grim-faced look over her shoulder.

And will He know ours before the day is out? The question pricked at Miriya's thoughts and she forced it away.

The stagnant air seemed to resonate, and her moment of distraction faded as the crackle of las-fire and bolter shots reached her ears.

'Inside–?' The question was still forming on Isabel's lips when a cloud of bone-dust billowed out of the closest hole in the wall, and from within it came a screaming, howling mass of people.

The Army of the Iconoclast were nightmare figures. A ragged mix of commoners, civilians, enforcers and guardsmen from every reach of the planet, all of them fallen to the blood-soaked madness of the Mark of Khorne. Their eyes were wide, lost to unreason and death-lust. Their clothing was coated in a slurry of congealed blood, organ meat and other body matter; some wore conical hoods made from the skins of those they had killed, some in crude armour fashioned from lashed-together human femur bones. They carried weapons of all kinds, from war-swords and makeshift stone clubs to lascarbines and autostubbers.

Their chants were a cacophony of dissonant shrieking, but one phrase repeated itself over and over as they boiled across the rubble towards the Battle Sisters. *'Blood for the Blood God! Skulls for the Skull Throne!'*

Miriya took careful aim at a chattering, flabby-faced man at the front of the group and fired a shot that turned his head into crimson mist. It was the signal for the rest of the squad to open fire, and as hostile rounds sparked off their armour, the Battle Sisters advanced and slaughtered their way through the enemy defenders.

The Iconoclast's devotees were so tightly packed together that some of the mass-reactive rounds over-penetrated their targets and ended more than one of them with a single shot. The following ranks hurdled the still-warm bodies of their dead brethren without pause, and as the slide on Miriya's bolt pistol locked open, she went to her buzzing chainsword. Revving the spinning tungsten teeth of the blade, she cursed the enemy and waded into their ranks with savage sweeps of the weapon, her face twisting in fury.

She killed a dozen in the span of a few heartbeats, opening torsos to the air, spilling out ropes of intestine and wet gushes of blood across the ground. A brutal kind of joy washed over Miriya as she briefly lost herself in the action. She felt herself being pulled towards the same berserker rage that her targets showed. Jetting streamers of red spattered over her armour and through the stale air, glistening brightly, daring her to wallow in the act of killing.

It lasted only a moment, but the feeling shamed Miriya and the Battle Sister expunged it brutally, mouthing a sacrament of protection to herself as she ended the lives of a group bearing heavy energy pikes. They were the last of the defenders at the entrance and they fell screaming, the echoes of their foul prayers fading away.

Miriya's heart pounded against the inside of her ribcage and she stilled her bloodlust with an effort of will. 'The power of the daemon Khorne is strong in this place,' she said aloud, her voice rough and cracked.

Rubria spat on the ground and made a sign of warding. 'I feel it. The beast does not care who wins in the wars that it creates, only that blood continues to be shed for eternity. Ours, or the traitor-kin's, it matters not.'

'Guard yourselves, my Sisters,' said Miriya, moving into the shadows of the ruined wall as she reloaded her bolt pistol. 'This will test us all...'

The horrors grew worse within.

Inside the chapel's devastated atrium, they came upon a heap of butchered bodies dangling from hooked chains, each of them milk-pale where they had been exsanguinated into troughs. The churn of thick, glutinous blood sloshed heavily along crude, jury-rigged channels into pipes along the walls, pumped upwards by chugging machines to then cascade down once more in a vast red waterfall. The curtain of hissing liquid acted like a shimmering partition to the vestibule beyond, and through it Miriya glimpsed more bodies – but these were lithe, armoured figures.

'The Celestians!' cried Verity, and she started forward, before baulking at the notion of pushing through the blood-fall. Danae and Ananke took the initiative and fired rounds into the mechanism of the horrific device, blasting the pumps into fragments. In moments, the rain of red became a trickle, and the scene within the vestibule was made clear.

The fallen Sisters of the Valorous Heart lay in a cluster. Miriya knew the circumstances of their fate immediately – the way most of them lay back to back, their guns all aimed outwards in a wheel of death, the cascades of spent bolt-shells scattered about their boots. When the end had come for them, they had been firing in every direction, and as she mentally tracked the lines of attack, Miriya's hard gaze found heaps of heretic bodies. A ring of dead enemies lay around the Battle Sisters, all of them carrying heavy man-portable autocannons of a type more suited to blasting through tank hulls than power armour.

'This.... This was butchery,' growled Marcia.

'This was an *ambush*,' corrected Danae, kicking at the headless corpse of a heretic fighter to turn it over. 'And curse Oleande, but she walked her squads right into it!'

Miriya nodded bleakly. The Celestians had fallen victim to a ploy that the Sisters of Our Martyred Lady had encountered on more than one occasion during this campaign. Her judgement was confirmed when she stooped and grabbed a fistful of heavy, slick material fashioned into a cover; a camo-cloak. The cloak shimmered as she tightened her grip, the colours of the material shifting and blurring, breaking up.

'Survivors here!' Rubria shouted from among the ranks of the fallen Sororitas.

Miriya tossed the ruined cloak away and ran to her side. She stood over an olive-skinned Celestian whose eyes were bloodshot and unfocused. At her side, a few others of her cadre were still alive, although their wounds were grave. 'Can you speak?' she asked.

The Celestian nodded, coughing up pink foam in a rattling wheeze. 'We... were undone by our own... arrogance.'

Miriya looked around, imagining how it had played out. The heretics, silently waiting in the shadows around the edge of the wide vestibule, concealed beneath the sensor-opaque cloth that mimicked exactly the shade of the blood-stained stonework around them.

'Oleande led us in...' the Celestian continued. 'The Iconoclast set a trap...'

'Eloheim,' Rubria said quietly. 'Sister Oleande... She is not here.'

The injured Celestian heard her and managed an agonised nod. 'My commander broke through while we... We held. Even now, she searches to find the Iconoclast and end... the mission.'

'Such a waste...' muttered Cassandra, standing nearby. 'If only they had waited! We would have known to watch for this tactic–'

Miriya held up a hand to silence her. 'No matter now. We must finish what was started here.' She beckoned to Danae and the Questor. 'Sister. Take Marcia and Aemilia, get the wounded back to the entrance. Nohlan, go with them.'

'What will you do?' said the adept. 'Without me to scry the way–'

'We will manage,' insisted Verity.

Miriya nodded at the hospitaller's words and turned away. 'Ananke. Cassandra. Rubria. Take the southern aisle across the way and search towards the reliquary. Signal via vox if you find anything.' The three women nodded as one and set off into the shadows. She turned to Isabel and Verity. 'You will come with me. We'll push forward down the nave towards the far side of the chapel.'

Verity frowned. 'You believe Oleande is still alive in this charnel house?'

Miriya nodded, checking her weapons as they moved off. 'I have seen her fight, Sister. She will not sell her life cheaply.'

* * *

Her words proved prophetic.

Crossing what had once been the ornate space of the main transept, skirting pyres made of bodies and desecrated artefacts, the clatter of blades and the skirl of weapons fire echoed off the high ceiling overhead.

Miriya broke into a run and Isabel kept pace with her. Verity was close behind, clasping a small-gauge holdout bolt pistol in her hands. She hid her hesitance well, considered the Battle Sister. Any other hospitaller might have asked to join the evacuation of the wounded, but not Verity. Her dedication remained exemplary.

They passed the low archway leading into the great chancel, and at last, the object of their mission presented itself.

The Iconoclast was in full flow of combat, fighting among a troop of traitor soldiers in debased Auxilia carapace armour festooned with spikes and kill-cult runes. Sister Oleande and a pair of her Celestians were giving them no quarter, but it was immediately clear that the enemy had them on the defensive. They were being toyed with, cut and bled with each surge of attack but not killed outright. The servants of the Blood God wanted to extend and savour the agony of their eventual defeat.

Miriya had never been this close to the arch-heretic before. Clad from head to foot in close-fitting wargear of porous white material that glistened like porcelain, the Iconoclast was rendered into a blank, indefinable human shape. She thought of a denuded mannequin or an artist's figure model; the Iconoclast had nothing to define it, no hint of identity or self. The only characteristics that broke the uniformity were the two weapons in the heretic's gauntleted hands – ancient *khopesh*-fashion sickle swords, wicked silver curves that flashed in the dull illumination filtering through chapel's stained glassaic windows. The ends of the hilts had concealed bolter magazines inside them, allowing the wielder to attack from range if needed. Miriya had witnessed the after-effects of those weapons up close, months before in a burning hive tower when they had arrived too late to prevent the heretic's escape. They were the grisly tools of a killer who revelled in bloodletting. A killer who could not be allowed to escape again.

'Attack!' shouted Miriya and she sprinted up over a pile of fallen masonry, leading with her bolt pistol. The Battle Sister killed three of the traitor soldiers with three shots from the weapon, and she saw Oleande react with shock at her arrival.

Still, her unexpected intervention was not enough to slow the Iconoclast's murderous assault. The white-clad figure leapt into the air and came down on one of the Celestians as the Valorous Sister scrambled to reload her bolter. The tips of the sickle swords went into the flex-metal mesh beneath her chin and around her throat, and into the point where her breastplate met her thorax. The weapons were aimed perfectly into the weaker spots of the Sororitas battle armour, and they went right through, bursting out the Celestian's back in a welter of red. Miriya could do nothing but watch as the Iconoclast tore the sickle swords away in opposite directions, opening up the Battle Sister, tearing her into rags.

A great liquid mass of the Celestian's blood seemed to rise up and engulf the Iconoclast in a wave, drenching the white armour until it was crimson. But then, to Miriya's horror, the porous surface of the wargear *drank in* the murdered woman's blood, soaking it away.

The heretic caught sight of the new arrivals and screamed out a command. One of the Iconoclast's surviving soldier-slaves turned a lascarbine on the Battle Sisters and opened fire, spitting shrieking bolts of yellow energy across the rubble-choked chancel. The shots went high, sizzling through the air over Miriya's head and she bobbed as she moved.

'Sister, beware!' Isabel shouted a warning and too late Miriya realised that the las-bolts had found a different target. Above them, a great brass ceremonial censer hung from a thick, dust-caked chain; in better times, it would have been filled with perfumed oils heated into vapour, to be breathed over the heads of the faithful penitents who visited the chapel to worship the God-Emperor.

Drained and dead, the censer was an empty vestige of the holy shrine's previous existence, and now the beam-shots severed the chain, bringing it down in a clattering rush. The brass orb, as big as a Land Raider, crashed into the mosaic floor and broke apart, the wreckage of it blocking the archway Miriya and the others had entered through.

The Battle Sister heard Isabel cry out and fall in the wake of the collapse. She spun, daring to disengage from the fight just long enough to find her scarred Sister lying a short distance away. A piece of bronze pipe thrown from the censer's interior had speared her in the back, her armour's artificial muscles sparking and jerking.

Verity sprinted to Isabel's side, waving Miriya away. 'I have her, Sister! Go!' Despite the energy bolts crackling around her, the hospitaller went to Isabel's aid, ignoring everything else.

Miriya shot her a nod and regathered her momentum, picking out and killing the cultist with the lascarbine before he could marshal himself for another salvo of fire. The few remaining members of the Iconoclast's retinue of killers were more focused on destroying Oleande's squad, and she saw another of the Valorous Heart ended in a flurry of sword strikes.

'Come at me, heretic!' bellowed Sister Oleande, drawing her own power sword and brandishing it at the enemy. She was now the last of her Order still standing inside the ruined shrine.

The Iconoclast's faceless visage inclined towards her, as if amused, and then the white-clad figure vaulted towards the Battle Sister with incredible speed. Blades clashed as they went into single combat.

Miriya moved quickly, trying to close the distance, but the other heretic soldiers anticipated her tactics and the three of them went at her at once, stub-guns and spiked power-mauls turned upon her.

Without the time to reload her bolt pistol, Miriya used the butt of the massive handgun to cave in the face of the first attacker to reach her, smashing through the bridge of a polymer visor and splintering bone, meat and cartilage.

Without losing a moment of potential, she let her chainsword extend and swing down, the blade's fanged teeth a blur of bloody metal as they cut into the thigh of the next attacker. The weapon sparked through dented armour and turned flesh into gobbets of red, opening up the man's femoral artery and setting him to gush his lifeblood into the dust.

The third attacker fired a stubber gun point-blank into her chestplate and the raw kinetic impact slammed her off-balance and into a stumble, the shock knocking the empty bolt pistol from her hand. Heat shunted from the impact site bloomed across her breast and throat, but she ignored it, thrusting herself back to her feet.

From the corner of her eye, she saw blades flashing as Oleande and the Iconoclast duelled back and forth, but she dared not shift her gaze from the shooter for even a moment. He threw back his head and laughed. *'Blood for the Blood God!'*

As he spoke the words, Miriya smelled the blood in her nostrils. The dark, heavy scent of it, lingering and potent. She could suddenly feel every single tiny droplet of spilled vitae that had spattered over her face as she made the chainsword kill moments earlier. The urge to lick her lips was so strong it took an effort of will to resist. 'Get out of my soul,' she growled. 'There is no place for your daemon king there!'

'Skulls for the Skull–!' The gunman's chant was cut dead when the dagger hidden in the Battle Sister's chaplet flew from her outstretched hand and arrowed through his jawbone, locking his mouth shut. He staggered back, trying to laugh, frothing and gurgling as his own vital fluids fountained out of a new, ragged wound in his face.

Miriya stepped to him in a single motion and grabbed him by the throat. She pulled the man to her, as if about to embrace him, but instead his body met the buzzing tip of her chainsword and she dragged him on to it. He jerked and screamed as the weapon made short work of his armour and the soft, yielding matter beneath it. When he was dead, the Battle Sister shoved him away and recovered her chaplet. She stalked back to where her pistol had fallen, shaking tainted liquid off the snap-dagger. Everything around her stank of stale, sour gore.

She blinked away ruby droplets from her eyelashes and events slowed around her. Miriya felt the tremor of unchained ferocity singing in her nerves, the thunderous pounding of her heartbeat. The raw need to do violence pushed at her psyche.

She stooped to grab her gun and froze. A few metres away, Oleande lay pinned to the ground with one of the sickle swords through her belly and her own blade lying out of reach. The Iconoclast stood over her, twirling the first weapon's twin, the spatters of red on her white armour trickling upwards against gravity into crevices across the torso and throat.

The blank doll-face turned to face Miriya and up came a hand to waggle a finger in her direction, like a parent giving a child a playful warning not to misbehave.

Miriya was too far away to attack with the chainsword, her bolt pistol was out of reach and empty, and she guessed that her tactic with the chaplet-dagger would be a waste, given that the Iconoclast would be able to kill Oleande in the second she drew back her hand to throw it.

But Oleande's life was worth the death of the heretic, and they both knew it. Miriya shifted slightly, readying herself to explode into motion.

Before she could commit to the act, soft, feminine laughter issued out from beneath the Iconoclast's mask. The porcelain sheath parted into quarters and retreated back off the face beneath.

I swear I will tear off the Iconoclast's mask and see the heretic's true face before I deliver the killing blow. Miriya's vow echoed in her memory; but here the traitor was revealing itself of its own accord.

It was a human face beneath the white covering, a woman's face. Scarred and florid with the rush of blood, but an aspect that Miriya *knew*. Severe green eyes. Ash-blonde hair. It was Oleande's face.

'What trick is this?' spat Miriya. 'Your mockery is meaningless, traitor! Whatever face you hide behind, you will still die!'

'I'm not hiding, Miriya,' said the Iconoclast. 'And it is no trick. Is it?' She looked down at the Battle Sister pinned to the ground. 'The only falsehood here is *her*.'

'Lies,' coughed the Sister of the Valorous Heart. 'Avert... your eyes. The daemons take on many forms...'

'No trick,' repeated the Iconoclast, becoming angry. 'I am no daemon, not yet.' She reached for the hilt of the other sickle sword and gave it a twist, causing the woman on the ground to cry out. '*I am Oleande*. I always have been. This one gave up her name to steal mine. So that none would know. So that *the lie* could never be seen.'

'No Sororitas has ever fallen.' Miriya said the words before she could stop herself. *Could it be true?* The possibility sickened her on a level she thought impossible to contain. 'I knew Sister Oleande! She would never give herself to the Ruinous Powers!'

'Fool,' said the Iconoclast. 'Liar.' She tapped her head. 'Think, Miriya. Didn't you wonder how it was my army could stay one step ahead of you for so long? Didn't you ask yourself how I could know the tactics of the Sororitas so well?' She let out a sigh. 'Remember the woman you fought with at the Icarus Front. You saw me. Even if you never wished to admit it, you saw how much I loved the cut and the kill.' She made a deep, purring growl. 'And after a while, the faith and fire our rancid corpse-emperor gave me wasn't enough. I wanted *more*. I wanted blood and skulls.' She leered at Miriya, her violent desire leaking into every word. 'Khorne answered my need...'

Miriya watched her lick the congealing blood off her sword and all doubt melted away. 'Is it so?' She asked the question of the wounded woman on the ground. When she didn't answer, Miriya went on. 'Tell me the name of the

Repentia who perished on the twenty-seventh day at Icarus,' she demanded, her voice rising. She felt betrayed. 'The one who saved the rest of us from a krak grenade. Oleande was there! She lit a candle in the name of the honoured dead that night!'

'I do… not recall!' spat the Battle Sister.

'Her name was *Adessa*,' said the Iconoclast, and part of Miriya's spirit died to hear the truth spoken by the heretic. 'Your Sister died in agony, but fear not. The Lord of Rage embraces such endings.' She pointed at Miriya. 'You wept for her, I remember. So soft then. But not so now. I think you hear the same clarion that I did. The rage, coming close to the surface.'

'No.' Miriya shook her head, turning inwards, concentrating on the Emperor's Light, grasping for it. '*No*.'

'You think I am the only one to fall?' The figure in white laughed and the harsh sound cascaded off the broken walls. 'The only one who *willingly* burned her oath for greater power? You know better than that, Sister Miriya. After all, it is *your* Order that carries the stain of being the first to give up a daughter to the Eightfold Path!'

'Do not… speak the name!' The wounded Battle Sister coughed up blood as she shouted out the words.

'Sister Superior Miriael Sabathiel!' shouted the Iconoclast. 'She of the Order of Our Martyred Lady! Given unto the embrace of the Lord of Dark Delights, and such a waste too…' She shook her head sadly, mockingly. 'As callow novices we were taught that no Sister ever falls, but Sabathiel is known. She is the cautionary tale. How do you square that circle, Miriya? *None fall, yet one fell*? How does it feel to know you are lied to?'

She reached for an answer and could not find one. The Iconoclast – *Oleande* – saw it in her eyes and smiled.

'Sabathiel was only the first. She built her own war band out of pious Sisters she enslaved herself from Order of the Argent Shroud, much to their shame… And then there were the others, quietly killed and cut out of history… Or *replaced*.

Like me.' Oleande strode back to her wounded double and glared at her. 'All to protect the great lie of the Adepta Sororitas, to shield its brittle heart and soul from the shattering truth of Chaos!' She drew back and spat in her own face. 'You see before you the blood-soaked shame of the Valorous Heart. So humiliated they were by my defection to the true gods that they made this lie. Took a Sister and gave her my aspect, so that none would know. And they've been following your crusade ever since, Miriya. Waiting for this moment to come and end me. To seal the secret forever and burn out the indignity that is the heretic Oleande. The Iconoclast who dared to disown them.'

And now the veil fell. Now it was all clear; the instinct that something was amiss about the woman Miriya had met at the head of the Sisters of the Valorous Heart; their insistence on executing the heretic and doing so alone; their inexplicable attack on Nohlan's adepts rather than waiting for the word of the Abbess. *They could not take the chance that the Abbess would rule against them*, she thought. *Their disgrace is too great for others to know of it.*

'You see the lie,' said Oleande, nodding towards her double. 'Cut it open, Miriya. And you will be reborn as I was–'

The heavy triple-report of a bolter on burst-fire setting cut through the stagnant air of the chancel and Oleande was slammed away into the dust and debris. The flat bang of the mass-reactive shells dragged Miriya back from the edge of reverie and into the moment once more. She spun and saw Verity standing a short distance away, holding on to Isabel's bolt rifle and shaking with adrenaline.

'I… I grew tired of listening to her pontificate,' she blurted out.

Miriya took a step towards the hospitaller, intending to take the rifle from her, but a high-pitched scream drew her back to the fray.

Oleande rose from the ashes, a bruise-purple impact crater in her chest where one of Verity's shots had hit home. Something unholy and monstrous was living in there, inside the heretic's chest cavity where her heart had once beat. She dragged herself up, advancing on the wounded Battle Sister who even now tried in vain to unpin herself from the ground.

Miriya broke into a run, and came in swinging her chainsword in a growling figure of eight, as Oleande screamed wordlessly at her twin. The bitter champion of Khorne brought down her curved blade in an executioner's blow towards the neck of the woman on the ground, intent on beheading her with a single strike.

The chainsword blocked the fall before the blade could bite, as Miriya closed the distance to her enemy. The sickle edge skipped off the churning teeth of the bigger weapon and a torrent of white sparks sprayed into the air.

Miriya put her weight into the parry and forced Oleande back and away from the injured Battle Sister. 'Your foul master will not take her,' she spat.

'Do not defy the will of the Blood God!' Oleande bellowed back. Her *khopesh* was slim and light, quicker to wield than the bulky engine of Miriya's chainsword, and she struck back hard and swift, trying to find a weak point in the Sister's defences. For her part, Miriya blocked each strike and kept up the pressure, forcing Oleande to back away in the face of the whirling blade-edge.

Their weapons met again and again, corrupted steel clashing with tungsten fangs, each blow ringing a bell-tone across the echoing space of the shrine's ruined chancel. A lucky swipe sang off Miriya's shoulder-guard but did little more than scratch the black ceramite. In return the Battle Sister jabbed at her attacker and almost connected with Oleande's chest, much to her incandescent fury.

As Oleande fought back, a sickly nest of pallid tendrils wavered out of the entry wound in her chest, each of them ending in a lamprey-maw that danced in the air in search of blood and meat. The sight revolted Miriya and she attacked again, chipping off a piece of her enemy's sickle sword with a particularly violent downswing – but every strike she threw at her target was blocked, every feint transparent to her. The fallen Sister knew her ways of war too well, just as she had boasted. Oleande had been trained by the same warrior-mentors in the same doctrines, and now she matched Miriya pace for pace in lethal deadlock.

Oleande gave a hollow, monstrous bark of laughter. 'You can't kill me. I have died a thousand times and the Blood God's gift always resurrects me...' She reached up to stroke the squirming mass of tentacle-things emerging from the hole in her chest. 'I will give him your bones as tribute!'

She reeled back, and Miriya saw the flood of motion before it came. Her foe was going to attack with all she had, and hold back nothing. The Battle Sister braced herself–

–And in the next second Miriya heard the *other* Oleande cry out in pain. The sound dragged the gaze of her corrupted namesake towards her and Miriya saw the Chaos champion's mouth open in hunger and avarice.

The woman lying on the ground had finally, agonisingly, pulled the second sickle sword from her side and tossed it aside. The sudden uprush of blood from her wound spilled over her armour and the scent of the fresh vitae drew Oleande's desire like a magnet. The Blood God's servant could not stop herself from licking her lips.

That split-second of inattention was all the opportunity Miriya needed. She roared as she brought the chainsword down in a snarling arc that severed Oleande's sword-arm above the elbow, cutting noisily through splintering porcelain armour, meat and bone with a grinding howl. Her foe was staggered, but to Miriya's disgust, the detached arm disgorged a bulk of pale tendrils at its severed end, which began to propel it across the ground towards her, like a fat maggot questing for carrion to consume. Without hesitation, she stepped forward and stamped the severed limb into a pulpy mess, grinding it into the broken tiles beneath until it stopped moving.

Oleande – *the other Oleande* – was on her feet now, ignoring the blood streaming down her belly and leg. Her power sword was in her hand once more, sizzling as its energy halo burned off the caked dust and fluids that coated its surface. Each step she took was torture to her, but she did not falter. 'This ends now,' she declared, aiming her blade at the fallen one.

The traitor whose face she shared opened her mouth wide and shrieked, vomiting unhallowed words into the air that curdled the blood in Miriya's veins. Tendrils grew out past her lips, from her nostrils, ears and through the orbs of her eyes. The shrieking came from hundreds of the tiny lamprey maws and the profane clamour made the air vibrate. Desecrated glassaic cracked and broke, dust and loose stones fell from the damaged ceiling above.

Miriya and the Sister of the Valorous Heart shared a look and they attacked the heretic as one. Blows from their swords rained down on the traitorous Sororitas, chopping off divots of armour, slashing away pieces of quivering flesh. But even as Oleande fell to her knees, she was still screeching, still kept alive by whatever daemonic parasite her blasphemous god had implanted in her.

'You are already His,' she brayed, her mouth choked with convulsing cilia. 'It is inevitable. The Sisters of Battle are drenched in blood! Your faith is a lie! You all walk the Skull Road!'

Miriya raised her chainsword and glanced at the other warrior. 'Together, then?'

The Battle Sister gave a weary nod. 'Together, aye.'

In a single united motion, both of them plunged their blades deep into Oleande's chest cavity and silenced her.

The heretic's body collapsed in on itself to become a mess of offal and warped bone. Whatever power from the warp that had kept the woman alive was suddenly gone, and all her deaths returned a thousand-fold.

Miriya did not grace the traitor with a second glance. She strode away, sheathing her bloodied chainsword on her back as she crossed to where Verity stood over Isabel's unconscious form. The hospitaller was still clutching the other woman's bolter, but clearly she had been unwilling to use it again for fear of hitting her friend in the turn of the sword melee.

But then the brief moment of relief on Verity's face crumbled and she raised the weapon, aiming it unsteadily past Miriya. 'Sister!' she called, her shout a warning.

Miriya halted and turned in place, knowing what she would see behind her. The surviving Sister of the Valorous Heart, the one who had subsumed herself in a traitor's identity to protect her Order's virtue, now aimed her power sword at Miriya's throat. 'You should never have come after us,' she said quietly. 'My duty is clear.'

'She won't let us live...' said Verity, drawing the bolter close. 'We saw Oleande... The *true* Sister Oleande... And what she had become.'

Miriya nodded. 'We are witness to her Sisterhood's greatest disgrace.' She cocked her head. 'That was the command you were given, was it not? Do whatever must be done to ensure that this secret is never revealed?'

The Battle Sister nodded. 'Just so. Anyone who learns of the shame must not be allowed to speak of it.' She shook her head sorrowfully. 'I am sorry, Sister.' The woman planted her sword in the dirt, and pulled a pair of krak grenades from her belt. 'But this is how it must be.'

'I disagree.' Miriya walked slowly towards the other Sister, and placed her hands over those gripping the explosive devices. She knew that if they detonated, the krak charges would bring down the shrine's ceiling and bury them all. 'You have sacrificed so much to this mission,' she told her. 'Your very self. And I have given much too. My service and my blood, my Sisters. But if we perish here today, that duty ends. And the enemy still endures.' Miriya nodded towards the remains of the heretic. 'Not just the foe without, but the foe within.' She closed her eyes for a moment and remembered the horrible sense of temptation ghosting at the edges of her thoughts. To live was to be in battle with it, day after day... But to live was also to defy it, and make each breath a victory against the darkness.

The injured woman's grip on the grenades slackened. 'But this is my failure,' she said quietly. 'I must sacrifice…'

'You must *live*,' Miriya insisted. 'Sister Oleande must live. Else, the archenemy will have their victory and all you have done… All *we* have done will be for naught.'

'We will not speak of what was seen here,' said Verity. 'I vow this, on the honour of the Order of Serenity. I will carry it to my grave unspoken.'

'I vow this,' repeated Miriya. 'On the honour of the Order of Our Martyred Lady and in the name of Saint Katherine. I will carry it to my grave unspoken.' She paused, and then met the other woman's gaze. 'What say you, Sister?'

At length, Oleande gave a nod.

They regrouped with Cassandra's team in the shrine's nave, finding Rubria grim-faced and bleeding, with Ananke supporting her weight. There had been a firefight, Cassandra explained briskly. None of the Iconoclast's army had survived it.

'What of the heretic?' she asked.

'Sister Oleande brought down our enemy,' said Miriya, before anyone else could speak. 'The treachery of the Iconoclast's existence is ended.'

Cassandra helped Verity carry Isabel towards the gateway in the energy field, and they passed through it with a flash of radiation. Rubria and Ananke were next, and then it was only Miriya and the Sister of the Valorous Heart.

'What do I tell my kinswomen when I return to our convent?' said Oleande. 'I was not expected to live beyond my mission.'

'Adversity is a test, Sister. We must never fail it.' Miriya strode towards the gateway, drawing herself up, her head held high as was fitting to a victor. She paused on the threshold and offered the other woman her hand. 'And only the God-Emperor can decide when our duty is ended.'

ABOUT THE AUTHOR

James Swallow is best known for being the author of the Horus Heresy novels *Fear to Tread* and *Nemesis*, which both reached the *New York Times* bestseller lists, *The Flight of the Eisenstein* and a series of audio dramas featuring the character Nathaniel Garro. For Warhammer 40,000, he is best known for his four Blood Angels novels, the audio drama *Heart of Rage*, and his two Sisters of Battle novels. His short fiction has appeared in *Legends of the Space Marines* and *Tales of Heresy*.